MEN LIKE THAT

MEN LIKE THAT

A SOUTHERN QUEER HISTORY

John Howard

The

University

of Chicago

Press

Chicago and

London

The University of Chicago Press, Chicago 60637
The University of Chicago Press, Ltd., London
© 1999 by The University of Chicago
All rights reserved. Published 1999
Paperback edition 2001

08 07 06 05 04 03 02 01   2 3 4 5

ISBN 0-226-35471-7 (cloth)
ISBN 0-226-35470-9 (paperback)

Library of Congress Cataloging-in-Publication Data

Howard, John, 1962–
    Men like that : a southern queer history / John Howard.
        p.   cm.
    ISBN 0-226-35471-7 (cloth : alk. paper)
        1. Gay men—Mississippi—History—20th century.   2. Rural gay men—
    Mississippi—History–20th century.   3. Afro-American gays—Mississippi—
    History—20th century.   4. Gays in popular culture—Mississippi.   I. Title.
    HQ76.3.U52M74   1999
    305.38'9664—DC21

                                                        99-24363

To Novid

Contents

Acknowledgments

FRIENDS AND ACQUAINTANCES generously shared in the work of this project. It began as a dissertation, and I owe thanks to the members of my committee—Martin Duberman, Catherine Nickerson, Mary Odem, and Allen Tullos—for their perceptive commentary and unfailing support. At Emory University, both in and outside the classroom, I benefited from discussions with fellow graduate students Meredith Raimondo, Amy Scott, Donna Jo Smith, Kim Springer, and my dear friend Nancy Koppelman. Other academic communities provided important venues for testing ideas. Particularly helpful were audiences at annual meetings of the American Historical Association, American Studies Association, and Organization of American Historians.

At a critical juncture, Rick Lester gave me just the push I needed; my father likewise helped revive my efforts that January of 1996. Nancy Bounds of the Mississippi Department of Archives and History; Patrick Cather of Cather & Brown Rare Books, Birmingham, Alabama; Gerard Koskovich of the Gay and Lesbian Historical Society of Northern California; and a host of other antiquarians, librarians, archivists, and public officials pointed me in the right directions. Staff at Lilly, Perkins, and Special Collections Libraries of Duke University warrant special mention. William Spivey and Saundra Anderson helped me navigate census data; Mark Thomas taught me computer mapmaking; Eve Himler persisted in innumerable interlibrary loan requests; Melissa Delbridge, Dale Edgerton, Robbin Ernest, and Eric Smith spurred me ever onward; and David Ferriero honored me with his affirmations.

At Duke, this project neared completion with the help and encouragement of my writing partner, Robin Buhrke; my comrade, Kathy Rudy, in the Program in the Study of Sexualities; and my colleagues in both the history department and campus community development, notably Maureen Cullins, Nancy Hewitt, and Alex Roland. Also, just across the hall, exuberant and uplifting, was Anita Mills. When I tired of talking of Mississippi, students continued to pepper me with smart questions. I'm most grateful to the Duke FOCUS participants in my course on the history of sexuality in America.

Institutional support of various kinds was provided by Emory, Duke, The National Faculty, and most recently the University of York. Further financial assistance was granted by the Southern Regional Education Board. In Mississippi, my parents, my sister and brother, and friends Stella Connell and Anna Callon Ayers facilitated countless trips and contacts. My mother also forwarded valuable clippings. Gifted southern writers and historians helped situate this study in relationship to a noble tradition of left scholarship and activism. I appreciate the words and readings offered by Connie Curry, Pete Daniel, and Steven Lawson. I greatly profited from James Loewen's reading of the entire manuscript.

About the time I began serious inquiry in gay studies, John D'Emilio published an essay titled "Not a Simple Matter: Gay History and Gay Historians." A pioneer and by then a veteran in the field, D'Emilio directly addressed the rising generation: "I encourage those of you reading this essay to persist, and"—more astonishing still—"I offer you my assistance." I picked up the phone to call; but, alas, my nerve failed. Now, a decade later, I perhaps have overstepped his marvelous invitation. John applied himself painstakingly to a rough early version of this book. When we differed— and we did, at various points—he persevered, ever diligent. For all of us trying to persist in this work, John continues to set the highest standards.

Heartfelt thanks go to Doug Mitchell at the University of Chicago Press. By phone, fax, letter, and E-mail, he gave sage editorial advice. On the conference circuit, he organized many an engaging restaurant roundtable and gallery viewing. Also at Chicago and on the road, "Cousin" Matt Howard repeatedly came to my aid.

Of course, I never could have undertaken this study had it not been for the kindness and generosity of the Mississippians who agreed to share their stories. And I may never have finished it had I not been so fortunate to spend the past few years with Novid Parsi. Far more than his unmatched close readings and constructive critiques, his love sustained—and continues to sustain—both the content and context of my writing.

Introduction

*So here it is: I'm putting it
down for you to see if our
fragments match anywhere,
if our pieces, together, make
another larger piece of the
truth that can be part of the
map we are making to-
gether to show us the way
to the longed-for world.*

—MINNIE BRUCE PRATT[1]

IN THE SECOND HALF of the twentieth century, male-male desire in Mississippi was well enmeshed in the patterns of everyday life. Men interested in intimate and sexual relations with other men found numerous opportunities to act on their desires, and did so within the primary institutions of the local community— home, church, school, and workplace. Never inherently hostile to homosexual activity, these institutions repeatedly fostered it.

Yet this activity was fraught with complications. From the 1940s through the 1960s, national media and medical advice literature depicted homosexuality as depravity or pathology. In Protestant evangelical Mississippi, most everyone took for granted that it was sinful, and it was legally proscribed by the 1839 state sodomy statute. But like so many other vices, homosexuality and gender insubordination were acknowledged and accommodated with a pervasive, deflective pretense of ignorance. At midcentury, to be labeled queer meant to be cast as different in any number of more or less threatening ways—from peculiarities of speech, manner, and daily habits to gender and sexual nonconformity. This ambiguity frequently benefited those willing to test convention because it often shielded them from accusations of a more explicitly sexual—and thus menacing—nature.

A compendium of superlatives, Mississippi was the nation's poorest state; its people, the least educated. A sparsely populated landscape with

TENNESSEE

ARKANSAS

LOUISIANA

ALABAMA

GULF OF MEXICO

Hernando
Corinth
Iuka
Ripley
Holly Springs
Tishomingo
Senatobia
Hickory Flat
Baldwyn
Crenshaw
New Albany
Sardis
Oxford
Marks
Batesville
Fulton
Clarksdale
Tupelo
Crowder
Water Valley
Bruce
Amory
Mound Bayou
Coffeeville
Houston
Tutwiler
Calhoun City
Rosedale
Drew
Aberdeen
Cleveland
Grenada
Ruleville
Shaw
Mathiston
West Point
Greenwood
Indianola
Winona
Eupora
Columbus
Greenville
Starkville
Hollandale
Vaiden
Tchula
Louisville
Macon
Belzoni
Lexington
Kosciusko
Rolling Fork
Durant
Noxapater
Shuqualak
Yazoo City
Carthage
Philadelphia
De Kalb
Canton
Walnut Grove
Union
Vicksburg
Forest
Meridian
JACKSON
Brandon
Edwards
Morton
Newton
Florence
Enterprise
Terry
Raleigh
Quitman
Mendenhall
Crystal Springs
Bay Springs
Port Gibson
Magee
Taylorsville
Hazelhurst
Union Church
Wesson
Laurel
Collins
Monticello
Waynesboro
Natchez
Brookhaven
Prentiss
Ellisville
Hattiesburg
Richton
Gloster
McComb
Tylertown
Camp Shelby
Leakesville
Woodville
Liberty
Purvis
Lumberton
Poplarville
Wiggins
Lucedale
Picayune
Gulfport
Biloxi
Pascagoula

Mississippi, selected cities and
towns

Two queer friends (three, including the photographer) in rural Rankin County, Mississippi, ca. 1940. Courtesy of Special Collections Library, Duke University.

grossly inadequate public services, it was readily available to ridicule. Its bigotry and its backwardness, many Americans felt, were unequaled. Mississippi, of all places, seemed least receptive to homosexuality. In her otherwise brilliant essay "Thinking Sex," theorist Gayle Rubin voices this commonsensical notion—both popular and scholarly—of sexual difference in the countryside: "Dissident sexuality is rarer and more closely monitored in small towns and rural areas. Consequently, metropolitan life continually beckons to young perverts, [who become] sexual migrants . . . instead of being isolated and invisible in rural settings. . . ."[2]

Queer sex in Mississippi was not rare. Men-desiring-men were neither wholly isolated nor invisible. From the most secluded farms in Smith County to the densest neighborhoods of the capital, Jackson, homosexuality flourished between close friends and distant relatives; casual sex between strangers was clandestine but commonplace. Androgyny, though doubly suspect, also thrived.

In contrast to urban-centered and identity-focused studies of American lesbian and gay history, *Men Like That* attends to queer desire, both identity based and not, in small cities, towns, and rural settings of meager economic resources. Informed by queer theory and spatial theory, the work argues that notions and experiences of male-male desire are in perpetual dialectical relationship with the spaces in which they occur, mutually shaping one another. This book examines sexual and gender nonconformity, specifically male homosexualities and male-to-female transgender sexualities in Mississippi from 1945 to 1985—from the end of World War II to the dawn of the age of AIDS.

While Mississippi has long been considered America's most repressive locale, the 1950s have long been assumed the most repressive period. And yet through internationally acclaimed works of "serious" literature published at midcentury, novelists Hubert Creekmore and Thomas Hal Phillips and playwright Tennessee Williams, for example, crafted wily individuals challenging the precepts of heterosexual normalcy. Like these fictional characters, their real-life counterparts fashioned circumspect relationships, prudently and judiciously sheltered from destructive forces.

Largely homebound, living in familial households, these Mississippians nonetheless traveled. With new and improved roads in the 1950s and 1960s, Mississippians had greater access to networks of homosexual desire. Hardly an exodus to the cities, queer movement more often consisted of circulation rather than congregation. In their cars, queers drove through complex, multidirectional avenues of interaction, prompting exchanges of ideas and affections. Still, many queer Mississippians, especially agrarian and working-class people—those with limited mobility—found companions as they always had, within the immediate vicinity. Though sometimes subject to intimidation and violence—as in the widely reported 1955 murder of Jackson interior decorator John Murrett—queer Mississippians proved adept at maneuvering through hostile terrain. They often remade material and ideological spaces and thereby regularly found themselves in the company of like-minded souls. This company, in keeping with broader cultural conditions, was racially polarized; on either side of the color line, black men and white men participated in markedly similar worlds of desire that rarely overlapped before the 1960s.

Indeed, pop culture representations, such as physique magazines of the 1950s and the more openly gay pulp fiction of the 1960s, promulgated norms of desire and standards of beauty based on distinctive racial hierarchies. These visual and textual representations of male sensuality emanated not solely from the assumed cultural capitals of New York, San Francisco, and Los Angeles. Rather, they were created and re-created by individuals dispersed across the American landscape. Often regional narratives like those produced by Florence, Mississippi, physique artist and pulp novelist Carl Corley instantiated more than a black/white dyad; they constructed complicated, pernicious strata of race, color, and ethnicity. Corley took up and elaborated an archetype of queer desire: the lusty (white) wild-eyed country boy. But Corley also specified the unique features of the Mississippi landscape and the demands it placed on queer life. As one of the most prolific and daring of pulp novelists, he pressed the limits of the genre, insisting on counterhegemonic happy endings and arguing for queer equal rights.

It was in fact not the "conformist fifties" but rather the "free love sixties" that marked the most strident, organized resistance to queer sexuality in Mississippi. This backlash resulted less from the tensions of Cold War domestic politics and fears of communism than from the increasingly successful African American civil rights movement and the vital role that queer Mississippians played in it. The state's most well-known black leader, Aaron Henry, as well as liberal white attorney Bill Higgs, repeatedly turned up in homosexual settings, as was exposed by intransigent white supremacists acting on sinister motives. Indeed, black and white activists from both inside and outside the state questioned sexual normalcy as they worked against racial inequality in Mississippi. Yet the state's mainstream media focused on the "dirty beatnik," the white male "outside agitator" who harbored perverse sexual instincts. Variants of this construction would surface again and again, from the 1960s through the 1980s, as official discourses attempted to put homosexuality at a safe distance, to characterize homosexuality as elsewhere.

But the mid-sixties police crackdown on homosexuality demonstrated its very prevalence within the ranks of upper-, middle-, and working-class Mississippians. In 1965—a turning point in queer Mississippi history— white men of all types were arrested in public lavatories, or "tearooms," at the Forrest Hotel in Hattiesburg and the City Auditorium in Jackson. As never before, authorities attempted to eradicate homosexual networks, literally forcing deviants out of the state. In a hysteria fueled by a crumbling archaic racial order, numerous lives were destroyed. Moreover, the postwar libertinism and accommodationism that fostered a white gay bar culture in the heart of Jackson during the 1940s and 1950s yielded to a massive resistance campaign designed to expunge notions of racial equality and sexual diversity. Those precious few gay establishments, the gay bars, went underground—specifically, they moved to the city's periphery and became highly secretive. The timing was hardly coincidental. The racist daily newspapers that reported the fate of one famous City Auditorium arrestee, Jackson Symphony Orchestra conductor Theodore Russell, begrudgingly marked the passage of the landmark federal Voting Rights Act in the very same edition.

Parallel black and white queer realms cautiously intermingled after the early sixties, as queer no longer denoted a nebulous eccentricity but was used as an epithet of sexual, gender, and racial nonnormativity. Whereas before, same-sex interracial intercourse usually involved advances by white men of privilege on their black class subordinates, desegregation enabled more—if seldom more egalitarian—interactions across the racial divide. Obstacles remained; racism persisted. In Jackson, though formal barriers eased, a queer boy out on the town could still expect to choose between the white bar and the black bar—located, at the end of the period, directly across the street from one another.

Just as *mainstream* representations of homosexuality in Mississippi—such as 1967's number one pop song "Ode to Billy Joe" and the 1976 film adaptation of the song, *Ode to Billy Joe*—traded on a prevailing homosexual suicide mythology, *mainline* Protestant churches were ever more obliged to denounce homosexuality as a mortal sin from the late 1960s onward. Yet in both the movie houses and houses of worship, oppressive discourses occasioned against-the-grain readings by those most invested in such narratives—queer Mississippians. In fact, to the surprise of national lesbian and gay activists, queer organizing in Mississippi increasingly relied on church tradition. The state's first sustained lesbian and gay political organization, the Mississippi Gay Alliance, founded in 1973, largely floundered for its first ten years, until its leadership began to acknowledge, respect, and finally harness the centrality of religion in the lives of queer Mississippians. These leaders helped form a local congregation of the worldwide Metropolitan Community Church, a Protestant denomination ministering primarily to lesbian and gay worshipers. A virulent right-wing opposition, headed by Mississippi Moral Majority president Mike Wells, mobilized grassroots xenophobia and warned of a homosexual invasion, while queer Mississippians found a new ease in melding queer sexuality with Christian spirituality.

Many queer Mississippians, however, continued to read and hear about their kind only as the objects of scandal. In the daily press and on television, one public official after another was branded homosexual. The heterosexual will to not-know, the pretense of ignorance, proved amazingly resilient. It thrived upon a perpetual reassertion of homosexuality as new. As noted, Aaron Henry, state president of the NAACP—the National Associa-

tion for the Advancement of Colored People—was arrested for homosexual sodomy or disorderly conduct on at least four occasions. Yet he was
reelected to office for a total of thirty-three one-year terms, from 1960 to
1993. U.S. congressman Jon Hinson, though he admitted frequenting Washington, D.C.'s homosexual sites, was reelected to a second term in 1980.
And attorney general Bill Allain, despite convincing evidence that he engaged black transgender sex workers, was elected governor of Mississippi
in 1983. The highly visible nature of these allegations meant Herculean efforts on the part of prudish Mississippians. As many stated over and over,
they just didn't *want* to believe the charges. The accused likewise ignored
or denied the allegations or—employing a familiar Sunday morning ritual
of conversion and redemption—successfully repented of wrongdoing.

Many did believe the allegations, of course. Across the state, queers were
empowered as they learned about the activities of gay cultural and political
organizations and about a gay presence in mainstream institutions. Other
Mississippians began to fear those very individuals they had long known
as fellow employees, church members, family members, and schoolmates.
As queer visibility threatened to destabilize the established order, public
officials tried to allay anxieties through a discourse of encasement. If deviancy was not new, if it was indeed among us, it was nonetheless cordoned
off, sequestered, encased within zones spatial—such as Jackson's racialized
"inner city"—and temporal—the dangerous late night hours.

Late-twentieth-century queer empowerment foreclosed the quiet accommodation of difference characteristic of the 1940s and 1950s. By 1965 homosexuality was linked to the specter of racial justice—what white authorities understood as the most serious threat to the status quo. Queer
Mississippians black and white found themselves in increasingly politicized positions. With the bravery earned in lives of local struggle and everyday resistance, they moved onto the public stage, determined to win a
legitimacy and equity so long denied them.

THE ABOVE IS A SUMMARY of arguments that I instantiate and elaborate in the
subsequent seven chapters, as I further attempt to refine one of the fundamental premises in the historiography of sexuality in the West. If, as has been
convincingly demonstrated, urbanization and industrialization enabled gay
identity and culture formation in the cities during the nineteenth century or
perhaps earlier, then the Western world witnessed what has been called the
Great Paradigm Shift, the articulation of a cultural binary undergirding
much dualistic thinking: the heterosexual-homosexual split. Homosexuality—and, by inference, heterosexuality—was no longer understood as a
set of acts, but as an identity; not as behavior, but a state of being.[3]

Men Like That complicates this schism by documenting the experiences both of men like *that*—which is to say, men of that particular type, self-identified gay males—as well as men *who like* that, men who also like queer sex, who also engage in homosexual activity or gender nonconformity, but do not necessarily identify as gay. Though I naturally have greater access as a researcher to the former, my project nonetheless unearths evidence to support my tentative assertion that throughout the twentieth century, queer sexuality continued to be understood as both acts *and* identities, behaviors *and* beings. It was variously comprehended—depending in part on race and place—along multiple axes and continuums as yet unexamined by historians.

The process of proving these queer histories is a story in itself. Obstacles in this project were considerable, not least of which, my own occasional reluctance to declare: "I'm researching homosexuality and gender nonconformity in Mississippi." Given persistent prejudices there as elsewhere, such a flat, unadorned statement would have assured a lack of cooperation from many I encountered—archivists, librarians, other historians, and interviewees/narrators among them. Like my queer Mississippi forebears, I relied on subtleties of language and markers of identity—in my case, whiteness, a mostly normative gender presentation, and a professionalized demeanor—to move in and across worlds of potential hostility and limited access. Thereby, I sometimes managed to win support for the project and, hopefully, achieve my purpose—which is not simply to recuperate past figures previously lost to history, but also to reassess sexual and gender meanings, practices, and regulations across time and place.

Chapter 1, "Ones and Twos," discusses my varied methodological approaches. It relies foremost on the power of personal testimony—oral history—as an introduction to the everyday life of queer Mississippians at midcentury. The principal oral history narrators introduce themselves via edited transcriptions of the interviews they kindly granted to me. Their stories are continued in chapters 2 and 3 and beyond. In chapter 1, I outline the geographical and historical parameters of my study, as well as its theoretical underpinnings. The chapter further positions this project in relationship to an American lesbian and gay historiographical tradition that is decidedly urban in focus. Along with the traditional concerns with identity, community, and politics—which surface most prominently in the later chapters of this book—my primary emphasis is on desire as an organizing category.

That emphasis, rare in queer history, requires an elaboration of terminology. I use the amalgam *homosex* to indicate sexual activities of various sorts between two males. *Queer* holds multiple meanings, in both the historical and theoretical contexts of this study. When writing of particular moments in Mississippi history, I use the widespread, contemporaneous understanding of things queer, as noted above. However, generally in referring to "queer Mississippians"—those who engage in queer sex or harbor queer notions—I am employing an expansive definition that goes well beyond homosex to encompass all thoughts and expressions of sexuality and gender that are nonnormative or oppositional. Though *gay* is always employed as an identity-based descriptor, *queer* may or may not be, depending on the individual. My focus is on *men* (who) like that, since women's experiences prove markedly different in this time and place; still, *lesbian* and *gay* are sometimes referred to jointly, especially in the later chapters, at moments of mutual effort and collaboration, in addition to moments of distinct but simultaneous phenomena effecting men-desiring-men and women-desiring-women.

Chapter 2, "Sites," locates male-male desire within the distinctive features of Mississippi's social and physical landscape. Along with chapter 3, "Movements," it points to a dialectical relationship between historical actors and their surroundings, suggesting that the two are perpetually at work shaping one another. Like chapter 1, chapters 2 and 3 are arranged more thematically than chronologically, privileging place and linking what little evidence may be available about particular sites across time. Informed by the interdisciplinary field of scholarship often referred to as the new cultural geography, this exercise in "militant particularism," as David Harvey calls it[4]—my articulation of regional specificities—should not be read as exclusivity. The extent to which queer genders and sexualities in Mississippi appear akin to those in other places is a question I leave to future writers of larger syntheses and surveys. Just as the existing histories of queer life in New York, San Francisco, and Los Angeles seldom discuss the rural countryside—except as hinterland, as a geopolitical closet from which sexual migrants flee—I feel no obligation to make mine a comparative history. I argue primarily for a *specific* queer Mississippi, which is not to say a wholly *unique* queer Mississippi.

Proceeding to a more chronological format, chapter 4, "Norms and Laws," traces a significant shift in sexual and gender norms and the policing of those norms over the 1950s and 1960s. Beginning with the John Murrett murder trial of 1955, I describe a climate of quiet accommodationism that gave way to overt hostility and legal persecution of difference as a result of the civil rights movement. As I assess mostly mainstream depictions of the mass of volunteers broadly and two key activists specifically, I concur with the oral history narrators' conclusions that crackdowns on deviant sexuality in Mississippi escalated not in the 1950s, as was the case elsewhere in America, but rather in the 1960s amidst violent white resistance to racial justice.

Chapter 5, "Representations," examines select cultural products aimed at detailing deviancy and, by extension, normalcy in Mississippi. The mid-century novels *The Bitterweed Path* and *The Welcome*; Carl Corley's artwork and fiction from the fifties and sixties; and *Ode to Billy Joe*, the homosexual suicide narrative popularized through song, film, and novel from the sixties through the seventies, all provide access to queer worlds real and imagined, historical and fictive. They cast light on varied constructions of gender and sexuality in mid- and late-twentieth-century Mississippi, in relationship to other American cultural arenas and avenues. They also point up race, class, and regional hierarchies structuring the narrative story lines, the historical conditions of their production, and the lived experiences of their creators. Further, journalistic accounts of these and other works and experiences—such as the lively column by *Jackson Daily News* arts editor Frank Hains—suggest startlingly candid engagements with homosexuality and gender subversion often assumed impossible during the first half of the period. Hains's own life history and its tragic end help us chart the blurring of the line between the mythic and real, the true and made up—a constituent element in the movement from modern to postmodern aesthetic concerns observable in cultural production in and about Mississippi.

Chapter 6, "Politics and Beliefs," tracks the development of gay identity politics in Mississippi, as it articulates a necessary component of queer institution building in the state—Christian spirituality. From the founding of the Mississippi Gay Alliance in 1973 to the establishment of a Metropolitan Community Church in 1983, this chapter examines organizational records, news accounts, and contemporaneous and present-day testimonies about that time to reconstruct a group of people increasingly under siege, increasingly understanding themselves as a community, a movement.

Finally, chapter 7, "Scandals," documents two political careers rocked by confessions and accusations of deviant sexuality during the early 1980s. These scandals provide windows on to experiences otherwise beyond the purview of official history. Also, they expose the attempts by the powerful to physically and ideologically marginalize sexual and gender nonconformists in Mississippi at the end of the period. Race again proves critical, as political leaders attempt to delineate and allocate spaces of varying qualities to individuals deemed deserving or undeserving. This chapter charts both the articulation and fallacy of discourses portraying homosexuality as elsewhere, homosexuality as new.

The book's first three chapters, which make up part 1, may strike the reader as markedly different from the four chapters in part 2. Oral history narratives are the predominant source material for the first part; the ephemera of so-called traditional historical documents—ostensibly more trustworthy, more tangible—contribute most to the second. Conversely, whereas the second part often reads like narrative legal and political history—with its emphasis on key individuals, major events, and important cultural products—the first has the sensate quality of social history, with an ear to the voices of ordinary Mississippians, an eye to their evolving environments. Like the wayward memories that give it shape, part 1 undulates back and forth over the entire era under discussion—a rich seedbed of sorts, on which historical agents might have tested many varieties of phenomena, from which they might have expected vastly differing yields. Part 2 more explicitly articulates transformations—the plowing, planting, and cultivating; the growth and harvest; or the withering and plowing under again of particular ideas and institutions, actions and representations. Thus, although both tradition and flux are shown to imbue all aspects of human endeavor, part 1 is perhaps best viewed as a set of contexts out of which develop, in part 2, a series of changes.

The result is a fragmented text. At times, I use the words of oral history narrators. Other times, I write a narrative in the third person. I also offer my own analysis, my conclusions, or my sense of unanswered questions. I occasionally appear in the first person, a reminder to the reader that I bring my own sociocultural positioning to this project, my biases, emphases, preferences, predilections—as any historian must. I'm a queer white southerner, a Mississippian interested in a group of men and women I somehow see as cultural predecessors. I try to remain true to their individual needs, wishes, and interests, while acknowledging my own investment in the subject matter.

A shift between these varied presentation styles is denoted for the reader with line breaks and occasional subheadings. The individual sections within chapters may be easily pondered on their own, while contributing, I hope, to an overall narrative flow, especially in the later chapters, where I do tend to move in chronological fashion. That doesn't mean, however, that—as suggested by the American progressivist tradition—I believe in the inevitability of events or the certainty that things are getting better and better over time. Quite the contrary, my story illustrates historical moments of extraordinary opportunity, often followed by periods of severe oppression, and vice versa. I attempt to explain why certain behaviors, networks, meanings, and sites are possible at some times and places and not at others; why these changes are accompanied by continuities; why today's demagogues like the American Family Association's Donald Wildmon of Tupelo, for example, eerily recall languages of hate employed by historical figures like U.S. senator James O. Eastland of Sunflower County. I believe that in today's movements for economic and social justice, we benefit from recounting and scrutinizing historical events, the distinctive matrices of forces that give rise to such figures and phenomena, along with their contrary social, cultural, and political forces—the concomitant resistances. Without apology, I concede that my academic explorations of the past are informed by my activist's will for social change in the present.

IN MANY WAYS, this project began in December 1986. Late that month, for the first time in my life, I walked into Jack's Saloon—the white queer bar in Jackson, Mississippi. I had come out of the closet, come out to myself, a couple of weeks prior in Washington, D.C., my adopted city, my proud cosmopolitan refuge. Back home for the holidays, visiting my parents in Brandon, Mississippi—the town where I grew up, where I grew to disdain and disavow all things unpleasant—I turned the melancholy lull of the family get-together to my advantage: "I'm going over to Jackson for a few hours."

I had driven into Jack's parking lot before. Drunken nights, I had sat there in my car, without resolve. This time I marched right in. One of my earliest encounters with queer culture in the Deep South, the outing was motivated less by an impulse to act on queer desire than by a need to witness a community organized around queer desire. Expecting to find a comfortingly anonymous, homogenous mass, like the crowds of Dupont Circle discos, I instead ran into old friends, a former next-door neighbor, a young woman I once dated. I saw Joe, who knew me by a false name and whom I knew only vaguely, through a sodden, faraway recollection: a car, a country road, a church parking lot.

Despite the awkwardness, I felt welcome in this space. There was a friendliness far more genuine than the "How are yas" and "Good to see yas" that marked my upbringing. No doubt, too, I exuded a newfound self-assuredness, a big-city swagger. I'm sure my fascination was tinged with condescension as I listened to a new acquaintance describe his monthly pilgrimage to Jack's. He drove up from Brookhaven, an hour to the south. Sometimes he stayed over; often he drove back in the dark of the wee hours. Soon we were talking about his job, his friends, his family, in Lincoln County. Sure enough, he knew my sister, who lived down in McComb.

Later that night I accompanied an old friend, Sam—a graduate of a tony parochial school—to Bill's Club, across the street. Bill's stayed open later than Jack's and, it was said, sold alcohol after hours. Sam led me past the door staff, apparently reassuring them with a nod, "He's OK." Besides one or two others, Sam and I were the only white folks in the club. Bill's clientele of African Americans—mostly men but also women, mostly young but also older—reminded me of a different aspect of my past. The nonwhite space evoked recollections of nonwhite Mississippians I had known, but only superficially, through the years. We had interacted mostly in hierarchical work environments, in worlds that remained—if not by law then certainly by custom—segregated.

Sam and I walked through the crowd, past the dance floor, to a hallway, at the end of which was a door. Sam knocked. The door cracked open, then swung wide. We were let in to what seemed an anteroom. A moment later we moved through yet another door to another room, where a young woman, perhaps once a man, declared with indifference, "That'll be a dollar." I gave her one; Sam did, too. In return, she reached into an old flip-top Coca-Cola refrigerator, fished out a couple of cans of beer, and handed them to us. "Enjoy your evening," I remember she said.

We withdrew back into the bar proper. Sam may have introduced me to one or two people, but I never really carried on a conversation with anyone. Dancing, playing pool, queuing up for the bathroom—black Mississippians at Bill's Club paid no particular attention to the occasional white patron. As in no setting I'd ever experienced, whether a predominantly white or black one, a white presence was of no consequence.

My memories of that night, of Jack's and Bill's—separated by a street and by greater divides—are still with me. The young man at Jack's from Brookhaven only partially dismantled my smug status as city dweller, reaching out to me through local networks of family and kinship; the young transgender person at Bill's, whose background I didn't learn, shared only a partial past with me, a history that separated us and offered us each different opportunities. Later I would realize what both he and she were far too polite or perhaps unconcerned to suggest that night in Jackson: that while I ran off to Washington to come out of the closet, under the protection of namelessness and economic advantage, they and others like them toughed it out in Mississippi, crafting lives of determination and grit.

I owe this study (and, I hope, a more mindful self-assessment) to these Mississippians. Though I now reside an ocean away, I cautiously align myself with them—in the hope that I never succumb to a haughty remove forged in exile's supposed luxuries, and in the belief that through their stories, American lesbian and gay history will be provided a needed refinement.

PART ONE

CHAPTER ONE

Ones and Twos

Although this play takes place in the state of Mississippi, I do not want it to drip with magnolias.

—MART CROWLEY[1]

MISSISSIPPI. SUMMER 1953. A teenager walks alongside a road in rural Jasper County. It's hot, and he needs a ride. He's on his way home, to the family farm. Or maybe he's headed to town, one of the few crossroads communities in the area—Louin, Bay Springs, or Hero. Cars and pickup trucks seldom pass. Only one every few minutes.[2] At last, a car approaches. He recognizes the driver, a Methodist preacher invited to lead a revival at the local church. The preacher stops. The teenager gets in. As they move toward their destinations, they exchange pleasantries, discuss the weather, the success of the church meetings, the number of souls saved.

Then, something happens. Slowly, the preacher begins to understand. Perhaps the teenager winks at him. He makes a not-so-subtle joke. Or, with right arm out the passenger side window, he puts his left hand in the preacher's lap.

It's impossible to know exactly what happened in the car. But somehow the teenager made it clear to the Methodist revivalist: he was sexually interested in the man.

The pastor deflected the advance. Ever hospitable, he sped on down the road, depositing the hitchhiker at his destination. He likely saw the teenager again, in church, and apparently never mentioned the incident. But he was so shaken that he discussed it with a friend, the Methodist pastor at Montrose, another Jasper County community. The Montrose pastor, Ted Herrington, found the story so compelling that—despite the revivalist's silences, his carefully chosen, suggestive phrases—he would re-member it distinctly over forty years later.[3]

THIS STORY, TOLD TO ME by Ted Herrington, is in many ways emblematic of homosexual experience in midcentury Mississippi. It broaches a number of issues central to the understanding of male homosexualities at this particu-lar time and place. These themes—fragmented subplots of my own delib-erately crafted narrative—repeat and reverberate throughout the following pages.

What unique features of the Mississippi landscape shaped and struc-tured homosexual interaction? What distinguished this predominantly ru-ral space from the urban areas previously explored by historians of sexu-ality? How was mobility—both physical and social—linked to sexual practices, meanings, and regulation? What institutions of everyday life fig-ured in the construction of sexuality—of homosexual desire, identity, com-munity, and politics? How were work and leisure organized to facilitate or thwart homosexual encounter? How was homosexuality represented in Mississippi, by Mississippians? What belief systems forged and were forged by notions of homosexuality? What was the nature of transgression? How were normalcy and perversity mutually defining and redefining in settings such as this? And perhaps most important: for human beings—the actors in the drama to follow—how was homosexual desire manifested? How did it shape and how was it shaped by a person's understanding of self and others, individual and community?

For the unnamed teenager—a young man sixteen or seventeen years old—a confluence of forces resulted in this brief attempt at sexual intimacy. He was momentarily in transit, moving between town and country. He likely was on his way to or from work. His path crossed that of another man—not a local, but neither a stranger. Both native and visitor under-stood one another within the context of a community of faith, connected to a complicated belief system. The automobile provided not only the means of transport, but also a place of interaction. The quasi-public space of the interior became the site for communication. Perhaps through a combination of verbal and body language, utterances and silences—utterances and si-lences that would be perpetuated and complicated in subsequent retellings, including this one—the young man communicated his desire. But like so many taboo expressions of sexuality at that historical moment, that desire was frustrated.

The story also, I hope, helps make visible some of the issues I wrangle with in writing history. I'm constantly reminded of issues of power. The institutional forces of oppression that made life difficult for homosexual men in midcentury Mississippi are related to the powers that control to-day's narratives about that life. Simply put, whose stories get told and how they get told are a function of power. I enjoy certain privileges—benefits of race, class, gender, and institutional affiliation—that allow me to undertake this project. Wherever possible, however, I prefer that the historical agents tell their stories for themselves, as I often enable through transcriptions of tape-recorded oral histories. Further, I solicit what might be called twice-told stories, such as the one above. This hearsay evidence—inadmissible in court, unacceptable to some historians—is essential to the recuperation of queer histories. The age-old squelching of our words and desires can be replicated over time when we adhere to ill-suited and unbending standards of historical methodology.

Also, particular methodologies tend to produce certain limitations and inevitabilities of outcome. For example, from over fifty sets of interviews I conducted or consulted, a few individuals like Ted Herrington implied their heterosexuality as they spoke of the past. But the vast majority of narrators are self-identified gay men. To have them speak only of their "gay" experiences would isolate sexuality and remove it from the realm of everyday life, which was its ordinary context. Also, it would privilege narrators' experiences of gay identity and community and their participation in definably gay organizations, which were few and far between in Missis-sippi. Thus, I ask my narrators to simply tell me their life stories, allowing them to place emphasis on what they view as most important (while recognizing that narrators' awareness of the very nature of my project tends to encourage a focus on "gay" phenomena). Also, I limit my questions so as to avoid scripting their responses. If we spin out yarns with minimal interruption, I have found, we are more likely to utilize the vocabularies familiar to us, to recall the words and phrases from the era described.

Yes, most of this volume's narrators are men like *that:* men who identify as gay or otherwise see same-sex desire as central to their being. And yet, as their stories demonstrate, many men with whom they had contact—men who experienced or acted on male-male desire, men who *liked* that—didn't identify as gay. These men probably predominated, though no one will ever be able to say with certainty. For obvious reasons, these men are unlikely to participate in a historical project such as mine. I can only get at them secondhand, as I refer to this phenomenon and illustrate it in this book—indeed, as many narrators themselves speak about the "straight men" they had sex with, "trade," "closet cases," and others. To insist on reading them, as some of my narrators do, as closeted, would unduly simplify complex self-conceptions. I only can assert that these men acted on queer desire, and thus I categorize them accordingly. For this reason—along with a number of transgender persons who further destabilize our easy notions of straight and gay, male and female—I have retained queer desire rather than gay identity as the principal analytic schema.

Queer is a useful rubric. Today it is often deployed idealistically, if sometimes problematically, to aggregate varied persons based on their myriad experiences of difference and outsider status—a coalition of the marginalized. I find that queer further opens up interpretive possibilities as we study the past. To speak of a gay history, to consult gay sources, and to query gay individuals often serve to perpetuate gayness as a category. To look for the queer, as variously conceived and embodied, in the past, might well result in richer and more accurate histories of deviancy and normalcy and might help denaturalize their present-day iterations.

We can never completely know what happened at any given moment in the past. What is *worth* knowing is an ongoing debate within and between the historical profession and the public at large. While all histories are speculative, this one may be even more so. My text is sprinkled liberally with words such as *perhaps, maybe, sometimes, likely,* and *probably.* Still, mine is informed speculation. I weigh evidence and attempt to be as accurate as possible, while creating what I hope are interesting, readily visualized depictions.[4] I consider many types of sources and often give authority to those previously denied it.

Chuck Plant: I am Charles William Plant. I was actually born in Slidell, Louisiana, but I have no recollection of it! My father was—I guess to be very fancy—a construction engineer on the highways that were being built in those days. I may have been born in a tent for all I know, because my brother tells me that he remembers living in a tent in those days because they moved around so much. Rural areas. My mother died six months after I was born. They weren't sure where I was going. My brother went to one branch of the family, and I went to another. Then after I was nine years old, the aunt and uncle that had taken me were having financial problems and had two children of their own, so I was taken by an[other] aunt, who brought me up from then on. She had been married, but by that time they were divorced, and he died soon after that.

I was born August 24, 1931. I guess I was a Depression baby. Things were rather bleak in poor ol' Mississippi at that time. The aunt and uncle who took me lived in Oakley, Mississippi. Blink your eyes and you'll miss it. Seven miles out in the country [from Raymond] is Oakley [in Hinds County]. This uncle I called Father and my aunt, Mother. They had two children older than I, and we grew up together. [Father] was working for a man who was quite a landowner and had horses and cattle. It was a big operation.

Our home burned. When you're a child, things just seem like they're enormous.

The fire from our home burning just seemed uncanny. That's one of my earliest memories. We moved to another house, still in Oakley. Then, this old prison that had hay stored in it also burned. This was probably during the period when fires just raged out of control in Mississippi. There was no way to stop the fire. If I thought our home burning was spectacular, this prison! We were quite a way off, but you could see the flames just going up into the air from maybe half a mile away. So these are big memories.

We went to school in Raymond. We went on the school bus. In those days, they decided to build a new school. And they rolled the old school to one side and built a new school. It's funny. The old school kind of went up like this, multilevel, and the new school was all flat, on one level. Must have been 1937, give or take. There was a new trend to keep it all flat, spread out, on one level.

Then in fifth grade I came to live with my aunt here in Jackson. I went to Bailey School. School was not that bad. In those days you had lady teachers, and some of them were sweet, sweet. I was kind of a dreamer. And the idea of studying something or paying attention or being very tied down to something was hardly my style, [unless] the teacher was the kind who read to you. I remember in the fifth grade we had a marvelous teacher who did a lot of reading. She would read things that would just make us cry. It was wonderful. She had everybody in the class drawing and painting things. That was right down my alley. I guess generally speaking I was never the greatest student. But I managed to get by.

[My social life] was fairly conventional until junior high, when I began to have some inkling of what my leanings might be. I remember being picked up and taken for a drive by an older man. It was titillating but frightening at the same time. And it only happened once. It was a hundred years ago. I remember it was a rainy day, and I thought, Oh, rainy day, what does that mean? I guess he offered me a ride, and I got into his car, and I think it was the hand-on-the-leg kind of approach. And one thing led to another. That's about all I remember. I remember being very sort of nervous. And wondering if I should say anything to somebody, but I finally decided not to say anything to anybody. I have no regrets about that. These people who now are exposing all kinds of people, forty years later, whatever, I just think, Why can't you just leave that alone?

I was in junior high. Fourteen or fifteen, something like that. It was like a small car with just two seats, driver and passenger. I was in the passenger seat; he was driving. I remember unzipping, but not too much after that. I don't even remember that it was oral sex. It could have been just handling. That was my first with somebody I didn't know. I guess there were playmates, you know, that you play around with. But that was the first thing with someone I didn't know.

Then, later, in high school, the realization of my sexual orientation sort of finally dawned on me. And of course I went through that—which I think is pretty standard—where you think you're the only one on earth. Will I never meet anybody else? Then finally you meet somebody else and then you're kind of introduced to the gay life.[5]

Fitz Spencer: My name is Fitzhugh Spencer, or Fitz that I'm known as usually. I was born in Natchez on March 11, 1926. We lived in Natchez until I was four years old. Then we moved to a little town about fifty miles [up and] across the river, Saint Joseph [Louisiana]. It was on a lake about five miles out of the town of Saint Joseph. I grew up in sort of a fairly isolated area, I guess you'd say. We lived right on the lake, which was marvelous in the summer. I had one older sister, a year and nine months older than I am, June. We sort of grew up together because it was fairly isolated. Of course, we attended the public school in the town.

My mother was from Vicksburg, and my father was from Natchez, so they were used to a more urban area. This was sort of different for them, particularly for my mother. They adjusted, and liked it. Saint Joseph was interesting because it was an old river town and it had many fine old families there. It was really similar to Natchez in a lot of respects.

My mother's family were from Vicksburg. Her father had the L. J. Parker Machine Works, which was a pretty big enterprise for Vicksburg. He did well, and they had a big Victorian house on Drummond Street that I remember as a child. We'd go visit. My mother was one of five, and she was the next to the oldest. She was a very responsible person. Her father died before she was married, so I never knew him.

My father's family were from Natchez. My father's family had come here about 1830. My great-great-grandfather. My great-grandfather, one of his businesses was plantations in Louisiana. And another was the steamboat business. One of his sons, who was my grandfather, he sent to Louisiana to manage the plantations. And that's where my father was born. But he would come over here [to Natchez] in the winter to go to the Catholic schools. He lived with his grandfather then. As a young man, he worked for his uncle, Oliver, on the steamboat line. They called him Captain Ollie. He lived here in Natchez, but he also had a small house in Vicksburg that just happened to be a few blocks from where my grandmother Parker's house was. So my daddy would spend time up there when he was working on the boats, and that's how he met my mother. So they married and lived here [in Natchez] until I was four.

I was fourteen, and I guess I had led a fairly protected existence up to that time. That was the year we had moved from out on the lake into town [Saint Joseph], which was an adjustment too. Also, I had started school when I was five, and so by the time I was fourteen, I guess I was a junior in high school. Because I graduated when I was sixteen, just was sixteen.

I was studying Latin, and at that time we got two resident priests. Before that we used to have priests that came [only] on Sunday to say Mass. That year we got two resident priests that lived there. I was going around to the priests' house in the afternoons after school to study the Latin responses in the Mass. The first couple of times I went, nothing happened. But then the third time I went by myself. We were sitting in the living room studying the Latin responses, and he was sitting right by me. He put his arm around me. Then he started running his hand in my pocket. Of course it got me excited. Then he said, "Well, why don't we go in my bedroom? I want to show you some of my Latin books." We did. And I followed along. Of course he had gotten me excited. Then the next thing I knew he had my pants down and I was on the bed. He blew me, or whatever you want to call it.

It scared me to death. I was terrified to be alone with the man after that. Not because of the . . . I guess what scared me was because I responded. I basically thought I shouldn't. So it was a guilt trip. The only thing I remember he told me afterward was, "Now, when you confess this, you can't go to me. You have to go to the other priest."

I know that the other priest was aware of what went on. He had to be. Even though it was a small town, and there weren't many Catholics, all the boys in my group happened to be Catholic. It was just one of those happenstance things. So I think it happened to all of them. I took it more seriously than the others did. They used to giggle about it. It affected me in a different way. Maybe because I was the homosexual and was frightened of it. I don't think any of the others were homosexual. I mean they all married and had children and all that. It was terrifying to me at the time. And needless to say, I never did become an altar boy that would go regularly. Now I would serve as an altar boy at Easter and those kind of times when all of us went. A lot of them would go every day. I don't know what happened to them after Mass. It really was wrong. But I guess he went through life doing that, and was never called down about it.

Well I guess in the era that I grew up, basically sex was not discussed. You just sort of learned through the other kids talking about it. Like I said, I had grown up in sort of an isolated existence, since I didn't live in town. In the summers, I would be pretty much by myself, unless I had friends that came to spend the day. I guess you were just taught that you didn't—sex was wrong basically unless you were married. By then, I guess I probably masturbated. I'm sure I did. I know I did. It was a secret thing.

I had one friend—he was later married—and we would spend a lot of the summer together in the water. We had a dugout canoe. It was really sort of idyllic. We'd go around the lake and go to the sandbars. I think the first time it happened was a sandbar. We docked on it and were just swimming around and took off our swimming suits, and the next thing you know, we were playing with one another. It was Russ Archibald. We used to spend Saturdays together, and go out in the woods. He liked to hunt. I didn't. I just sort of went along. Then, we were always on the lake, in a boat, in the summer. It was a very pleasant experience growing up on the lake. It was a beautiful lake.

I read a lot. I didn't play baseball and all that kind of stuff, much to my father's disappointment. I was more artistic, you might say [laughs]. And liked to draw and paint [laughs] or try to. Like I said I started [school] when I was five so I was always the youngest. I really didn't find myself, I guess, until I was a freshman in high school. Then I started making straight A's. Now in grade school I didn't. I was a C student. But then I had a seventh-grade teacher who I later found out was a lesbian. I was very special to her. I think she basically taught me how to study. With her, I started making good grades. And the next year I was in high school. Louisiana had seven elementary and four high [school grade levels]. That was all the grades they had. So in seventh grade I had her, and I was crazy about her.

When I got to college I was only sixteen. Of course I was like a fish out of water because I was younger than most of them. But I could compete in the classroom. So I did study, and I made good grades.

Then I went into the navy right before I was eighteen. It was called D5. Navy air force. They sent me back to college because the flight schools were full. I had already finished four semesters of school, Louisiana Tech in Ruston, when I went in the navy. They sent me back to Tech for two semesters. By then I had had six semesters of school. That fall when I was eighteen I was sent to the seamen's school on Long Island for about three months, in order to go to the midshipmen's school. I transferred to supply corps, because they said the flight schools are always going to be full. I guess I was young too. So I transferred to supply corps, and their midshipmen's school was the Harvard Business School. And in order to enter the January course, I had to leave school in November, and so in that interim time I was stationed on Long Island.

We used to come into New York on the weekends. I went with a couple of other guys. We were living in a big dormitory. So there wasn't any sex. But you know you just sort of found people you palled around with. And we used to go to New York on the weekends. I had an aunt that lived there. She was, I'm sure, my lesbian aunt. She lived at 340 East Fifty-second. And I would see her. But then I'd try to get away to go with my friends. We used to stay at a little hotel that had sort of a dormitory-type arrangement. Of course this was wartime and all the hotels were full. They catered to servicemen. And they had a Turkish bath downstairs, which was very interesting. We'd go down to that. I remember the attendant, who was probably about forty-five. He would offer to dry you off when you got out of the steam room. He'd get sort of personal when he was drying you off [laughs]. Of course the others, it didn't bother them. But it bothered me. It bothered me because it excited me. I liked it.

Then I moved to midshipmen's school at Harvard. Then I got my commission as ensign. I was nineteen by then. That was 1945. So the war ended right after I got my commission, while I was en route. I was between Hawaii and the Philippines when the war ended. But I stayed in the Philippines for a year.

I had a guilt feeling when that priest seduced me at fourteen, but I think mainly because he was a priest. At that point I didn't know what my sexual inclination was. I sort of instinctively knew that what I was doing would meet with disapproval. In the next few years my biggest problem was with the Catholic Church. Because I would confess, if I had an experience, and was told that it was absolutely wrong and that masturbation was wrong. So the confessional gave me a lot of inhibitions and was a real problem to me. Going in the navy probably helped some, because I was out from that sort of influence. Whereas I would still go to Mass, it didn't have me captured, I guess, as much as when I was home.

I didn't have time to read any. The experiences that happened, I just had to deal with them. Later on when I got out of the navy and finished college, which I did when I was twenty-one, then I started reading as much as I could. Trying to get books about homosexuality. Which you know weren't too many at that time, in the late forties. Kinsey Report—god, I bought that as soon as it came out. I think I was about twenty-two then. I had graduated from college, I had been to art school in L.A. for three months, then I came back and was working in Baton Rouge. I bought that book. I think it helped me a lot. Because Kinsey said that it wasn't that unusual, that one out of ten had a homosexual experience, maybe it was higher. That made me feel that I wasn't so abnormal.

But I was never aggressive as far as sex was concerned. I had a lot of sex, when I finally acknowledged it to myself. I'd say I had a fair amount of sex, almost a lot. I usually didn't initiate. I guess I put myself in a position where I would be approached.

Then my mother was killed in an automobile accident when I was twenty-two. I had come back home to work for my family in the automobile business. And I had only been back about a month when my parents and my sister went on an automobile trip to New York and Boston, because my father wanted to go to the World Series, which was both in New York and Boston that year. And she was killed in an automobile accident coming back.

Of course, I was very close to her. It was a big adjustment for me, more so for me than for June or my father. Anyway, at that point, without my mother's looking over my shoulder, so to speak, that was when I made up my mind that I was going to accept that I was a homosexual and live with it and try to do what I wanted. So within a year after—my father remarried in a year and a half—so within a year from that I decided to go back to school and study interior design. I was entering a field where it was fairly well accepted. Expected [laughs]. From then on, I had no problem. When I went back to school—first in Atlanta, then in Houston—I had lots of sex then. I was very busy. And my doorbell rang a lot [laughs].[6]

Histories

New York. San Francisco. Los Angeles. Philadelphia. Washington. Buffalo. Many early works of American lesbian and gay history read like a roster of the United States' most populous cities.[7] Initially an East Coast–West Coast phenomenon, the bicoastal bias prevalent in many modes of cultural production is in this case now a simple matter of mass: recent community studies examine lesbian or gay life in Atlanta, Birmingham, Chicago, Detroit, Flint, Louisville, Memphis, and New Orleans.[8] Where many are gathered there is the historian.

The history of gay people has often mirrored the history of the city. As currently crafted, the predominant theoretical model of American lesbian and gay historiography scripts gay identity and culture formation as linked to capitalist industrialization and urbanization, as most convincingly put forward by John D'Emilio.[9] The four primary areas of focus—desire, identity, community or culture, and political movement—are arrayed in chronological fashion, such that the history of the group becomes an analogue for the individual. That is, as historian Allan Bérubé scrutinizes it, our history is a "coming-out" narrative writ large: Persons of ambiguous sexuality, experiencing inchoate emotions (desire) out there in the hinterlands, move to the city for economic reasons. There they find themselves (identity) and each other (community). They become aware of their collective oppression and act to resist it (movement).[10] This linear, modernist trajectory—at least partially at work in Fitz Spencer's narrative—proves highly descriptive of any number of lives over time, but it also effects a number of exclusions.[11]

What's more, the pattern becomes self-perpetuating. While scholars have identified a genuine historical phenomenon, the disproportionate attention given it reflects certain contemporary realities. Sociological studies show that urban dwellers in general publicly articulate a greater tolerance of sexual nonconformists.[12] Today most practitioners of American lesbian and gay history are strongly self-identified as lesbian and gay. We speak of our own political commitments, our activist scholarship. Such scholarship and such scholars often find homes in urban colleges and universities, where the work garners tentative endorsement; where support from deans and archivists is more forthcoming; where traditional historical documents related to taboo sexualities have been kept and cataloged. Thus, historians in New York write about New York. Graduate students explore histories of the communities around them.

Ours is an opportune and participatory history, as evidenced by one of the most vital methodologies of the enterprise: oral history. Gay persons who have gone through the stereotypical trajectory—from country to city, from "closetedness" to "awareness"—those who are strongly self-identified as gay and highly politicized make *excellent* oral history narrators. They understand the need for such studies. They feel compelled to participate and often do so via urban-centered, community-based oral history projects, some of the earliest of which were undertaken in Boston, Buffalo, San Francisco, and Toronto. Key movement leaders, business owners, literary figures, and celebrities appear in more than one study. Popular history writers follow on the heels of narrators first interviewed by scholars and vice versa.

As part of this exercise of "giving voice" to the marginalized, as life stories are spoken and tape-recorded and played back for one another, a commonplace personal narrative is not just uncovered—an unmediated account ready to be told. It is also produced and reproduced in the process. Through these community efforts, we dialectically tell one another *how* the story goes, the constituent elements of the individual coming-out narrative (for example, "I didn't know before. . . . Now, I know."). Replicated, these stories are then aggregated to form history's coming-out narrative writ large.

What exclusions result? Scott Bravmann warns that race, class, and gender biases can be perpetuated when we look to urban enclaves and traditional gay political and cultural institutions as exemplars of queer life. For example, the physical and social mobility requisite to urbanization and culture formation was more available to whites than blacks, who for most of this country's history were literally bound to place. Nonetheless, in his analysis of sex districts in Chicago and New York, Kevin Mumford makes a compelling case for linking the Great Migration—the early-twentieth-century exodus of black southerners to northern metropolises—to changes in sexual mores in urban culture.[13]

Other racial and ethnic minorities likewise faced checks on mobility and likewise often overcame them—migrating and grouping such that queers felt torn allegiances between home communities and a lesbian/gay culture frequently perceived as white.[14] Women of all colors were similarly restricted in many cases. But historians such as Madeline Davis and Elizabeth Kennedy adeptly demonstrate the possibilities for working-class lesbians who staked claims on the streets and in the bars, while anthropologist Esther Newton well articulates the privilege and access purchased by lesbian and gay home owners and tourists in one resort community outside New York City.[15] Fluidities and rigidities of socioeconomic class functioned across all these groups, either to facilitate or to thwart homosexual interaction. Access to public space, a potential site for encounter, was often prescribed by class.

While these various factors overlap and figure prominently in this work, the regional bias—specifically, the exclusion of rural people from much

American lesbian and gay history—is what I most hope to redress. I don't want to examine individuals who "remained behind" in the "great gay migration." Rather, I attempt to look at persons who chose or found it necessary to make their homes on farms, in the woods, on rivers, in small communities and towns in Mississippi. Recognizing that those lives are never completely "isolated," as Fitz Spencer refers to it, that those with means often move into and again out of cities, I look at densely populated spaces *in relationship* to sparsely populated ones. Circulation is as important as congregation, avenues as important as venues.

While I document the spell, sway, and influence of Jackson (and New Orleans, Memphis, and other cities) on many Mississippians, I argue for an understanding of urban centers not only as centripetal, but also as centrifugal forces—locations from which emanate any number of forays and journeys, many of which are short term, leading to a variety of opportunities for encounters, meetings, and rendezvous. Of course, such spatial movements and interpersonal connections need never involve cities at all.

Indeed, the historiographical concern with identity and culture formation, as tied to cities, must remain a secondary but underlying focus of this study. Though Fitz Spencer valued, as many historians have, the freedom from parents, church, and local community allowed by mobility, other stories emerge if we listen and look closely. By examining desire, not only can we hear the words of those who utilized privilege to craft a gay life away from home, but we also can see the interactions between men who experienced and acted on queer desire within a small, localized realm, men who never took on a gay identity or became part of a gay community or culture. I resist essentialist notions that would find a certain percentage of gay people—a presentist category—among all peoples, across vast expanses of time and place. Instead, I would argue that homosexual desire is possible, to varying degrees, in all persons in all places.[16] I attempt to chronicle the expression of that desire in this particular place across a narrow historical period. And I hope to enhance a theoretical model that at times has denied agency to rural folk, that has assumed that non–urban dwellers can't attach meanings to, can't find useful ways of framing, their nonconforming attractions and behaviors.

For my purposes, human interactions are conceptualized and described less in terms of community or culture, than in terms of networks—often organic and incohesive, but sometimes consciously well structured. For example, a narrowly place-based, sustained, urban gay enclave—in which gay men regularly interacted with other self-identified gay men, mostly patronized gay establishments, and frequently participated in gay community rituals—did not pertain in Mississippi. Instead queer networks stretched across broader expanses of terrain, overcome at times by car or other transport; queer men with stealth and cunning moved in, across, and out of these spaces, local and long distance, usually retaining normative personae in work and leisure routines.

In Mississippi, spatial configurations—the unique characteristics of a rural landscape—forged distinct human interactions, movements, and sites. Gay community, thus, is not simply a *phenomenon* lacking at this place and time. Rather, it is a *concept* lacking in explanatory power, a notion that incompletely and inadequately gets at the shape and scope of queer life. Gay culture certainly existed, increasingly flowed into and out of this region, especially with the reproduction and dissemination of queer texts and images. Gender-nonconforming Mississippians learned about surgical and therapeutic options through the internationally reported Christine Jorgensen story, as mentioned later in this chapter; sexual nonconformists discovered the great range of erotic practice in American culture broadly through 1948's influential Kinsey Report, which not only lent a social science legitimacy to homosexuality but also underscored its prevalence, with fully 37 percent of male respondents reporting at least one homosexual experience to orgasm.[17] Also, Mississippians didn't have to read about urban gay communities: New Orleans was but a short drive away. But generally in Mississippi, as we shall see, a more sporadic, on-the-ground, locally mediated queer experience prevailed. Tracking this experience and integrating the concept of networks with desire and pleasure finally allow a consideration of the human desires for friendship, companionship, love, and intimacy, as well as often unrelated, overtly sexual contact—homo*social* as well as homo*sexual* realms.

A focus on (in this case, male-male) desire points up another current in American lesbian and gay history. It often glosses over the erotic interactions of queer historical subjects. Concerned with identity, culture, and politics, it sometimes politely overlooks the arguably defining feature of the enterprise, homo*sex*.[18] It's as if a desire for respectability, a will to have our besieged scholarship legitimized, prevents us historians of lesbian and gay sexuality, practitioners of queer history, from writing about sex acts. It's as if the present-day experience of AIDS, the scapegoating of gay male promiscuity, and the homophobic attacks on explicit safe sex guidelines give rise to a similar silencing in contemporaneously constructed historical monographs.[19] Moreover, of the four foci—desire, identity, community, politics—desire is the most elusive, in terms of traditional historical methods. There is a conspicuous lack of tools for the historical recuperation, the uncovering, of desire and its expression. As Martin Duberman has said, "I don't think . . . that historians are very good at dealing with motivation. I don't think psychologists are very good at it. Since we get it secondhand, we are probably worse." Like Duberman, I try instead "to let the portrait emerge from a description of the behavior, the career, the events."[20] Mississippi's queer oral history narrators do not shy away from detailing historically situated sexual practices; and neither will this study, in hopes that, among other things, these practices will shed light on the varieties and limits of today's.

As previously noted, the formal geographical and historical parameters of my study are Mississippi from 1945 to 1985. Having found both Allan Bérubé's and John Dittmer's arguments convincing—that is, that World War II was, respectively, a signal moment in the forging of gay worlds and a watershed for the state of Mississippi, marking dramatic socioeconomic change[21]—I begin my period at the close of the war. Again, while hoping to challenge the theoretical framework of culture and identity formation, I acknowledge that the coming together of people—one to one in a rural setting or as part of a massive mobilization like the war effort—enables homosexual activity. Indeed, Fitz Spencer's experiences in rural Louisiana and in New York City support both scenarios. I close my study in 1985 for two reasons. First, the year could be defined as the onset of the AIDS crisis in the state. The demographic characteristics of the plague meant Mississippi felt the effects—that is, experienced large numbers of cases of AIDS—after urban centers such as New York, San Francisco, and Los Angeles.[22] Still, the impact of AIDS in Mississippi was and is enormous, and it has markedly transformed homosexual meanings, practices, and politics there. Second, according to the U.S. Census, 1985 roughly demarcated the culmination of a rural to urban drift in Mississippi, such that its tradition as a predominantly rural society remained secure. Population increases in urban areas were more than offset by population increases in rural areas. A plateau was reached. Whereas 47.3 percent of Mississippians resided in towns, suburbs, and cities in 1980, 47.1 percent did so in 1990. Most Mississippians, it seemed, would continue to live in small communities and in the countryside.[23]

C. Vann Woodward has referred to the South as the "perverse section."[24] Within that section, Mississippi has been seen by a number of observers as the worst of the worst; chroniclers of the civil rights struggles—Branch, Carson, and Kluger, for example—have described the extent of racial bigotry and resistance in Mississippi as unparalleled.[25] One movement volunteer said Mississippi was "a synonym for hell."[26] Statistical figures supported the claims: economic and educational indicators in particular ranked the state dead last on a number of scales over the period.

Indeed, Mississippi held an exotic place in the American imagination—the Third World within the First World.[27]

Yet my purpose is not to describe the most alien people in an alien land. Nor is it to exalt a privileged few who—like the tormented elite male characters of Tennessee Williams's plays[28]—struggled within a glamorized planter-class world that Mart Crowley derides, in this chapter's epigraph, as dripping with magnolias. Too often and too easily, perverse sexuality has figured in outlandish representations of a cartoon South, in which overdrawn, hyperbolic characters play out tortured scenarios against a backdrop of mist and hanging moss. Real life for most is difficult enough in the South. Rather than participate in this mythologizing, my goal is to understand the extraordinary opportunities and challenges facing certain desired and desiring Mississippians, their oppressions and resistances. While highlighting homosexuality and gender insubordination, I want to grapple with all the complexity of the lives of these men. I want, in as broad a way as possible, to understand their changing social, cultural, and political contexts over this particular historical period.

Given the pervasive influence of race in all realms of human endeavor in this place and time, the study engages with the lives of both black and white men and their distinct but interwoven worlds. Power differentials structured by race are shown to prescribe and proscribe particular homosexualities and transgender sexualities. Though lesbians and gays often found a sense of shared concerns and struggles—late in the period especially—the experiences of women-desiring-women and men-desiring-men strike me as sufficiently dissimilar to warrant separate treatment of the latter group, to which I have greater access. Nonetheless, women of all kinds appear as narrators and as vibrant historical agents in this story.

As a framing device, Mississippi is a somewhat arbitrary set of geopolitical boundaries. My study often retreats well within those lines to examine closely specific regions—the Yazoo-Mississippi Delta or the Piney Woods, for example. As already seen, the study spills over state lines—not only into Louisiana, but also Tennessee and Alabama—on other occasions. Yet, in that my primary interest remains the rural, I take Jackson—Chuck Plant's home for a time—as the one city with which to confirm, counter, and add complexity to urban gay histories. To the extent that the Gulf Coast counties of the south, outside New Orleans, and the increasingly suburban counties of the north, outside Memphis, reflect the influences of those cities, I give those areas less attention. The orbs of Bourbon and Beale Streets—the subjects of numerous straight popular accounts—merit their own histories of sexuality.[29]

Desires and Genders

There are remarkable similarities between the early life histories of Chuck Plant, raised in working-class conditions, and Fitz Spencer, a son of privilege. Using almost identical language, they describe a naturalized, seemingly unproblematic sexual interaction between young male friends in the thirties and forties. Fitz Spencer regularly went swimming and—despite his distaste for it—went hunting with his friend Russ, just so they could "play around with one another." Chuck Plant found it so commonplace that he only mentioned in passing his "playmates"—those "that you play around with." *Play*, like *queer*, was an expansive term that could suggest both the sexual and nonsexual behavior of male youths. As several narrators describe it, play regularly and matter-of-factly slipped across this distinction. As Fitz and Chuck both experienced it, play often helped reveal to them the nature of their desires.

Likewise, Ronald Knight describes growing up in Terry, Mississippi, during the 1930s as a bawdy time of male-male sexual *and* gender experimentation. Across the railroad tracks from town, a creek spilled down a small, rocky waterfall into a deep swimming hole, bridged by a fallen tree. There, a number of white boys played together. They swam naked, played leapfrog on the banks, and regularly "ended up corn-holing." On any given occasion, this casual "fool[ing] around" continued until the friends "just got bored with it" and chose other games to play. These "gang bangs" began when the boys "were too young to come," but continued into their late teens, when some of the friends—no longer interested in such sex acts—drifted away from the group. Still, during Ron's "teenage years, there were about five boys in this town of less than a [few hundred] people who were actively gay, really."[30]

Anal sex proved easier after Ron discovered Vaseline. Paradoxically, he remembers hiding the Vaseline from his mother, while nonetheless having no sense of shame around his sex play. Dressing up with a friend in their mothers' clothes was even more public and carefree. The two happily "priss[ed] around town, you know. Everybody thought it was so funny, so cute and all."[31] Even as late as the mid-1960s, the gender experimentation of male youths was accommodated if not encouraged by adults, especially women. Patrick Garvey passed numerous summer days playing in a family friend's dress shop in Brookhaven. "I spent hours dressing the windows and rearranging the costume jewelry and hat displays," he recalls. "As a rather dyed-in-the-wool cross-dresser, [I] also tried on some of the wears. . . . I don't recall as much as a raised eyebrow from the girls. If anything, they egged me on."[32]

While Ron Knight, Fitz Spencer, and Chuck Plant often participated in sexual intercourse with other adolescent males, an encounter with an older man—well remembered as a "first"—marked a turning point for both Fitz and Chuck. And it evoked feelings of guilt and a sense of furtiveness more acute than in Ron's secrecy around Vaseline. Homosex between boys was tolerated, expected even. To continue in homosexual activity as a teen or young adult, however, was more problematic—as was intergenerational interaction.

Fitz's and Chuck's "first" involved an advance by an adult toward a legally underage but postpubescent teen. The encounter between the unnamed Methodist preacher and the aggressive teenager in Jasper County conversely involved the younger's desire for the elder. Or might we reasonably speculate that the Methodist revivalist, like Fitz's priest, initiated sexual activity and subsequently concocted the story for his friend and colleague Ted Herrington, in case the teenager later came forward with accusations against him? Just over a decade prior, around 1940, the Methodist Church quietly transferred a young minister to California after allegations that as a camp counselor at Roosevelt State Park near Morton, he had inappropriately approached a youth.[33] Though the case was not widely known, those within the clergy probably would have been familiar with it. At a minimum, the revivalist likely would have been aware that—around the very same time of his preaching engagement in Jasper County—a fellow Methodist pastor from Mississippi was arrested in Atlanta on sodomy charges after engaging in oral sex with a man in a public rest room. As a result, Robert Billings lost his assignment as director of youth work for the church's south Georgia conference.[34]

This is not to suggest that young Mississippians were not capable of sexual advances on older men, that they did not want advances from older men, nor that such intergenerational activity could only be exploitive. Indeed, many young Mississippians actively sought out older men for sex. From the age of fourteen, Pascagoula native Ben Childress looked for "hot guys in their twenties and thirties" at local cruising areas during the 1970s.[35] In referring to the 1930s and 1940s, Fitz Spencer's partner later in life, Texas native Bill MacArthur, lamented, "I don't know where all the child molesters were when I was a child. Because I would have loved every minute of it. I didn't meet a child molester, unfortunately. At Catholic [summer] camp [in Texas], we did see these two priests have sex together one night. The other kids thought it was funny. I thought it was fabulous. I knew I was gay."[36]

It was during MacArthur's childhood that popular media increasingly equated adult male homosexuals with child molesters.[37] Fostered by cultural anxieties over youth and dating, automobiles and lack of parental control, such stereotypes followed on the heels of changes in age-of-consent laws affecting young women. During the early twentieth century, jurisdictions like Mississippi raised the legal age of female discretion from ten to eighteen.[38] In a state where many women had traditionally married in their teens—indeed, once had legal sanction to marry as preteens—the intergenerational aspect of some homosexual intercourse carried little added taboo. Queers willing to break the sodomy statute, a felony, often seemed not to care that they also crossed generational bounds, even after age-of-consent laws were amended to cover not just young "girls" but any "child."[39]

Whereas Chuck Plant's experience with the older motorist made him "nervous," Fitz Spencer's encounter with the priest was "terrifying." It "scared [him] to death." The two youths' different reactions suggest some of the complex and contradictory contours of desire in midcentury Mississippi. They also help describe both men in relationship to three primary institutions of community life—church, school, and home. Interestingly, both men felt they were lackadaisical students, though particular female teachers were powerful influences in their lives and, in the case of Fitz, helped make him a better student. The teacher Fitz later "found out was a lesbian" and his "lesbian aunt" opened up possibilities for him within the otherwise restrictive realms of educational and familial systems. But especially for Fitz, a Catholic in an overwhelmingly Protestant state, church, school, and home represented sites of contestation. His homosexual desires were explicitly forbidden by the church; they had to be confessed as sins. That he had engaged in homosexual activity with a member of the church hierarchy—further, his tutor in Latin—left him in an ambiguous position. While officially church and school seemed to condemn, their agent—the priest—lived out Fitz's desires.

Chuck Plant is the only person I interviewed who failed to mention the church.[40] He never discussed attending, nor did he express an understanding of homosexuality shaped by religious thinking. His family structure— namely, his adoption by an aunt, who alone raised him—allowed him a freedom that others lacked. Answerable only to her, he could frequently and easily make excuses for time spent away from the house, out from under her watchful eyes.

It is significant that Fitz Spencer "made up his mind . . . to accept" a gay identity after his mother died. Though he doesn't say it directly, he clearly felt her presence a constraining force. She wouldn't approve, he suggests. She couldn't understand. Her passing made the point moot. Combined with increasing residencies outside the region, in large cities like New York, Los Angeles, Houston, and Atlanta, Spencer found more and more opportunities for homosexual encounters, and he felt increasingly at ease about acting on them.

The stories of Chuck Plant and Fitz Spencer are in many respects familiar to us. They bespeak the unhappy, furtive side of difference, the sense of isolation and repression that many of us recall all too well. Chuck Plant felt, despite his interactions with other boys and men like that, that he was "the only one on earth." He recognizes in retrospect that *many* felt as he did. Fitz Spencer harbored considerable self-loathing, terror even, at the notion of same-sex intercourse. The church in particular and the fear of parental reproach fueled his guilt—indeed, a very common emotion among young men experiencing queer desire.

But Ron Knight's adolescence and young adulthood fly in the face of these familiar and at times clichéd narratives of sexual difference in the countryside. (And, indeed, Plant's and Spencer's own stories grow more complicated as they are elaborated in subsequent chapters.) Ron and his friend not only dressed up in women's clothes but paraded around town, eliciting not sympathy nor punishment but delightedness and endorsement. Of course, Ron's class position as the son of a wealthy white landowner and businessman shaped societal reactions to him, likely giving him more leeway for gender transgression. And yet he also participated in a markedly open, cross-class (but racially exclusive) network of boys who enjoyed queer sex.

Some would opt out of this network when adult expectations forced heterosexual dating and matrimony. Still, for Ron Knight and for men of all races and classes, it is clear that parents, married relatives, and other adult heterosexual couples were *not* "their only model[s] of intimate erotic relationships," as historians sometimes assume. Queer youths were *not* "unaware of sexual alternatives . . . [with] no encouragement for same-sex eroticism." Further, "resources even for naming their desires" were *not* meager.[41] Gang bangs and corn-holing, while linguistically unscientific and not altogether intimate in practice, nonetheless loomed large in the minds of those seeking sexual options. The sanctioned sexual and gender experimentation of boys and young men in small towns and rural communities, as well as the clandestine but commonplace adult and intergenerational queer acts, provided a tradition with which men like that could craft viable alternatives (or complements) to the marriage paradigm.

Rickie Leigh Smith: I was born November 16, 1939, in Smith County, which is about forty, fifty miles southeast of Jackson. The town was Mize, although we lived out in the country. Grew up on a farm. Like the Waltons. It was a close-knit family. Two brothers and three sisters.

Wonderful childhood. Great childhood, great parents. Good solid values. There was nothing really unusual too much about it. Just perfectly normal kind of childhood. The only thing was this gender problem. That was the major thing. Of course at that time, I was too young and naive. I didn't understand what was going on.

When I was growing up, this was the age of sexual repression. You didn't ask or talk about sexual matters. It was all hidden or suppressed or just not talked about. In the early fifties when the Christine Jorgensen case came out, everybody was talking about it. Immediately something clicked in my mind. I identified with her. I was just so fascinated with her. I didn't understand why until years later. I didn't know what was going on in my head. I really did not know. All I knew was, when I was a child, all I wanted to do was be with the little girls and play girl games. I did not want to play with the boys. I wasn't interested in sports and rough-and-tumble things. I wanted to play with dolls.

I was very feminine. And of course I suffered at the hands of other kids, my peer group, because they constantly made fun of me because of the way I sat and talked and acted. So I tried to hide this. But the need is so strong to express that, that it's going to come out some way or another. It's that constant battle. I remember my mother—very, very concerned about it. They didn't know what to do about it. Some people advised them they needed to administer physical punishment to me to make me stop playing with dolls. But I thought at the time how cruel that was. I don't ever recall being punished physically for having those feelings.

I remember cross-dressing. I'd sneak around and put on women's clothes, and play in women's clothes occasionally. [Age] five, six, seven, like that. I would just get very stern disapproving looks from my parents if they caught me doing it. [We would play] childhood games, cowboys and Indians, the usual stuff. I always had to be the girl. I was Dale Evans, never Roy Rogers, you understand. I remember my mother or father would say I should be more like my older brother because he was so masculine. [My brother] would try to get me into fights with other kids my age, other boys, try to toughen me up.

Second and third year [of elementary school] they wanted to hold me back both years. My father wouldn't let them. I seemed to have some problems there. [Other students asked,] "Why do you sit like you do? You have fingers like a little girl. Why do you play with girls all the time? And [why do] you want to play with dolls?"

I can remember having erotic dreams about men when I was a child. That disturbed me. I just remember this intense attraction to men, intense attractions, sexual attractions to men, before I really understood what sex was all about. So that was disturbing to me then.

When I was about nine or ten, there was a little boy that lived next door to us. There was some homosexual-type behavior between us. More in the nature of curiosity, experimentation. It didn't leave any lasting imprint on me. Just playing together. We would undress and just fool around with each other. He would want me to perform certain acts [oral sex], and I wouldn't do it, because something didn't feel right about it. I was scared. I didn't know how to handle it. I couldn't, I wouldn't suck. I felt physically excited, but I couldn't handle it. I think he and I were distantly related, maybe distant cousins on my father's side. When I was a child, it was the only sexual experience with another person. The only one.

My self-image, my self-esteem was so low by the time I reached my teens, it couldn't have been much worse. I knew nothing, zero, nothing, about sexual matters. I didn't know why I had these feelings. I was made to feel bad about them. So, it was all very negative.

My father owned about sixty acres. He farmed cotton, corn. We worked. At the time, I thought I hated it. But now I look back and wish I could go back to it. In the summertime, going to the creek, going swimming in the creek, walking to town to go to the movies on Saturday, to the matinees. We did chores. We all worked very hard. Feeding farm animals, working in the fields, from five or six years old, until I was well into my teens. My father stopped farming when I was about fifteen or sixteen, except for having a garden every year. He had some livestock. And he did other things. He had another job. By that time, nobody was growing cotton anymore. It wasn't profitable.

When I entered puberty, I had a terrible case of acne. A horrible case of chronic acne developed on my face, back, arms, chest. I still carry the scars from that today. That affected me just as bad as the transsexual situation. That compounded it, made it worse. It lowered my self-esteem. Had no confidence. I never dated in high school, was never interested in anything like that. I got crushes on boys. And that scared me. I didn't know how to deal with it. I didn't dare talk to anybody about it.

When I got on up in my teens, I still was very naive. I had never heard the word—well we didn't use the word—*gay* then. They had all the usual derogatory terms. I think I was like a senior in high school when I first found out about gay people. I heard some boys talking about it: "This guy come on to me, and he wanted to you-know-what," dah-de-dah-de-dah. I thought, My god, do men do that to each other? I thought, Oh this must be what I am. OK. That must be what's wrong with me. That's what clicked in my mind. But I didn't tell anybody, of course. I kept it to myself.

One case was a nightmare. I was in ninth grade. This guy moved to our school from around Magee, Mississippi. He seemed so much more mature and older than the rest of us. I adored him. I worshiped the ground he walked on. I could not get enough of him. I was around him as much as I could. He was tall, but he had an air of maturity about him for his age. He couldn't have been more than fifteen or sixteen. He liked me. He was very nice to me. I developed a really strong crush on this person.

I finally got up the courage to write him a letter, to explain these feelings to him. I put it in his locker at school. I don't remember if I signed my name or not. I think so. That was a bad mistake. It was the need to express that, to talk to somebody. I was telling him in this letter how I wished I were a girl. I didn't realize in my mind that for all practical purposes I already was. He didn't find the letter. I don't know if he ever actually saw it. It fell out of his locker and was on the floor of the high school corridor there. One of the guys in my class found the letter, picked it up and read it, and spread it all over the school. So I was the disgrace of the entire school. A very traumatic experience. The person that it was addressed to never said anything to me about it. He never made an issue of it. His name was Monroe.

I was called to the principal's office. I was dressed down thoroughly about this. The principal wasn't rude or mean to me: "Did you write this?" And I said, "Yes, but it was just kind of like a joke. I didn't mean any harm." So he kind of let it go. He didn't want to make a big issue about it. My mama and dad found out about it. My mother chewed me out royally. She was very upset about it. But it all died down. The boy moved when I was in tenth grade. I was depressed about that for a while. When I was in high school, that was the only major attraction to someone else. I graduated from high school at seventeen. Very naive.[42]

Rickie Leigh Smith—born Ricky Lee Smith—views her boyhood attraction to other boys as a "gender problem," suggesting that the taxonomy of sexual orientation, specifically the category of gay male, is not applicable. A biological male according to her birth certificate, she was, she clearly states, sexually drawn to other young males. But how did her gender behavior delimit and frame her access to queer sex? How did Fitz Spencer's or Chuck Plant's gendered presentations of self open up or close off prospects for queer sex?

To understand the meaning of transgender as it relates to lesbians and gay men (homosexuals) and bisexuals requires an understanding of today's popular and theoretical distinctions between sex and gender. Biological sex—legal and medical designation of individual human beings as male or female—is deceptively absolute and consequently resistant to change, even though there are perhaps as many as two in one hundred persons who don't fall squarely into either category, including intersexuals—individuals once called hermaphrodites—as well as those with chromosomal or hormonal "anomalies."[43] Gender, according to theorist Judith Butler, is akin to a performance. It is the set of predominant societal expectations around sex, such as the so-called masculine and feminine behaviors, that are scripted, that we rehearse, that we inculcate through constant repetition.[44] Boys do this; girls do that. Gender, therefore, can be considered more malleable than sex.

The term *transsexual*, which Rickie today uses to describe herself, and the term *transvestite*, which will prove significant in chapter 7, preceded

Ricky Lee Smith, age seventeen, 1957. Courtesy of Rickie Leigh Smith.

today's notion of transgender, often used as an umbrella term for both and for much more. Since the late-nineteenth-century conceptualization of a male homosexual or invert as "a female caught in a male body," transsexualism had become a distinct and separate category by the mid-twentieth century, used to refer to anyone who wanted to alter or modify his or her biological sex or, more to the point, the *markers* of biological sex such as genitalia, breasts, body hair, musculature—hormonally, surgically, or through some combination of the two.[45] Extensive media coverage in 1953 of Christine (formerly George) Jorgensen—"the first American man to undergo a 'sex-change' operation"—greatly increased public awareness of the availability of sex-reassignment surgery. And it greatly influenced Ricky Lee Smith.[46]

Transvestitism, Marjorie Garber shows, names any range of gender nonconforming activity. Indeed, it occasions a "category crisis." But it ordinarily referred in this time and place to someone who cross-dressed—perhaps for sexual pleasure—without ever taking on a permanent or primary identity as someone of the opposite sex. Drag queens, for example, typically had stage names but often did not choose to live day to day as members of the opposite sex, as women. Transvestitism thus was more explicitly connected to performance in the nontheoretical sense, to the stage—as in the radio, television, and stage acts of Jack Benny, Milton Berle, Flip Wilson, and Little Richard, all wildly popular in Mississippi and throughout the United States.[47] As we shall see, Rickie performed in drag at a popular gay bar in Jackson at the same time that she considered hormone therapy and surgical options and increasingly identified as transsexual.

But as a youth in Smith County, Ricky initially was marked as a boy with girlish ways, even a girlish physiognomy. Fitz, in contrast, sometimes went along with traditionally inscribed masculinist pursuits, cultivating manly styles and preferences of his own. Though he didn't like to hunt, he said, he went hunting to be near his friend. Further, he developed distinct predilections in friends and partners: "I never did like nelly queens." Men like *that*— those with markedly nonconforming gender presentations—often were not desired by men like that. Thus, even within the related and intertwined worlds of gender and sexuality, conformity in one often facilitated deviancy in another. For Fitz, though he was "never aggressive as far as sex was concerned," he was inscribed as masculine and he "had a lot of sex." Though he "usually didn't initiate," he "put [him]self in a position where [he] would be approached"—gendered spheres such as the navy, the Turkish bath.

Due in large part to gender nonconformity, Ricky Lee Smith often felt alone and sheltered. Smith sees herself then as cut off from vital vectors of knowledge regarding transsexualism—hopelessly naive, an innocent. Her hindsight at times seems incongruous. "You didn't ask or talk about sexual matters," and yet "everybody was talking"; young Ricky "heard boys talking." It was a "wonderful childhood" that was "all very negative"; he "suffered" and was "scared." Unlike Ron Knight's, Ricky's cross-dressing brought surveillance, threats of punishment, "disapproving looks." "At the time, I thought I hated [farm life]. But now," she says from her mobile home in a working-class town near Jackson, "I look back and wish I could go back to it."

Such is the power, Raymond Williams suggests, of a prevailing cultural myth that casts "the transition from a rural to an industrial society . . . as a kind of fall, the true cause and origin of our social suffering and disorder." The "structure of feeling" that dwells even in the person of Ricky/ie, a thoughtful queer boy with a painful past, reflects partially a tenacious "perpetual retrospect to an 'organic' or 'natural' society."[48] But the retrospective gaze is not only temporal—a nostalgia for a golden age located somewhere in history. It is also spatial, played out at infinite numbers of historical moments in the dialectic of the country and the city:

On the country has gathered the idea of a natural way of life: of peace, innocence, and simple virtue. On the city has gathered the idea of an achieved centre: of learning, communication, light. Powerful hostile associations have also developed: on the city as a place of noise, worldliness and ambition; on the country as a place of backwardness, ignorance, limitation.[49]

Gay writing has often imbibed a neat half-portion of these ideas. If not always explicitly, many late-twentieth-century gay tales of the city, fictional and historical, implicitly have borrowed on and extended the hostile associations of the country and the hospitable associations of the city. Under such representations, the dirt-road-cum-boulevard to gay self-actualization —to identity, community, and political movement—begins in the dark hinterlands of naïveté and deprivation, and ends, happily, in the bustling corridors of wisdom and illumination. As one dissatisfied writer puts it, "Gay is a grand narrative—come out of the darkness into the light."[50] The stories of physical migration from rural to urban spaces employ the same metaphors as those describing the individual ideological shift of the coming-out narrative. This tradition might well benefit from a dialogue with Rickie Leigh Smith, whose worldview can encompass all the complexities and contradictions of these conceptions and can further—as we shall see— craft new ways of thinking about life and landscape, gender and sexuality, in rural, urban, suburban, and exurban worlds.

Silences

If historians seem skilled at recounting past events—assumptions (or "facts") that can be corroborated (or "proven") by contemporaneously produced written documents—we are less adept at explaining the human motivations behind historical incidents. If today I can scarcely understand my own nebulous, slippery, contradictory impulses, how can I assess the motivations of someone else decades ago? Of all human emotions or feelings, how can I explain desire? How can I describe someone else's experience of it, given the gaps in the so-called record, given the silences then sustained in the historical literature?

Ed Foreman remembers experiencing his "first feelings for another boy" in 1961 when he was four years old. A fifteen-year-old cousin, Stan, visited Ed's home outside Taylorsville, where Ed's father raised beef cattle and farmed soybeans, corn, wheat, "whatever was profitable." Stan, Ed, Ed's sister Jill, and several young friends were all piled on Jill's bed as Stan read stories from a book. Ed now has only distant recollections of the precise emotions, but he vividly recalls wanting to be inside Stan's clothes—*with Stan*, between Stan and his shirt.[51]

Equally vivid, Randall Sawyer's memory of desire in his early teens focuses on his friend Jimmy, specifically his "hard body." After some initial awkwardness, the two had sex regularly during the mid-1970s. What at

first for Randall was a visual sensation—an unspoken admiration, a stirring for Jimmy's physique—became an all-too-tactile phenomenon: Jimmy
"screwed" him. Randall found it both pleasurable and painful, "because he
was huge." There was frequently "hurting, bleeding, pain."

Also, there was secrecy. Family members were all about. Five or six
households of relatives, headed by Randall's parents, aunts and uncles,
grandfather, and others, sharecropped the same tract—a Mr. Giordano's
land near Edwards, Mississippi, thirty-five to forty-five acres altogether.
Even when occasionally left alone, Randall found that schoolwork and
chores left little time for sex. Though a "small guy"—"teased" and "picked
on," he says, for helping his mother in the kitchen, for buying himself a Ken
doll at Christmas—Randall pulled his weight on the farm. He fed the
horses, cows, and chickens; got the eggs; harvested cucumbers; tended the
cotton and soybeans; picked up pecans; and fished in the pond for catfish,
bream, and bass.[52] His hectic schedule precluded frequent opportunities for
same-sex intercourse; his circumstances precluded frequent discussions of
same-sex desire.

But these two scenarios suggest that as we look at the past, at moments
of desire, silence can not be equated with *absence*. Historical projects, by
their very methodology, tend to access and privilege the spoken (or written) over the unspoken (or unwritten). Thus is presented a challenge in
queer history: to read the silence. Such reading, in order to offset the
multitiered biases against queer historical inquiry, must assume from the
beginning the *presence* of queer desire.

The two scenarios and the many others that precede and follow them are
meant to lend support to Valerie Traub's assertions that "like all forms of
desire, homoerotic desire is implicit within all psyches."[53] I share Traub's
view that what we now call homosexual desire is ever present and ever
possible, across time and place. Rightly, Traub offers several caveats, however, that bear repeating:

> I do not mean to dispute the evidence that homosexuality in the modern
> sense (as a distinct mode of *identity*) came into being under the auspices of
> sexological discourse. Nor do I mean to imply, as some "essentialists" do,
> that the "experience of homoeroticism" is unproblematically available to the
> historically inquiring eye—that it exists in some pure form, unmediated by
> language, political discourse, and the process of historical narrativiza-
> tion. . . .[54]

Yet, she implies, it—or *something*—exists, if not "in some pure form," as
she puts it. What's important is how it exists in varied forms, how it is expressed in varied ways, how it shapes and is shaped by culture:

Whether and how [homoerotic desire] is given cultural expression, whether and how it is manifested as anxiety, is a matter of culturally contingent signifying practices. What is culturally specific is not the fact or *presence* of desire toward persons of the same gender, but the meanings that are attached to its expression, and the attendant anxieties generated by its repression.[55]

Valerie Traub is careful to speak of historical specificity because the period about which she writes—early modern England—greatly predates the historiographical location in time of the emergence of the modern homosexual, usually ascribed to the late nineteenth century and usually attributed, in part, to particular medical discourses. To believe that homoerotic desire is ever present is not to believe that such desire remains fixed or culture-independent over time. Social constructionism contributes most to the history of sexuality, as Eve Sedgwick describes it, by "radically defamiliarizing and denaturalizing not only the past and the distant, but the present."[56]

Traub's project of specificity, like Sedgwick's, is temporal. To upset notions of past sexualities has the potential to destabilize present ones—and, further, to question our ability to know, now and then. How homosexual desire might be manifested at any one time in vastly different *places* should be of equal concern, as Sedgwick only hints at with her reference to the "distant." Traub shows social construction theorists as focused on—Sedgwick might say obsessed with—a particular historical moment, the late nineteenth century; but neither addresses precise spatial dynamics.

Because of particularities of place, rural Mississippi in the 1950s might have been just as foreign to this dominant historiographical narrative—the coming-out narrative writ large—as early modern England was. More to the point, early modern English configurations of sexualities, like rural Mississippi manifestations, should be examined on their own terms—to the extent those terms can be articulated, understood, and comparatively assessed, silences and all. When compared to the midcentury United States as a whole, at least as thus far described by historians of sexuality, what is apparent is that gay identity in Mississippi (surely as elsewhere) existed alongside multiple queer desires that were not identity based or identity forging. Such desires should not be labeled or maligned as premodern; they don't demonstrate that Mississippi was backward or that it lagged *behind* other regions in fostering gay community. They simply specify certain lived experiences, neither inherently positive nor negative. These desires and experiences of midcentury Mississippians might serve to upset and denaturalize what is often universalized in the scholarly circles of the Western world as "homosexuality in the modern sense."

To that end, one pertinent category of analysis in Mississippi would certainly be race. How might Ed's story and Randall's story be construed under repressive regimes of strict racial segregation? How might their stories be construed *differently* under different racial codings: if Ed and his partner are black and Randall and his partner are white? Or if, as is the case, Ed and partner are white and Randall and partner are black? How is desire "given cultural expression," to use Traub's phrase, in these settings? How, in short, can we examine the intersection of race, desire, and discourse? While these questions must await fuller discussion in the chapters to come, the two stories already imply that just as the *presence* of same-sex desires should be presumed from the start, so too *differences* in same-sex desires should be presumed across discrete cultural groups—especially across races in Mississippi, and attendant issues of physical and socioeconomic mobility and public articulation of identity.

Traub's use of the word *expression* is interesting, in that Rickie Leigh Smith describes a near compulsive incitement to discourse, "the need to express that, to talk to somebody," to write a note to her beloved, a note that held nightmarish consequences. Yet discourse is far more than speech or text—and, it should be added, far less than the totality of lived experience. Indeed, silences and silencing seem as much a part of the shaping of anxieties around homosexuality in Mississippi as expressive or repressive languages and vocabularies. If, as Fitz says, "basically sex was not discussed," how was it understood or manifested? How did Mississippians *conceive* of sexuality or, as is assumed, condemn *homo*sexuality if, as Rickie asserts, "you didn't ask or talk about sexual matters," if they were "all hidden or suppressed or just not talked about"?

Philosopher Michel Foucault convincingly overturns what he calls the "repressive hypothesis"—the idea that sex in Western cultures has been marked by (a progressively eased) repression over time. Deceptively and ironically, he says, our society "speaks verbosely of its own silence, takes great pains to relate in detail the things it does not say. . . ."[57] "Around and apropos of sex," says Foucault, "one sees a veritable discursive explosion."[58] Indeed, Fitz Spencer's experience of the confessional—recounting his sexual activities to "the other priest," naming them as sins—illustrates what Foucault sees as a key system in the discursive production of sexualities. The more typical southern variant of the Catholic confessional might be the well-thought-out, well-planned, but hush-hush dismissal of accused homosexuals from Protestant organizations, epitomized by the Methodist youth director defrocked in Georgia.

But what about silence? Why do so many of Mississippi's oral history narrators refer to it again and again? Why do they conceive of the past in this way? Whether understood as a non-polar-opposite part of discourse, problematically subsumed within discourse, or as a technique somehow outside of discourse, silences are best illuminated by Foucault in their multiple, multifaceted states.[59] Also helpful, Foucault's mention of "strategies" implies the importance of will and motivation. Yes, individuals and institutions are sometimes forced into silence based on power relations, but they also might choose to utilize silences or silencing. These strategies are evident among queer men in Mississippi, and they help us reconceive silence, which too often is portrayed either as a cowardly denial of gay identity or as a successful institutional suppression of gayness.

First, silencing need not be unidirectional. That is, silence should be seen as something more than a state *imposed* by dominant groups or authorities on subordinate groups.[60] For example, though Fitz understood homosexual acts as sins because priests told him to confess them, many churches within and outside the predominant evangelical Protestantism in midcentury Mississippi were remarkably silent with regard to homosexuality. On either side of the racial divide within the United Methodist Church, pastors report they never addressed the topic in sermons and never heard it addressed by colleagues, though derogatory references to homosexuality appear in both Old and New Testaments.[61] Similarly, a Cleveland native, whose husband pastored both Methodist and Episcopal congregations in northeast Mississippi, says she never heard homosexuality denounced or even mentioned from the pulpit.[62] Two women who grew up in Baptist churches during the 1950s and later self-identified as lesbians report a dearth of church proscriptions. As Betty Dudley says, "I don't remember anyone ever saying that it was horrible or wrong."[63] Though Victoria Bolton intuited that "everything I did was a sin" as a child and teenager, sermons she heard in Magee and Columbia never broached homosexuality specifically.[64] Instead, like most Mississippians, she deduced that homosexuality must be wrong, given that premarital and extramarital sex *were* expressly forbidden by church leaders.

Perhaps queer and questioning youths like Betty, Victoria, and Ricky put school administrators and church officials, concerned as they were with propriety, in uncomfortable and sometimes untenable positions. This discomfort likely increased in direct proportion to gender-nonconforming behavior, which typically was, by definition, more readily legible than a proclivity toward homosexual intercourse. A highly public reckoning with these problems might only exacerbate them, community leaders seem to have reasoned. Consequently, in dealing with Ricky's note—discursive *proof* of homoerotic desire, a written *text*—the school principal "let it go." Monroe, the boy Ricky had a crush on, "never said anything . . . about it, . . .

never made an issue of it." In this sense, Ricky had the power to silence those around him—his potential adversary *and* his would-be lover.

Second, self-imposed silences by persons in positions of power often purposefully or unwittingly enabled homosexual practices. Or at the least, they foreclosed the likelihood of censure for homosexual persons. The Methodist counselor accused of making a pass at a camper was quietly shipped off to California, where he may well have continued to engage in homosexual activity. Having met with only the mild reproach of the politely hushed revivalist, a powerful authority figure, the hitchhiker in Jasper County likely made his desires known to others over time.

In another case, silencing and frivolity combined to accommodate one conspicuous local bachelor. After his brief tenure in Jasper County, Methodist minister Ted Herrington was assigned to a charge in neighboring Jones County—again a small rural church. Soon Buchanan, a gentlemanly insurance agent in his fifties, invited him to lunch. The two went to lunch again and again. Buchanan was not seeking pastoral counseling; he didn't attempt to sell an insurance policy—the interest wasn't professional. Initially unaware, Brother Herrington welcomed his new friend—*until* some teenagers in the church choir made fun of him and told him suggestively, "We saw you with ol' Buck." Buchanan, it seemed, had something of a reputation in Jones County. But the choir members, Herrington recalls, said nothing expressly derogatory about it. They just "seemed to laugh it off." And Herrington, soon to be married, fended off any additional overtures. When Buck continued telephoning the boardinghouse where Ted lived, Ted had the landlady instruct him not to call again.[65] While the teenagers' laughter and Herrington's aversion clearly indicate a marginalization of homosexuality, they also suggest a lack of serious retribution. As historian Pete Daniel has written, despite a trademark xenophobia and propensity to violence, "Southerners often accepted (or forgave) almost any eccentricity so long as it posed no threat to the established order."[66]

Finally, rural southerners experiencing male-male desire utilized silence as a resistance strategy. In many cases, silence not only deflected the sometimes harmful repercussions of disclosure, it created psychic space for individual contemplation and affirmation—and, on occasion, action. While Ed's silence provided space for fantasy, Randall's secrecy made sex with Jimmy possible.

Whether still figuring things out or highly self-aware,[67] queer boys—on their own and in pairs, singles and couples, ones and twos—felt desire and thought it through. Not simply momentary manifestations or unthinking impulses, queer desires permeated ongoing internal dialogues. Again, as Rickie remembers:

I heard some boys talking about it: "This guy come on to me, and he wanted to you-know-what," dah-de-dah-de-dah. I thought, My god, do men do that to each other? I thought, Oh this must be what I am. OK. That must be what's wrong with me. That's what clicked in my mind. But I didn't tell anybody, of course. I kept it to myself.

Whereas Ricky heard others describe homosexual acts and privately found their snide remarks useful, Bill MacArthur witnessed the acts with friends: "We did see these two priests have sex together one night. The other kids thought it was funny. I thought it was fabulous. I knew I was gay." Bill's momentary silence allowed personal affirmation as he watched his desires being carried out. Further, his silence well positioned him to observe the boys around him—to locate adversaries, to identify potential allies. And, as for so many others in the rural South, it safeguarded him from individuals and ideas that might work counter to his aims.

HOMOSEXUAL MEN IN THE United States were hardly the sick, self-absorbed, psychotic perverts suggested by most midcentury popular media.[68] Likewise, men like that in Mississippi, though often deeply conflicted, were hardly the ignorant, un-self-possessed hayseeds assumed by some late-twentieth-century American urbanites. Quite the contrary, they were savvy in their methods, skilled in their machinations. Experiencing desire, they pondered the best means for its expression. They wrote their desire; they spoke it. They sheltered their desire; they sometimes used its power to silence others. For individuals in rural spaces—connected to others through home, church, and school; work, consumption, and leisure—desire pervasively structured the experience of everyday life. Within complex systems of race and class, gender and sexuality, queer Mississippians explored their desires in relationship to landscape, ready to locate the critical *where* of sex.

Sites

PLACE IS SIMULTANEOUSLY a physical and social
phenomenon. As I drive through central Mississippi, over smooth, low hills, I'm likely to notice
the trees—cedars and oaks, magnolias and pecans—along the older roads; quick-growth pines
on the interstate. I see them clearly in the winter,
on cool, crisp days. In summer they blur in the
oppressive heat and haze. On my way home to
Brandon—to my parents' home, that is—passing through Pelahatchie, I recall watching Johnny
Carson on the *Tonight Show* with Mom and Dad
in the seventies. Somehow, perhaps because of
the unusual name, Johnny fixated on Pelahatchie
(pee-luh-HATCH-ee) and often made it the butt
of his jokes. He wouldn't be caught dead in Pelahatchie, he once said. And if he had occasion
to fly over it as he jetted around the country,
he'd be sure to go to the lavatory and flush. In
Pelahatchie, people fumed. I remember it vividly. Little wonder Mississippians were defensive about their place in the world.

As I look at my roadmap, these memories slip.
I'm simply on a road, the symbols tell me—either Highway 80 or Interstate 20. I'm moving
westward, between two municipalities, in the
county known as Rankin, in the state known as
Mississippi. These are political entities formed
by governmental officials, maintained through
laws and jurisprudence, subdivided into tracts
for individual ownership (I notice the barbed-
wire fences). So these are also economic entities.
And they are social and cultural locales, places

to which people attach meanings, associations, experiences, feelings—and allegiances.

Space is produced and reproduced over time through complex forces seemingly beyond the control of any one individual. This is "your place," society dictates. You should "know your place." Such scripts shape and are shaped by gender, as in the sexist declamation "A woman's place is in the home"; by race, as in the place to which Richard Wright felt the white South had assigned him; and by class, your place in society, your position—lower or higher—on the metaphorical, hierarchical socioeconomic ladder.

The mutually constitutive categories of normativity and difference, normalcy and deviance, likewise shape and are shaped by place. That is, certain acts and behaviors are acceptable in one place, unacceptable in another. What's right here may be wrong there. Notions of propriety and transgression thus shift with the site—especially across spaces we call public and private.

And yet homosexual activity in Mississippi during the post–World War II period was transgressive everywhere. With the sodomy law, legislators had criminalized sexual intercourse between persons of the same sex. Regardless of where it occurred, homosex was illegal. In language that remained unchanged since its initial adoption in 1839, the statute against "unnatural intercourse" held that "every person who shall be convicted of the detestable and abominable crime against nature committed with mankind or with a beast, shall be punished by imprisonment in the penitentiary for a term of not more than ten years."[2] The public—the people, through their elected representatives—expanded the public sphere. Wherever it was practiced—indoors, outside, at home, in the woods, on the streets— homosex was a concern of the state. State intervention thereby helped break down the public/private distinction, and queer sex pervaded spaces traditionally understood as public.

Place affected sexual meanings and sexual practices in other ways. Some sites enabled homosex; others hindered it. Conversely, homosex altered sites. Men contemplating queer desire and men engaged in queer sex remade spaces for queer purposes. Their imprints and gestures, their movements and actions, modified particular places, contributed to the ongoing evolution of the built environment. Queer lives were constructed by place, as they likewise constructed place.

As I attempt to examine history—change over time—as forged and experienced by queer Mississippians, I try to remember that change happens across place as well. As Edward Soja puts it, "Life-stories have a geography too; they have milieux, immediate locales, provocative emplacements which affect thought and action."[3] Also, these geographies have life stories.

Within ever-shifting landscapes are human beings at work, modifying and adjusting their physical and psychic places. Distinct locales in the Mississippi landscape forged attitudes and sexualities as yet unexamined by queer historians. Queer Mississippians—with attitudes and sexualities of their own—changed Mississippi. They transformed the sites they occupied, the sites through which they moved, and they remade themselves, marking off space for insurgent conceptions of sex and everyday life.

Mississippi

How is it that different people are made to feel united? How are they brought together around a shared sense of common interests? How did vastly different individuals and families scattered sparsely over a geologically and topographically diverse set of regions all come to see themselves as similar—as Mississippians? What linked them? What connected African American families of sharecroppers, working the rich, flat-as-a-pancake Delta farmland in the northeast quadrant of the state, to white lumber mill operatives and their families in the southeast's Piney Woods region? How did garment workers outside Jackson feel themselves akin to shipbuilders and dockworkers on the Gulf of Mexico?

Legally, Mississippians were so defined by the state. The Constitution of 1890—a racist post-Reconstruction effort to disempower blacks—decrees that "all persons, resident in this state, citizens of the United States, are hereby declared citizens of the state of Mississippi." But a sense of belonging was generated in other ways. Literate people throughout the state often read the same newspapers, the morning *Clarion-Ledger* and the evening *Jackson Daily News*. At public buildings, Mississippians hoisted the same state flag, a banner adopted in 1894, incorporating the Confederate battle flag in the upper left-hand corner. They dubbed a particular tree and flower—the magnolia—as officially representative of the state; they chose a bird—the mockingbird—as somehow symbolic or emblematic. As Benedict Anderson has written of the nation and nation building, so too it was with statehood. With a variety of symbols and rituals, customs and beliefs, groups of people began to *imagine* themselves as part of one political community, as a part of Mississippi: "It is *imagined* because the members . . . will never know most of their fellow-members, meet them, or even hear of them, yet in the minds of each lives the image of their communion."[4]

Such not-knowing was complicated in Mississippi by the fact that many persons felt they could "know of" a number of persons, often associated by family and place. "Are you related to the Joneses of Smith County?" (Or the Smiths of Jones County?) In this manner, a black Mississippian might try to "place" another black Mississippian, a white another white. Given persistent racial stratifications, whites might try to identify blacks by employment relationships as well. Just as black slaves were forced to adopt the surnames of white owners in the antebellum South, black identity in twentieth-century Mississippi sometimes could be subsumed within white families: "Doesn't your family work for the Joneses of Smith County?" Such placements smacked of encasement, confinement. Because black and white Mississippians were regularly locked into such limiting vocabularies and their attendant power dynamics, all Mississippi history must necessarily be examined in light of racial categories and inequalities.

Mississippi is a collection of places, peopled by African Americans and European Americans, along with much smaller numbers of Chinese Americans and Choctaws. In a segregated but fluid black-and-white world, the Chinese occasionally stepped over to the privileged side, as when they attended "all-white" public schools in the Delta.[5] Choctaws, heirs of the area's indigenous peoples, were sometimes grouped with blacks, as when playing America's favorite pastime, baseball, in Mississippi's Negro leagues after World War II.[6]

More so than in any other state, African Americans made up a large proportion of the population—nearly half of the over two million residents in the 1940s, better than a third of the almost two and a half million during the 1980s. But blacks were concentrated in certain regions, whites in others.[7] Whites were sizable majorities on the Gulf Coast, where shipping and tourism were promoted, and in the sandy, cretaceous Northeastern Hills—the foothills of the Appalachians—where generations of self-sufficient farmers maintained small plots. In the (Mississippi) River Lowlands, most farmers— as distinct from large landholding "planters"—were black, the descendants of slaves who worked the antebellum plantations from Vicksburg south to Natchez and beyond. Blacks also predominated in the Delta—a vast, flat region of rich alluvial soils, located not at the mouth of the Mississippi River, but rather between the Mississippi and Yazoo Rivers. Here, blacks made up significant majorities in every county. But a white elite controlled the economy through a postbellum plantation system, made possible around the turn of the century by the clearing and draining of the swampy overgrowth and the construction of levees along the Mississippi.[8]

With violent intimidation and disfranchisement mechanisms insuring that only 6.7 percent of eligible blacks were registered to vote before 1965, these elites controlled state politics for much of the period, forwarding narrow racial (racist) and economic (plantation agriculture) agendas. In many ways, they had a considerable say in national politics, too—especially in the person of James O. Eastland. An overfed, cigar-chomping, intransigent segregationist, Eastland garnered seniority and influence as he

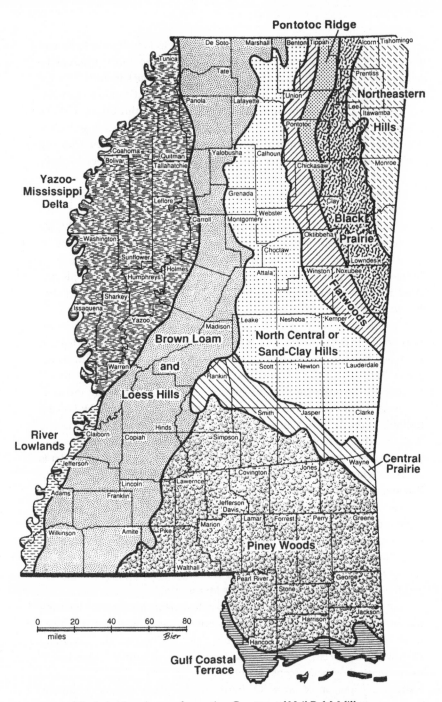

Mississippi, regions and counties. Courtesy of Neil R. McMillen.

rose through the ranks of the U.S. Senate from 1956 to 1978. He became chairman of the powerful Senate Judiciary Committee and thereby blocked federal attempts to bring racial justice to the South. During his three-year tenure as head of the Civil Rights Subcommittee, Eastland proudly flouted the law and called not a single meeting of the group, effectively killing all legislation.[9] Not surprisingly, at the time of the Supreme Court's *Brown v. Board of Education* ruling, forcing the desegregation of public schools, massive resistance in the form of white Citizens' Councils—"the businessman's Klan"—originated in Sunflower County, home to Eastland's vast plantation.[10] However, skilled and courageous organizers, heroes of the civil rights movement, would also emerge from the Delta region.

Though always powerfully represented in Jackson and emotionally resonant throughout the state, agriculture and its preeminence in state policy making were on the wane late in the twentieth century. Whereas nearly a third of new state senators and representatives were farmers or planters in 1951, only one-fifth were in 1983.[11] This reflected a precipitous decline in family farming, as land and wealth were increasingly concentrated in the hands of a privileged few and in the portfolios of corporate interests. At the close of World War II, there were 260,000 farms in the state, averaging 74 acres; four decades later, 34,000 farms averaged 315 acres each.[12]

Leaving race aside, Mississippi ranked as the most homogeneous of all states on at least one diversity index.[13] Very few people hailed from outside the state, almost no one from outside the United States.[14] Religiosity seemed strikingly uniform and pervasive.[15] From the 1930s, when Charles Angoff and H. L. Mencken began measuring the states' relative merits and they ranked Mississippi "worst" on a quality-of-life scale,[16] "poor ol' Mississippi," as Chuck Plant called it, became a compendium of superlatives. It regularly generated the lowest per capita income, with the highest percentage of children living below the poverty level. It had the smallest percentage of dentists, and the largest percentage of federal aid recipients—those surviving off food stamps, Medicaid, Aid to Families with Dependent Children, and Supplemental Security Insurance. It had the second lowest percentage of physicians, and the second highest infant mortality rate. Large numbers of people had no health insurance coverage.[17]

The legal system was markedly unprofessionalized. When the legislature revamped the justice of the peace system in 1975, it instituted a minimum educational requirement for the renamed justice court judges—not a law degree, but a high school diploma. Further, the judges were finally to be paid by salary as opposed to fees, a method shown to be rife with abuse. Little wonder, then, that Mississippi ranked last on a scale of state public policy innovation.[18]

Mississippians were poorly fed and poorly led; they were poorly educated and poorly cared for. In short, they were poor. But these indices and averages mislead. They elide the human experience of suffering, and they eclipse and aggregate individual lives with numerical calculations. They also suggest uniform deprivation, across-the-board desperation. They smooth out wild disparities within these *ostensibly* homogeneous and insular communities. They erase the gross inequities—the stark contrasts between the haves and have-nots, whites and people of color, men and women—that were at the heart of societal tensions. If Mississippi was a contentious, near-mythical place, it was because of the outrageous extent of race, class, and gender oppression (and subtle fragmentations *within* race, class, and gender groups). Virulent racism and a thinly veiled misogyny supported much of the fabric of a once-agrarian, increasingly industrial, capitalist economic structure. A minute portion of citizens lived well at the expense of others.

Historically, these elites under siege generated "a passion for uniformity of thinking, . . . an overpowering demand for conformity within the white ranks," as professor James Silver describes it.[19] In the view of one visitor, certain Mississippians became noticeably "defensive about their reputation."[20] Outsiders—perhaps observing the worst of America, perhaps projecting their own anxieties—described Mississippi as unreal, otherworldly. But as historian James Cobb shrewdly notes, Mississippi must be "reexamine[d] . . . within the context of its interaction with, rather than its isolation from, the larger national and global setting." Then it can be understood as "a part of the world rather than a world apart."[21]

To undo generations of injustice, to learn from Mississippi's history of racism, classism, sexism, and heterosexism, we must engage with those distinctive aspects of local life that both promoted and prevented tolerance and equality. We must be able to sit with the complexities and contradictions of these individuals and the institutions to which they felt tied. As scholar Tal Stanley prompts us: "If collective struggles for social justice are to be effective, we must first give attention to those traditional institutions and concepts too often glibly and condescendingly dismissed as conservative and reactionary: country, God, church, home, family, community."[22] It was in these very sites—physical and conceptual—that queer notions, queer individuals, and queer resistances were to be found.

Home

Queerness began at home. Queer boys conceived of difference while sitting alone or with family; they gazed upon and thought about their bodies—

and other like bodies—while in the bathroom. In bed, they dreamed of men; relaxing or doing household chores, they daydreamed about things seen and unseen. Wherever they were, at any given moment, they might experience desire.

For boys growing to manhood in Mississippi in the second half of the twentieth century, the home was the premier queer site. It was the stage for playacting, for imagining nebulous scenarios. It was also the platform for real-life expressions of desire. In and around the house, men felt desire *and* acted on it. The bedroom—the bed, especially—as routine site for fantasy and autoeroticism, could easily become a site for realizing fantasy through alloeroticism. If, as Aaron Betsky hypothesizes, "the goal of queer space is orgasm," then of all possible spaces, Mississippians first and foremost queered the home.[23]

Fitz Spencer: My sister was engaged to this young man from the next town. They had a plantation, and he was farming. Anyway, he would come up to see June frequently, and that Thanksgiving he asked if he could spend the weekend. I know that he knew that if he did, he was supposed to sleep with me. Because that was the only place for him to sleep. Because we only had three bedrooms: one was June's, one was Mother and Daddy's, and one was mine. I had a double bed.

I was home from college, so I was out with kids. And I came in late. Everybody was already in bed. So I sneaked in my bedroom, didn't turn on the light, and put on my pajamas and crawled into bed. Then the next thing I knew, I felt a hand on my dick. I responded.

And I had sex with him several times. I was in school, and when I would come home, he would try to arrange it. The next year my sister went to school where I was. And he would come over to see her, and so . . . .[24]

The familial home should be understood not only as an ideological space—about which certain politicized assumptions are made or within which related assumptions are formed—but also as a material site with distinct propensities. John Brinckerhoff Jackson has observed, "The house as a space or a composition of spaces and walls and doors . . . makes certain relationships possible and impedes others."[25] To be sure, the home might not be at all amenable to homosexual interaction. The exterior walls, its boundaries with the outside world, might be jealously guarded. Controlling movement in and out could be a key method of parental surveillance, as Andy Hechinger recalls of his late teens in Ellisville: "My father was very strict, and I could only go out on Saturday night, and I had to be home at eleven o'clock. And he had to know where I was going, who I was going with, and if I was one minute after eleven getting home, I got grounded for two weeks."[26] To disobey parents often meant severe punishment: confinement to the home. And yet homosexual encounters frequently happened within those very walls, often between distant relatives.

The historical partitioning of upper- and middle-class dwellings into discrete, monofunctional rooms is often credited with enabling diverse sexualities behind closed doors. The rich, we are told, can afford their indiscretions, can better conceal them. Correspondingly, historians have described the public sphere as an inevitable social and sexual space for the working classes, due to overcrowded conditions in the cities.[27] But growing up poor in Vicksburg during the 1970s, Darryl Jeffries—like many other Mississippians—found that cramped quarters meant numerous opportunities for sex. Though he was already sharing a bed with his mother in their "tiny" one-bedroom basement apartment, relatives were welcomed when they fell on hard times:

> My aunt moved in with her three children—her two sons and her daughter. Both of these [older] male cousins I had sex with. It was mutual. The first time, [another] cousin from out of town was there; she was asleep on the sofa. And my male cousin wanted to do something, with her right there in the room. The lights were on and everything. We went over and stood behind this chifforobe, and he gave me head. It was real exciting. I liked it immediately.[28]

For rich and poor, black and white, family life shaped sexual possibilities. During the second half of the twentieth century, Mississippians on the whole had a distinctive way of living. As compared to other Americans, they were much more likely to live in detached houses and mobile homes on larger tracts of land. Despite persistent tenancy and sharecropping, they were more likely to own their homes, which were ordinarily of very low cost. Though the homes might be small, the households were large, often with more than one person per room. The majority of housing units were located in rural areas. And the vast majority of people lived in *family* households—more so than in any other state, save one.[29]

Under these conditions, not only married couples shared a bed. Children and youths did, too—with each other, with their parents, or with unmarried or widowed adults in the extended family, especially those of the same sex. In the same fashion that a young black Georgian until the age of twenty-three slept with his grandfather,[30] a young white Indianola, Mississippi, native often slept with his father around midcentury. Such physical closeness prompted intimacies that sometimes became sexual in nature. As in the Indianola case, these sexual encounters often involved coercion and deceit, since sex between parents and their children was strictly taboo.[31]

But for young males, sex between cousins provoked scant consternation by comparison. Boys were expected to experiment with their young friends and neighbors, and cousins were included among these. Still, even slight differences in age or strength could result in coercion. In the late fifties in rural south-central Tennessee, Robert John tried to repel the advances of his older cousin Kenny, who would regularly procure a handful of lard from the kitchen and lead Robert to a wooded area beyond the cow pasture. Robert didn't think these dalliances wrong; he simply didn't enjoy them. "I don't want to," he pleaded with Kenny. "It makes me feel like I have to shit."[32]

Though sexual experimentation between boys was expected, it was not fully condoned. The young feigned innocence; the old feigned ignorance. Parents and other adults in authority commonly turned a blind eye as young males found momentary havens in the home and reliable spots just outside. For wealthy whites, a homestead might include several outbuildings well suited to sexual privacy, as was the case in Fitz Spencer's youth.[33] Other boys had sex together, as a rural Rankin Countian remembers the 1930s, "in the open fields, . . . on [the] sandy banks of a river, or on the hay in a barn."[34] Such sex regularly grew out of the ordinary interactions of boys at play. However, racial distinctions structured these interactions. While black and white boys often swam naked together at the local creek, sex play across the color line was rare.

As males grew up, they approached the age at which same-sex play was frowned upon. Though imprecise, at some point in the teen years, sex between boys proved problematic, as the interests of many young men remained with or turned to young women. For some, a period of bisexuality followed. In the Vicksburg area during the late 1940s, Mark Ingalls recalls that

> there were about three or four of us [white boys] that decided we'd just play with each other and see how it was. You know, it was jerking off together, sometimes a little anal intercourse, whatever. You know, we'd get together and do it, after school before our parents got home. So we did that, and we did that for quite a while until we were up about thirteen or fourteen. And then we decided we were supposed to like girls. But I kept on with it because I thought it was fun. I must admit I was attracted to girls. I dated. I experimented with touching women and all that. And I would get very excited sexually. I remember that guys attracted me more.[35]

Ingalls and others chose to ignore the stricture against same-sex involvements beyond adolescence, and consequently they learned to exercise caution in conversation and in their choice of partners. As a youth, Ed Foreman regularly got himself invited to spend the night at his best friend Jim's house, near Taylorsville. There, the two took showers together. And Jim performed oral sex on Ed. (Ed didn't like to "give head.") In fact, they had sex so often that when Jim casually began to mention their exploits to others, Ed felt compelled to break it off.[36]

While boys and young men surreptitiously brought friends into their parents' home to have sex in a bedroom or bathroom,[37] parents sometimes unwittingly brought potential sex partners into the home to meet their sons. Once, Mark Ingalls met "a guy who was the son of one of my mother's friends. I was like seventeen or eighteen; he was twenty-one or so. He came with his mother to a cocktail party that my mother gave. I picked up on him, and he picked up on me. And my mother said, 'Well, why don't y'all go to the movie?' We went to the movie, and then of course we hopped into bed."[38]

But Ingalls's sex partners were not limited to the sons of his mother's friends. They included one of her friends as well—a rather famous friend, theater maven and writer Frank Hains. Again, they met in the home:

> In the fifties, he used to come visit my mother—because she was big in the theater guild. I remember I was home from college. They [had been] out for dinner. I remember scoping him out. And then I remember her going up to bed, and me doing everything I could to seduce him. And I finally did. We just jerked each other off. In my home. Downstairs. In the living room. Hoping my mother wasn't going to hear.[39]

Even away from home, familial relationships often enabled homosexual relationships, as Fitz Spencer realized during his navy service at the close of World War II:

> Once in Manila, a man from my hometown—the Exec Officer on a ship in port at that time—looked me up. He was older, but our families had always been friends. He asked me to have dinner with him, and he also asked a cousin of his who was in the army and also stationed in Manila. He took us to an old galleon in the harbor that had been made into a restaurant. When I went to the men's room, the cousin came in and stood next to me at the urinal. You can guess what happened. By then I had a room by myself, and several times when he had a pass, he came to see me.[40]

Within a web of familial ties and commitments, boys and men inevitably experienced same-sex desire in relation to home and hometown networks.

However, while some found home a useful site for clandestine encounters, others found it a lonely, solitary space. For many Mississippians, especially young men struggling with difference, the private home—the parental household—was a site of internal conflict and despair. Jonathan Odell experienced a painful adolescence during the 1960s, as he began to realize he "was different from everyone else"—his brothers, "the kids at school." He "didn't know how" he was different, but he knew he was. What's more, he knew he couldn't talk about it with anyone. He "became more reserved, quieter, distant." When he began to see a psychiatrist, his father asked, "You don't like boys, do you?" In this way, in countless other ways, Jonathan learned that he "couldn't tell [his parents] the truth." He spent nights "crying alone in [his] room."[41]

Just as homosexuality prompted a variety of familial responses, gender nonconformity among youths evoked multiple reactions from parents in the Deep South. As previously described, Ron Knight of Terry, Mississippi, regularly cross-dressed, and community members found benign amusement in it. In Elora, Tennessee, Robert John's parents let him dress up in his sister Faith's clothes and high heels. They let him sit in the porch swing on Sunday afternoons, a sight for all to see as cars and trucks passed on the highway.[42] In Mize, Mississippi, however, when Ricky Lee Smith's mother discovered that her son wished he were a girl, she "chewed [him] out royally." Generally, cross-dressing was tolerated as a childhood game; a transgender identity was verboten.

The home was a vital site in the circulation of received wisdom regarding gender and sexuality. Throughout the century, it was a site for teaching and learning sexual knowledge. In the same way that Protestant precepts guided understandings of homosexuality while Protestant pulpits remained largely silent on the topic, parents could negotiate silence and still get particular messages across to their children. Ben Childress recalls that in the 1970s his mother, quite indirectly, gave him an instructional manual on puberty and sex. It was "a birds-and-the-bees book [called] *Almost 12.*" It was a "cheap, probably sixty-page text [with] hand-drawn diagrams, cross sections of genitalia." She "left it on the bed for me, for me to find. And it was completely understood. I would look at it, but say nothing about it."[43] Similarly, several decades earlier, Ronald Knight's mother gave him a book on sex. It was the same one she had given to Ron's older brothers, and it dated from the turn of the century. Even in the 1930s, as an adolescent, Ron thought it retrograde. But he dared not discuss it with his mother.[44]

Almost 12 and its Victorian predecessor conveyed derogatory messages about homosexuality within broader normative portrayals of procreative marital heterosexual intercourse. Both Ben and Ron—and perhaps generations of young Mississippians—were left to wonder: Did their mothers simply want to teach them the ropes in advance of an assumed marriage? Or did they suspect that their sons might succumb to the deviant desires tangentially mentioned? Regardless, these guides to a normal sex life inevitably and ironically prompted thoughts of nonnormative sex as well.

Of course, many of these young Mississippians would indeed marry. Adult males who engaged in homosexual activity often lived in traditional nuclear and extended family households—patriarchal households that they "headed," as husbands and as fathers. In what by midcentury standards was a bizarre love triangle, one married man invited his male lover to live with him and his wife in the same home. Though all were southerners, they attempted this short-lived experiment in Massachusetts, presumably a more amenable environment.[45] Much more common was Mark Ingalls's fate. In 1957, though he was "not in love," Ingalls married. After his divorce in 1969, he quickly remarried and remained so for another decade. During this time, he had four children. And he had "lots of boyfriends on the side."[46]

More than his homosexuality, Mark Ingalls's mother disapproved of his second marriage. The two had never discussed homosexuality, observing as so many others did a system of "mutual discretion," as historians Elizabeth Kennedy and Madeline Davis have called it.[47] But avoidance of the topic did not indicate a lack of awareness on either side. As Ingalls's mother demonstrated, her views could be communicated when the situation warranted. "Knowing what you know," she said to her son, "why are you doing this?"—why are you getting married a second time? According to Mark Ingalls, this was "the closest she ever came to naming it."[48]

For queer southerners who didn't marry, discretion was all the more important because the freedom associated with independent living in the cities rarely pertained. A young man typically resided with his parents until marriage, which was expected. If he didn't marry, he remained in his parents' home—or perhaps in a separate dwelling on the same or an adjacent plot of land—often until old age. Even in the big city, men otherwise identified as gay lived with their parents, who—though never told—"knew" about their sons. Such was the case among white upper-class Birminghamians in the 1950s and 1960s,[49] and among black working-class Memphians in the 1970s and 1980s.[50]

On occasion a daring Mississippian might bring his parents into his own home, even if he shared that home with a male lover. Stan Watson lived in Hattiesburg with his partner James and with James's parents, who were nearing death: "His mother and daddy were ill. . . . He had to look after [them], and so I just stayed too, and they never said anything about it. They depended on me almost as much as they did him toward the end."[51] Even more daring, one fifty-year-old rural southerner who lived with his ailing mother invited his acquaintances over to the house for sex, confined as he was to the homestead. One December day he persuaded a young man named Matthew to ride by on his horse. After a conversation about the good ol' days bathing nude in the local "swimming hole," the elder man "went down" on his friend. A first for Matthew, the act left him wracked with guilt: "Had I committed a terrible sin? Was this behavior acceptable in the eyes of God?" Years would pass before he would become convinced it wasn't sinful.[52]

Opportunities multiplied for a man who could afford a home of one's own. Especially for white upper-income men strongly self-identified as gay, the private domicile was more than a privatized refuge from an antagonistic world. It was a site for building gay networks. Though some well-to-do same-sex couples like Fitz Spencer and Bill MacArthur entertained a mostly straight circle of friends,[53] others very consciously and purposefully threw house parties designed to bring together gay men and sometimes lesbians from across broad stretches of countryside. Hattiesburg resident Frederick Ulner, along with his partner Melvin Hunt, "gave large parties" that were often "three-day affairs." Hundreds attended. Most partygoers were from "Laurel, Columbia, Richton, the surrounding area." But others came "from all over the state of Mississippi. . . . Some stayed over[night]."[54] Friendships were forged, liaisons arranged, and relationships developed at these parties and at others like them.

Still, a single man could own a home all to himself without enjoying the full benefits of its usage. One Florence, Mississippi, native held only "small, quiet gatherings" of friends, so as to limit the attention of locals. He rarely brought dates home either: "[I was] very careful about inviting a sex partner into my home, mainly because my home was located in an area with people I had known all my life."[55] If a man chose to live openly with his partner, he could be spurned by his community and his family. And yet during the 1950s, at least one Alabama man, when silently rejected by his own family, regularly spent his Saturdays and holidays, Thanksgivings and Christmases, with his partner at the home of his partner's sister or brother.[56]

Thus, the family home in Mississippi was a complicated site of multiple sexual meanings and practices. At home, young men could learn to loathe their sexual desires; they could also find ways to act on their desires there. They could have sex with other young men in and around the house; they could masturbate there while fantasizing about boys and men. As adults, they could have homosexual liaisons there and elsewhere, while constructing a normative home life with a wife and children. Some men remodeled the standard Mississippi domicile, building a family around a same-sex partner and, at times, one or more relatives and friends.

At a time when the home stood as the fundamental building block of society, in a place where most people lived in a family household, men necessarily experienced same-sex desire in relation to the precepts and dynamics of the home. Home wasn't always an exemplar of heteronormativity. Rather, it was most commonly a site of contestation, a place for fluid and shifting conceptions of sexuality and a stage for varied, fortuitous, and opportune sexual encounters. In myriad configurations inflected by race, class, and religion, desires of all kinds found their home in the home.

Church

Joe Holmes: I'm one of four children born to parents from Winona, Mississippi. My maternal and paternal families both go back a long way in that area of Mississippi, the Montgomery County area. My daddy was captain of the football team at Winona High School, and my mother was homecoming queen. They dated in high school. My dad sold insurance. He was a business major at Ole Miss. My mother taught English in Tchula before [they] married in 1949. I was born in 1953. I went through the first grade in Winona, Mississippi. Then our family moved to Jackson in 1960, where I spent most of my life from then on. I went from the second through the twelfth grade in the Jackson public schools.

I was outgoing and popular as a kid. I liked to stand up in front of the room and read stories to the class—my latest Dr. Seuss book. I liked school. I was a happy person until about the fifth or sixth grade. As I approached puberty and began to grow older, there were certain conflicts and anxieties that made life more difficult. I was not as much at ease with people. In junior high school and high school, I did well academically, but I didn't excel athletically—which doesn't bother me. I wasn't real turned on by sports.

I became aware in junior high that I was attracted to males. In the gym class and in the locker room, I thought, Hmmm, this is something I need to find out more about! But I dated a girl for about two or three years in high school and had a lot of fun.

I grew up Southern Baptist, in a Baptist family that was real strict. We were made to go to church. We were there Sunday morning—Sunday school and church—and then Sunday night for Training Union and church. Every Sunday. It was a rare occasion that we ever got to see *The Wizard of Oz*, because it came on on Sunday night. Or *The Wonderful World of Disney*—that was one of the first color shows that came on. We were there for all the Sunday activities. And as I got into junior high school, that also included Sunday afternoons even, going to choir practice. Wednesday night we had prayer meeting and supper.

During the sixties, we went to Broadmoor Baptist, one of the largest Baptist churches in the state. My parents weren't quite as Bible thumping and conservative ideologically as a lot of other people in the church, with reference to drinking and dancing. I could tell that my parents pooh-poohed some of these ideas. They and their friends liked to have fun and cut up. Religion wasn't drilled into me a lot at home.

I remember the annual summer revivals, where some evangelist, usually from Texas, somewhere, would come in and have the whole church rededicating their lives by the end of the week. Everybody in tears. By that time, most of us had been baptized and joined the church and accepted the Lord as our savior and all you're supposed to do. We were saved. But he came down one by one, and he would go, "Son, are you saved?" And everybody would go, "Yes, sir." Then, he would say, "Are you *really* saved?" And by the end of it—of course, you weren't—you'd go, "No sir." By the end of that hour, hour and a half, or two hours, he had every one of us convinced we weren't saved, and we had to do it all over again his way. Everybody goes home saved again. Got to walk the aisle again.

Broadmoor Baptist has a recreation building, over on the east end, constructed during the late sixties. When I was in the ninth or tenth grade, about the time we were starting to drive cars, we had a weekend indoor camp-out. I took this best friend of mine, who was a member of Trinity Presbyterian right across the street. We all took sleeping bags and slept in this game room, where the pool tables were. There were these two guys there who obviously were into pairing off. When the lights went off, they were in the same sleeping bag. At first, it just looked like they were sharing stories. But then they wanted to go off into the next room by themselves. It was one of those rooms that has a[n interior] window with wire mesh. All the rest of us were wondering what they were up to, kind of laughing and joking at them. Then somebody cut the light on in the room where they were. And they were both naked as jaybirds.[57]

The hometown of Joe Holmes's youth, Jackson, Mississippi, has been called "the 'buckle' of the Bible Belt" by one cultural geographer. H. L. Mencken, in characteristically sardonic fashion, once dubbed Jackson "the heart of the Bible and Lynching Belt."[58] Up until the 1960s, white Protestants in Mississippi found little hypocrisy in their piety and white supremacy. Their churches, like their schools and neighborhoods, were strictly racially segregated. In fact, the churches were more exclusionary than commercial establishments. Whereas stores and movie theaters accommodated whites along with blacks—who were restricted to certain spaces and treated to second-class service—Sunday morning from eleven to noon remained, as the saying went, the most segregated hour of the week.

At the center of black life in Mississippi were the black churches. As Eric Lincoln and Lawrence Mamiya attest, "Historically, black churches have been the most important and dominant institutional phenomenon in African American communities."[59] Especially in rural areas, churches served as critical gathering places. Like the large white city church described above, rural black churches held services several times on Sunday and often at midweek as well—though the pastor, charged with serving several rural congregations, might be in attendance only on alternate weeks. "Revival season" came in "the late summer months and sometimes the early fall [during] the slack period when the crops ha[d] been 'laid by.'"[60] Black Mississippians, just like Joe's best friend "who was a member of Trinity Presbyterian," were known by the church they "belonged to."

Churches—black and white alike—abounded in the Mississippi landscape. Whereas Mississippi had the third largest proportion of Christians (94 percent) as compared to other states, it had more churches per capita than any state.[61] Thus, churches were smaller in Mississippi, a reflection of both its rural nature and the fractious nature of religion in Mississippi. Almost a third of Mississippians labeled themselves Baptist, but this name group consisted of a wide range of evangelical beliefs and traditions, sects and splinter groups.[62] Methodists were the second largest denomination.

Willie Morris's description of the hierarchy of white churches in Yazoo City might apply equally well to most Mississippi towns:

> The town Baptists were both more numerous and more aggressive, given to wilder exercises, inured to a form of baptism calling for heads to go under the water (the Methodist joke being, "I have nothing against the way the Baptists baptize, except it should last forty seconds longer.") and as a body, not so solidly middle class as the town Methodists. . . . Next up the scale from the Methodists were the Presbyterians, who had more "prominent" people, and more dues-paying members of the country club; at the top of the scale, smaller and more exotic and more willing to mix a cocktail, were the Episcopalians, who rivaled the Presbyterians in money, and surpassed both the Methodists and Baptists in respectability if not in numbers.[63]

Black Mississippians had their own Baptist churches, as well as segregated congregations of the United Methodist Church. But many belonged to various African Methodist Episcopal, or AME, churches, along with the charismatic bodies, such as the Church of God in Christ (COGIC)—the nation's second-largest black denomination after the National Baptist Convention, U.S.A.[64] Small-town African American class hierarchies were reflected in these denominational preferences. In Indianola during the 1930s, for example, Baptists and Methodists looked down on members of COGIC —known also as the "Sanctified" or the "Holy Rollers." Their "noise and dancing, . . . their powers of healing and the gift of 'tongues'" were considered "somewhat heathenish."[65]

Across lines of class and race, Mississippians felt impelled or compelled—by the family, by the community—to attend religious services. Among black farm families in east central Mississippi, for example, Sunday worship was one of many weekly communal routines—like farming, hunting, fishing, and swimming.[66] These routines were difficult to defy. One white queer Mississippian "attended church merely to go along with a churchgoing community." Though he "always thought the Jesus story a fairy tale," he faithfully accompanied his parents' to their rural church, Richland Methodist, well into his thirties.[67]

Though most Mississippians believed the church to be made up of the "body of believers"—the people, the membership, the followers—church buildings were important as symbols of collective endeavor (since many were literally built by the members); as signs of status (as wealthy or populous congregations like the Baptists used tithes and offerings to construct additional classroom buildings and recreational facilities); and as places for community meetings both sacred and secular (of tremendous value for black communities during the civil rights era). For queer boys, too, the church as a physical structure proved significant.

Many church events were sex segregated. Congregations often organized Sunday school classes, for example, by both age and sex. At midcentury a few continued the practice of seating women on one side of the sanctuary and men on the other during worship. At social occasions especially, men might cluster together informally or formally, as part of established church procedure. The bonding that was allowed, indeed endorsed, in the name of godly fellowship fostered an intense physicality and closeness, a mixing of the "homopastoral" and the "homotactile," as historian D. Michael Quinn refers to it in the Mormon church. These affinities and affiliations might also lead, Quinn demonstrates, to homoeroticism.[68]

Women outnumbered men in most Mississippi congregations.[69] Although men held pastoral roles, women were often lay leaders, as part of matrons clubs, missionary societies, circles, and other educational and social groups. In a sexist world, gendered notions of churchgoing might have thrown male believers' masculinity into doubt, at the same time that church life opened up possibilities for creative manipulation of gender roles. Among weeknight black church socials and fund-raisers in Indianola, the women's "style show" competed in popularity with a male drag variant of it, as anthropologist Hortense Powdermaker observes about the 1930s:

The "Brideless Wedding" is a mock wedding in which all the parts are taken by men. The "hit" is the matron of honor, one of the foremost citizens. He is a large, portly man, costumed in a coverall apron, a kimono, and a broad-brimmed hat. As he walks up the aisle, hands clasped behind his back in his usual masculine fashion, he rouses shouts of laughter. The "groom" is the smallest boy that could be found and the "bride" the tallest. The parody is carried off with great gusto and *éclat*.[70]

Like World War II military drag shows designed to further the cause, sanctioned church drag—as well as school-sponsored male beauty contests and womanless weddings[71]—offered a space for multiple interpretations of gender, performance, sex, and sexuality. While parody of the premier heterosexist institution was viewed by many as good clean fun, for others it gave rise to complicated thoughts and feelings, many of which went against the grain. Identifying the tallest (most masculine?) man to play the bride might have instilled pride in the one so chosen. But how did the groom feel? Did he see what the others saw? What about those men who adhered to prescribed gender roles in daily life but found the performance curiously liberating? As Allan Bérubé concludes about GI drag, "Reveling in dresses, makeup, and wigs, [gay men] called up the magic of drag and double entendre to subvert the moral order that otherwise rendered them silent and invisible."[72] While church teachings might alienate those outside the orb of procreative heterosexual marriage, church social events like this one, church gender distinctions, and even church architecture participated in the construction of queer concepts and queer sex.

The primary church edifices—the sanctuary and the education building—were well utilized on Sundays and Wednesdays and, as in Indianola, on other nights of the week as well. But they stood quiet at other times. Pastors occasionally kept the doors unlocked, so that parishioners could have a place for reflection and prayer. Yet with the preacher usually out visiting the sick, ministering to the homebound, or serving other congregations, and with churchgoers busily carrying out their daily tasks, these peaceful settings were propitious sites for queer sex.

During the 1960s in Centreville, Alabama, boys repeatedly had sex with one another in the houses of worship and in one particular parsonage, where the preacher's son entertained his friends.[73] Such occurrences between boys and between men were not uncommon in other parts of the South, including Mississippi. Among the few communal spaces in rural areas and small towns, church grounds attracted young men both during and outside the hours of worship. In the 1930s and 1940s in Terry, Mississippi, rowdy Pentecostal services were "considered entertainment" by Ron Knight, who listened from the wooded area surrounding the church. On other occasions, Ron brought companions there to have sex under the trees.[74]

Though one Mississippian I talked to insists that any couple—heterosexual or homosexual—would have been "tarred and feathered" had they
been caught having sex inside church buildings,[75] another Mississippian I
talked to took the risk himself, with great frequency in the 1970s. Mark
Ingalls, married at the time, belonged to the little Episcopal church, Saint
Albans, in tiny Bovina, Mississippi. As Ingalls describes it, he "knew that
one of the windows did not lock, [and] there was no alarm system." He and
a male partner would crawl through the window at night and "would do it
in the parish hall." Once, Ingalls and a friend even did it in "the main
church"—the sanctuary proper.

Though over time he led several different friends to his secret rendezvous, Ingalls was nonetheless conflicted about the site. "I remember once
as I was raising the window to get in, I was bitten by a wasp. I decided that
God was telling me not to defile his 'house.' That little adventure was not
as good as I expected, because I had the sting to deal with plus my conscience."[76] But the guilt that was inculcated in church settings did not prevent Mississippians from using the church as an arena for expressions of
same-sex desire.

In the seventies and early eighties, Pascagoula native Ben Childress attended church youth social events similar to Broadmoor Baptist's indoor
camp-out. A "lock-in" was a popular form of entertainment, often involving young people from more than one congregation. Youths, along with a
minister of youth or other adult guardians, were "locked" inside a church
building or other facility for round-the-clock "twenty-four-hour fellowship" that could last an entire weekend. Lock-ins typically included a sleep-
over, though some specified that participants stay awake for the full agenda
of activities. Childress remembers a lock-in held at a skating rink in Esca-
tawba, but he was most impressed by the lock-in at Dauphin Way Baptist,
a wealthy white church in Mobile, Alabama. Dauphin Way's "Family Life
Center . . . had a bowling alley, outdoor pool, gym, basketball court, Ping-
Pong, locker room—and showers . . . with no dividers." Childress, who
from the age of fourteen had sought out other boys for sex, lingered in the
locker room as one young Baptist took a shower. Danny "worked out [and]
had a good body." Childress watched him for a long time, then "asked to
use his spigot, because his water was already warm." Such ruses were
transparent. Yet the good-natured fun of these religious outings often precluded contentious encounters. The two didn't have sex, but neither did
Danny seem to take offense at Ben's flirtatious gaze.[77]

Moreover, church activities often extended well beyond the local community. Many churches were affiliates of large denominations organized at

the district, conference, state, and national levels. Two African American leaders in the United Methodist Church recall meetings at Gulfside Assembly in Waveland, Mississippi, in the 1950s that brought together young people from throughout the conference. Some of the youths exhibited distinct "homosexual tendencies." As a group, they were seen as "very smart, very outgoing. . . . All of the people liked them."[78] In fact, "one particular young man"—clearly marked as homosexual by "the way he walked, the way he talked"[79]—was so well respected that the conference youth organization elected him president. The Methodists financially supported his attendance at national meetings.

The summer months in particular drew youths and adults into church-supported endeavors. In addition to revivals and camp meetings, young believers and their elders participated in Vacation Bible School at the local church. Prizes went to those who brought along the largest number of "guests," or nonmembers. Outdoor social activities, such as picnics and hayrides, also increased in the warmer months, as did the possibilities for homosexual interaction. "Especially during the summer," one Mississippian recalls of the 1940s, "gays made friends with other gays" at these church events.[80]

Within the local community church, queer men also met one another in the choir. They found friends in the black church choirs of Memphis.[81] They found lovers in the chorales of even the smallest white chapels, as in Shuqualak.[82]

The opportunities expanded when choirs went on the road. For those congregations with enough funds to maintain a bus, summers meant choir tours and mission trips. Ben Childress remembers that his church youth choir prepared new music months in advance of their annual excursion. He recalls with humor the one summer he spent "spreading the good news through song" in the "small country churches of east Tennessee." Mixing faith and fun, the group also visited the amusement park at Gatlinburg, Tennessee, and shopped at the Metrocenter Mall in Jackson, Mississippi, on their way back to Pascagoula. At all these places, in the churches and in the commercial establishments, Ben was ever on the lookout for "cute guys." He found one at the mall. As a result, Ben almost missed the bus. While his fellow passengers waited, wondering where he was, eager to return to Pascagoula, Ben was "getting a blow job in the mall bathroom." He returned guiltily to the parked bus, to his disgruntled friends, "scared that they knew."[83]

As scholar Gayle Graham Yates has written, "Christianity matters in Mississippi—for good and for ill." Whereas she "loved religion" and found "great comfort, warmth, and belonging" as she learned Bible verses;

whereas her white rural east Mississippi youth was profoundly shaped by "the gracious style of church life" offered by "MYF"—Methodist Youth Fellowship[84]—many Mississippians loathed the church. They participated in its rituals begrudgingly. Richard Wright writes of his Mississippi upbringing in *Black Boy*, "Wherever I found religion in my life I found strife, the attempt of one individual or group to rule another in the name of God. The naked will to power seemed always to walk in the wake of a hymn."[85] Similarly, gay black southerner Max C. Smith sees southern religion as the primary perpetrator of homophobia among African Americans: "American Blacks' bias against gays is due to our forced socialization into Dixie Christian culture during slavery."[86]

Indeed, many black churches in twentieth-century Mississippi had been constructed on the orders of white plantation owners in nineteenth-century Mississippi. True, many young men, black and white, prayed to God—as Vicksburg native Darryl Jeffries says he did[87]—to be changed, forgiven, cleansed of homosexuality. And yet the picture is quite complicated.

While most Mississippi Christians were evangelical Protestants who believed in the "inerrancy of Scripture" and in the literal interpretation of it, they ignored many biblical passages (such as proscriptions against eating pork). They overlooked contradictions between discrete passages. And when their views differed from those of church leaders, they relied on their own reading and understanding. The widespread belief in an unmediated relationship with God, in which pastoral intercession was unnecessary, fostered an independence of mind among some. The faithful might find the few biblical references to homosexuality as condemnatory,[88] but the emphasis they placed on them depended on a host of factors.

Undeniably, Protestant pastors wielded enormous influence in Mississippi. Some garnered extraordinary political power. Douglas Hudgins—regarded as "the state's preeminent Southern Baptist preacher"—led numerous civic and political organizations as he pastored Jackson's massive all-white First Baptist Church from 1946 to 1969. Hudgins's indifference to black civil rights struggles pleased parishioner-patrons such as Thomas and Robert Hederman, owners of the "militantly segregationist" *Clarion-Ledger* and *Jackson Daily News*. Hudgins further spoke out as early as 1953 against "the rise in perversion" and in the 1960s against "homosexuality." He castigated "social tramps and admired libertines" to audiences that extended beyond the pews of downtown Jackson to the radio airwaves reaching out across the state.[89]

But Hudgins was the exception not the rule. Pastors in Mississippi rarely spoke publicly about homosexuality prior to the late 1960s. In the small rural churches most Mississippians attended, homosexuality was "a taboo subject," as one Methodist remembers. "Deacons skirt[ed] around sodomy and leapfrogged [over] Sodom and Gomorrah." At "the big Baptist church in downtown Brookhaven," nothing was "ever . . . said about homosexuality."[90] Still, most Mississippians took for granted that queer sex was forbidden as part of the wider ban on premarital and extramarital sexual intercourse.

Others could find within Scripture a vocabulary and ideology for understanding and accepting homosexuality. Stan Watson and his partner James earned the respect and admiration of James's parents, whom the two men invited into their home and cared for in their old age. James's parents referred to Stan and James as "Jonathan and David," the two Old Testament figures who shared a "great love" for one another.[91] Indeed, the Jonathan and David story would inspire fictional as well as real-life conceptualizations of homosexuality in Mississippi, as we shall see in chapter 5.

Religious structures exerted contradictory influences on queer sexuality in Mississippi in the second half of the twentieth century. Although Protestant doctrine would more explicitly condemn homosexuality along with a rising gay activism after the 1960s, houses of worship nonetheless proved useful meeting grounds throughout the period. At church events, men met; in church space, they got to know each other better. Though congregations rarely extended clear-cut support to male-male couples, they were often aware of the men in their midst who might act on male-male desire. Within the complicated interstices of theologically inflected thought and within the opportune spaces of local church life, queer men could effectively maneuver.

School

Schools and colleges were not merely places of learning in Mississippi. Nor were they simply sites of child and young adult socialization. Schools and colleges were among the most contested, politically embattled public arenas, especially around issues of race. From 1945 to 1985, education underwent enormous transformations in the state, reflecting dramatic shifts in social and cultural norms.

As white Mississippians at long last were forced to reevaluate their tortured concepts of supremacy and dominance, black Mississippians pushed for equal rights, equal access, and an equal share of public services. Black claims were hard to refute: at midcentury the state spent $117 per pupil on its white schools, $35 per pupil on black schools. The state paid black teachers roughly half as much as white teachers.[92] Equalization—a term of widespread use but divergent meanings—would require constant struggle by black Mississippians. Even when schools were integrated, at great human cost, the process destroyed many black schools and traditions; it involved layoffs of large numbers of black teachers; and it was largely controlled by intransigent whites bent on maintaining privilege.[93]

Brown v. Board of Education didn't desegregate public schools in the South. The 1954 ruling *ordered* the desegregation of public schools without setting a timetable for implementation. The U.S. Supreme Court directed local authorities to proceed "with all deliberate speed." White officials in Mississippi interpreted the phrase loosely to mean "when hell freezes over." For example, during the 1965–1966 academic year, only 7,258 of the 295,831 African American students in Mississippi, or 2.5 percent, attended desegregated schools. It took another Supreme Court case, brought by blacks in Mississippi, to desegregate public schools. At last, fifteen years later, in *Alexander v. Holmes County Board of Education*, the Court decreed that implementation must begin "at once."[94]

For this reason, the South's fledgling all-white private schools—the segregation academies—experienced exponential growth in late 1969 and early 1970. Already organized in Mississippi by white Citizens' Councils as early as 1954 and propped up by the state government's devious Sovereignty Commission, which funneled public school texts and funds to them, the segregation academies insured that many Mississippi children would continue to receive segregated educations. Communities and counties unable to adequately fund one school system now funded two—the public school and the private school, as they were commonly known. The academies lacked the niceties typically associated with private education. These one-story facilities tended to be hastily built of cheap slab and cinder-block construction, vulnerable to the region's persistent, violent tornadoes. Library collections were woeful, laboratory resources meager. Fees were low, such that poor whites could attend but African Americans—faced with subtle obstacles and overt intimidation—would not.[95]

In classrooms, public and private, official ideologies proliferated.[96] In schools, perhaps as nowhere else, children learned that they were Mississippians. They learned that the name was a Choctaw word (or perhaps Natchez or Chickasaw or Ojibwa, depending on the source) meaning "father of waters." They were taught, with a sense of pride and ownership, that the river bounding the western edge of the state was the longest in North America. It neatly divided the continent, such that American places were either "east of the Mississippi" or "west of the Mississippi." Students played games that helped them remember how to spell the name: "M-I–crooked letter–crooked letter, I–crooked letter–crooked letter, I–humpback-humpback, I." At spelling contests a distinct rhythm could be heard: "**M-I**-S-S, I-S-S, I-P-P, **I**." And when, in 1962, the state song ("Way

Down South in Mississippi") was deemed too lackluster, too unfamiliar, "Go, Mississippi" was adopted and children sang it at school. As if defying all traditions, the new anthem offered, as its last stanza, a new rhythm for spelling out the state's name: "**M-I-S, S-I-S, S-I-P-P-I**."

Also, a principal lesson learned in Mississippi classrooms was the centrality of gender in everyday life. Girls were different from boys, students learned; with countless cues, explicitly and implicitly articulated, young Mississippians were instilled with distinctive notions of maleness and femaleness, masculinity and femininity. These basic assumptions were embedded in the very curriculum they studied. And they were reflected in the expectations they developed toward their future places in the world.

In the 1940s at the Piney Woods Country Life School in rural central Mississippi, students' perceptions of appropriate male and female professions evidenced the values imparted in class. Though their thoughts might defy Victorian norms relegating men and women to public and private spheres respectively, students nonetheless delineated clear limits to women's work outside the home as well as men's work inside the home. As student Ruby Nell Kelly opined, "Along with housekeeping, a girl should learn some kind of business, such as shorthand, typing, bookkeeping and filing. A boy should learn carpentering, blacksmithing, mechanics, printing, farming, and dairy work." A disciple of self-help and accommodation advocate Booker T. Washington—after whose Tuskegee Institute in Alabama he modeled Piney Woods—headmaster Laurence Jones inscribed racial boundaries to economic activity by advising his predominantly African American student body to become, in the case of boys, "good farmers, honest mechanics, welders, bakers, and agricultural experts; the girls to become teachers, nurses, homebuilders, dressmakers, typists, stenographers, and homemakers." [97]

Black public school curricula differed little from this private course of study, even after the advances of the civil rights movement. While many public schools remained racially segregated into the 1970s, both predominantly African American and predominantly white schools maintained gender-segregated coursework to varying degrees, especially in the agricultural, technical, and industrial courses more commonly found at black schools. For example, Randall Sawyer took classes in basic English, math, typing, biology, and PE at Hinds County Agricultural High School in Utica, whereas the neighboring all-white Raymond High School, located at the county seat, offered its students more advanced courses and equipment. At Utica, female students were expected to take two years of homemaking; males took two years of agriculture or one year of agriculture and one year of "family living for men." Randall chose the second option. Already skilled in horticulture and livestock from working on the family farm (and already labeled gay by his classmates because he "liked to stay with girls"), Randall preferred the family living class, which was designed to "teach the single man how to live—to do grocery shopping, cooking, living." Until the age of eighteen, the school and this class in particular were Randall's primary means of meeting other guys, his potential sex partners.[98]

If curricula and coursework instructed students in gender norms, school social circles further dictated acceptable and unacceptable comportment. Among classmates, queer Mississippians regularly felt the sting and stigma of stepping out of line—literally. Gender nonconformists commonly received taunts based on their manner of walking. As Greg Brock describes his youth in 1960s Crystal Springs: "At school, I was made fun of. The kids mimicked the way I walked, the way I talked. I was petrified. I'd go home and cry myself to sleep a lot of nights." Still, Greg "managed to be[come] a student leader."[99]

Similarly, queer students could find protection behind the guise of an artistic or intellectual life, as one oral history narrator, an accomplished painter, explains: "My art formed a shield from local criticism. I was a genius, an artist! Therefore odd or eccentric." Other boys he knew, however, bore the brunt of adolescent male animus. Shy and unprepossessing, they were "cowed down" by the taunts of school bullies.[100]

Though southern boys like Robert John might be allowed to dress up in girls' clothes while relaxing at home on the porch swing, they endured ridicule at school if others found out. Robert's chums "would hoot" at him after such an escapade, teasing him mercilessly for cross-dressing: "Was that you wearing that red dress and those shoes?" Engaging in homosex was a different, if related, matter. As one of Robert's friends would later describe it:

> Corn-holing, in the rural South, doesn't imply homosexuality. . . . [I]t's just a little something among the boys. . . . Still, the one who gets repeatedly corn-holed is bound to be called a fairy. Soon the boys at school would let John go down on them, by the creek, behind the gym, but never spoke to him in the school hall except to chant things like, "There goes John, the softest cheeks my balls ever laid on."[101]

Lots of young men participated in homosex. To be too willing, to be too often penetrated, to be further feminized by dressing in drag, meant a greater likelihood of being labeled queer. And yet to be clearly defined as queer at school could mean a greater likelihood of connecting with other queers—and arranging dates for later.[102]

As early as the 1940s, athletics eclipsed academics in importance at many Mississippi high schools. PE class served as a training ground for sex-segregated competitive team sports like track, basketball, baseball, and—most important—football. The state passion was football. (Surely it's no accident that during practice, when waiting to rush the quarterback, the defensive linemen were made to count out a full five seconds as "one Mississippi, two Mississippi, three Mississippi, four Mississippi, five Mississippi.") At racially segregated public schools in the Delta and throughout the state, social life for teens and adults alike often revolved around school sports events.

Jan Terrence remembers that well-attended sock hops took place after almost every Friday night football game during the 1950s. They were held in the school "gym, the VFW [Veterans of Foreign Wars meetinghouse], or the American Legion hut." Students danced in socks to a record player or a jukebox, or on special occasions, two or three times a year, to live music. The good times continued at "juke joints" located on the outskirts of town, where young men could procure liquor in what was otherwise a dry state. Away games involved travel by bus and car for the team, the band, and the fans, and it involved momentary interaction with students and adults from nearby towns and communities.[103]

Queers, Terrence says, were known by their lack of participation in or exclusion from this world. They were most readily marked as "effeminate, not athletic." The sure sign was a "pronounced prissy walk." Terrence's classmates would identify queer boys with a distinctive gesture. To lick your pinkie finger and run it over your eyebrow, from nose to temple, meant you had spotted one.[104]

Yet the sites of these sex-segregated sports activities—the locker rooms, the playing fields, the training grounds, the PE classes—proved likely sites for homosexual intercourse. As Joe Holmes attests, recalling his early epiphany in the junior high boys' locker room, they were certainly sites for homosexual desire. Josh Holland, another southerner who while at school "realize[d] what it meant to be gay or homosexual," states it flatly: "I always liked to watch the boys in the shower after gym class. I guess I really knew for sure I was different then." Ron Knight didn't just watch. At the school gym, in the showers, Ron often had sex with a teammate after practice or after a game. Players who lingered, when all the others had left, were always likely candidates. On rare occasions, Ron even participated in "small group sex."[105]

Like the probabilities for self-understanding, the opportunities for homosex increased in these and other homosocial environments, such as the ever-popular 4-H clubs and Boy Scout troops, as boys and men regularly played, showered, traveled, and bunked together. In these settings, homo-

social posturing and vocabulary sometimes even enabled homosexual posturing and vocabulary. As one southern writer has noted, "Gay talk is
enough like good-ole-boy talk to be nonthreatening to many Southern men.
And some of the motions—bear hugs, ass patting, shoulder blows—are the
same, differing only in the degree of overt sexuality."[106]

In addition to poor and working-class black youths at Laurence Jones's
Piney Woods Country Life School, middle- and upper-class white boys attending venerable old private schools, especially residential military academies like Chamberlain-Hunt in Port Gibson, found numerous occasions for
male-male interaction and intercourse.[107] As rumors circulated about which
cadets at Chamberlain-Hunt were queer inclined, physical closeness alone
seemed destined to nurture queer interchange at Piney Woods and at another Laurence Jones project, the Oakley Training School, founded with
state support as a home "for delinquent colored boys" in the 1940s. At the
Oakley dormitory as at Piney Woods' Harris Hall, boys boarded together
in tight quarters—in the latter case, in a building constructed in part by the
students.

Harris Hall was completed in 1923, "all the brick made by the boys in
hand molds, ten bricks at a time." The spotty extant files of the Piney
Woods Executive Committee give only blurred glimpses into the sex lives
of students there. At one meeting, the officials alluded to a "disturbance in
the Boys Dormitory," during which a twelve-year-old Mexican youth used
"foul language in Mexican tongue" and committed unspecified "other obsence [sic] actions." Male youths at Piney Woods, their superiors noticed,
had a habit of "slipping out of the Boys Dormitory" late at night, against
school regulations. Principal Jones was dismayed to discover "a pallet upstairs in the Auditorium off the stage, which some boys used as a meeting
place"—he perhaps too readily assumed—"with girls." No corresponding
cases of girls slipping out of their dorm were recorded.[108]

As proximity fostered intimacy inside and outside the dorms, a willingness to participate in queer sex was influenced by distance from home and
the institution's tolerance. As Warren County native Mark Ingalls describes
it, homosexuality thrived at some single-sex schools:

At age seventeen, I went to boarding school. My parents got a divorce in
1951; I needed to get away from home. I was sent to Saint Andrew's School
in Saint Andrews, Tennessee, two miles down the road from Sewanee, Tennessee, where the University of the South is. I also went there. Saint Andrew's School was owned by the Order of the Holy Cross, which is a monas-
tic order of the Episcopal Church. That was like a revelation, like coming

Mark Ingalls, 1952, at age eighteen. Courtesy of Mark Ingalls.

home. This is where I belong; this is where I should be. I got very interested in schoolwork. I seemed to fit in better. Father Spencer decided I should be a thespian. He put me in plays. That was wonderful.

At boarding school, that was when I really met people who were gay and who knew they were gay. I thought it was pretty horrible for someone to kiss me. They could jerk me off, but they certainly couldn't kiss me; I *certainly* wouldn't kiss them. After a while, I found out how much fun that was. Both my roommates—there were three of us in a room—were gay. I explored that whole side of my nature. I had several guys that I was romantically connected with. What was unusual about it, we were also dating women at this time too. We would go to a dance at Saint Mary's School, which was on the other side of the mountain, and rub up all over them and have a big time, and then come home and do each other.

About half the faculty was gay. So long as you didn't flaunt what you were doing, you were all right; no one said anything to you at all. No one was ever kicked out of that school for being gay. And it was going on all over the place. It was not a hotbed of sedition. But when the lights went out at night, people got together and did it.[109]

Similarly, around the same time back in Vicksburg, at All Saints Episcopal School for Girls—where Ingalls's mother taught English and where he later would teach history—the potential for homosex was ever present.

Sites for homosex had to be carefully sought out and, once identified, protected. After many furtive encounters, twenty-one-year-old Toni McNaron, who also taught English, was "determined to find a more private, preferably lockable place" for herself and her lover, a high school senior:

> My classroom was across from the library in the basement of the main building. It opened on to a narrow corridor [with] two doors: one to a toilet and the other to some unknown space. Inside the second door, I found a tiny room full of trash, part of an oil furnace, and a small metal box just inside the door in which lay a lead key. . . . [I]t had neither lights nor a window. . . . There, in that literal closet, in constant fear of the curious or fatal knock, my gentle and loyal first lover and I talked and cried and made love.[110]

Like so many inventive Mississippians working within and against societal limits, McNaron invented a new queer space from the raw material of existing spatial arrangements.

IN THE ORDINARY personal coming-out narrative, the closet is a trope of repression and self-loathing. It is "a place to hide, . . . a dark and musty place."[111] It must be escaped. To reach gay self-actualization, the closet must be overcome. In the historical collective coming-out narrative—the theoretical model on which American lesbian and gay history rests—the rural landscape functions as an analogous space. The countryside must be left behind to reach gay culture and community formation in the cities. Thus, the South—rural space generally—functions as gay America's closet.

Architectural critic Aaron Betsky rehearses and reinscribes these narratives as he describes the closet as "the ultimate interior, the place where interiority [preconsciousness?] starts. It is a dark space at the heart of the [rural, parental?] home." And yet, Betsky hints at oppositional readings of the closet. While it is a "harrowing, spooky space," it is "also one that is free from outside constraints."[112] More precisely, the closet is in dialectical relationship with forces that are simultaneously outside and in. It is, metaphorically and physically, a space that can be cordoned off *within* existing structures, ideological and material. It is not solely imposed but can also be (re)created, a space of queer agency. In the same way that silence—too often read as repression, as a discursive closet—was embraced as an effective strategy of resistance, as described in chapter 1, the manipulation of physical closets or shelters enabled not so much hiding as resistance, a refashioning of a seemingly inflexible environment into a site of perverse pleasure.

Physically, a closet is understood as a space, usually smaller than a room, demarcated by four walls, a floor, a ceiling, and a door. It exists *within* a larger edifice, a house or other building. Symbolically, a door connotes opportunity. Indeed, we are told, "opportunity knocks." A door must be opened. The step is usually outward, into another space. However, a closed door can likewise open up opportunities. As Toni McNaron demonstrates, queer space can be created and claimed; it can be made from given forms. McNaron monitored her "literal closet" for signs of janitorial entry and exit; she noted the times it was otherwise in use; she slowly removed the debris over the course of several weeks so as to minimize suspicions; all this before she and her lover occupied it.[113] Moreover, the door had a lock and key; and the room had no windows. The door and the site proved opportune to the extent that they could be secured.

But walls are not impenetrable. Though the two boys at Broadmoor Baptist's indoor camp-out identified a site for sex—a room within the most hallowed of community structures, a church building—the interior window meant the space could be violated, outsiders could peer in, when someone turned on the light. For Fitz Spencer, his bedroom door could be secured, but darkness was required before he and his sister's fiancé could engage in what they both knew to be forbidden sex. Likewise, McNaron brought flowers to her lover, "though it was too dark to see them."[114] And yet Darryl Jeffries and his cousin could ignore the light, could elude the sleeping girl on the sofa, by simply positioning themselves just to the other side of the chifforobe, a freestanding closet within the living room.

Successful to the extent that the outside world remained ignorant, these sexual liaisons illustrate ever-shifting notions of inside and outside, invisible and visible, hidden and exposed. In these settings, queer Mississippians created usable spaces that could momentarily be made inside by turning aside or shutting the door to the outside. While hidden from others, they were exposed to one another, more or less visibly engaged in the most intimate of interactions. In these spaces, hardly lonely, hardly alone, queer Mississippians understood and voiced their passions; they shared them with one another.

The rural landscape was anything but empty, devoid of sexuality. Rather, it was peopled with resourceful sexual beings. The three key institutions of community life—the school, the home, and the church—harbored diverse sexual proclivities. And, they housed workable spaces for sexual encounters. These spaces were never inherently averse to homosex; rather, they often fostered homosex.

College

White obstinacy, black persistence, and tragic deaths marked the integration of public universities in Mississippi. In 1959, when Clyde Kennard tried to gain admission to Mississippi Southern—later, the University of Southern Mississippi—local officials arrested him on false charges. He would die within weeks of his release from prison in 1963. Meanwhile, James Meredith finally succeeded in integrating Ole Miss—the University of Mississippi—when he enrolled in 1962, amid riots that left two dead. The showdown over state versus federal use of National Guard troops, between demagogic Governor Ross Barnett and "the Kennedys"—President John and Attorney General Robert—further elevated racist political discourse in the state.[115] For decades afterward many black Mississippians would prefer the state's three publicly funded HBCUs—historically black colleges and universities—Alcorn A & M (later, Alcorn State) in Lorman, established shortly after the Civil War; Mississippi Valley State in Itta Bena, opened after World War II, despite its location scarcely thirty miles from Delta State; and Jackson State, founded in 1877.

With the exception of Jackson State, Mississippi's public universities embodied the pastoral ideal, as did most two-year and private colleges. Located in small towns and farm communities, these schools often sequestered students from the outside world. Still, like elementary and secondary schools in the state, they provided key opportunities for rural youths and others to come into contact with large numbers of people. New ideas were shared, and new conclusions were reached.

In the 1950s and 1960s especially, the college experience brought many Mississippians into association for the first time with organized struggles for racial equality. On campus, what previously had passed for common sense—the ordinary, the taken-for-granted—was held up for scrutiny and targeted for change. Local action increasingly was perceived as part of larger national transformations. Yet despite the political tumult, despite the campus protests and demonstrations characteristic of the 1960s and 1970s, everyday life for Mississippi's students mostly consisted of learning and growing, studying and socializing. The mundane often obscured the momentous as young people went about their daily routines.

Both before and after integration, a college education was available to only a few in Mississippi. At the end of the period, only 64 percent of adults over the age of twenty-five held high school diplomas, the lowest percentage of any state. Only 15 percent—a distinct elite—held college degrees. But many more enrolled than graduated. Many attended the state's numerous junior colleges, which numbered roughly one for every five counties. At the middle of the period, however, all-white junior colleges, such as Itawamba and Copiah-Lincoln, greatly outnumbered all-black institutions, such as Coahoma and Utica. As compared to their percentage of the overall state population, black students had significantly fewer slots available to them in higher education classrooms—and, thus, lesser access to an important queer site.[116]

For those lucky white students and even luckier black students who could attend, college helped widen their sphere of friends and acquaintances. While high school social circles persisted at in-state colleges and universities, a curious student could meet dozens of new people. Often, though, the campus became its own tight-knit community of a few hundred or—at five or six institutions—several thousand. Privacy was rare. "Because Natchez College was so small," Anne Moody writes of the early sixties, "most of the relationships between girls and boys were a public thing. Everybody knew everybody else's business."[117]

Like these heterosexual relationships, homosexual couples were frequently acknowledged—and occasionally accepted. They were accepted at Rust, a Reconstruction-era Methodist college for black students. Around 1950 at least two men were understood to be homosexual. Though no one "came out of the closet," these two were known to have "all the signs"—a particular walk, "a fine voice." According to one student on the Holly Springs campus, the two "were not treated any differently" from their classmates. Indeed, the housing office insured that the young men roomed together throughout their entire time there—in consideration of the couple and perhaps also of reluctant potential roommates.[118] At another southern university in the late 1950s, two white men happened upon one another and fell in "love at first sight. We met in class, and our eyes kept meeting, too." Like the couple at Rust, these young lovers were able to secure a dorm room together, beginning the following semester.[119]

Queer men regularly congregated in particular dormitories, suites, or wings of dorms, most of which remained sex segregated throughout the period. They even managed to secure adjacent room assignments, sometimes creating large blocks of safe space. At Jackson State in the 1970s, men's residence halls had distinctive, well-recognized gay and straight areas. While the latter predominated, the former usually proved more cohesive and united. On small and large campuses, from Millsaps in Jackson to Southern in Hattiesburg, an entire residence hall could earn a reputation as queer space. Though such labeling often reflected homophobic aspersions cast by fraternities at marginalized "independent" students, many of those outside the orb of "the Greek system" happily and willfully chose queer dorms.[120]

At Mississippi Valley State in Itta Bena, gay and transgender students were a lively presence during the seventies. Bonita Garrett, who grew up in Louisville, Mississippi, considered her queer friends at Valley a fascinating lot: "They had a world of language all their own. They had a code going." And they turned any ridicule they faced to their own humorous advantage: "They used to dance around, make jokes, right out in the open. If a good-looking guy passed by, they'd say, 'Oooh, gotta have that,' or, 'I sure want that guy with the big butt.' . . . They rolled their stomachs. It was entertaining." For Garrett, city sophistication was not prerequisite to accommodating difference. On the contrary, because "those of us from small towns" were taught very little of homosexuality, "because we were not conditioned to hate it . . . , we were able to form our own opinions."[121]

"Becom[ing] more aware" of homosexuality characterized the college experience of both straight and queer.[122] At coed colleges and universities, black and white, women discussed "bulldaggers" and "funny" women in their dorms.[123] Bisexuals were said to be "fifty-fifty."[124] Mississippi University for Women, one of the nation's most enduring state-supported all-female colleges, was not only known by its moniker, "the W"; it also gained a reputation as "that queer college."[125] Male students on Mississippi campuses noticed the homosexuals in their midst, calling them "faggots," "queers," "sissies," or "punks."[126] Or, more flatteringly, homosexual men were sometimes referred to as "talented."[127] Self-acknowledged gay male friends spoke of one another as "true sisters."[128] And perhaps most characteristic of the language of southern indirection, queers were simply understood as being "that way" or "like that."[129]

As students engaged in frank and sometimes hostile conversations about homosexuality in the halls and unions, on the quads and walkways—and as homosexuality was anxiously negotiated in the sexually charged same-sex environments of dormitories and fraternity and sorority houses—classrooms were distinguished by a careful silence over most of this period. "While quite liberal," Tougaloo College, according to one long-time faculty member, "never offered a full platform for the discussion of homosexuality."[130] At Tougaloo, as elsewhere, rumors were rampant about particular faculty members, and hiring committees even went so far as to weigh faculty candidates' sexual histories.

Given the need for discretion, queer professors' influence over students was never so great as alarmists feared. Any homosexual interaction or even discussion of sexuality between student and teacher usually happened in one-on-one settings and followed a lengthy period of testing the waters— measured disclosure, hints, innuendo. While a scholar might trust his ability to detect a queer student, he still found it difficult to measure that student's particular interest in him. In the early sixties in Brookhaven, for example, a Whitworth College piano instructor felt a strong attraction to— and, he thought, a certain affinity with—his newest pupil. "About my third visit," the student remembers, "he started playing with my hands, doing things with my hands, putting my hands on his crotch." Unwilling to act on the advance, Vince Jones selected another sheet of music and proceeded to play the piano as if nothing had happened. As yet, Jones says, "homophobia" tinged his own budding homosexuality.[131]

Generally, faculty opinions about queer genders and sexualities were seldom heard, and if so, only outside of class. These views could rank among the most bigoted. Even celebrated scholars, widely respected, showed streaks of reactionary politics. For example, in her biography of fellow Mississippian Richard Wright, Margaret Walker—author of the acclaimed novel *Jubilee* and a longtime faculty member at Jackson State— wrote the following: "There are many indications of [Wright's] bisexuality. He had small delicate hands and feet, a very slightly bearded face, and a pipsqueak voice—high, shrill, and sometimes grating." Perpetuating a common stereotype, Walker says Wright "learned . . . who controlled the artistic fate of the cultural world," and consequently, she asserts, he struck a Faustian bargain with these evil men.[132]

Administrators at several universities attempted to suppress homosexual activity, especially sexual activity in campus rest rooms. Not all men's bathrooms on campus were sites for queer sex. But location and floor plan, secrecy and accessibility, made certain lavatories more conducive than others. Once a particular rest room became well-known, men from on and off campus would gather there. According to a professor at one large southern university, "In one month [around 1960], with guards posted near the only entrance" to a popular lavatory, "three hundred and fifty homosexuals were caught, and only two had any connection with the university."[133]

During the seventies at the University of Southern Mississippi, security officers were stationed outside one notorious "tearoom" in the George Hurst Building, jokingly renamed "Patty Hearst" after the kidnapped California heiress turned revolutionary activist.[134] Several individuals were arrested at the University of Mississippi.[135] While college officials conducted sweeps of public cruising areas, they forbade formal queer socializing and organizing. As of 1985 not a single university campus in Mississippi recognized a lesbian and gay student group. Indeed, in the seventies, the administration at Mississippi State went all the way to the United States Supreme Court to block formation of a group near its campus.[136]

A queer student in Mississippi need not be caught with his pants down to be expelled from school. As Frederick Ulner describes it, the University of Southern Mississippi regularly rounded up suspected homosexuals and kicked them out. He attributes these crackdowns to sinister motives: "What they were doing was running a scam. They got all their goddamn money for four years then wouldn't give them a [degree]." Though Ulner vaguely remembers these events as occurring with some frequency, "about every spring," he clearly recalls "the purge" of 1964, during which, he says, numerous students were forced out.[137]

Under adverse conditions, queer college boys had to stick together. Like the couple who roomed together at Rust College, homosexual men utilized the facilities at hand to mark off safe spaces for themselves. At Jackson State, Mississippi State, and Southern, among other campuses, men petitioned the housing offices so they could share rooms, suites, and wings of residence halls.[138] These queer homes away from home usually shielded them from the sanctions associated with queer organizing and the arrests associated with sex in public places. As Kerry Hartley describes queer groups at Southern during the seventies, "There wasn't anything organized. . . . It just wasn't really that cohesive of a community that I encountered. I guess people felt like they had to be pretty careful."[139] Nonetheless, through a complex web of friendship ties, queer residential quarters, campus cruising areas, and off-campus networks of house parties and nightclubs, male college students constructed worlds of same-sex desire and intimacy, love and camaraderie. The overall spirit of inquiry at college enabled some students to question prejudices and to explore sexualities. For those in Mississippi fortunate enough to attend college, these experiences well equipped them to expand their gay circles and to safeguard their queer desires in the cutthroat working world.

Work

Along with the social mobility afforded by a college education came a physical mobility enjoyed by degreed Mississippians. Job prospects took many workers out of the state. Yet most Mississippians felt impelled or compelled to remain. Though, as we shall see, migration was sometimes the last resort for the economically desperate, many could not leave precisely because of economic reasons. They couldn't take the gamble. They couldn't jeopardize the minimal safety net they had in place. Largely impoverished, Mississippi put its residents in a double bind. They could stay and try to eke out a subsistence living; or they could go—leave the support of family and friends—and run the risk of unemployment.

Like so many Mississippians during the middle of the twentieth century, a large number of queer Mississippians were tied to the land, earning meager amounts of money. In rural central Mississippi daughters and sons, like their mothers and fathers before them, worked as "farmers, dairymen [sic], cattle, horse, and pig raisers. . . . [F]ew held public jobs." Of necessity, children and teens "did field work, picked cotton, sold peas in Jackson for school money." Most queer Mississippians, like other agrarian and working-class adults, were as "poor and ragged as church mice." Contrary to latter-day assumptions of the great wealth and disposable income of purportedly childless gay couples, in midcentury Mississippi it seemed one "never found a well-off gay."[140]

George Albright: I was born January 15, 1960. My mother was born in Soso, Mississippi, and she moved to Eastabuchie in 1937, and she's been there since. My father was born in Eastabuchie, and he lived there until his death [in 1989]. I grew up in the same household. I grew up in the late sixties. We lived out in the country.

I farmed a lot when I was coming up. Now I still do a little farming, not as much as I did when I was growing up. And when I was coming up, we all, back then, worked as a community, instead of just one family trying to do everything. Everybody knew who was who. Once one farmer got through with his crop, he'd go help others finish their crops. It was more together back then than it is now.

We'd all go to church together, we'd all fish together, and some of us even hunted together. And we also went swimming together, during the summer when we were taking a break from farming. Everybody kind of pitched in and did things together, which made it a whole lot easier than it is now, because everybody's going their own separate ways. [Farming was] how we made our money for school—school supplies and clothes. My parents provided for us, but they taught us all how to work and take responsibilities at an early age—so when we got older, it wouldn't be a total shock to us and we'd all know how to deal with it.

I went to high school at South Jones High School in Ellisville. We really didn't have much time to date in high school, because working on a farm took a lot of our time. When we came in from school in the afternoon, we had chores. In the fall we had to get the cotton out of the fields, the corn had to be gathered, and the sugarcane had to be cut down and ready for syrup. It really kept us pretty busy.

Then I went to Jones Junior College for one year and took automotive machinists' training. Graduated in '79. Then in '79 I went into the U.S. Navy, where I took propulsion engineering school in Great Lakes, Illinois. A steam operator. We generated the steam for the boats. Once we were out to sea, our electricity and everything came from steam. The ship was moved by steam. Which was an easy job. [After four years], I returned back home, where I'm still at home. Same house, same road. Most of [my friends] have moved away, the ones that haven't gotten killed in car wrecks. Over half of my high school classmates are dead, either got killed in automobile accidents or drowned swimming. So I'm just blessed to be here.

[I was] one of the fellas. We all got along. Everybody treated everybody as they wanted to be treated. [When I came back from the navy,] they were glad to see me as I was glad to see them, especially my old drinking buddies. Went back to the old hole in the wall—that's what we called the old local bar. We had a good time.[141]

In black communities in rural Jones County, the never-ending cycle of farm labor hindered George Albright's social life—at least heterosexual dating. But after a hard day's work in the fields, he often made time for drinking, in mostly male worlds of camaraderie and commiseration. Friends in leisure doubled as fellow workers during the peak periods of harvest. But through the years, as more and more families were squeezed out of farming, a communal spirit diminished.

On and off the farm, the situation was dire. Elected officials regularly snubbed the poor and working class. Mississippi's state legislature was the nation's first to institute a sales tax, the most regressive of governmental income generators; it was the last to adopt a workers' compensation act.[142] Antilabor sentiments were perpetually in evidence. Legislators passed a sweeping right-to-work law in 1954 and inserted a right-to-work clause into a 1960 constitutional revision.[143] These union-busting measures coincided with the drastic decline in farm employment. As planting and harvesting were mechanized and even onerous tasks like chopping cotton were made obsolete by sprayed chemical pesticides, family farms withered and large-scale agribusiness grew.[144] Dispossessed agricultural workers sought jobs in industry, while state officials—in attempts to lure outside capital—touted low production costs and made conditions unbearable in factories. Onetime farmers of cotton, soybeans, and timber struggled as underpaid operatives in apparel, food-processing, and furniture plants. Caught in a downward spiral, Mississippi ranked worst of all states in all income categories—median household income, median income of families with children, average annual worker pay, and per capita personal income.[145] One-quarter of all Mississippians lived in poverty.[146]

In this bleak employment picture, queer workers held precarious positions. With jobs scarce, competition among applicants and employees increased, as did the pressure to conform on the job. Though they landed positions in the public realm—as soda jerks, bellhops, clerks, jewelers, hospital orderlies, theater ushers, and short-order cooks, among others[147]—homosexuals and transsexuals usually were not welcome in the workplace. As Rickie Leigh Smith remembers, for gender nonconformists it was difficult to determine who was more eager to "get you out": your boss or your coworkers.[148] If homosexuality was "a frequent topic [of conversation] among employees," it was most commonly as "a ridiculing or threatening discourse."[149]

For queers in both the working and professional classes, job discrimination often was subtle, difficult to detect. In the sixties a well-trained white architect in Hattiesburg spent years in a respected firm and yet never made junior partner. Convinced the principal "didn't want a gay partner"—even though he had never revealed himself to be gay—he finally "went out and started [his] own practice." [150] Dr. Ben Folk, a widely respected physician in Jackson, similarly was urged out of his practice after he divorced his wife and increasingly identified as gay.[151] The success of his subsequent individual practice attested to the potential of serving a gay clientele. But most queer workers didn't have the financial wherewithal to strike out on their own.

In the seventies a black bank teller in Pelahatchie never may have realized that his "sissified ways" were a subject of concern and discussion among his superiors. And he never may have been told that he was fired for this very reason.[152] This epistemology of not-knowing perpetuated anxieties. Having never spoken about his gender and sexual positionalities, an employee seldom had confirmation of an employer's knowledge nor, consequently, his motives in personnel decisions.

Other queer workers, however, knew full well their employers' views on gender and sexual nonconformity. Most employers, either as a matter of personal opinion or as a necessary public posture, disapproved. Especially after the growth of gay identity politics in the 1970s, antigay stances were publicly articulated such that Larry, an organist, felt the need for secrecy. Larry knew that the black Pentecostal churches where he worked would no longer hire him if he was openly gay on the job.[153]

Even businesses and institutions explicitly linked to queer worlds practiced discrimination based on sexual orientation or gender performance. Indeed, the linkage oftentimes fostered discrimination, as owners and administrators sought to protect their organization's standing. In the seventies Kerry Hartley worked for a beer distributor that supplied, among its numerous clients, Hattiesburg's gay bars. Because Hartley was rumored to be gay, he suffered harassment from his fellow employees.[154] As same-sex educational institutions earned reputations as queer spaces, administrators there attempted to purge homosexual staff members. At both All Saints Episcopal School for Girls in Vicksburg and Mississippi University for Women in Columbus, lesbian instructors were found out and forced out.[155] Likewise, men like that were susceptible to bias and employment discrimination at both all-male and all-female schools and colleges. Mark Ingalls, for example, thinks his stint as instructor and administrator at All Saints may have been cut short in the sixties due to rumors of his bisexuality.[156] At times the well-known connection between same-sex institutions and queer worlds—such as the homosexual activity prevalent in homosocial spheres—fueled an even more virulently outspoken homophobia than otherwise would have been observed.

However, as the site where Mississippians spent the majority of their waking hours, the workplace too was a site of homosexual desires, behaviors, identities, and networks. In large organizations particularly, small queer groupings were possible, though not readily apparent to the uninitiated. At times queer networks even facilitated queer employment, and certain units became queer bastions. In one government agency,

> the small post office located in the lobby . . . hired only gays. Not purposely. But if one gay quit his job there, he always recommended a person to take his place, who was always gay! I worked [at that agency] for the state . . . for twenty-six years and I saw literally hundreds of gays coming and going in that small cell at the end of the lobby. It was an accepted thing. . . . Every employee there, eight hundred and fifty, knew but turned their backs and kept their mouths shut. Of course that was [the sixties and seventies], not the Depression thirties.[157]

Queer workers not only helped one another find work; they also imagined, arranged, and experienced homosexual encounters on the job. As we shall see in chapter 5, for legendary Mississippian Billy Joe McAllister, the momentous first time happened with a complexly positioned partner, his employer. And as we shall see in chapter 3, for hairstylist Ricky Lee Smith, a beauty supply vendor was a logical sex partner and the back room of the beauty parlor a logical site for sex, even in the little crossroads community of Mize, Mississippi. Indeed, while recognizing the potential for discrimination and harassment—here as elsewhere—queer workers appraised vendors and clients, bosses and subordinates, colleagues and fellow laborers, as possible partners. Contingent on the time and occasion, queer sex could be pursued in work settings.

Though Chuck Plant considered the workplace "too risky" a site to approach other men,[158] others took the chance. Managerial-level employees and the self-employed especially utilized privilege to pursue sexual encounters at work. Mark Ingalls, for instance, never had intercourse at the office; but as personnel director for a large government agency, he set up dates with colleagues and subordinates there, even—in the 1970s—with a black associate. If his wife was away from home, Ingalls and a partner might go to his house for sex. Otherwise, they rented a motel room.[159]

In a racially stratified society, sexual encounters on the job were more fraught for black workers than white. Blacks were underrepresented in the professional classes, overrepresented among the poor and working classes. They seldom enjoyed the protections of economic independence; their employment often was at the whim and under the supervision of prejudiced white Mississippians. Especially early in the period, demands on black workers proved all too high. Under a pernicious system of white dominance, under a scrupulous and painstaking set of codes and customs, transgression was too easy, punishment too swift. If queer white workers were cautious on the job, queer black workers were even more so. The risks were greater, the retribution quicker, the penalties harder.

On the job, class and racial positions often effected sexual outcomes. Financial autonomy helped some individuals, including black entrepreneurs, maneuver around accepted codes of behavior. But those less well-off were more bound to these codes. While queer workers of color—blacks, Choctaws, and Mississippians of Chinese descent—suffered the multiple biases of their white supervisors, white businesspeople often moved successfully within and across social, sexual, and physical boundaries.

Fitz Spencer: It was the national interior designers convention.

Bill MacArthur: And it was in Dallas. Fitzhugh was there, and I was there. About a month before that, there had been a little magazine in Austin[, Texas]. I was in Austin, in a hotel. I can't remember what the name of the little magazine was.

S: *Go.*

M: *Go.* But anyway there was a picture of Fitz in his house [in Austin]. I knew who he was. And I thought, God, he's good-looking. He's a real hunk. I thought I'd like to meet him sometime. Then about a month later we were in Dallas for this meeting.

S: It was a festivity for the evening. Big tent.

M: The night before I had seen him at another party. I sent this guy that he knew and I knew too over to invite him to come to an after-party party. He was very nice. He didn't even see me, didn't even look at me. He said no he had other plans.

S: Had a hot date *[laughs]*.

M: Had a hot date with another decorator that I didn't think was very cute.

S: I didn't either *[laughs]*.

M: Not nearly as cute as I was. Anyway, the next night we were at a big picnic under a tent.

S: In the Dallas Decorative Center.

M: In the Dallas Decorative Center. They tented the whole parking lot. He was at a table about two tables over from me.

S: There was probably, what, seven or eight hundred people there—

M: I'm sure there was seven or eight hundred people there. I just turned around to look at him—

S: —from all over the country.

M: —and he was looking at me. And I winked at him. And he winked back. And we got up and sort of met in the middle of the tent, and discussed where we were going afterward. We were going to a party, happened to be invited to the same party. We went. We didn't go together, did we?

S: Uh-uh.

M: But we met at the party. Immediately we met on the landing of the stairs and started kissing. We had nothing to do with anybody else at the party. Had a couple of drinks and went back to his hotel room. I didn't need a hotel room because I was living in Fort Worth. That was on a Tuesday. And we were together that night, and then the next night, and then Thursday he went to Austin, went back home. I came [to Austin on] Friday. We spent the weekend together. Monday morning he sold me half his house and half his business. I didn't have that much cash.

S: I wanted the cash [laughs].

M: I had some stock, but the stock was in my father's safety deposit box in Odessa [Texas]. So I had to go out there. I went out and told my father. My mother was in their summer home in New Mexico. My father happened to be at home, thank goodness. And I went out and told him I wanted to talk to him. Of course, he didn't have any idea what I wanted to talk to him about. I told him what I wanted to do, and he thought I had lost my mind. We had a knock-down-drag-out. This was about eleven o'clock at night. I said, "The stock is mine. Admittedly you gave it to me, but it's in my name and you can't change it." I said, "If you won't get it out and give it to me in the morning, then I will get a court order in the morning to get it out." So he slammed his door and went to bed. And so I slammed my door and went to bed. The next morning at breakfast, he said, "You're crazy. You've lost your mind. I'm never going to give you another thing. But I have to give you the stock." He gave it to me. Some of it was bank stock. I wanted to sell the bank stock. He was a director of the bank, so he arranged for me to sell the bank stock. I got that. Then I sold the rest of it, which was in an oil company that he owned. It was a publicly owned company, but it was still his company.

S: He makes it sound like it was a million dollars.

M: It wasn't. Oh no, it wasn't that much money. It was like—how much was it?

S: Like about twenty thousand dollars.

M: Oh, it was more than that. The house was worth more than fifty thousand dollars. Anyway, whatever it was, it was not a great amount of money.

S: That was 1964. My friends thought that I had lost my mind, as Bill's family thought he had lost his mind. Because I had been in business for about eighteen months and it was very successful. And I had built a new house, which Bill and I later had in Architectural Digest. So I sold him half of each. They thought, you know, I was just giving it away. But he knew it would work, and I knew it would work. And we knew it was right. So we just said, you know, the hell with them.[160]

A college education, a break with family, and the economic opportunity of the city led many a queer Mississippian like Fitz Spencer out of the state. For those who stayed, those who felt viscerally tied or materially bound to place, the obstacles were significant but not insurmountable. Mississippians understood the difficulties as they thoughtfully made their choices. While persons of all sexual types departed the state for a variety of reasons, home had a hold on many. As one black Mississippian described it:

> You know, Mississippi got a bad reputation as being backward, and when I go up north, if I say I'm from there, they automatically think they know more than me and that everyone from Mississippi is dumb and stupid. But Mississippi is changing a little bit—it's got a long way to go, but it's changing. . . . You just got to stick in there in Mississippi and if you see something wrong you got to let people know about it and try to straighten it out. Mississippi is home for me and I want to stay.[161]

Queer boys who stayed generated sexual and gender realms diverse and distinct, discreet and divulged. These realms functioned within and occasionally against mainstream structures and discourses decidedly local in nature. Mississippi's patriarchal, racist, heterosexist institutions and inclinations shaped thought by and about the sexually marginal. Antiqueer sentiment extended from Ku Klux Klan directives on stoning perverts to subtle biases in everyday work and leisure environments.[162]

Male ambivalence over gender insubordination ranged from callous sexism to pride in uppity women. On the one hand, state agricultural commissioner Jim "Buck" Ross unselfconsciously asked the nation's first female vice presidential contender, Geraldine Ferraro, if she could bake blueberry muffins. (When Ferraro replied, ever feisty, "I sure can. Can you?" Ross was not to be outdone: "Down here in Mississippi," he dared to speak for the entire state, "the men don't cook."[163]) On the other hand, in 1975 Mississippians elected Evelyn Gandy—"Miss Gandy," as she was known, since she never married—as lieutenant governor, admittedly an acceptable "number two office."[164] Gender nonconformity of other stripes likewise provoked varied responses. While cross-dressing might be tolerated among the young, transgender identities and activities among adults elicited hostility in Mississippi.

Conservative notions of sexual propriety and gender normalcy imbued all aspects of daily life. These notions were frequently reinforced on the job and in the principal social environments of every Mississippi community— the home, the school, and the church. If at times these institutions resisted a queer presence, if they appeared decidedly antagonistic toward queer notions, they also served as malleable sites for queer interaction. Home, church, school, and workplace, for some, were suitable sites for queer activity. With limited resources but unlimited inventiveness, queer Mississippians reconstituted dominant environments, making everyday places into useful queer locales.

Male-male desire foremost was experienced and acted upon at home. Most Mississippians lived in rural family households, markedly different from the independent single life associated with urban gay ghettoes or even urban family life.[165] When men prepared for sex, the question was not "my place or yours?" Rather, "our place or y'all's?" Within the house, sex was negotiated spatially and temporally. At certain times of day and night, when wives or other family members were away, men invited other men into their homes. Or with family members all about, men sequestered their desires in momentarily protective spaces. Fitz Spencer and his sister's fiancé had sex with the bedroom door closed, the lights out. For resourceful youths like Mark Ingalls or Darryl Jeffries, a sleeping mother upstairs or a sleeping cousin on the couch did not prevent them from getting off with a partner under the very same roof or even in the very same room. Thus, given their situation, Mississippians cultivated a distinct form of *home*-osexuality.

Home inspired loyalty, as a distinctive built structure, as an imagined, conflicted refuge, and as a broader cultural space. Home, for Fitz Spencer, was Natchez, Mississippi. Spencer and partner Bill MacArthur moved their successful interior design firm from Austin to Houston in 1965 but ultimately bought a grand old antebellum home back in Natchez, weathered a relatively short three-and-a-half-year separation in the mid-eighties, and retired there. Many other queer boys like George Albright lived nowhere else but Mississippi, even residing in the same house and working the same land for their entire lives. For these boys and men, and for countless other men like that, male-male desire existed not *apart from* but rather as an inextricable *part of* everyday home and community life.

CHAPTER THREE

Movements

The constant query of my childhood was "Where you been?" The answer, "Nowhere." . . . The truth was that I did go nowhere— nowhere in particular and everywhere imaginable. I walked and told myself sto- ries, walked out of our sub- division into another, walked all the way to the shopping center and then back. . . . [W]hen I walked, I talked— story-talked, out loud— assuming identities I made up. Sometimes I was myself, arguing loudly as I could never do at home. Some- times I became people I had seen on television or read about in books, went places I'd barely heard of, did things that no one I knew had ever done, particularly things that girls were not supposed to do. In the world as I remade it, nothing was forbidden; everything was possible.

—DOROTHY ALLISON[1]

WHERE YOU BEEN? Where you going? How long are you here for? Need a lift? Can you give me a ride? Excuse me, do you know where I might find the Tropic Bar? Want to get in the backseat? Want to see the back room? Our place or y'all's? Available?

As queer Mississippians queried one another, as they exchanged inquisitive gestures, as they communicated with each other using eye contact and body language, their overtures and prop- ositions all shared one underlying, sometimes unstated element: movement. Queer interaction presupposed transportation. Friends and sex partners, longtime acquaintances and strangers relied on technologies of transport to enable not just congregation but circulation. These modes of transit proved more or less advantageous depending on the moment, the place, the condi- tions. Negotiating fractious terrain, queer Missis- sippians gauged an environment in flux. Perceiv- ing hostility as well as hospitality, they moved into available spaces, pressing them into the ser- vice of queer desire.

In mid- and especially late-twentieth-century Mississippi, gay communities existed along- side and within broader queer networks; self- identified gay men shared spaces with pre- sumably larger numbers of non-gay-identified queers; men like that came into contact with men who also liked that. These exchanges and inter- changes mirrored and occasionally countered dominant cultural trends. They evinced six important traits well-known to queer Mississippians.

First, movement was constant. Though perhaps slow paced as compared to the big cities of the North and West, life in Mississippi reflected a perpetual process of change. Old institutions passed away; new mechanisms arose to replace them. Second, queer movement was multidirectional. For hours, days, or years at a time, men moved back and forth between areas rural and urban, intimate and anonymous, familiar and unknown. As family farming declined and urban living increased across America, queer Mississippians nonetheless returned with frequency to the land, if only a quarter of an acre in suburbia. Third, queer movement, long term and short, was enabled by multiple means of conveyance. Queers met and gathered on foot and on horseback, via buses, trains, and planes that were racially segregated through the 1960s. The act of walking itself—a person's gait, his manner—became a means of eliciting and finding queer companionship. Some were more daring than others: "One black gay in Jackson, around 1935 to 1938, wore white rice powder on his face and hands when he walked down Capitol Street at night and wore a wide-brimmed yellow leghorn hat, Scarlett O'Hara style. Boy! He was one nervy gay!"[2]

Movements were both large scale—transforming society as a whole—and small: momentary, idiosyncratic, at times inconsequential. Some queer Mississippians lived and died without ever traveling beyond the bounds of their county. Others were a part of massive migrations, mobilizations, and movements for social change. Fifth, movement encompassed institutions as well as individuals. Queer spaces changed over time; they flourished then floundered. Gay bars ceaselessly picked up and moved, relocated, ever in search of the most receptive and responsive site. Generally over the period, gay and queer-friendly bars shifted from locales evenly dispersed across the landscape in the forties and fifties, to peripheral spaces on town and city outskirts in the sixties, to ostensibly abandoned inner cities in the seventies and eighties. Cruise areas evidenced a related pattern, though rural spaces remained strong throughout, with the aid of improved highways. Even stationary structures were transformed, as their neighboring structures changed, as the people who utilized them changed.

Finally, movement was delimited by race, class, and gender, in keeping with mainstream values and attitudes. Especially at midcentury, Choctaws and Chinese Mississippians were granted few of the liberties enjoyed by whites. African Americans even less so. Since racial hierarchies often dictated class hierarchies, mobility decreased for people of color, those with diminished financial resources. As compared to whites, access to queer networks was circumscribed, and queer desire remained closer to home. And just as men were freer to move about than women, so too male homosexuals by and large got around more than male-to-female transsexuals. "Straight-acting" gay males had entrée where gender-nonconforming queers did not.

Ease of mobility reflected one's station in life.

Chuck Plant: I went to high school at Central High [in Jackson]. I had an older friend. It was not a sexual relationship, but really a friendly relationship. As we talked, things came out. He kind of introduced me to the life, the gay life—that things were going on, that you could go to a gay bar, and meet another gay man. And it might involve a sexual encounter—which was very titillating. The Tropic Bar was on the street behind the old post office on Capitol Street. I think it was Pearl or Pascagoula, one or two streets over. I was very apprehensive. I thought, I hope no one that I know in the outside world is seeing me, or that I'm going to run into anyone that I know in here. That never occurred, fortunately.

It was on street level, you went in, and it went way back. There was a long bar and a jukebox. It was kind of on the dark side. It was like a restaurant that had been converted. I met a lot of gay guys, all types of people. You know, you met the regulars who came. But if you made contact with a stranger it was great, because he was the new blood, not the run-of-the-mill, the old crowd. Because I was quite young, still in high school, they seemed older, which was attractive to me. Or some of them were attractive. Just men. This was way back yonder, so it was just white. Like 1948, '49, somewhere around there.

My main time to go was in the afternoon. That was the time that was available, convenient for me. In those days you could only have beer in Mississippi, so generally speaking you never saw drunkenness. If someone came in who was straight, he might have a quick beer and leave. But the regulars were sort of there for a long stretch. It got to be fairly well-known. And I guess maybe that's what happened to it. It sort of faded out. The circumstances I don't know. It may have become too notorious.

During that period the bus stations were quite active places, Greyhound [on Lamar Street] and Trailways [on Pascagoula]. In the Trailways [men's room], there was a glory hole. In the Greyhound there was maybe a peep hole and I think a glory hole, too. But sometimes those things would be shut up and then reopened. They came and went. Also, there were hotels that had active men's rooms. The Robert E. Lee Hotel was right up the street from the Greyhound bus station on Lamar. It was back of Central High. There was a way to get into the men's room from the street, from the parking lot, so that you didn't have to go through the lobby. It was on a level below the lobby, which made it ideal. There was always eye contact. You know, it was kind of like looking, and show me. One thing led to another.

Another place that was very active—believe it or not—in the new Capitol build-ing, there was a men's room that was flagrant. And it had glory holes. There were two booths. You could go into a booth and sit down and wait for, you know. And I guess you were satiated. There seemed to be a steady stream of people coming. I used to go there quite often. It got so bad that they put metal sheets over the sides of the stalls. I don't recall [anal sex] happening, and yet anything is possible.

There was not a lot of crackdown, you know, legal intervention. Things were kind of wide open. And now that I look back on it, I kind of wonder why. That may have happened later, like this business at the old City Auditorium. That happened after I had left Jackson and was in New York.

I graduated from high school in 1949, but I went to school for a year and a sum-mer at Hammond, Louisiana—Southeastern Louisiana College. I was having trouble adjusting to being away from home, and I was going through a flagrant period. I guess I wanted a good many people that I saw in those days. In the dormitory set-ting, I suppose I was sort of reckless. You're in the showers, all that sort of thing. Sometimes it worked out; sometimes it didn't. I guess I was always fairly obvious. If you've got to pick out someone who's gay, the finger would stop at me. You can get a bad reputation, which of course I did. There are some who come on to you in oblique ways; there are some who are just downright insulting and almost threaten-ing. Guys come on to you, and you think, I'm too afraid. I don't know whether he might become violent. That's a risk you take all your life.

I remember being called by feminine names. A girl's name was sort of common. Once I said that I had a sister whose name was Patricia, and I was called Patricia right away. And I was called Myrtle. Somebody calls you a name and it sticks. Those were the two. Also, fag. And gay.

I lost my scholarship in music. So my aunt said you better come back home and just go to Millsaps [College]. So I went to Millsaps and lived at home. The house we lived in is gone. It was 708 North Street. There are buildings there now. You know, Millsaps is a very difficult school, and I thought, Lordy. I received a draft notice. At Millsaps they said, "We can get you out of this." But I thought I'm not doing any-thing here but just going down the tubes. So I decided to go ahead and go into the army, which may have looked like jumping out of the frying pan and into the fire. But I'm glad I did, because in the army you come in contact with so many, many guys. I saw that though I certainly was not the ideal man in this group, neither was I the . . . You find that you're somewhere in the middle, is what I'm trying to say. That you're neither the glowing example, nor are you the tail end of the group. It gave me confidence that I needed, that I lacked.

I went in in January of '52. I went overseas to Korea in June. Came back June of '53. I think I was separated in September. Then when I came out of the army, I went to Mississippi Southern. It was a college then and is now a university, in Hattiesburg.

There was another bar in Jackson, a block or two from the [Illinois Central] railway station. That may have been Pearl Street, but on the other side of the overhead, the elevated railway. It was a very small, tiny place, and it had a small bar that had stools. Hardly room to walk between the tables and the bar. Maybe three tables. It had a jukebox. And again just beer. I was at Southern then. The bartendress, a woman, was named Connie. And she did not like me at all. I used to think, Why doesn't she like me? Because I was a student, I had no money to spend, and I was not tipping her anything. There were guys younger who had jobs and I'm sure were leaving her generous tips. They were her favorites. Not me.[3]

I don't remember any bars in Hattiesburg. Some of my gay friends lived off campus, and we used to go to their apartment, but it was very hush-hush. We tried to be very nonconspicuous, if that's possible. We were very scared of being known, though I'm sure I was fairly well-known. But you needed to be careful. You could meet behind closed doors with the drapes drawn with your friends, but you didn't want it known. Now I remember going to a hotel there that had a glory hole down

Chuck Plant, *right*, and a friend on the streets of Columbia, South Carolina, 1952. Courtesy of Chuck Plant.

in the men's room. The Forrest Hotel. Also, the Trailways bus station, though I didn't go there as often, because you could run into students coming and going, having gone home maybe for the weekend, coming back to school. That was not too smart to be seen cruising the Trailways bus station, unless you were legitimately going home for the weekend or the holidays or something. I didn't have a car, and I really did not come home that often.

I still had one year of GI bill [after Southern]. My aunt thought I should go to art school, and a very close friend of hers was pushing for Pratt Institute, which is in Brooklyn. So I went to Pratt Institute for four years, and I have a degree from Pratt. Graduated in '60. Then New York was like opening the door on the world, of course. When I first got out of Pratt, I knocked around at any number of jobs. Then I went into social work because you could take the test and get in, and you were kind of frozen in. And it paid better than most of these other knock-around things. So I did that for a good long time. But I worked for banks and a whole lot of stuff. I worked for Manufacturers Hanover Trust for six years I think. But I can't say that I was ever just crazy about what I was doing. Even social work in New York is ghastly. But you gotta do something.

In New York, I lived on Christopher Street, and the Stonewall thing happened, and I was totally unaware of it.

I would come back for holidays. When I got far enough along in my work, I would get summer holiday, and then I used to come maybe for a week in the summer, and every time at Christmastime. So sometimes I was coming back maybe twice a year. Then when my aunt was getting to be an old lady, I knew that she was forgetting things. So I said to one of her friends, "You know, it might be a good idea for me to come back and look after her." And this friend of hers says, "*I know it would*" [shouted]. Just about like that. And I thought, Uh-oh. I haven't moved fast enough. So I did come back.[4]

Cities and Towns

For some, Jackson is home. For others, it is a destination—a place to visit or one day settle down. Situated near the center of the state, Jackson is the capital and largest city in Mississippi, though its population has only ranged between 100,000 and 200,000 during the second half of the twentieth century.[5] It is almost midway between the larger Mississippi River cities of Memphis, Tennessee, to the north and New Orleans, Louisiana, to the south, along the 340-mile greatest length of the state. On an east-west axis—never more than 180 miles wide in Mississippi—Jackson is closer to the port of Vicksburg, on the west, than to Meridian, near the state border with Alabama, on the east.[6]

Chosen and developed expressly as the capital in 1822, Jackson was laid out on a grid, as suggested by Thomas Jefferson. Though ten miles from the nearest road, the Natchez Trace, the city was well perched—for a low-lying coastal state—along the Pearl River, near LeFleur's Bluff. By mid-twentieth century much of the economic and social life of the capital was still carried out within and around the thirty blocks originally platted. On the highest point of the west bank, with its back to the Pearl River, the by-now "old Capitol" building sat at the east-center edge of town. From the front steps Capitol Street ran westward, forming a T intersection with State Street. Most street names chosen during the 1820s remained in the 1950s. North-south streets running parallel to State were West, Congress, President, and—commencing at the Capitol's north side—North Street. Perpendicular to State and parallel to Capitol Street were Mississippi, Yazoo, Amite, Pearl, Pascagoula, and Tombigbee.[7]

The downtown core was so neatly contained that a wandering queer boy like Chuck Plant could easily survey the major queer spaces within a few minutes' walk. From his home at 708 North, Plant began an ordinary day by walking south and west to Central High, an impressive two-story Gothic structure of brown brick, fronting on West Street. If he could get away over lunch, he might check out the rest room at the Robert E. Lee Hotel, behind Central across the street, or the new Capitol, only a block away. Next door to the hotel on Lamar—one block off West—was the busy Greyhound bus station, and just three and half blocks down, at the southern terminus of Lamar, on Pascagoula, was Trailways, also known as Continental Southern. Plant often dropped by the Tropic at the end of the school day, one block back up Lamar on Pearl. From there, two blocks east on Pearl, at Congress, was the City Auditorium—where Plant practiced his viola and performed with the Jackson Symphony.[8] He also cruised the rest room there on other occasions.

Other oral history narrators confirm the popularity of the bus stations and add that queers also gathered during the 1950s at Walgreens, the coffee shop at the Heidelberg Hotel, the Jackson Zoo, and Poindexter Park.[9] Likewise fertile grounds, the city's principal movie theaters were located along Capitol Street. Whereas moviegoers could make homosexual advances from the seats of a darkened theater, sex in public buildings chiefly occurred in the rest rooms. As Laud Humphreys explains in his on-the-ground sociological studies and as Lee Edelman elaborates in his provocative theoretical treatises, public rest rooms have provided ideal settings for homosexual interaction.[10] As a lavatory gained a reputation as a tearoom, those interested could identify one another by distinctive gestures and eye contact, while others went about their business undisturbed. Hand jobs at urinals and blow jobs through glory holes cut in stall partitions often happened quickly and quietly. However, if police went looking for queer

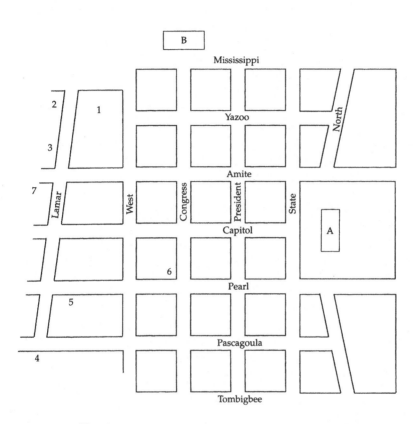

B

Mississippi

2   1

Yazoo

North

3

Amite

7

Lamar   West   Congress   President   State

Capitol

A

6

Pearl

5

Pascagoula

4

Tombigbee

N

DOWNTOWN JACKSON, 1949

A   Old Capitol
B   New Capitol
1   Central High School
2   Robert E. Lee Hotel
3   Greyhound Bus Station
4   Continental Bus Station
5   The Tropic Bar
6   City Auditorium
7   Hotel Heidelberg

sex, they could find it. As will be discussed in chapter 4, in addition to the widely discussed raid at the City Auditorium, police also made arrests at the Forrest Hotel in Hattiesburg, long after Chuck Plant's tenure at Southern.[11]

Men nonetheless took the risks, in municipalities large and small. Public sex flourished, from Atlanta, where a McComb native was jailed along with nineteen others in 1953; and Dallas, where one Mississippian was arrested at the airport a year later; to Jackson, Hattiesburg, and even Vicksburg, where homosexuals, as early as the 1950s, dubbed those hotels with active tearooms as "silver tray" establishments.[12]

Hardly a metropolis, Vicksburg was home to twenty-eight thousand at midcentury.[13] Still, its movie houses proved logical sites to meet men, and its municipal library, like those throughout the state, served a dual role for questioning men and youth. Though they often searched unsuccessfully under "H" for affirming representations of their condition, they sometimes found sexual activity in the men's room. While Mark Ingalls "snuck into" the library stacks in a futile quest for useful information, others acted on their desires, just the other side of the wall, within the helpful space of the library toilet. By the 1960s Ingalls found another popular downtown site: "There was a wonderful tearoom in the Hotel Vicksburg. Nice glory holes, the whole nine yards. You go down on an afternoon, just sit there and wait. Somebody always came in. And you'd be surprised. You could be walking along a street and see somebody. You could follow them or they could follow you, and you could figure out what was going on."[14] Even in Mississippi's smaller cities and towns, queer sex seemed to be going on with great frequency.

Rickie Leigh Smith: I left home at seventeen to come to college in Jackson. I was taking business courses for a year at a business college. I had my first—I'd say I lost my virginity—my first homosexual or gay experience. I went to a movie theater. At that time, I didn't have a car. I lived close to the downtown area, and I walked down there [to] the old Royal Music Hall on Capitol Street, right close to Capitol and State. It was one of my favorite haunts. I would go there and watch movies. I would go and sit in the dark theater. This man sat down. He must have been probably in his early thirties. Quite young, but much older than I. In the dark, he reaches over and touches my hand. I touch his, and I get extremely excited. It was the most pleasurable thing I can remember. It seemed so natural. We just held hands, and played with each other's hands, and rubbed legs, that sort of thing. We were having a lot of foreplay right there in the theater. I was extremely excited. I mean aroused to a fever pitch. Finally, he suggested we leave. So we did. We got up and walked out. And I remember I had this really enormous erection. It was embarrassing, because I had on tight pants. Anyway, his car was parked close to the theater. We went and got in his car, and we drove off. Being young and naive, I didn't even think about the dangers of that. But I went with him willingly. He was a professional person, something in mental health. We drove out to some wooded area close to the city, not too far away. And we had sex in the car, in the front seat. They were big in those days—big, roomy cars. I was more on the receiving end of that deal. I was passive, and he was active. At that time, I still did not engage in [take the receptive role in] oral sex. The thought of it was just too much. I couldn't deal with it. But, oh god, with that man, it was just the most pleasurable experience.

Very guilty. I was torn between the pleasure I felt and the guilt I felt. I was very confused. I had a lot of crying jags. I could see hell opening in front of me. But I kept going back and doing it again and again with different people.

[Also around 1957,] I picked up a guy at the old Paramount [Theater]. He was not much older than me. Probably he was twenty-four; I was about seventeen or eighteen. Very good-looking, physically very appealing. His name was William. Dark hair, tall, well-built, very handsome. We went to his mother's house, where he lived with his mother. She was a nurse. She was working that night, so he was home alone. He wanted to engage in anal sex. I had never done that before. It was very painful. I went along with it to please him. It was not a pleasurable experience [for me]. I was very tense; I couldn't relax. I remember I was very excited with him, but he didn't like to kiss. And I do. And that really upset me. He was one of those types that anything was OK but not the kissing. He could not go for that. He was engaged to be married. That was something he could only do with a woman. So I felt let down, very much so. So that was not a good experience.

I was living in a boardinghouse at the corner of George and President Streets [one block north of the new Capitol]. Most of the guys who lived in this rooming house were very rough, masculine-type guys, beer-drinking, honky-tonk-carousing types. But I do remember one guy. He was my hero. I loved him so much. He was maybe a couple of years older than I. He was a football player, and he was in college. But that summer he was working for the Mississippi Highway Department. He was from Wesson, Mississippi. And he was one gorgeous hunk of man. Not just physically; he had the most wonderful character, personality. All these other guys, they would all get together and go out honky-tonking and doing their little thing, and they'd want him to come with them. He wouldn't. He'd stay with me. He said, "I'm going to stay here with Ricky, and help him with some work." I was going to college at the time. And if they went anywhere, he insisted they let me come. He would take me to the movies with them—wherever they were going. Needless to say, I needed that. And I don't know why he took up so much time with me—this tall, gangly, underweight, ugly person, ridden with acne. But he loved me, and I loved him. It was the most marvelous friendship.

But I crossed the line. I would call him affectionate little pet names like "darling" or "sweetheart," and he would get very upset with me about that. "Don't call me that." You know, "You act like a woman." I said, "Well, I feel like one—a girl." He wouldn't really push the issue that much.

But he and I would just have the best time when we were together. He would go in the bathroom to take his bath, and I would prop something against the door so when he opened the door it would fall on him. Just practical jokes. And he would chase me down the hall in the altogether. He just ran around nude in front of me all the time. He had a great body, but I never made a pass at him physically. I never did come on to him that way. I guess maybe I had sense enough not to, realized he would not take it very well. He left at the end of the summer to go back to college. I remember crying. I almost had a breakdown. It was terrible.

[After] Jackson Commercial College from '57 to '58, I went to cosmetology school, the old Fritz Marinello Beauty School on Pearl Street. I went there for almost a year, graduated, got my license, started working in the cosmetology field. I moved home to Mize for a while and worked down there for a lady, a friend—'59, '60, '61, along in there. I was there for about a year and a half.

There was this salesman that came through. He was extraordinarily good-looking. He was a sales rep for one of the beauty supply companies in Jackson. He'd come in occasionally. I made a pass at him one day. In the beauty shop. I was in there alone when he came. No customers right then. It was a frustrating attempt at a sexual encounter with him. It did not work. He was willing to go along with it, [but] he wanted to be very passive about it. At that point, if it wasn't a mutual thing I wasn't interested. He was trying to explain something to me. He was standing next to me. And I just started brushing his leg and playing with his leg and moving up his leg with my hand. It was very obvious. I took his hand, and he followed me into the back. We had a little room in the back of the shop. He unzipped his pants, said, "OK, I'm here, do your thing." And that was a turnoff. I said, "Uh-uh, no, I can't go for it like that."

There was this lady hairdresser. I worked with her, and she and I became good friends. She was a beautiful, beautiful woman. I mean Elizabeth Taylor beautiful. Black hair, gorgeous. She was always trying to match me up with girls. She insisted I had to start dating. So she fixed me up with this girl who used to come in. She'd do this girl's hair. "This girl's interested in you." She wanted me to date her. I was terrified. I did ask the girl, she said yes, and we went to a drive-in. I remember we went in the pickup truck, my father's. I was miserable. It was the most miserable night I spent in my life. It wasn't the girl's fault. It was me. It was the way I was. I didn't want to be with a woman; I wanted to be with a man. And she was a sweet person. And I just thwarted every attempt of hers. I wasn't interested. Couldn't wait for that date to be over with and get her home. I must have made that poor girl feel horrible. I think about that to this day. It was so unfair to her. If I had been a red-blooded American-type man, I would have been all over her. I wasn't interested. I just wasn't. I wanted a man.

In the early sixties after I moved back to Jackson, Miss Tullos owned a boarding-house on High Street—the old Magnolia House right behind the [new] Capitol. We had a lounge upstairs where the boys used to go up and sit and watch TV and smoke or whatever. And two of us were sitting on the couch one night, and he started playing hands with me and came on to me, and I went to his room with him.

That's what it was like until I got married. From the time I was seventeen until I got married at twenty-six, it was like that. At the movies, at the boardinghouse. I was in and out of little sexual encounters here and there with guys, but I never was super-promiscuous. It wasn't like a two or three times a week kind of thing. It was like once a month, once every six weeks. I didn't date [women]. That was the only date I had before I got married.

I met [a woman] who also worked at the beauty shop [where I worked in Jackson]. She was from Prentiss, Mississippi. We became good friends, and I let it go beyond friendship. I carried it far beyond that because I was getting on up in my twenties, I wanted children, and I knew I could never have children except as a father. I think that was the primary motivation for me marrying her. I cared about her, but I wasn't in love with her. So I went along with the courting and the engagement ring, the whole bit. I let her think it was OK. So we got married in '66.

I left the beauty shop business and went [back] to college. Went home and lived with my father and mother and helped him in his chicken business. I also went to school for two years at a junior college, then transferred to Southern for two years and got my B.S. degree, graduating in '68. We lived in married student apartments on the campus.

Then we moved to Jackson County to the Pascagoula area. I started teaching school down there. Our first child was born, our second child, then we had twins. So we had four sons. The marriage, the sexual part of it, lasted about ten years, although we were together legally about twelve or thirteen years. The last two or three years she knew the score. It was kind of an armed truce. And we of course just stayed together until she got tired of the situation and said I had to leave. I tried very hard for ten years to make that work, but I just could not do it. It got progressively worse. I went along with it for a while, played the role, almost fooled myself into believing I was having a wonderful time. It just wasn't so.

Sooner or later you have to have that showdown with yourself. That to me is the most frightening thing we'll ever have to face in this world: we have to face ourself and look at ourself squarely. You've got to be yourself. You have to go where your heart leads you. There's a great deal of peace that comes with that. There's no longer that struggle, that confusion.

I ended up hurting her badly because it didn't work. I fell in love with this guy

I taught school with. The tenth year of our marriage. He started teaching school there. He hit me like a ton of bricks. I loved this man so much. It was just consuming. I couldn't think about anything else but him. I went and I had a talk with this guy's brother-in-law, who was teaching school down there too. He said, "The problem is not Tom. The problem is your transsexualism." He said, "You've got to do something about it. You've got to face it." I said, "Bill, I'm married and have four children." "That does not matter. You've still got to do it for yourself, regardless. Because if you don't, you're never going to be happy." So Bill was the one who gave me the pep talk and got me started on this. He made me see that I really had to go through with this.

So that's when I went and faced my wife. And she had pretty well figured it out by then because the Renée Richards story had come out.[15] It was in all the news, and we talked about that. And she was really on my side in the whole matter. She was hurt by the marriage coming to an end. Of course she was. But she was very much for me and what I wanted to do. She was my champion. For a while. Her parents caused a lot of problems, her family. They got real upset, of course, when they found out. It caused a big rift in the family.

I went to Baltimore, Maryland, in '76, after I confronted my wife with this. I was in touch with a psychologist in Pascagoula and also up there. And I flew up there to confer with her about all this. She worked with transsexuals. At that time, Johns Hopkins Hospital was treating transsexuals and doing the surgery. As I understand it, that was the first place in this country that actually did the surgery. They had a strict set of prerequisites. First step you do this, you do this, you do this, you do this. You clear all these hurdles before they will even consider doing the surgery. You've got to pass all these tests. This is a serious step, and you have to be sure. Once the surgery's done, it's irreversible. So you better be damn well sure you know what you're doing. Well, I knew. Still do. There's no doubt. I mean there's no way I would ever regret it.

Anyway, I went up there and talked with her and spent the whole day with her. It was a very enlightening day. I enjoyed it. So when I came back home, the first step was to find a physician who would administer hormones, get me started on hormone treatments. Because you have to have those a minimum of two years before the surgery.

We moved to Jackson [from Pascagoula]. We moved back in '77. It was the week that Elvis died, as a matter of fact. And I started working in September [as a ticket agent] at the [Greyhound] bus station. Could not find a doctor in the whole Jackson area. They didn't even want to talk about it. They all had a very negative attitude. "Uh-uh. We don't treat people. Uh-uh. No." Rather like homophobia. They just didn't want to discuss it. This went on for three years. I was beside myself trying to figure out what to do. Very depressed.

I had in the meantime gotten involved in the gay community here. I made gay friends. I started going to the gay discos. I started hobnobbing around with all the gay people. And my whole life was wrapped up with them to the point where I didn't even know what the heterosexual world was anymore. I felt comfortable with gay people; I was having a great time. It was like I was liberated. But I still had this problem. I couldn't get on the hormones. And I didn't want to be a drag queen. I wanted to live as a woman and have the feelings.

I had never been in a quote gay bar until 1977. The Myers owned two bars at that time—Mae's Cabaret and Mama and Papa Jack's, they called it, out on North State. Eddie Sandifer—who was the spokesman for the gay people at that time here—I went and met with him and he was telling me all about it. I went out to Mama and Papa Jack's and started hanging out there, before that place closed. This was a small bar. They had a little dance floor and a bar. It wasn't too bad. It later became a redneck bar. Somebody bought it out. Mae's Cabaret was big, very big. It was the main bar in town. They had a big disco scene there with the dance floor and everything. It was where the old Wagon Wheel used to be, the old nightclub called the Wagon Wheel, a country-and-western honky-tonk, which was on the corner of Capitol Street downtown right near the Mayflower [Café]. And I went there, before they moved over to the old Amite Theater on Amite Street, before it burned. That was going strong about the time of John Travolta and *Saturday Night Fever* and all that. And I got involved in sexual experiences with gay people. I became part of the scene. Most of it was very frustrating. Because I didn't want any one-night stands. I wanted a relationship. I couldn't find that.

I started doing the drag shows. I loved it. It gave me an excuse to dress up and have a good time. It was a novelty. It was something I enjoyed for a while. But I didn't realize I was doing myself a disservice by doing all that stuff. Because I was building a reputation, and I didn't like, didn't really want to be a part of that. I went in for the old Broadway show tunes. My drag name was Lady Gay Chanel. I went in for all the glitter and the sequins. The Ethel Merman numbers, that type of stuff.

It was during the drag shows one night [in 1980] I met this person who was a transsexual also, who was on hormone therapy, who was anticipating having the change. I said, "I can't get anybody to give me the hormones." "Oh honey, no problem. Go to Dr. Ben Folk up here on State Street." Her doctor. She sent me to Dr. Folk. He put me right on the hormones. I've been on them ever since. Ben Folk came on to me right in his office, tried to have sex with me right in his office. A sweet, eccentric old man. And I went along with a lot of his crap because I wanted to get the hormones. I never was sexually involved with him. It wasn't that. It never got to that. But he flirted around and carried on with me one time. Well, Dr. Folk was murdered two years after he retired.[16] His office referred me to a Dr. Allen off Lakeland Drive that I went to for six years. He finally decided he didn't want to treat transsexuals anymore. I said, "What?!" I got real upset. They referred us to another doctor.

New Year's Eve [1980] was the night I threw a terrible drunk and almost never got home. I lived out in Rankin County. My father owned some property out here; he had a mobile home, and I was living out there. And how I got home that night I will never know. I was as drunk as one human being can possibly be and still drive. If I had gotten picked up, they would have never let me out of jail. I woke up the next morning, got out of bed. There was panties and bras and this and that and the other all the way down the hall. I didn't take my makeup off; I had passed out. And ought to have died. I had a hangover that you wouldn't believe, for two or three days. I told my wife about it, and she laughed. She said, "Good, it's what you deserve." It was horrible, terrible. I never did that again.

[In the early 1980s], I was still going to the bars, doing the drag shows. I was not living twenty-four hours a day as a woman. It was a once in a while thing. It was getting to me. And people told me, "Rickie, you've got to stop this. You're trying to straddle the fence. You're trying to live two different lives. It won't work." My boss was giving me a lot of pressure at work. He was trying to get me out. I have to look at the good things he did for me, not for the other. I think he was unfair, and on occasion he was cruel. But he came through for me; he was there for me when nobody else was. Because if a lot of those people I worked with down there had their way, I would have been fired. He would not hear of it. Because he told me, a bunch of them were trying to get rid of me. But he stood up for me, and he would not fire me. He would also give me a bigger Christmas bonus than he would the rest of them. He told me, "You try harder, you work harder, you give more down here than they do."

I left there on my own—I wasn't fired—because I couldn't stand the pressure anymore. Everybody was at me. Do this; do that. Finally, I just decided that it was time. If I was ever going to, I needed to move on. So I went ahead and got my name changed legally, got my birth certificate changed, my school records changed, everything changed to reflect the new gender in fall of '86. Then I started going out and looking for different jobs and gradually worked my way up to where I am now, building up my experience and building up a work history as a woman.

I have not been able to have the surgery, which is very hard. Physically I have fully developed breasts, and still I have male genitals. The only difference is the hormones have totally eradicated almost the testicles. I don't have them anymore. What's left of them, they have drawn up so tightly inside the body, they're just almost not there. That's the only difference. Sexually, it's just as intense, the feeling's just as intense sexually as it ever was. I can have just a powerful orgasm, but it's a dry orgasm mostly. There's no ejaculation hardly. They talk about the calming effect of the hormones. It hasn't calmed me down too much. I'm still very intense, very driven, high-strung. It hasn't calmed me down that much, and I've been on them for sixteen years.

All my friends now are heterosexual. When I'm with my girlfriends, they treat me

Rickie Leigh Smith, 1995. Files of the author.

just like one of them. I'm no different. I'm just a woman like they are. They don't discriminate in any way. I'll still go out to bars, but I go to so-called straight places, gambling casinos, places like that with them, on occasion.

My children just adjusted to it. They had a good mother, and she taught them some good values. I attribute that to her, although I feel very bitter at her for a lot of things. She turned against me in later years. She got in with Jehovah's Witness religion, she went gung ho for that, and so suddenly I'm this monster. That's OK. I never put her down in front of my children. I don't want them to ever hear me say anything derogatory about their mother. Ever.[17]

Bars

Like many, Rickie Leigh Smith's experience of the Jackson bar scene was both "liberat[ing]" and "frustrating." Gay bars seemed a safe haven, a place where—as nowhere else—she could be herself. And yet gay bar culture had its own norms and rules of comportment. As Smith discovered, gay-owned bars serving an explicitly gay clientele tended to structure and normalize both a particular form of gay identity and certain queer desires based on race and gender presentation. For Smith and others perhaps, identity and desire were more fluid and dynamic than bars could readily contain and countenance.

Smith entered the bar realm in Mississippi at a pivotal moment in its evolution. As was the case for commercial property holders of all types, gay bar owners diligently heeded one overriding real estate maxim: location, location, location. The placement of a gay bar—its relation to other spaces, its position within existing avenues of movement—made it more or less desirable to patrons, more or less susceptible to infiltration. Police might crack down on, concerned citizens might report on, and ignorant passersby might stumble into a gay bar, if the establishment didn't strike the right balance between accessibility and invisibility. Care was taken to attract customers but ward off meddlers.

As early as the 1930s and 1940s, white queer-friendly establishments were situated both in town and outside the city limits, primarily to the west. At least one Jackson supper club allowed men to dance together, as the state's principal gay activist, Eddie Sandifer, recalls.[18] Further out, road-houses like Toler's, on Clinton Boulevard between Jackson and Clinton, were operated by "broad-minded" owners who hosted a handful of gay patrons. Ron Knight was friends with one waitress—a "regular fag hag"— who often loaned him her shoes: "I'd put on her high heels and dance with the straight guys there." Though "way out in the country," Toler's was "close enough" to the terminus of a streetcar line to be within walking dis-tance. Of the numerous roadhouses on U.S. Highway 49, "past Five Points, going toward Flora," Knight frequented one that although not as welcom-ing as Toler's, likewise was accessible by streetcar, near the end of the Bailey Avenue line.[19] Still, a roadhouse's chief attraction lay in its out-of-the-way location, best reached by car. Patrons looking for a good time thus could be assured some level of anonymity.

No-tell motels along U.S. Highway 49—then also known as Delta Drive—took care to shield their customers' identities. Many motels were built behind roadhouses, away from the road. For those not attached to a bar, other safeguards were taken. The Oaklawn Motel, which to this day stands in the 6800 block of the renamed Medgar Evers Boulevard, evinces its builder's concern for privacy and its owner's willingness to capitalize on the bounce-on-the-bed trade. Constructed in the thirties, the Oaklawn, like so many others, is a set of one-story structures arrayed around a driveway, roughly twenty units in all. Its thin wood siding and screen doors reflect a world without the comforts of air-conditioning. But the Oaklawn boasted an extra feature: after pulling up to the detached office and paying for a room, the patron could drive his car into his own garage, adjacent to each motel room. He then could close the garage doors and escort his partner— a mistress, perhaps, or another man—directly into the room. The partner need never be seen.[20]

In the 1940s gay bars in Jackson occupied viable spaces in the heart of downtown. After the war the Cracker Box served a clientele of white, mostly working-class homosexual men. Located in an old railroad building along the tracks—behind the old Capitol and down the hill—it was ac-cessed only by an unlighted footpath.[21] Later in the decade the Tropic Bar served teenagers just out of school, adults just off work, and men out on the town in the evenings. A long, narrow space discreetly sandwiched between office buildings, it attracted significant queer foot traffic, whereas it rarely drew an oblivious outsider. Police surely knew of its existence, but they seemed a threat only when bars became "too notorious," as Chuck Plant put it.

Another would-be tavern owner from the late 1940s solved this dilemma in a different way. He opened up shop in that originary queer bastion—the private home. As Ron Knight recalls, this unnamed bar, perhaps predating the Tropic, was operated out of a house on a steep lot on High Street, between North and Jefferson, slightly north and west of the new Capitol. Patrons walked up the front steps, crossed the front porch, and entered the house proper in the living room, which functioned as the bar. There were ten stools and a jukebox. The owner offered beer as well as mixers for those who brought their own bootleg liquor.[22]

The wide-open attitudes of World War II persisted in Jackson, and white gay bars operated downtown into the 1950s. Bars like the Wagon Wheel changed locations, mostly up and down Capitol Street, and their clientele fluctuated between an explicitly gay and a gay/straight mixed crowd. But their reputation remained—sufficiently perceptible to attract men like that, sufficiently ambiguous to allay police officers who patrolled the area.[23] Cottonpickers on Mill Street, near the Illinois Central train station, was "not gay," one patron remembers. But for queer locals and men wandering off the train, it regularly served as a "pickup bar."[24]

When Connie's gay establishment, the Cellar, opened some time shortly after 1950, a distinct pattern was emerging. This bar was situated a little farther away from downtown. Still walkable from the boardinghouses around the new Capitol, it nonetheless occupied a marginal space, on the other side of the tracks, under the trestle, beyond the western edge of the downtown business and shopping district.[25] In response to police raids in the sixties, this trend of bar locations continued well into the seventies.

Gay bars were clandestine operations situated on the city periphery in the sixties and early seventies. In 1964 *The Lavender Baedeker*—a U.S. gay tourist guide—showed only one entry under Mississippi: the Cellar Bar. By now the Cellar had moved, and the new owner provided no address to the *Baedeker* editor, given a "reluctan[ce] to have the place known to more people."[26] Secrecy did not imply lack of activity, however. As Joe Holmes recalls of the late 1960s:

> There was a lot of activity if you wanted it and knew where to go. I never went there, but there was a place in those days apparently called the

Raincheck Lounge out on Northside Drive. I heard enough reports to know. Do you know where that big power station is out there on Northside, right by Lake Hico, if you're going out Northside toward Clinton? Before you get to 49. There's a railroad crossing there by Lake Hico. Right along in that area there's a big open space on Northside. If you turn left and go back in there, apparently there was a pretty active little gay bar called the Raincheck Lounge. I think I heard a time or two [about] it. Like we would be out on Friday nights after a football game and a bunch of you in a car. Maybe something like, "Oh, there's the Raincheck Lounge, a queer bar." [27]

Queer locations generated speculation and intrigue. Though purposely removed, they nonetheless fostered curiosity and fascination, for those both likely and unlikely to enter.

Victoria Bolton remembers that by the time Jack Myers got into the gay bar business, he was careful to locate on the city's outskirts. As of 1974 Myers's mostly white, mostly male Mae's Cabaret stood on Delta Drive— that is, the aforementioned U.S. Highway 49, in an increasingly black section of town.[28] Similarly, adult bookstores, well-known for gay male cruising in the film screening booths, operated west of downtown on Terry Road and elsewhere.[29]

Through the 1980s Jackson never supported more than three or four gay bars. Most commonly, one or two operated at any given moment, usually owned by Jack Myers. When Rickie Leigh Smith returned to Jackson in 1977 and started "hobnobbing" at gay discos, some dramatic shifts had occurred. Gay bar life was transformed. Not only were bars like Mae's bigger and glitzier, they were again located in the center of the city. Also, black gay bars emerged. Marginalized from white gay bars, African Americans previously had lacked the capital and critical mass to sustain gay commercial establishments of their own in Mississippi. More importantly, black businesses of any kind were subject to closer police scrutiny. Law enforcement's benign neglect, which shielded white gay bars in the forties and fifties, did not pertain.

By the 1970s and 1980s, however, Key West and then Bill's Disco drew black patrons from all over the state. From the communities of the Delta to the north and towns as far away as Gloster to the south, men and women came to downtown Jackson to dance, play pool, watch the drag shows, and make new friends.[30] In response to a variety of factors, social and economic, queers black and white began to dominate downtown after dark.

Suburbanization was not solely a white flight phenomenon in the capital city, as public spaces integrated in the sixties and seventies. Black Jacksonians, many of whom grew up in rural areas, preferred the larger plots and greater seclusion found outside the urban core. Segregation endured in most neighborhoods; residential developments—black or white, middle and working class—sprung up in newly annexed portions of Hinds County, to the south and west; in Madison County to the north; and in Rankin County, across the Pearl River to the east and north. The business district became just that—an area utilized almost exclusively during business hours. Downtown movie theaters, department stores, restaurants, and hotels closed up; many buildings stood empty. Real estate rates went down, especially for nighttime establishments. Spatially and temporally, queers filled the void.

However, bars frequented by male homosexuals—whether or not explicitly gay owned—were not confined to Jackson and environs. In the sixties in Hattiesburg, as elsewhere, queers found space within a beer bar culture that often defied binary sexual categorization. A "trashy bar" in the eyes of some, the Ritz was "run by an ex-stripper," as a former patron recalls. Carla "was very sympathetic" to her bisexual and homosexual clientele.[31] A sex radical in Mississippi, she shared an affinity with them, the common bond of outsider status.

The beer bar at the Holiday Inn also "was a great pickup and meet place, for gays and straights" alike.[32] Indeed, it was difficult to distinguish one group from the other. At both the Ritz and the Holiday Inn—at bars and clubs, roadhouses and juke joints throughout Mississippi during the first half of the period—men and women maneuvered through conversations, advances, and pickups that seldom observed the neat labels with which narrators retrospectively explain them. Further, these fluid taxonomies made surveillance difficult. Bar owners knew that they could avoid police altercations by confounding rigid notions of gender and sexuality. According to one Hattiesburg Holiday Inn lounge patron, police officers "did not do any hassling, like coming into the bar and, 'Let me see your ID,' and all that. . . . I mean you had football players and their dates. You had gay guys and their lovers or their pickup. If you're going to go in and arrest, you're going to have to take everyone. And you can't take Johnny Good Kickoff and his girlfriend."[33]

Nonetheless, owners took added precautions. At the Boiler Room, a basement establishment in Hattiesburg, an employee was positioned upstairs, at street level, to look out for cops who were known to walk through. If an officer approached, the employee let him in, but simultaneously flipped a switch. A blue light flashed on the dance floor, alerting certain patrons to swap partners. As straight couples proceeded as usual, lesbians paired off with gay men to support the illusion of heteronormativity.[34] This performative switching symbolized much of queer experience, which required constant, vigilant negotiation in Mississippi. That the switching occurred in sight of some "straight" patrons and out of sight of official surveillant forces, the police, does not necessarily mean that tensions with the former were any less than with the latter. Rather, they were more complicated. As one Mississippian explains it, up until the sixties most queer-frequented bars "were not gay bars intentionally. Gays through word-of-mouth would frequent a certain bar, there would be trouble—fights, robbery, etc.—then gays would automatically migrate to another bar."[35]

At some bars, a blurred hetero/homo dyad functioned in decidedly spatial and temporal ways. Near the Ritz, a local lesbian and her lover opened the Townhouse. It was a "mixed" bar, "gay and straight." Patrons delineated—but regularly crossed over—segregated spaces within. As Frederick Ulner recalls, "Downstairs was gay, and then about three steps up was straight. And straight [males] would have their dates up there, and then they would run downstairs and make a date for later, after they took the girl home."[36] Further, like "mixed" bars in midcentury Birmingham, Alabama,[37] the Townhouse served distinct clienteles at distinct hours of operation: "If you were in [the owner's] good graces, you could stay. She would go—she'd point. That meant you could stay after the bar closed. And we'd stay sometimes [until] three or four in the morning. There was a piano bar there, of course. We'd have a hell of a good time. Met a lot of [gay] people through that. . . . That's where [my lover] and I first met."[38]

White Hattiesburg residents describe the definitively gay establishments that developed downtown in the late seventies and early eighties as remarkably egalitarian spaces. According to one patron, the Boiler Room "was terrific. It really was, because guys and the girls were together and really got along well. . . . It was half and half [men and women]. We'd have two, three hundred people from the surrounding areas at some times. It was really good. Then it became the Townhouse."[39] As "the only [gay] bar in town," the new revamped Townhouse "was pretty much an equalizer" with regard to race, class, and gender. Both men and women patronized it, though the lesbians often were outnumbered; both black and white were there, though African Americans were in the minority. Black patrons felt welcome to greater and lesser degrees at these establishments. Some white owners discouraged black patronage; some white queer boys displayed openly racist sentiments.[40] Fleeing these and countless other injustices, queer African Americans who moved out of Mississippi discovered urban gay bar cultures that likewise were segregated, in cities such as Memphis and Detroit, along the traditional migration route north.[41]

Within separate racially homogenized realms before the 1970s, queer

Mississippians negotiated sexually heterogeneous zones. Like the all-white roadhouses outside Jackson at midcentury and the all-white beer bars in Hattiesburg during the sixties, black drinking establishments in Mississippi, while open to the entire African American population of a given county or region, attracted queer boys looking for like-minded companions—or, at a minimum, willing partners. At midcentury a "punk" could "blow" an otherwise heterosexual male, if the mood was right. With the help of good beer and good cheer, many a rural black man dropped his pants "behind a nightclub."[42] After 1966, when liquor could be legalized by local referendum, bars, clubs, and roadhouses became even more raucous and potentially obliging. In communities like Itta Bena, there was only "one place to party" for African Americans, says Bonita Garrett. "Everybody went." The result was a "mixture of things." There was drinking and smoking "reefer." And there were people of all kinds. Men-desiring-men were apparent. Though discouraged from dancing together, they regularly detected one another.[43] At the right moment, in the right place, they could fulfill their desires.

From 1945 to 1985, few Mississippi cities other than Jackson could support an exclusively gay bar, especially for African Americans. Late in the period, predominantly white gay bars emerged in small cities like Hattiesburg, Meridian, and Biloxi—the latter two near military bases. Much more commonly in the second half of the twentieth century, queer Mississippians went out to local watering holes, black or white, and commingled with individuals of all sexual persuasions. This fluid sociability and, in particular, the relative ease of same-sex relations in nightspots during the 1940s and 1950s "raises questions" for southern scholar Donna Jo Smith "about regional variations in the rate at which binarized conceptions of sexual identity were culturally transmitted."[44] More specifically, it suggests that a heterosexual/homosexual dyad prevalent throughout American culture during the twentieth century functioned in some regions alongside other conceptions of sexuality that did not privilege sexual object-choice, or the biological sex of one's partner, as a primary technique of categorization. Certainly in mid-twentieth-century Mississippi, sexual regulation followed other mechanisms as well, such as race and gender performance. Over time the relative importance of particular sexual categories varied greatly. Such variations were well reflected in the movement of institutions such as gay bars and of individuals such as queer Mississippians.

Cars and Roads

Throughout Mississippi during the second half of the twentieth century, from large gatherings of people to one-on-one encounters, the critical conduit was often the automobile. If America had a love affair with the automobile, Mississippi had an obsession. Comparatively speaking, Mississippians relied more heavily than others on the car and light truck: in the half decade following the Second World War, they registered more than 160,000 new vehicles. By the end of the 1980s, only three other states licensed more drivers per capita. And poorly maintained roads meant that Mississippi tallied more deaths from car wrecks per capita than any other southern state.[45]

For all southerners, automobility had a profound effect. Automobiles and highways expanded the reach of rural people, "literally broaden[ing] the horizons of the region."[46] As railroads once brought self-sufficient agrarian people into broader national markets (and made them more dependent thereon), so the automobile through innovations such as truck farming linked country folk to consumers in ever more faraway places. Urbanites also used new roads for regular excursions out of town and for more permanent relocations to the city's edge, in suburbia. Increased automobility in the South meant cities tended to grow outward rather than upward, putting people in complex, multidirectional patterns of daily movement between work, home, and leisure destinations. More so in the South than elsewhere, even in destitute Mississippi, commercial and industrial expansion after World War II fueled new automobile purchases as well as new road building, which pumped state and federal dollars into local economies urban and rural.

In his fascinating study of postwar Flint, Michigan, Tim Retzloff argues that "the car allowed gay and bisexual men to assemble like never before, and these men gave new meaning to the concept of driving for pleasure." Indeed, the "instrumental significance of the automobile" for queers cannot be overstated, especially in rural locales.[47] While my research confirms a number of Retzloff's conclusions concerning the car as a queer space and as a carrier between queer spaces, I would like to further explore relationships between identity and mobility. As Rickie Leigh Smith attests, cars were sites for queer sex in Mississippi; as both Chuck Plant and the Methodist revivalist demonstrate in chapter 1, cars drew hitchhikers aiming to get sex; and as is apparent in Jackson, Hattiesburg, and Vicksburg, cars helped bring large numbers of men-desiring-men together, often in one queer space. However, as the primary means of travel to church, home, school, and workplace, cars enabled much of everyday life, individual and collective. Further, they participated in new modes of movement—social and physical—as they shaped new spaces. As such, they helped mold distinctive sexualities in Mississippi.

Retzloff focuses on commercial establishments: bars, hotels, restaurants, theaters, bus stations, and their parking lots—queer sites he sees as "fixed" or "stationary."[48] Yet queer sites are ever a part of built environments—in the country and the city—which are themselves constantly in flux. Sites exist in perpetual relationship to other shifting spaces, such that even urban-rural dichotomization begs complication, as theorist Henri Lefebvre reminds us.[49] These relationships suggest dynamism and movement. The primary vehicle of movement in Mississippi, the car, could scarcely function without roads. And just as the car both moved between sites and was itself a site, roads both served as avenues and venues, as arenas of circulation and congregation. Moreover, cars and roads participated in synergistic processes of social, cultural, political, and economic development, crucial in the formation and reformulation of desire and difference.

Postwar road building was a boon to queer networking. While the federal government introduced the interstate highway system in the fifties, paved state roads linking county seats were completed in Mississippi, greatly increasing mobility for many.[50] But at both the county and state levels, road and highway construction was marked by corruption. Where roads were placed and who got to build them depended on powerful political forces. As in no other state, Mississippi's three-member Highway Commission was elected—that is, chosen by voters, who were almost exclusively white until the 1970s. Further, the commission administered a large pool of gasoline-tax receipts specially earmarked for highways and thus "immune from budget cuts." With large pools of funds at their disposal and their longevity dependent on a fickle electorate, commissioners were susceptible to influence peddling, kickbacks, and favoritism.[51] Just as white town councils regularly left black sections with inadequate dirt roads, state officials built new highway interchanges that often did not reach into predominantly black areas. Not only was it financially more difficult for blacks to own cars than whites; the racial dynamics of road construction suggest just one of many other subtle checks and restraints on black mobility in Mississippi.

The problem was particularly acute at the county level. Each of Mississippi's eighty-two counties elected five supervisors on the "beat" system. Voters within each beat chose a supervisor, who received a neat one-fifth portion of the county road budget, with virtually no oversight. A *Newsweek* exposé at the end of the period reported that FBI agents had uncovered a variety of kickback schemes in county contracting. And as analyst Gerald Gabris summarizes, the favors granted (white) friends and supporters included digging graves and wells on private property, graveling and grading private drives, and blacktopping county roads near supporters' property.[52]

Mississippi's scant resources thus were drained through corruption and mismanagement. In the early seventies, a corridor plan designed to link all major Mississippi cities with four-lane limited-access highways—places like Tupelo, Corinth, Columbus, Starkville, Vicksburg, and Jackson—went underfunded and consequently was reduced to a widening and overlay program.[53] Uneven development meant uneven access and mobility. Across the state's three highway districts, across each county's five beats, roads could vary dramatically in quality, scope, and usage. Queer boys, though willing, might find it difficult to drive to gay establishments in Jackson or elsewhere. Thus, queer networks thrived locally.

Surveying and road-building crews were ordinarily all-male environments, often sexually fraught. Before the Second World War, a group of surveyors rented rooms in Terry as they prepared rights of way for a new highway. At least one crewman got friendly with the locals, as Ronald Knight recalls:

> One night, a big blond hunk, Butch, got a little drunk on beer. Peter and I started walking home with him after Waldo's [restaurant] closed. He kept bragging about being known to have the biggest prick in the survey. We got up to a dark area, about a block from our house, and he said he had to take a leak. So he pulled out this big thing, and wanted us to play with it. So I was playing with it, and so was Peter. He kept on; he was trying to get us to go down on him. Well, I would have, except I didn't want to do anything in front of Peter. Peter was the same way. So we kept making excuses. You know, the grass was dewy and too wet for us to lie down on, for him to screw us. That's what we were thinking. But he just wanted a blow job. Anyway, nothing happened, other than just playing with it. I think he was very disappointed.[54]

Road builders paved the way for new levels of interaction between and among locals and transients. As they laid out roads, they tied rural people together, making possible a number of homosexual encounters.

Anthony Greene of Cleveland says that in the late seventies, Delta queers carpooled and drove as much as two hours to the black club Key West, a former movie house in downtown Jackson. In the early eighties, they drove to Bill's Club, on Amite Street. For many the ride itself—swapping stories, sharing sorrows, and singing along to WJMI—was all the fun, as they took on passengers in Leland, Shaw, Midnight, and Louise.[55] Rural whites also shared rides to Jackson, to Jack's Saloon, the white bar across the street from Bill's. But roads didn't just lead to bars in the cities. They enabled friendships as well. Many nights during the eighties, Ed Foreman drove an hour north from Taylorsville to go to the gay bar in Meridian, the Talk of the Town. But he would just as frequently travel thirty miles east to visit his *closest* gay friend, in D'Lo. "Often," he says, "I was on the road every night."[56] Sometimes it seemed that being in the car and being on the road epitomized queer travel in Mississippi.

Indeed, the automobile and identity were inextricably linked. In a poor state, not everybody owned cars. But in Mississippi almost everybody could drive: though there were seventy-five registered vehicles for every hundred people, 99 percent of those eligible to drive were licensed.[57] Mississippians not only shared rides, they shared cars. Thus, Ricky Lee Smith drove his dad's pickup truck on a date, while others took streetcars, where available, and walked to get to queer spaces. As the century progressed, however, and the great majority of Mississippians acquired autos, it was a widely held adage: You are what you drive.

This proved problematic for queer boys. Hattiesburg business owner Melvin Hunt complained that *both* of his cars were one of a kind. Either auto—"the only one in town like it"—would "stick out like a sore thumb." More to the point, it would be readily recognizable as his. Consequently, Hunt stopped going to the gay bar, for fear his customers would see his car parked there.[58] Furthermore, Hattiesburg police were said to keep lists of license plate numbers taken from the Townhouse parking lot in the 1970s.[59] Nosy townspeople also monitored cars to identify patrons of gay bars and, in some cases, to threaten them with exposure. In 1986 ten to fifteen Tupelo residents attempted to close the Tulip Creek Estates Clubhouse Disco & Show Bar by harassing its clientele. Led by Morality in America's T. K. Moffett and Christian talk radio host Bob McCustion, the group patrolled the parking lot, wrote down license plate numbers, obtained the automobile registrants' names and addresses from public records, and mailed out at least fifty messages not in sealed envelopes but on postcards—insuring that the text was read by any number of people. Purporting to help homosexuals "break out of the vices of immorality," McCustion discovered that customers would drive from near and far to find kindred spirits. Those receiving postcards lived as near as adjacent counties and as far away as neighboring states.[60]

Not only where you parked, but also where you drove might brand you as gay. In towns and cities across Mississippi, certain blocks and streets gained reputations as queer spaces at certain hours. Queer introductions relied on automobile *and* foot traffic. Hardy Street in Hattiesburg was "out of control" in the 1960s:

At the time the Townhouse and the Ritz were in full swing—I swear to god—if you wanted to pick up a trick and didn't want to be seen downtown picking up one, drive out to the university. Turn around and start back downtown. You could fill your car up with them. . . . I used to park my car, and [two of us] would walk around the block. As they were cruising us, I'd say, "Well, which one do you want? You want the one in the green car?" "I think the one in the red car is cute." "OK, I'll wait on this corner. You go around. Let's meet back here at twelve o'clock or two o'clock at our car, and then I'll take you on home."[61]

In Jackson in the 1980s, at least one man—the governor of Mississippi— had to explain why his car was seen at a disreputable downtown cruising area, as we shall see in chapter 7.

Few wanted to be publicly identified as gay. As one government official stated in 1986, "Accusing someone of being gay these days is like being accused of being a leper."[62] So a full decade prior, the director of the state motor vehicle license plate division should not have been surprised at the extraordinary bitterness of some Hinds County drivers. Before the advent of vanity plates, in a state that marked tags with three letters followed by three numbers, many were incensed in 1976 when their new license plates spelled out "GAY." The state refused to offer replacements, but in a bow to popular sentiment, officials apparently quit distributing the "GAY" plates.[63] Though one atypical Mississippi artist went so far as to paint scantily clad men onto the body of his automobile—as described in chapter 5—most Mississippians queer and straight bristled at having their cars *explicitly* marked as GAY.

Mississippi motorists moved about as a part of work and leisure rituals highly conscious of their vehicles' identifying propensities as well as their sexualized potentialities. Cars, pickup trucks, vans, and buses shunted men around a rural landscape of dispersed sexual actors. Racially, these men had differing levels of freedom and mobility. In addition to horrific violence, black Mississippians suffered white discourtesies beyond the withholding of honorific appellations—Mr. and Miss, Sir and Ma'am. An adult male was infantilized as "boy" (just as the sexually nonnormative was called "queer boy"). Indeed, the proper place of the African American— socially and physically—was stringently regulated, especially around midcentury: "Courtesies of the road are among those withheld. Negroes . . . are very cautious drivers, and have need to be, since white drivers customarily ignore the amenities toward a car driven by a colored person."[64] In the barbarous white supremacist South, many deadly altercations between blacks and whites began as or were framed as automobile mishaps.

Automobiles nonetheless helped black Mississippians transgress, to move out beyond the "place" white Mississippi had "assigned" them, as Richard Wright refers to it in the epigraph of chapter 2. By custom and often by choice, this movement tended to remain within segregated black realms. But the few interracial homosexual encounters that took place before the 1960s were entangled in and filtered through the politics of motoring. Black men had to carefully gauge their own desire and safety as white men sought to engage them in homosex. Greenville writer and plantation heir William Alexander Percy had several black boyfriends, up until his death in 1942. Among his favorites were his cook's son, Ford Atkins, and his chauffeur, Ernest. Percy paid for Atkins's education as a mechanic in Detroit. Upon his return, Atkins turned the tables. One observer noted, "After [Atkins] got a taste of city life . . . , things didn't click too well." Atkins eventually left Percy.[65]

At a time when black and white men would rarely commingle outside working relationships, the automobile provided a unique semiprivate space for interaction. Baton Rouge, Louisiana, native Allen Bernard remembers picking up a group of hitchhikers along U.S. Highway 90, between New Orleans and Mobile, in the 1950s. Bernard singled out the oldest youth to sit up front with him, while several climbed into the backseat. As they headed east toward Bay Saint Louis, the young black man was vexed and distressed by the white driver's increasingly bold advances. Finally, unnerved, he insisted Bernard stop the car, and the teenagers all got out, miffed at having lost the ride.[66]

Black-white homosexual interaction sometimes accompanied black-white heterosexual contact, again made possible by the automobile. In 1958, for example, two white motorists, brothers Richard and Joey Myers, approached three black pedestrians on Mill Street in Jackson, at 2:00 in the morning. Johnny Murphy, James Rodgers, and Mary Lee Smith got in. The group then drove out toward Delta Drive, parking on the more secluded White Rock Road. One after another, the new acquaintances undressed. Hours later, near daybreak, this "negro-white sex party [was] interrupted" by police. Though some white men may have expected unfettered access to black bodies, both of the Myers brothers and their passengers ended up in the Hinds County jail.[67] Years would pass before interracial liaisons between heterosexuals, much less between homosexuals, would fail to attract legal attention.

Intimate and erotic exchanges *within* racial groups likely multiplied along the state's byways, as Mississippians traveled distances short and long ever more frequently over the period. Even in areas without U.S. highways or, later, interstate roadways—in counties like Calhoun, Leake, Smith, and Winston—traffic volume more than doubled between the 1950s and 1970s, while population levels stabilized.[68] Much traffic involved short trips across one or two counties. The "liquor run" was a common means of bringing men together in cars. Before midcentury, Ron Knight regularly rode with other Hinds County queer boys across the river to the "Gold Coast" of Rankin County. Known for illicit alcohol, gambling, and (perhaps not exclusively heterosexual) prostitution, the establishments along the east bank of the Pearl were eventually shut down by the National Guard.[69] Still, bootleggers could be found in remote locations all over the state.[70] And even after liquor was legalized at local option in 1966, as some counties voted to remain dry and others went wet, many an early evening and late night carload journeyed across the county line to purchase alcohol. These boisterous road trips sustained both homosocial and homosexual networks, as did more wholesome amusements.

A significant portion of sports culture in Mississippi existed apart from educational institutions and broadcast professional athletics. Vital components of Choctaw life, intratribal baseball competition and *toli*, or stickball, relied on cars and roads as conduits. With seven Choctaw communities spread across five counties in east-central Mississippi, teams chose a manager "not only for his knowledge of the game," as anthropologist Kendall Blanchard notes, "but also because he had some form of transportation by which the team could make the often lengthy trip to scheduled games." Interestingly, in documenting localized Choctaw women's sports, Blanchard asserts that a "healthy female athlete self-concept [wa]s reflected in the language. The Choctaw term for a masculine girl (*alla nakni iklanna*, 'half boy') reflect[ed] essentially the same meaning as that for a feminine boy (*alla tik iklanna*, 'half girl'). Neither ha[d] stigmatizing overtones." Indeed, Blanchard convincingly shows that "strong women" were revered and found sexually desirable in Choctaw culture. He provides no evidence to support the assertion about "feminine boys."[71]

Black and white semipro baseball leagues owed much to the proliferation of good roads, if not good playing fields. At midcentury, the Highway 80 League brought men into competition from towns across Scott and Rankin Counties. Forest, Morton, Pelahatchie, Brandon, and Pearl teams piled into cars, drove a dozen miles or more, and vied for regional championships on diamonds that were little more than cow pastures.[72] These all-male road trips and athletic gatherings may not have guaranteed homosexual interaction, but they certainly didn't hinder it. As oral history narrators have explained, automobiles and locker rooms were among Mississippi's most prolific queer sites.

Joe Holmes: One summer my best friend from college, Francis, and I went out west on a three-week Greyhound Ameripass, back in the summer of '74, and went to all these gay bars in different cities—San Francisco and Los Angeles. We got to

San Francisco. I was drinking every night in every hotel, in every bar, having the time of my life. I would a lot of times, some nights, I might just stay in the hotel room and watch TV and drink, and he'd be out in the baths.

I hadn't even been in the [gay bar] in Jackson yet. Nashville was the main one [I went to while I was in college at Vanderbilt]. I don't believe I had been to many others. I'd go home with Francis sometimes, spring break or something, and we'd go to the ones in Florida, like Jacksonville. They had a pretty good one there in the early seventies.

We had just within the year before that [trip west] told each other we were gay. I think that was a big reason for the trip. We just wanted to celebrate having another friend who was gay, go out and see the West, go to bars. We had a ball. Within a year, he went right back alone on the same trip and went to some of these places he wanted to find out more about.

We met in New Orleans. He came over from Florida, I went down from Jackson, and we spent the first night in New Orleans, a good place to kick it off. We stayed at the Sheraton Saint Charles, an old downtown hotel with high ceilings. Went to some gay bars. We got on the bus in New Orleans the next day. Went to San Antonio, Texas, and spent one or two nights there. Francis had a gay bar guide, knew where to go. We had sex for the first time [with each other] in San Antonio. You see why I want this to be anonymous. He loved giving blow jobs. And I learned to start liking them. By then we had established such a good friendship for several years that the sex was fun and all, but I wasn't really attracted to him physically.

After San Antonio we got back on the bus and went all the way through to Las Vegas. We didn't have a lot of money to spend, so we'd ride straight through on the bus overnight. On the way into Las Vegas, we met this kid who lived there and had an apartment. He was about eighteen or nineteen, and we started talking to him. I don't think he was gay or even the question of being gay came up. He offered us a place to stay and we ended up staying with him. We went to the casinos during the daytime. Hot as hell out there. I played the slots. I got so mad at Francis because he would always win on the slots next to mine, and I'd lose.

Then we headed to L.A. I remember the bus broke down in Barstow, California, in the desert. We saw *The Exorcist*. It was just coming out. Gerald Ford was in the White House. Watergate had already happened. We stayed at a downtown L.A. hotel, the Alexandria. There's not a lot to do in downtown L.A. But we caught buses—L.A. had pretty good transit—so we caught buses out to Hollywood. Saw the stars in the sidewalk. Went out to Venice Beach. Did a few touristy things, but I was not really impressed with L.A. I was getting a little weary from my drinking habits.

One day we went down to San Diego, went over to Tijuana for the day. Then we went up to San Francisco and stayed there for two or three days. San Francisco was chilly. The hotel didn't even have air-conditioning in it. We were on foot. We'd get off at the damn bus station, not knowing where to go. The handle on my suitcase broke. I remember lugging that thing, carrying the suitcase through most of downtown San Francisco. And you know there are some hills in that city. I was so tired and short of breath. I smoked then too.

We went out to the gay section, Castro. We went to Haight-Ashbury. I remember guys with earrings and stuff, their hair slicked back. Walking hand in hand. You could tell it was a really big gay community.

Something was happening then that I was not really attuned to. I've never been that much into casual sex. It's not that I didn't really want to or I felt above it. Sometimes I'd use what they call the yellow lemon rationalization: Oh, it's better that I didn't anyway [given the subsequent AIDS crisis]. I never fit in to much of the culture of casual sex and the sex clubs and the baths that much, but Francis was really into it. I didn't know the extent. He just didn't share a lot of that with me. On the side, out there, he was doing a lot of that. All I know is—this is after we got back and compared notes of our experiences—he absolutely loved San Francisco. He saw what he liked there.

To me, San Francisco was not that great. More gay bars and discos. I still remember this good-looking go-go boy standing up there at one of the gay bars; I remember the song actually. [Hums the tune.]

We left San Francisco, coming back the northern route. Went to Salt Lake City. Took a shower at the YMCA. Got back on the bus and went all the way to Chicago. By then we were running low on money and antiperspirant. Chicago, I loved it. Bars on the northwest edge of downtown. What I liked, even more than bars, I liked the buildings. We went on top of the Sears Tower; it had just opened. We went on top of the John Hancock building. I saw these buildings I had only seen in the *World Book Encyclopedia*. The Wrigley Building, the Tribune Tower.

Then, I think he went his way again, and I went mine, back to Jackson.

I'm sort of sad when I talk about that, 'cause he's passed away. He died of AIDS. Was he actually the first guy I ever had sex with? He was one of the people I probably hurt. Not real bad. But he later shared that with me. He wanted to get closer to me than I had allowed him to get. There was no romantic tie from my end. We were young and learning.

He was always down. He was sort of depressed about his lot in life. He was frustrated about being gay. And he was very much into a lot of casual sex. But he was very much conscious of how old he was and how old he was getting, even though we were only around eighteen at that time. Once at Vanderbilt, he had said he was depressed because he was over the hill now. He had read somewhere that men peak at eighteen and women, like, at thirty-five. And he was nineteen and he was over the hill. He was serious. He was depressed about that.

Plus he was real bitter. I didn't know one thing about who I was or what I believed in politically. I had been sucked into the traditional conservative Southern Baptist [upbringing], and I still defended that. And didn't even know yet that I didn't go along with all that. And people like him tried to tell me. God, I wish I could tell him how grateful I am now. His influence. He was ahead of me in many ways. He used to tell me, "How can you not be for somebody like George McGovern with the way you are?" I voted for Richard Nixon. Can you believe it? He knew where he stood politically, and he lived it out. He had a profound influence on who I am today.[73]

Many a Greyhound and Trailways bus took Mississippians out of the state —often not just for a summer vacation, but for a lifetime. Mississippians black and white felt the push of dire social and economic conditions; the pull, the promise of life in the big city, the allure for some of gay neighborhoods and bars. But for many like Joe Holmes and Rickie Leigh Smith, gay enclaves were less a refuge than a mirage—more problematic, less fulfilling than they seemed.

Urban gay culture produced its own biases and exclusions. Though often gay communities readily welcomed and freely incorporated country boys fresh off the bus, other rural visitors were repelled by urban provincialism—the snide, condescending rebuffs. Where a youthful masculinity was prized, ageism and transphobia resulted. Thus even a nineteen-year-old such as Francis could nurture obsessive notions of having passed beyond his prime in life. Transsexuals such as Rickie Leigh Smith would look forward to giving up the momentary satisfactions of drag shows in order "to live as a woman," day to day. Further, as both Smith and Holmes attest, many queer Mississippians clung to a belief in monogamy and to the values of a committed long-term relationship with a single life partner. Just as Smith "didn't want any one-night stands" with bar-goers in Jackson, Holmes determined that he "never fit in to much of the culture of casual sex and the sex clubs and baths" of larger urban areas. Joe Holmes returned home to Mississippi and devoted his life to psychiatry, working with patients at a mental health facility. He continued to harbor a love of travel.

Interstate buses and other means of public transport were hybrid spaces neither local nor foreign. Bus interiors offered a place suspended from community laws and norms. In the same way that days of bus travel allowed a complicated intimacy between Joe Holmes and his friend Francis, short excursions often permitted behavior otherwise unattempted. For those with the means—like Vanderbilt student Joe Holmes and, two decades before him, Sewanee student Mark Ingalls—movement along roads afforded new sorts of human interaction. Also, time away often amounted to a "moral holiday," a momentarily loosening of the restrictions of community mores.[74]

In the early 1950s, on an evening bus between towns in eastern Tennessee, Mark Ingalls discovered the sexual potential of spaces in motion. A soldier sat down next to Ingalls and put his hand on Ingalls's leg. Soon, the serviceman was "stroking me and stroking me."

> So I was sort of playing with him [too]. He was pretending like he didn't know what was going on, and I was pretending like I didn't know what was going on. You know we kept doing it until we got each other off. You can imagine what a mess that made. They didn't have bathrooms on buses at that time. So you're having to find a handkerchief and go through all this stuff, and then pretend you didn't know that he was doing you and you were doing him.[75]

Such pretending allowed an anonymity usually associated with big cities— a freedom from familial and community restraints. For some queer Mississippians, such freedom necessarily was found very close to home, just down the road a bit.

As landscape historian John Brinckerhoff Jackson rightly concludes,

> Roads and streets and alleys and trails can no longer be identified solely with movement from one place to another. Increasingly they are the scene of work and leisure and social intercourse and excitement. Indeed, they have often become for many the last resort for privacy and solitude and contact with nature. Roads no longer merely lead to places; they *are* places. . . . In the modern landscape, no other space has been so versatile.[76]

And yet, Jackson can't or doesn't imagine all the multifarious transgressive uses to which the road could be put. Chief among them in Mississippi were the homosexual valences of the roadside rest area.

Roadsides

Homosex at roadside rest areas was predated by a tradition of back-roads parking. In the thirties in Mississippi, "there were many lonely dark roads and lanes. And locating a safe place was no problem." These roads were in poor condition, made of dirt, "wide enough just for one car or wagon," as one queer motorist remembers. Traffic was scarce and an approaching car was easily heard well in advance—sufficiently so that clothes could be put back on or a better hiding place could be found. "My first car was a Model-A Ford with a rumble seat, but too crowded for sex. I always parked, and we lay on the grass."[77]

Roadside parks emerged in the 1930s as community endeavors. Women in local garden clubs persuaded farmers and landowners on a town's outskirts to donate an acre or two of land, which the club then maintained. These "safety rest areas," on two-lane primary roads, consisted of a short gravel access and a few benches and tables made of wood and concrete.

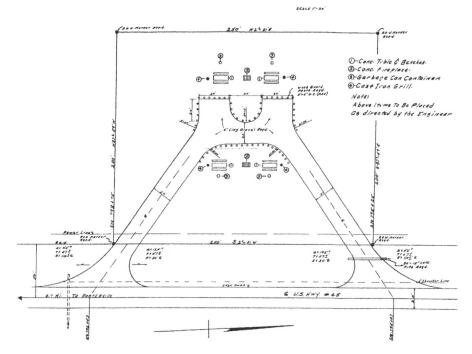

Roadside Park No. 75, U.S. Highway 45, Kemper County, before 1967 renovation. Files of the author.

Heavily utilized during the day, especially as lunch and picnic spots, they mostly were open to white residents and travelers.[78] Though rural homosexual men surely cruised these parks and the adjacent woods and farmland, especially after dark, during these early years, their traces were more pronounced from the 1950s on. As a longtime Mississippi highway department official notes, things changed drastically when the state took over operations. Work crews added rest rooms to these sites and built extensive new facilities on new interstate highways.[79]

When roadside park number 75 was spruced up in 1967, distinctive new features made it more and less conducive to homosexual cruising. First, the site's preservation—three and a half miles north of Portersville and a mile and a half south of Electric Mills on U.S. Highway 45—insured that rural Kemper County queers had at least one public venue at their disposal. The twenty-foot-wide clay-gravel access was overlaid with a dense, graded, hard surface, making entry and exit—and, occasionally, eluding the law—quicker and smoother. Since men often waited hours at night for another passerby, new drinking fountains were hospitable; new mounted lighting inhospitable, given the need for stealth. Most importantly, new brick rest room facilities promised accessible shelter of limited visibility. Toilet stalls proved especially beneficial. At parks across the state, glory holes appeared in the partitions. Maintenance officials "replace[d] the stalls, but holes would be there again within a couple of weeks."[80]

Outside Electric Mills, as workers added more benches, tables, and barbecue grills—including one set sheltered from the elements and the lights—highway patrol officers elsewhere caught glimpses of men having sex "right out there on the picnic tables."[81] At the brand-new interstate rest stops, elaborately landscaped grounds meant more opportunities for sex. One site rendered by architects Godfrey, Bassett, Pitts, and Tuminello included a brick rest room building, two brick and columned pavilions with tables, and fifteen more tables with metal barbecue grills, all set amid luscious greenery and footpaths.[82] Though the Electric Mills renovation called for "clearing, grubbing, thinning, and underbrush removal," presumably to the detriment of cruising, new sites and new growth boded well for men-desiring-men.[83]

Rest areas on Interstate 59 not only served rural men in southeast Mississippi; they replaced Hardy Street in Hattiesburg as the main drag for queer college students, townsfolk, and area residents. According to Melvin Hunt, the pair of rest areas on either side of the four-lane concrete superhighway, located south of Hattiesburg toward Purvis, drew countless locals, despite law enforcement attempts to clean it up: "They put a highway patrolman sitting out there in his car, and it still didn't faze them. They still went out there, and they still went out in the woods and tricked. . . . And the [median] crossovers are so deep and rutted. They [drove] from one rest area to the other."[84] Even at basic rest stops with only parking spaces and trash cans, like the I-55 pull-off near Johnstons Station, men walked the surrounding woods for sex and found it.[85]

Warren and Hinds County men drove to the rest area on I-20 outside Vicksburg to meet one another and to meet travelers taking breaks on their journeys. "All the time I was married," Mark Ingalls reflects, "if I wasn't seeing anyone, I could drive out and get a trick anytime I went out there." Men also took friends there to have sex in their cars or on the trails. By the late sixties, these spaces were well integrated racially such that a black and white male-male couple drew little added attention. But automobiles with Warren or Hinds County plates raised the doubts of highway patrolmen. An officer was more likely to question a local than a transient, whose purpose at a rest area seemed self-evident.[86]

As dispersed commercial developments and retail strip-mall establishments predominated across America in the sixties and seventies, city and town centers declined. Car culture reigned. Increasingly, men looking for sex had to hit the road. Those accustomed to pedestrian life—to sidewalk cruising in Hattiesburg, Jackson, Vicksburg, or larger cities—were forced to adjust, as the Mississippi landscape dictated specific forms of mobility and sexuality. As Chuck Plant recalls:

> Smith Park [in downtown Jackson] has been, in the past, very active. In more recent times, there's a park that's south of town. . . . After I came back from [living almost twenty years in] New York, which was 1979, I thought, Well, I've got to have my own car. And in driving around, then for the first time, I discovered places like that. I used to stop at all of the roadside rest rooms. If I went anywhere I would just stop to see what was going on. And sometimes they were active.[87]

Most likely at all two dozen rest areas and state-border welcome centers, along north-south I-55 and I-59 and east-west I-10 and I-20, men came together in the rest rooms and on the picnic tables, in the woods and on the trails. Contrary to J. B. Jackson's assessment, the road for queer Mississippians was less an escape to the seclusion of nature, than a material ingress to a busy network of men and would-be women, homosexuals and transsexuals, persons of varied identities and sexualities.[88]

As older Mississippians adapted to shifting means of social and physical mobility, those who came of age in the seventies and eighties learned early the value of mechanized transportation. Interested in cruising from his early teens, Ben Childress roamed the streets of Pascagoula by whatever means available: "first, the bike, then the moped, then the car." He moved up from two wheels, "a little red Honda," to four wheels, a Ford Mustang, when his dad, an auto shop owner, helped him buy his first car and fix it up. Childress got his learner's "permit at fourteen, driver's license at fifteen." He regularly drove two miles to the beach, walked up and down, and periodically checked out the "little cinder block rest room." "Eighty percent of the time," he says, he "wouldn't get any." But sometimes he bumped into strangers, with whom he had quick sex. And on other occasions, he ran into people he knew and trusted. Once, he saw his former math teacher there and followed him home to his apartment.[89]

Rural and small town analogues of the city park and downtown tearoom included roadside and beachfront areas, county and state parks, forests and lakes,[90] riversides and other gathering places. Homosexual meanings and readings, desires and actions could surface at most any roadside get-together. Consider white musicologist Alan Lomax's humorously homophobic and unselfconsciously homoeroticized account of an African American fife-and-drum performance at a community picnic in north Mississippi, 1978: "In the cleared space in front of the barbecue stand," drummers and dancers "entwined, face to face, their thighs interlocked, their hips rocking and bucking. [One man was] behind one of the lads, symbolically screwing him from the rear." Several were "simulating sex, balling the jack as part-ners, holding on to each other so as not to fall." Overall, Lomax found it "a very anal performance." But he concludes:

> The normal American audience might mistake this sexually hyperactive, virtually all-male dance for a homosexual orgy, which it most certainly was not. All-male erotic dancing has always been a part of African tradition. . . . Mixed-couple dancing is rare except in Europe. In most agricultural regions, as in Africa, the sexes dance in separate choirs, dramatizing each gender's particular concerns. That was what these young Panola County drum danc-ers were doing—competitively showing off the steely muscles of their backs, loins, and buttocks, as well as their skills at winding their hips, just as they had that afternoon exhibited their mastery of baseball on the local diamond. The young women watched with appreciation, as well as anticipation, I presume. . . .[91]

Some young and not-so-young men also watched with appreciation, as well as anticipation, I presume.

Often in Mississippi, people met where roads converged. Over time so-called crossroads communities grew or declined depending on traffic to or through the area. County seats, no less than the state capital of Jackson, prospered or languished based on the movement of people—and their commodities. An amiable but nonetheless competitive form of exchange, harkening back to premodern agrarian economies, were the county and state fairs held annually at numerous locales. Once a year, usually in the summer or fall, rural and town folk came together, country and city dwell-ers intermingled, at the fair—a temporary commercial venture that was part amusement park, part agricultural (and later industrial) exposition. As early as the 1930s and as late as the 1960s, oral history narrators remember fairs as boisterous occasions to meet new people and make new friends. With hundreds, sometime thousands, of people on parade—walking the midway, riding the rides, comparing their livestock, sizing up their fruits and vegetables—many men like that gazed upon more men than they had ever seen assembled in one place. They not only experienced desire for some of these men; they also acted on their desires with them.[92]

Cars and roads didn't simply make these places more accessible. They reciprocally shaped the contours of ever-evolving, never-static entities. Though symbolically fixed on a map, a single place—a rural juke joint, for instance—could vary greatly from one moment (say, midnight on Saturday) to the next (9:00 A.M. on Monday). It could change radically when a bridge or road leading to (and from) it was washed out; when regular spring downpours temporarily made of it an island; when a new highway made it more or less visible, by directing traffic to it or diverting traffic from it. Of course, a significant flood or violent tornado—neither uncommon in Mississippi—could, as they say, "wipe the place off the map." Such was the course of change in the built environment over time *and* across place.

Migrations and Mobilizations

Intricately interwoven with American success ideology, car culture ostensibly lent credence to age-old notions of individualism and mobility, self-reliance and autonomy. You could get about and get ahead by going it alone, working your way up. Yet while many viewed the automobile as an individualistic means toward a physical and socioeconomic end, queer Mississippians demonstrated the collective potential of motion. Queer boys were driving not for solitude but communion. Indeed, while small gatherings of two or more facilitated homosexual encounters in rural space, large-scale ventures further prompted thoughts and actions at odds with hegemonic beliefs and practices. In particular, in postwar Mississippi, military mobilizations, social movements, and population shifts portended enormous consequences for male-male desire.

As Allan Bérubé perceptively demonstrates in his landmark study of World War II, the armed forces drew men and women into surveillant, sex-segregated worlds that both constrained and liberated homosexual potentialities.[93] After the war the armed forces in Mississippi remained an important means of employment and service, as the nation ambivalently readied for combat in Korea, where Chuck Plant served, and Vietnam. With a strong military ethos and powerful hawks in the U.S. Congress, Mississippi supported several large federal facilities, including the Columbus Air Force Base, Meridian Naval Air Station, and Pascagoula Naval Port; U.S. Army Corps of Engineers Waterways Experiment Station, for which Mark Ingalls worked most of his life, in Vicksburg; and Camp Shelby and Camp McCain, two massive army training grounds in Forrest and Grenada Counties.

Soldiers, sailors, pilots, and corpsmen were pressed into new ways of living and thinking. As both a means of escape (from family, from hometown) and a place of confinement (to barracks, to base), military life rearranged ordinary patterns of existence. In intimate quarters, enlistees encountered other men from all over the country. They also encountered civilians who lived near their facility. One of these, Ben Childress, "was gutsy and horny" as a young teen. On occasion he went to the Pascagoula station, "locked his bike to the fence, walked right past the guards, went into this eight-floor dorm-style facility, and hung out in the bathrooms."[94] Similarly, military men on leave came into contact with area residents interested in sex. Within the ranks, queer boys experienced the naked physicality of drill and leisure as both disconcerting and consoling—and sometimes titillating. Although many, like Chuck Plant, sensed their difference, they likewise realized they were no better nor worse examples of manhood than the others around them. Also, they discovered they were not alone in the ranks.

Still, homosexuality was under intense observation in these all-male environments. Depending on the particular base and commander, battalion

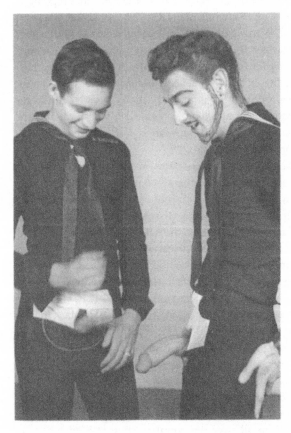

At the close of World War II, navy veterans Ron Knight, *right*, and a friend posed for pictures in the Manhattan studio of Harry Eastern, a student of Louise Dahl-Wolfe. Knight returned home to Mississippi with what he assumed were the only prints. He so feared their discovery that he disguised his face by penning in a beard and mustache. Other copies of the photos, however, apparently circulated in informal pornography circles. In 1988 a shot of the two sailors kissing appeared on ACT UP/ Gran Fury posters and T-shirts in New York, with the caption "READ MY LIPS"— a reference to George Bush's presidential campaign slogan. Courtesy of Ronald Knight.

and leader, homosexual men could be quietly tolerated or loudly drummed out of the service with a traumatic, dishonorable discharge. Memphis, Tennessee, resident Oye Apeji Ajanaku apparently was thus "separated" from the U.S. Navy and the "Black masculine multitude" in 1963.[95] In the fifties Neil Simon presumably witnessed two dismissals at Keesler Air Force Base, as recounted in his semiautobiographical play *Biloxi Blues*.[96]

Purges at Keesler became legendary. As Damien Martin reflects:

> I very seldom did anything on base. Most of the time I would go away to areas where people weren't likely to know me. . . . You have to understand that I was in the middle of some of the worst antigay purges the air force has ever known. I remember in about 1952 at Biloxi, Mississippi, there was a purge where people were committing suicide. The air force finally had to stop because people were turning people in just to get revenge for one thing or another.[97]

Difficult to trace, narratives of suicide persist in southern gay male folklore. For those deaths prompted by fears of disclosure and dishonor, the responsible authorities are as invested in historical erasure as queer cultural descendants are in recuperation.[98]

If caught up in a military raid or purge at midcentury, there were generally two options: the accused either could accept summary dismissal or could accept the "help" of professionals. Treatment varied. Military hospitals and psychiatric wards were staffed by physicians and nurses of disparate methods and sensibilities. Robert Coles credits himself and other liberal-minded doctors with making life easier for many homosexual patients in Biloxi during the fifties.[99]

Markedly similar to the military experience, Mississippi's state penitentiary system locked men into race- and sex-segregated compounds rife with homosexual possibilities. A twenty-one-thousand-acre working plantation in Sunflower County, the infamous Parchman Prison housed fifteen hundred convicts in over a dozen semiautonomous camps at the middle of the period. Caged sleeping facilities consisted of approximately sixty "beds arranged two or three feet apart in the pattern of a military barracks." Up to 50 percent of the inmates engaged in homosex, camp sergeants reported. Used as a rationale for heterosexual conjugal visits—pioneered in the United States by the Mississippi system—homosexuality nonetheless persisted at Parchman. In the early sixties, sergeants observed "wolves," "jockers," and "top-men" interested in penetrative oral and anal sex. Receptive partners, consenting and not, were known as "kids," "punk kids," "boys," and "gal-boys." In one black camp, "sissies act[ed] just like high school girls, prissing around, plucking eyebrows," as their guard put it. Interestingly, even across the relatively short distance of a couple of miles, across and within racial groups at Parchman's scattered camps, queer vocabularies differed. "Fag," "punk," and all these labels carried multiple assorted meanings.[100] Like the sexualities it described, queer terminology was fluid, flexible, imprecise, and versatile.

As poverty and crime persisted in Mississippi and as inequities were magnified across the color line, dissatisfaction and unrest grew among African Americans. Building on a long tradition of resistance, black Mississippians in the postwar era pushed harder and yelled louder for dignity. The civil rights movement emerged not because Democratic presidents finally took up the banner; not because northern white liberals pressured unrepentant white southerners; not because advocates in the national media brought attention to southern beatings, bombings, and lynchings; and not because fiery black orators and figureheads such as Martin Luther King Jr. stepped forward to lead. While all of these individuals figured prominently, it was the collective struggle of ordinary southerners—local black organizers and followers—that ultimately generated twentieth-century America's grandest movement for social change.

Manifestations of movement were both broad and localized, colossal and minute. In Mississippi—where white bigotry loomed and black tenacity prevailed—courageous African Americans risked life and livelihood by asserting themselves and by activating their friends and neighbors. By registering to vote, by protesting economic injustices, by demonstrating against segregated facilities, these local people set an example of perseverance and power. Setbacks were numerous, but key victories were won.[101]

As civil rights activists questioned assumptions about justice and equality, they created an atmosphere conducive to queer thought and, sometimes, queer desire. Many who fought for racial justice harbored these thoughts and desires—and not just those like Aaron Henry and Bill Higgs who were widely recognized as leaders of the movement. In Hollandale in 1963, one registered black voter boldly took up the torch. He housed out-of-state organizers and carried local residents to the courthouse to pay their poll taxes. A respected member of the Masons, he was also known as a bisexual and an operator of two houses of prostitution.[102]

Among those in need of housing, black and white college students poured into the state for organized campaigns such as 1964's freedom summer. Many white volunteers later understood their commitment in terms of shared struggle, as solidarity in difference. Amber Hollibaugh's "naive anger" at racial oppression propelled her into the Mississippi project from California. She soon was conflicted, however, over the potential problems she posed for black households in the Delta: "We [white female volunteers] brought down the wrath of God: we were staying with Black families, frequently lovers of Black men, and certainly their friends, which was horrific in the eyes of the surrounding white community." According to Hollibaugh, who later self-identified as lesbian, she and her college student friends "put the Black community in even more danger because of that heterosexual racism." [103]

Yet interracial intercourse enabled by the massive mobilizations of the civil rights movement was also homosexual in nature. As a few national figures like Bayard Rustin were urged to cloak their homosexuality, [104] locals and volunteers cautiously explored sexualities across the color line. Burton Weiss, a nineteen-year-old Jewish student from Brooklyn, went south in 1964 to Fayette County, Tennessee, just across the Mississippi border. While registering voters, he lived with seventeen-year-old Jonah Jenkins and his grandfather in a "two-room shack." With Jonah, Burton developed a "special friendship." "Practically naked" due to the heat, they shared a narrow bed at night, such that their legs often became "entangled during sleep." "A few nights things became sticky" for Burton, but he never let on to Jonah. Though "nothing was ever said," the two clearly "loved each other." Weiss wryly remembers the one time they kissed, while working in the garden, eating a cucumber together. [105]

The experience of sexual difference attuned many whites to the intricacies and injustices of racial difference. [106] While hardly a reliable barometer of homosexuality, the later marital status of volunteers nonetheless proves interesting. Doug McAdam found that twenty years after freedom summer, only half of the project veterans were married—compared to 79 percent of a nonactivist comparison group. Though it is "tempting to attribute some of the disparity to differences in sexual preference," McAdam states, "the answer . . . would seem to lie in the volunteers' continuing allegiance to a politicized view of the world"—a worldview that apparently narrows the field of potential spouses. [107] My findings might suggest otherwise, especially as we consider further the implications of the civil rights movement in chapter 4. As the academy just begins to complicate the intersections of race and sexuality in the civil rights movement, we may find some surprising results. What is certain is that the movement fostered egalitarian principles and idealist settings, engendering frank discussion of topics controversial and challenging. As civil rights were won, queer rights issues resounded just beneath the surface.

Blacks and whites, queer and straight, participated in dramatic population shifts over the period. Black out-migration from Mississippi during the forties, fifties, and sixties followed on the heels of the Great Migration before, during, and after World War I. Harsh employment conditions and severe racial hostilities forced many to pick up and head north or west. Increasingly, generations of black Mississippians settled outside the state at distinct and distant locales.[108] Families were sometimes split, some members stayed behind, such that Ricky Lee Smith sold hundreds of Greyhound bus tickets to Chicago, Detroit, and East Saint Louis, Illinois—one-way *and* round-trip. Less frequently noted but no less sizable, white Mississippians left the state in droves. After the close of World War II, the percentage of white natives not in residence was the same as that of blacks, roughly 30 percent.[109] Black and white exiles alike, from upper and lower socioeconomic strata, sought commercial and cultural opportunities in major American cities, while state officials fretted over "brain drain."

As James Loewen and Charles Sallis summarize, "in every decade between 1890 and 1970, more people left Mississippi than came in. . . ." However, "in the 1970s, this out-migration finally came to a halt."[110] The reverse migration evident from 1970 on—the attraction of many to the South—didn't impact Mississippi as prominently as other Sunbelt locations. Indeed, many queer Jacksonians and rural Mississippians chose other cities in the section: Houston, New Orleans, Memphis, and Atlanta. Leaving behind parents and extended families, many men left on their own, lured by the economic and sexual promise of cosmopolitan life. For black Mississippians in particular, Atlanta beckoned. With its well-established black middle class, black political leadership, and distinct black gay male cultures, the self-professed capital of the New South drew both Anthony Greene of Cleveland and Randall Sawyer of Edwards in the 1970s.[111]

Some Mississippians went farther afield. And their reasons were often explicitly sexual. At the close of World War II, white Mississippian Craig Claiborne was compelled to move, though he didn't know exactly where:

> I knew better where I didn't want to go than the direction in which to travel. I didn't want to go home [to Indianola] to the cares of cotton and boarding-house living and live burial in a family bosom. I had tasted enough personal freedom in the service. An important factor as well, I felt that my sexual needs would be poorly served in a small town in the Mississippi Delta.[112]

Claiborne ended up in Chicago, and eventually moved on to New York, where he prospered as food editor for the *New York Times*.

In 1971 Vietnam draft resister Scott Smith followed two fellow gay Jacksonians to the Big Apple. As reporter Randy Shilts condescendingly describes it: "Hip life in Jackson . . . was less than scintillating. There are only so many times you can take LSD, listen to the same Moody Blues songs, and stare at the three-dimensional cover of the Rolling Stones' *Satanic Maj-*

esties Request album before a lusty young man yearns for greater things."[113] Contrary to this representation, most émigrés' decisions involved deeply held convictions and complex thoughts and emotions. For example, in the late seventies, after he "dated girls, almost got married, went to psychiatrists, [and] tried to drink it away" and after he "tried just about everything to deal with being gay," Jonathan Odell decided to leave Mississippi for Minnesota at the age of twenty-nine. Reflecting on that time, when Christian discourse in Mississippi was increasingly hostile to homosexuality, Odell speaks of his choice in spiritual terms: "I knew that I needed to get away and try to find out who I *really* was—not worry about if it was good or bad, right or wrong, acceptable or unacceptable. . . . I know without a doubt that God led me here because he loved me. I feel better about myself than I have *ever* in my life."[114]

OUT-MIGRANTS BENEFITED not only from the material advantages of life in the city—the greater economic opportunities and varied social institutions. They also cultivated an intrinsic satisfaction, a sense that personal values and beliefs were better served by metropolitan living. For Mississippians who chose to remain, the attitudes of the dominant culture invariably shaped the range of queer possibilities.

In a sexist society, homosexual practices sometimes reflected mainstream notions of gender roles, as we have seen in and across various queer sites in Mississippi. When male-male sexual intercourse implicated one of the men in "womanly" acts, the other could feel his heterosexual masculinity uncompromised. In both oral and anal sex, the insertive partner's manhood was rarely called into question; the receptive partner was the queer. Thus, many young men who would later self-identify as gay found it unsettling early on to be penetrated. Ed Foreman was happy to get blow jobs from his boyhood friend Jim, as we saw in chapter 2. But Ed wouldn't "give head." For Ricky Lee Smith, the first homosexual encounter was necessarily penetrative oral sex. That is, he wouldn't suck, or "take the active role," as he put it.[115] "The thought of it was just too much." But he was excited about getting sucked. Similarly, Mark Ingalls's first few homosexual partners at Saint Andrew's School could "jerk [him] off," but Ingalls wouldn't give a hand job or blow job. A variant on this, Ron Knight and his friend Peter would "play with" the surveyor's penis—that is, give him a hand job—but they would not be penetrated in each other's company, orally or anally.

Kissing carried distinct connotations. Ingalls says that initially he wouldn't allow his partners to kiss him. Even more emphatically, Ingalls "*certainly* wouldn't kiss them." Such kissing betrayed too much interest in homosex and in romance, which was culturally scripted as heterosexual. When he was old enough to accept and pursue his interest in men, Ricky Lee Smith was willing to get fucked by William, but ultimately he couldn't be bothered with him: "He was one of those types that anything was OK but not the kissing. He could not go for that. He was engaged to be married. That was something he could only do with a woman." Similarly, the beauty supply vendor "was willing to go along with" Smith's advance, but "he wanted to be very passive about it. At that point," Smith says, "if it wasn't a mutual thing I wasn't interested. . . . He unzipped his pants, said 'OK, I'm here, do your thing.' And that was a turnoff. I said, 'Uh-uh, no, I can't go for it like that.'"

The unspoken rule of manly impenetrability (and, in some sense, passivity) was respected by self-acknowledged homosexual men who preferred "trade"—*trade* defined as straight men who perform penetrative homosex, or *trade* defined as the act itself. Ron Knight was a self-described "trade queen" in the forties because he liked to have sex "with straight guys all the time":

> We were out in all these roadhouses and things trying to make out with supposedly straight guys. And we did. A drop of sissy come would choke us. If we were going to go down on anybody, they would have to be *men*, trade. And if we went down on some sissy queer, some gay thing, it would choke us. So most of my sexual encounters in those days were one-sided. I was always on the receiving end. You might say active if it was oral sex. And to get my own rocks off, I would jack off a lot of times.[116]

Men like that often desired men who liked—but were not like—that. As Ron Knight testifies, queer eroticism was framed not solely as "orientation"—an essential drive for a partner of a particular ("the same") biological sex—but also as an appetite for a particular gender performance. Depending upon the individual, however, the preferred gender performance was not inevitably masculine. As the sexual partners of Rickie Leigh Smith and Robert John demonstrate, effeminate gender performances were also desired. To complement the above formulation: men like that often were desired by men who liked—but were not like—that.

Impenetrable, unkissable men involved in homosex—men that Knight describes both as "supposedly straight guys" and as *"men"*—should not be understood within the present-day psychoanalytic frame of *denial* or the identity politics category of *closeted*. They should not be read as essentialized gay men unable to accept it. As this and the prior two chapters show, in midcentury Mississippi male-male sexualities happened within complicated worlds of myriad desires. To experience or act on homoerotic appetites did not necessarily define the person as gay. Male-male desire functioned beside and along with many other forms of desire—all at some times, in some places, privileged, oppressed, ignored, overlooked, spoken, silenced, written, thought, frustrated, and acted upon. As sociologist Steven Seidman puts it, "The very possibility of framing homosexuality as a site of identity and ethnicity presupposes sexual object-choice [the gender of one's sex partner] as a master category of sexual and self-identity."[117] For many in this time and place, this master category may not have been at work as an identity mechanism; although certainly, sexual object-choice functioned more broadly in American culture in the framing of acceptable and unacceptable, normative and nonnormative sexual practices.

Rickie Leigh Smith used the available categories in Mississippi to describe herself—at different points in life—as a boy who wanted to be a girl, as a gay male, a married gay male, a married man who wanted to be a woman, a drag queen, a transsexual, and a straight female. One Crystal Springs intersexual, who was labeled female on the birth certificate, lived as a boy, then a gay man, for the rest of his life.[118] Mark Ingalls had sex with young men and women in high school and college; twice married and had children, while occasionally having sex with men "on the side"; and settled into a long-term gay relationship at the end of the period. He remembers midcentury homosexual identity this way:

> The [men] that I had sex with, we didn't discuss it. We did not sit around and have intellectual conversations about being gay. Today, that's what you have to do to validate yourself. When you meet someone, you have to go through all this crap about how you knew you were gay, and then how you reconciled it, and now we sit around and tell each other how wonderful we are, because we're OK. That didn't go on then. You just did it, and didn't do too much speculating.[119]

Where you did it mattered. Mississippians were both migratory and place bound, wanderers and homebodies. For many who left Mississippi, their queer desires were increasingly understood within a mass media construction of the gay. For those who lived in Mississippi, distinctive features in the rural landscape resulted in particular sexual desires, behaviors, identities, and networks. Queer boys *did it* in abandoned cabins, beside streams, among the trees;[120] in haylofts, in the fields, in ponds;[121] in cars and pickup trucks, at roadside parks, at summer camps; in hotels, bus stations, theaters, bars, city parks, and roadhouses; in prison, in the military; at church, at work, at school, and at home. Queer desire permeated all aspects of everyday life, such that it could not be relegated to leisure hours; it would not be confined to the cities.

As Will Fellows characterizes the Midwest, so too queer life in Mississippi might be comprehended in terms of "rigid gender roles, social isolation, ethnic homogeneity, suspicion of the unfamiliar, racism, religious conservatism, sexual prudishness, and limited access to information."[122] While certainly relevant, these taxonomies focus on mainstream hegemonic forces and tend to negate queer agency. In Mississippi I see gender subversion; social dispersion and convergence; racial stratification and, late in the period, integration; varied religiosities among greatly varied sexual types; and perpetual social and physical movements—networks transmitting multiple ideas, desires, behaviors, and identities.

And, like so many, I feel a continuing ambivalent attraction to my birthplace, Mississippi. After twenty years in New York, Chuck Plant returned home to Jackson and cared for his aunt until her death; he continued to play viola in various local chamber ensembles. Ron Knight, after a successful career in film production in Los Angeles, again set up house in his hometown—tiny Terry, Mississippi, population 655. Countless others like George Albright, Joe Holmes, and Rickie Leigh Smith chose to live nowhere else but Mississippi. With these men on my mind, I reside irresolutely across the Atlantic—an expatriate returning again and again, turning page after page, to Mississippi.

PART TWO

CHAPTER FOUR

Norms and Laws

The sharply drawn perimeters of normalcy created its opposite, the grotesque. If some people must be normal, then some must be different from normal, or freaks. In reality, everyone is a freak because no human can cram her/himself into the narrow space that is the state of normalcy. But all have to pretend that they fit, and those closet freaks choose the most vulnerable among them to punish for their own secret alienation, to bear the burden of strangeness.

—MAB SEGREST[1]

Chuck Plant: THERE WAS A TERRIBLE CRIME [in Jackson]. A guy that was gay in interior decorating here. The story was that he had gone to the Heidelberg Hotel with two army guys, and they had murdered him in the hotel room. That was probably '54 or '55. This was not the Second World War, but later on, the war that I was in.

I actually had met the guy, and I knew he was in the gay community. In fact I heard through another gay guy that he was badly, badly beaten, that you couldn't recognize him he was so badly beaten. He was very, very tall, I remember, unusually tall. This story hit Jackson. It was known in every household, this horrible thing that happened. Known to one and all. My aunt [who raised me] had heard it in her office. She worked in the post office [building]. She was in the Internal Revenue Service. She had the grand title of administrative assistant. She had no children at all.

A group of [college] friends of mine came home with me from Southern, five of us. We were at the breakfast table, and she was fixing breakfast for us. She was telling the story. She said, "I understand that that young man was a practicing homosexualist." We all had to clap our hands over our mouths to keep from giggling at her phraseology. He was a practicing homosexualist. I think I said, "Well, I had heard that too." And we just let the conversation drop.

[Several years later, in 1965,] my aunt came to New York to visit me. And she [told me], in her own way, [about another incident]. Mr. Russell was caught in the men's room of the City Auditorium. I had cruised there when I was younger. It was open all the time, so that I didn't use it when we were rehearsing, but I used it at other times. I had played in the symphony when I was a late teenager, before I went off to school, and the conductor was Theodore Russell.

Apparently it got to be so active that the police put a camera in the ceiling, and they filmed activity going on. A lot of people were involved. She said he was the leader of a homosexual ring. And I thought, Not so; I know full well that he was not. But when his name came out in the paper, it appeared—I think she knew him, and she thought he was quite important, and she assumed, I think—that he may have been the ringleader. He was the conductor of the symphony. He had founded it. It was his baby. And he had nurtured it. He played at the very large church on Capitol Street; he was the organist there. He was on the faculty of Belhaven [College]. And when this broke, he was out of a job.

When I came back [to Jackson to visit], I spoke to friends who were straight and gay, and of course to the straight ones I'd say, "What is this I hear about" such and such? So I got more information than from what my aunt had said. I thought her story was probably very fuzzy. I don't remember, but I think it was quite a number [that were arrested]. I think it all appeared in the paper, though I never saw it.[2]

For ordinary Mississippians, the concerns of everyday life centered on work and family, friends and leisure: how to pay the bills, how to maintain good relations with kinfolk, how to make time for recreation and entertainment. For queer Mississippians like Chuck Plant, these were also the principal concerns of the daily routine. The experience of difference, the sense of being queer, was negotiated as part of these commonplace interactions. In the armed services, in college, through friendship networks, and at home with his aunt in Jackson, Plant learned the appropriate rituals and demeanors, phrasings and silences, for maintaining a life at odds with prevailing sexual norms.

Just going about one's business, these norms were comprehended and tested, adhered to and resisted. But on occasion out-of-the-ordinary events —notorious public episodes—reminded Mississippians of the laws of the land and the limits of the possible. Home and local community were the day-to-day proving ground; but society at large was the context. Societal values were sometimes most revealingly articulated and adjusted through media coverage of scandal and upheaval.

In addition to print sources, knowledge of queerness also got around by word of mouth. Queer Mississippians hesitantly engaged in such discussions, while others, such as Plant's aunt, seemed rapt with speculation. An effusive conversationalist, she demonstrated the ways in which queer discourse extended associations of place or defied in-state/out-of-state and rural/urban borders. As Chuck Plant's narrative suggests, queer discourse circulated far and wide, and it relied on a careful etiquette of revelation and (dis)identification.

Chuck Plant's precise recollections of two queer events in postwar Mississippi—well corroborated by other sources—not only give evidence of the importance of these events in the lives of queer Mississippians at the time. They also suggest a critical shift in attitudes toward homosexuality in the state over this period. Though both events involved white men and the exposing of white queer sites to a larger public, the differing legal handling of the incidents—the John Murrett murder of 1955 and the Jackson City Auditorium arrests of 1965—illustrate a significant change in mainstream notions of deviant sexualities, a change resulting from broader sociopolitical transformations forged primarily by black Mississippians. As we shall see, over the course of ten years, a vibrant, ever more successful civil rights movement would become connected in the minds of many Mississippians to queer sex, among other suspect practices and ideologies. Consequently, police and judicial responses to queer Mississippians would prove increasingly hostile and punitive.

Murrett and Murder

In 1955 the murder of John Murrett reverberated throughout Mississippi. From the moment the statewide daily *Clarion-Ledger* carried the banner headline "JACKSON MAN SMOTHERED BY ASSAILANTS IN HOTEL" until the Mississippi Supreme Court ruled on a defendant's appeal almost a year later, Mississippians speculated about the victim and his assailants. As Chuck Plant said, the incident "was known in every household."

For John Murrett the nightmare began on Saturday, 23 July 1955.[3] Late that afternoon, around 6:00, the lanky six-foot-seven-inch twenty-nine-year-old interior decorator—labeled a loner by many—got off work at the Sid Jones furniture store. From there, he went to a small basement café on the west end of downtown, the Cellar, located on Pascagoula near Gallatin Street. After a couple of beers, Murrett walked up Capitol Street to the Mayflower Café, where he chatted with an acquaintance and, after eating, cashed a check for $20. Farther up Capitol Street, at roughly 11:00, Murrett entered the Wagon Wheel. "A place serving beer and juke box music to its customers," as the state supreme court later described it, the downtown tavern was also known as a gay gathering spot.[4]

Inside the narrow second-floor bar at 109-1/2 East Capitol Street, several armed service members drank and conversed. Wagon Wheel owner Houston Barnett noticed Murrett, a regular customer who came in two or three times a month, "always by himself." Murrett was talking with three uniformed Missouri Air National Guardsmen on bivouac in the area. When

the Missouri airmen left, Murrett sat down at the bar next to five other air
cadets. He discovered as he conversed with two of them that they were on
leave from Keesler Air Force Base in Biloxi, over three hours' drive to the
south. Murrett further learned that the men, short on cash, planned to sleep
in their car that night.

Perhaps emboldened by the alcohol, Murrett offered overnight accommodations to the two sitting closest to him, twenty-two-year-old Lawrence
Burns of Cincinnati and seventeen-year-old Warren Koenig of Chicago,
known to his fellow cadets as "Chi." Burns and Koenig informed their companions that Murrett would put the two of them up for the night. The other
three would have to drive to the city outskirts, park, sleep, and meet the
two at the Elite Café the next morning at 8:00.

Around 1:30 that morning, Murrett, Burns, and Koenig left the Wagon
Wheel. They had coffee at the Mayflower, then walked back up Capitol
Street to the east. The two men later said they assumed Murrett was taking
them home. But Murrett, a boarder in an elder lady's house in tony Woodland Hills, well outside downtown,[5] led them into the elegant Walthall
Hotel lobby. W. C. Dear was the clerk on duty that night at the Walthall.
Dear, who also served as justice of the peace in the nearby town of Florence,
didn't like the looks of the three men. Murrett asked for only one room, a
request that the other two men clearly heard. All three men then signed
the registration card with false names, and Dear, of his own prerogative,
quoted them a high rate, a late-night premium of $12. The men refused.
They walked out of the Walthall, and Dear marked the registration card
with the letters "NDG," indicating his "interpretation of the crowd." The
men were, in Judge Dear's view, "no damn good."[6]

Next, the three men walked down Capitol to the Hotel Heidelberg. This
time the two airmen waited outside while Murrett secured a single room
with one double bed. The rate was $6. It was now 2:02 A.M. Murrett asked
the clerk where he might buy cigarettes, then walked outside and turned
onto the sidewalk, the clerk noticed, in the opposite direction.

Moments later the three men walked through the lobby and took the
elevator up to the seventh floor. Inside room 709 Murrett, Burns, and Koenig each undressed down to his shorts and washed up for bed. Murrett
carefully put away his shoes and hung his coat, shirt, and trousers on a
hanger in the closet. As the men smoked cigarettes, he took off his watch
and placed it neatly along with his wallet, tie clip, and necktie on top of the
dresser. Koenig got in bed next to the wall, then Murrett climbed in. Meanwhile, Burns placed his own clothes over the sole chair in the room and
sat down.

Burns would later claim that he intended to sleep in the chair, but that

Murrett insisted he get in bed too. Regardless, Burns likewise ended up in the bed, next to the edge, with Murrett in the middle. Sometime thereafter, Burns struggled with Murrett. Then, as Burns held Murrett from behind, Koenig beat Murrett "terribly," in the words of the supreme court justices, "breaking his nose, hitting him in the abdomen sufficiently hard to cause a hemorrhage in the abdominal wall, knocking a tooth out, lacerating the face, scalp, nose and jaw." With Burns's help, Koenig continued to beat Murrett, "finally knock[ing] him out, unconscious."[7]

Burns and Koenig then tied up the victim. They bound his hands behind his back with the lamp cord and strapped his feet together with his own belt. Though Murrett remained unconscious, Burns and Koenig stuffed a pillowcase into his mouth and partially down his throat. They then secured the gag with a sheet, wrapping it around his neck and over his mouth.

The two washed the blood off their bodies, put their clothes back on, and on their way out, rifled through the items on the dresser. Burns took Murrett's money; Koenig took his Bulova watch. Murrett seemed to be regaining consciousness as Burns and Koenig turned to go. The airmen left Murrett sluggishly grappling to free himself.

Rather than take the noisy elevator, Burns and Koenig walked down the seven flights. Nonetheless, the Heidelberg night clerk noticed them leave the lobby, sometime between 3:15 and 3:45. With the money they took from Murrett, the two men checked into another hotel, then met their friends as planned after sunup. The friends noticed blood on the clothing of both Burns and Koenig, who told them what had happened. The five airmen spent Sunday afternoon with some young Jackson women, then drove back to Keesler Air Force Base that night in Burns's 1948 Chevrolet.

At 9:30 A.M. that Sunday, Heidelberg housekeeper Acie Stiff discovered the body of John Murrett, bound and gagged, on the floor of room 709. Police arrived, then called the coroner, Forrest Bratley. Bratley's autopsy, conducted that afternoon, showed that in the early morning hours of Sunday, 24 July 1955, John Murrett died—not from his wounds, but rather by strangulation, "suffocation from lack of oxygen in the body."[8]

The city's chief detective initiated what he called "the most extensive investigation the Jackson police department has participated in."[9] Following a single slim lead—the fact that the assailants were servicemen—detectives embarked on an all-out manhunt. Locally, they retraced Murrett's steps, noting the places and enlisting as witnesses the people he had seen that night. Detectives then fanned out across several states, worked collaboratively with the FBI and congressional offices in Washington, and finally located their suspects two months later at Keesler Air Force Base in Biloxi. On 27 September 1955, the *Jackson Daily News* trumpeted the results in their all-caps banner headline: "POLICE SOLVE MURRETT MURDER WITH ARREST OF FIVE AIRMEN."

Even as the case took on a decidedly queer cast, as the newspapers revealed Burns's contention that Murrett had "made a pass" at him,[10] the *Clarion-Ledger* praised police investigators in a gushing editorial.

> Our hat is off again to the efficient and tireless efforts of the Jackson Police Department. . . . Many, many times, in the face of almost hopeless odds, they have continued to sift through the most meager of clues in search of the "little something" that might lead to the solving of a case. Such was true in the latest efforts of officers in a most baffling murder case. . . . It is comforting . . . to know that [there are] trained personnel capable of conducting and successfully concluding such a difficult investigation.[11]

Despite the prevalence of sanctioned racially motivated white mob violence in Mississippi at this time, reporters professed abhorrence for murder. Regardless of the sexual proclivities of the deceased, John Murrett, Jackson journalists first and foremost wanted his killers captured and convicted.

AT THE NOVEMBER 1955 MEETING of the Hinds County Grand Jury, the eighteen-man body indicted Lawrence Burns and Warren Koenig for the murder of John Murrett. Their three fellow cadets and Keesler electronics students—Willard Dougherty, age twenty-one, of Hoosick Falls, New York; Joseph Fernandez, seventeen, of New York City; and Joseph LaRocco, nineteen, of Brooklyn, New York—were not charged but remained in custody as material witnesses. Though Burns and Koenig had confessed the murder to Jackson detectives and to members of the air force Office of Special Investigations, or OSI, they pleaded innocent before Circuit Judge Leon Hendrick. Hendrick appointed attorneys W. W. Pierce and William Waller— later governor of Mississippi—to represent the men at trial.

The men were tried separately, Burns first. During jury selection on Monday, 28 November 1955, defense attorneys revealed what would be their primary strategy at trial. In determining whether or not to accept a prospective juror from the seventy-eight-man venire, W. W. Pierce posed a key question: Would the potential juror find the defendant Burns innocent if it were shown that Murrett was killed while trying to commit a felony on Burns? That is, would Burns be held less accountable for his actions if Murrett were proven to have attempted a "crime of nature" upon Burns?[12]

Burns's attorneys would rely on a by-then familiar legal tactic: they asserted that Burns committed "justifiable homicide" because Murrett "attempt[ed] to assault [Burns] in a homosexual manner." The homosexual panic defense, to this day employed in many American courtrooms, has been and continues to be quite effective.[13] Burns seemed well positioned to benefit from it. He was a serviceman, a vocation of great respect in military-minded Mississippi. Murrett, on the other hand, had been employed in a variety of gender-suspect professions. Before moving to Jackson over a year prior, Murrett had worked at Rich's department store in Atlanta, and before that, he taught painting and sculpture in South Carolina. Though local jurors might have viewed the defendant and his fellow air cadets as outsiders or renegades, Murrett—originally from Silver Creek, New York—seemed no less so.

Undaunted, prosecuting attorney Julian Alexander indicated that he would seek the death penalty against Burns.

The trial proceedings, followed in close detail by Mississippi reporters and newspaper readers, not only illuminated the lengths to which Jackson detectives went in pursuing Murrett's murderers; they also disclosed witnesses' perceptions of the victim, his assailants, their activities, and their respective culpability. In the process, varied understandings of queer sexuality surfaced. In light of strident homosexual crackdowns under way in numerous American locales, police and prosecutors in the Murrett case proved strikingly benign in their views on homosexuality. Whereas cities large and small—San Francisco and Sioux City, Baltimore and Boise— "witnessed sudden upsurges in police action against gays" during the 1950s,[14] Mississippi law enforcement demonstrated a tacit acceptance of homosexuality. In crafting their case against Lawrence Burns, district attorneys clearly hoped that jurors likewise would choose to disregard aspersions cast upon Murrett, to find sexuality irrelevant to the case.

On Tuesday morning, 29 November 1955, Lawrence Burns appeared for trial deftly attired in a "neat blue shirt, tie, and khaki pants."[15] His silver-haired attorney, W. W. Pierce, immediately set about the task of discrediting the victim, John Murrett. After Jackson police detective Paul Stribling described for prosecuting attorney Alexander the events on the evening of Murrett's death, Pierce went on the counteroffensive.

Pierce: Was [John Murrett] a single man?
Stribling: Yes, sir, he was. As far as we could find out he was a single man.
P: Do you know about how old he was?
S: Approximately twenty-nine.
P: Did you make any investigation to determine whether he had ever been married?
S: Our investigation showed that he had only been in Jackson approximately fourteen months. He hadn't been married while he was in Jackson.

P: Well, in making your investigation, did you determine whether or not he had any lady friends, women that he went out with regularly?

S: We worked on that angle and came up with nothing, as far as his lady friends.

Despite Stribling's reluctance to engage the issue of Murrett's dating habits, Pierce persisted. And, intervening in the exchange, Judge Hendrick demonstrated that he would resist defense deprecations of Murrett.

Pierce: In other words, as far as your information was, the only people he associated with were men.

Stribling: He wasn't—as far as our information was, he wasn't doing too much associating; his boss told us he was a very quiet man and stayed to himself. The information we got from his landlady was that he never brought any visitors to his room. He was very quiet and stayed to himself most of the time.

Pierce: Well, if a man was going into an act of debauchery, he wouldn't like to take a person to his room.

Alexander: We object, Your Honor. That's argument; he can save that for the jury.

Judge Hendrick: I sustain the objection. You are asking for facts, Mr. Pierce, so far as the witness knows.

Pierce: If the court please, here's an experienced police officer.

Judge Hendrick: Mr. Pierce, I sustained the objection to your question, so I don't care to hear any argument on the question of debauchery at this time.[16]

Indeed, from the very beginning, Jackson detectives knew that their victim, John Murrett, was considered queer, as was revealed in Pierce's cross-examination of detective James Roy Luke.

Pierce: In making your investigation, . . . did you get any information as to whether or not [John Murrett] was a sex pervert?

Luke: No, sir, we didn't.

P: Didn't you, Mr. Luke, when you went down to Keesler Field report to the commanding officer down there that this man was a sex pervert?

L: I did not.

. . .

P: In making your investigation, you say you didn't get any information with reference to this man being a sex pervert?

L: There were some opinions of other people, but, no, I disregarded that.

P: You disregarded that because that was against—in favor of this boy [Burns], didn't you?

L: No, sir, it was immaterial to me.

. . .

P: Tell this court and this jury whether or not you made any effort to tie that down, to find out if that was a fact or not.

L: I wouldn't know where to start.

. . .

P: Mr. Luke, you will just have to admit to this jury that you didn't put in [your reports] something that [an informant] said.

L: (No answer.)

Like fellow detective Stribling, Luke was reluctant to elaborate upon this line of questioning, as he had been reluctant to pursue this particular lead during the investigation. And again, Judge Hendrick narrowly delimited Pierce's queries:

Pierce: Now, Mr. Luke, you—did you know that a male person who tries to have sex relations one way or another with another male person is guilty of a felony?

Alexander: Your Honor, I object to that.

Judge Hendrick: I sustain the objection. That's not the witness's province.[17]

Though enforcement of the state's sodomy law presumably *would* have fallen within detective Luke's province, Judge Hendrick suggested that in this case such considerations were, as Luke had testified, immaterial.

Air force investigators Marcus Atkins and C. E. Flanagan also eluded Pierce's stubborn explorations into Murrett's sex life. Each man told Pierce that such speculation and investigation were beyond the scope of their duties.[18] Further, the medical examiner, Forrest Bratley, skillfully handled Pierce's questions. Relying on a model increasingly dominant in more liberal strains of midcentury American medical discourse, he depicted homosexuality as a condition readily observed in human populations, a state of being for a definable minority of individuals. Moreover, Bratley refuted societal stereotypes of queer promiscuity and pathology, as voiced by Pierce.

Pierce: Doctor, for my own information, the information of the court and the jury, there's such a thing in the human race as a homosexual?

Bratley: I have heard of homosexuals.

P: Tell the jury what a homosexual is.

B: A homosexual is out of my line of work. We don't see them pathologically. In performing an autopsy one cannot differentiate between a heterosexual or a homosexual. I don't have a good definition for a homosexual.

P: Would a homosexual or a queer differ materially in his physique, in ordinary behavior in public from the average individual?

B: In physique or appearance there would not be any difference. In behavior among the general public there would not be any difference. How they might act before an individual, which I wouldn't consider public particularly, I don't know.

P: Doctor, sex has a great deal to do with the behavior of a good many people. You know that as a medical man, don't you?

B: Sex does determine some of our behavior patterns.

P: And in some instances it can be an uncontrollable urge in the individual. Don't your medical books teach that?

B: I am sure some of the specialized books do. I haven't had that specialized training.

P: Doctor, would a person who would engage in sex perversion, would he be a person who might be aggressive if the sex urge was strong enough?

B: I am sure the sex urge would be just as strong as if he wasn't a homosexual.[19]

Despite their knowledge—or, their pretense of ignorance—of Murrett's homosexuality, Jackson detectives pursued Murrett's assailants with a dogged persistence greater even than Pierce's. Though the very crime scene suggested sordid homosexual overtones in the case, the Jackson Police Department nonetheless conducted a lengthy and expensive investigation unprecedented in Mississippi crime fighting, as the police chief boasted—an investigation that placed far more emphasis on reconstructing the murder than revisiting Murrett's sexual past. As the trial of Lawrence Burns continued into a second and third day and as journalists continued to share the particulars with readers, radio listeners, and TV viewers, Mississippians learned just how complicated the detectives' task had been, relative to their usual workload, and just how intricate the prosecutors' case would be.

By questioning hotel clerks, barkeeps, and other people out on the town that Saturday night, Jackson detectives ascertained that their suspects were military personnel. They scoured local hotels and discovered that a group of five such men had registered at a cheap lodge that weekend, apparently under false names: Larry Alloway (later determined to be Burns), Warren Bradley (Koenig), Will Ryan (Dougherty), Joseph Baccardi (LaRocco), and, most importantly, J. Fernandezson (determined to be Fernandez).

After reaching several dead ends, detective Paul Stribling began to speculate that "J. Fernandezson" might be a not-so-creative pseudonym for a J. Fernandez. Consequently, Jackson police requested a search of the entire United States military roster. U.S. congressman John Bell Williams of Raymond—also later to become governor of Mississippi—coordinated the effort from Washington. After a list was developed, OSI agents detained Joseph Fernandez at Keesler, then called on Jackson detectives, who rushed to Biloxi. Fernandez and his friends had used fictitious names, he easily explained, because their trip to Jackson had violated the base's one-hundred-mile pass limit. But as investigators stepped up their questioning, Fernandez broke down. He implicated Koenig. A search of Koenig's personal effects then revealed a repair slip for a Bulova wristwatch, traceable to Murrett. Koenig, in turn, implicated Burns, whose fingerprints, specialists proved, matched a bloody print found in Hotel Heidelberg room 709. Finally, both men confessed to detectives.

On the stand, however, Burns and Koenig, as well as fellow cadet Dougherty, helped construct a justifiable homicide defense by portraying Murrett as queer. In so doing, they had to balance an ability to identify a queer against the possibility that they too might be labeled queer. This tension first arose as defense attorney W. W. Pierce questioned Dougherty about the Wagon Wheel.

Pierce: Now tell the jury what [Murrett] did that makes you say that he tried to get chummy with you [five men].

Dougherty: Well, it was just the look about him.

P: Well, tell the jury how he looked.

D: You could tell the man looked queer. He would just look at you that queer way.

P: And did he say anything at all to you . . . three boys . . . sitting at the end of the [bar]?

D: No, he didn't.

. . .

P: Did you join in the conversation in any way?

D: No, sir.

P: Why didn't you?

D: I didn't—I didn't want to have anything to do with the man.

. . .

P: Had you had any experience with that kind of people before?

D: No, sir.

P: Well, then how could you tell?

D: Because I had seen many of them.[20]

Contrary to Dougherty's testimony, it was incumbent on Koenig and Burns to profess ignorance of Murrett's queerness, at least upon their initial meeting and during their first interactions. As a consequence, district attorney Alexander attempted to show that the two men were either the worst rubes or the most unrepentant liars.

Alexander: Did you size that fellow up in your mind and in the mind of Burns, size him up for being a queer?

Koenig: No, sir.

. . .

A: You thought it was perfectly normal for a man to take both of you boys and jam you up in a hotel room for the night and give you money in the morning and wish you happy traveling?

K: Thought he was a nice guy helping us out.

A: And nothing out of the way—nothing appeared out of the way to you?

K: (No answer.)[21]

Defense attorney Pierce tried to help Burns put this aright when, in the trial's closely studied climax, the defendant finally took the stand.

Burns: [Murrett] took all the money he had and laid it out there [on the dresser] and said that we could have it in the morning, when we left. He wouldn't need it. He could get some more early and he knew we were short. . . .

Pierce: He told you he was giving that to you?

B: Yes, sir.

P: Well, up to that point he had played along sure 'nuff in the role of a jolly good fellow, hadn't he?

B: Yes, sir. I have had things like this happen to me before in the service as far as giving me night's lodging and being given a couple of dollars as I went along. . . . I didn't think there was anything unusual about this.

Most significantly for the defense and for the success of the justifiable homicide claim, attorney Pierce had to show that around 2:30 A.M., on 24 July 1955, Burns was fending off a homosexual assault by Murrett—specifically, a felonious act of sodomy. Thus, on this the third and final day of the trial, the defendant offered a detailed and dramatic recounting—or revising—of the events in room 709, the struggle between the three bedmates.

P: How long, according to your best judgment, Lawrence, were you in the bed then before anything started?

B: It was three or four minutes.

P: What, if you recall, was the first thing that attracted your attention?

B: Well, . . . I was just laying there. I was more or less trying to get . . . settled down and the first thing I knew he was—his hand was rubbing across my body, my chest.

P: What did you do then?

B: I turned back around towards him to tell him about it and as soon as I turned back around on my back he laid himself across me and started to kiss me. He tried to kiss me but I kept twisting away. He kissed me along side of the neck and cheek on both sides and he started running his hands, one hand, down my body. And I took one hand and pushed his hand away and he reached down and tried to grab a-hold of my penis, but I pushed his hand away and grabbed hold of it myself. At this point he was still on top of me and still trying to kiss me and calling me "honey" and kept saying things like that. . . . I didn't know what to do. I was scared. I didn't even think about anybody else being in the room like Koenig or anybody. And all this time he kept struggling with me and the more I pushed him the more he kept on struggling and after a little while I remembered Koenig was in the room and I looked over at him, twisted my head around to where he was, and he called me and I said, "Help me" or something like that, at which time he sat up in bed and I told him to hit him, or words similar, and he did. Soon as he hit him he rolled off of me. As soon as he rolled off, he grabbed, he rolled around more or less off my body facing Koenig. When he did I grabbed him and Koenig grabbed him, started to hit him, and we fell right off the bed in a couple of seconds. He was tussling there on the bed with me trying to hold him.

Pierce continued to question Burns about the altercation, but the most important element remained unsaid.

P: Now after this thing started did he continue or not to progress in his efforts?
B: Yes, sir, he persisted. . . . [T]he more I would try to push him off the more he would stay on or try to stay on, to increase his, I guess you would say, his love-making, but he kept trying to kiss me and everything and slobbered all over me.
P: Tell this court and this jury whether or not he slobbered and rubbed his tongue all over your neck.
B: Yes, sir.
Alexander: Your Honor, I object to leading the witness.
Judge Hendrick: I sustain the objection. The question is what was done.
P: I beg your pardon. Tell this jury what was done.

And still, Burns did not provide the key evidence needed to sustain the defense argument. Pierce thus was forced to lead Burns further. After much subsequent questioning with no appropriate response from Burns, Pierce virtually put the words in his mouth. Uncharacteristically, district attorney Alexander raised no objection.

P: Lawrence, speaking of sex perversion, do you know what the expression "to go down on a man" means.
B: Yes, sir.
P: What does it mean?
B: It means to try to blow a man.
P: Tell this court and this jury whether or not that tried to happen to you [sic] at that particular time.
B: Yes, sir.
P: How did he try to accomplish that?
B: Well, he tried to get a-hold of my penis with his hands and then get his face down to it before I had a chance to pull his hand away and cover myself with my hands.
P: You tell this court and this jury that's what happened to you there?

B: Yes, sir.

P: If the court please, that's all.[22]

As testimony ended, Judge Leon Hendrick instructed the jury. Despite his impatience during the trial with these sexual chronicles, the judge allowed the jurors to consider the justifiable homicide defense. But, in a matter of timing that would figure prominently in deliberations, he specifically authorized them to ascertain only whether Burns's murderous acts "were done to *prevent* the commission of a felony [sodomy] upon him."[23]

Further, the judge told the jury to weigh the prosecution's own crafty argument. In his closing statement, district attorney Julian Alexander used minute details of the crime and subtle points of the law in a bid to thwart Burns's defense. The gagging, he reminded the jurors, was the proximate cause of Murrett's death, according to the medical examiner, not the beating. Burns and Koenig had gagged Murrett *after* he was beaten unconscious. The alleged attempt at sodomy, even if assumed true, had already been successfully resisted.

Moreover, Burns had stolen money from Murrett, the $4.50 he lifted as he left the room with Koenig. Though Burns insisted Murrett had promised them what little money he had left that night, Burns at minimum was an accomplice to Koenig's theft of the watch. Thus, the wristwatch not only provided a critical link between Murrett and his slayers in the police investigation; it also proved the linchpin in this complicated legal strategy designed to insure Burns's conviction. Prosecuting attorneys had produced two witnesses in connection with the watch. The owner of Juniker Jewelry in Jackson testified that two or three days before the killing, she had sold Murrett a watchband similar if not identical to the one found in Biloxi. Her repairman, Free Loar, identified markings within the watch itself as ones he had made when he repaired it earlier that year.

The watch was crucial. A related but obscure state statute held that if a suspect killed an individual while "engaged in the commission of the crime of robbery," that suspect was guilty of murder, regardless of intent. Thus, if the jury determined that Burns gagged Murrett, which he had admitted in court; that the gagging killed Murrett, which Dr. Bratley testified; and that Burns robbed Murrett, either by theft of the money or as accomplice to the theft of the watch—then Burns must be found guilty of murder.

In five hours, the jurors reached just that conclusion. Late on 1 December 1955, they filed back into the courtroom, and the foreman delivered their verdict: guilty as charged. The jury recommended life in prison for Burns. The judge concurred. The ruling later would be upheld by the Mississippi Supreme Court.

In his separate trial two weeks later, Warren "Chi" Koenig struck a deal, a plea bargain. In exchange for his guilty plea, prosecutors suggested—and Judge Hendrick begrudgingly accepted—a reduced twenty-year term. "If you were older," Hendrick told Koenig before he was led away, "I don't think I would accept it."[24]

The sophisticated interpretations of law that insured the Burns conviction were especially generous in Mississippi, where, as previously noted, the judicial system was notoriously substandard; where white vigilantes were regularly acquitted of lynching black men, often for purported sexual misconduct with white women; where, during that very same September in which the airmen were apprehended, two white men were acquitted of the murder of black youth Emmett Till, though international media monitored the trial and the two later confessed; where the fourteen-year-old Till, found strapped to a weighty cotton gin fan at the bottom of the Tallahatchie River, had done nothing more than flirt with a white woman; and where the sixty-eight-minute verdict in the Till case was, in the words of historian John Dittmer, "generally well received."[25] In comparison, the legal establishment in Mississippi seemed remarkably sympathetic to white male homosexuals. As the Till case and the Murrett case literally shared the headlines in the Mississippi press, bold contrasts emerged. Though queer Mississippians would long cite the Murrett murder as a reminder of the horrific violence that at any moment could befall them, the police and the court system—at least in this one, pivotal case—sided with them.

We can only speculate about the aims of murderers Lawrence Burns and Warren "Chi" Koenig. Maybe robbery was their motive, as police chose to craft it. However, such starkly drawn arguments in the adversarial space of the courtroom tend to smooth out the tangled motivations at work in the human psyche. How can we account for the cadets' presence in the Wagon Wheel, a club not explicitly gay owned but nonetheless gay frequented? Why did they agree to sleep in a single room, with only one bed? Did their own pretense of ignorance extend even to one another? Were they testing one another's propensities? With fine shadings of conversation and subtle nuances of body language, the men may have proceeded ever uncertain and equivocal about the night's final outcome, about the fellow cadet's take on the situation. Perhaps in a genuine homosexual panic, Burns discovered only at the moment of sexual intercourse with Murrett that Koenig found it detestable. Perhaps it was only then that Burns along with Koenig had to reaffirm their masculinity by bashing the queer.

For those who participated in, reported on, and talked about it, the John Murrett murder trial of 1955 made visible a social compact that, as a rule, functioned invisibly. Around deviant sexuality, a quiet accommodation was the norm. Whether they believed homosexuality to be an immutable state of being for certain individuals, as Dr. Forrest Bratley asserted, or a set of behaviors deemed sinful but forgivable, most ordinary Mississippians overlooked expressions of queer sexuality all around them. Of sexual deviance, they were not *ignorant*, in the traditional sense of the word. They were aware, but rather *chose* to *ignore*—much as Jackson police detectives, air force OSI agents, the eighteen grand jurors, the twelve trial jurors, Judge Hendrick, and the state supreme court justices found Murrett's sexuality immaterial or irrelevant. Perhaps this all-male legal brotherhood found Murrett's queerness not wholly irrelevant but rather a point of identification and even empathy with him, as part of a common, tacit understanding of queer acts past, especially among male youths.

For their part in the social compact, queer Mississippians maintained low profiles. In day-to-day life they went about their routines, as did others. They simply avoided discussions of their sexual activities and fantasies—again, as did others. Even as interracial heterosexual interactions, real or alleged, fueled or retrospectively justified the most heinous mob violence in the state, same-sex same-race intercourse yielded comparatively little open hostility. Indeed, as numerous oral history narrators describe conditions in the 1950s, the homosexual homicide that was John Murrett's fate spoke less about the state of things than did the legal vindication of the homosexual murder victim.[26] As Chuck Plant put it, before the 1960s there was "not a lot of crackdown, you know, legal intervention. Things were kind of wide open." Between Mississippians, normative and queer, a careful equilibrium prevailed.

This rapprochement was soon to end.

Higgs, Henry, and Freedom

Ever since the end of Reconstruction and the reestablishment of minority white rule under the 1890 state constitution, black Mississippians had resisted Jim Crow, the inhumane structure of racial segregation extending to every facet of daily life. Especially after the Second World War, African Americans insisted on the right to vote. They demanded equal access to education, housing, and public accommodations. Their long strivings eventually yielded the civil rights movement's most significant, tangible achievements, the federal legislation aimed at breaking segregation: the Civil Rights Act of 1964 and the Voting Rights Act of 1965.

The civil rights movement at its heart was a struggle of local people, as historians John Dittmer and Charles Payne convincingly demonstrate in Mississippi.[27] Though the struggle was largely quashed by white terrorism in the state during the late 1950s—including at least ten murders of black men by white men, none of whom were convicted—black Mississippians in the early 1960s conducted visible, nonviolent, direct-action campaigns akin to the lunch counter sit-ins that mobilized students and organizers across the South.[28] In Biloxi activists sponsored a wade-in at the segregated public beach in 1960. Tougaloo College students staged a sit-in at the Jackson Public Library in the spring of 1961. These and other demonstrations across the state were soon eclipsed, however, by a large-scale integrationist operation known as the freedom rides—a nationally publicized protest movement that triggered severe official opposition, coupled with a sexualized rhetoric of racial anarchy and decline.

For centuries white supremacists had portrayed blacks and, to a lesser degree, their white supporters as sexual miscreants. To justify their sexual assaults on black female slaves, for example, white male slave owners had depicted their victims as lusty Jezebels with voracious sexual appetites. Following the Civil War, a panicky white rhetoric fabricated a hypersexualized black male rapist, whose retrogressive bestiality threatened a mythical southern white womanhood. Throughout the years white liberals were branded as traitors to the race, "nigger lovers" prone to race mixing and miscegenation.[29] Post–World War II resistance to the civil rights movement, to the freedom rides of 1961 and the freedom summer campaign of 1964, furthered this discursive tradition, while it also elaborated and extended the range of sexual deviancy.

Among varied white propaganda machines, the publications and broadcasts of the Citizens' Councils were particularly potent and pervasive. Since its founding in Indianola, Mississippi, in 1954, the Citizens' Councils organization had grown regional in scope and national in influence. By the early 1960s, most southern counties had a chapter or loose affiliate. Though often referred to as the businessman's Klan, these groups were made up of white citizens both male and female from across the socioeconomic spectrum. They lobbied elected officials, many of whom were members; punished blacks and white dissidents with economic reprisals; and stirred opposition to civil rights, in the guise of support *for* "states' rights," through sustained media blitzes, sometimes publicly funded.[30] State identity, in this sense, always implied a (white) racial identity. Deviations from racial—and, as we shall see, sexual—customs were an assumed consequence of outside interference.

Greenwood, Mississippi's Association of Citizens' Councils churned out flyers and leaflets chronicling the social deviancy of African Americans. Citing FBI statistics, this literature warned of the "menace of integration" with pseudoscientific data on "negro crime." Blacks, as a proportion of the population, were more frequently arrested for murder, gambling, and "dope violations," the councils asserted. They also committed more acts of prostitution, rape, and "other sex offenses."[31] Perpetuating a siege mentality and a language of titillation, Citizens' Council founder Robert Patterson claimed that national media were covering up the prevalence of black-on-white rape: "In the North, newspapermen and other molders of public opinion writhe in an orgy of 'perverted brotherhood and tolerance' and hide the crime of rape and its sordid facts from the Northern public."[32]

Even as they adopted slogans from the poet laureate of libertinism Walt Whitman,[33] the councils warned of the dangers of "amalgamation." They looked back in history for inspiration to the rabid, racist governor Theodore Bilbo, whose World War I and Depression-era vitriol they repeatedly recirculated: "If the blood of our white race should become corrupted and mingled with the blood of Africa, then the present greatness of the United States of America would be destroyed and all hope for the future would be forever gone."[34] With the Citizens' Councils' help, such thinking persisted into the 1960s, as ordinary white Mississippians echoed these sentiments. As Dovey Johnson Boydston of Water Valley asserted in a letter to a local paper, "mixing the two races is as unacceptable, as astonishing and as UNGODLY as . . . lower animals mixing with another [sic] of a different species."[35]

When freedom riders first came by bus to Jackson on 24 May 1961, testing the recent Supreme Court decree against segregation in interstate transportation facilities, they were subjected to similar smears and denunciations. But names could not hurt the activists who had survived the sticks and stones of Alabama mobs. On their way from Washington, D.C., to New Orleans, the activists from CORE—the Congress of Racial Equality—suffered mob violence in Birmingham and Montgomery and outlived the firebombing of a bus in Anniston. When some riders gave up, additional riders were recruited from the ranks of SNCC—the Student Nonviolent Coordinating Committee, or "Snick."[36] The first two busloads to arrive in Jackson and attempt to integrate the waiting rooms and rest rooms included mostly black male southerners, with only two whites and but a few females among the twenty-seven volunteers.[37]

When police jailed these freedom riders, the floodgates opened. Volunteers poured into the state. Though they remained a mostly male squadron, they were drawn increasingly from the ranks of white college students from outside the South. White supremacist pundits would occasionally comment on the black activists who initiated these efforts, but their attention was captured by white male "dirty beatniks"—outsiders whose nonconformity confounded local whites.

White "freedom rioters" in particular drew the ire of Jimmy Ward, the egomaniacal editor of the *Jackson Daily News*. Never content to limit his observations to the editorial page, Ward penned a daily "Covering the Crossroads" column and placed it prominently along the left-hand edge of the front page. In it, he circulated racist jokes, castigated political moderates and liberals, and helped construct and disseminate the dirty beatnik stereotype, the personification of the "invading latrine-sniffers," "the scummy people . . . trying to destroy law and order in the nation."[38]

In random musings, reportage, and editorials, Mississippi journalists depicted the "gay crowds" at the bus and train terminals as a marauding criminal element.[39] The *Clarion-Ledger* noted the activists' "past police records," the vast majority of which contained arrests only for similar protests.[40] Ward and others insisted the "CORE crumbs" and "crackpots" and "muddled punks" and "nuts" were atheistic dupes of a broader communist plot.[41] Indeed, the 29 June 1961 headline of the *Jackson Daily News* declared that "SOVIETS PLANNED 'FREEDOM RIDES.'"[42]

Even as Jimmy Ward pushed his reporters to pursue leads in the communist conspiracy theory, he was fixated on the young white men who counted for but a portion of the multiracial battle against segregation. On 21 June he dedicated half of the editorial page to an enlarged photo of a representative freedom rider, accompanied by a scathing commentary. Ward felt it necessary, he wrote, to "let the dignity drop" and provide readers with "a clear close-up of a 'freedom rider,'" in this case, Buron Lewis Teale, of Albany, California. Today the photo seems harmless enough. Teale sits on a bench with his knapsack. He wears a jacket and trousers, even a tie, slightly askew. His hair is unkempt and his eyelids are narrowed, but with almost four decades' hindsight, he looks like a run-of-the-mill thirty-two-year-old white male. Ward sarcastically derided this "distinguished gentleman" as "typical of the hordes . . . creat[ing] violence [and] racial friction . . . in a patriotic, clean and honorable society of the South."[43]

Cleanliness and patriotism were the distinct markers of normalcy, as journalists exhibited a continuing fascination with the dirty beatnik. Cleanliness symbolized whiteness and dirtiness symbolized blackness in this racist and occasionally anti-Semitic discourse. Thus the beatnik, if not already identified as Jewish, became "dirty" through his association with African Americans. As over two hundred volunteers arrived during the summer of 1961, Jackson papers compiled a periodic "box score," tallying the numbers arrested, awaiting trial, convicted, released on bond, in Jackson jails, and in Parchman, the notorious state penitentiary.[44] When nationally syndicated columnist Westbrook Pegler interviewed freedom riders in prison, he more directly but shrewdly laid bare their subversion—social, political, and sexual.

Pegler perpetuated the racist and misogynist Jezebel stereotype as he described twenty-two-year-old Catherine Burks, "a self-confident, bantering little number" he visited in the Hinds County jail. Burks was "a deep brown Negro girl" who "had a lively effect on the male Negro inmates." To her eternal shame, Pegler reported, she planned to "marry for love." Her future spouse's "color would not matter."[45]

Pegler, however, was most taken by the young white men at the Jackson city jail. He expended copious quantities of ink describing their habits, their physical attributes, and their demeanor, all of which suggested gender insubordination and, by extension, sexual nonconformity. Though several riders came to the state from New York—"a mysterious labyrinth of sinister strangers who fear one another"—Pegler chatted first with Charles David Myers of Noblesville, Indiana. Myers was "a pale, frail boy" of twenty-one, with "sprigs of wispy whiskers and the start of beatnik sideburns, although they all are allowed to shave." Negroes certainly would not benefit, Pegler insisted, from assimilating with the likes of Myers.[46]

In a gendered rhetoric of military might, Pegler characterized Myers and his fellow rider David Fankhauser as "pallid fellows with pallid voices and the watery passiveness of the conscientious objector. They wouldn't fight for anything," Pegler expounded, "but they didn't think it wrong . . . to affront a local social system and kick up riots and civil war [sic]." This reasoning—with a cultural resonance now greater than the homosexual panic defense of 1955—linked men with violence and cast a movement billed as nonviolent as therefore unmasculine and perhaps queer. "Negative weaklings" such as Myers and Fankhauser would never even make "good Gandhis, for they were beginning to wail already. The jail is hot, the inmates have B.O., and they don't believe in cards or dicing."[47] These clearly were not real men.

Along with these print descriptions of social and sexual deviants, Mississippians would long remember the photographic images that circulated during this time. As one Mississippian recalls, pictures of freedom riders and other civil rights workers appeared in "lengthy tableaus," most of which were sexually suggestive. In addition to the racialized Jezebel and her race-mixing, dirty beatnik friend—who sometimes, it seems, preferred the company of other white men—these "shocking" photos also documented black men "relieving themselves in the presence of young white girls" and "hugging and kissing white girls" at demonstrations and protests.[48]

Civil rights volunteers didn't just flout southern miscegenation laws, which until 1967 forbade cross-racial heterosexual unions—purportedly commonplace in the movement; they also disregarded the sodomy statutes, as these tableaus hinted. Distributed in Ku Klux Klan literature, and perhaps as inserts to Citizens' Councils publications and even mainstream newspapers, the photo spreads further showed "young black and white boys hugging each other" on marches. Also, in a vivid shot, well remembered, two young men sitting by the side of the road "groped" one another: the white man held his black friend's arm, while the black man had one hand on his partner's leg, the other hand on his partner's crotch. This exceptionally alarming picture was printed and distributed with two separate captions. One asked, "What is this guy trying to do?" And the other more explicitly queried, "Is this some kind of sex act?"[49]

Though the freedom rides of 1961 drew the nation's attention to racial inequality in the South generally and Mississippi specifically, they did not succeed in desegregating bus, train, and air facilities in the Magnolia State. They did, however, set the stage for future action aimed at black voter registration and the integration of state schools. They also set the tenor of discourse. By the time James Meredith integrated the University of Mississippi in 1962, after riots in which two died, right-wing radicals had fully adopted a sexualized vernacular. They branded liberal white faculty as "racial perverts," "prostitutes and libertines." They castigated U.S. marshals as "sadists and perverts." And though they urged their fellow white male students, first and foremost, to protect the "Flower of Southern Womanhood," they implied, as did more and more observers, that the proponents of racial justice harbored deviant sexual practices that went beyond interracial heterosexual intercourse to include interracial homosexual intercourse.[50]

The white supremacist lexicon of sexual deviance was in full bloom when Mississippi witnessed the next large-scale influx of outside activists. From June through August 1964, over one thousand volunteers—mostly white college students from the North—participated in SNCC's Mississippi Summer Project, or freedom summer campaign, to educate and register black voters across the state. Again sounding the warning, Jimmy Ward reminded his readers that national movement figure Bayard Rustin—a subject of great scrutiny by the Mississippi Sovereignty Commission, the state segregationist coordinating body—had been convicted back in 1953 for "sex perversion and lewdness" in Pasadena, California.[51] Rustin had been caught late at night with two white men in a parked car.[52] As late as 1968, the *Clarion-Ledger* would refer to him in headlines as a "sex criminal."[53]

Many anxieties about black-white sexual interaction focused on the housing for "leftniks" and civil rights volunteers. The *Jackson Daily News*, for example, highlighted a Michigan convention of the Students for a Democratic Society (SDS). In this "bohemian atmosphere, . . . sleeping accommodations and restroom facilities were assigned without regard to 'race, sex, or creed.'" Moreover, the newspaper reported that "the majority of delegates went barefoot and were dirty. The men were unshaven and needed haircuts."[54] Of freedom summer accommodations, even U.S. senators James Eastland and John Stennis publicly worried, citing local precedents as well as the case of Bayard Rustin. In Mississippi—as in Tennessee, where volunteer Burton Weiss shared cramped quarters with sharecroppers Jonah Jenkins and his grandfather—"beatniks and below that group . . . a very low-class, common trash [of] white boys and white girls would live in Negro homes," the DeKalb attorney Stennis declared. Further, "they would sit in the courthouse square on park benches, and they would love and hug and go down the streets holding hands." Eastland told his fellow senators that back in his hometown, "a Negro woman cut her husband up because of his attention to one of those white girls." Many of the volunteers, he added, were "syphilitic."[55]

Interaction with African Americans endangered white sexual health, Sovereignty Commission director Erle Johnston felt. "One of the biggest concerns of the era, aside from threatened school integration, was the public accommodations section" of 1964's Civil Rights Act. "Many white Mississippians cringed at the prospect of Negroes invading what they thought to be their restaurants, public rest rooms, swimming pools, libraries, or lunch counters." Writing a quarter of a century later, Johnston indicated with parenthetical interjections that he still shared *some* of these anxieties:

> There . . . was a fear (unwarranted) that venereal disease could be contracted from public toilet seats, as well as a fear (warranted) that crabs, that invade the genital area, could be transferred from toilet seats. This apprehension developed chiefly in the Delta area, where most Negroes worked in the cotton fields and were vulnerable to crabs, which caused itchy sensations until they were controlled by a salve known as Blue Ointment.[56]

Though any link between cotton cultivation and crab lice is insupportable, the era's linkage of African Americans and a diseased sexuality was an all too frequent concoction of racist thought.

Jimmy Ward still railed against white "weaklings" and the "motley groups of dissenting civil rights workers [who] tramp the streets."[57] He felt the effeminized "youthful offenders ought to be inducted into the Marines, where trained and experienced officers know the art of subduing the unruly sort and making men out of striplings."[58] Throughout freedom summer of 1964, Ward's "Covering the Crossroads" column persisted in diatribes against the filthy bodies of activists: "One of the four-letter word [sic] that the beatnik-types who have invested [sic] Jackson in recent weeks don't seem to understand is SOAP."[59]

Even publisher Percy Greene of the *Jackson Advocate*—a conservative black newspaper—faulted the "summer project workers" for fomenting "racial antagonism and confusion." He felt that many were communists, blindly pursuing "some kind of utopia." Perhaps too in resistance to the savior mentality of many white liberals, Greene urged them to return "to their own states where much work on the Negro question is still needed, and leave the affairs of Mississippi to the White people and Negroes of the state."[60]

While Mississippi's U.S. senators berated the "cunning, vigorous, and persistent" agitators, the "crumbs" who affronted local standards with their public displays of affection and their interracial dating,[61] and while the state Sovereignty Commission looked into the lives of "convicted sex pervert" Bayard Rustin as well as organizers closer to home,[62] the White Knights of the Ku Klux Klan of Mississippi most explicitly linked civil rights activism and communism to male homosexuality. In an open letter to President Lyndon Johnson, the Klan mocked his "Great Suicide" program as "full of treason, blood, and perversion." They attacked his "homosexual associates," the "sex perverts and atheistic murderers . . . engaged in the deliberate, criminal destruction of this Nation under color of unConstitutional, unLawful [sic] statutes and decrees."[63] Johnson was in league with commies and queers, even Satan himself, and the Klan vowed to resist until the end. In Mississippi that meant in part resisting northern volunteers. As Imperial Wizard Sam Bowers saw it, "The heretics, the enemies of Christ in the early spring of 1964" were the "false prophets . . . from the pagan academies, with 'the whores of the media' in tow. Communists, homosexuals, and Jews, fornicators and liberals and angry blacks —infidels all."[64]

White Mississippians afraid of change harassed and punished local civil rights organizers through traditional legal channels and through entrenched institutions such as the mainstream Citizens' Councils and the reactionary Ku Klux Klan. White Mississippians fearful of life's uncertainties ever more strenuously scapegoated non-Mississippians, the ubiquitous outside agitators whose humanitarian impulses and liberal sentiments brought them into the struggle during the 1961 freedom rides, the 1964 freedom summer, and throughout the decade. White Mississippians bent on maintaining privilege utilized strategies of red baiting, sex baiting, and queer baiting, in efforts to discredit the movement and isolate dissenters. Conformist pressure was intense, and during the early 1960s, homosexuality was transformed into an insidious and subversive emblem of nonconformity.

QUEER CIVIL RIGHTS ORGANIZERS were not simply figments of a paranoid white Mississippi imagination. Queer sexuality was not an import, brought into the region by an invading army of misfits. Support for sexual difference existed alongside varied reformist tendencies within the movement. And in the heart of the lynching and Bible Belt, queer Mississippians were at the forefront of the civil rights struggle.

Visiting college students sometimes learned this even before they arrived in the state. When Coe College in Cedar Rapids, Iowa, sent a fourteen-student work-and-study team to Mississippi in the summer of 1962, nineteen-year-old volunteer Phil Ensley knew the reputation of one key movement operative. An associate of Ensley's father had attended law school at Harvard University with a well-liked Greenville, Mississippi, native—a tall "Southern gentleman [of] awkward rural grace [known to] drawl slowly and easily, smile often, [and] listen courteously."[65] Also known as homosexual by his classmates at Harvard Law School was William L. Higgs.[66]

Bill Higgs, though first in his undergraduate class at the University of Mississippi, proved an average student at Harvard. When he graduated with his law degree at the age of twenty-two in 1958, he returned to Mississippi, settled in Jackson, and within little more than a year waged an unsuccessful campaign for the state legislature on a prototypical prosegregation platform. He somehow underwent a remarkable conversion on the race issue, however, for by the time Phil Ensley and his Coe College classmates arrived in Mississippi in 1962, Higgs was among the most hated white men in the state. Public officials, watching him closely, now counted Bill Higgs outside the "ninety-nine per cent plus of the white people" in Mississippi who believed wholeheartedly in apartheid.[67]

After his failed bid for the state legislature, Higgs tried to unseat beloved racist, U.S. representative John Bell Williams. Failing that, he became a pro bono legal adviser to other political campaigns, including those of black office seekers. Though Mississippi was home to a larger percentage of African Americans than any other state, disfranchisement methods assured the lowest black voter registration rate in the nation. These black candidacies thus were not only long-shot efforts; they were also dangerous. Black registrants, voters, candidates, and their supporters endured subtle intimidation, economic reprisals, and violent resistance in civil rights—era Mississippi.[68] Indeed, reporters hounded Higgs for merely employing a black typist.[69]

But Higgs persevered. With a courage born of conviction and, at times, a naïveté born of privilege, he launched a vital movement newspaper, the *Mississippi Free Press*, with black grocer Robert L. T. Smith Jr.[70] Higgs helped coordinate demonstrations. He served on the legal team of Jackson State student James Meredith, the black applicant to Higgs's all-white undergraduate alma mater—widely known as Ole Miss, a slave term for the plantation mistress. On a Lasker fellowship at Brandeis University, Higgs authored a political handbook for organizers in Mississippi. And in 1962 he headed an important summer high school and adult education program at Mount Beulah Christian Mission, near Edwards, Mississippi. With a multiracial staff of black, white, and Chinese Mississippians, Mount Beulah was owned by the Disciples of Christ, based in Indianapolis. Its 1962 summer project, supported by SNCC, would enlist movement veterans Julian Bond, Anne and Carl Braden, Jim Dombrowski, Myles Horton, and Bob Moses, among others, and would be staffed by college student volunteers. It was under constant state surveillance.[71]

Most controversial, in January 1961 William L. Higgs had joined with Robert L. T. Smith Jr. and two union officials in a lawsuit against the Mississippi Sovereignty Commission and its chairman, Governor Ross Barnett.[72] The Sovereignty Commission was established in 1956 to maintain segregation or, as more obliquely phrased in its enabling legislation, to "do and perform any and all acts and things deemed necessary and proper to protect the sovereignty of the state of Mississippi and her sister states [from] encroachment thereon by the Federal Government or any branch, department or agency thereof."[73] The Sovereignty Commission fulfilled its mission by investigating and harassing civil rights workers and other political dissidents, by coordinating and sharing information with varied federal, state, and local officials, and by mounting an extensive public relations campaign. Their speakers bureaus and print, television, and film programming were designed to counter integrationist appeals and to improve the state's reputation nationwide.

As part of this propaganda effort, the commission gave as much as $5,000 per month, up to a total of almost $200,000, to the Citizens' Councils to support its monthly periodical and its own radio and television series, *The Citizens' Council Forum*, aired over fifteen hundred stations in fifty states.[74] Higgs and Smith—minus the union officers, who withdrew under pressure—said such public funding for a private organization was unconstitutional. Their class-action lawsuit was intended to open up the files of both the underhanded Sovereignty Commission and the violence-courting

Citizens' Councils, while halting the flow of taxpayer dollars from the former to the latter.[75]

A few liberal journalists voiced support of the suit. In Greenville, Hodding Carter praised Higgs for taking action, "despite the sneers, harassment and intimidation which will surely follow."[76] Most editors, like Jimmy Ward of the *Jackson Daily News*, however, denounced the plaintiffs. The *Holmes County Herald* disparaged their "left-wing labor socialistic action" as "a vicious and absurd attack," "ill-conceived and dastardly."[77] The *West Point Times-Leader* bemoaned the "disgruntled do-gooders [who had] cried wolf."[78] Such rhetoric followed Higgs, as did Sovereignty Commission investigators. As a white man who regularly associated with African Americans, as a companion of young out-of-state visitors with "northern brogues," Higgs was not difficult to track.[79]

While the Sovereignty Commission case wended its way through the courts, Higgs served as tour guide and coordinator for visiting student delegations. On 9 June 1962 he, Phil Ensley, and two of Ensley's fellow Coe College students were traveling through the Mississippi Delta when they took it upon themselves to stop and examine a "Negro shanty" in Yazoo City. Coe College summer missions to Indian reservations in South Dakota, to Mexico and Puerto Rico regularly entailed such random, pseudo-anthropological observations. Higgs and the three young white men approached Minnie Pearl Collins on her front porch and asked to see her home. She hesitated, declaring the house was a mess. Higgs persisted, then escorted students through the structure, as Collins waited outside. Before leaving, Higgs questioned Collins about her water and plumbing. She told them her family's "rest room was in the back yard." She said, "we got our water from a water hydrant in the front yard."[80]

So unusual was this cross-class, cross-racial interaction that somebody called the cops. Yazoo City police chief Art Russell arrived at the home of Minnie Pearl Collins just after Higgs and company had moved on, driving north on Highway 49. Russell radioed ahead to Belzoni police chief M. L. Nichols and told him to "watch out" for a group of four white males "acting suspicious." So uncommon was a red Volkswagen Beetle with Iowa license plates that Nichols apprehended the group with ease. (Indeed, another pair of students driving a pea green VW with Massachusetts tags would later prompt a testy encounter with Chief Russell when they attempted to photograph "the Negro slum area of Yazoo City.")[81]

Belzoni chief Nichols "accosted" Higgs and the Coe College group "in a threatening manner," according to the students. After pulling them over, he searched the men and their car. And he warned them not to "fool with the

Negroes" on the remainder of their journey. Phil Ensley and friends were scared. They sent a telegram to U.S. attorney general Robert Kennedy.[82]

During their short stay in Mississippi, Coe College students would have a second run-in with the law, this time under perilous circumstances. Apparently out to get Higgs, Coahoma County officials tracked him down after he, Ensley, two female Coe students, and a male Oberlin College student left a conference at a black church in Clarksdale, scarcely a week after the Belzoni incident. Around 7:30 P.M. on 17 June 1962, the Coahoma Sheriff's officers stopped the biracial group in their car on Highway 61 at the Clarksdale town limits. They arrested all five "on suspicion" and took them to jail. Whether the state Sovereignty Commission instigated the detention is uncertain. But, as spotty evidence indicates, director Albert Jones and investigator A. L. Hopkins clearly were aware of it from the very beginning. With either their blessing or their restraint, they permitted the sheriff's office to detain Higgs and the students through the night.[83] Higgs repeatedly begged to make a phone call but was denied. "We were held incommunicado for almost twenty hours," he said. "It was just like a Russian police state."[84]

Indeed, the interrogations were fierce, often focusing on deviant sexuality. Officers asked Vicky Burroughs, a white Coe student, if she had ever dated any Negroes. With courtesy, she "answered all their questions about [her] relationships with Negroes except their last—did [she] ever have sexual relations with a Negro?" More daring, white Oberlin undergraduate David Campbell readily proclaimed that he "dated Negroes," at which point he was threatened with violence. As the deputy hissed, "We have a man in jail that would cut your throat or stab you in the back. All we got to do is put you in a cell next to him."[85]

Sheriff L. A. Ross personally supervised Higgs's interrogation. He told Higgs it was illegal "to have that Negro girl"—Coe student Jean Johnson— "in the car." When attorney Higgs corrected him on the point of law, Chief Deputy Fitz Farris threatened Higgs with his life. All he need do, he reminded Higgs, was tell some of the "dangerous inmates . . . to get you, and they would take care of it." Higgs's companions also could be killed. Farris could "easily have [them] taken care of." "This shook me," Higgs later testified. "Knowing the situation in Mississippi, I knew that the man could do this without fear of a successful prosecution in a state or federal court."[86]

After a harrowing night and a long morning that stretched into the afternoon, the group was released. They filed a complaint with the U.S. Justice Department. They wired protests to President John Kennedy and the governors of Iowa and New York, home state of Phil Ensley. And they reported their story to the state advisory committee of the U.S. Civil Rights Commission. National media again focused attention on Mississippi. While Ensley and friends resumed their duties "staffing YMCA and YWCA day camps, teaching swimming to Negro children at a municipal pool in Jackson, conducting vacation Bible school classes, preparing a Boy Scout camp, and participating in seminars and interviews with Tougaloo students and community leaders"[87]—Bill Higgs emerged as the state's most visible white integrationist.

This visibility came at a price—to Higgs and to the black Mississippians whose cause he championed. After Higgs's presumably benign interrogation of Minnie Pearl Collins at her Yazoo City home, Police Chief Russell and a Sovereignty Commission investigator questioned her under more grave conditions. Her position untenable, she found it necessary to justify her actions under oath. She said she had been afraid to deny the men entrance to her house because "they said they were inspectors." She was six months pregnant, and the intrusion "excited me so I did not get straightened out for over a week." Fully two weeks after, she was "still nervous from their prowling though my house." Illiterate, she signed her sworn statement with an X.[88]

Similarly, Coahoma County prisoner Dewey Peters—heralded by Higgs as a long-forgotten freedom rider who had integrated the Clarksdale bus station[89]—received a visit from Sovereignty Commission investigator Tom Scarbrough at the jail.

Scarbrough: William Higgs testified to the Civil Rights Commission in Jackson, Mississippi, [that] you came to Mississippi as a freedom rider. Is this true?

Peters: It is not true. I did not come to Mississippi as a freedom rider.

S: Did you tell William Higgs anything which could have sounded like that?

P: I did not. I did not know who William Higgs was until I read in the newspaper and heard on the radio who he was.

. . .

S: What are you being held for here?

P: I am being held for contributing to the delinquency of a minor and false pretenses.

S: What did you do?

P: Spent the night with a girl the city officials claimed was under age. . . . I was just traveling through. My mission here was to see [the all-black town of] Mound Bayou, Mississippi. I met the girl I spent the night with on the bus, and I got off the bus to stay with her and got into my present trouble in Clarksdale.[90]

The culture of investigation that permeated Cold War America, the belief that subversion and insubordination could be uncovered through "reasoned" inquiry and deliberation, was the context for Sovereignty Commission inquisitions. The state's secret police, patterning themselves after J. Edgar Hoover's FBI, probed the intimate details of their subjects' lives as they attempted to prop up precarious structures of racial inequality. Their work also mimicked the earlier techniques of U.S. senator Joseph McCarthy and the House Un-American Activities Committee, leaders in the fight against communism and sexual perversion in American social, cultural, and political institutions. The Sovereignty Commission, like its Sunshine State counterpart—the Florida Legislative Investigation Committee—conjoined anticommunism and homophobia with white supremacy. But while the Florida body, known as the Johns Committee, explicitly targeted homosexuals and suspected communists as a principal strategy in combating civil rights activism, the Sovereignty Commission seemed to stumble across alleged communists and homosexuals—and begin to vilify homosexuality—only as a secondary outgrowth of its broader mission to maintain racial segregation and discredit activists for racial justice.[91]

Also, Sovereignty Commission efforts sprang from local and regional traditions that promoted white scrutiny of black lives. Over and over again, blacks were made accountable to whites in the South. They were forced to endure constant questioning. While questions posed seldom went unanswered, resistance sometimes was subtly reflected in those very answers, such as Minnie Pearl Collins's responses to both Bill Higgs and Art Russell. Nevertheless, under Jim Crow, African American's predicament often involved deference—or, the performance of deference—to white authority.

Bill Higgs and other white liberals participated in this system. However well intentioned they might have been, their race and class positionings meant a freedom to speak to, interrogate, and occasionally speak for African Americans with whom they were unacquainted. By striding onto Minnie Pearl Collins's front porch in Yazoo City, by insinuating himself upon Dewey Peters at the jail in Clarksdale, Bill Higgs brought about unforeseen consequences not only for himself and his traveling companions, but also for these black Mississippians and their friends and families. Though himself the subject of reprehensible surveillance and intimidation, Higgs wielded considerable investigative capacities of his own, as he and other Mississippians were variously situated in hierarchies of power inflected by race, class, gender, and sexuality.

As his lawsuit against the Sovereignty Commission and Citizens' Councils now languished in the courts, as his wife of only six months filed for a divorce that summer of 1962,[92] Bill Higgs continued to lead local and out-of-state activists, often housing them in his own home. Neighbors informed on Higgs, reporting his comings and goings to the Sovereignty Commission, who in turn infiltrated many movement strategy meetings.[93] Local parents forbade their sons and daughters from consorting with Higgs, and they assured Sovereignty Commission investigators that their automobiles would never again be seen parked outside Higgs's home. The Sovereignty Commission watched Higgs's every move.

By January 1963, with awards and accolades from various national civil rights and civil liberties organizations, Higgs seemed headed for a fall. That month he met a white sixteen-year-old runaway, William McKinley Daywalt, at the Jackson YMCA. Daywalt had hitchhiked into the area from his home in Collegeville, Pennsylvania. Higgs invited Daywalt to dinner, then to his home. Ever the good Samaritan, Higgs arranged appointments for Daywalt with both a black physician and an (apparently white) optometrist, then paid for necessary medication and prescription eyeglasses. He outfitted Daywalt in new clothes, introduced him to his parents in Greenville, and according to Daywalt, shared a bed with him at night.[94]

Driving Higgs's car, Daywalt was involved in an automobile accident in Jackson. Police questioned Daywalt about the incident. They further asked about his living arrangements, his relationship to Higgs. Shortly thereafter Jackson police arrested Higgs for contributing to the delinquency of a minor. Higgs swore he was being framed. He was out of town, accepting an award, when the trial was called.

In court, District Attorney William Waller—who seven years prior had helped defend the murderers of John Murrett—accused Higgs of having "unnatural relations" with Daywalt, by "placing his (Daywalt's) private parts in his (Attorney Higgs's) mouth." Daywalt testified that over the two weeks of their friendship, he and Higgs usually slept in the same double bed and regularly had sex. However, when Higgs had other company, Daywalt slept "on the couch in the living room or on a bunk bed" in another bedroom.[95] Among those overnight guests, the trial proceeding disclosed, was Jerry Brown, son of the governor of California—later governor himself. As a result, rumors spread like wildfire that Brown and Higgs were lovers.[96]

On the stand, the doctor and pharmacist confirmed that they had seen Daywalt. A spying neighbor—a Sovereignty Commission informant—likewise testified to observing Daywalt at Higgs's home. A more reluctant witness was Higgs's housekeeper, Syerella Van Buren. She insisted she always made up two separate beds for Daywalt and her employer. When other guests slept over, she made beds for them as well and remade them the next morning. She likewise cooked for them all.[97]

On 15 February 1963, an all-white jury found William L. Higgs guilty of contributing to the delinquency of a minor. He was sentenced, in abstentia, to six months in prison and a $500 fine. Though his attorneys later moved for a new trial, Judge Russell Moore denied the motion. Bill Higgs never returned to his home state of Mississippi. If he dared, District Attorney William Waller promised "unlimited jailings."[98] Though he produced an affidavit in which Daywalt recanted—alleging coercion by the Jackson police Department and its chief (who had spearheaded the 1955 John Murrett murder investigation)—Higgs soon was disbarred.[99]

Jackson police, perhaps with the help of the Mississippi Sovereignty Commission, succeeded in ridding the state of its preeminent white dissident, William Higgs. "No question about it," says one longtime political observer: "Step by step," Higgs was "run out of town."[100] Like his friend University of Mississippi historian James W. Silver, who also helped James Meredith enroll at Ole Miss, Higgs unwillingly turned away and moved north.[101] Though they forced him into exile, they could not break his zeal nor diminish his efforts on behalf of the movement. From Washington, D.C., Higgs recruited new student activists, who in turn became targets of Sovereignty Commission surveillance.[102] He served as attorney for SNCC and for the Mississippi Freedom Democratic Party as they challenged the old guard all-white "boll weevil" Democrats, most stunningly at the 1964 and 1968 Democratic National Conventions. Higgs was a consultant to CORE and SDS; he contributed articles to *The Nation* and other liberal publications. His anti–Vietnam War organizing provoked the wrath of J. Edgar Hoover and sealed his friendship with SNCC comrade Stokely Carmichael. Of most lasting significance, Bill Higgs drafted key provisions, ultimately passed into law, of the monumental Civil Rights Act of 1964.[103]

The exiled Higgs would later relocate to Acapulco, Mexico, where both he and his mother died, five days apart, in 1988. It seems they lie buried there, to this day, in unmarked graves.[104]

Though there is no conclusive evidence that Bill Higgs was framed in early 1963, history has concluded that he was. In the same phrasing used to describe incidents involving a prominent black leader in Mississippi, Higgs is said to have been arrested on a "trumped-up morals charge."[105] Such conclusions result from legitimate assertions, well corroborated, of duplicity in the Jim Crow legal establishment. Further, they seem reasonable given the timing of the Higgs arrest—just hours after he petitioned a federal court to force enrollment of another black applicant, Dewey Green, at the University of Mississippi.[106] But assertions of a framing or a conspiracy also reflect historians' restraint and reticence around deviant sexuality, particularly homosexuality and intergenerational intercourse. For too long, we have disavowed queer leadership in the movement.

Bill Higgs may never have had sex with William Daywalt. But apprised as they were of Higgs's homoaffectionalism and homosexuality, Sovereignty Commission officials, Jackson police, and other Mississippi residents could use or misuse that knowledge in an effort to silence him. When civil rights leaders evinced propensities toward queer sex, their enemies were never far behind, ready to capitalize on any misstep.

CLARKSDALE NATIVE AARON EDD HENRY was accustomed to arrest. Especially after he assumed the presidency of the state conference of the National Association for the Advancement of Colored People, or "N-double A-C-P," in 1960, promising aggressive new action toward desegregation, Henry received recurrent visits from law enforcement officials. "From the very beginning," he stated, "I had been an 'uppity nigger.'" However, "until 1962, most of the harassment and intimidation of me and my family had been relatively minor. Threats consisted mostly of anonymous telephone calls and occasional verbal abuses on the streets." [107] Even the police kept a certain distance. All that changed in 1962.

Aaron Henry was well loved in Mississippi. Countless black Mississippians felt beholden to him for the assistance he readily and repeatedly provided. In Clarksdale the Xavier University–trained pharmacist dispensed wisdom along with prescription medications from his Fourth Street Drug Store, a popular local hangout and makeshift museum, with copies of the Declaration of Independence and Emancipation Proclamation on display. Throughout the state, he spoke before church groups; he wrote letters of recommendation; he interceded with local and state officials on behalf of prisoners; he loaned money to relative strangers. Most of all, Henry was an inspired and inspiring leader of the civil rights movement, known to volunteers as "Doc." After the assassination of Medgar Evers in 1963, he became and would remain for three decades the leading advocate of racial equality in the state. [108]

Such respect came at the expense of white enmity. Especially in the 1960s, authorities resented Henry and his efforts to combat the state's pervasive, systemic racism. Even those few white liberals who admired him were occasionally made uncomfortable by his personal style and self-presentation. Whereas black friends enjoyed his "cheery countenance" and "deep resonant voice," some white cronies bristled at his warm physicality, his habit of "rubbing heads"—that is, rubbing his head against the head of another person. [109] According to James Silver, Henry was "an easily met fellow, rather aggressive and certainly very cocksure. You have a tendency to like him at once. That is, in spite of the fact that he assumes an intimacy . . . that you may find hard to take, at once that is." Henry remained "a real optimist. . . . As a man who is in constant danger, he seems not to be aware of it, and laughs about our hoping to live forever."[110] To others, Henry's demeanor was prissy, as evidenced by at least one anonymous prank: someone sent him a gift subscription to *Ms.* magazine and billed it to one of Henry's friends on the University of Mississippi faculty.[111]

When white authorities went after Henry in 1962, they used an emergent tactic of incrimination and reproach. They accused him of homosexuality. Specifically, the Clarksdale police chief arrested Henry at his home on 3 March 1962, as his wife, Noelle, and daughter, Rebecca, looked on. At the Clarksdale jail, where Higgs and company would spend a frightful night three months later, Aaron Henry noticed several white officials— perhaps Sovereignty Commission investigators among them. Shortly thereafter Henry was turned over to Bolivar County officers. "It was becoming quite clear," he later wrote in his unpublished autobiography, "that nothing about the matter was following any established legal procedure." Henry was bound in an "elaborate set of chains" and driven to the Cleveland jail. "The hostility I had noted in Clarksdale had settled to a silent somberness, and it was beginning to be a little frightening."[112] Denied any phone calls, Henry was cut off from family and friends. He wouldn't be told the allegations until the following morning.

Meanwhile, Clarksdale officials claimed no knowledge of Henry's whereabouts, and Henry's associates called Attorney General Robert Kennedy, who in turn dialed Coahoma County sheriff L. A. Ross. Kennedy told Ross that "the U.S. government was holding him responsible for [Henry's] safety."[113] The next day Medgar Evers and roughly twenty others retrieved Henry from the jail and took him back to Clarksdale. By this time, Henry "was able to gather the essence of the charges."

> I was accused of picking up a young white hitchhiker near Mound Bayou and asking him to find me a white woman. When the boy said he couldn't do that, the conversation had allegedly moved to other forms of sex. I was supposed to have told the boy that he would have to play the role of substitute if he couldn't find a white woman for me.[114]

Whereas Henry's version of events, written well after the trial, emphasized an interracial heterosexual taboo, most Mississippians read or heard versions that focused only on Henry's "reaching over and touching" his accuser, eighteen-year-old Memphian Sterling Lee Eilert, in the car.[115]

Indeed, at trial no one claimed that Henry asked for access to white women. Rather he was accused of first inquiring about Eilert's sexual relations with women and then establishing physical contact with Eilert against his will. Further, Eilert claimed that whereas the offense occurred down the road near Shelby—near Eilert's ultimate destination, his former hometown of Cleveland—Henry first picked him up not in Mound Bayou, but in Henry's hometown of Clarksdale, at the very time Henry got off work.

Henry's car was being washed on the afternoon in question. Several individuals could attest that from 10:00 that morning until 5:30 that afternoon, the automobile was parked at Delta Burial, "a funeral establishment where several of the employees made extra money by washing cars in their spare time."[116] Moreover, Henry produced another bevy of witnesses to testify to his good character and to affirm that the pharmacist had worked at his drugstore all day and was seen at home shortly thereafter. But a police dispatcher produced records indicating that she had received and transmitted calls about the alleged offense at 5:56 and again at 6:04 P.M.

As Henry explained it, an eighty-year-old justice of the peace in Shelby, Mississippi, found him guilty on a general count of disturbing the peace. But a subsequent jury trial also found Henry guilty—specifically, of "us[ing] obsence [sic] language [with] . . . and placing his hand on the leg and private parts of the said Sterling Lee Eilert." Henry was fined $500 and sentenced to six months in jail. Henry later said he was informed that unknown white conspirators planned to hang him while in custody, "with an official explanation following that I was so disgraced over the arrest on morals charges that I had committed suicide."[117] At a time when homosexual suicide mythology pervaded the popular consciousness and when civil rights activists often paid for their activism with their lives, such a scheme seems entirely possible.

After his release, Henry accused Clarksdale police chief Ben Collins and district attorney Babe Pearson of fabricating the entire incident, of crafting a "diabolical plot."

> I was convinced that they were trying to destroy my effectiveness in a movement where most of the participants at the time were men. I felt that the arrest was an attempt to prevent people, particularly the young men who were so very important to us, from participating in a movement where they might be accused of homosexuality. . . . My anger was over the deviousness of the plot—intended not only to render me completely ineffectual, but also to assassinate the character of the entire movement.[118]

The officials sued Henry for libel and won.

Tenacious, Henry appealed both convictions all the way to the U.S. Supreme Court. In 1965 the highest court in the land cleared him of the libel charges.[119] But in 1968, after numerous appeals, the justices let stand the conviction in the Sterling Lee Eilert case.[120] Nonetheless, at least two historians would refer to Henry's arrest as a "trumped-up" morals charge.[121]

Within a year of the arrest, Noelle Henry was fired from her job as a Coahoma County public schoolteacher. Aaron Henry's drugstore was later bombed. Their house was set afire. In the course of a long, productive lifetime, Aaron Edd Henry would survive countless beatings, bombings, shootings, and jailings.

The Sovereignty Commission was, at minimum, a willing spectator in the Sterling Lee Eilert incident. More likely, the commission may have helped orchestrate the inquisition. The commission's concerns extended beyond "fixations on 'Communist influence,' and on the threat of 'intermarriage' and interracial sex," as historian David Garrow calls them— "obsessions that most civil-rights opponents shared."[122] Investigators also fretted over male sexual deviants and "strong females" in the movement. Though homosexuality and gender insubordination were not among their primary targets, they relished the utility of such phenomena as tools of scandal.[123]

Like the Bill Higgs–William Daywalt incident of a year later, the Aaron Henry–Sterling Lee Eilert scandal evidenced a shift in legal strategies of white resistance. The queer baiting of freedom riders in 1961 established a precedent for tarnishing the movement's image. As Aaron Henry described it a few years afterward, his arrest in 1962

> marked an interesting point in the history of intimidation of civil rights workers. No longer were bigoted officials satisfied with trying to brand us as communist. That charge, along with the claim that our goal was to put a Negro in every white woman's bed, had lost its punch. Standard charges were getting old and even those who screamed them the loudest were beginning to feel foolish. So they picked a new charge—one detested equally by whites and Negroes—homosexuality.[124]

But were the accusations against Aaron Henry so far-fetched? Even if assumed a setup, why did officials choose this particular plot as opposed to any number of others? Perhaps, as in the Higgs case, authorities believed Henry was uniquely vulnerable around issues of sexuality. Perhaps, as in the Higgs case, they had additional information based on covert observations. Perhaps, too, they concluded, as Henry suggested, that blacks "detested" homosexuality every bit as much as whites. However, throughout his life, as allegations continued to follow Aaron Henry, black Mississippians seemed willing to shrug them off. Whereas Higgs was driven out, Henry remained firmly in power.

Henry repeatedly evaded charges of homosexuality, but as the years progressed, he became more careless or carefree in his interactions with men. Instead of destroying or discarding evidence of these encounters, he kept many letters that might well have implicated him in homosexual acts. In fact, his files quickly filled up with correspondence from men—often young, often white—whom he met on his numerous trips both inside and outside the state.

Among the most revealing was the letter Washington, D.C., resident Gerald Epworth sent to Henry at his home address in Clarksdale. In the letter, dated 17 April 1972, Epworth thanked Henry for the "great and enjoyable time" the two had had "a few days ago . . . in Washington." He marveled at how quickly they had become such close friends, after having first "met in your hotel room." Epworth, a southerner working as a page on Capitol Hill, spoke to the interracial nature of their friendship, a bond that transcended the ordinary difficulties: "Us white folks just don't know how to talk with blacks." [125]

Upon receipt of the letter, Henry drafted a lengthy reply. Continuing a conversation the two had initiated in D.C., he sketched out his ideas for achieving justice through brotherhood. "My belief," he wrote, "is [that] the best way for members of either race to get to know each other is to have associations that cause each to lose race consciousness." "The major . . . desire on my part," he added, "is to be your brother." Weeks shy of his fiftieth birthday, Henry acknowledged the difficulties in pursuing this particular relationship, given persistent societal barriers to black-white as well as male-male and intergenerational intimacy. But he insisted it was possible. "This kind of getting to really know each other in Washington can be handled in a way that it causes no problems," provided the seventeen-year-old Epworth wouldn't mind getting together in "a common hotel room. While you are quite young, I was impressed with your maturity." Finally, suggesting that their interracial relations might (continue to?) include sexual relations, Henry wrote, "The next time I am in town, I will try to let you know far enough in advance so that you can inform your host and roommates that on a particular night in the immediate future you will be spending the night with a friend." [126]

It was during one of Henry's next trips to Washington that he again was arrested for soliciting sodomy—this time from two undercover policemen. On 18 October 1972, Henry encountered the men at Eleventh Street and New York Avenue, Northwest, just after midnight. He was jailed, as the Associated Press reported, after he "offer[ed] to take them to his hotel room for a sex act" and after they accompanied him there. He additionally was charged with possession of narcotics. [127]

Henry convincingly refuted this latter allegation. One of his physicians, Dr. L. W. McCaskill of Mound Bayou, provided Washington authorities with the original prescriptions for all drugs confiscated.[128] But Henry felt an added investment in fighting the sex charge. As he wrote to his D.C. attorney Ronald Goldfarb, the "morals or soliciting charge . . . needs clarifying, exposing, and countering [since] the press and some other persons have become involved in the case." Defying Goldfarb's advice to downplay the incident, Henry had already fashioned a possible rejoinder (and performed it for his secretary, to whom he dictated the letter to Goldfarb): Henry said that under the morals allegation, he was "suppose[d] to [have] be[en] getting men for some of the girls in our group or soliciting for myself."[129]

Seemingly defensive, Henry was on the offensive, albeit with subtlety. Press accounts mentioned only the homosexual charges, as had been the case in the Eilert incident. But both then as now, Henry willingly rewrote the charges, adding to them, giving them at least a partial heterosexual makeover. To deflect attention, he said the allegations stemmed from his requests, first, that his accusers—Eilert in 1962, D.C. policemen in 1972—broker an arrangement involving women. Such allegations seem never to have been made against Henry. Henry may have taken them on as a shield against the more damaging queer accusations.

Eventually, in D.C. both the sex and drug charges were dropped.[130]

Though Henry's obfuscations seem consistent with queer Mississippians' cagey habits of dissembling, by the time he was elected to the Mississippi House of Representatives in 1979, he had dropped most pretenses. Though he remained committed to his wife, Noelle, in Clarksdale, life in the state capital provided other opportunities. Henry's well-known relationship with Gullum Erwin only confirmed what many had long suspected: Henry was, at the least, bisexual.

Gullum Columbus Erwin, known to many as Pedro, was born of mixed white, Choctaw, and Cherokee descent near the Jefferson County community of Union Church in 1960. Aaron Henry met Pedro's parents when they became active in the 1964 freedom summer movement. A few years later, in a tragic automobile collision with a freight truck, Beatrice Erwin died and her son Pedro suffered severe head injuries that left him with recurrent medical problems. After Pedro's father, Whitfield Erwin, was murdered in 1971, one black family after another cared for Pedro.[131]

Henry was reacquainted with Pedro Erwin in the early 1980s. As Henry explained it to Mississippi's most widely circulated black-owned newspaper, the *Jackson Advocate*, "I did my best to assist him. . . . Pedro is now an employee at the Burger House, a restaurant [on Monument Street in Jackson] operated by my daughter, Rebecca, and her husband, David."

State NAACP president Aaron Henry, *left*, laughed as he leafed through a Ku Klux Klan newspaper and walked through a Klan rally in Jackson's Smith Park, 1980. The new Capitol is visible in the distance. Courtesy of UPI/Corbis-Bettman.

Henry described Erwin as a part of his family. "I consider Rebecca, David and Pedro, all three, as my children." And yet, Henry pointed out, Erwin had "his own apartment in a nice residential section of Jackson. We see each other often; I eat at least one meal a day at the Burger House." [132]

In truth, Henry lived with Erwin. When the legislature was in session and Henry was in residence in Jackson, the two shared a room at the Sun-N-Sand Motel, near the Capitol Building. For the motel clerks, it was obvious. Over a period of years, both Erwin and Henry received mail there, addressed to the same room number; [133] each received phone messages there, often from the other. [134] Among the local business community, their relationship was common knowledge. Erwin wrote merchants checks that were countersigned by Henry and imprinted with Erwin's name and address: Sun-N-Sand Motel, Room 132. [135] Henry's fellow legislators knew it, too. Senators who likewise had set up their Jackson home at the motel on Lamar Street regularly saw the two together. Representatives and reporters often spotted Erwin in the House gallery, waiting for Henry. [136]

For Henry, to familiarize was to familialize. That is, he used familial relationships as a model for his relationships with first Gerald Epworth, whom he wanted to call brother, and then Pedro Erwin, whom he called his child in the *Jackson Advocate* interview. Interestingly, Erwin's girlfriend from nearby Flowood referred to Henry as "Dad." But in private, Erwin and Henry—as evidenced in reams of intimate notes and messages they exchanged—referred to one another lovingly, by their familiar names, Pedro and Aaron.

Henry's continued acceptance and effectiveness as a public official and as president of the state NAACP did not depend on denials, for under systems of mutual discretion he was rarely asked point-blank about his sexual habits. Instead, Henry and Erwin—like so many other Mississippians, queer and straight—participated in the crafting of plausible, if highly improbable, alternative rationales. The *Advocate*'s aforementioned 6 June 1985 feature story on Erwin, for example, provided not just a rationale for a "young white male['s] working in a Black restaurant"—the ostensible occasion for the story—but also a reason for a sixty-two-year-old black man's spending so much time with a twenty-four-year-old "white" man.

Like Henry, Native American Gullum "Pedro" Erwin slipped across racial boundaries, across worlds queer and normative. He received love letters from his girlfriend, even as Henry received birthday and holiday cards from his wife, Noelle, addressed "To Precious." That both Henry's cards and Erwin's letters ended up in Henry's files seems illustrative of the male-male partnership. In fact, as numerous men like that attest, to have a wife or girlfriend was the norm. Throughout the period, homosexual relationships most commonly coexisted— "on the side," as Mark Ingalls put it— with heterosexual relationships.

The *Advocate*'s readership understood this ritual of public disclosure and discretion. Though Henry was arrested as many as four times on sex-related charges with men,[137] he would continue to be reelected to the state's highest black office for thirty-three consecutive one-year terms: he served as president of the state conference of the NAACP from 1960 to 1993. In 1963 he was elected president of the umbrella group, COFO, the Council of Federated Organizations—the community pot, of sorts, for the alphabet soup of civil rights groups at work in Mississippi: CORE, NAACP, SNCC, and SCLC—the Southern Christian Leadership Conference, headed by Reverend Martin Luther King Jr. Henry was voted chairman of the Mississippi Freedom Democratic Party in 1964 and named chairman of the state Democratic Party when the national organization finally disavowed the "boll weevils," the all-white "regulars"—who were led by the defense attorney for Burns and Koenig; the prosecuting attorney against Higgs; and by 1972, the governor of Mississippi, William Waller.

If Henry's so-called private life seemed a little suspicious, little harm came to his public life. He remained black Mississippi's elder statesman until his death in 1997. Still, as Henry apparently saw it, discretion was necessary, dissembling was required. At any time, political enemies might attempt to use his nonconforming sex life against him, as they first had done, although with limited success, in 1962.

Russell and Arrests

As a cumulative effect of the 1961 freedom rides, the 1962 Henry arrest, the 1963 Higgs arrest, and the 1964 freedom summer movement, deviant sexuality loomed ever larger as a menace to the state. Queer Mississippians, who once quietly had been accommodated within local systems of discretion, indirection, and complacency, now seemed positioned within the front ranks of civil rights activism. Among law enforcers, laissez-faire sensibilities gave way to explicit contempt for homosexuality and gender nonconformity. No longer would police assertively *combat* violence *against* homosexuals, as they had done in the John Murrett case of 1955. Instead, they carried out their own violent actions against the sexually marginal in Mississippi.

Simultaneously, there was a change in notions of the queer: not just the queer as a figure or personage but the queer as an arena of thought, action, and imagination—the so-called unthinkable, undoable, or unimaginable. Ten years after the Murrett case, the sociopolitical climate was markedly different. In 1965 police raids on men's rest rooms or tearooms in Hattiesburg and Jackson pointed up an increased state oppression of homosexuals. At the Forrest Hotel in Hattiesburg and the City Auditorium in Jackson, authorities relied on new techniques of surveillance to establish definitively the identities of men engaged in homosexual acts. When influential and cherished citizens turned up among them, an official ambivalence resulted.

Theodore Russell had helped form Mississippi's first symphony orchestra over two decades prior in 1944. Under his direction, the orchestra "really grew and matured" over the years, as a founding violinist, Delia Janacek, remembers. By the 1950s, in addition to a full season of performances, the Jackson Symphony Orchestra (JSO) offered children's concerts in the schools, special concerts for black audiences, as well as numerous run-out concerts—road shows at towns and campuses throughout the state. In 1965, as the JSO reached ever more widely dispersed audiences, its Jackson subscriber base also continued to expand. Soon Ted Russell would move the orchestra into a new home, to be constructed at the site of the old Trailways bus station, on Pascagoula Street at Lamar.[138]

Russell well trained his musicians, who early on were all volunteer. "He was extremely patient" with them. Plus, he was "socially equipped to mingle with the people" who funded the operation, the donors who eventually amassed enough resources for player stipends. "He had an ideal, a dream, and he worked hard to make it a reality." [139] Also, for Maestro Russell, the orchestra was a family affair. His wife played cello; his daughter Elaine, violin. The three faithfully attended Saint Andrew's Episcopal Church, where Russell directed the boys, girls, and adult choirs. Holding a master of arts in music from Northwestern University, Russell further enjoyed a prestigious appointment as chair of the Belhaven College music department, where the symphony offices were located. [140] Colleagues there considered him "nice-looking" and "energetic." [141]

But problems were reported at the City Auditorium. As violist Chuck Plant recalls, since at least the late 1940s, the men's room had been very "active." When not rehearsing with the orchestra, Plant regularly found his way back to the rest room, where he awaited opportunities for sex, as did many other men. By 1965 the site was notorious. Alerted to the situation, Jackson police took action.

The same department that once turned a blind eye to John Murrett's sexual proclivities now installed a hidden camera in the City Auditorium men's room to identify the culprits. Over a period of days, their films recorded any number of white men—young and old, indigent and well-to-do—engaged in homosexual acts. Among them were men of great power

Founding conductor Theodore Russell rehearsing with members of the Jackson Symphony Orchestra, ca. 1957. Courtesy of Mississippi Department of Archives and History.

in Mississippi. Though these men were arrested along with the rest, they later succeeded in having their police records cleansed. Also, they assured that media coverage was kept to a minimum. Contrary to Chuck Plant's assumption, the news never made it into the papers.[142]

Nonetheless, word got out. With the help of Plant's aunt and a talkative multitude, Mississippians discovered that JSO conductor Ted Russell had been caught. As a regular at the City Auditorium, he was even assumed by conspiracy theorists to have been a "ringleader." Russell's purpose, however, surely was no different from anyone else's. He now and then went to the rest room to have sex. When cops nabbed him and three others on 29 July 1965, he could foretell the consequences. Indeed, he tried to escape. Though he and others ultimately paid fines for an imprecise count of disorderly conduct, Russell was further fined for resisting arrest.[143]

The symphony's board of governors insisted he tender his resignation. Russell likewise had to give up his post at Belhaven. True to form in Mississippi, the farewells were dressed up for the press. Belhaven president Howard Cleland said Russell's resignation, ostensibly for "health reasons," was accepted "with sincere regret." Symphony president Ralph Hester went one subtle step further, asserting that Russell's decision to step down was due to "health *and personal* reasons."[144]

News of the Russell resignation concluded a week of spectacular and tumultuous events, as reported by daily and weekly papers across Mississippi in early August 1965. Racial and sexual fault lines appeared on the verge of fissure. In Washington, D.C., "in a grandiose ceremony televised from the Capitol rotunda,"[145] President Lyndon Johnson signed the Voting Rights Act into law, forever changing electoral politics in the South. In Brandon the Ku Klux Klan staged a rally of resistance. At Tougaloo integrated audiences watched the Free Southern Theater's production of Martin Duberman's play *In White America,* a historically informed commentary on contemporary race relations. Meanwhile in Jackson and throughout the state, many had already learned the real reasons why Maestro Russell had left his jobs and soon would leave the state.[146]

The City Auditorium arrests and the growing climate of racial upheaval apparently occasioned a heretofore rare and hostile medical dispensation on homosexuality in Mississippi's daily press. An article from the syndicated column "Dr. Crane's Clinic" appeared prominently on the editorial page of the 5 August 1965 *Clarion-Ledger.* In sharp contrast to the Murrett coroner's assertions that homosexual persons made up a distinct and fixed minority of individuals, the advice columnist Dr. Crane sought to reassure parents that male-male sex play could be confined to childhood and that when properly supervised, the process of "growing up cure[d] abnormal emotions." To drive the point home, editor T. M. Hederman placed the piece underneath an editorial cartoon that depicted a skinny, goateed beatnik in flip-flops, picketing for "WEIRD-O CAUSES." The *Clarion-Ledger* cartoonist apparently shared *Jackson Daily News* editor Jimmy Ward's belief that armed service, or the threat thereof, could put these pallid protestors back in their place. A military figure, on whose back was emblazoned "STEPPED-UP DRAFT," symbolized the appropriate official response to race and sex perverts. The beatnik fled: "Sorry . . . I've got to get back to the old books."[147]

Like many others arrested, Theodore Russell was shunned: "For a while, nobody spoke of him." But "his wife stuck by him." The two "had built a nice home" for themselves and their daughter on Sleepy Hollow Drive. They had contributed much to the city and the state. But after the arrest and the firings, they knew they "had to leave" Mississippi.[148]

Gossip spread from home to school, from the church to the workplace. Teachers were rumored to be among the City Auditorium arrestees,[149] men of all types. A sense of paranoia took hold. The perverts were everywhere.

They were in Hattiesburg, police surmised. The university town and Forrest county seat, almost a hundred miles south of Jackson, had clearly gotten out of hand. Even gay residents were "shocked about the number of [male] hustlers lining the street in Hattiesburg, leaning on the cars." As one traveler measured it, "There was a lot more here in Hattiesburg than there were even in Atlanta, being that much larger."[150]

Queers held dominion over certain public rest rooms as well. In particular, the "men's room in the old Forrest Hotel [was] infamous. For miles around, they would come there to have sex. The businessmen downtown would make it a practice to go there at noon, either to get a little sex or give a little sex." Easily accessed by both hotel guests and locals, the facility was off the lobby, below ground level, and thus relatively inconspicuous. Once inside, the stalls allowed "no privacy," as Frederick Ulner remembers, "because what they called glory holes were [enormous]. You could walk into the next booth, you know, and you didn't have to do anything. You didn't have to stick anything through. You didn't have to look through a little pin hole, because you could just [say], 'Hey, how are you?'"[151]

By the mid-sixties, police and the district attorney's office began to monitor the rest room. They took photographs. And they discovered, as in Jackson, that not only ordinary folk but also trusted community leaders relied on public lavatories for quick anonymous sex. When Hattiesburg police rounded up their suspects, an aide and several acquaintances of Governor

Paul B. Johnson Jr. were among them.[152] Although Johnson, a Hattiesburg native, urged the police to call off their raids, crackdowns continued elsewhere. As never before, the legal system in Mississippi and the sentiments of average Mississippians turned toward punishment of sexual and gender nonconformists.

WHAT BROUGHT ON THIS HYSTERIA? Why in the mid-sixties, seemingly more than ever before, did the state take such severe steps to harm and humiliate homosexuals? The answer lies in the relationship between queer sexuality and the African American civil rights movement.

The year 1965 crystallized both a successful civil rights movement and a nascent queer visibility in Mississippi. The two were commingled—both in practice and in alarmist rhetoric designed to thwart them. Portentous movements, physical and sociopolitical, enabled homosexual acts, thoughts, desires, and ideas at this historical moment. As the dirty beatnik figure emerged as official Mississippi's bogeyman, his presumed views of racial justice and sexual freedom proved to be shared by many real-life Mississippians. The backlash against queer sexuality in 1965 and the massive resistance campaign against black enfranchisement, redoubled in 1966, signaled a watershed in Mississippi.[153] Many battles were yet to be fought. But racial and sexual minorities appeared ever more prepared and inspired for struggle.

The period 1945 to 1985 in Mississippi would be mischaracterized if I applied here Edmund White's somewhat flip yet widely held assessment of American homosexuality as "oppressed in the fifties, liberated in the sixties, glorified in the seventies, and wiped out in the eighties."[154] Contrary to this seemingly irrefutable trajectory, it was not that the fifties invariably evidenced overt hostility to queer Mississippians—though cadets Burns and Koenig symbolized the potential for violence—or that the sixties were wholly freeing. Rather, as the Murrett murder trial illustrates, ordinary Mississippians and legal authorities could identify and even sympathize with a man commonly known as a "practicing homosexualist," as Chuck Plant's aunt called Murrett. Also, as many oral history narrators attest, while witch-hunts proceeded in American locales as nearby as Memphis and New Orleans in the 1950s, Mississippi was understood to be a relatively safe harbor.[155] Conversely, in the 1960s, official Mississippi was in pitched conflict, in turmoil: practicing homosexualists not only evoked a potentially dismissable if unsettling question of sexual deviancy; they also now were helping to lead the civil rights movement and thus presented the undeniable threat of racial unrest.

If in our popular imagination the early sixties beatnik represents a politically passive free love advocate, a hep cat tuned in to experimental music and antiestablishment rhetoric, in early sixties Mississippi he represented a headstrong sex *and* race radical, mobilized en masse to overthrow the system. Thus, it was the 1960s, not the 1950s, when the force of the state was actively brought down on queer Mississippians. This shift was fully realized by 1965, the year when police raided tearooms in Jackson and Hattiesburg and began to aggressively enforce the nineteenth-century sodomy law—regularly pleaded down to a disorderly conduct conviction. This shift was also materially manifested in the movement of gay and queer-friendly bars, such as the ones John Murrett visited the night he was killed, from downtown Jackson to the clandestine and peripheral spaces on the city's edge, such as Joe Holmes's legendary Raincheck Lounge.

This turbulent era not only meant changes for men like that. It involved transformations in broader notions of the queer, as explicated in the media and as understood in everyday realms. Maintenance of societal values in Mississippi proceeded from the experiences of rural community and small-town life, which nonconformists often found confining, limiting. True, rural life tended to narrow norms, at least as officially articulated. But at the same time, an all-in-the-same-boat mentality—a sense that community members were bound together, like it or not, over the long haul—broadened tolerance in day-to-day practice. It fostered an unwillingness to pry about certain matters deemed private: how neighbors raised their children, what they did in bed. About such things, people didn't want to know.[156] As so many oral history narrators recall of the 1940s and 1950s, these issues just weren't talked about—or, more accurately, they were cautiously discussed, with vocabularies of deflection. Most resisted knowledge of wrongdoing, turning their backs rather than being placed in the position of accuser. To accuse might open them up to counteraccusations, which weren't worth the trouble. Besides, everyone had flaws and peccadilloes they hoped to leave unremarked. Reciting Scripture, Mississippians reminded themselves and their neighbors, "Judge not, lest ye be judged." Understood another way, there was a cultural *need* of the queer, the unusual, the abnormal—conditions into which anyone might fall.

If forced to the surface, however, if held up to the light, transgressions were indeed punished. If someone boasted of perceived licentiousness— like the white Oberlin college student who bragged about dating African Americans—or if he was caught in the act—then boundaries were firmly drawn, and deviants like Theodore Russell and Bill Higgs were run out of town. White folks could get along fine without a queer orchestra conductor. Most would happily do without an agitating liberal attorney.

But for black Mississippians, Aaron Henry was indispensable. Though they might profess abhorrence of homosexuality as much as their white counterparts did, their station was more complicated. An odious tradition —white scrutiny of blacks, African American answerability to whites— imbued and tainted the accusations against Henry. Even when the charges emanated from a more trustworthy source, a District of Columbia government soon to be headed by Itta Bena, Mississippi, native and civil rights veteran Marion Barry, forgiveness was readily offered. African Americans in Mississippi, a people under siege, could not allow a proven leader to be sacrificed. Overlooking sexual and gender nonconformity amounted to cultural self-protection, social self-preservation.

Civil rights activism had always suggested a queering of norms, accompanied by "perverse" interracial interactions, both sexual and not. Racial equality was threatening in its very cross-racial relations, deemed "queer" by both straight and queer alike in Mississippi. During the 1960s, ideologies shifted. Queerness—an expansive category, a nebulous eccentricity sanctioned but mostly unspoken in every community, black and white—narrowed. Now, interracial relations were used to suggest the queer, and the queer was reformulated to suggest interracial relations.

Interactions with outside agitators characterized many constructions of deviant sexuality in Mississippi during the early 1960s. Homosexuality was depicted as alien, as elsewhere, despite the overwhelming evidence of local white queers, made manifest in subsequent raids on tearooms. As black and white civil rights activists came to the state in increasing numbers, culminating in the influx of over one thousand mostly white college students during 1964's freedom summer project, official discourses perpetuated fears of interracial heterosexual intercourse and increasingly referenced homosexual relations as well, however coded the language. Because white Mississippi women were assumed pure, the daily press focused on sex between black men and out-of-state white women and between out-of-state white men and black women—acts that, while no doubt grossly overreported, were illegal under the miscegenation statute. Still, in 1964 the vast majority of non-native volunteers were white, and the outside agitator became personified in popular representations as the white male dirty beatnik—a figure sullied by his associations with blacks.

As we have seen, the dirty beatnik was the subject of news and feature stories, editorials and humor columns, during the early and mid-sixties. With visceral language and morbid frequency, papers throughout Mississippi commented on the bodily smells and the disgusting personal habits of the beatnik, a white pervert who might as soon bed men as black women. And yet insurgent voices were also apparent. By the time the freedom summer hordes had left Mississippi and the U.S. Congress supplemented the landmark Civil Rights Act of 1964 with the equally earth-shattering Voting Rights Act of 1965, defenders of sexual difference within the state were beginning to emerge, as we shall see in chapter 6.

And black Mississippians generally were turning the tide in Mississippi. Long denied the vote, with the nation's lowest registration rate—6.7 percent of eligible African Americans in 1964—they now elected black and white candidates committed to racial justice and social reform. By 1980 fully 64 percent were registered, the highest rate among states covered by the Voting Rights Act.[157] With federally mandated reapportionment of polling districts, black leaders like Aaron Henry, constantly arrested on myriad counts as lawbreakers, became duly elected lawmakers.

Though liminal, queer Mississippians in the forties and fifties had been well enmeshed in the patterns of everyday life. In the sixties, dissatisfaction with the status quo both energized a queered insurgency and activated state apparatuses of oppression. Thus, by 1965 queers more forcefully and visibly troubled social norms—both sexual and racial—and experienced a strident legal effort to ferret them out, punish them, and banish them.

CHAPTER FIVE

Representations

Bobbie Lee: I wish I could understand.

Billy Joe: I wish I could understand.

Bobbie Lee: I always thought that men like that were easy to see.

Billy Joe: Oh, Jesus. Men like that.

Bobbie Lee: Well, I know you're not a man like that. So you're wrong. You've conjured it all up for some reason that I don't understand. Because I couldn't be wrong about the only boy in the world that I'd ever permit to love me. I couldn't be wrong. I couldn't.

Billy Joe: Well, you are wrong.

—HERMAN RAUCHER[1]

A SURE AND EARLY DEATH awaits the homosexual, or so it's been told over the last several decades. Carriers of cultural traditions—playwrights, poets, novelists; journalists, historians, filmmakers; pastors, orators, storytellers—have replicated and embellished the myth that the sexual deviant rightly will be erased from the earth, either at the hands of others or by his or her own final action. Homosexual suicide and homosexual homicide mythologies are as old as the modern homosexual.[2] Yet successive generations of increasingly self-identified and politicized lesbians and gays attest to the resiliency of an ostensibly self-destructive and nonreproductive people. Hence, the early 1990s movement slogan "We're here, we're queer, get used to it" takes on added significance. Nonetheless, the myths persist.

How have narratives of lesbian and gay self-destruction been told and retold over time? How have they come to structure and symbolize so-called mainstream conceptions of queer life? More importantly, how have queer Mississippians incorporated such stories into their own worldviews? In what ways has suicide mythology created, influenced, reflected, and/or contradicted their understandings of societal strictures against homosexuality and gender nonconformity, their understandings of themselves? How have counterdiscourses and resistances been cast? How might the homosexual suicide narrative be seen as a representational homophobic *homo*cide narrative? How have broader narratives of queer *life* been shaped by and about queer Mississippians?

Further, as gay cultural products have multiplied nationally, what regional differences have been manifested or effaced, explored or erased? As this chapter suggests, an expanding queer cultural production was multidirectional, proliferating from and reaching into varied sites across the American landscape. Queer Mississippians thus would seek not only means for reconfiguring dominant, homophobic narratives, but also methods for creating and circulating queer stories true to their place.

Song and Screen

I first examine these questions in light of one discrete, relatively recent iteration of the homosexual suicide narrative—the legend of Billy Joe McAllister. As told through song, film, and novel, the story describes a confused country boy who in 1953, at the age of seventeen, jumped to his death from a bridge over the Tallahatchie River in the rural Mississippi Delta. As retold by a variety of cultural producers, the tale is a regionally specific configuration of the standard suicide myth plot elements. Though global in its reach, due to its origins in mass media, it is particularly resonant and, at times, discordant with the experiences of those living in the locality depicted. Queer Mississippians are most invested in the legend of Billy Joe McAllister. For them, this story, which materially enriched its creators, carries a symbolic currency that must be exchanged for a more affirming sense of subjectivity. The narrative must be reshaped and subverted, retold and reinterpreted, as marginalized Mississippians negotiate for material and discursive space.

THE LEGEND OF BILLY JOE MCALLISTER originated with Bobbie Gentry, whose meteoric rise to pop music stardom followed the 1967 release of her first single, "Ode to Billy Joe."[3] With both lyrics and music written by Gentry, the song described 1950s farm life in Mississippi and the suicide of Billy Joe McAllister, who, in the words of the haunting refrain, "jumped off the Tallahatchie Bridge." Accompanied only by Gentry's acoustic guitar and a six-violin arrangement, the folksy ballad, an enormous crossover hit, was sung in the first-person singular and suggested that the narrator, perhaps Gentry herself, was Billy Joe's girlfriend. The song's success was due at least in part to this and other mysterious qualities of the narrative. Equally mysterious was the uncertainty over Gentry's background, key aspects of which her handlers apparently instructed her to manipulate or withhold. Where exactly did this new sensation come from?

Bobbie Gentry was the stage name of Bobbie Lee Streeter, a white southerner born 27 July 1944, on a farm in the Flatwoods of northeast Mississippi.[4] A region characterized by broad hills and flat-bottomed, poorly drained valleys covered in forests, the Flatwoods had been home to relatively few slaves in the antebellum era, and the black population remained small over the years. Increasingly over the course of the twentieth century, Flatwoods residents traveled east or west for work, unable to scratch out a living on tenant farms. Gentry grew up on the same farm where she was born—located between the tiny communities of Woodland and Mantee and owned by her paternal grandparents, Mr. and Mrs. H. B. Streeter. She also spent some time during her early years with her father, Robert H. Streeter, in Greenwood, Mississippi, where she attended school.

Greenwood, scarcely fifty miles west, differed markedly from Gentry's Chickasaw County birthplace. The seat of Leflore County and one of the larger towns in the Yazoo-Mississippi Delta, it was situated in the heart of the rich, flat alluvial basin formed from Mississippi River flood deposits. The Delta landscape was marked by large cotton-producing plantations after Reconstruction and large numbers of black workers ever after. Even after the great out-migrations of the early and mid-twentieth century, counties like Leflore retained majority black populations and the state's highest rates of farm tenancy.[5] Heirs of the Delta planter class coexisted with the descendants of slaves, and income disparities between rich and poor, between politically empowered whites and disenfranchised blacks, were staggering. From Chickasaw to Leflore counties, Gentry was exposed from the youngest age to divergent geographies and cultures.

Back in Chickasaw County, Gentry taught herself, from age three, to play piano by watching Ginnie Sue, the pianist at the Pleasant Grove Baptist Church. Though their home lacked electricity and indoor plumbing, Gentry's grandmother reportedly traded a cow for an old upright for Bobbie to play. She composed her first song at age seven, and by age ten, she sang in the church choir, occasionally soloing.

Little has been written of Gentry's mother or her whereabouts during this time, though Gentry apparently moved to suburban Los Angeles at age thirteen to live with her mother and stepfather. Residing first in Arcadia, California, they relocated to Palm Springs two years later. Bobbie graduated from Palm Springs High School and then apparently discarded her family name Streeter for Gentry—after the 1952 film *Ruby Gentry*, starring Jennifer Jones and Charlton Heston.[6] Gentry briefly attended UCLA and the Los Angeles Conservatory of Music, before drifting between secretarial and nightclub jobs. She staged, acted, and danced in various revues and eventually found herself in Las Vegas working as a showgirl.

The archetypal trajectory from farm to fame reached its climax when Gentry approached Capitol Records in early 1967. Short on confidence in her vocal ability, Gentry "wanted to sell song[s], not myself as a singer."[7] She proposed two tunes, "Ode to Billy Joe" and "Mississippi Delta," which producer Kelly Gordon insisted *she* record. After the recording session, however, Capitol executives had difficulty choosing the headliner. Which of the two songs would have greater popular appeal? Ultimately, they decided to make "Mississippi Delta" the B-side, and "Ode to Billy Joe," despite its lengthy four minutes and thirteen seconds, was released on 10 July.

Country, rhythm and blues, and top 40 radio stations repeatedly played the song, making it an immediate hit. With a sparsely instrumented melody, its greatest interest derived from the story line, which promised intrigue from the opening stanza:

It was the third of June, another sleepy, dusty Delta day.
I was out choppin' cotton and my brother was balin' hay.
And at dinnertime we stopped and walked back to the house to eat,
And Mama hollered at the back door, "Y'all remember to wipe your feet."
Then she said, "I got some news this morning from Choctaw Ridge.
Today Billy Joe McAllister jumped off the Tallahatchie Bridge."[8]

At the dinner table, the narrator's father discussed Billy Joe's death in a shockingly offhanded manner: "And Papa said to Mama as he passed around the black-eyed peas, 'Ol' Billy Joe never had a lick of sense, pass the biscuits please.'" The ballad further revealed that "a girl who looked a lot like" the narrator was seen with Billy Joe, shortly before his suicide, "throwing something off the Tallahatchie Bridge." What they threw was never disclosed, nor was Billy Joe's reason for ending his life. But the two questions opened the song up to much speculation.

Listeners thought the second question could be resolved by answering the first. What had the two presumed lovers dropped into the Tallahatchie River? Radio stations held contests, and many guessed it was a fetus or a baby.[9] But in an early interview with a Seattle station, before Gentry and her agents realized the publicity value of secrecy, she said they tossed some trinket, perhaps a ring or a locket, symbolizing the breaking off of an engagement. Later, she consistently answered the question with an elusive "no comment."[10]

By the end of summer 1967, "Ode to Billy Joe" had climbed to the number one position on all three major American music charts—Billboard, Cashbox, and Record World. At least one commentator recognized the key to the song's popularity—its diversionary appeal in a time of great national upheaval. "The burning question of the day," wrote *Jackson Daily News* arts editor Frank Hains, "is not how to un-snarl ourselves from Vietnam or how to un-uppity H. Rap Brown. . . . It's what did Billy Joe and that girl throw off the Tallahatchie Bridge."[11] Gentry clearly chose not to engage pressing social, cultural, and political issues. Unlike many folk balladeers, such as Joan Baez, Bob Dylan, and Arlo Guthrie, whose melodic styles she emulated, Gentry eschewed protest: "People are trying to read social comment into the song, but none is intended." Advocacy, she said, meant "impos[ing] a whole philosophy on the public," which she didn't want to do. The song was simply about human indifference. And she "wasn't even protesting indifference in 'Billy Joe,' just describing it. I'm not so sure indifference isn't a good thing. If we were all totally affected by tragedy, we'd be afraid to go anywhere or do anything."[12]

Moreover, the "Ode to Billy Joe" narrative, despite its perceived genuineness and its use of actual place-names, was "not true," Gentry insisted.[13] Yet, she conceded that of all the bridges spanning the Tallahatchie River, she referred in her song to the one just outside Greenwood, her father's place of residence. Choctaw Ridge was also located in Leflore County, she noted, near the former home of Greenwood LeFlore [sic], the Choctaw leader accused of selling out his people during the Indian removals in the 1830s.[14] The movie house—the "Carroll County picture show," where Billy Joe "put a frog down my back"—stood only a few miles east of Greenwood in Carrollton, before it burned in the 1950s.[15] And the Mississippi town of Tupelo (the birthplace of Elvis Presley) was also mentioned.

Print media coverage regularly hinted that the story might indeed be factual, as writers, especially those outside the South, commented again and again on the song's authenticity, as well as Gentry's. *Newsweek* called her "a true daughter of the Mississippi Delta who can vividly evoke its pace and poetry and smells and style." The song proved "just right" in "every detail."[16] *Time* reported that "Ode to Billie Joe" was "based on [Gentry's] recollection of life around Greenwood, Miss.," and that "millions of puzzled Americans coast to coast [were] ready to start dragging the Tallahatchie."[17]

The *Life* magazine team was particularly ebullient in its own depictions of "real" southern persons, while wholly unscrupulous in the melding of distinct southern places. In its glossy photo-essay, shot with Gentry in Mississippi, *Life* relied on numerous clichés and awkward appropriations of colloquial language. The writer swooned over Gentry's "grits-and-gravy voice," noted that the star knew "this backwoods corner of the South from the bottoms of her bare feet on up," and marveled at "an old slave hex that a Negro family servant once taught her." Gentry was described as "galumphing away in her Granpa's pick up, . . . riding along the dirt back roads." Such roads apparently took her, in the course of producing the piece, from Chickasaw to Leflore County, though no such distinction was made. Paired with a photograph of Gentry eating "a dinner of butter beans, corn, fried steak, cornbread and fried apple pie" with her grandparents in Chickasaw County, the lead image showed Gentry "cross[ing] the Tallahatchie on the bridge she wrote about in her hit 'Ode to Billie Joe.'" [18] But the particular bridge depicted, as the caption indicated, was in Money, Mississippi—a few miles upriver from the Greenwood bridge. The latter had been modernized since Gentry's youth and apparently didn't look authentic enough.[19] In no case did the story differentiate between the two Mississippi locales in which Gentry spent her childhood, much less the varied sites within Leflore County.

On the heels of her smash single, Bobbie Gentry released an album titled *Ode to Billie Joe* in August 1967. Nine of the ten cuts were penned by Gentry, and they mostly traded on the Billy Joe formula. Story lines were set in Mississippi in songs such as "Sunday Best," "Chickasaw County Child," and "Papa, Won't You Take Me to Town with You."

Gentry appeared on American television's most popular variety shows—hosted by the Smothers Brothers, Ed Sullivan, Bob Hope, Perry Como, and Carol Burnett—while she piloted a BBC series that subsequently enjoyed some success in other countries.[20] She honed an increasingly sophisticated business sense. In March 1968 Gentry formed her own publishing and production company, and by the end of the summer observers commented on her "fiscal wizardry."[21] She cut deals that assured large royalties, taking advantage of the more than fifty offers to remake "Ode to Billy Joe." Moreover, she arranged for more drawn-out production schedules on her future albums, under the assumption that "fast-flowing output . . . jeopardize[d] prolonged success through inferior artistry."[22]

Nonetheless, Gentry's fame subsided, as subsequent releases generated lukewarm responses. Though she was said to be dating TV's Gomer Pyle[23]—actor Jim Nabors, an Alabama native later rumored to be gay[24]— Gentry married William Harrah in late 1969, wedding her considerable fortune to that of the renowned casino owner. News reports focused on the couple's thirty-year age difference and on the bride's $150,000 pear-shaped diamond ring.[25] The marriage lasted four months.[26] Throughout the early seventies, Gentry's concert dates were infrequent and often limited to Las Vegas gigs.

While Gentry's rise seemingly replicated many elements of American success ideology—it was, or at least it was represented as, a rags-to-riches story—it also was proving dangerously analogous to the flash-in-the-pan phenomenon. Gentry appeared headed for obscurity by the mid-seventies, having produced one monumental hit record and a string of inconsequential follow-ups. A void developed, such that Gentry had to return to and trade on her one popular success. The resulting collective effort to squeeze additional revenue from Billy Joe would mean a significant doctoring of the narrative. The legend was now ripe for the mapping of additional ideologies onto its basic plot line.

AFTER FIELDING NUMEROUS offers—after waiting, she said, for just the right opportunity, the most sensitive treatment of her by-then classic song—Gentry finally signed away the rights, and both a film adaptation and novelization of "Ode to Billy Joe" appeared in 1976, nine years after the hit single. They were enormously popular. Issued only in paperback, by Dell, the book enjoyed over a dozen print runs in 1976, tallying several hundred thousand copies sold; the movie ranked fifteenth in earnings among all films released in the United States that year, grossing $10.4 million.[27] The sensitivity of the film's production, release, and subject matter, however, remained open to interpretation.

The film premiered in Jackson, Mississippi, with much fanfare on 3 June, the "anniversary" of Billy Joe's swan dive. Mississippi governor Cliff Finch proclaimed it "Bobbie Gentry Day," while Lieutenant Governor Evelyn Gandy presided over a dedication ceremony at one particular bridge over the Tallahatchie, designating it, in the words of *Boxoffice* magazine, "the official Billy Joe leap site." A three-day "celebration" ensued. The picture opened as well in 550 theaters across the South, followed by national distribution. Riding the latest crest of the legend's periodic popularity, Gentry became the first woman to be inducted into the Mississippi Hall of Fame.[28]

The concern with specifying the exact date and the precise site of Billy Joe's demise ironically eclipsed the questionable truthfulness of the story. Was it fact or fiction? The legend eluded such easy categorization. As Janet Maslin pointed out in *Newsweek*, though the first frames of the film included a title explaining that it was shot on location in the Mississippi Delta, "where this story actually took place," the final frames contained the standard disclaimer that all individuals and incidents depicted were fictitious.[29]

Other reviews and promotional materials nonetheless focused on the film's perceived authenticity and successful evocation of place, owing in part to the producer-director. Max Baer Jr. was not a southerner—but he played one on TV. Born in 1937, in Oakland, California, son of the boxing champion, Baer was best known for his role as the dimwitted Tennesseean Jethro in the popular television series *The Beverly Hillbillies*. Baer, *Time* magazine insisted, had "a good, close feeling for the rural South."[30] Judy Stone of the *San Francisco Chronicle* concurred: "What is . . . unusual in the film is the way producer-director Max Baer has captured the feeling of the dusty, Mississippi Delta country. . . ."[31] Ever since *The Beverly Hillbillies* and just prior to *Ode to Billy Joe,* Baer had met with increasing success as a movie actor, producer, and director, working on other films set in the South—*Macon County Line* and *The McCulloughs* among them. Perhaps this experience helps explain Gentry's selection of Baer—a "cocky, bull-headed," sexist, conservative Republican, as described by *Rolling Stone*—to give sensitive treatment to her narrative. But Baer outlined his motives directly and crassly: "I came to L.A. broke, made money in the TV show, then lost it all in my divorce. This time I'm going to make so goddam fucking much they can't take it away from me. Not even Uncle Sam."[32]

Meanwhile, the writer chosen to do the screenplay and novel, New Englander Herman Raucher, appeared no more competent to render this particular region of the South than Baer. Most notably, Raucher blundered in his concoction of Billy Joe's workplace, a lumber mill. Some of the richest cotton country in all the world, the Delta's vast, flat alluvial plain mostly had been deforested to allow maximum cultivation. Perhaps Raucher drew his ideas from Gentry's Flatwoods birthplace as opposed to her girlhood home and site of the legend, the Delta. Still, Jonathan Rosenbaum of *Monthly Film Bulletin* credited the screenwriter with having "create[d] a remarkably persuasive portrayal of a back*woods* Mississippi community in the early Fifties."[33] Another account more accurately, but no less condescendingly, labeled the locale a back*water* (but also, in the same piece, utilized the term *backwoods*).[34]

In tandem, Baer and Raucher crafted characters hardly "free of cliché," as *Variety* asserted.[35] These figures were lost in a confusing sea of southern stereotypes, just as the place depictions were fused into an unschooled mishmash of rural imagery. The young leads, Billy Joe and Bobbie Lee—played with awkward accents by Robbie Benson and Glynnis O'Connor—were prone to stilted conversations of incongruous verbosity and formality. The early portions of the film featured a stock hillbilly chase scene, precipitated by a two pickup truck standoff on the one-lane Tallahatchie Bridge. While such demeaning portrayals typically adhered to residents of the upper South, specifically Appalachia, in this film a caricatured rural Mississippi youth curiously blamed the incident on neighbor-state yokels in the other truck—"Alabama rednecks," he called them. Set in a region of Mississippi with a majority black population, the film had not one African American character. And equally surprising, for a film based on a song, the music also was uprooted and displaced. When characters attended a jamboree, they were treated not to Delta blues but rather to upcountry bluegrass.

No doubt even many southern moviegoers took little notice of such inconsistencies. But what could scarcely be overlooked or wished away—especially in light of a southern filmic tradition that included little more than Tennessee Williams's veiled references to male homosexuality—was Billy Joe's frank admission to Bobbie Lee, the upshot of which occasioned his suicide. After a furtive, unsuccessful attempt at intercourse, after being assured by Bobbie Lee that "it's alright," Billy Joe insisted: "It *ain't* alright. *I* ain't alright. Bobbie Lee, I have been with a man—did you hear me?—which is a sin against nature, a sin against God. I don't know how I could have done it, I swear."

This episode, Billy Joe's startling confession, was preceded by an even more curious scene that condemned southern backwardness while it unquestioningly reaffirmed a seemingly taken-for-granted social more—abhorrence of homosexuality. Employing a retrograde Freudian analysis of arrested development, the screenplay depicted Billy Joe as a victim of the incompetence and prudery of Bobbie Lee's parents. Had they not interfered in the young lovers' relationship, had they not in their moral righteousness blocked a heterosexual union that was as "natural" as the "squirrels" and "cottontails," Billy Joe would not have been forced to opt for a homosexual liaison, the "sin against God."

Now, after nine years, Billy Joe's death made sense. Back in 1967, as the pop song reverberated across the radio waves and resounded in the minds of listeners, "everybody was trying to figure out what he was throwing off the bridge, why he committed suicide," as Joe Holmes recalls. "It was only . . . with the movie—I can remember with the movie coming out, thinking, Oh, *that* was what was going on."[36] Every bit as memorable was the eerie ballad, the first verse of which Holmes could still sing—word for word—over three decades later.

Did this rationale for Billy Joe's suicide, the resolution of the question left unanswered by the pop song, originate with the screenwriter, Herman Raucher? Or was the legend of Billy Joe McAllister somehow based in reality? Was songwriter Bobbie Lee Gentry, who would have been nine years old in 1953, a model for the screen character Bobbie Lee Hartley? Did Billy Joe have a real-life analogue? While Gentry had learned the public relations benefit of evading such questions, Herman Raucher confided in a *Jackson Daily News* reporter that "the lyric (in the song) is not quite all fiction. We've got an odd combination of fact and fiction in it."[37]

If Raucher fabricated the motive for Billy Joe's suicide, his plot line was not an original one. As Vito Russo points out in *The Celluloid Closet*, after the 1961 lifting of the Motion Picture Code ban on homosexuality in film, homosexual characters had predictable screen outcomes: "Once homosexuality had become literally speakable in the early 1960s, gays dropped like flies, usually by their own hand. . . . In twenty-two of twenty-eight films dealing with gay subjects from 1962 to 1976, major gay characters onscreen ended in suicide or violent death."[38] Raucher took up a theme that was in the air. That is, his screenplay traded on representations of gay men that were quietly omnipresent. Raucher, Baer, and perhaps Gentry perpetuated a homosexual suicide mythology pervasive in American culture—in film, literature, and other cultural products, not least of which were actual documentary accounts of suicide. Homosexual suicide narratives reflected both a haunting historical reality and a grisly fictional cliché.

Also, the reworking of the Billy Joe narrative corresponded to a narrowing of notions of the queer in Mississippi. Whereas *queer* as a conceptual space—the undoable, the unimaginable—long connoted varied, nebulous, individual differences akin to Billy Joe's indeterminate alienation in the ballad, *queer* in post-sixties Mississippi specifically named the sexually subversive. Thus, the rewriting of the pop song's ambiguity as "really" about the queer—specifically queer suicide—is not just coincidental. Rather it arises from this larger cultural context.

Just as Gentry, during the era of Joan Baez and Bob Dylan, produced a folk-styled ballad comfortably stripped of political content, Raucher created a screenplay that while broaching the highly charged issue of homosexuality, defused its impact in imagery of an untroubled, bucolic, indeed nonexistent place and time. He presented a 1950s Mississippi without the problems of race or extreme poverty. In elaborating on Gentry's narrative, he depicted a white Delta people whose simple lives and churchgoing sensibilities were only slightly ruffled by the occasional comic fistfights, the unpleasantries of benign prostitution (of the heterosexual variety, of course), or even the suicide of a native.

Raucher's reputation helped. As *the* screenwriter of teen love—whose credits included the classic *Summer of '42* and would soon include *The Other Side of Midnight*—he could frame a film about homosexuality within a broader all-encompassing heterosexual love story. Indeed, critics described *Ode to Billy Joe* as a "date movie," a "Mississippi Romeo and Juliet."[39] Publicity stills featured Billy Joe and Bobbie Lee embracing under the Tallahatchie Bridge. And surely a large portion of these summer moviegoers consisted of young heterosexual couples.

However, the movie spoke, and spoke differently, to an array of audiences. What of queer audiences? More specifically, what about young Mississippians coming of age and grappling with sexuality at the time of the film's release? What about male teens, close to the protagonist's age, who would eventually self-identify as gay? Critics from gay publications in North America's urban centers could smugly dismiss the film as silly or homophobic.[40] They could find "good things" in it, such as a regional accuracy.[41] But they could also attack it for the messages conveyed; as Paul Trollope of Toronto's *Body Politic* wrote, "The most important and dangerous thing this film is saying is that homosexual experiences are so traumatic, unpleasant and frightening that they drive a fairly together young kid to suicide."[42]

Such messages were not lost on young Mississippians. But they were weighed against other emotions, other readings. Philadelphia, Mississippi, native Kelly Walls was only twelve when *Ode to Billy Joe* was released in theaters, but he remembers seeing it on television shortly thereafter. Walls thought that Robbie Benson was "cute." He *recognized* his attraction to the star. However, in retrospect, he says the film proved "frightening . . . because I identified with the character and probably didn't *know* it."[43] Cognition is slippery, sometimes contradictory.

Some engaged in disassociation or willful disregard. John Riley and Ben Childress—born at opposite ends of the state, in Oxford and Pascagoula, respectively—both noticed the skill with which particular audiences, especially parents, could ignore queer content. And each witnessed a silencing with regard to the film. Riley saw *Ode to Billy Joe* with his mother. While the two talked about the film afterward, Billy Joe's death and the homosexual incident were carefully avoided.[44] According to Childress: "There are a lot of movies like *The Color Purple*, which had a lesbian thing going on, and to my amazement, . . . there are lots of people who totally didn't see that. And I think a lot of people . . . wouldn't see something that's not thrown in their face, . . . a lot of people like my parents."[45] Both Riley and Childress speculate that their parents may have sensed something in their sons that foreclosed discussion of queer plot elements. Also, a tradition of quiet accommodationism—forged during their parents' formative years—dictated that queer sexuality, while acknowledged and understood, would not be talked about.

Jake Woods grew up near the site of the legend, in Carrollton, Mississippi, home of the Carroll County Picture Show referenced in the song. He says there was an aura of adventure and excitement surrounding the film production, especially since local people were used in supporting roles and in crowd scenes. That summer in 1976, Woods was on hand for the movie's opening night in Greenwood. At fifteen, he was "confused" by Billy Joe's death: "One minute Billy Joe couldn't make out with Bobbie Lee, and the next he was being pulled out of the water." With a precocious curiosity and an increasing self-confidence, Woods was spurred on to read the novel, in which "the homosexuality was made much more clear." He came out two years later at the age of seventeen.[46]

For many young Mississippians struggling against hegemonic conceptions of teen romance and heterosexual life, *Ode to Billy Joe* amounted to an oppressive force. It represented a hurdle that had to be overcome on the road to self-acceptance. For Stuart Wilkinson of Belzoni, when "growing up in a small town, growing up in that whole environment, you kind of think that you're the only one. You *really* think that you're the only one, and that you are very isolated, and that it is extremely wrong." The movie echoed those feelings and profoundly affected him at age sixteen:

> I don't know that I ever thought, Well, if I ever act on this, then I'll have to kill myself. . . . I think it was more disheartening than anything else, because at that young of an age, you do try to struggle for that something, some image, or someone to go, "That guy's gay, and that's what I'd like to aspire to." I think it was very disappointing. It was like, great, he's gay, he killed himself, what for me? What does life hold, what's in store for me? [47]

Wilkinson, like many other Mississippians, would continue to search for "that something, some image" to affirm him in his difference. Such images were sometimes hard to find in the Mississippi of his youth and early adulthood.

Yet, available representations were open to multiple, sometimes counterhegemonic readings. Jake Woods, for example, followed up on his viewing of the film by locating and securing his own copy of the novel, which he still retained decades later. Though pessimistic, the account corroborated his budding sense of self with its depiction of queer sex between *two* white southerners. For after nine years of probing those two vital questions—What did Bobbie Lee and Billy Joe throw off the Tallahatchie Bridge? [48] Why did Billy Joe jump?—audiences were now presented with a third question. Bobbie Lee posed it immediately after Billy Joe confessed his sin, after he admitted having sex with another man. She seemed to step out of the part and ask coldly, matter-of-factly: *Who was it?*

Answering that question entailed the subversion of suicide mythology; it pointed up the fallacy of isolation as "the only one." For suddenly, it became apparent: *It could have been anybody.*

The compelling funeral service scene enacted the question and summoned up its tensions. While the Baptist minister, Brother Taylor, insisted that someone in his congregation must know why Billy Joe killed himself, viewers were offered, in succession, shots of male suspects shifting uncomfortably in the pews. Was it Bobbie Lee's father? Maybe her brother James? [49] Or another coworker at the sawmill, Tom? After all, James and Tom had camped it up on the job, effecting effeminate gestures as they directed queer gibes at Billy Joe. Was it the sawmill owner, Dewey Barksdale? [50] Or

Brother Taylor himself?[51] Maybe it was one of the two state troopers who pulled Billy Joe from the river.[52] Alternatively, viewers may have heeded Billy Joe's conclusion. When Bobbie Lee asked him, "Who was it?" his answer was unexpectedly poignant: "It doesn't matter."

Indeed, the uncertainty over Billy Joe's sex partner necessitates what Eve Sedgwick calls "a universalizing view" of "homo/heterosexual definition." While homo/heterosexual definition can be seen "on the one hand as an issue of active importance primarily for a small, distinct, relatively fixed homosexual minority (. . . a minoritizing view)" of men like that, it also can be viewed—or, in the case of Billy Joe, *screened*—"as an issue of continuing, determinative importance in the lives of people across the spectrum of sexualities."[53] Making homosexuality available to all, positing a bisexual potential in all, or suggesting means of categorization other than sexual object-choice, helps embroider sexuality with all its complexity and diversity, just as gender inversion, transgression, and androgyny offer multiple identifications and disidentifications, alliances and ruptures.[54]

As demonstrated by the bounded and boundless lived experiences of Mississippians, such multiple understandings are essential to the accurate re-presentation of historical figures, mythic and real. In Mississippi, as I have recounted, queer desires existed alongside and in relation to infinite, untold other desires. Those desires didn't always mark the subject as gay. Similarly, gender transgression—while certainly that, transgressive—didn't inevitably result in scorn or liminality. It didn't necessarily summon up an either/or decision, a sense of a mismatch, a rush to surgery—an option Rickie Leigh Smith still had not exercised at the close of the twentieth century.

As Bobbie Lee Hartley learned all too well, men like that were *not* always "easy to see." They represented subtle, sometimes illegible differences of various types, reflected in the ambiguity of the phrase itself. They aligned themselves with one another or not; they conceptualized themselves as similar in their differences or not. All too frequently, men like that appeared decidedly normative in their habits and life choices.

Bobbie Lee Hartley made a decision. She would let the local people think she was pregnant. She would leave the county. Billy Joe might become known as the virile (heterosexual) teenager who, having dishonored himself and his beloved with an unwanted pregnancy, took the gentlemanly way out. Or, the legend might be retold in other ways. But she was leaving, running away, letting the myth unfold as it would. She packed her bag, snuck out before dawn, and started across the Tallahatchie Bridge. There she encountered Dewey Barksdale, Billy Joe's employer. He was on his way to see her daddy, he said. He had something to tell him, something that would let her off the hook.

Why? Bobbie Lee asked. Why should Mr. Barksdale alter the course of the narrative? Billy Joe was becoming a legend. What good would be served if a respected leader of the community—a husband and father—was thrown in jail? Shouldn't he best keep silent? Shouldn't he quietly persist in his normative home life with wife and family (as so many men like that did)?

So it was that homosex—in the fictional Delta, in the movie theaters of America, in the towns and rural communities of Mississippi—remained occluded or illegible to some, transparent or legible to others. Dewey Barksdale took Bobbie Lee's advice. He turned around, escorted her toward her destination: the bus station. And the unusual couple, man and woman, walked off into the sun*rise.*

CLOSURE AND COHERENCE are the storyteller's tools. Scholar Henry Nash Smith has written that "history cannot happen—that is, men cannot engage in purposive group behavior—without images which simultaneously express collective desires and impose coherence on the infinitely numerous and infinitely varied data of experience." [55] The screen imaging of the legend of Billy Joe McAllister expressed a certain collective will, the will of many, to squelch the liminal incidences of homosexual desire as experienced by some. These were not new images. *Ode to Billy Joe* was merely a southern iteration of a homosexual suicide narrative that was steeped in tradition, long since having taken on mythic status. But as Richard Slotkin warns, mythologies carry consequences. For queer Mississippians viewing *Ode to Billy Joe*, Slotkin's words could not be more instructive or cautionary: "Myths reach out of the past to cripple, incapacitate, or strike down the living." [56]

Interestingly, though it was one of the most widely watched narratives of queer life at the time, few elder oral history narrators saw the film, though they well remember the song on which it was based. [57] And of the younger men I interviewed—the ones who eagerly attended the initial screenings in Mississippi—only a few interpreted Billy Joe as evidence of the fact that they were *not*, in the words of Stuart Wilkinson, "the only one." Though generally they remembered *why* Billy Joe jumped, most couldn't recall with *whom* he had sex. The existence of homosexual desire in Billy Joe's community seemed elusive. But against-the-grain readings were possible and did occur. Indeed, for Jake Woods, reading about Billy Joe in novel form made clear the queer undertones; and for him, that animated consciousness.

Ode to Billy Joe functioned as one of many complex, often oppressive discourses at work around homosexuality in Mississippi, especially during the 1970s. Among others were broader pop culture representations of deviants, as well as religiously based diatribes, so well symbolized by the ever-watchful figure of Brother Taylor in the song, novel, and film versions of the legend. Though narrators assert that such diatribes were virtually nonexistent during the setting of this story—Mississippi, 1953—they were ever more common at the time of its telling on screen.

In Mississippi during the 1960s and 1970s, everyday queer resistances included subversive readings and retellings of media depictions and public pronouncements. As *Ode to Billy Joe* demonstrated, when represented by others to mass audiences, queer Mississippians sometimes appeared doomed, tied to a mythology that perpetuated notions of perversity, helplessness, and despair. Yet queer Mississippians, embedded in local community and family institutions, clung to insurgent reconceptions of normative models and practices. Resilience marked queer struggles; endurance characterized queer lives.

Physique Art and Fiction

While popular representations of queer Mississippians elicited multiple readings, representations of and *by* queer Mississippians summoned multiple means of conveyance. If hegemonic discourses treaded both clumsily and carefully over queer territory, if they enlisted subtleties of language and silence to both reveal and obscure (from would-be censors) their potentially subversive subject matter, how did queer-identified, queer-generated narratives reach audiences? Did audiences distinguish between the queer-made and queer-inflected? Was "authenticity" even a concern? Whose stories got told? How and where were they told?

New York–published "serious fiction" funneled dissident ideologies to largely elite readerships.[58] Fitz Spencer remembers reading Kossuth, Mississippi, native Thomas Hal Phillips's first novel, *The Bitterweed Path*, when Rinehart put it out in 1950. Spencer loved the book, which helped him "come to terms" with himself. Raised in plantation country, Spencer identified with the main characters—wealthy Mississippi landowner Malcolm Pitt; his son Roger; and the son of a tenant farmer, Darrell Barclay—involved in a love triangle. Yet author Phillips, a lifelong bachelor, personified the complications of queer authorship. He never self-identified as gay; yet he wrote a novel of striking significance to gay (and other) readers.[59] How would different readers identify the text? How would queer readers find it?

Of course, even so-called highbrow fiction could be differently packaged for multiple audiences. For example, Phillips's *The Bitterweed Path* was sub-

In the 1950s author Thomas Hal Phillips of Kossuth, Mississippi, penned five well-received novels, two of which explored queer themes. He appears here in a publicity still for his daring first effort, *The Bitterweed Path*, 1950. Files of the author.

sequently released by Avon in paperback, or "pocket book," form—a publishing technology scarcely ten years old at that time. But the first paperback edition's decidedly lowbrow cover depicts a steamy heterosexual advance and only hints at more lurid homosexual interactions. A later British paperback reprint made it clear: "Thomas Hal Phillips' brilliant novel tells of three men and the strange and beautiful relationship that grows up between them . . . and the homosexuality common to them all." By this time, however, the cover evinced an elite sensibility, perhaps necessarily so. It noted that the novel—actually, the author—was "winner of the Julius Rosenwald Fellowship and the Eugene Saxton Award."[60]

Phillips believes that the controversial nature of *The Bitterweed Path* may have foreclosed broader success as a writer. Though he published four more novels within the span of six years, by the late 1950s he had given up writing for varied pursuits. He worked in a number of capacities both in Hollywood and on location during the production of several major motion pictures, including those of director Robert Altman. But he continued to make his home in Mississippi, and he helped his brother manage two unsuccessful campaigns for governor. Years later, as the first head of the Mississippi Film Commission, Phillips was a principal project consultant for the 1976 filming of *Ode to Billy Joe*.[61]

I was somewhat disappointed to discover that after *The Bitterweed Path*,

Phillips's subsequent four novels from the fifties—peopled by numerous never-married men—rarely engaged explicitly queer themes. *Kangaroo Hollow*, however, broached the limits of subtlety dictated by Cold War–era cultural standards. This elegantly written portrayal of two generations of a northeast Mississippi timber milling family gestures to homoerotic yearnings among characters seemingly secondary to the central cross-class heterosexual pairing. In the masculinist world of timber cutting and woodworking, Jesse Shannon stands out as a quiet fellow given to musing alone in his bedroom. When, in a case of mistaken identity, he is shot and killed— a not uncommon homicidal fate—his sister Anna speculates that he may have killed himself—likewise, a not uncommon suicidal fate. She confides to her Sutpenesque working-class husband, Rufus Frost, "Last week I found his diary. I found it before then, but I read it last week. The strangest, queerest things went through his mind."[62]

As the novel's setting shifts from the World War I years to the pre–World War II era, a subsequent generation of the mill-owning family accommodates its own nonconformist figure. Jesse's nephew Bayard, the son of Rufus and Anna Frost, is frequently but elliptically compared to his long-lost uncle. After an abortive schoolhouse tussle, for example, Bayard recounts the events to the incredulous Anna:

> "I know why you said you didn't expect me to get in a fight. It's because I'm different. [. . .] People say it all the time, even when they don't say anything. [. . .] All the others are like Papa, and I'm not. I never will be. I'm like . . ." But he would not dare say it. Both of them were relieved that he had broken off sharply and got up.[63]

As he reaches manhood, Bayard meets and develops a profound affection for Dean, whom he eventually discovers to be Rufus's son by another woman.

Thus, *Kangaroo Hollow* instantiates the fraternal relationship that author Phillips first relies on as metaphor for the primary homoerotic bond in *The Bitterweed Path*—wherein the planter, Malcolm Pitt, claims both his biological son, Roger, and his tenant's son, Darrell, as his own; and Darrell expresses his desire for Roger as a desire to be Roger's brother. Indeed, for Phillips, the great love between the Old Testament characters Jonathan and David served as model for the Darrell-Roger relationship in *The Bitterweed Path*, as the author told me.[64] Just as the indigent but valiant giant-killer David becomes his beloved's brother-in-law when he marries Jonathan's sister, the daughter of King Saul, so too the field hand Darrell becomes his beloved's brother-in-law when he marries Roger's sister, the daughter of planter Malcolm. As we have seen, historically the notion of brotherhood often stood in for, or alongside, queer desire among Mississippians of Phillips's and later generations. The trope of brotherhood was for Aaron Henry, for example, the means for categorizing a same-sex, interracial, and intergenerational relationship (even as another of his partnerships mirrored the sexualized, paternalized pairing of Malcolm with Darrell). The trope of brotherhood, particularly as expressed in biblical lore as the "covenant" of love between Jonathan and David, also served as an interpretive mechanism for parents and other family members of Mississippi men in committed relationships with other men, as discussed in chapter 2.[65]

As *Kangaroo Hollow* nears conclusion in Memphis, Bayard's love for Dean is shown to mirror the love between two ancillary characters, Bill and Cleve. When Bill leaves Memphis for Cleve's funeral in Cleveland, Dean dies in an automobile accident—and Rufus Frost now must disclose his paternity. Anna learns the truth about her husband's son Dean and, perhaps too, the truth about her own son Bayard. As Bayard returns home to northeast Mississippi, his mother, Anna, finally burns the diary of her brother Jesse, dead now for almost twenty-five years.

Though Phillips's subsequent novels—*The Golden Lie* (1951), *Search for a Hero* (1952), and *The Loved and the Unloved* (1955)—like his first novel, *The Bitterweed Path* (1950), were each published by a respected New York press and received generally favorable critical attention, the author's second flirtation with queer subject matter, *Kangaroo Hollow* (1954), was never published in the United States, but published only in Great Britain.

Hubert Creekmore, a white writer from Water Valley, Mississippi, offered a provocative critique of small-town procreative heterosexual marriage in his 1948 novel, *The Welcome,* published by Appleton-Century-Crofts of New York.[66] The story, set in a fictional Mississippi town much like Water Valley, details an intense, volatile friendship between two men—a friendship readily available to queer readings. Indeed, one later critic flatly labeled it homosexual.[67] But as with much serious fiction that dealt with homoeroticism at midcentury, homosexual intercourse, not to mention homosexual identity, could only be inferred from the story line.

Perhaps revealing more about themselves than their subject, two New York critics reached remarkably similar conclusions in their reviews of *The Welcome.* While a stifling small-town life proved wholly credible to these reviewers, queer desire in a small town—a dissatisfaction with the imperative of heteronormative marriage—seemed overdrawn, if not impossible. Warren E. Preece of the *Herald Tribune* found that "as a novel [*The Welcome*] is a highly readable production; . . . as an examination of modern marriage [it] fails." In particular, "Jim Furlow . . . remains unbelievable throughout"—both in his love for Dan and in his "unhappy marriage."[68] Coleman

Rosenberger of the *New York Times* felt that "Mr. Creekmore's second novel is most rewarding in those passages, almost incidental to his main theme, in which he probes searchingly into the pervading sterility of life in a small Southern town, . . . the town's emotional and intellectual barrenness. . . . Mr. Creekmore is considerably less successful," the critic surmised, "in dealing with what is here his major concern, . . . modern marriage."[69]

As in Phillips's *The Bitterweed Path*—and as was the case with many men like that in midcentury Mississippi—queer main characters in *The Welcome* choose marriage, thereby complicating today's readerly notions of gay identity and community. For us, reading the author's life poses equally complex identifications and disidentifications. In the forties and fifties, Creekmore lived in New York and Jackson. When in Mississippi, he socialized with other well-known, never-married artists and intellectuals. These included his friend Frank Hains, *Jackson Daily News* arts editor, and acclaimed author and photographer Eudora Welty, a relative by marriage (Welty's brother married Creekmore's sister). From his chair in the viola section at Jackson Symphony Orchestra concerts, Chuck Plant often spotted Welty on Creekmore's arm.[70] Ron Knight remembers meeting Creekmore, an avid bourbon drinker, at several Jackson parties. Creekmore was, in Knight's view, "a closet case."[71]

Creekmore's two other novels, *The Fingers of Night* (1946) and *The Chain in the Heart* (1953), evidence a deep concern respectively for the plight of poor white Mississippians in the grip of religious fundamentalism and for black Mississippians under the strictures of Jim Crow. These critiques further alienated him from elite southern audiences, and he lived the bulk of his latter years as an exile.[72] Creekmore worked for a major literary agency in Manhattan and, for a time, was employed by New Directions publishing house, whose unconventional list included early works by Tennessee Williams. Though he published only three novels, Creekmore was wildly prolific as a critic, translator, librettist, bibliographer, and poet, for which he was best known. Still, with the exception of *The Welcome*, Creekmore's voluminous body of work only obliquely references homoeroticism—or, more to the point, it utilizes a subtlety, like that of Phillips, which not only comports to elite literary codes but also best exemplifies the lived experiences of queer men in midcentury Mississippi who finessed their way through the dominant order. Hubert Creekmore died in New York in 1966.

IN MY SEARCH FOR Mississippi predecessors, I wanted these authors to more forcefully articulate a queer agenda. But was I simply projecting presentist identities and cultural models on to historically situated actors? Was I not attending to the exigencies and specificities of their time and place? Might

I, on the other hand, piece together an observable historical trajectory by identifying cultural producers in the interim and on the periphery? Could these narratives from the forties and fifties be better viewed in relationship to other Mississippi stories from the sixties and perhaps seventies? Would these other narratives be easily located in the well-cataloged world of high literature, or would I have to search elsewhere?

Partial answers to these questions presented themselves in the person of Carl Corley. I learned from a friend—a gay southern antiquarian, a dealer in rare books and manuscripts[73]—that this obscure gay novelist had set some of his fiction in Mississippi. Indeed, the first Corley novel I found was set almost entirely in Rankin County, where I was raised. I wanted to find out more. *Lives of Mississippi Authors, 1817–1967*—which included essays on Creekmore and Phillips and lengthier tributes to famed Mississippi authors William Faulkner, Eudora Welty, and Tennessee Williams—had no entry on Corley. The Mississippi Department of Archives and History had only a single newspaper article about him, from the 25 September 1960 edition of the *Clarion-Ledger/Jackson Daily News.* But that article proved invaluable in tracking Corley.

Carl Vernon Corley grew up in the 1920s and 1930s on a farm near Florence, Mississippi, where he attended high school. The proximity to my hometown—about ten miles away—connected me viscerally to him. I was interested in him as a seemingly out gay man and as a writer. My curiosity was piqued by his appearance, his sensibilities. But I was drawn to him, attracted to his life story, primarily because he was a fellow Rankin Countian, a local boy.

The newspaper article answered many questions. It raised many more. Corley clearly was a writer: one of the two photos accompanying the piece showed him posing next to several leather volumes embossed with his name and the titles. But these particular titles yielded no results in my search of library databases (though a few other, later works surfaced). If the books mentioned in the 1960 *Clarion-Ledger/Jackson Daily News* were widely distributed, they certainly didn't make their way into any major American libraries. Though Corley told the reporter that MacMillan and Comet published five of his novels—one, he conceded, "wasn't good enough"[74]—I began to suspect they were self-published or printed by so-called vanity presses. I doubted Corley for two reasons.

First, a key motive behind this 1960 newspaper exposé was transparent. Compared to Mississippi authors like Welty, Faulkner, and Phillips, Corley was a complete unknown. Why feature him? Why would Corley consent to—or perhaps invite—a lengthy interview? The answer was obvious: Corley was leaving the state, and he wanted to sell his home.

It wouldn't be easy. He had decorated the square pink house elaborately and idiosyncratically. At worst, it might be called tasteless. At best, it reflected a variety of tastes. Every interior wall was "covered with art," mostly by Corley, including "a silhouette of an ancient Egyptian queen" and "his interpretation of famous Michelangelo statues." On the living-room floor was painted a huge circle, above which sat "a gigantic white leather hassock with dozens of rainbow-colored satin pillows." In detail, the reporter (perhaps a friend of Corley?) described the space-age kitchen; an "underwater-green" bathroom painted with murals of "sea-monsters"; and "the most unusual room in the house . . . the bedroom"—"with velvet tapestry, . . . more marble-topped tables and even more Venetian glass. Completing the decor [was] a bird cage holding almost everything except birds." On whole, the effect was dizzying, "your eyes . . . frantically trying to sort out the myriad of colors."[75] A buyer would have to take on expensive renovations or accept the property "as is"—the latter option made easier if the house were understood to be the work of a creative mind, a noted writer. The article simultaneously legitimized Corley as author, as it helped to market his real estate. To me, Corley seemed duplicitous.

Second, Corley purportedly was moving to Hollywood to oversee Columbia Pictures' filming of his novel *Goddess in Amber.* I could find neither the novel nor the film—nor any reference to them—among U.S. libraries and archives. If Corley wasn't lying, he was playing a little too fast and loose with the truth. Self-promotion notwithstanding, the facts didn't add up.

Indeed, I was soon to discover that fact and fiction regularly blurred in Corley's life work. He didn't seem to accept the two as distinct. Corley engaged the performative not as artifice but as reality, or as one and the same. He crafted written narratives, I began to ascertain, that both took on the rubric of fiction or fantasy *and* served his own need for self-disclosure and outness. He told stories (in both the narrative and deceptive senses) in order to tell his own story. But before I could understand those stories, I had to learn more about the genre Corley most frequently relied upon, the genre that would eventually, in the mid- and late 1960s, prove amenable to his writing—pulp fiction.

TWENTIETH-CENTURY PULP FICTION had its origins in 1830s story weeklies. The advent of the steam printing press, expanded postal and rail distribution, and a growing working-class readership insured viable markets for the cheap four-page newsprint publications. Relying first on plagiarized copy from higher-priced American and British magazines, then on stolen original manuscripts, weeklies eventually cultivated their own pool of poorly paid writers who worked under tight deadlines. Thus, Lee Server notes, "the hack fiction writer was born."[76]

Though an individual writer's serialized work was often strung together into dime novel form, magazines began to dominate the market at the turn of the century and reached their zenith in the interwar period. Purchased at the local drugstore or supermarket, train or bus station, or through the mail, a single magazine issue ordinarily offered several short pieces by a variety of authors around a central theme. Distinctive magazine genres included Westerns, adventures, mysteries, detective fiction, hero and superhero legends, horror tales, science fiction, weird menace stories, and—"the only rough-paper category aimed specifically at women"—romances.[77] Women's romance pulps like *Love Story* and *Thrilling Love* often were read alone, in secret, as young Bobbie Lee Hartley did atop her bed, door locked, in the film *Ode to Billy Joe*. "Reading the good book?" her mother later asked. "Yes, Mama. It was a *very* good book," she replied.

The masturbatory potential was not lost on publishers. To male consumers, they marketed racier sex pulps or "Spicy" stories of heterosexual encounters. Again, low-paid writers provided quick, often reworked copy. Lee Server speculates, "It is likely that many a Spicy detective and adventure story was a reject from the straight [that is, serious fiction or nonsexual pulp] markets, recycled with a few hastily added sex scenes."[78] Though popular sex pulp magazines rarely, if ever, wove homosexual yarns, underground operations produced typewritten queer "fuck stories" that probably circulated, Roger Austen assumes, from the 1920s through the 1960s.[79] Yet queer representations made their way into other "straight" pulp. During the 1920s, for example, famed publisher Harold Hersey devoted the bulk of his debut *Courtroom Stories* issue to "The Trial of Oscar Wilde."[80]

Pulp novels of the mid-twentieth century borrowed on the magazine formula—sensational cover, cheap paper, and cheap copy. Because the pulp novel emerged simultaneously with pocket book versions of serious fiction, critics carefully distinguished between "real" writing and the "lowbrow and throwaway." As Woody Haut notes, the result was "a class-based separation between writers who [had] the status of literary artists and those . . . relegated to the status of literary workers. Tied to contracts and deadlines and obliged to include obligatory scenes of sex and violence, these writers, many of them refugees from other professions, were subject to the vagaries of the market."[81] And yet the distinction was never so clear. The murky line was repeatedly crossed. Highbrow hardcover fiction—like Thomas Hal Phillips's *The Bitterweed Path*—could be dressed down for the pocket market. Serious writers penned pulp novels under pseudonyms, while pulp writers sometimes worked their way "up" to the New York market. However, literary slumming—and the recognition of it as such, marked by the use of the pseudonym—was much more common than bootstrap cultural ascendancy.

These cross-cutting, male-dominated professions also generated lesbian pulp—"trashy novels produced cheaply . . . for heterosexual men's titillation as much as for lesbians' pleasure." These novels' story lines were "often ludicrous and improbable and frequently internally inconsistent."[82] Yet, women-identified-women read them. And, increasingly, they wrote them. Though the genre imbibed prevailing myths of lesbians as sterile man-haters, inverted and pathological, it also provoked against-the-grain writings and readings. For example, Diane Hamer notes that the "emphasis on the fluidity of sexuality" in Ann Bannon's five novels from the late 1950s became "a critique of heterosexuality." Though usually denied happy endings, lesbian readers, like some queer audiences for *Ode to Billy Joe*, enjoyed "the pleasures of . . . identification and recognition. . . . What Bannon did was to provide a range of possible trajectories to lesbianism . . . and to insert an element of choice into becoming a lesbian."[83]

Though several Supreme Court pornography rulings contradicted and clouded one another during the late fifties and sixties, the net effect was an easing of restrictions over time. From the repressive *Roth v. United States* ruling in 1957 to the liberatory *Redrup v. New York* decision in 1967, the Court found it ever more difficult to label nude photography or textual renderings of sex acts as "utterly without redeeming social value."[84] All the while, pulp publishers kept one eye on the Court and another on profits. Editorial choices reflected the latest legal decision, but to publish or not to publish was seldom a question. The number of new lesbian-themed novels peaked at 348 in 1965 and fell off thereafter.[85]

Yet it is *from* 1965 that both critics Roger Austen and Tom Norman date the "explosion" of gay male erotic fiction.[86] Gay pulp proliferated from the late sixties through the seventies. It was not, however, without its antecedents. William Talsman's *The Gaudy Image* (1951) was one of many sexually explicit American novels from the fifties first published in Paris. (Others included Henry Miller's *Tropic of Cancer*.) Though most of Olympia Press's American copies were seized, it's possible that Carl Corley read *The Gaudy Image*. Set in New Orleans, this "unabashed novel," Austen argues, made "homosexuality neither perplexing nor regrettable but 'worthwhile.'"[87] Likewise, Corley probably encountered the "wish-fulfillment fantasy" of Jay Little. Little's two novels, *Maybe-Tomorrow* (1952) and *Somewhere Between the Two* (1956), set in small-town Texas and New Orleans, may have been unconvincing or unsophisticated, as Austen suggests;[88] but they clearly influenced latter-day gay pulp writers of the 1960s, when stock characters and story lines were developed and elaborated. And, they established New Orleans as a queer urban hub in perpetual reciprocal relationship with adjacent rural populations, a relationship Corley would explore in his own work, a relationship many oral history narrators experienced, returning again and again to the gay world of the Crescent City.

Readers of gay erotica—often published as part of larger lists addressing controversial but timely "social issues"—were akin to and often the same as buyers of physique magazines. These pictorials emerged in the 1940s and 1950s, Tracy Morgan argues, with "cloaked," racialized representations of "gay desire" and "a veneer of respectability."[89] By the mid-fifties, there were at least twenty such pocket-size magazines, and their audiences were spread across urban and rural locales. As one southerner remembers, "I was living in a little bitty town. . . . Apparently the town homo ran the drugstore, and he carried the Athletic Model Guild['s *Physique Pictorial*]. I was only twelve, so they wouldn't sell something like that to me, not in 1957. I stole that . . . issue."[90] Chuck Plant also secured numerous copies of physique magazines in Mississippi, building up "quite a collection."[91] As they balanced a normalized fitness culture with a growing—and growing up—queer audience, pictorials reached production levels of 750,000 by 1965.[92]

Gay pulp output likewise skyrocketed. Among the more provocative titles and noms de plume were *Summer in Sodom*, by Edwin Fey; *Gay Whore*, by Jack Love; *Hollywood Homo*, by Michael Starr; *The Short Happy Sex Life of Stud Sorell*, by Orlando Paris; *It's a Gay, Gay, Gay World*, by Guy Faulk; *Gay on the Range*, by Dick Dale; *Queer Belles*, by Percy Queen; *Gay Pals*, by Peter Grande; and the widely recognized classics *$tud*, by Phil Andros, and *Song of the Loon*, by Richard Amory.

Given this campy, explicitly sexual array of narratives and personas, I was startled to learn that Carl Corley wrote pulp fiction under his real name. And as I collected—with great difficulty—most of his twenty-two novels from 1966 to 1971,[93] Corley's works stood out as more sober, more earnest. Though maudlin, titles like *A Fool's Advice, Cast a Wistful Eye*, and *A Lover Mourned* evoke literary aspirations. Still, on the surface, the lightweight novels looked no different from all the others: 4¼ by 7 inches; approximately 150 (now yellowed) pages; a brightly illustrated cover with sensational teaser; and the moniker of an unfamiliar publishing house and series name—for Corley, usually the French Line by P.E.C. (Publishers Export Company) of San Diego. These Corley novels begged closer analysis. And they motivated for me a reconciliation of binarized notions of highbrow and lowbrow writing.

*

THEORIST PIERRE BOURDIEU examines processes of classification in *Distinction: A Social Critique of the Judgment of Taste*. Social and cultural labels, divisions, and classifications are inherently hierarchical, Bourdieu says, and they proceed from a primary duality—high/low, superior/inferior, fine/crude. Those who control representations and other forms of cultural production are materially invested in their structures. As Bourdieu puts it, "Position in the classification struggle depends on position in the class structure."[94]

Classifications become solidified as they are naturalized. The dominated are complicit in domination, as "the social order is progressively inscribed in people's minds." That is, "a sense of one's place"—one's limits—is instilled such that it is not merely accepted, but is taken for granted and *forgotten*. "Primary perception of the social world . . . is always an act of cognition . . . but at the same time it is an act of miscognition."[95]

> Nothing is further removed from an act of cognition, as conceived by the intellectualist tradition, than this sense of the social structure, which, as is so well put by the word *taste*—simultaneously "the faculty of perceiving flavours" and "the capacity to discern aesthetic values"—is social necessity made second nature. . . .[96]

In 1960 many readers of the *Clarion-Ledger/Jackson Daily News* might have unquestioningly concluded—indeed, taken as self-evident—that Carl Corley's home was tasteless, garish, outlandish, gauche. Further, they might well have accepted Corley's own assertion that some of this, his early writing, "wasn't good enough" to be published. In so doing, they were participating in the reproduction of social and cultural hierarchies, in the (re)attribution of distinction and "stigmata."

The relationship between counterposed classes and classifications can be further examined by comparing two cultural producers, Mississippians Carl Corley and Hubert Creekmore, and the ways in which they are represented in one particular genre: the famous author newspaper feature. Such features don't merely represent or assess authors; they produce them. Further, they normalize and legitimize certain ways of being an author.

To begin with, the previously mentioned exposé on Corley and the discovery of it as the sole item in an archival file put it decidedly at odds with a 1954 feature on Creekmore from the same newspaper.[97] The Creekmore piece I likewise found in a Mississippi Department of Archives and History subject file. But this file was filled with other indicators of success: numerous reviews of Creekmore's work from revered publications, other famous author features on Creekmore, and obituaries by local as well as national media. Corley's life—and, I presumed, death, since I had no evidence to the contrary—had escaped notice.

The two pieces, written only six years apart, depict two markedly different authors. Creekmore's credentials were unassailable, the report implied. He had written for *The Nation*, the *New York Times*, and the *Yale Review*. His poetry and fiction were published by the major houses of New York. Corley, on the other hand, needed to provide tangible evidence of his literary output—the leather-bound volumes, subsequently photographed. Creekmore had studied at Mississippi, Columbia, and Yale; no reference was made to Corley's education. Creekmore's volunteer activities were recounted. Corley worked as an illustrator for the state highway department; his writing amounted to moonlighting. Both apparently lived alone— Creekmore at a tony Jackson address, Corley across the river in Rankin County, near Florence, in the unfortunately named crossroads community of Plain (later renamed Richland). Corley's fantastical art hung all over the walls and even covered the floor. Creekmore admitted an interest in the cutting-edge art movement of the day: "I dab at painting abstract things." Further, Creekmore was linked to good food and fine music. Well traveled, he was anticipating his next trip to Europe. Elsewhere in Creekmore's file, I found assertions of his family's elite status. Though it was not commented upon, I imagined a refined "literary" manner of speaking, especially as compared to Corley, whose "thick Southern drawl" the reporter noted. A curious description, given the locale.

Neither article mentions homoeroticism as among the subject matter addressed by the author.

Author photographs accompanying the pieces also inscribed distinction(s). Both men are half shot, depicting the upper body; both are positioned to the viewer's left. Corley's picture is tight, claustrophobic. His right shoulder is cut off. He wears a casual short-sleeve shirt, a thick gold chain around his wrist. Other than the books, only the rendering of the Egyptian queen is visible. Creekmore stands confident in buttoned-up shirt and fine jacket, his arm on the bas-relief mantle, a cigarette poised between his fingers. A few other markers of class are in evidence. Atop the hearth is a candelabrum and vase. Above it, a mirror with ornamented gilded frame. Artfully shot, the photograph further captures the author's profile in the reflection.

In tandem with the text, each photo documents and exhibits what Bourdieu calls "bodily hexis"—a physical taking up of space not unrelated to the metaphorical space to which marginalized Mississippians like Richard Wright felt "assigned." As Bourdieu describes it:

One's relationship to the social world and to one's proper place in it is never more clearly expressed than in the space and time one feels entitled to take from others; more precisely, in the space one claims with one's body in physical space, through a bearing and gestures that are self-assured or reserved, expansive or constricted ("presence" or "insignificance") and with one's speech in time, through the interaction time one appropriates and the self-assured or aggressive, careless or unconscious way one appropriates it.[98]

Indeed, Creekmore is portrayed as "a very engaging personality, whose zest for living is smoothly projected. . . ." Corley, by contrast, is "a very soft-spoken man." Whereas Creekmore's is a commanding presence, easily labeled handsome by the prevailing standards, Corley peers warily at the camera. He sports "a blue star tattoed [sic] on his right cheek as a permanent momento [sic] of his tenure in the Marine Corps." An oddity, this blue star—like the author, like his home, the piece implies. Moreover, this bodily adornment or tattoo, as of midcentury, still connoted class—that is, it marked Corley as working class. Corley's star, for me, proved an important clue to understanding him and his writing. It became a guidepost, a marker in tracking Corley and in locating his later published work.

CORLEY'S INITIAL WORK, the six novels pictured in the 1960 newspaper story, I never did find. But I identified eighteen pulp novels he published from 1966 to 1968—an astonishing number even for a so-called hack fiction writer. Also, I found four more published from 1970 to 1971, for a total of twenty-two.[99] Given this extraordinary output, I assumed Corley relied on and reworked the earlier manuscripts.

The star appeared everywhere I searched for Corley. Most notably, it cropped up on the paperback covers. To supplement the $250 Corley was likely paid for each of the novels[100]—which in turn sold for 95 cents a copy in 1966; $1.25 in 1967 and 1968—he produced the cover art for several. On most, his distinctive signature appears. Always at a downward angle, the signature could be viewed as a depiction of the author's face. The capital C's in Corley's first and last names double as his eyes or eyebrows. The remainder of his first name suggests the line of his nose; the last, the right edge of his face. Corley embellished the *y* with a crescent moon, the arch of which forms the right cheekbone. Within the crescent is the star.

These covers further illustrate the settings and thematic concerns of the narratives. As a body, the novels oscillate between the country and the city. The early pulp novels are set in rural Rankin County, Mississippi, during the first half of the twentieth century. *A Fool's Advice,* for example, takes place entirely around Corley's hometown of Florence, 1926. (Customarily,

Cover art for *A Fool's Advice*, 1967, and *Jesse: Man of the Streets*, 1968

Corley uses actual place-names.) On the cover, main character Cutlar "Cutty" Ragan, the first-person narrator, leans against a split-rail fence, shirtless, chewing on a weed. In the background is young Cutty's connection to the outside world—"a little store and filling station . . . papa put up . . . next to our house" (10). Indeed, the illustration's prominent gas pump would seem to portend visitors from afar. But Cutty's local friendship network grows because he holds the popular position of clerk at the store. As he tends the merchandise—including "pulp editions of . . . Amazing Stories, and Love and Romance magazines printed on rough yellow paper" (11), an obvious gesture to the cultural antecedents of Corley's own pulp genre—Cutty finds his sex partners among the farm boys. His most alien—indeed, exoticized—partner is Mingo, a Choctaw from northeast Mississippi who shows up one day "looking for work" (63).

Many later novels are set in the city. *Jesse: Man of the Streets* takes place in Baton Rouge and across the river in Port Allen's Goldcoast red-light district, depicted on the cover—a nod to Jackson's Goldcoast in Rankin County. Part Choctaw, the twenty-six-year-old bisexual hustler Jesse is from Mississippi. So is his unwitting client, the first-person narrator Lily—who, along with Attala Rose from the novel of the same name, is one of only two *female* first-person narrators in Corley's work. An artist and decorator of elevated sensibilities, Lily forges a bond with Jesse by confessing she too "was born on a one mule farm in Mississippi" (71).

Despite its female protagonist, *Jesse* was published, like the majority of Corley's P.E.C. novels, as part of the French Line series, a decidedly gay one. Corley's 272-page magnum opus, *Attala Rose*, on the other hand, is aggressively heterosexual and was published as a P.E.C. Classic. As I will argue, Corley's work eroticizes the first-person male butch bottom and his partners, all butch tops, often racial others. It obsessively attempts to disown any implied femininity in the narrator's receptive sexual role by referencing again and again his masculinity. Indeed, in this economy of desire—corroborated historically by Fitz Spencer's and Ron Knight's expressed preferences for so-called real men—femme men are both debased and undesirable. One way of interpreting the gender of the occasional *female* first-person narrator is as a vehicle both to eroticize the femme—necessarily the penetrated—and to own a desire to be the femme.

Mel and Rusty, the main characters of *Cast a Wistful Eye*, grew up in rural Louisiana and Texas, respectively. But they live and love and eventually thrive in New Orleans. They hang out in "Cafe Demonde" and across the street in Jackson Square, the park Truman Capote claimed as queer.[101] Mel need never return to his idealized pastoral home in Golden Meadow, the cover suggests. He holds the sun in his hand in New Orleans. The dazzling illustration—evoking the square with its statue of Andrew Jackson and the spires of Saint Louis Cathedral—foretells a rare pulp happy ending. "Forget Golden Meadow," Rusty tells Mel in the concluding passage. "Come on, Lover. . . . Let's see what's cooking in the square" (153).

Despite *Cast a Wistful Eye*, ordinarily for Corley the urban connotes evil. Though his first novels mostly take place in an idyllic Rankin County, an occasional protagonist makes a regrettable foray into the city. This lapse of judgment or, more commonly, a banishment from the Garden of Eden marks a turning point, a descent. Corley's cover for *My Purple Winter*, for example, depicts a key moment prior to expulsion. This moment and this novel—in many ways representative of Corley's oeuvre—merit closer attention. *My Purple Winter* is one of two novels I will discuss in some detail, given their value in interpreting not only Corley's body of work, but also his own life story—his fictionalized position within these narratives and his historical position within processes of queer cultural production.

In the cover illustration for *My Purple Winter*, first-person narrator Brut

 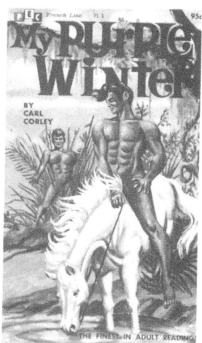

Cover art for *Cast a Wistful Eye*, 1968, and *My Purple Winter*, 1966

"Bru" Toro, naked, parts the underbrush, which covers his pelvic area. An only child—the fifteen-year-old son of a classically Freudian overbearing mother and aloof, brooding farmer—Bru tries to sneak a glance at the hired hand Dany Buck. Dany, nineteen, also is naked, astride a stallion, the mane of which obscures Dany's penis. In the text, Dany proceeds to bathe himself and the stallion in the pond. Bru joins them. Drying off, the bigger, stronger Dany—"so utterly of the earth"(24)—eyes Bru and snaps his shirt on Bru's butt. Dany rubs the red spot and tells Bru, "You got a cute little ass. . . . You shoulda been a girl." Dany kisses Bru "full on the lips" and locks him in "his primitive embrace" (28). Then, like a horse, he "mounts" Bru (30). Bru is now "slave" to the "master" Dany (36). Dany promises never to leave Bru or the farm.

Bru's "happiest" summer is spent working with Dany on the farm (39). They have sex daily, "in the corn-ricks, in the hay-loft, in the dark woods on the carpet of pine needles" (82). When Bru's aunt Roxie dies in Kosciusko, Bru and Dany are left alone in the "big house" for four days, like "man and wife" (51). In the evening, Dany "smoke[s] his pipe" while Bru "washe[s] the dishes and clean[s] up" (51). Less hurried in their love-making, Bru marvels at "the great size," the "gargantuan dimension" of Dany's "organ" (52), which he again compares to a horse, "savage" and "primeval" (52–53).

Bru's father ultimately catches Bru playing with Dany's dick in the barn. Papa, a Greek immigrant, sends Bru away to New Orleans, to live with a relative, "a huge man, gross and be-whiskered as a genii [sic] from the Arabian Nights" (60). Bru forever remembers "my father's cowman-shepherd" (65); he harkens back to the golden summer with Dany, first set in motion by their encounter at the pond.

Bru refuses to live with his grotesque relation, Blaize Salario, especially after Blaize refers to Bru's beloved Dany as "a half-nigger plow hand!" Bru belligerently counters that Dany is "Creole . . . French and Spanish." On behalf of his lover, Bru disavows any non-European lineage. Indeed, throughout Corley's fiction, the racialized desired other repeatedly suggests a black race that the narrative acknowledges but denies by gesturing to other nonwhite—yet nonblack—races and ethnicities. If, as *My Purple Winter* increasingly suggests, fraternization with queers makes one dirty, filthy, scummy, then as in the contemporaneously constructed dirty beatnik of dominant discourses, queers and blacks become ever more conceptually entangled in a racist language that figures whiteness with cleanliness, blackness with dirtiness.

On his own, Bru must now fend for himself in Depression-era New Orleans (72). Inevitably, he slides into the French Quarter's seamy world of prostitution. He's ensnared innocently enough when he meets Cecil Jarreau at the "Cafe DeMonde" on Decatur Street. A good-looking "Cajun" boy with "girlishly-red lips," Cecil has recently quit "the C.C.C.'s"—the federal Civilian Conservation Corps (79).[102] As to making a living, Cecil reassures Bru: "You ain't got nothin' to worry about—not with your looks and your build" (81). Soon Bru is trapped.

Though he successfully gets Cecil off the streets and supports both of them with his earnings, Bru lets his trade become a compulsion. Though his tricks are uniformly odious—"sodden, debased beings" (136)—Bru works harder in

> an endless nightmare of groping hands in the darkness—along Dauphine and Bourbon Streets and along the waterfront—hiding below some low-hanging roof, or in the shadow of thick hedges—beneath the pilings of the wharf or the canvas of a wharfed boat—in public toilets, or in dingy, deso-

late rooms—in the rear of barbershops, in parked cars, narrow stairway entrances, storage rooms and vacated warehouses. (135)

Bru sinks ever deeper. He begins to seek out "masculine young men . . . purely for my own sexual pleasure, not for money" (140). His fateful "purple winter" hits bottom when three men beat the "friggin' kid fairy" nearly to death, in a scene replete with sadomasochistic fervor (145).

Bru hitchhikes home to Rankin County. With little clothing and a blanket, he walks to his father's stone house from the highway. At the door, the father says Bru's mother is dead. She agonized over Bru until sickness set in, and she died. Bru promises he's "not a child of sin, anymore" (148). But Papa knows Bru is no more than a "common whore," and he turns his son away (149). Bru stumbles to Dany's small tenant house. Through a window, he watches Dany in a rocker before the hearth. Bru knows himself to be "trash—filth—scum—dirt" (153). With increasing hyperbole, he compares himself to Dany, who is "pure and sweet and noble." Bru is nothing more than "gutter ooze and slimy worthlessness" (154). Bru walks away; whispers good-bye to Mama and to Dany; and returns to the highway to hitchhike back to New Orleans—to the "dark sewer peopled by the long, dim, never-ending line of old men, bold men, young men, harsh men, revolting and dirty men like animals, with fetid breath and stinking repulsive bodies." (156). Exhausted, completely bereft of energy or will, he rests a moment in the roadside ditch, sheltered from the winter wind.

At this point, the narrative (and the narrative structure) takes a startling turn. Scarcely three pages from the end, there is a line break—the first in the text. What was, throughout, the protagonist's first-person account becomes here at the conclusion a third-person narrative.

Dany awakes. He sees "something in the ditch beneath the rails, . . . something wrapped in a blanket." Then, Dany is on his boss's front porch, "bearing a blanket-wrapped burden" (158). Bru's father comes to the door. "It's tha son, little Bru," Dany says, "frozen to death in the ditch beside the road. . . . His death is on our hands. I got him turned out, and you turned him out again—to die. We'll share a spot in hell together for this" (158–159).

MY PURPLE WINTER, perhaps more than any other gay male pulp novel, evinces what John D'Emilio calls the "tack[ed] on unhappy ending"[103]— both in its third-person appendage and in the inconsistencies of tone and action immediately preceding the shift in voice. Though author Corley clearly depicts urban gay life as seedy, the publisher appears obligated to magnify that seediness; though Corley crafts a narrative of rural return, a seeming peripatetic way back to a pastoral partnership, the publisher interrupts that would-be blissful reunion.

Pulp publishers like P.E.C.—whose other titles included *Vietnam Underside* and *Was Oswald Alone?*—skirted moral objections to queer content by packaging the narratives as socially responsible, cautionary tales. Homosexuality, they warned as they reworked authors' narratives, led to ruin. Editors forced these constructions on writers like Corley, altering the plot in obvious ways. The radical shift from first-person to third-person voice at the close of *My Purple Winter* is particularly conspicuous—and incoherent, given that early on, the narrator is portrayed as speaking from the present day about his past experiences, the events of the novel. "To this day, when I [visit] the stores of New Orleans"—he confesses in the reminiscent voice, in the present tense—Bru Toro pines after his mother. But he pines because "I do not know where she is—I know not if she is alive" (9). The editors incongruously kill her off in the final passages. She dies, Bru *learns*, of "grief . . . over" his wretched lifestyle (150). In this way, the editors capped a morality play ending onto an otherwise unacceptable work of gay porn.

Corley's 1967 novel *A Lover Mourned* similarly contains an abrupt aboutface at the conclusion of a nonetheless regionally and temporally precise narrative. First-person narrator Bebe Tarver and his lover Deke Baxton are kicked out of Hinds (County) Junior College in Raymond, Mississippi, for kissing in the dorm. They cling to one another in pastoral isolation in Rankin County—in a lakeside cabin, the Tarver family's second home—before their parents find out. The two never feel "guilt, or shame from our relationship. It [i]s too divinely wondrous for that" (25). Bebe traverses (and author Corley thereby documents) numerous queer sites in Mississippi— from college to Sunday school, sports facilities to roadhouses, roadside to homestead. Bebe experiences homosex in cars, among other places. He tracks down his father, also a lover of men, at the Robert E. Lee Hotel on Lamar Street in Jackson. Bebe's love for Deke—and, by extension, his father's love for Barry—is compared to the apostle John's love for Jesus. Yet, by the novel's end, Barry dies, the young marine Deke is killed in the South Pacific of World War II, and father and son renounce their love for men. Together they return—an ambiguously eroticized couple, a homosocial pair—to Bebe's mother.

These reversals, marked by a discrepant language of debasement and loathing in the closing passages, signal aggressive editorial intervention in *A Lover Mourned* and *My Purple Winter*, both published by P.E.C. So incongruous are the passages, so out of keeping with the prior tone, that many readers likely discounted these disavowals and deaths, longtime hallmarks of homophobic representation. Many readers undoubtedly saw through the editorial ploys. Counterhegemonic readings surely accompanied these textual interactions. Moreover, sexual arousal surely sometimes accompanied phobic imagery, as suggested by the queer-bashing/sadomasochistic fantasy of *My Purple Winter*'s marine fight scene and throughout Corley's work. Author, editors, distributors, and readers, along with a varyingly engaged legal system, participated in a complex web of meanings and desires that both reinscribed and challenged prevailing standards along the uneasy dividing line of pornography and literature.

A Chosen World, the second novel I will examine in depth, was released by Pad Library of Agoura, California, in 1966. It provides us with clearer access to Corley's vision, given its greater length, autobiographical content, and relative lack of editorial mediation, and given that it was his first published work—likely a pastiche of his prior unpublished or self-published titles. Roughly seventy thousand words, as compared to fifty thousand for most P.E.C. titles, *A Chosen World* contains striking parallels to Corley's life history (which I began to reconstruct from scant sources). The events chronicled in *A Chosen World* might prove "truer," I speculated, since Pad Library apparently reproduced Corley's manuscript without editing. Every page is filled with misspellings and typographical errors. "Chapter One" is followed by "Chapter One," which is followed by "Chapter 3." Though the tale is rife with violence and riddled with corpses, the ending is anything but tragic.

Protagonist Rex Polo narrates *A Chosen World* in the first person. Rex resembles the author, as do most Corley protagonists, even the female character Lily, who narrates *Jesse*. Indeed, the first-person fictional narrator of *Fallen Eagle* (P.E.C., 1967) is named Carl Corley. *A Chosen World*'s Rex is born in Florence, Mississippi, in 1921, as was Corley. Now fifteen, in 1936, Rex embarks on a homosexual odyssey, the geographical components of which match Corley's movements across place and time. I uncovered these bare outlines of Corley's life in two short bios, taken from his self-published works of nonfiction, *The Agony of Christ* (1967)—a subtly subversive, sadomasochistic text in its own right—and *Carl Corley's Illustrated History of Louisiana* (1983). (The preservation of these two books—ostensibly about Christianity and traditional state history—in a few Louisiana libraries demonstrates that they were considered more reputable than the pulps.)

In Corley's autobiographical novel *A Chosen World*, Rex discovers homosex in Florence High School's "tin shower house" with the football player Norman, "a big ox of a boy" (6). The two meet almost every night in Norman's father's cow pasture. Soon Norman catches Rex with Maurice. He pulls Rex from Maurice's convertible—apparently a setup—and assaults him, forcing Rex into a submissive act of anal sex. Rex and Maurice have sex regularly, sometimes along "the sand on the inward cline of Pearl River" (24). When Rex refuses a blow job from Maurice, Maurice beats him. Rex next takes up with Luther. Luther is "profoundly masculine, with none of the gestures, thank God, of those I would come to know later in that lavender world of anarchy" (32). With Luther, Rex spends the "happiest summer of my life" (49), passing hours together at a little-used hunting lodge on Hoover Lake in Rankin County. When Luther's parents force an end to the relationship, Luther joins the merchant marine and Rex joins the marines.

After Rex finishes boot camp in San Diego, Japan bombs Pearl Harbor. Rex is sent to the South Pacific, as Corley was during World War II, and works in intelligence as a quick-sketch artist. Stationed in various parts of the South Pacific—Guadalcanal, Guam, and Iwo Jima, as was Corley—Rex chronicles his lovers in rote succession: Cisco, the baseball player from Texas; Myrka, the farm boy from Ohio, from whom Rex receives his first blow job; and Stanley, an art student from New Jersey, to whom Rex gives his first blow job. In anal sex, Rex is always the penetrated partner, as are most all of Corley's first-person narrators.

Rex's refusal of oral sex from Maurice, his delay in experiencing it as either the insertive or receptive partner, suggests a hierarchy of homosexual roles at odds with those explained by most oral history narrators in Mississippi. In Corley's world, anal sex—regardless of the role taken—seems preferable, less culpable than oral sex of any kind, even as this world recirculates a commonplace desire for masculine gender performances. As part 1 of my book suggests, however, in Mississippi of the 1940s, 1950s, and 1960s, anal or oral homosex appeared societally endorsed for the penetrative partner, whereas the receptive partner was more definitively marked as queer and transgressive. This discrepancy might result from an authorial impulse to legitimize autobiographical scenarios of desire. Yet a tension remains; the penetrated first-person narrator holds an insecure position in gender-connotative sex-role hierarchies, as will be further assessed.

In the sadomasochistic climax of his war service, Rex is gang-raped by drunken soldiers on the concrete floor of the communal shower. The rapes continue, sometimes nightly. The recurrence—truly, the centrality—of rape in Corley's writing hints at a brutish world in which the author lived. Imagining or reporting rape, I speculate, might have been a way for Corley to take on, eroticize, and libidinize the ubiquitous specter of violence that may have characterized his life as a soldier and as an out gay writer in the Deep South of the civil rights era.

The rapes cease as the men are called into combat. In the space of a single chapter, across various parts of the South Pacific, all three of Rex's marine lovers are killed in battle; and Rex learns that Luther "drowned in a sunken battleship off the shores of Normandy" (112). Rex returns home at war's end; Corley was discharged 15 October 1945. On the ship bound for the United States, Rex commemorates the rapes and the deaths:

> I tattooed a tiny star directly beneath my right eye, my eternal brand for an old bitterness, an oath against mankind and of the love of mankind. A star, which was to later be my label, to be incorporated in my name on all my paintings—that word, which was to resound again and again in those lavender alleyways, in those dimly lit lairs, in those strangely illuminated bars and lounges where those of my kind will seek out their loneliness, will search for their counterparts, their own fascmiles [sic], the things they will both love and abhor, in searching out their own. (111)

Back in Florence and now twenty-four, Rex encounters Suny, "a boy not over sixteen." Presaging the pivotal moment in My Purple Winter, Suny is "shirtless, astride a white stallion." Suny worships the war hero; he begs Rex to paint his portrait. Soon Rex has done a number of "pencil sketches," "pen and ink" drawings, and "Tempra" [sic] paintings of Suny, "posed in a bathing suit" in outdoor farm settings (123). Rex and Suny sell these to "the physique magazines," and Suny receives fan mail from all over the world.

CLEARLY, CARL CORLEY perused the physique and fitness magazines of the 1950s and 1960s. Their influence is evident in his visual art, in the cover illustrations for his pulp novels. Physique magazines regularly included reproductions of hand-drawn and painted work as well as photographs of near-naked men. Though the readers of Physique Pictorial preferred photos over paintings by a margin of three to one in a 1953 survey, this particular magazine ran nonphotographic illustrations from the opening issue in 1951 until the late 1970s.[104]

Physique Pictorial—published by the Athletic Model Guild, a one-person operation in Los Angeles—made famous the artwork of George Quaintance in the fifties, Tom of Finland in the sixties. Unlike Tom's meaty he-men with outsized organs, Quaintance's figures are muscled but svelte. These most closely resemble Corley's and surely informed them. Quaintance trained would-be artists through the mail and through the magazine, with articles such as "How to Draw from Projected Color Slides" in the February 1952 Physique Pictorial. Corley must have observed carefully. Corley's cover for My Purple Winter seems to mimic Quaintance's cover for the November 1951 Physique Pictorial—"Dashing," which depicts a nude man riding a white horse. The male figure on the cover of Corley's *Fallen Eagle* mirrors the form of Quaintance's "Island Boy," on the back cover of the May 1952 issue. In each study the figure's genitalia are discreetly covered by the wing of a bird—an eagle and a seagull, respectively.

But Corley didn't merely emulate Quaintance. With others, the two developed and extended thematic concerns at a vital moment of visual—and, in the case of Corley, textual—foment in queer representation. Indeed the gay erotic archetypes outlined in 1991 by veteran pulp writer "Ace"—"awakening books, college boys, jocks, working men, family, between generations, and white collar men"[105]—have antecedents not only in sixties gay pulp, but also in fifties physique art. Another staple, horsemen—farm boys and cowboys—appear in Quaintance's earliest work, set mostly in the American Southwest. Corley frequently used backdrops of southern and Mississippi landscapes for his portraits and multifigure studies of farmers, among others.

Corley's work circulated in dialectical relationship with expanding queer media. Homoerotic magazine illustrations, posters, prints, flyers, advertisements, and other works of visual art (including physique movies) emanated from various regions of the country and the world during the fifties. Unlike the static, nonnarrative quality of many portraits, multifigure studies reproduced in physique magazines suggested libidinous plot lines to queer viewers and queer writers. "[Fraternity] Initiation Week" by Fred Mathews of Beverly Hills, California; "[Football] Locker Room" by "former marine-combat artist" William MacLane of Seattle, Washington; "Moonlight [Skinny] Dip" by Lloyd Steel of Metarie, Louisiana; "Finnish Sauna" by Andrew Kozak of Los Angeles, California; as well as a variety of sailor fight scenes by Ronald McCann of Chicago, Illinois, resonated in queer representation for decades to come.[106]

Cross-racial representations, particularly depictions of Native Americans, imbibed dominant cultural stereotypes (for example, the noble savage) even as they defied easy categorization. As Tracy Morgan points out, men of color did appear—in underrepresented numbers—in the Eurocentric and Greek mythology–inflected pages of fitness magazines.[107] But paintings in *Physique Pictorial* inverted the racial subject positions Morgan finds in *Grecian Guild Pictorial* photographs. In George Quaintance's "White Captive," for example, a blond fey "Spanish conquistador is held hostage by Aztec King Cuauhtemoc."[108] In "Slave Market," a hairy dark-skinned man with helmet prepares to whip two smooth white men in chains and togas.[109] While Quaintance professed a dubious interest and expertise in the folklore of indigenous peoples, Carl Corley took up Native Americans in both his *Illustrated History of Louisiana* and most problematically in the historical pulp novel *Sky Eyes* (1968), set in early nineteenth-century Mississippi. The cover of *Sky Eyes* depicts a regal blond man, naked, back to the viewer. His crown and cape are discarded. A scantily clad Choctaw approaches with a white horse, positioned above the white man, looking down on him. This image and Quaintance's slave pictures reverse ordinary depictions of the "colonial fantasy," in which whites dominate and subjugate various peoples of color. Corley and Quaintance nonetheless reinscribe "scenarios of desire . . . which trace the cultural legacies of slavery, empire, and imperialism."[110] In these cases, as in the others, white supremacy is assumed, historically normalized. The difference here is that white figures and their white creators narrate a desire for masochistic submission to a righteous retribution or rebellion, a slave-system role reversal.

This is apparent in an advertisement I discovered from the late 1950s, a loose flyer found among an elder gay southerner's files, a mailer typical of the surreptitious distribution of homoerotic posters and other imagery during that era. The first of the ten Carl Corley posters offered by Sir Prise Publishers of Chicago—roughly a decade before Corley began publishing gay pulp—epitomizes the slave-system role reversal.[111] Entitled "Persian Prince," the image depicts two men—one seated, the other standing—inside an ornate tent. The standing man sports only a thong, a necklace with medal, and a majestic flowing headdress—the tail of which obscures the midsection of the naked seated individual. The standing man is several shades darker than the reclining figure, whose feet are propped on velvety cushions and whose right hand fingers a lyre. Though both men exhibit princely demeanor, the direction of desire is obvious. The darker man's eyes are cast down at the seated figure. The white man stares out, directly engaging the viewer. In this economy of desire, the white man—a seemingly willing captive—is the male to be gazed upon.

The slave-system role reversal, the racial inversion of the colonial fantasy, is a masochistic discourse not unlike Corley's textual scenarios of rape. Additional Corley posters from the 1950s articulate a variety of queer prototypes as they foreshadow narrative moments from his later pulp novels. And, as in the novels, the posters suggest autobiographical concerns in Corley's visual art. Though "Gladiator," "Triton," "The Slave," "Persian Prince," and "Secluded Garden" rely on mythological and mythologized pasts, the remaining five images hint at moments from Corley's past. In "Silver Moon," a single male figure reclines in a rural setting suggestive of Mississippi, replete with hanging moss and a patient horse. Male couples in "Hunters' Lodge" and "Rustic Shower" call to mind *A Lover Mourned* and *A Chosen World*, respectively. "Atoll"—with three servicemen variously entangled, a military frigate at harbor in the background—clearly was inspired by Corley's experience in the South Pacific. And "Campus Retreat"—an iteration of the college-boy genre—may have arisen from Corley's (unconfirmed) brief stint at Millsaps College. Corley never mentioned that period in his bios. He consistently described himself as a self-taught artist and writer.

AS SUNY'S PHYSIQUE modeling career wanes, *A Chosen World*'s first-person narrator, Rex Polo, gets work at the Mississippi Department of Highways— where Carl Corley was employed as a draftsman/artist, city directories confirmed, through 1960, the year of the newspaper exposé and the year Corley made preparations to move out of Mississippi. Meanwhile, Rex gives in to his desire for Suny, despite the age difference. Rex's description of their union flatly recalls for the reader his six prior lovers: "The brutality of Norman, the clumsiness of Maurice, the perfection of Luther, the depravity of Cisco, the boyishness of Myrka, the hunger of Stanley, all, were no more than childish hyperboles compared to this powerful novice turned professional" (141).

Rex leaves Suny to accept a job in Baton Rouge. (After fourteen years with the state of Mississippi, Carl Corley worked for the Louisiana Department of Transportation and Development in the art and model unit for twenty years. He never lived in Hollywood.) In Baton Rouge, Rex first experiences an urban gay bar culture. In the closing passages of *A Chosen World*, he describes its habitués. And he delineates his position in "this shadowy world [of] which I had become a member" (167).

With his new friend Erik, Rex makes note of two broad types of patrons at the Looking Glass Lounge. "Masculine homosexuals" sit at the bar, proud and self-assured (160). Hanging around the jukebox are the "faggots, queens, nellies, aunties," for which Rex harbors a "fascination" (162). Still, he and Erik reside squarely in the former camp. Though Rex is "short of stature"—indeed numerous Corley first-person narrators weigh in at only 120 pounds—he is a manly miniature, masculine enough to pick up two marines on the streets of Baton Rouge. In the novel's denouement, the two assault Rex. Insisting he could never have been a marine, they beat him nearly to death. Rex thus has a stake in the schema Corley develops: "I wanted to call the gays, the faggots, the gueens [*sic*], the nellies—those of exaggerated femininity—these I wanted to call mannequin. . . . And I wanted to call the masculine homosexual[s] TOROS, for, to me, this is the most masculine word in the human language today" (167).

In so doing, Corley asserts his rights to representation. He becomes a "classifying subject," as Bourdieu calls it.[112] We are not powerless in the face of hegemonic cultural forces, the theorist suggests. Yet by classifying,

Corley must inevitably work within—and sometimes against—dominant discourses of sexuality and gender. The fact of homosexuality Corley celebrates. In fashioning queer taxonomies, he dismisses the importance of the role taken in the sex act—the "sexual aim" in Freudian terminology. His focus instead, like that of so many other narrators, is on gender presentation.

A mainstream stigmatization of gender nonconformity and a physique culture will-to-manliness lace Corley's construction of the mannequin.[113] Not terribly inventive, the toro/mannequin dichotomy mirrors butch/femme classification as it perpetuates mannequin-femme marginality—that is, as it replicates Bourdieu's primary duality: high/low, superior/inferior. The dichotomy is further fraught by a central tension running throughout Corley's body of written work. Does the main character—usually a bottom; a small, but insistently masculine, war veteran—belong among the toros, the bulls? The protagonist's perpetual reassertion of his masculinity only heightens the uncertainty, as when Rex is challenged by fellow marines at home and overseas. The attempt to dissociate sex role from gender presentation—especially in the delinking of the bottom and the femme—seems a justifying impulse. Are the mannequins worthy of liberation, as are the toros?

Corley's manifesto at the close of *A Chosen World*—a defiant, seemingly unexpurgated assertion of queer rights—waxes ambivalent:

> The society that has bred [the Toro], and is constantly attempting to exile him, has failed. The Toro refuses to be exiled. . . . As long as I live, no one is going to put me down, to accuse me, nor try to make me feel inferior again. I am going to be more than merely tolerated. I am going to be accepted. At last, my mind recalls an old saying of my great aunt's, one which I think appropriate fo rall [sic] the mannequins and Toro's [sic] in this world. "Love is like water in a cup. It shapes itself to the vessel that contains it." (187)

Corley's call for liberation exceeds the limits of gay male pulp fiction, at least as of 1966. Yet his oeuvre redeploys hierarchies of gender, race, and class prevalent in American life, thereby situating his desires firmly within those of the broader culture and the emergent culture of his readers. Gender-bending males prove undesirable—even the radiant, resilient drag queen of *Brazen Image*, whose partner insists s/he abide by rigid on- and offstage roles. To be womanly is to be more definitively queer—a sometimes loathsome classification in Corley's schema.

Corley delineates intricate racial striations, frequently casting Asians and African Americans in subservient, domestic roles. While Asian and Choctaw men become the exoticized objects of desire for a few of the invariably European American protagonists—and stereotyped carpet seller Blaize Salario, of indeterminate Middle Eastern ancestry, embodies the sexually repulsive—black-white interracial intercourse proves the great taboo. Not only does it seem to violate homosexual (not to mention heterosexual) convention in the Jim Crow South; it also parades as distasteful for the white characters. While an exaggerated African American anatomy captivates certain white characters, to act on the desire—as Augie does with Cheka in *Brazen Image*—is to endanger the subordinate and debauch the dominant. Cheka tells "Mist' Augie," "I'm afraid to play 'round [with] you white boys, . . . with all this . . . burning crosses and hangin's" (65, 70). When Augie buries his face "in the huge dark hollow of Cheka's twitching thighs, his lips slipping lovingly over Cheka's gargantuan organ," first-person narrator Dewy recoils in disgust. "I couldn't believe! I wouldn't believe! Augie, my best friend, . . . doing this with a negro" (72).

Within a European American continuum, "darker" figures are cast as desirable in their "savage earthiness," notably characters of Greek, French, and Spanish descent and Creole figures, like Dany Buck. Their physical attributes, particularly genitalia—while probably subject to editorial embellishment—attest to their textual hypersexuality. Still, normalized, unlabeled Anglo-Saxon white men hold the ascendant status. Indeed, Corley's (and other white Mississippians') desire for whiteness seems, among other things, a way to distinguish "the queer" from those who represent difference from other norms—that is, blacks. With whites at the helm of queer cultural production and with queers, as we have seen, embedded in struggles for African American civil rights, there was an awareness and a seeming resentment—on both sides—that the two, queerness and blackness, evoked one another.

Lest they be feminized, white characters—no less frequently than nonblack darker characters—act as top to the narrator's bottom. And their strength and vigor are authenticated through an agrarian upbringing. Corley's (re)circulation of this gay archetype, his awareness of an outside urban queer audience, is particularly evident in the cover art and copy for *A Fool's Advice*. Hayseed main character Cutty, the rural Rankin County youth depicted on the front cover, delineates in the back cover text those males "who awoke me," who "arous[ed] within me the [homosexual] passion": they are "those hot-eyed tantalizing *country boys*."[114] Cutty seemingly would have no need of such a referent. He and his creator are no less country boys themselves. Indeed, the romanticized rural ethos of Carl Corley novels is reflective as much of an authentic Mississippi experience as of the expectations of outside editors and a national audience with urban footings.

As Carl Corley's work demonstrates, textual interactions between writer, readers, characters, and archetypes occasion a layering of stories, real and fictive. Queer readers such as Chuck Plant and Fitz Spencer experienced erotic relationships to and varied identifications with the characters of the genre-crossing pulps. Part memoir, novel, and political treatise, pulp fiction like Corley's allowed readers to assess their own understandings of queer desire while in dialogue with widely circulating queer media. Just as Corley layered his own life history over those of his first-person narrators, readers in both the country and the city further layered and compared their own stories with those of fiction—then, in the sixties, as I do now. Regional identification and racial categorization, then as now, prove salient.

Composed at home, submitted by post, published in California, and purchased through the mail and at the newsstands, Carl Corley's fiction employed regionally specific idioms and locales in reciprocal exchange with growing queer mass media and dominant, mainstream conceptions of gender, race, and class. Corley's production neither emanated unidirectionally from cultural capitals to the provinces nor depicted queer urbanites as refugees from the blighted hinterlands.

Though occasionally tied up in pastoral utopianism and elitist Old South mythologizing, Corley's work complicates queer cultural studies by unsettling its urbanist roots. Whereas Angela Weir and Elizabeth Wilson, for example, see the Greyhound bus station as the purchase point for lesbian pulp and the starting point for a (fictional and historical) lesbian migration to the cities,[115] Corley's life and work exposes such a contact point as but one of many complex nodes of circulation, not just aggregation. Movements of queer texts and queer bodies prove multidirectional and multidimensional. While Corley's painted and textual figures wander across myriad terrains of sexuality and gender, Corley tells his own story within and against the grain of the forms available to him, a resistant memoir of queer life in Mississippi and Louisiana.

CITY AND SUBURBAN DIRECTORIES as well as telephone directories from the Jackson and Baton Rouge areas corroborated the two short bios I had on Carl Corley.[116] He had relocated to the Louisiana capital from Mississippi in 1961. He moved to rural Zachary, Louisiana, in 1971, apparently commuting the roughly fifteen miles to and from his state job in Baton Rouge— much as he had done between Florence and Jackson. He continued to reside in Zachary after leaving the Louisiana Department of Transportation and Development in 1981, with nearly twenty years of service. Why then would it be so difficult for me to locate Carl Corley? Though we were of different generations, we had grown up in the very same county. Surely I could find him.

At the end of the twentieth century, none of the Corleys in Rankin County, Mississippi, knew of Carl Vernon Corley. They were not related to him, they each told me by phone. Since Carl Corley's name and number no longer appeared in the Zachary, Louisiana, telephone listings after 1986, I assumed he died that year. The Louisiana Office of Vital Statistics released death certificates only to family members, none of whom I had identified.

Corley left few of the traces that remain in the wake of the famous. His obscurity reflected elite biases in literary criticism and in historical methodology—biases of focus and selectivity that privileged those already deemed culturally worthy and that resulted in a perpetuation of worthiness over time. Negated at the time of production, definitively queer work and queer life histories would residually inhabit liminal spaces outside the canon, outside the archives. These distinctions were exacerbated by an increasingly palpable logic of queer representation in post–World War II America: explicit depictions of homoeroticism were foreclosed from the realm of literature and art. While Thomas Hal Phillips and Hubert Creekmore novels—and even popular films like *Ode to Billy Joe*—exemplified the requisite subtlety of highbrow engagements with homosexuality, Corley's work perforce was relegated to the world of pulp, porn, and cartooning.

Finding additional information on Corley proved nearly impossible. Though generous with their time, staff members at the State Library of Louisiana, parish libraries, and other organizations unearthed few leads. Publishers of Louisiana's *Eunice News*, which printed Corley's spiral-bound *Illustrated History of Louisiana*, seemed to be brushing me off. Was homophobia at work? Did they resent Corley? After all, into his otherwise straight history of Louisiana, he had inserted some not-so-subtle queer imagery—Native Americans eating phallic sugarcane, French American settlers sporting lavishly androgynous garb, military men ogling one another, and war veterans modeling tight-fitting uniforms, taut at the crotch.

The people at the Louisiana Department of Transportation and Development (DOTD) were much more friendly. A few remembered the "little white-haired man" and his tattoo. Several recalled his car. That Ford Pinto, they said, was painted with all sorts of colorful human figures. One employee had even complained about it. "You see," said a printer who worked closely with Corley and seemed to admire his automobile, "the people he drew were all muscular built." The printer's name was Blaise Salario.[117]

Blaise Salario looked nothing like the odious Blaize Salario of *My Purple Winter*. He was astonishingly youthful and vital for a thirty-eight-year veteran of the DOTD. He knew he appeared—at least by name—in Corley's fiction, but he professed little knowledge of the subject matter. Corley had kept his private life at home, Salario said. "He was a good man, a nice man."[118] He was, perhaps, a trickster as well.

Florence Watson, the DOTD's human resource manager, kindly retrieved and summarized Carl Corley's employee file for me. It shed more light on Corley's life story. In his 1961 application, Corley wrote that parental illness forced his resignation from the Mississippi State Highway Department after fourteen years. Corley was hired at the Louisiana DOTD in late 1961 and quickly worked his way up to head of the art and model shop, supervising three staff members. Though marred by wage garnishments in the

Carl Corley surrounded by the staff of the art and model shop, Louisiana Department of Transportation, ca. 1965. Files of the author.

early 1970s—apparently for failure to pay furniture debts—his file other-wise was exemplary. It was filled with numerous commendations: from the public relations officer, from the director, from a Bicentennial Commission officer, from a U.S. Treasury Department official, and from the governor, Edwin Edwards.[119]

Why, then, did the Louisiana Department of Transportation and Devel-opment fire Carl Corley on 1 July 1981, just a few months shy of the twenty-year-service mark, less than six months away from his sixtieth birthday? As I pondered this question, Watson made a few phone calls. She did some-thing that all my traditional historical methods had failed to do: she located Carl Corley. It seemed he was alive and well, still residing outside Zachary. This came as a shock to most DOTD employees who remembered him. Hadn't he resigned due to ill health? Didn't he succumb to liver disease?

The directions to Mr. Corley's residence were carefully given. He lived on a small tract off the side of a highway. You could easily miss it, I was warned. It was, after all, no more than a . . . "Shack?" I asked. Yes, some-thing like that.

I did miss Mr. Corley's place on the first try. Eventually, I found it. After a few yells and a few honks on my car horn, I saw him. He greeted me at the gate, wearing a soiled white T-shirt, white shorts, sandals, bandannas, Mardi Gras beads, and several rings, including a U.S. Marine Corps signet ring. On his right cheek, above white beard and mustache, was a faded blue star.[120]

Mr. Corley agreed to an interview, and I returned a few days later. He led me in through his ornate gardens of swept dirt, pebbled walkways, lawn statuary, profuse plants, and shade trees. We talked inside his home, a tiny but commodious half-trailer or camper, as his companion, a three-year-old Boston bulldog, barked at this rare visitor.

I found Mr. Corley hospitable, warm, and generous. But also embit-tered—by former publishers, by former employers. He was proud of his work and confident of its import. He gave me several copies of his by-now scarce pulp novels, including one title I didn't know, *The Different and the Damned* (1968). The editors had insisted it be published anonymously, given Corley's employment in state government.

I would later read its contents. Issued as a documentary and perhaps more confessional than any Corley novel, it chronicled a state employee falsely accused and acquitted of a morals charge in the 1960s. It detailed the subsequent harassment at home, on the streets, on the job. The threat of violence seemed at every turn. The author pleaded for social change. Fur-ther, this work suggested both a persecution complex and a messiah complex that I had intuited in other Corley works. Indeed, the main character of *Carl Corley's Illustrated History of Louisiana*, Pe'pa Paree—juxtaposed in profile against a matching photo of the author—bore a striking resemblance to the cartoon Jesus of *The Agony of Christ*, which was billed, with scant humility, as the author's "legacy to mankind."

Was Corley's work autobiographical, as I suspected? Yes, he told me, much of it was. But he had only one lover in the marines, a baseball player who died at Iwo Jima. It was the most significant relationship of his life. Mr. Corley didn't want to talk about his tattoo.

Yes, in Mississippi, he purchased physique and fitness magazines at newsstands in Jackson: "One of my ambitions [was] to be the greatest male physique artist of all." He devoted more time to writing once he relocated to Louisiana. By phone and mail, he had battled with pulp editors. They often butchered his texts, discarded his artwork. Corley got rid of his telephone when it no longer seemed necessary.

Somber in old age, hoping to see his eightieth birthday, Mr. Corley reflected on his primary wish in life: "I wanted to be a serious writer and a serious artist."

Carl Corley's desire for recognition—the proud use of his real name in an industry marked by pseudonyms—clashed with standards of conduct at his day job. Though often unspoken, fellow employees knew of his writings and speculated about their content. Undoubtedly, Corley's termination was the product of discrimination, as he explains:

> I was dismissed. The department had a new director. He wanted young people, and he was just dismissing the old ones. He dismissed me five months before my official retirement. I lost my complete retirement. I lost my $50,000 life insurance policy with the state. I was devastated. I put in some good years there. I had to start drawing Social Security ahead of time, three years in advance—which cut the Social Security income down. It was quite shocking. I had given so many years, and now I was denied. I bet you I have drawn up and lettered a thousand retirement certificates. And I didn't even get one for myself.[121]

Today, Louisiana DOTD employees remember the director's purge, the removal of several workers. But as at least two recall, Corley's termination likely involved not only age discrimination but also an ambiguous "personality conflict," which I interpret as heterosexism—a discrimination based on sexual orientation so well documented by oral history narrators in Mississippi. Though Corley's employment file says his termination was predicated on an "abuse of leave," it further notes his liver disease, the reason for his absences. As Blaise Salario comments, "Everybody knows the cure for hepatitis is extended bed rest."[122]

Carl Corley's life has been marked by struggle. He battled conventional hierarchies of cultural production as he generated narratives and images that both informed and were informed by prevailing representations of queer desire. He engaged and sometimes clashed with cultural mediators, those empowered to make or break careers in writing and the visual arts. To support his art, he toiled for almost thirty-five years in state bureaucracy that ultimately turned its back on him. In everyday life, he grappled with interpersonal hostilities and perceived threats of violence, graphically realized and reimagined in his novels.

Interweaving personal narrative, liberationist politics, queer fiction, and painting, Carl Corley told stories. Within and along the limits of cultural hegemonies, he elaborated racialized histories of queer Mississippians—himself and select others—in relationship to broader realms of queer cultural production and representation. The persistent partiality of their circulation, the ongoing negation of queer life, required constant struggle—to convey, extend, interrogate, and expand these notions of the past and the possible.[123]

Press and Plays

In midcentury Mississippi and beyond, the daily press was a principal source of information on gender nonconformity and homosexuality. More than highbrow fiction, soft-core erotica, or even popular film, newspapers reached audiences in urban, suburban, small-town, and rural locales. In addition to the weeklies published in most county seats, Jackson papers such as the morning *Clarion-Ledger* and evening *Jackson Daily News* were delivered throughout the state, on rural routes that often followed those of postal carriers. For the literate in Mississippi, reading normally involved the newspaper.

Press accounts of queer sexuality ordinarily fell into two categories. First, and most sensational, were hard news stories, usually of political scandal or homicide, as in the 1955 murder of John Murrett. Along with arrests for public sex, ever more common from the mid-1960s, these bits of information would produce a history of criminality, a history of calamity, if relied on exclusively. But second, and more subtle, were representations of representations. That is, in newspaper entertainment sections, feature writers described and critiqued cultural products that often imagined—on screen, on stage, and in print—scenarios of queer desire otherwise infrequently spoken or discussed. Critical reviews of fiction, film, song, and drama intimated and engaged the queer content of the subject in question.

In some cases, journalists evinced a need to smuggle out information not only about particular queer representations, but also about access to other sources, about developments in queer cultural production.

Over the two decades forming the middle of my period of study, 1955–1975, Mississippi's premiere cultural mediator, broadly, and principal queer medium, specifically, was Frank Woodruff Hains Jr. A native of Parkersburg, West Virginia, Frank Hains had graduated from Marietta College in Ohio, served two years in the military, then embarked on a radio career back in his hometown. That career eventually took him in 1951 to Vicksburg, where he met and had a brief fling with the young Mark Ingalls, whose mother Hains had befriended in local theater circles.[124]

After the *Jackson Daily News* hired Hains in 1955, he continued to volunteer as an actor and soon as a director of local stage productions, often with the Little Theatre of Jackson. When in 1956 Hains was given a daily column in the *Daily News,* he not only had the opportunity to promote amateur theater, but he also had occasion to comment on the myriad offerings of American mass culture. For the almost twenty years he penned his "On Stage" column, until his death in 1975, Hains demonstrated not only his impressive skills as a writer, but also his uncanny and venturous ability to locate and promulgate queer narratives.

To engage with such seemingly unspeakable subject matter and to remain in the employ of right-wing reactionaries Jimmy Ward—the editor-in-chief—and the Hederman brothers—the publishers—Hains had to develop and cultivate a loyal readership. This he did with a witty and charismatic style. Moreover, he willingly took on his role as taste maker, as cultural arbiter, with bravado and hyperbole. "Toscanini is dead," he wrote in 1957. "There is no other."[125] Hains also passed along to his readers a reverence for particular Broadway shows, holding up for special mention those productions he would see on his regular pilgrimage to New York. In the fifties, he boasted that he had been able to secure cherished tickets to "My Fair—uh, set that in caps please—MY FAIR LADY. Nuff said."[126]

Aside from his reviews, Hains spoke often of his favorite stars, noting the shrine in his home to Ethel Waters; his fascination with Talullah Bankhead, Bette Davis, and Judy Garland; his appreciation for the "muscular young" Tab Hunter. He drubbed his least preferred. He regularly carped on the inadequacies of Tupelo native Elvis Presley, and he even maligned Billy Graham, whose televised religious crusades once preempted local broadcast of the Metropolitan Opera. For this, Hains was forced to apologize.[127]

Honest and self-revealing, Hains shared select details of his personal life with his audience. His cat George made frequent appearances in his columns and was even depicted in a photo in a 1960 edition. Hains and

George received numerous fan letters from cat lovers, including one signed "Sam Cat." When a neighbor apparently poisoned George, letters of sympathy poured in. Mrs. J. L. Shields, wife of the Tchula mayor, urged Hains to "find another pet. . . . [I]t will be company to you, and you will love it."[128] Mrs. Shields not only lamented the loss of George; she lamented the loss of companionship for Hains.

Readers knew Hains lived alone. When a local TV celebrity—one of the first women to forecast the weather in Mississippi—prepared to wed a young engineer with a name similar to Hains's, the columnist's colleagues kidded him about the impossibility of his marrying. Sharing with his fans this preposterous notion, Hains penned a satirical column about his "non-engagement."[129] And yet, Hains still had to keep up certain appearances of masculinity—or at least join in the ribbing with self-deprecating humor. In 1964 he devoted a lengthy column to his first manicure, imploring his readers with an ironic, secret-revealing subhead "NOW, DON'T LET THIS GET AROUND."[130]

But such campy disavowals and indirections characterized much of Hains's writing, as it did much twentieth-century queer representation.[131] Hains regularly called upon the adjective *gay* to describe any number of phenomena, and he coded his queer desire in even more tantalizing puzzles. His unflattering but lengthy review of the 1958 film *The Vikings*, for example, focused on the mostly male cast and the lead, Eric, played by Tony Curtis. The column included a subhead, in bold lettering, conceding, "WELL, THE SCENERY'S NICE ANYWAY . . ." The line directly underneath read, "This means that Eric is—" (The sentence continued on the following lines: "by maternal descent at any rate—heir to the throne.")[132]

But Hains didn't evade queer subject matter. Quite the contrary, he sought it out, labeled it, and, in a sense, thereby produced it. Under the prevailing Motion Picture Code, screen engagements with homosexuality were characterized by nuance and finesse. Hains took pleasure in de-Coding. As theorist Novid Parsi notes, up to the present day "ambiguity of meaning . . . gets decoded by the knowing critic as not ambiguous at all."[133] While this creates unnecessarily fixed distinctions between the homosexual and heterosexual, the queer and the normal, Hains apparently found it necessary in 1950s Mississippi to call attention to what he saw as queer relationships in film. What seemingly couldn't or wouldn't be said on screen, Hains stated baldly in his column.

"Here is the major problem which the screen has had," Hains wrote in his review of the "tremendously exciting film" *Cat on a Hot Tin Roof*: "to imply without clearly stating it, the homosexual relationship between the husband and the friend." [134] When the Jackson Little Theatre staged its own production of the Tennessee Williams play in 1959, Hains took another occasion to address the topic—in the program notes. About the toned-down film version of the play, he wrote, "Some felt that the allegation of a homosexual relationship between Brick and his football player friend [Skipper] was so glossed over as to be lost completely. I felt that it was made as tastefully clear as the films are permitted to do." [135] Indeed, if it wasn't made clear, Hains was doing his part to clarify.

In his 1959 review of *Compulsion*, based on the Leopold and Loeb case of 1924, Hains made clear that the Loeb character was "the strong man in the king-slave fantasy which was the keynote of the youths' homosexual relationship." [136] Hains went all out in his coverage of the 1956 film *Tea and Sympathy*. He not only gave it a complimentary review and spelled out the central tension of a "tortured youth who is convinced by [his classmates'] tauntings and derision that he is the homosexual that they believe him to be"; he also decried the "thoughtless cruelty of the herd." [137] Further, in an additional day's coverage of *Tea and Sympathy*, he told his readers how to secure a copy of the novel on which the movie was based: he gave them the publisher's name and told them the price of the inexpensive paperback edition, a rarity in his column. [138]

Nothing got Frank Hains riled up like censorship. Indeed, cries of censorship proved a viable liberal strategy for safeguarding representations of radical queer sexuality. In early January 1957, Tennessee Williams's troubling film *Baby Doll*—about the psychosexual dynamics of a married couple in Mississippi—was banned from Jackson to Brookhaven, where a committee representing eleven thousand Lincoln County Baptists branded the film "degrading" and where the mayor "vow[ed the] police w[ould] enforce the ban on the 'dirty' movie." [139] Censorship was not limited to Mississippi, however. New York's Cardinal Spellman denounced *Baby Doll* as "revolting," "deplorable," "morally repellent," and "grievously offensive to Christian standards of decency." The Catholic Legion of Decency rated it "condemned for all." [140] National media generally deplored it. Writing for the *Saturday Review*, Arthur Knight asserted that "Williams's story smelt of the sewer," though "it had at least the virtue of being authentic sewer." [141] Worse still, Williams's playwriting as a whole was "an unconscious attack on heterosexuality." [142] *Time* magazine called *Baby Doll*—shot on location in Benoit, Mississippi—"possibly the dirtiest American-made motion picture that has ever been legally exhibited. . . . [T]he language of Tennessee Williams, no less than his subject matter, often seems to have been borrowed from one of the more carelessly written pornographic pulps." [143]

While *Time* castigated writer Williams and director Elia Kazan, and applauded in a related story the Motion Picture Code's continued ban on film depictions of "perversion," Frank Hains gave *Baby Doll* a highly favorable notice in his "On Stage" column. Moreover, he wrote a valiant defense of the film, appearing on the *Jackson Daily News* front page, under photographs of combatants in the city council deliberations. *Baby Doll,* Hains insisted, was "in fact, a moral sermon—an outspoken indictment of ignorance." Suppressing its showing would "be in flagrant abrogation of the rights of free choice which Mississippians have so long and so vehemently claimed. [It] will make all future protestations of belief in personal freedom mere lip-service to a hollow hypocrisy and a barren lie."[144]

Little more than a year after he was hired by Jimmy Ward and the Hedermans, Frank Hains was brave enough to pen this and other defenses of perverse sexuality—or, more precisely, of representations of perverse sexuality. Indeed, this was the very crux of Hains's approach and success. Whereas homosexuality and gender nonconformity were often considered taboo subject matter in 1950s America—even in the pulpits of 1950s Mississippi—they were nonetheless obliquely written and screened. Hains could further engage queerness by filtering it through criticism of those plays and films that only alluded to it. Hains's criticism was candid where movies were subtle, direct where plays were sometimes circuitous. In a manner not unlike the coded films of the fifties, moreover, Hains wrote about himself—as an unmarried aesthete, living in the context of Mississippi's quiet accommodationism.

As Chon Noriega has noted of movie media at midcentury, "Censorship incited and multiplied discourse within the field of 'non-filmic events'— literary sources, film reviews, editorials, and advertisements."[145] Controversy bred discussion; discussion bred controversy. As a purveyor of non-filmic events, Frank Hains helped promulgate queerness. As critical readers of these media, Hains's audience helped destabilize any given, pat, official, or unitary reading of queerness, as portrayed in print and visual culture.

Though the queer cast of his columns became more muted over the years—perhaps a reflection of increased hostility to queer sexuality from the 1960s onward—Hains still consistently defied official ideologies. Just days before the 1965 City Auditorium arrests, he devoted three separate stories in the *Jackson Daily News* arts pages, which he now edited, to the University of Southern Mississippi production of Lillian Hellman's *The Children's Hour.* Though the play in Hattiesburg, Hains wrote, "is generally considered, of course, to be about Lesbianism, [it] is not, per se." Rather, "it

Theater director and *Jackson Daily News* arts editor Frank Hains with cast members from *Annie Get Your Gun*, 1958. Courtesy of Mississippi Department of Archives and History.

is about the damage done by a lie."[146] Nonetheless, by explicitly stating the lesbian theme or subtheme, Hains pointed queer audiences to yet another queer performance, at the same time that he urged all his readers to see the work. Also that same month, Hains included yet another of his covert references to things queer in his "On Stage" column—a review of the "interesting and genuinely inventive" films of Kenneth Anger, which he had viewed on a recent trip to New York.[147]

More than a Mississippi mediator of mainstream and alternative cultural production in American, Frank Hains was a cultural producer. Through his own columns and feature stories and those of his staff, he crafted a coherent editorial stance that rewarded artistic works of ingenuity, innovation, and daring. He espoused freedom of expression, and he particularly defended works on queer sexuality.

Also, Frank Hains helped stage his own dramatic and musical productions in cities and towns, at schools and universities, across Mississippi. With the mantle of director or critic, Hains could create and interact in distinctly queer settings while drawing scant consternation. Indeed, among numerous plays, Hains would mount several, mostly male productions at Jackson's Little Theatre; he would make casting calls for young men in the pages of the *Jackson Daily News*. And yet, at a time when male homosexuality was equated in the popular imaginary with child molestation, Little Theatre executive director Jane Petty would proudly declare (and justify) in the stage-bill notes the fact that Frank Hains "likes teen-agers. Frank's mature sympathy for and understanding of the problems, attitudes and interests peculiar to the almost-grownup brought him merited national recognition . . . when he was picked for a Warner Award, given for service to young people."[148]

Readings, rehearsals, performances, and cast parties generated an intense but festive milieu that gave Hains and others reprieve from the limits of the everyday. Theater gatherings fostered the envisioning of alternative realities. In the world of make-believe that theater inspired, actors and audience members suspended convention and played out fantasy. Under such conditions, queer interaction was enabled among the gay- and non-gay-identified. As lighting technician and bit-part actor Eddie Sandifer recalls: "There were quite a few gays that were involved in the Little Theatre, even though some of the men laughed and talked about getting rid of the queers. They'd say it right in front of me. They never got rid of them. Some of the ones doing the talking were guilty of doing things too. Had wives and fat kids, but that's OK."[149] No matter how queer friendly the theater appeared, as in real life unfriendly colleagues had to be negotiated. They might sneer one moment; they might pursue male-male desire the next.

Participating in and commenting on a uniquely Mississippi queer dramatic tradition—a tradition spanning from film and Broadway versions of Tennessee Williams's *Cat on a Hot Tin Roof* and Mart Crowley's internationally acclaimed *The Boys in the Band*[150] to local runs of these and other works—Frank Hains interjected queer renderings into a broader normalized discourse over the state of the arts in America. He directed, acted in, or wrote about plays that reached audiences and engaged cast members from throughout the region. Most poignantly, his daily column, read by Mississippians from the country to the city, produced and circulated queer argot, representations, and experiences. Whether identifying and creating queer texts or recounting his own queer narratives, Hains helped point the way for innumerable queer Mississippians.

TRAGICALLY, FRANK HAINS became the subject of that most clichéd of journalistic accounts of homosexuality: the homosexual homicide narrative. As the *Jackson Daily News* and papers throughout the region reported in mid-

July 1975, Hains was the victim of a brutal murder at the age of forty-nine. His body was found in his 616 Webster Street home early on the morning of 14 July by Kevin Sessums, a nineteen-year-old "theater associate who was residing temporarily with Hains."[151] According to police, Hains was naked, bound, and gagged, facedown on his bed, apparently killed by a blow to the back of the head.

Jackson police arrested former janitor Larry Bullock, twenty-four, a native of Louise, Mississippi, and—as one newspaper article made clear in the first line—"a black man."[152] Bullock previously had been arrested for sodomy, other "sex offenses," and first-degree murder in Indiana. At trial, Bullock's attorneys argued that Hains's "indiscriminate associations" meant that "anyone" could have committed the "sadomasochistic" murder.[153] The judge instructed the jury to disregard Hains's alleged homosexuality, unless the killing was in response to a homosexual attack—the ever-present legal defense of homosexual panic. In less than three hours, the jury found Bullock guilty. He was sent to Mississippi's notorious state penitentiary, Parchman prison, in the Delta.

A few months later, Larry Bullock was stabbed to death by a fellow inmate. There was scant speculation as to the circumstances or motive in the newspaper accounts of this killing.[154]

Obituaries and memorial articles described Frank Hains as a widely loved community member and a respected writer. Famed Mississippi author Eudora Welty, a longtime friend, said "he was a positive critic, and never a defeating one," possessed of a mind that was "first-rate—informed, uncommonly quick and sensitive, keenly responsive." His life, she wrote, was "made up of thousands of unrecorded kindnesses."[155] Hains's *Daily News* colleague Charles B. Gordon penned a more dubious memoriam. While he expressed sympathy for the "poor fellow who stood charged with Hains' slaying," he characterized Hains's life of "books, art, music, literature" as "slightly constricted." Hains, Gordon wrote, had "devoted himself to [that life's] ramifications."[156]

But the lead editorial in the 15 July 1975 issue of the *Jackson Daily News*, perhaps offered by Jimmy Ward himself, spoke with pride of Hains's accomplishments and of the admiration he earned in life.

A man of extraordinary talent and writing ability, Mr. Hains always maintained the highest level of devotion to his profession. His energetic and faithful performance of duty gained for him [a] reputation [as] one of the most respected arts editors in the South. . . . Ever a gentleman, he represented the epitome of graciousness. Violence, by which he died, was not of his being. He abhorred it.[157]

Reprise

On Wednesday morning, 23 March 1988, at the stately Cathedral of Saint Andrew, on Capitol Street in Jackson, friends and family members gathered for the funeral service of Dr. Benjamin P. Folk Jr. With the Episcopal priest, the congregants recited Psalm 121: "I lift up my eyes to the hills—from where will my help come? My help comes from the Lord, who made heaven and earth." They were read the words of Jesus, which reverberated off the bricks and stained-glass windows of the Gothic structure: "Do not let your hearts be troubled. Believe in God, believe also in me" (John 14:1).[158] At that moment, throughout the state, Mississippians again opened their papers to find out the latest news in this particular iteration of the homosexual homicide narrative: the arrests of two suspects in the Ben Folk case. An increasingly clear picture of the murder began to emerge.

Three days prior at 5:00 P.M., on Sunday, 20 March, in his pricey East-brooke condominium in northeast Jackson, Dr. Ben Folk, age seventy, was found dead by "two male houseguests returning from lunch." Folk's throat had been cut from "ear to ear." Folk—a graduate of Vanderbilt Medical School, a fellow of Johns Hopkins School of Medicine, and a decorated World War II veteran—was well-known in Mississippi. Among the state's most distinguished physicians, he had retired after a thirty-six-year practice; he had helped found the exclusive River Hills Tennis Club, just up Lakeland Drive from his home.[159] Relying on Folk's two sons for corroboration, reporters were reticent to mention Folk's failed marriage, his coming out as gay, the forced withdrawal from his medical partnership, and his later sole practice, tending to the needs of, among others, gay and transsexual clients, including Rickie Leigh Smith.[160]

The *Jackson Daily News*, however, did not shrink from publishing sensational developments in the murder case on the morning of the funeral: "Jackson police," the story began, "finding leather straps hanging from bedposts and sex devices scattered around the townhouse of a slain physician, are investigating whether homosexuality and drug use played roles in his Sunday throat-slashing."[161] Two unemployed twenty-four-year-olds, Kenneth Overby and John Tyler—whom the doctor apparently knew—were arrested. Police said robbery was the motive.

Overby and Tyler lived together in nearby Brandon, but they blamed one another for the murder, as their attorneys attempted to arrange plea bargains. Since Overby was HIV-positive, Tyler's attorney offered to "help authorities and the state Health Department" by providing them with a list of all those individuals with whom Overby had had sexual relations. Overby, who first turned himself in to police, said Tyler committed the murder while he waited outside repairing their car, which the two pushed away from the crime scene. Overby further led police to stolen goods, the murder weapon, and Tyler's bloodstained clothing.

Overby consequently was allowed to plead guilty to accessory charges; Tyler was convicted of robbery and homicide.[162] Like Frank Hains's murderer, Larry Bullock, Ben Folk's murderer, John Tyler, would die while serving time.[163]

DR. BEN FOLK'S DEATH, like that of Frank Hains, generated significant media and popular interest, as did the John Murrett case decades prior. Such interest reflected the race and class biases inherent in news reporting and police inquiry over the second half of the twentieth century. Whose murder got covered? Whose murderer got pursued? At the end of the period, law enforcement in Mississippi—homophobic though they may be—would be expected to track down and prosecute the killers of a twenty-year columnist for the state's leading newspaper and a venerable white physician from a long-standing elite family. No longer, however, would they aggressively pursue more difficult, legally complicated cases involving ordinary queer victims—say, a lower-middle-income one-year resident, as was John Murrett.

Further, the lengthy, prominently placed television and press accounts of these more notorious crimes and trials produced and reproduced insidious notions of homosexuality in the American imagination: Gay men were among the established artistic and professional elite, yet they led shadowy double lives. They engaged in risky behaviors and consequently paid the price when they came into contact with a younger, fully debased, homicidal queer underclass. The popular fascination with and the dominant discourse of homosexual homicide functioned alongside and in conversation with the homosexual suicide mythology previously discussed. Thus, long before the onset of AIDS and its own politically charged metaphors, Mississippians perceived homosexuality as deadly dangerous.

Such hegemonic discourses are easily replicated over time. These narratives are retold as lore, but they are also institutionally guarded and, if we allow, resuscitated and recirculated. That is, because these are the most respected and revered citizens, their stories are reported; because these are the most visible and available accounts, they are collected; the newspaper stories are clipped and maintained in the archives, waiting for the historian to (re)discover them and (re)document them. With ambivalence, I choose to retell these narratives, in order to critique them. Such stories must always be understood as tiny slivers, incompletely documented fragments of a complex, but necessarily partial and biased mosaic of queer life.

CHAPTER SIX

Politics and Beliefs

God made man in his own image; and if the world is badly run, it is because we have not used our divine intelligence to our natural desire and need to love and be loved.

—AARON HENRY [1]

AS CHRISTMAS 1982 APPROACHED, readers of *This Month in Mississippi,* published by the Mississippi Gay Alliance, took notice of an exceptionally vitriolic article in the December issue. Entitled "Christianity's Intolerance of Gays," the piece opened in a deliberate, rational tone:

> Today, there seems to be an attempt on the part of many Gay people to accommodate Christianity into their lifestyles. This seems . . . like . . . fitting round pegs into square holes. Unfortunately, many Gay people find it difficult to take an honest look at the history of Christianity. They have been so thoroughly indoctrinated since childhood that to question these dogmas can be compared to renouncing one's parentage or even truth itself.

A historical enumeration of church abuses followed. By the conclusion, gay Christians were dubbed (oxy)morons, as inconceivable as Jewish Nazis or black Klansmen. "Some Gays may consider themselves Christians," the author surmised, "but when I think of what Christianity has done to Gay people, I can only regret the lack of lions in the Roman Empire." [2]

Written by Don Sanders, vice president of the Gay Atheists League of America, Houston, Texas, the article likely drew few sympathizers. While Christianity, especially Protestant evangelicalism, increasingly fueled much of the bigotry directed at them, many queer Mississippians were reluctant to fully relinquish ties to their religious past. Brought up in the heart of the Bible Belt, often in communities so small that the church served as the primary sociocultural institution, they sometimes drifted away, especially when acknowledgment of their sexuality left them feeling alienated, but they rarely severed all connections.

In fact, the institutional merging of Christian faith and homosexual orientation was about to attain a watershed in the state. Just after the new year, 1983, in the capital of Jackson, organizers announced plans to form a local congregation of the Metropolitan Community Church, a Protestant denomination ministering mainly to lesbian and gay parishioners. Founded by a southerner in Los Angeles almost fifteen years earlier, MCC boasted a national and international following. Affiliated churches flourished in urban centers across the country, such as Nashville and New Orleans. Yet their spread had only lately reached many smaller cities in the South. Political and popular resistance in Mississippi would be fierce, just as allegiance from spiritually inclined lesbians, gays, bisexuals, and transgender persons would be intense. By December 1983 *This Month in Mississippi* reported that after a "long, rough row . . . things [we]re definitely looking up for the Metropolitan Community Church of Jackson."[3] In its wake, public discourse on homosexuality had mushroomed in Mississippi. The state's fledgling gay movement—scarcely twenty-five years old and only ten years active—was radically altered in its direction. And for a couple dozen members of MCC and many more across the state who followed the events, personal religious reconciliation had begun.

Protestant Christianity became the center around which lesbian and gay life and politics turned. Whereas since the 1960s persecution had been directed from religious sectors and patterned on scriptural references, perhaps a majority of queer Mississippians clung to other aspects of church doctrine and ritual. These queer Christians, black and white, rarely responded to a narrow gay movement driven by identity politics. Instead, they joined only when a more expansive definition of gayness was fashioned. Leadership came to recognize this phenomenon and eventually encouraged MCC's entry into the local arena. The backlash from religious right fundamentalists and mainline churches meant an increased level of hostility in the short run; but the discourse it fostered and the attention it focused on lesbians, gays, bisexuals, and transgender persons forged greater levels of community solidarity and political power over the long run. With the successful establishment of the Metropolitan Community Church in Jackson, a new era dawned on lesbian and gay organizing and institution building in Mississippi.

Homophile Rights, Civil Rights, Gay Rights

Queer organizing in Mississippi began as early as 1959, with the establishment of a local branch of an Austin, Texas–based organization. Wrapped in the language of science and education, Wicker Research Studies was the brainchild of college student Randy Wicker. Wicker had met Mississippian Eddie Sandifer in the summer of 1958 at a New York meeting of the secretive Mattachine Society;[4] and by early 1959, Sandifer was an officer of the tristate Wicker Research Studies, convening meetings in Jackson. In this sense, Wicker Research Studies was a southern manifestation of a national "homophile movement," of which Mattachine was but a part. Wicker Research Studies took its credo verbatim from the San Francisco–based lesbian organization Daughters of Bilitis, as printed in DOB's monthly publication, *The Ladder*.[5]

No less than Mattachine and DOB, Wicker Research Studies relied on secrecy—false names and clandestine operations. Such measures well suited the quiet accommodationism characteristic of queer life in fifties Mississippi. As Eddie Sandifer remembers:

> The founder, the one that started it—Randy Wicker, who uses that name still, Charles G. Hayden Jr.—he was in Texas at the university at the time. There was Randy one, two, and three. Randy was number one, a [college student in] Louisiana was number two, and I was number three, Randy Wicker three. We had a local meeting here at my house, and the mail came down on McDowell Road here to Meadowlane Station, a little store. That was the mailing address. We had a pamphlet [and] only one paper we put out.[6]

Wicker Research Studies quickly passed. The state of Mississippi denied its request for incorporation. Worse still, "it was hard to get blacks *or* whites to come to meetings," Sandifer remembers. Upon graduation, Wicker left Texas for New York. Sandifer toughed it out in Mississippi.

As civil rights activism took Mississippi by storm in the 1960s, police targeted homosexuals in and outside the movement. Queer organizing all but ceased. On occasion a coalition of leftists—not specifically gay-identified—protested antihomosexual initiatives, utilizing broader calls for free speech and freedom of expression. Queer writing found outlets in late-sixties left-wing counterculture publications such as the underground newspaper *Kudzu*, printed in Jackson and distributed on high school and college campuses throughout the state. But Sandifer remembers it as a time of retrenchment, a time of great repression as compared to the forties and fifties.

Longtime gay rights activist Eddie Sandifer, *center*—convener of the Mississippi
branch of Wicker Research Studies (1959) and head of the Mississippi Gay Alliance
(founded in 1973)—shown here unusually dressed up for a minor role in a Jackson
Little Theatre production, 1955. Courtesy of Mississippi Department of Archives
and History.

In 1968, when the Jackson Federation of Women's Clubs forced the city
council to ban a local screening of *The Fox*, pickets formed outside city hall.
Women and men carried signs reading: "THE TRUTH SHALL SET YOU FREE."
But official Mississippi dug in its heels. *Jackson Daily News* editor Jimmy
Ward acknowledged that he had "not seen the film." Nonetheless, he understood its hazards: "All the reviews by responsible critics I have read
describe the movie as a sack of trash featuring the love affair between two
women. . . . Few mature persons would want to view sordidness of that
nature unless afforded the facilities to take a shower before, during and
immediately after the show. . . ." *Kudzu* editors made fun of Ward's puritan-
ism: "Mr. Ward, if you need a shower after thinking about a movie on homosexuals, if you get *that* sexually excited, we suggest that you see a psychiatrist, or can the crap and go enjoy the movie!"[7]

However, in late-sixties Mississippi, counterculture advocates of free
(heterosexual) love and a particular kind of gender nonconformity rarely
espoused homosexuality, at least in public. More commonly, male long-
hairs resented the fact that their parents and other authority figures called
them "fruits." Many white left-wingers—supporters of sex, drugs, rock 'n'
roll, and radical politics—disavowed queer tendencies.[8]

Like lesbian and gay movements in other American sections, concerted and highly visible gay political activity in the South emerged in the early 1970s. Partially informed by New York's Stonewall Riots of June 1969 and descended from the civil rights, women's, and student movements, early organizations such as the Gay Liberation Front (GLF) championed a holistic radical politics encompassing a wide array of leftist causes.[9] The South harbored high-minded revolutionary sentiment, as a core group of Atlanta organizers started a vibrant but short-lived local cell of the GLF in 1971. Weekly meetings, one former member recalls, borrowed from feminist consciousness-raising techniques. Participants discussed "the evils of sexism, racism, capitalism" and learned "a smattering of Marxism." However, they mostly "focused on the plague of sexual objectification, sexist language, and oppressive looksist standards running rampant among gay men."[10]

Lesbian and gay political dissent in Mississippi was no less radical in its tenets. In 1973 the Mississippi Gay Alliance appeared on the scene with its founding chapter in Starkville, led by lesbian faculty and students at Mississippi State University. Soon headquartered in Jackson and spearheaded by the daringly outspoken Eddie Sandifer, the group's stance on many issues inevitably reflected his own political worldview. A self-described Trotskyist, Sandifer was born in Cotton Valley, in rural Webster Parish, Louisiana, in 1929, the son of a Baptist preacher. He moved to McComb, Mississippi, in 1945. Involved from that time in the American Communist Party, he attracted considerable attention. "It was out and about town," he says, "that I was a Commie, a queer, and a nigger lover."[11]

Sandifer, like Randy Wicker, was involved in civil rights protests in the South and, like so many early homophile activists, participated in a range of left causes, including equal treatment initiatives for senior citizens and the disabled. Sandifer's experience, perhaps more than any others', demonstrates how queer rights were linked to and thwarted in the wake of the black struggle for equality, a struggle consistently red-baited as well. Though he was well-known since the 1940s as a communist, homosexual, and civil rights activist, Sandifer never suffered harassment based on his sexual orientation until the 1960s, when he hosted freedom riders in his Jackson home. As historian Donna Jo Smith concludes, "His account of the ways in which his sexuality was used as a weapon in local battles to maintain white dominance parallels similar reports surfacing in research on lesbian/gay experience throughout the South during the 1960s. [It] reveals how ideologies of race and sex have been inextricably intertwined in the South."[12]

Though he was "a strong believer in armed revolution," Sandifer also possessed enough political savvy to moderate his statements during the

MGA's early years.[13] In 1975 he told a reporter that MGA's official position was that "homosexuals have the same rights as heterosexuals. This includes the right to sexual acts between consenting adults . . . [and] the right to show affection in public—kissing and holding hands."[14] In a state with a strict sodomy code, Sandifer alluded to the specter of civil disobedience by supporting sexual intercourse between women and between men, but he tempered his words with references to public displays of affection—acts that, while no doubt repulsive and confrontational to many Mississippians, at least were not illegal. Moreover, Sandifer characterized the alliance's primary purpose as alleviating prejudice through education, a common programmatic method in traditional liberal interest–group politics. The alliance supported "educational programs on campuses and [on] radio and television, counseling for members, and activities including gay pride week"[15]—again, a local manifestation of a broader gay cultural phenomenon.

The same reporter questioned an unofficial and unnamed spokesperson for the Gay Activist League of Mississippi (GALM), a Jackson organization that didn't enjoy the longevity of the MGA. In a rare mainstream press engagement with issues of religion and homosexuality, the GALM member responded directly and caustically. Persecution of lesbians and gays amounted to a violation of the First Amendment protection of freedom of religion because, he said, "anti-homosexual statutes [we]re based on Judeo-Christian moral codes" and as such they represented "an imposition of religion on the majority of us." While not defining its parameters, he referred to a monolithic "Judeo-Christian culture . . . that is unequivocally anti-sexual."[16] He pointed out several European and Latin American countries that, though no less devout, had decriminalized homosexual practices, and he suggested that the United States, collectively and individually, follow suit.

The MGA attacked religious fundamentalism in the person of Anita Bryant. After her successful campaign to overturn Dade County, Florida's antidiscrimination ordinance, the pop singer and orange juice spokesperson took her antihomosexual "Save Our Children" message on the road to Southern Baptist conferences and various other public engagements in 1977. "Once you allow special privileges for a radical group like that," she chimed, "then you have to do it for the prostitutes, you have to do it for the one who has a sexual preference with [sic] a German shepherd. . . ."[17]

While hundreds, sometimes thousands, protested her appearances in major American cities, the MGA was able to mobilize twelve for a rally when Bryant came to town for the Mississippi State Fair. In his speech to those assembled on 12 October, Eddie Sandifer, state president of the MGA, said: "I feel the same way towards Anita Bryant that I do toward any fascist right-winger that is oppressing other people."[18] A few months earlier, a group of MGA members had driven three hours south, where they took part in what *Workers' World* called "the largest lesbian and gay demonstration ever in New Orleans," in reaction to Bryant's appearance there.[19] The MGA was said to be one of the largest contingents among the estimated three thousand marchers.

More typical of MGA activities during the 1970s was the monitoring and reporting of police harassment of queer Mississippians, especially in the Smith Park area. Covering one city block directly behind the governor's mansion, between it and the new Capitol Building, Smith Park had long been an after-dark meeting place. It sometimes attracted Jackson's gay bar-goers. Known for drag shows and dancing, the predominantly white Mae's Cabaret (later renamed Jack's) and the predominantly black Bill's Club were located just three blocks down Amite Street, across the street from one another. But more commonly, the park was frequented by persons who couldn't or wouldn't support the bars. Some refused to patronize Mae's, calling it "a social club run for friends of the owner."[20] "Smith Park People"—mostly white but also black males—cultivated varied styles of identification and visibility. At one end of the spectrum, they included married, middle-class, middle-age men who circled the park in their cars, hoping to discreetly meet a partner for the most anonymous of sexual encounters or for ongoing relations of many kinds. For many such men, being seen in a gay bar was unthinkable. At the other end were out-of-the-closet gay men, cross-dressers, and male sex workers. Estranged from the self-acknowledged but circumspect bar crowd, they were often young, from lower-income groups, willing to hustle for a living. Still, this spectrum simplifies. Smith Park harbored a queer miscellany of individuals, marked by diverse configurations of age, race, class, gender, identity, desire—and place. As many oral history narrators attest, rural and small-town motorists regularly "checked out" such notorious queer haunts whenever driving through the area—just as city dwellers frequented the park's rural equivalent, the roadside rest area.

The Jackson Police Department (JPD) targeted the men at Smith Park. According to one gay member of the JPD, superiors instructed officers to "give hell" to "those queers at the park."[21] Implicit in these orders, in the view of many gay men, was a proviso to lay off the bars, which they said made payoffs to the police.[22] Thus, Jackson law enforcement lent legitimacy to the quasi-private, sequestered spaces of gay commercial establishments while attempting to cordon off public spaces from use by so-called undesirables.

Eddie Sandifer personally was the victim of police harassment in Smith Park on the night of 25 September 1976 (two weeks after Aaron Henry was caught up in a JPD sting operation there). Three uniformed policemen confronted Sandifer, William McLemore, and Steve Pond around midnight and threatened to arrest them for disturbing the peace and interfering with an officer in the line of duty. As described in his formal complaint against the department, Sandifer and his two friends were patrolling the park as part of a safety and visibility campaign by the MGA and its supporters—"ministers, lawyers, reporters, young and old, from babes in arms to 75 years old, male and female, black and white, gay and straight."[23] Volunteers cleaned the park, monitored police activity, and advised persons against sleeping there or making disparaging remarks to officers. Sandifer had informed the department of the MGA patrols, adding that volunteers could be readily identified by the pink triangles they wore. Despite (or perhaps due to) the triangles, Sandifer and his two friends, one in a wheelchair, were forcibly removed from the park that September evening.

A U.S. Civil Rights Commission adviser labeled the incident one of "a series of police department maneuvers to harass members of Jackson's gay community."[24] In assessing these reports, along with an unrelated case of police brutality resulting in wrongful death, the official concluded in 1977 that the department's complaint process was shrouded in secrecy, completely closed to outside review, and that internal investigation procedures remained undefined. Not only queer citizens, but a significant portion of the city's residents—especially African Americans—had come to distrust the police force. Disputes raged in the local newspapers between Jackson mayor Russell Davis and police chief Lavell Tullos, on the one hand, and Civil Rights Commission regional director Bobby Doctor, on the other.

Thus another explicit linkage between gay rights and civil rights was manifested. That a U.S. Civil Rights Commission official addressed gay issues and that its regional body consciously focused on bias against queer Mississippians were particularly significant, given that the principal enabling federal legislation—the Civil Rights Act of 1964—did not cover discrimination based on sexual orientation. Still, racial bigotry and queer baiting, as we have seen, had long been entangled. Indeed, Eddie Sandifer became a target of queer bias in Mississippi not for his communist sympathies, but for his involvement in the African American struggle for equality. It was Sandifer and the MGA that subsequently pressed the Civil Rights Commission to intervene in Mississippi on behalf of lesbians and gays.

In September 1979 Sandifer again appeared before the commission charging Jackson police officers with soliciting and entrapping gay men in illegal sex acts in Smith Park. Specifically, he singled out Officer David Pinson, the subject of numerous complaints. Captain Joe Alford, head of the vice and narcotics division, defended Pinson. "You can't entrap somebody who starts playing with your legs," he said. "We don't have to approach anybody up there [in Smith Park]. You can't stay there for five minutes any night without one of them trying to play with you."[25] Alford thereby confirmed the considerable police presence in the small Jackson park. And chief of detectives J. L. Black acknowledged "furnish[ing] the bait" by utilizing undercover officers. Black was intransigent in the face of criticism: "The officers are already performing an unpleasant task and don't deserve this kind of abuse. We are going to enforce the law against homosexual acts, and we will not be intimidated."[26]

Mississippi Gay Alliance activities also included occasional legal actions, educational forums, and hate group monitoring through its Jackson headquarters and through a handful of local chapters elsewhere in the state. In 1976 at the U.S. Circuit Court of Appeals in New Orleans, MGA unsuccessfully challenged the refusal of Mississippi State University's student newspaper to print an MGA advertisement.[27] (As recently as 1990 the newspaper, *The Reflector*, rejected an ad from the newly organized campus group Gays, Lesbians and Friends.) MGA found a reliable ally in the American Civil Liberties Union of Mississippi, which sponsored a forum on sexual privacy in 1975, but this and other events garnered relatively little support from lesbian and gay Mississippians.[28] Though he did amass a protest group of thirty in 1976—fewer still in 1979—in response to police harassment allegations, Eddie Sandifer was the sole MGA observer at an antigay Ku Klux Klan rally held on 10 October 1981, in Smith Park. The lead speaker, Grand Dragon Gale Gordon, advocated the caging of homosexuals, and he encouraged listeners to take back "Queer Park." Robed member Jessie Sanford snapped photographs of Sandifer.[29]

Though constantly under siege, the Mississippi Gay Alliance proved a vital lifeline for queers in Jackson and across the state. Its mere existence gave heart to those who, due to a sheer lack of numbers, felt alienated in the countryside. Its high profile meant greater ease in connecting previously disparate and sometimes incohesive networks of men like that. Even official Mississippi had to own up to MGA's determination and resilience. Jimmy Ward's *Jackson Daily News* received queries of its advice columnist as early as 1974 from readers who wanted to contact the MGA. "I can't reveal my name," one letter writer confided, "because of the small town in which I live." The columnist supplied the invaluable data to the writer, who signed his letter "One of them."[30]

But Sandifer candidly recalls the frustrations of mounting a gay political movement in Mississippi, a movement he continues to lead as director of the renamed Mississippi Gay and Lesbian Alliance: "You have a few people that'll do all the work, and you have a lot of people willing to pay dues if you ask for dues, but they're not willing to get politicized."[31] In the 1970s MGA membership never totaled more than a few dozen, with white membership always vastly outnumbering black. Influenced as it was by identity politics, most notably an increasingly national lesbian and gay movement, gay organizing clashed with local sensibilities, queer and nonqueer. For decades, sexual deviants and gender nonconformists in Mississippi had functioned quietly but effectively within rural and small-town contexts, outmaneuvering hostile forces. Queer Mississippians even in remote parts of the state were nonetheless visible and available *to one another*. Gay politics required a *different* sort of visibility. Most disturbingly, it required clear-cut identity statements, individuals' open and *public* avowal of homosexuality, a speech act that some belligerent lawmakers and law enforcers interpreted as a felony in and of itself (attempted sodomy). And many queer Mississippians—even those like Baptist Joe Holmes, who renounced the teachings of his youth, embraced liberal politics, and identified as gay— found Sandifer unkempt, his methods brusque and shrill.[32]

Further, the category *gay* didn't well encompass the range and inventiveness of sexual and gender nonnormativity in Mississippi. And it made few allowances for those whose sexual and gender nonnormativity served as a relatively insignificant component of identity. For African Americans, for example, to participate in gay organizing meant to participate in yet another white-controlled, white-dominated institution. Though homosexuality and gender insubordination clearly weren't just a white thing, gay political organizing for the most part was.

As the seventies gave way to the eighties and as the effects of the Reagan revolution began to be felt, the Mississippi Gay Alliance languished. Administration policies crippled the U.S. Civil Rights Commission. Hopes for lesbian and gay political struggle in Mississippi reached their nadir. Despite Eddie Sandifer's diligence and what must have seemed at times his single-handed effort, MGA failed to attract a wide following. The mainstream press mostly ignored their activities; state attorney general Bill Allain, citing the sodomy statute, denied their bid for incorporation and a potentially lucrative, nonprofit status.[33] And as attitudinal surveys showed that southerners' feelings toward lesbians and gays were akin to those toward radical student activists and marijuana users, queer Mississippians appeared destined to languish on the political margins.[34] For the most part, this liminality would remain intact until interrupted by stirrings of religious activism initiated by southerner Troy Perry.

Gay Churches

Troy Perry was born in 1940 to a Pentecostal family in north Florida.[35] After running away from home in his early teens, he lived with relatives in south Georgia before becoming an itinerant evangelist in Alabama. In his late teens he married a preacher's daughter just graduated from high school. Perry passed a high school equivalency exam, and despite his denomination's distrust of seminary training, he attended a nonaccredited Bible college. At the same time, he pastored a Church of God congregation in Joliet, Illinois.

Church officials excommunicated Perry after they learned of his adolescent affair with another boy, but he was able to secure preaching engagements at the rival Church of God of Prophecy when he, his wife, and their two young sons moved to southern California. After his refusal to disavow homosexuality, clerics again forced Perry out. This time his wife left him, taking the children with her. In 1965 the U.S. Army drafted Perry, by now a seasoned pastor at the ripe old age of twenty-five. (The military, according to Perry, was less concerned with his sexual orientation than was the church.) Still attending Pentecostal worship services, he came under the influence of a fellow gay enlistee, an Episcopalian who posed a prophetic question: "Why don't you think about starting your own church?"[36]

The Metropolitan Community Church was founded on 6 October 1968 when Perry and his partner Willie Smith hosted twelve people at an afternoon service in their Los Angeles home. Vowing to preach a three-pronged gospel of salvation, community, and Christian social action, Perry saw his following expand rapidly. Initially conceptualized as "not a homosexual church, but a special church that [would] reach out to the lesbian and gay community," only 5 to 15 percent of the membership was heterosexual. The church's appeal, according to Perry, was its doctrine of acceptance, its belief in a God of unconditional love: "We were the first Christian bulwark against a determinedly ignorant society whose homophobic cruelty masked a callous indifference to humanity."[37]

MCC became the Universal Fellowship of Metropolitan Community Churches in 1969, with Troy Perry as general moderator. In the wake of a splashy, impromptu service/demonstration in Washington, D.C.'s dignified National Cathedral, congregations continued to spring up throughout the United States. Thirty-five were represented at the Third General Conference, held in 1972 at the "Mother Church" in Los Angeles. Such ecclesiastical gatherings, in stark relief to in-your-face activism, could generate the support of some liberal politicians. California Assembly member Willie Brown delivered a well-received speech at the MCC conference, though a small faction, dismayed over the so-called politicization of the church, walked out.

Congregations attempted to incorporate elements from various Protestant traditions into their worship services, but usually the format and tone mirrored those of the more middle-class, mainstream, "mainline" Protestant faiths. Troy Perry attempted to distance himself from inherited Pentecostal customs—speaking in tongues, shouting, and a healing ritual known as the "laying on of hands"—though they sometimes were practiced at MCC meetings. Heeding the advice of gay Congregational minister Revel Quigley, Perry wore liturgical robes at his first service and was commonly seen thereafter in clerical collar. Furthermore, as Perry later stated, Quigley helped raise his "parochial Pentecostal view of religion to a more sophisticated level where individuals worshipped God with a devotion similar to mine, but without the great public display of emotion I had previously assumed was the only way to be a good Christian." [38] Like that first gathering, a typical MCC service, held on Sunday, opened with singing; included communion, along with prayers for various concerns, personal and public, local and national; and featured a sermon by the congregation's pastor. Services were conducted in private homes, in gay bars, in public spaces, or in facilities owned by other religious or secular organizations. Over time, MCCs in many cities came to occupy their own houses of worship.

MCC's growth was not without its setbacks. Nor was it immune to criticism from within and without lesbian and gay circles. Its overwhelmingly male laity and leadership left it open to charges of sexism. Not until its fourth year did MCC license a female minister, Freda Smith, then assistant pastor at MCC-Sacramento. Yet it was hardly surprising that even a gay church would mirror the patriarchal structure of mainstream social, cultural, and political institutions, given the inherently patriarchal biases of Christian teaching. Intense hostility from outside forces surfaced in 1973, when three worship sites burned. Presumably the results of arson, fires consumed meeting places first in Los Angeles and then Nashville, without personal injuries. But a fire that summer in New Orleans claimed thirty-two lives. Perhaps not directly aimed at MCC, the deliberately set fire engulfed the Upstairs Bar, at the corner of Chartres and Iberville in the French Quarter, where the congregation often met. The bar was filled with revelers, as it was the last day of gay pride weekend, held in June on the anniversary of Stonewall. Many of the dead were MCC members. Perry says seventeen such blazes have been set over the years, including a fall 1982 firebombing in Atlanta.

In terms of doctrine, the Metropolitan Community Church suffered from a perplexing identity crisis. MCC bylaws lacked any reference to homosexuality, and as of 1974 the church had made no official statement on lesbian and gay sexuality.[39] "We are *not* a gay church," said MCC-Boston pastor Larry Bernier. "We worship God like anybody else worships God, and the fact that we're gay has very little to do with it."[40] Sociologists Ronald Enroth and Gerald Jamison refute such claims in their disparaging but informative 1974 study, *The Gay Church*, for which Troy Perry declined to be interviewed. While acknowledging the church's importance in the lives of its parishioners, the two self-described heterosexuals condescendingly chided MCC as "merely an extension of the gay life-style clothed in religiosity."[41]

Enroth and Jamison nonetheless were astute in their observation that "the straight church is, in part at least, responsible for the emergence of the gay church. Gay churchmen *[sic]* are correct in the charge that conventional churches fail to minister to homosexuals. The attitude of many Christians toward gay people is one of repugnance and even contempt."[42] Indeed, beginning in the late 1960s, primarily as a result of rumblings made by ever more politicized lesbian and gay members, the Catholic Church and major Protestant denominations issued increasingly condemnatory proclamations and doctrines. Despite the concomitant growth of lesbian and gay affiliate groups, such as Episcopal Integrity and Methodist Affirmation, mainline church policy proved decidedly antagonistic.

Mainline Churches

The nation's largest religious body, the Southern Baptists, published relatively temperate articles on homosexuality during the late 1960s and early 1970s. While hardly accepting of homosexuality, Baptist writers advanced a policy of benevolent caretaking. Seen as either psychologically maladjusted or especially prone to sin, lesbians and gays could be accommodated within the church given they had humble attitudes and repentant hearts. By the late 1970s, however, as gay activism spread inside and outside the church, ecclesial statements became more caustic, focusing on biblical injunctions against homosexuality. The 1976 meeting of the Southern Baptist Convention pronounced its "commitment to the biblical truth regarding the practice of homosexuality and sin," and discouraged congregations from hiring homosexual preachers or church employees.[43] The 1977 convention members lauded fellow Baptist Anita Bryant for her "courageous stand against the evils inherent in homosexuality."[44] State conventions joined in: thirteen issued condemnations of homosexuality in 1977, and of those, Mississippi and six others further expressed their support for Bryant's campaign to stop gay rights legislation in Dade County.[45] Bryant delivered the opening address to the Southern Baptist Pastors' Conference in Atlanta in 1978, but she lost her bid for first vice president at the denomination-wide convention that followed. By this time, Baptist ministers and church members were leading the backlash against numerous local initiatives designed to recognize or protect lesbian and gay citizens. Baptist sentiments continued to harden through the 1980s.

Ordinarily more liberal minded and less reliant on concepts of scriptural inerrancy, United Methodists, America's second largest Protestant denomination, were scarcely less hostile to lesbians and gays. The 1972 General Conference declared "the practice of homosexuality . . . incompatible with Christian teaching," in what one Mississippi minister described as the "famous paragraph 71F" of the denomination's *Book of Discipline*.[46] He and others would rely on it through the years to guide their interpretations of homosexuality. The 1972 conference also recommended against marriage between two persons of the same sex. The next quadrennial conference, held in 1976, exposed a developing rift between national officers of the United Methodist Church and local church clergy and laity. The former attempted to add a conciliatory clause to the otherwise condemnatory "Social Principles" doctrine. But the statement "we welcome all persons regardless of sexual orientation" was soundly defeated by the evangelical "Good News" wing, as was a proposed study of human sexuality. The grassroots elements further forbade the ordination of lesbian and gay clergy and forced through a resolution that would cut funding from any church agency using money to support homosexual organizations or to "promote the acceptance of homosexuality."[47] In 1979 the Mississippi Conference of the United Methodist Church voiced strong support for these positions, which the national body reaffirmed in 1984.[48]

Among smaller religious denominations, responses covered a broad range. As summarized by Robert Nugent and Jeannine Gramick:

> Other churches, such as the Moravian, the Friends, and the Unitarian Universalist Association, not only have voiced official and strong support for lesbian and gay people in the area of civil rights, but also have endorsed same-sex genital expression as fully compatible with Christian morality and human sexuality. Not surprisingly, many Evangelical, Pentecostal, and smaller, independent Bible churches remain adamantly and vociferously opposed both to homogenital behavior and to any support for societal or ecclesial recognition of what they see as a moral or psychological evil and a serious threat to family values.[49]

The latter churches greatly outnumbered the former in the South, a section that, according to sociologist David Greenberg, was less tolerant of homosexuality and more opposed to gay rights than any other in America, at least as publicly articulated.[50] Moreover, Baptists and Methodists, who pre-dominated in Mississippi, described homosexual relations as "always wrong," in survey proportions of 88 percent and 77 percent respectively.[51]

In his otherwise perceptive study of American churches and homosexu-ality, Thomas Hewitt mistakenly asserts that "there was no struggle within any Christian denomination over the issue of accepting or rejecting homo-sexuals until after 1969," the year of Stonewall.[52] Methodist quadrennial conference attendees debated homosexuality at least as early as 1968, though it was not officially taken up by the entire assembly until 1972.[53] More impressive still, Southern Baptists' "Brotherhood Commission" grap-pled with church responses to homosexuality as early as 1908.[54] As in all histories of sexuality, a dearth of readily accessible sources should not be construed as an absence of concern.

Over the course of the twentieth century, Protestant denominational en-gagement with homosexuality likely waxed and waned in the South. My research shows a hushed church in Mississippi during the 1940s and 1950s. As Methodist minister Ted Herrington recalls, homosexuality then "wasn't viewed in any sense [as] a great threat, a bugaboo."[55] He and his colleagues rarely if ever preached against it or counseled members about it. Even as late as the early 1960s, Loyd Star native Vince Jones heard not a single con-demnation of homosexuality from clergy at his rural Baptist church, nor at the Baptist college he attended in Clinton.[56] Still, most assumed this quiet reflected certain unspoken understandings: The "love that dare not speak its name" was clearly forbidden by church proscriptions against extramari-tal sex.

By the 1970s and 1980s, a significant change had taken place. Even a parishioner ill attuned to church doctrine as adopted by the national body could not fail to learn the prevailing attitudes toward homosexuality from within the local church. A survey of Southern Baptist, independent Baptist, and Assemblies of God pastors—half of whom were attached to congre-gations in the South—found that of all "public issues addressed . . . in ser-mons," homosexuality was among the most frequently mentioned. It was matched only by pornography and surpassed only by the more generic category "Christian attitude toward civic responsibility." It superseded prayer in schools, abortion, equal rights for women, and the state of Israel, among others.[57]

Now some of the most influential and persuasive discourse flowed from preachers' sermons, which in many Mississippi Protestant congregations tended toward the "hellfire-and-brimstone" variety.[58] In rural north Missis-sippi in the 1980s, one eighteen-year-old churchgoer, Bud Thomas, felt the wrath of a fanatical pastor after he confided his homosexuality to the pastor's son. When the friend in turn told his father, the preacher confronted Thomas during the Sunday morning worship service, in front of the entire congregation. Thomas was kicked out of his church and told never to return.[59] Papal hostility made it difficult for others. As one gay Mississippian, a self-described "ex-Catholic," put it, "An awful lot of the Catholic Church will fuck you up."[60]

Religiously inclined lesbians and gays in Mississippi were at an impasse with the state's major churches, at the same time that the Universal Fellowship of Metropolitan Community Churches had come to a standstill in relations with national denominational bodies. In 1983 the National Council of Churches, to which most major Christian faiths belonged, again denied membership to MCC and moved to postpone indefinitely any future vote on their eligibility.[61] Yet MCC was undaunted. With 150 U.S. congregations—including new southern groups in Little Rock, Shreveport, Memphis, Montgomery, and Birmingham—and thirty more in seven foreign countries, they were determined to continue their expansion, with or without ecumenical support.[62] They found fertile soil in Mississippi.

Mississippi Churches

Palm Sunday services of the Metropolitan Community Church of Jackson, on 27 March 1983, resembled those held at other Protestant sanctuaries across the state that morning. The service began with hymn singing: "Amazing Grace" and "Jesus Loves Me." The Reverend Gilbert Lincoln of Nashville, coordinator of MCC's South Atlantic District, delivered a brief sermon to nine women and men. The group celebrated Holy Communion, eating crackers and drinking grape juice—a common substitute for wine among teetotaling congregations in the South. And Lincoln offered a prayer for "Mr. Wells and all of the Moral Majority, . . . for everybody who fears . . . and mistrusts us."[63]

Since Lincoln had first come to Jackson over a month prior to initiate meetings and plan for this, MCC's first worship service, the Reverend Mike Wells, pastor of Mountainview Baptist Church in nearby Raymond, had emerged as the church's most adamant opponent. President of the state chapter of the national Moral Majority, founded by Baptist minister Jerry Falwell of Lynchburg, Virginia, Wells had been stirring controversy, trying to raise money to combat homosexuality in Mississippi. Indeed, homosexuals were popular scapegoats for what Kathy Rudy calls "the 'new' Christian Right." Highly influential in "setting the agenda for national Christian politics," this movement sprang up prior to the 1980 election with the advent of four conservative organizations—the Christian Voice, the National Christian Action Coalition, the Religious Roundtable, and the Moral Majority. These and other conservative Christian organizations "did not limit their political organizing tactics to television," Rudy demonstrates. "Radio, mass mailings, rallies, book and sound recordings sales, telephone, leafleting, and personal contacts . . . helped."[64] Mike Wells and the Mississippi Moral Majority utilized most of these methods.

Wells's initial salvo in the battle against Mississippi's first MCC congregation was a letter dated 7 March 1983, sent to ten thousand people throughout the state. In their mailboxes, recipients found an envelope with a red computer-generated "handwritten" message on the outside. In all capital letters, it read: "PLEASE, OPEN AT ONCE. HOMOSEXUALS INVADE JACKSON, MISSISSIPPI."[65]

In the letter, Wells told readers he "just couldn't believe" the recent news that "a sodomite church" was forming in Jackson. Raising the looming specter of homosexual teachers and public officials, he denounced lesbian and gay attempts at "disguising this perverted life style in a normal light by building a homosexual church." Compelled to "alert God-fearing Mississippians statewide," Wells insisted that he needed support to prevent Jackson from becoming "another San Francisco or Houston." "With a massive budget," he warned, "the homosexual pressure groups are gripping our city now. Perhaps your home town is next." Opposition had to be rallied, and he was the person to lead:

> I have prayed to God, "Lord, someone needs to go on local radio and television across Mississippi and call forth the God fearing people to do all, then stand." Then God called me to do just that. But He calls you to stand with me. Take a stand now, before it's to [sic] late.

Wells asked for three things. First, he needed suggestions. On which radio and TV stations should he buy airtime? Second, he needed prayers. Would God make audio and film equipment available to him in order to produce radio and television programming? Third, he needed money. Would the recipient "help in paying for these specials to expose the truth to the people of Mississippi"? In a "handwritten" postscript, he made an offer: "If you will send a gift of $29.00, I will send by return mail a casett [sic] tape of a message preached in my church and broadcasted on Radio." In yet another postscript, he said he would accept "whatever you can send" as a show of support, for he knew that "most Mississippians view the practice of homosexual sodomy among the worst imaginable form [sic] of perversion."

Clearly, sodomy was a problem of the imagination. For something so alien, so unimaginable, homophobes in Mississippi seemed to think a great deal and in detailed, projective fashion about homosexual acts. Beyond hypocrisy, this contradiction was fueled by an epistemic dilemma. Preachers and police needed to know about homosexuality in order to combat it. Yet too great a knowledge compromised the moralists' integrity and masculinity (for, with the exception of Bryant, there were few female leaders among the opposition). Such knowledge might implicate them, especially when so corporeally involved. Jackson police captain Joe Alford described the sexual interactions between "Smith Park People" and his officers—presumed heterosexual—in infantile language reminiscent of queer youth. They *played*. That is, Smith Park people allegedly played with officers' legs. Wells, on the other hand, deployed a rhetoric of deception. A gay church could only be a disguise—worship in drag, masking what any right-minded person *knew* to be inherently sexual activity.

Wells's letter was effective. A media bonanza ensued. Never before had Mississippi's lesbian and gay communities received such attention. Both Jackson newspapers, the morning *Clarion-Ledger* and the evening *Jackson Daily News*, carried stories, as did the Memphis *Commercial Appeal*. On 23 March, the *Jackson Daily News* published an editorial cartoon by Jimmy Johnson, who attempted to frame the principal combatants in the debate. In the foreground, Johnson depicts an elderly minister clad in Puritan hat, small round spectacles, and lengthy black frock, labeled "MORAL MAJORITY." Wielding a smoldering hot branding iron with the letter Q, the zealot chases a stereotypically gay figure—a limp-wristed, frailly slender young man wearing flip-flops, tight pants, and a tank top reading "MISS. GAY ALLIANCE." Pinky finger outstretched, he attempts to fend off his pursuer by swinging his handbag. In the background is a middle-aged couple, presumably married and representative of average Mississippians. While the woman stares in fright, hand to her chest, her husband begins walking away. With the classic will to ignorance, he declares: "I'm not sure I want to know what's going on here."[66]

Johnson seriously misread and oversimplified the discourse. Opposition to the MCC was hardly limited to a radical right fringe. Leaders of various well-established local and regional church bodies weighed in with derogatory remarks. Reverend F. L. Langley, superintendent of the Assemblies of God Mississippi district, stated, "We are dynamically [sic] opposed" to a gay church. Bishop Joseph Brunini of the Catholic Diocese of Jackson said homosexuality was "condemned by all Christian people as a way of life." He acknowledged lesbians' and gays' right to form a church —"It's a free country" after all—but he felt they needed to be "ministered to." He emphasized the importance of salvation.[67] Reverend Michael

Editorial cartoon by Jimmy Johnson, 23 March 1983. Courtesy of the *Jackson Daily News*.

Schneider of Saint Paul Presbyterian Church in Jackson said that "biblically speaking, a church for those who engage in homosexual acts is the equivalent of a church for practicing adulterers, prostitutes, murderers, drunkards or thieves."[68] An editorial in the *Baptist Record* made a backhanded swipe at MCC, ironically proposing that a church for lesbians and gays, "a group that has openly embraced a sinful lifestyle," might not be such a bad idea: "After all, where would the gospel find a more needy audience than this?"[69]

Cartoonist Johnson correctly surmised that the Mississippi Gay Alliance was at the forefront of support for the Metropolitan Community Church. The leadership of the two organizations was intimately intertwined, as MCC's first worship coordinator, Kathy Switzer, recalls: "Many of us who were on the board of the church were also on the board of the alliance."[70] Notable among those was Eddie Sandifer, who, along with Switzer, Johnny Estes, Bryan Homeyer, and Denita Claypool, had first solicited MCC expansion into Mississippi. Regularly contacted by reporters, Sandifer attempted to discredit Mike Wells's letter, saying it was "just something to raise funds."[71] As the rhetoric heated up through April 1983, MGA issued a press release that compared Wells's mailings and flyers to fascist pamphlets and Hitlerian edicts from Nazi Germany.[72]

Johnson inaccurately gauged the level of feeling among ordinary Mississippians. Many reacted with anything but indifference to the issue. The pretense of ignorance and quiet accommodation suggested by the cartoon's middle-aged male passerby was now eclipsed by the fascination and shock of his wife, the willful onlooker. The *Clarion-Ledger/Jackson Daily News* reported that "a heavy stream of letters—pro and con—poured in" after their own liberal columnist Raad Cawthon urged the Moral Majority to lay off MCC.[73] Cawthon had scoffed at assertions of a homosexual invasion, saying that such language implied "the homosexuals are from somewhere else. Perhaps Wells thinks citizens of Mississippi are immune to homosexuality." While carefully pointing out his own heterosexuality, Cawthon clearly sided with MCC, echoing the MGA argument that "the Moral Majority is just using this issue as a straw man to be set up, screamed at, and knocked down for monetary gain."[74]

Even the *Jackson Daily News* ombudsman/advice columnist "Jack Sunn" fielded letters from concerned Mississippians. Normally prone to folksy conservatism, his response was surprisingly sympathetic to MCC, reflecting a libertarian strain in his thinking. When Mary wrote in, declaring homosexuality a "deformity," Jack Sunn good-naturedly demurred. "Now that's a new one on us," he wrote. "We think folks have the right to believe just about anything they want to, and to worship just about any way they want to, as long as it doesn't interfere with anybody else."[75]

In his crusade to "go on . . . television across Mississippi and call forth the God fearing people," Mike Wells was beaten to the punch by adversaries, the People for the American Way. The New York–based advocacy group, founded in 1980 by TV producer Norman Lear, had created a half-hour documentary about the national Moral Majority's attacks on First Amendment rights, previously aired in thirty-six American cities. Donors in Mississippi paid to have the show broadcast on the biracially owned NBC affiliate, WLBT, Channel 3, at 6:30 P.M. on Saturday, 19 March 1983. Because the local telecast purportedly was funded only by individuals, neither the Mississippi Gay Alliance nor the national Urban League was allowed to contribute.[76] Yet its timing, during the midst of the MCC controversy, was a clear indication of both national and local support for queer Mississippians and their quest for a church.

Many Protestant pastors denounced the People for the American Way documentary. Reverend Don Patterson castigated WLBT the next day during Sunday worship services at First Presbyterian Church, a large downtown congregation filled with white middle- and upper-class families. He said the telecast "maligned" the Moral Majority, "a Christian organization seeking to alert the American people to the trends in our country." He insisted that Mississippians must "take seriously the teachings of scripture," especially proscriptions against homosexuality.[77]

The Mississippi Moral Majority's rebuttal was less than swift. While president Mike Wells reported "a tremendous response" to his direct-mail campaign,[78] months passed before he completed his video project. When he did, its reach apparently was limited. Perhaps for lack of funds, the documentary seems mostly to have been aired in bits and pieces. Portions were shown in Jackson on at least one local evening news program, but it may never have been broadcast in its entirety. More likely, copies of the tape were distributed to church groups and other organizations. Evidence of any radio broadcasts by Mississippi Moral Majority remains inconclusive.[79]

Most importantly for advocates of lesbian and gay rights in Mississippi, the debate over the Metropolitan Community Church fostered a print media discourse that ultimately aided organizing efforts and promoted community development. According to Eddie Sandifer, the Mississippi Moral Majority campaign and the subsequent press coverage did "more to solidify gays in Jackson and throughout the state" than "even Anita Bryant."[80] Moreover, in the wake of the controversy, the *Jackson Daily News* ran a crucial series of stories on Mississippi lesbian and gay cultures. Published in early June, these features addressed lesbian and gay spirituality, bar culture, committed partnerships, employment discrimination, Smith Park cruising and socializing, hate crimes against lesbians and gays, and—two years after the initial report in the *New York Times*—the spread of AIDS cases, at that point numbering only two in Mississippi.[81]

The liberatory potential of such news accounts should not be underestimated. Though hardly celebratory, often serving to further marginalize lesbians and gays in the consciousness of many Mississippians, the coverage often empowered its subjects. As we have seen, queer Mississippians had long employed against-the-grain readings of even the most phobic representations in print and song, on film and stage. As John D'Emilio writes about an earlier period in American life:

> Systematized oppression . . . exerted contradictory influences on gays. In repeatedly condemning the phenomenon, antigay polemicists broke the silence that surrounded the topic of homosexuality. Thus the resources available to lesbians and homosexuals for attaching a meaning to otherwise dimly understood feelings expanded noticeably. The attacks on gay men and women hastened the articulation of a homosexual identity and spread the

knowledge that they existed in large numbers. Ironically, the effort to root out the homosexuals in American society made it easier for them to find one another.[82]

This certainly was the case in Mississippi, where never before had issues surrounding homosexuality been afforded such a public forum. Suddenly, valuable information abounded in the daily press. Queer Mississippians contemplating their first forays into lesbian and gay cultures learned the locations of gay bars. They read the names of community leaders and activists, organizations and working groups. They found out about Smith Park. They were informed that committed relationships were a common complement or (normalizing) alternative to the relative abandon of the bars and parks.

But such information did not *clarify* "dimly understood feelings"— for as oral history narrators attest, their feelings and those of non-gay-identified queers were regularly acknowledged and acted upon. Rather, this discourse *channeled* queer feelings into particular modes of gay being and homosexual identity. Undeniably, this discourse promoted or expanded gay community, enlisting new individuals into the ranks and shoring up the allegiances of old guard activists such as Sandifer. But even more so, it shaped that community, setting boundaries, parameters, standards of conduct. While the enumeration and articulation of gay institutions appeared an invitation to many, it seemed a barrier to others, a signal that an identity-based community, by its very nature, excluded some as it smoothed out differences among the elect.

Now more than ever before, however, those with deeply held religious faith—a vast majority in Mississippi—were welcomed into a gay community. Queer Mississippians learned that a new congregation existed to address their spiritual concerns. They learned that their spirituality and sexuality were not antithetical.

Darryl Jeffries: I had met one gay person through my cousin's wife. A waiter at Tuminello's [in Vicksburg]. He wasn't really a sexual partner. More like a gay confidant. Somebody that I could talk to, that could give me information on something that I knew nothing about, but I knew I was a part of. He really enlightened me a whole lot.

But what *really* gave me the message that it was OK to be gay was when I was nineteen. I looked in the *Clarion-Ledger*. And it was really strange, because I *never* looked at the *Clarion-Ledger*. I had no interest in it. It didn't mean anything to me. Jackson was a place that I had been maybe two or three times in my life; I had no reason to even look in it. But I looked in it this one Sunday. There was a write-up. There was the Baptist Church, I think, opposing the Metropolitan Community

Church on the same page. I called the gay minister out in California and started talking to him on the phone.[83] I called him; I got information from him on my sexuality. He wanted me to move out to California. I was too afraid to, of course.

So at that point I got the message that it was OK to be gay. That God loved me regardless. It was not a sin to be homosexual. So I started developing a whole new belief about myself. That's when I started coming out to other people. It was like, I'm not bad, you know. All this shit that I've believed all my life is bullshit. It's just bullshit. It's a bunch of lies that people have concocted out of their own fears and their own ignorance. That's when I really started coming to life, really. I used to be a very shy person. And after that, it was just like *boom*. The energy was in me then to live, actually. My depression started lifting. I had a reason to live then.

I felt like an alien up to that point. Then I found out there were people like me. This was a very big turning point in my life. It was so strange that I happened to pick up that paper at that point. It was like a God thing, you know. It was meant to happen.[84]

Jackson's Metropolitan Community Church appealed to queer Mississippians who personally had felt the sting of church-sponsored oppression yet had retained the commitment to Christian spirituality. Ever larger groups of men like *that*—a category given to occasional dissembling and disidentification—began to band together with, as Darryl Jeffries put it, people like *me*—a distinctive form of identification and association. Where gay identity politics flagged, a gay social gospel flourished.

MCC reached Harold, a conflicted fifty-five-year-old who, having been kicked out of his church and told he would be barred from heaven, still considered homosexuality a sin. Kathie likewise was told she was destined for hell. However, after "going from church to church, counselor to counselor," she concluded that "it's not me that's screwed, it's them." Young Johnny Estes so thoroughly absorbed fundamentalist teachings into his psyche that "I prayed to God that he would allow me to be straight." Estes later overcame his guilt, even after a painful divorce. He became one of the five founding members of MCC-Jackson in 1983.[85]

After the success of their Palm Sunday gathering, MCC began regular Sunday services two weeks later on 10 April 1983. The first lesbian and gay organization to be incorporated by the state of Mississippi, the Metropolitan Community Church met thereafter at two o'clock every Sunday afternoon, just two doors up North State Street from First Baptist Church downtown. The Human Coalitions Building, which housed various nonprofit organizations including the Mississippi Gay Alliance, remained their home throughout the early period. Membership expanded from the initial five to twenty-two within five months. Thereafter, it grew exponentially.

The early numbers were deceptively small. Truly, they promised MCC's continued presence in Mississippi for years to come. Many who worshiped at MCC never transferred their letter of membership from their home church, ordinarily their parents' church. Many people visited and took part in services and activities without ever becoming members. Of these, many went on to help strengthen local gay affiliates of mainline Protestant churches, such as the Methodist group Affirmation, and the even stronger Episcopal Integrity, local founding of which predated MCC of Jackson.

Some visitors to MCC felt particularly unwelcome. As Kathy Switzer recalls, the congregation was entirely white. Though African Americans visited, "they would always go back to their home churches because they felt more comfortable there." One black worshiper explicitly stated the dilemma to the group: "It's hard enough to be black. You want me to be gay too?" "Yes," came the response. "You play with the boys, honey. Don't you think it's time to identify yourself?"[86]

Indeed, identity was the issue. Just as gay organizing privileged a particular form of outness as a primary and sometimes prerequisite political act, gay worship mandated and affirmed a gay identity that in theory was stable and thus in practice was often inflexible. Further, as we have seen, particular styles of worship were valorized. If MCC in Mississippi minimized emotive and charismatic elements of the liturgy, as even Pentecostal Troy Perry did, then the resultant complexion of the membership should not surprise. Gay worship, we can assume, not only excluded African Americans; it also alienated those whose desires and self-conceptions did not comport to these gay standards.

Of those who did join MCC, most shied away from leadership roles, given the degree of disclosure entailed—for example, signing official papers of incorporation. Under Kathy Switzer, Johnny Estes became assistant worship coordinator and Denita Claypool served as secretary. The founders tapped as treasurer longtime gay activist, MGA president, outspoken revolutionary, and committed communist Eddie Sandifer.[87]

Sandifer's involvement was less a reflection of his own religious values and upbringing—as son of a Baptist minister—than an indication of the nature of lesbian and gay politics in Mississippi. Sandifer, who first invited MCC officials to come to Jackson, realized that after ten years of MGA activity, political organizing would falter if it did not address the spiritual concerns of a vast number of queer Mississippians. For these individuals, Protestant Christianity, while the source of much oppressive activity in the state, nonetheless informed their identity as much as, if not more than, sexuality. According to Switzer, the Metropolitan Community Church offered them "a place where they could actually be themselves, where their faith was validated and their lives were affirmed."[88] Just as parishioners came to MCC from throughout Mississippi, gay people of faith in Jackson and across the state formed their own informal religious groups, prayer circles, and gatherings.

So pervasive was Christianity in Mississippi—the state with the third largest percentage of self-declared Christians[89]—that one's existence was fairly predicated on one's adherence to a Christian worldview. *To be*, in many ways, meant *to be Christian*, as Darryl Jeffries's narrative suggests. Jeffries said that he "had a reason *to live*" once he discovered "that it was OK to be gay," "that God loved [him] regardless." His very sense of having or being a self was informed by a particular religious culture of meaning. Before, he had "felt like an alien"—in a sense, a nonbeing. The struggle over a gay church was consequently a struggle over gay existence, over *being* as defined by a broader culture. Queer Mississippians' spiritual need was a conflicted need for assimilation, no less or more so than the needs of other Mississippians, including members of the religious right.

The strident backlash against MCC suggested the nonetheless subversive potential of queer religious organizing. Right-wingers like Mike Wells no longer enjoyed the comfortable distance constructed between us and them, the devout and the sinful, the saved and the damned. Early MGA activity had never occasioned this level of reactionary diatribe. Wells and other religious and political figures felt more threatened by MCC because it muddled lines of distinction. Gay people now seemed startlingly similar to average Mississippians in their desire for safe communities, work environments, and houses of worship—in short, in their desire for normalcy. Once a danger from without—Wells presumed the "invasion" originated elsewhere, say San Francisco or Houston—homosexuality proved a hidden threat from within. When Sandifer asserted that "we are everywhere including [Wells's] Mountainview Baptist Church," the reply of the Mississippi Moral Majority president rang conspicuously hollow. While Wells professed having counseled and "reformed" lesbians and gays in Christian congregations, he paradoxically denied the possibility of homosexuals at Mountainview: "[That] is the most ridiculous thing I ever heard."[90]

Finally, the MCC controversy demonstrated that the discourse of lesbian and gay rights could no longer ignore religious right arguments, but would have to refute them on moral grounds. Organizers could not presuppose that the taking on of a lesbian or gay identity was accompanied by the shedding of a spiritual identity. Queer Mississippians, as a group, were not atheistic, as Don Sanders of Houston's Gay Atheists League assumed logical. Instead of discarding their religious upbringings, many were learning to accommodate them to new ways of living—and also to accommodate their new ways of living to their religious upbringings.

As Meredith Raimondo writes of Atlanta during the 1980s: "While [Christian] religion clearly fueled homophobia . . . it also energized AIDS [and gay] activism. Actions often took the form of memorial services, prayer services, and protests in which ministers spoke. . . . Religion served as a basis for political organization as well as personal strength." [91] Likewise in Mississippi, this historical moment signaled the necessity for a complex change in tactics for political movement and institutional development. Though the shift was not a wholesale departure from radical left systemic critique—as in Sandifer's early communist alliances and Atlanta's Gay Liberation Front—it clearly was a turn toward an articulation of aims and objectives within Christian discourses. Given the life histories of members like Sandifer and the recent regional history of a church-based African American civil rights struggle, the time and place were opportune. Queer Christian community building was not a mere rhetorical reaction to religious persecution. It was instead an enunciation of the rich, intricate spiritual convictions of many Mississippians.

The most effective affirmation of queer life in Mississippi could no longer preclude Christian faith. Instead, it would increasingly comport itself to a different model. That model was elaborated in a 5 June 1983 op-ed piece for the *Clarion-Ledger* by Reverend Ken Martin—a Mississippi native, pastor of MCC–North Hollywood, California, and long-distance telephone mentor to nineteen-year-old Vicksburg resident Darryl Jeffries. To the paper's point-counterpoint query "Is it possible to be homosexual and still be a Christian?" Martin responded with a series of supportive biblical interpretations and answered the question with a vigorous, reassuring "YES." [92]

In Mississippi, MCC's fate mirrored that of so many denominations. As it expanded, it splintered. Differences developed. In the big rift of 1987— based as much on personal political power as theological doctrine—a portion of the flock left and formed a new church. [93] Other gay churches appeared. By the late 1990s Eddie Sandifer—leader of Mississippi's foremost gay political organization for over a quarter of a century—had to acknowledge that congregations were the strongest gay institutions in the state. [94] In their meeting spaces, under their aegis, religious bodies supported varied lesbian and gay community groups and initiatives.

Coda

In 1998, as the files of the Mississippi State Sovereignty Commission were finally opened, as Mississippians learned of the dastardly deeds of the taxpayer-supported, segregationist spy agency, a curious name surfaced from the files: Eddie Sandifer. Sandifer, it seemed, was not just a target of Sovereignty Commission surveillance in the 1960s and 1970s. Moreover, he was one of their paid informants.

Though most friends and associates stood by Sandifer, others were appalled. Ken Lawrence, who once shared an office with Sandifer, said, "It was emotionally devastating to discover that one of my closest friends in all my years in Mississippi was working for our enemies, the people who were trying to destroy our movement."[95]

But to say that Sandifer was "working for" the Sovereignty Commission seems to overestimate the involvement and underestimate the persuasive reach of the inquisitional agency. Sovereignty Commission investigators —as state employees, backed by the state's highest elected officials— demanded the deference that Mississippians would give to police or sheriffs. Patterned after the FBI, the commission both ran roughshod over individual civil liberties and expected complete cooperation from all persons questioned. Furthermore, Sandifer counted himself among the many who not only were framed on various charges, but also were subject to legitimate arrest on any number of counts, given the state of the legal code.[96] If he did not comply—or did not at least appear to comply—officials could have him detained indefinitely.

The payments were small; they mostly covered conference registration fees; they were exchanged for information about meetings that Sandifer no doubt would have attended anyway. But Sandifer didn't do it for the money, he said. He offered no excuses.

"It's something I will regret for the rest of my life."[97]

CHAPTER SEVEN

Scandals

When desire lives constantly with fear, and no partition between them, desire must become very tricky; it has to become as sly as the adversary, and this was one of those times when desire outwitted the enemy under the roof.

—TENNESSEE WILLIAMS [1]

Jon Hinson *(Jackson, Mississippi, 8 August 1980):*

THERE ARE FEW who would find it easy to engage in a public discussion of that within us which strips bare our human frailty. . . . However, with great regret I must risk affronting the sensibilities of many who would also prefer to leave the discussion of past personal problems and difficulties within the privacy of close relationships and share with you a difficulty of mine from several years ago.

As a preface, let me offer a few insights involving the period during which I underwent a personal crisis. It is well known that I chose public service as a career early in life, and it is also well known that my largest ambition . . . was to be the United States representative for this district. However, early in 1976, I came to believe that this ambition would never be a reality. For one thing, I was working for a man holding the Fourth District Congressional seat for whom I had the very highest admiration and who was serving this district with great competence and distinction. In addition, other political factors within the state seemed to disallow any hope for the realization of my ambition.

To be quite honest, I had to that point lived a life amazingly free of disappointment and adversity, but during this twelve-month period I was visited with every fear and self-doubt ever conceived. It seemed that all my aspirations, my hopes, and my efforts began to evaporate. . . . My reactions during these months reflected completely my great sense of disappointment and subsequent sense of purposelessness and isolation with which I wrestled unsuccessfully for this time.

In September 1976, I was accused of a misdemeanor of committing an obscene act in Arlington, Virginia. This accusation was never brought to trial. For a number of personal reasons I determined it was best to dispense with the matter by paying a $100 fine for creating a public nuisance.

In October 1977, slightly over one year later, a fire occurred in a Washington, D.C., theater which showed X-rated films. Although I was not seriously injured, nine people lost their lives. I was one of the four survivors of that fire. Subsequently, civil suits were filed in the District of Columbia by the survivors or by the families of those who died. I am not a party to those suits, but I was asked to provide a deposition relating to my knowledge of the event. I did so in June 1980, voluntarily and without subpoena.

I must be totally frank and tell you that both of these incidents were in areas frequented by some of Washington's homosexual community.

In all personal crises the reasons are difficult for even the individual to perceive and are convoluted and deeply hidden, requiring great personal introspection and thought. Needless to say, I have invested a considerable amount of time in struggling to understand what happened to me.

What I would like you to know is that from this period of such great stress, I have discovered strength, resolve, and a renewed, strong sense of purpose. I have learned one of the greatest lessons life has to offer—that disappointments are not irreversible, and that, without question, the good Lord does indeed work in mysterious and miraculous ways. There is one piece of advice that I would emphasize time and time again to others who find themselves facing their own crisis. Seek the advice and counsel of one's minister as I did.

I will also tell you that this was not accomplished alone. Blessedly, I rediscovered my basic religious values, and thankfully I had Cynthia, who has been, through it all, my confidante, my friend, and now my wife. She was there through this entire spiritual crisis and to my great good fortune she was there when it ended. The most positive recollection I have were her words after the fire. She said to me, "Today we start putting it all back together." The other solid recognition I had is that I survived. I believe I lived for a reason.

As you might imagine, Cynthia and I engaged in a considerable amount of discussion at the time of these circumstances. Frankly, it was our mutual determination to put this period firmly and irrevocably behind us. We resolved to ourselves and to each other to make every day count from that point forward. At the same time, we did not place these matters behind us to be buried and wrapped in secrecy. We have shared this information with a good number of our family, friends, and members of my staff. We were always prepared to deal with these matters publicly. . . . We never considered hiding, but decided instead to live with courage and commitment. . . .

In a sense, this press conference offers both of us some relief, and I think you will understand that we find comfort in being able in a complete sense to put these incidents behind us—finally. We both still feel a deep sense of commitment to that new beginning upon which we embarked. While we still seek our privacy in this personal matter, we have embraced enthusiastically our convictions and our desire to share ourselves and our blessings. It is the highest privilege of my life to represent this district in Congress. I shall continue to offer my services, and my service will continue to reflect the genuine love and regard I feel for this district and its people.

In as much as this personal matter is wholly unrelated to my record and service in the Congress, I am going to respectfully decline to answer any questions. I do wish to thank you for your attention.[2]

With those final words, first-term Republican congressman Jon Hinson "quickly left the room."[3] And reporters quickly went to work. The Tylertown, Mississippi, native—representing twelve counties stretching from the capital to the state's southwest corner—had left much unsaid in his Jackson press conference. Johanna Neuman at the *Clarion-Ledger's* Washington bureau worked late that Friday night to ferret out the details. She was accustomed to tracking Hinson. In a late 1979 story, she had chronicled "a day in [the] life" of the congressman, from 8:00 A.M. to 5:00 P.M., noting everything from pending legislation to the needlepoint on the office wall, a gift of U.S. representative Robert Bauman of Maryland.[4]

Neuman found nothing on the September 1976 incident in Arlington, Virginia. The courthouse where the arrest records were kept was closed over the weekend; she and others would have to wait until later. However, because the October 1977 fire had been extensively reported in D.C. newspapers at the time, she had a trail to follow. She found enough material to sketch out the events, and her story appeared the next day in the statewide Saturday joint edition of the *Clarion-Ledger/Jackson Daily News*.

The theater in question was the Cinema Follies, "less than a mile from the Capitol" Building. It featured "X-rated male homosexual films 24 hours a day." But it "was more than a movie theater": it housed a "first-floor discotheque," and on the second floor, adjacent to the "viewing area," were "empty rooms." A gay rights leader told the *Washington Post* that in those rooms, "'a full range' of sexual activities [was] conducted."

The multipurpose Cinema Follies had "an estimated membership of 22,000 homosexuals," Johanna Neuman reported. Though the names of the nine men who died in the fire were released to the press back in 1977, "the names of the survivors were not."[5] Thus, Hinson—a top aide to then–Fourth District representative Thad Cochran, his predecessor—had been able to maintain secrecy, Neuman implied.

Indeed, it seemed Hinson's confession was designed as much to conceal as to disclose. Made on a Friday, the revelations would appear in the less widely read weekend newspaper editions, on the less widely watched weekend television newscasts. Those Mississippians who did learn of the events that Saturday and Sunday were more likely to discuss them first with family members than with coworkers, with churchgoers than with schoolmates. As observers would soon note, Hinson appeared calculating, cunning.

Some nagging questions remained. Why, the *Jackson Daily News* editors asked, did Hinson choose to "fess up" now? "Was Hinson the victim of a blackmail attempt? Was he tipped off that someone in the news media was about to 'expose' his past? Or was he—as he said—simply easing his conscience by telling voters something he had understandably kept hidden from them?"[6] Most importantly, why had he "pretty well eliminated himself" from contention in the upcoming election, only three months away?[7] Why had he willingly ruined his chances for a second term, as most all commentators assumed? Why had he "committed political suicide"?[8]

A close reading of Hinson's five-page statement suggests his motives, conscious or not, were multiple, complex, and contradictory—as were the results. These events—examined in state and national arenas—shed light on the local experiences of queer Mississippians caught in the perpetual tensions between secrecy and disclosure, silence and discourse. At a time and place where homosexual desire was often understood to be—indeed, was *"understandably"*—hidden, it was nonetheless in myriad ways acted on, talked about, and known. Its persistence and its reception reflected not only the opportunities and challenges facing queer Mississippians, but also the values and attitudes of Mississippians variously sexually identified.

The scandal that engulfed Jon Hinson in 1980—especially when measured against a subsequent 1983 scandal involving working-class Mississippians and another public official—exposed the fluidity of sexuality in twentieth-century Mississippi, as linked to hierarchies of race, class, and gender. The gender of one's sex partner, or sexual object-choice, was not always the primary means of sexual categorization or marginalization, as the cases demonstrate. The role in the sex act, or sexual aim, was sometimes preeminent, with penetrated partners more readily marked as queer than penetrative partners. In this way, male gender insubordination—linked to sexually passive or receptive roles—fueled heterosexism, as effeminacy not only signaled queer sexuality but also political marginality. Simply put, the unmanly were unfit for the highest political offices.

Race—as tied to class—often proved central, as interracial intercourse continued to loom as taboo in a culture shaped by legacies of slavery and racial domination. If similar black and white queer realms intermingled with increasing frequency after the civil rights years, individual encounters between African American and European American men occasioned virulent reactions from mainstream cultural mediators. As strategies of oppression cast homosexuality as new and homosexuality as elsewhere, spatial zones were elaborated such that the dirty faraway big city—even the nation's capital—was said to harbor deviance and perversity, into which the most innocent of rural denizens might fall. Similarly, if queer sexuality appeared to be evident among their own, ordinary Mississippians felt it contained and containable, encased, within a zone of race and class marginality, such as the physical and metaphorical locale of Jackson's so-called dangerous inner city.

In Protestant evangelical Mississippi, religious principles guided understandings of the queer as more a range of sinful but forgivable behaviors than an identity or way of being. Conceptions of sexuality and gender nonconformity did not comport easily to dyads of homosexual versus heterosexual behaviors, homosexual versus heterosexual identities, straight versus queer gender performances, or even penetrative versus penetrated sex roles. Myriad configurations served to marginalize or normalize gender and sexual proclivities. Getting at those configurations—determining which acts had taken place, determining which acts and identities would be marked as transgressive—involved surveillance and retribution that served as much to produce as to uncover the truth. Confession and denial—techniques of lying and truth telling—made desire tricky, elusive. As a historical quiet accommodation of queerness gave way to explicit persecution of the sexual and gender nonnormative in Mississippi, queer habits of dissembling, long inculcated as second nature, often proved effective. Observing the scandals through press and television representations, ordinary Mississippians—denied complete access to an unmediated truth—had to choose what they *wanted* to believe.

Confession, Class Work, and the Congressman's Race

From his opening remarks at the Jackson press conference in August 1980, Jon Hinson both engaged with and disengaged from what he knew would be a public scandal. He acknowledged it while distancing himself and others from it. Hinson had brought the reporters together to tell them something, but he felt obliged to apologize for the telling. He spoke in terms of binarized public and private spheres and insisted this issue belonged in the latter,[9] repeatedly referring to it as "personal," "a personal problem." He had rightly told his close associates and advisers, friends and family members, but it was irrelevant in the public realm. Although he paradoxically was "always prepared to deal with these matters publicly," Hinson said the two incidents were "wholly unrelated" to his career—what John Diggins describes as the embodiment of classical republicanism's civic life, formal service to the body politic as an elected representative.[10]

Many Mississippians shared the view that this was a private issue. *Jackson Daily News* editors *understood* the reasons for keeping it secret and hinted that Hinson should have continued to keep it secret.[11] *Clarion-Ledger* humorist "Crazy Murphy" Givens chided Hinson for "lick[ing] his wounds in public," and he aligned Hinson's confession with a decidedly queer, nationally popularized, spatially conceptualized presentation of the self: "Rep. Hinson came out of the closet, so to speak." Givens perhaps reflected many Mississippians' sensibilities when he wrote that Hinson's "gay adventures would not have concerned me at all, except for the fact that he made a big deal of telling about them."[12] Mississippians could live with homosexuality, like other unpleasantries, as long as it went unremarked.

So, again, why the disclosure? Though an aide declared "it was a very personal decision, not a political decision,"[13] Hinson's past concern for his political life was everywhere apparent. And a concern for his political future seemed to undergird his statement, surfacing only at the conclusion in his expressed willingness to "continue to offer my services" to the district. As a politician, Hinson had to be—or appear to be—honest. Though he clearly had been hiding something, he asserted that he "never considered hiding." Though he undoubtedly had shrouded these events in secrecy, he insisted he had "not . . . wrapped [them] in secrecy." Indeed, as he now revealed selected portions of the past, he continued to cloak other portions. Hinson resorted to the Foucaultian confession— "the West's most highly valued technique for producing truth," particularly around sex.[14] But this truth was necessarily partial, shifting, fragmentary. Hinson frequently prefaced his sentences with "frankly" and "to be quite honest," though he often was not "totally frank" or honest. Much remained unclear.

Hinson chose to disclose so that the disclosure would be on his own terms. He had to refute any potential attempts—like Givens's—to link him to things "gay" or "out of the closet." He repeatedly referred to the incidents as a "crisis" or "difficulty," not an affirmation of self or a statement of identity—much less a liberationist avowal of public sex.[15] Hinson consistently spoke of that time—an assiduously bounded "twelve-month period" from 1976 to 1977—in the past tense, a period that had "ended," that was "firmly and irrevocably behind us." It all happened "several years ago," he said, though the latest incident was less than three years past.

The need for temporal distance became all the more apparent when Hinson astonished political observers the following week by officially opening his reelection campaign headquarters in Jackson. Hinson must have real-ized, as the astute pundit Bill Minor did, that the "majority of the people . . . don't know anything about the supposedly shocking news on Hinson."[16] Again strategically scheduled on a Friday, Hinson met with reporters for the first time since the confession.[17] He kicked off his campaign (as quietly as was then possible) at the start of a weekend, hoping to rely on the power of incumbency and the collective capacity of Mississippians to ignore or forget homosexuality.

But reporters persisted. They were finding out more and more about the "nice-looking, red-haired" thirty-eight-year-old "baby-faced ex-Marine."[18] The 1976 incident in Arlington, Virginia, they soon disclosed, occurred at the U.S. Marine Corps War Memorial, better known as the Iwo Jima Me-morial—a nighttime homosexual cruising area, on a hillside across the Po-tomac River from Washington.[19] With a sinister edge, *Jackson Daily News* cartoonist Jimmy Johnson sketched the widely recognized statue of several marines erecting a U.S. flag. Two shadowy human figures, dwarfed by the monument, faced each other on the margins. Scrawled at the statue's base: "JON HINSON WAS HERE."[20]

Guilt by association. Observers used it again and again. As Crazy Mur-phy Givens put it, Hinson's carefully orchestrated confession in Jackson never explained "why he went to those places, unless you can figure that he went to homosexual hangouts so he could *not* commit a homosexual act."[21] Following her leads on the Cinema Follies fire, Johanna Neuman dug ever deeper, uncovering more incriminating evidence on Hinson. Just as she assumed that all twenty-two thousand members of the theater facility were homosexuals, she implied that Hinson must be one, too, in her 28 August front-page banner headline: "HINSON A FREQUENT VISITOR TO THEATER, DEPOSITION SHOWS." As his sworn statement about the fire had demonstrated, "U.S. Rep. Jon C. Hinson was a regular customer during 1977 at the Washington Cinema Follies Club."[22] When the fire erupted, Hin-son had *known* the location of an alternate exit.

Likely aware that these facts would arise, that doubts would linger, Hin-son found it necessary to make a more forceful declaration, a clear-cut iden-tity statement, at the opening of his reelection campaign headquarters on 15 August 1980. A week after the initial confession, pressed by reporters, Hinson recalled a McCarthy-era language of disassociation, stating, "I am not, never have been, and never will be a homosexual." He reiterated, "I am not a homosexual. I am not a bisexual." Of those directing questions at him, Hinson consistently ignored the Mississippi Gay Alliance's Eddie Sandifer.[23]

Jon Hinson's confession and his disclamation, reporters' counterasser-
tions, and my own current re-presentation of the Hinson saga share a certain inability to "deliver the unquestionable truth," as theorist Novid Parsi
asserts. More productive, for my purposes, is "to explore how who we
'are' or, more precisely, who we perform ourselves to be— . . . with all our
contradictions and consistencies . . . —writes, is written by, and (above all)
matters in what we do, in what we write, and in how we write, perform,
and confess."[24] A distinction between seeming and being becomes moot.
"If [in this case, Jon Hinson] thinks he can confirm his own straightness by
only now-and-then seeming to be and not 'really' being a fag, then I want
to argue, as a fag, that being a fag, like being straight . . . , means seeming
to be so as well."[25]

Determining what constitutes queerness and queer sex across time and
place is a useful, multifaceted ethnohistorical project. That project, however, often flounders in its inability to categorically document—to turn up
traditional written historical sources of—queer sex, understood in presentist terms as same-sex genital contact. Parsi proposes an alternative to this
bind, an alternative that is particularly cogent in the Hinson case:

> Although I'm interested in reading how this text [let's say Hinson's state-
> ments and reporters' and voters' observations] desires and narrates sem-
> blances of queer sex while its homophobic assumptions and maneuvers
> attempt to separate its desire from that sex [more telling than Hinson's "pro-
> testing way too much" is Johanna Neuman's investigative reporting and
> Mississippians' avid consumption of it], it seems to me that gay sex itself is
> not some essential or fixed thing. Rather, (gay) sex acts are themselves also
> the semblances of (gay) sex acts.[26]

If Hinson could not be shown, by custom or lack of evidence, to have
engaged in queer sex, semblances abounded. And looks were not deceiv-
ing. The *Clarion-Ledger/Jackson Daily News* staff published increasingly
vivid accounts of the Iwo Jima Memorial incident, and Hinson felt compelled to respond. Though early on he refused comment in televised debates and interviews—except to say that he had not been entrapped[27]—he
called a 9 October *Jackson Daily News* story "utterly untrue," and his campaign produced TV advertisements to refute it. The newspaper said Hinson
had "made a blatant homosexual advance to an undercover officer."[28] As
was further reported nationally through the Knight-Ridder newspaper syn-
dicate, Hinson had "exposed himself to [the] policeman": "The congressman groped at the officer's groin area, placed his hand on the officer's head,
and tried to coax him toward him."[29] Coax him *down* toward Hinson's
crotch?

Reporters for the *Clarion-Ledger/Jackson Daily News* and the Memphis *Commercial Appeal*, sources at the National Park Service, and officials of the Jon Hinson campaign continued to dicker over details of Hinson's apparent attempt at penetrative oral sex. In a strange twist, the Hinson campaign tried to elicit voter sympathy by now claiming, contrary to the confession, that Hinson had indeed feared blackmail, specifically that Democratic opponent Britt Singletary had knowledge of the arrest and might have used it against him. Underlying a Hinson campaign press release was contempt for Singletary and a disingenuous assumption that Mississippians would pity Hinson: "The public may make a judgment as to whether Congressman Hinson had reason to believe that Singletary knew of the Washington matter prior to the news conference on Aug. 8." [30] Suddenly, it was the Singletary campaign that was acting deceptively. As the *Jackson Daily News* put it, "There's an old saying that the best defense is a good offense." [31] Such wranglings obscured the reality of the arrest, which Hinson tried to "put behind" him from the moment of the confession.

Though he had confessed to amorphous misdeeds, Hinson more to the point disidentified from those deeds. Hinson took on the difficult task of proving that although he'd been caught in "areas frequented by some of Washington's homosexual community" and indeed may have engaged in homosexual acts, he was "not a homosexual." Clearly Hinson was, as Novid Parsi describes another context, *worried*—about how he looked and how he seemed, as opposed to how he "really" was: "A way out of this dilemma . . . is to imagine an interiority at variance with our exteriority. And not just to imagine it ourselves but to let everyone else in on it by actively giving off signs of that 'inner' conflict or, in other words, by making external that 'internal' struggle. Letting everyone else in on the inside means producing an inside." [32] In Mississippi, producing an inside meant producing a spiritual life. And this Hinson did masterfully.

Hinson's "personal crisis"—"requiring great personal introspection and thought"—was foremost a "spiritual crisis." He both exposed *and* produced, that day in Jackson, an interiority—a soul in the continual process of change. But change though it might, one constant remained: that inner life was understood (perhaps retrospectively) in religious terms. Hinson described his "fear and self-doubt," his "purposelessness and isolation." These were not static states. He "wrestled" and "struggled" with them, albeit "unsuccessfully for this time."

Overcoming the crisis was likened to a spiritual reawakening. Hinson did not come out. Rather, he was born again. His conversion, his turning from his former ways, was marked by a "rediscover[y] [of] my basic religious values."

"The good Lord does indeed work in mysterious and miraculous ways," Hinson asserted. And as was common among the evangelical Protestants who predominated in Mississippi, Hinson posited direct divine intervention in his life. In the same way that Darryl Jeffries assumed God had led him to read the newspaper that day in 1983 and thereby learn about Mississippi's gay Christians,[33] Hinson saw his surviving the fire as an omen: "I believe I lived for a reason." Such a statement further, callously, distanced Hinson from those *other* Cinema Follies members who (rightly? apocalyptically?) perished in the blaze.

Hinson may have cynically understood the ascendancy, dating from the late 1960s, of religious discourse over queer sexuality in Mississippi. Or perhaps his "struggle" was truly marked by a personal relationship with God. Either way, or both, Hinson made clear to Mississippians that he sought not the psychiatrist's couch but rather the minister's chambers for confession. He advised others to do likewise.

Intentions aside, Hinson's shrewdest political device was a 19 August letter to the editor of the *Jackson Daily News*. The letter was penned by Reverend Robert Troutman "on behalf of Riverside Baptist Church of Washington, D.C., its members and pastor." The letter, Troutman wrote, was not an endorsement of any "political position," but instead "an endorsement of the lives of Jon and Cynthia Hinson." Relying on metaphors of spatial and temporal distance, he said, "We know how far [Hinson] has come in these past few years, and we proudly stand with him now." The congregation had "watched" Hinson—a "member of our community of faith"—in his "growth" from "self-doubting" and (perhaps a reference to the [hellish] fire) "almost self-destruction to a . . . purpose-filled life through a new found faith in Christ." What Hinson surmised and what Troutman insinuated was that their audience, mostly rural Mississippians, did not necessarily conceptualize homosexuality as a state of being for a distinct, definable minority—or if they did, they cast homosexuality as elsewhere, as an otherworldly, urban phenomenon (an alarmingly large one, Johanna Neuman suggested with her Follies membership roll). Homosexuality was a set of acts that were sinful. Universalizing its potential, Troutman noted that "apart from the Grace of God, all of us are weak and prone to failure."[34]

Thus again, Mississippians were offered a means for understanding (that) men like that. If, as has been discussed, a minoritizing view of queer sexuality held its import to apply primarily to a discrete substrata of society—to men like that—Reverend Troutman voiced the belief of most Mississippians in a universalizing view, a view that men liked that. That is, men, women, all persons, were susceptible to the allure of deviant behavior. As such, however, all could be redeemed.

Additional testimonials were offered for Hinson. The names of almost five hundred Walthall Countians appeared in an advertisement in the *Tylertown Times.* "Your hometown folks," it read, "those who know you best, are backing you all the way!"[35] At least eighteen signatories, however, didn't authorize the use of their names and were later listed in a retraction. But Melba Bufkin may have best summarized the mood of local residents: "I think most of the people are for Jon. I know he has fine parents and a good background. Some of that good had to rub off on him."[36] Cast as one of us, Hinson's primary identification as a God-fearing Mississippian (and voters' identification with him through that) could dismiss his (and, by association, their) potential queerness. Homosexuality was not in my backyard.

But when asked by a reporter about her former student's dalliances in Washington, Hinson's fifth-grade teacher, Mrs. Preston Dampeer, colluded in Reverend Troutman's universalist sentiments. She engaged the unnameable act, even as she reinscribed notions of the corrupt, culpable city and the decent, innocent countryside: "I know he did that thing, but we all make mistakes," she said. "He was a little country boy who got up there and got into something he couldn't handle."[37]

Handle it he did, however, with the help of Cynthia. The former Cynthia Johnson—a native of Statesboro, Georgia, and a secretary to that district's congressional representative, Democrat Ronald "Bo" Ginn—had married Hinson a year prior.[38] Indeed, the couple's first anniversary fell during the week between Hinson's public confession and the opening of his reelection campaign headquarters. At the opening in Jackson, Cynthia accompanied her husband to the podium. Their picture, Cynthia's head on Jon's shoulder, her hand clutching his arm, took up a quarter page of the Saturday *Clarion-Ledger/Jackson Daily News.*[39]

Hinson's heretofore bachelor status had not gone unnoticed in Mississippi. The *Capital Reporter*'s "Behind the Scene" column had called it the most incongruous aspect of Hinson's initial election to Congress. That the "unknown, untested" Hinson could defeat John Hampton Stennis—son of the popular longtime segregationist senator John C. Stennis—was remarkable enough. That Hinson "bombed out as a law student at Ole Miss in his freshman year" and Stennis was "a graduate of Princeton and a law graduate from Virginia" was stranger still. But above all else: "Hinson changed the time-honored [and, I hardly need to note, sexist] rule of Mississippi politics that the candidate has to trot out the wife and kids on TV to show he is a family man." Hinson was "a bachelor at the age most Mississippians are settled-in marrieds."[40]

The *Reporter* moreover hinted at a cover-up: "The fact that Hinson had left the employ of Cong. Thad Cochran over a year ago [the time of the arrest] under somewhat less than amicable conditions never got into the picture."[41]

Thus, it's neither unusual nor incidental that Congressman Jon Hinson's 1980 reelection campaign handbills described "The Man" with a bullet list that declared him:

- Native of Tylertown, Mississippi
- Member of Tylertown Baptist Church
- Graduate of the University of Mississippi, 1964
- United States Marine Corps Reserve, 1964–1970
- Nine years experience as Legislative Assistant in U.S. House of Representatives

But preceding these, and preeminent, he was

- Married, 38 years old[42]

I don't want to suggest here that Hinson's marriage to Johnson was solely, consciously the self-serving act of a jaded, closeted politician—though it hardly harmed his continuing political aspirations. Hinson's ambitions and desires, his postures and maneuvers, were locked into an inevitable reciprocal relationship with the mores and values of his culture, his constituency—the people of southwest Mississippi. Ostensibly private inner workings of the psyche meshed with public—the people's—attitudes, as Hinson performed and occasionally resisted societal scripts and rituals.

Tracing a Victorian ideological lineage, ethicist Kathy Rudy suggests that the American religious right's promotion of "traditional family values" flows from a "Christian nationalist" perspective on "specific gender roles, gendered theology, and sexual purity"—the latter relying heavily on women's influence.[43] In their genuine search for relationship with God, evangelical Christians feel "neither men nor women alone have complete access to God. Men need women to have a successful relationship with God, and women need men to support the family so that they may stay at home and develop their spiritual and moral sensibilities. The single life, therefore, is rarely seen as a viable and permanent choice."[44] Thus, Jon Hinson's bachelorhood signaled not only the possibility of homosexual deviancy, but also, more seriously, a particular type of gender nonconformity. Religious life in Mississippi carried distinct gendered roles and responsibilities reliant on the institution of marriage. Single men and women, those who refused marriage, endangered their access to God.

Though Cynthia Hinson worked outside the home, she still was embedded in a cultural tradition dependent on an idealized white female virtue. Jon Hinson expressly tied the rediscovery of his "basic religious values" to his confidante, friend, and wife, Cynthia. "Blessedly," he said, she had been the conduit for his spiritual reckoning. Though vital in the production of Jon Hinson's inner spiritual life, Cynthia Hinson's interiority was never discussed. It was assumed. Likewise, male profligacy was a given. In this sexist construction, a domestic, privatized female moral rectitude existed to prop up and support a civic, public male obligation to service—exemplified by the photograph of Cynthia leaning *into* Jon leaning *on* Cynthia.

Just as Jon's life had been miraculously spared, Jon and Cynthia's union had been divinely ordained. It was "blessed." And the two—with certain caveats of privacy—were ready to "share [their] blessings." Their model: the personal testimonials of salvation and redemption so common in Protestant evangelicalism.

HINSON HAD A RACE to run and, he still hoped, win. More than God, he needed money. Would his financial backers, the wealthy Republican elite in Jackson, desert him? *Daily News* staff writer David Hampton assumed so. Though Hinson's "conservative credentials" were impeccable, so were those of white Democrat Britt Singletary. By omission, Hampton apparently dismissed black independent Leslie McLemore, a liberal, as a long shot. How could conservatives now support Hinson over Singletary? Hinson's "admissions" were "likely to offend the very people who provided his strongest backing in the past."[45] As one Republican leader unselfconsciously punned, "Some of these Presbyterians in Jackson had to swallow real hard about this thing."[46]

Two key Presbyterians were oil producer W. D. "Billy" Mounger and insurance executive Wirt Yerger, the former state Republican Party chairman. The Mounger and Yerger families belonged to Jackson's First Presbyterian Church, a large, powerful white congregation founded in 1837 and housed in an imposing set of columned orange-brick buildings north of downtown on State Street. The influence of "First Prez" pervaded Mississippi business and politics. Of its two most visible Republican Party leaders, Mounger was "dead neutral for about three weeks" after the Hinson confession.[47] But ultimately Hinson's House voting record and his positions on the issues lured Mounger and Yerger back into the fold—and their money back into the campaign coffers. As Yerger said, "He has had an outstanding record as a congressman, and the [again, unnameable] things he referred to took place before any of us had ever heard of him."[48] Mounger concurred: "You'd think a man who had acknowledged frequenting a homosexual theater would have been run out of Mississippi. But he's got a great record. There are folks who think we would rather have a queer conservative than a macho liberal, and they may be right."[49] In effect, Hinson defied queer *identity* by speaking—and repenting—only of queer *deeds*. Hinson's identity was shaped most by a tried-and-true conservatism.

Hinson's congressional record had yielded him a 100 percent approval rating from the American Conservative Union, a zero rating from the Americans for Democratic Action; a hundred from the U.S. Chamber of Commerce, zero from the National Education Association; zero from the National Council of Senior Citizens, ninety-two from the Christian Voice.[50] Mike Wells and the Mississippi Moral Majority chose not to make an endorsement in the race, but after a "behind closed doors" meeting with Hinson, "the preachers seemed impressed."[51] A group of Pentecostals, by contrast, publicly reneged on their support for Hinson.[52]

Overall, however, Hinson's views met with receptive audiences, especially among white Mississippians. In his first campaign for Congress, Hinson had papered towns like Crystal Springs, Port Gibson, Brookhaven, and Magnolia with promises to cut taxes, thwart "socialized medicine," fight the Humphrey-Hawkins national jobs program, and—proudly and overtly at odds with his father, a Walthall County supervisor—oppose the Panama Canal "giveaway."[53] Along the way, Hinson gained few black supporters. His opposition to the Martin Luther King Jr. national holiday was "obnoxious" and "archaic" in the eyes of longtime civil rights activist Fayette mayor Charles Evers. NAACP field director Emmett Burns labeled Hinson "young, brash, and very inexperienced."[54] Summit resident Joy Adams was more direct: "Hinson speaks as, spoke as, and indeed is an old time racist!"[55]

As Hinson further alienated black voters with his opposition to affirmative action, to many public assistance provisions, and to the extension of the 1965 Voting Rights Act[56]—the very act that had enabled anything more than token black voting in Mississippi—he shored up support from moneyed Republicans like Yerger and Mounger. In the 1980 reelection bid, Hinson espoused military growth and tax cuts; he opposed federal deficit spending and the Equal Rights Amendment.[57] Indeed, in a last-ditch solicitation of funds, a 25 October 1980 letter to donors, the Hinson campaign portrayed the pending election in stark ideological terms: "Those who believe in good, sound conservative government . . . cannot afford to sit idly by. . . . The Liberals are giving it their most serious shot." God and conservative politics were explicitly linked: "We urge you to give the most prayerful consideration to making the maximum financial contribution."[58] The dollars poured in.

*

HINSON WON. Far more shocking than his 1978 "come from nowhere" defeat of a household name in Mississippi politics, John Hampton Stennis,[59] Hinson had overcome two separate queer episodes to win reelection to the U.S. Congress from Mississippi's Fourth District. On 4 November 1980 Jon Hinson garnered almost 40 percent of the vote in the three-person contest.[60] That Leslie McLemore placed second, ahead of Britt Singletary, attested to increasing black voter strength in the majority white district and to Hinson's naïveté or disregard around issues of race in Mississippi. In early 1980, scarcely fifteen years after passage of the federal Civil Rights Act and Voting Rights Act—won at the cost of lives in Mississippi and throughout the South—Hinson declared "racism is past in Mississippi, and it ought to be."[61] He said on another occasion that "the problem in Mississippi is not black/white, but green."[62] The 1980 election results suggested that Hinson's racism—even if the type that minimalizes race—was more important to white *and* black voters than his dormant queerness.

A variety of factors resulted in Hinson's surprise victory. First, like so many others around the country, Hinson benefited from the landslide presidential victory of conservative Republican Ronald Reagan, who before the confession had campaigned for Hinson.[63] Second, in a racially polarized vote, conservative and liberal Democrats split their numbers between Singletary and McLemore, allowing Hinson to win with a plurality but not a majority of ballots cast.[64] Third, regardless of Reagan, Hinson's own right-wing politics—proven during his first term in Congress—appealed to many voters in southwest Mississippi.

Most importantly, Hinson dissipated the cloud of homosexuality by portraying it as an act, not an identity; a temptation, not a state of being; a sin, not a lifestyle. Hinson convinced voters and financial backers that this murky "thing" was "behind" him, in the past. His righteous economic and racial conservatism overshadowed his prior moral lapses. As much as sexuality, his politics, his class, and his race shaped his identity. Yet Wirt Yerger's summation showed that Jon Hinson would remain subject to scrutiny, that Cynthia Hinson would be required to certify his allegiance. "He has a happy marriage," Yerger noted; "he's done a super job as a congressman. I think that's all there is to say."[65]

Hinson mastered a religious rhetoric that designated homosexuality a sin. While sins were baleful, even repugnant in this case, they were forgivable. Indeed, Hinson considered his win a sign of Mississippians' "forgiving" nature—while he acknowledged, at the same time, that "if this had happened ten years ago, I would have been driven from office."[66] National and local church bodies had been openly and frequently discussing homosexuality for well over a decade. Though this "thing" continued to evade precise vocabularies of hegemonic depiction, it was understood to fall squarely within the spiritual realm in Mississippi. Hinson capitalized on spiritual discourse. As south Mississippi farmer Harold Patterson best explained it, "Most of the people in this district are churchgoers. . . . And remember, Baptists love a repentant sinner." [67]

Hinson's public confession mirrored the staple of Sunday morning worship services, the concluding "altar call." In Protestant churches throughout Mississippi, preachers asked congregants again and again to get up from their pews, step down the aisle, and in front of God and everybody, profess they needed to be saved. Like those Sunday penitents, Hinson had seen the light, he said. And Mississippians believed.

In a culture of manners obsessed with appearances and demeanor, looks and performance, queers perpetually performed within and along the boundaries of what Judith Butler calls "historically delimited possibilities." Hinson's confession wasn't so much a deceit (though as Neil Bartlett notes, "we [gay men] all . . . grow up as liars");[68] it could perhaps better be understood as a parody—a parody, as conceived by Butler, not reliant on any unmediated "original." Hinson's mea culpa seemed yet another example— albeit a highly public one—of dissembling, a habit that was second nature to most ordinary queer Mississippians. Rather than "disruptive," "subversive," or "troubling," the confession was "domesticated and recirculated as [an] instrument of cultural hegemony." [69] Hinson, in producing and performing a spiritual inside, ensured that he wouldn't be relegated to a stigmatized cultural outside.

AND YET, HINSON'S performance faltered. Just three months after reelection to Congress, Hinson slipped. The stage was vividly set, the characters colorfully drawn, and the tragic downfall graphically depicted in the Jackson papers in a trademark Johanna Neuman minute-by-minute, voyeuristic reconstruction. I provide an abridged version below.

Johanna Neuman: There was a phone call on hold Wednesday morning [4 February 1981] when Congressman Jon Hinson tossed his jacket and tie on a side chair, grabbed a sweater and left his office by a private door. The drama started in a men's restroom in the Longworth House Office Building. At 1:15 P.M., U.S. Capitol Police arrested Hinson for giving oral stimulation to Harold Moore, a black employee of the Library of Congress.

Hinson's first call went to his $50,000-a-year administrative assistant, Marshall Hanbury. The congressman asked him to go to the office of U.S. Rep. Bo Ginn. He wanted Hanbury to be there when he called his wife Cynthia, a bride of eighteen months.

[Around 2:30] Hanbury and Cynthia Hinson wandered upstairs at the Capitol police station. They were directed to the office of Capt. Richard F. Xander, the arresting officer. Hinson was sitting in Xander's office. Quietly. Expressionless.

Hanbury and [Jon] Hinson agreed that the congressman should call his friend and pastor in Tylertown, tell them what had happened, and ask them to go to the congressman's parents' home so they could be there when he called. Hinson did. Then he called his parents.

By then it was after 3 P.M. Hinson [went] to the central cell block to be finger-printed and booked. A clerk set bail at $2,000, the standard rate for felony sodomy.

Back at the office, Hanbury called a staff meeting. The seven employees sat in Hinson's office. The jacket and tie left on the side chair were hung up. The staff sat stunned. They would bear the brunt of it, fielding obscene phone calls. Cynthia Hinson walked in. The female employees hugged her, told her they loved her and were praying for her.

The staff left to begin the work that would leave them drained and hurt. Their boss had brought shame to his office. At 4:30 P.M., the *Washington Post* called. No statement, said the staff.

A series of calls would broaden the circle of the informed. Hanbury called Billy Mounger, he tried to reach ten or twelve other key financial backers. Their reactions were identical. "I guess it's all over," Mounger said.

At 5:30 P.M., Hinson reentered his office by the private door from which he had left so few—or so many?—hours before. He hugged Cynthia, shook hands with [Reverend Robert] Troutman. For three hours they sat and talked. Hinson, quiet and dazed, did very little of the talking. It was decided to make an appointment for him the next day with a local psychiatrist.

At 8:30 P.M., the Hinsons left. Hanbury stayed to write the first draft of a statement that would make national news of the psychiatric term "dissociative reaction."

[The next day] Hinson decided to admit himself voluntarily to Sibley Hospital for treatment of "dissociative reaction." The doctor explained that the disease was a "success reaction," a delayed reaction to the rigors of the campaign. Hinson had no immediate plans to resign. There were the financial considerations of unemployment to consider.[70]

Reactions were swift in Mississippi. The day after the arrest, *Jackson Daily News* editors called for Hinson's resignation. "Gaiety," they said, "is no laughing matter."[71] An editorial in the *Clarion-Ledger* the next day insisted, "Hinson should resign immediately."[72] Three of the four other members of Mississippi's House delegation publicly called for Hinson's ouster. While one Baptist minister in Jackson, John Claypool of Northminster, adopted a "wait-and-see attitude"—after all, Hinson was "innocent until proven guilty"—another, Leo Touten of Calvary, "suggest[ed] he resign."[73] Across the political spectrum, four out of five southwest Mississippians agreed.[74] Ku Klux Klan members rallied on the old Capitol steps to express their "disgust";[75] Eddie Sandifer said Hinson should resign for his failure to support gay rights.[76]

Perhaps most incensed over Hinson's latest turn of fortune were Republican Party financiers Billy Mounger and Wirt Yerger. The pillars of First Prez felt betrayed, deceived. Yerger said he had acted "in good faith" when he stood by Hinson after the confession. "Through a spiritual commitment we gave him the benefit of the doubt," Yerger insisted. "We trusted him, and he just didn't play the game straight with us. I think he should resign."[77] Mounger felt Hinson had at least *initially* played the game straight. "He has a very attractive wife," Mounger noted, "who has a good job and isn't just a flighty lady."

> They'd gotten married and we thought nothing was wrong with Jon. . . . Who [we]re we to say anything? . . . We've all done something wrong. . . . [There was] a degree of Christian forgiveness. . . . He was convincing. Jon looked at me in my eyes and said he was not a homosexual. And I believed him.

But for Mounger, this rest room incident was the last straw: "I think he's sick, and I think all he can do is resign."[78]

Holed up at Sibley Hospital in Washington, Hinson waited five weeks before calling it quits.[79] On 13 March 1981, he sent a one-sentence letter to Mississippi governor William Winter, copied to House Speaker Thomas P. "Tip" O'Neill: "This is to advise you that I resign from the United States House of Representatives effective at the close of business on Monday, April 13, 1981."[80]

Why had Hinson been unable to shirk the latest charges? Why had Mississippians evinced a willingness to forgive in one instance and not in another? As Joe Holmes noted of Jackson's Broadmoor Baptist Church, Mississippians were accustomed each and every summer to hosting fiery revivalists and getting saved "all over again." On Sunday mornings and evenings and in Wednesday evening services, too, Mississippians repeatedly turned from their former ways. Being baptized, saved, or converted often implied an inaugural experience—a once-in-a-lifetime transformation from "lost" to "found," in the terminology of the popular altar-call hymn "Amazing Grace." But even regular churchgoing folk, pious and upstanding, could acknowledge their ongoing struggles with sin through the ritual of "rededicating" their lives to Jesus. Why couldn't Hinson rededicate his life even now?

Kathy Rudy sees the scandals that soon would be visited upon televangelists Jimmy Swaggart, Oral Roberts, and Jim and Tammy Bakker as not "the downfall of conservative Christianity." Quite the contrary,

> the scandals reminded the evangelists' followers that sin could erupt at any moment into the lives of clean-living Christians. . . . The circle of conservative Christianity could include those like Swaggart who had repented of their sins, but not those who persisted in what the Right saw as unclean living. While it might have *former* sinners, *former* adulterers, *former* homosexuals, *former* militant feminists in its ranks, the Right contained none of these undesirable elements who still practiced their sins.[81]

Hinson maybe delayed resigning in an attempt to gauge how much Mississippians could forgive, how readily they might let him put this latest episode behind him. He could not have been encouraged.

When Hinson was reelected in November, fellow representative Robert Bauman, the four-term self-described ultraconservative from Maryland, lost his reelection bid. Fighting charges that he engaged the services of an underage male sex worker, the Catholic family man who had needlepointed a welcome gift for Jon Hinson learned the limits of forgiveness (though he tallied an impressive 48 percent of the vote in his two-person race).[82] Like Bauman's escapades, Hinson's latest breached other taboos. And the details were becoming all too vivid for the folks back home.

Johanna Neuman of the *Clarion-Ledger*'s Washington bureau ran a story on Hinson's sex partner, Harold Moore—"a black man" known as "a good worker and a nice guy." The Washington bureau also offered a story on the Longworth House Office Building men's room: "INSIDERS KNOW WHICH RESTROOM." Even Cynthia Hinson became the subject of a *Clarion-Ledger* biographical sketch that dredged up old allegations of financial improprieties against her father, a Georgia banker and politician.[83]

Even after Hinson resigned, Johanna Neuman felt obliged to offer Mississippians one final blow-by-blow replay of "the Hinson drama." In her Sunday *Clarion-Ledger/Jackson Daily News* feature, Neuman took readers back in time to that fateful day and site. She enticed readers to "picture the bathroom." She bid readers to imagine "the 28-year-old black Library of Congress employee who sports a frail look and a cultured demeanor."[84]

Though hardly unusual among the mainstream press of the day, the tendency to specify the race of only nonwhite individuals proved vital in this second Hinson arrest. White Mississippians especially would remember over a decade afterward that Moore was, yes, a Library of Congress employee; but foremost, he was "a black guy."[85] Whereas Hinson would suggest years later that interracial intercourse—homosexual as well as heterosexual—was often a class prerogative of elite white Mississippians,[86] most Fourth District residents felt differently in 1981. On this much, blacks and whites agreed. Together they evinced Mississippi's characteristic collective defensiveness. Betty Robinson, a thirty-two-year-old African American telephone clerk, called the scandal "a disgrace to Mississippi"; John Hulsebosch, a forty-six-year-old European American personnel officer, termed it "an embarrassment to the state."[87]

"That he did it in the bathroom" upset one voter "the most."[88] Another angrily fired off a letter to Washington, urging the director of federal personnel to deny Hinson's petition for medical disability benefits.[89] While many hometown folk in Tylertown described a "stunned," "sad feeling about it," around Jackson reactions were much more visceral. One middle-aged woman bitterly mimicked Hinson: "I am not, I never was, and I never will be!" Another young woman said she "wanted to vomit."[90]

Hinson's second arrest differed from the first in important ways. The sex acts contrasted sharply. At the Iwo Jima/Marine Memorial, former marine reservist Hinson attempted to engage in penetrative oral sex, it seemed. As the accounts suggested, he was an overworked, stressed-out young man looking for any receptacle for his pent-up desires. Such male profligacy was understood and often accepted in Mississippi. As we have seen, this particular act historically did not always mark Mississippi men as queer. In the second case, Hinson donned drag, of a sort. Epitomized by the coat and tie left draped across the side chair, Hinson cast off the markers of office, of public service, of *manhood.* He put on a sweater, walked from his own Cannon House Office Building into another, and entered a well-known tearoom. There, he presumably got down on his knees to give oral stimulation to a *black* man. Indeed, he was caught in the act, found out, whereas in the first incident, his stepping forward allowed the structure of the confessional previously discussed.

Hinson's homosexuality was now undeniable. His gender nonconformity—his feminization and consequent degradation—complete. Not only was he penetrated. Not only was he the receptive partner in the sex act. He was penetrated by a black male, someone still viewed by many white Mississippians as his inferior—if not racially, then professionally and economically. Moreover, Hinson's cross-racial intercourse discounted his conservative racial politics as it evoked the sixties cultural amalgamation of queer sexuality and African American equal rights. Sex perverts in Mississippi were also known to be race perverts. Another central figure in the cultural imaginary of white southerners across time, the black male has been vilified and scapegoated for a carefully fabricated hypersexuality. Historian Joel Williamson charts the invention of this "black beast-rapist" from just before the turn of the century.[91] While antebellum slave owner–slave heterosexual relations are to this day evidenced by mixed-race descendants, postbellum white southern men hypocritically tracked down and murdered black men *said* to defile white womanhood. This cultural imagery likely was not far from the minds of Mississippi readers as Johanna Neuman seduced them into picturing the scene between Hinson and Moore.

Neuman's sensationalism further participated in the ongoing construction of homosexuality as a new phenomenon. For decades observers had noted homosexuality, usually via public scandals, and straightaway forgotten about it, heralding its novelty again and again. Neil Bartlett shows that even the novelty of Britain's infamous Oscar Wilde trials of 1895, the ostensible origin of public homosex scandals, was subverted *at the time* by Mr. Justice Wills's comments. "I have tried many similar cases," he conceded.[92] Likewise, Mississippians learned about police surveillance of men's rooms at the University of Mississippi in the eighties, at the University of Southern Mississippi in the seventies; they heard about the tearoom busts in Jackson's City Auditorium and Hattiesburg's Forrest Hotel during the sixties; Mississippians were arrested in rest rooms from Atlanta to Dallas in the fifties. Why then would Johanna Neuman assert that after the Hinson scandal, the word "bathroom" was *"no longer* [a] synonym for a mundane habit of everyday life"?[93] Though some might wish it away, Mississippians would continue to find evidence to defy the homosexuality-as-elsewhere model, the homosexuality-as-new phenomenon.

Meanwhile, Jon Hinson pleaded no contest to a reduced misdemeanor charge of sodomy and was put on probation.[94] Hinson resided the rest of his life in the Washington area. Tragically, his parents died in a predawn fire at their Tylertown home in 1984.[95] Jon and Cynthia Hinson separated in 1987, divorced in 1989. Hinson relied increasingly on psychiatrists and finally "realized I was living a lie."[96] In its 1995 obituary, the *New York Times* noted that Hinson was a founder of the Fairfax [County, Virginia] Lesbian and Gay Citizens Association. Shortly before his death, he made a visit to Mississippi to lend support to gay causes.[97] At fifty-three, Jon Hinson died of respiratory failure resulting from AIDS.[98]

ULTIMATELY, JON HINSON was exiled. In the dialectic of the country and the city, under the strategy of oppression that cast homosexuality as elsewhere, he was relegated to a queer urban domain, a physical and metaphorical remove that belied the realities of queer Mississippians who chose life in their native land. In a gender system that espoused heterosexual marriage as the conduit to Christian faith, Hinson performed a spiritual life and confessed queer sex as wrongdoing but finally found himself outside the requisite familial relationship after he transgressed gender conventions, most notably in the receptive, interracial sexual role. Though he took on the trappings of elite political life with the appropriate markers of race and class privilege, he ceded those rights when he consorted with those near the bottom of race, class, and sex hierarchies.

A time-honored pretense of ignorance had been broken. Tacit agreements now were useless. Relying on the mode of public confession, Hinson could not feign innocence and thus his constituents could not feign ignorance. Queer sexuality had been explicitly summoned up and spoken. In 1980 Hinson's repenting was rewarded, but in 1981 his dissembling was punished.

In the view of most Mississippians, Jon Hinson's career ended in 1981. He would thereafter be unknown to many. But during the six-month period from Hinson's initial confession on 8 August 1980, until his ultimate downfall, on 4 February 1981, the Tylertown transplant to Washington severely tested mainstream coping mechanisms. Though Mississippians might conveniently attempt to forget or ignore, homosexuality and gender nonconformity would repeatedly resurface in public discourse—in the early eighties even sooner than Hinson scandal aficionados could imagine. Another political intrigue was yet to break. And this time, queer sexuality would hit even closer to home.

Denial, Sex Work, and the Governor's Race

In the words of the Donna Summer tune then popular in gay discos from Biloxi to Jackson, Hattiesburg to Meridian: "She work[ed] hard for the money."[99] In 1983 David Holliday worked at the upscale Walthall Hotel on Capitol Street in Jackson. But he rarely interacted with the downtown executives who lunched in the dining room or the out-of-town guests who slept upstairs. Holliday labored behind the scenes, laundering towels and bed linens, perhaps, or washing dishes.[100]

After a hard day's work, Holliday often walked over to Bill's Disco, just a few blocks away. The predominantly African American gay nightclub held elaborate drag shows after midnight, and Holliday was a well-regarded entertainer there. Of the numerous soloists that black drag queens chose to emulate—Gladys Knight, Patti LaBelle, Melba Moore, Dionne Warwick[101]—Holliday picked superstar Diana Ross.[102] Of all the great singers, Diana Ross was many a queer Mississippian's top choice. Gloster native Jeremy Powell, who regularly went out to Bill's in the 1980s, called the former Motown sensation his "favorite gal."[103] And David Holliday gave a convincing portrayal. Backstage at Bill's, he threw off his Walthall uniform and slipped into an elegant evening gown. He applied makeup and falsies, donned jewelry and wig, and emerged into the spotlight as Devia Ross.

In rotation with other performers, Ross lip-synched classics such as "Ain't No Mountain High Enough," "Upside Down," and "Love Hangover." Audiences cheered the queer appropriation and double entendre of "I'm Coming Out." And sometimes, I imagine, Ross effected bouffant and pedal pushers for retro-hip renditions of songs from the sixties, from Diana's days with the Supremes. Devia Ross gladly grabbed one-dollar tips or the occasional five offered from the edge of the stage as she crooned "Baby Love," "Love Child," or "Stop! In the Name of Love."

Glamour was expensive, as Ross knew well. Try as she might, it was difficult to build a wardrobe from tips at Bill's and minimum wage at the Walthall. Moreover, salesclerks eyed her warily when she shopped for dresses; they made her uncomfortable. Once, in 1980, Ross got caught for shoplifting. Another Diana Ross impersonator from the same period described the experience this way:

> We pick[ed] up things we would want, like eyebrow pencil or a tube of lipstick. Might steal a panty girdle. Things that we were going to use, you know. . . . We would like take two or three outfits in the dressing room. Wrap up two of them or either we would even put them on underneath our clothes and walk out the stores with them . . . so we would have outfits.[104]

For shoplifting, the Jackson municipal court judge sentenced Devia Ross to six months' community service at the Salvation Army[105]—cutting severely into her paid working hours, not to mention her rehearsal time.

In the early morning hours, after the Bill's crowd went home, before she retired to the broken-down Bloom Street Apartments,[106] Ross often "strolled" the area with her friends. Unlike Smith Park—a mostly white male world of nighttime cruisers on foot and in cars—the Farish Street district was largely a black realm of women and cross-dressing men walking and men driving. As in Smith Park, some of the casual sexual encounters there were paid; others unpaid. Devia Ross both wanted and needed to be paid.

In the 1980s Jackson's residential housing was racially segregated, such that blacks, as in the larger Southeast regional center of Atlanta, lived primarily to the south and west, whites to the north and east—bending with the Pearl River. More precisely, Jackson evinced what urban historians refer to as a checkerboard pattern of irregularly alternating white and nonwhite squares or sections, even within large sectors known as black or white.[107] One such black section was the multiblock district at the edge of the downtown core bisected by Farish Street and bounded by Capitol and Monument Streets on the north and south, Lamar and Mill on the west and east.[108] Mill Street, running alongside the railroad tracks, had been home to cotton and lumber mills in the nineteenth and early twentieth centuries. In the late twentieth century, the remaining mill housing—narrow cookie-cutter dwellings known as shotgun shacks—looked as dilapidated as the apartment house David Holliday called home. A few businesses remained, like Bill's at the corner of Mill and Amite. But the Farish Street district, once a hub of black life in Jackson, had certainly seen better days.

Jackson police considered the Farish Street district a high crime zone. Patrol officers frequently counseled late-night motorists to avoid it. White drivers were so rare that five years later Shelby Johnson would remember having seen one over several nights in 1978. Officer Johnson eventually pulled this motorist over and "asked him to leave the area."[109] Devia Ross remembered the white driver too. They met around Christmastime 1982, at the corner of High and Church Streets. He approached her in his shiny new Oldsmobile. When Ross asked if he needed a "date," he said yes. She got in.[110]

The man gave Ross a blow job at the Jacksonian Inn, on Interstate 55 North. He also gave her money. They had sex three more times over the next several months—once in the Oldsmobile, twice on the back steps of a Church Street home in the Farish Street district.[111] The home was occupied by William Francis, a friend of Ross. Madame Francine, as she was known, would later deny to reporters that the man "had ever been *in* her house."[112] Ross last talked with the white driver one September night in 1983. But the man told her he "could not transact . . . business" for fear that "something heavy" was about to come down.[113]

ACCORDING TO FRIENDS, millionaire oil developer Billy Mounger had "very strong convictions" against homosexuality. As Mounger described it, homosexuals gave him "a crawling sensation in my skin."[114] So in 1983 he was both repelled by and drawn to the rumors he was hearing—rumors that state attorney general Bill Allain was queer. Allain, a Democrat, was running for governor; Mounger had made over $14,000 in campaign contributions to Allain's Republican opponent, Clarksdale farmer and businessman Leon Bramlett.[115]

Mounger heard the rumor again. This time from his pal, Jackson lawyer Bill Spell, who heard it from his wife, who heard it from her gay hair-

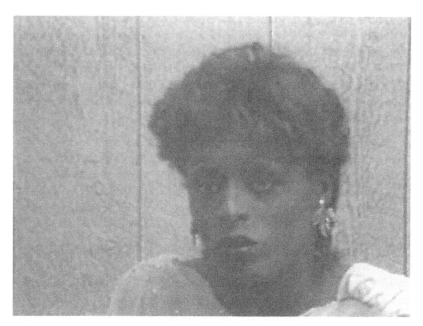

Devia Ross, 1984. Courtesy of ABC News.

dresser.[116] Mounger and two other self-acknowledged "big, rich oilmen" decided to check it out. "The group," as they came to be known, funded an investigation by the private firm Pendleton Detectives. Attorney Spell co-ordinated the effort. "We kept hearing these rumors, and we're all in the oil business," Mounger said, "so we decided to sort of drill a wildcat well."[117]

On 12 October 1983, their well-funded explorations paid off when a Pendleton detective found Devia Ross and took her to meet Spell. As Ross described it:

> He gave me one hundred dollars when we got in the car to get ready to come downtown to Mr. Pendleton's office. . . . He said, "I'll give you the other when we get down there." We got down here in the Deposit Guaranty building in the elevator. He gave me another hundred-dollar bill. . . . Upstairs . . . they went to asking me about had I had Bill Allain.[118]

After "promises of plane trips to soak up some sun" and assurances that "the information was for confidential files" only, Ross agreed to a polygraph examination, which was administered two days later in New Orleans.[119]

Pendleton detectives also took statements from two other sex workers, Nicole Toy—given name Grady Arrington—and Donna [Donald] Johnson.

Toy and Johnson, aged twenty-four and twenty-two, were longtime friends. Members of their extended families lived in the same trailer park on the city's northernmost edge. In the Farish Street district, Toy and Johnson had moved in together. Their decaying house on Oakley Street was just around the corner from Devia Ross.[120] With others, the three made up what East Coast transgender sex worker Shontae calls a "family-hood." As sociologist Leon Pettiway elaborates:

> These women live their lives in community, not in isolation. . . . The family-hood provides support, advice, imitation, and friendship; it connotes far more intimacy than "neighborhood." It implies a more porous boundary between one's home and others' homes as well as between one's family space and the spaces of the streets. It is a rich term and it indicates the geography of connection through which the women move and live.[121]

And work. Like the subjects of Pettiway's study, Toy, Johnson, and Ross pooled resources of necessity. Toy barely eked out subsistence wages as a dishwasher at the Sun-N-Sand Motel restaurant up on Lamar Street. Johnson, on the other hand, hadn't been able to maintain a steady job since moving to Jackson from Rankin County, where he worked as an orderly in a nursing home.[122] Ross brought in the most earnings, but they all relied on sex work to stay afloat. At home, on the streets, the three looked after each other. They swapped stories and lessons; they developed trust in one another. A collective, they "shared laughter, money, and clothes."[123] And they were about to spend three of the most unusual weeks of their lives together.

"The group"—oil executives Billy Mounger, Victor Smith, and Neal Clement—compiled the results of the Pendleton investigation and through attorney Bill Spell made them available to state newspapers and television stations. Spell dangled the bait before one journalist, then another. No one was biting. The culture of quiet accommodation, though considerably diminished since the 1940s and 1950s, still held sway on occasion. *Hattiesburg American* editor Frank Sutherland said the group "wanted to set conditions on what we would print concerning where we got (the documents)." News director Frank Morock of WJTV, Jackson, said, "I wanted somebody coming forth and making statements in front of a camera. I wasn't going to do their dirty work for them."[124]

For over a week, the group played the media against one another, asserting that the competition would get the scoop if they didn't act quickly. The *Clarion-Ledger* chose not to print the charges but began its own investigation. The paper sent reporters and a polygraph examiner—retired Memphis Police Department veteran Tom Harlan—to Vicksburg, where the group had boarded the three sex workers ostensibly to protect them from "harassment or pressure." A Pendleton detective was also staying at the motel to watch over them. After separate pretest interviews and tests of thirty-five to forty minutes each, Harlan concluded that the three sex workers' "responses were not indicative of deception." That is, they had told Spell and *his* polygraph examiner the truth.

Despite this, despite "dozens of post-midnight interviews in the Mill [and Farish] Street area," the *Clarion-Ledger* still refused to run the story, as did all other media.[125] Finally, Spell called a news conference for 25 October. He would break the story himself.

Appearing "smug, arrogant, and self-righteous" to at least one journalist,[126] Spell read a brief statement before television cameras, radio microphones, and newspaper reporters. He alleged that "Attorney General Bill Allain, over a period of years, frequently engaged in homosexual acts with male prostitutes." Further, Spell said, "the evidence includes the following":

1. Sworn statements of persons who state they engaged in homosexual acts with Mr. Allain.

2. Polygraph or lie detector tests . . . that indicated the persons who state they participated in homosexual acts with Mr. Allain were truthful.

3. Statements of police officers and former police officers that they observed Mr. Allain in a pattern of conduct consistent with solicitation of male prostitutes and inconsistent with conduct reasonably for any other purpose.

4. Statements of persons who say they have seen in Mr. Allain's apartment pornographic items and activities consistent with homosexual activity.[127]

Shock. Disbelief. Cynicism. Humor. Horror. Mississippians reacted in a variety of ways to the new scandal.

Those reactions and the events suggested in the group's allegations provide a useful window on to a nexus of experience, discourse, and spatiality as imagined and felt at this particular place and historical moment. While I want to illuminate and assess the disclosed sexual acts and the "truth" of those acts, variously perceived, I am also interested in examining the production of spatial configurations that—through circulations of power in Mississippi—assigned certain individuals, groups, acts, identities, and classes within and without prescribed social, economic, and political boundaries. While these boundaries were, as geographer David Harvey understands them, part of the dialectical processes of change characterizing all social forces, they had achieved and sustained at that time a relative permanence, the undoing of which requires but is in no way coextensive with a linguistic unpacking, which I undertake here.[128]

After Spell's news conference, Mississippians looked for specifics in the daily press. Most looked in the *Clarion-Ledger* and *Jackson Daily News*, the capital city's morning and evening papers, distributed throughout the state. On 26 October 1983, a front-page *Clarion-Ledger* story spelled out the allegations and—after the page break—detailed the sex acts: "Holliday [Ross] said Allain would always perform oral sex on him. Arrington [Toy] said he would perform oral sex and anal intercourse on Allain. Johnson said he would perform oral sex on Allain and that Allain would perform anal intercourse on him." [129]

As previously mentioned, notions of active and passive get confused in such linguistic constructions, especially when applying phallocentric terminology to persons whose self-presentations defy gender norms. The active verb tense—for example, to suck, to perform oral sex—does not necessarily connote an "active," "aggressive," "masculine" role. To suck, seemingly an active engagement in sexual relations, is to be penetrated, which was often conceived as a "passive," "submissive," "feminine" role. While some might say that all these variations implicated the participants in homosexual intercourse, the acts were not so uniformly perceived at this time and place, as evidenced by prior oral history testimony and the Hinson episodes. Indeed, all alleged behavior was "detestable and abominable" under the state sodomy statute, as Spell pointed out, and was punishable by up to ten years in prison. Yet, as widely imagined, some acts were more reprehensibly queer-identified than others. For men in Mississippi, to fuck and get sucked—that is, to be the oral and anal insertive, penetrative partner—reflected an often acceptable, masculinist practice, regardless of the biological sex of the receptive, penetrated partner. So it became necessary for Allain's accusers to implicate him in all conceivable variations of oral and anal sex [130]—which the *Clarion-Ledger* politely phrased in a popularized dissociative language of *performance*.

With three sexual actor-confessors, the group entangled Allain in behavior that cast him as the oral and anal insertive and—more suspect—the oral and anal receptive partner. All these acts, furthermore, were criminalized under state and local prostitution ordinances, since cash changed hands. Ross had dubbed Allain "a good trick": he was friendly, and he paid well. [131] Still, the group relied on gender and racial transgressions, spatially coded, as even more definitive evidence of Allain's debasement.

Allain's feminization was manifested not only in receptive sex acts—analogous to Jon Hinson's final abdication of sexual and political power in the Longworth House Office Building men's room. It was not only evidenced by his sucking Ross or getting fucked by Toy. But also, as the group's polygraph examiner asked Ross to confirm, it was indicated by Allain's willingness to engage in intimate nongenital relations with the gender ambiguous: in the language of the examiner, retold by the *Clarion-Ledger,* Ross admitted that s/he had "kissed Allain all over the face while wearing lipstick."[132] This gender transgression was amplified—and its uncertainties, it was hoped, tamed—by the repeated press and television representations of Ross, Toy, and Johnson categorically as "males," as men "who dress as women."

That Allain did it, engaged in homosex, mattered. How and with whom he did it mattered more. As was the case in the Hinson arrests, transgression adhered more readily to some acts than others—and some partners than others. Ross, Toy, and Johnson—like the "nice," "frail" Library of Congress employee, Harold Moore—defied gender norms. In the given ideological landscape of sex and gender, political leaders Hinson and Allain might use these individuals as receptive sex partners. But to submit to the partners' insertive potential violated prevailing standards of manhood. Hinson and Allain were doubly feminized in that their kissable, penetrative partners were black.

The racially transgressive nature of these acts paraded as common sense, as understood, in a state whose ban of interracial heterosexual marriage had been overturned by the Supreme Court only sixteen years prior.[133] Again, most press accounts referred to Ross, Toy, and Johnson as "black"; Allain and his wealthy accusers were assumed to be, were unwritten as, white. Overt and opaque evocations of racial and class crossings and (mis)alliances occasioned increasingly precise spatial identifications, as Democrats and Republicans, blacks and whites, questioned the veracity of stories, as they considered the credibility of the group, the gubernatorial candidates, and the collective of sex workers.

For three weeks Ross, Toy, and Johnson were shunted from motel to motel in Louisiana and Mississippi as the group and its investigators, Pendleton Detectives, attempted to control their public appearances. Long days were passed in motel rooms; others were enlivened by interviews and tapings for nightly newscasts. Ross and her friends watched the news together; they read the papers to one another. With care, they prepared their statements. They wanted to get it right. Still, they heard the derisive undertones; they read between the lines. TV and press depictions of the family-hood were highly derogatory; campaign rhetoric—Democratic and Republican—was insulting to Ross, Toy, and Johnson.

Candidate Bill Allain denied knowing the three. He counterattacked. He accused Republicans of "damnable, vicious, malicious lies." He maligned their informants: "There is no confirmation of the statements of freaks and weirdoes upon which they rely." "I'm no sexual deviate," he insisted, "and Leon Bramlett knows it."[134]

The Republican candidate Bramlett attempted to distance himself from the group, although they contributed large sums of money to his campaign. By claiming no involvement in the investigation, he appeared deceptive to reporters. After all, two weeks before Spell's press conference, before the news broke about Allain's nighttime wanderings, Bramlett had launched a political attack predicated on the "family issue." "My opponent is a bachelor," Bramlett said of Allain, a Catholic who divorced in 1970. "I have reared a family, educated three children, and operated a business."[135] "Blessed with a family," Bramlett added, he could better address issues of education and health care.[136] Virginia Bramlett, his wife, joined in the offensive: "I'm running for First Lady," she told an audience in Natchez, "and I'm unopposed."[137]

Perhaps fearing where it all might lead, Allain scolded his opponent for engaging in "smears and innuendo" and for inciting "rumors and rumors of rumors," which Allain declined to specify for reporters. Allain responded on Bramlett's terms, moreover, when he declared he had helped raise three sons from his ex-wife's previous marriage. He appeared at a rally in Jackson with his two sisters, a nephew and two nieces, whom he introduced from the dais.[138] With neither wife nor kids of his own, Allain had to "trot out" members of his extended family.

Since his surprise Democratic primary victory over former lieutenant governor Evelyn Gandy—repeatedly referred to in the press as "Miss Gandy"—Allain had stepped up his masculinist rhetoric of "fighting" for Mississippians. The populist campaign highlighted his defeat of telephone and utility rate increases as attorney general. He promised to "continue the fight" for consumers, against crime, against drugs, and "against high utility rates which are a heavy burden on our people and are hurting our economic growth."[139] Some laughed it off as a campaign for cheap air-conditioning. Others bemoaned as a line-in-the-sand ploy Allain's promise to "fight against the dumping of nuclear waste in Mississippi," reflected in his country music campaign jingle "Don't Mess with Mississippi." (As yet, the state had stored no such refuse.) But these issues resonated with middle- and working-class voters, who traditionally discounted effete, intellectual leadership styles.[140]

Of his multifaceted personal history, campaign leaflets pointed up Allain's military credentials, his service in Korean "combat zones"—although, the candidate conceded, hostilities had abated over much of his tenure. Allain grew up in rural Adams County, attended public schools, graduated from Natchez High, the University of Notre Dame, and the University of Mississippi Law School. Of his many professional affiliations, he forefronted his memberships in the American Legion and Veterans of Foreign Wars.[141] Similarly, Bramlett tried to convey what one reporter called "a masculine, All-American image" at his campaign headquarters. The walls were covered in "huge posters showing the candidate as a Navy cadet, in his football uniform or his boxing shorts."[142]

In a still predominantly Democratic state, Republican strategists capitalized on hegemonic notions of leadership and white masculinity to dispute Allain's ability to assume the state's highest elective office. Their attack on his manhood invoked material and metaphorical spaces dissonant and consonant with social and political authority. As Allain attempted civic ascent, an upward class mobility, "Republican kingmakers" reiterated and reinscribed boundaries of political power and cultural normalcy.[143] Their articulation of otherwise unspoken, accepted forms of manliness "turned" masculinity, as Homi Bhabha describes it, "from an innate invisibility, a normal condition, to a compulsive interrogation"[144]—exemplified in this case by the reliance on a polygraphed discourse.

Voices of resistance likewise were heard, though often contained. Together, the competing voices—hegemonic and counterhegemonic—did not emanate from preexistent, solidified classes of Mississippians. Rather, they participated in the ongoing formation and transformation of social borders. The voices and *practices* of queer Mississippians and their interlopers help us reconceive the flux of class structures and sexual categories. As Andrew Parker notes of left academic undertakings, "While we have begun to appreciate how class impinges upon sexual formations, we still have nothing resembling what might be called a sex-inflected analysis of class formations."[145] The events surrounding the Allain candidacy point us in the direction Parker suggests. As we see, struggles to (re)define the so-called lower- and upper-most echelons of society in early-eighties Mississippi demonstrate that sex and gender were among the most salient of properties. These properties were grounded in everyday life and discourse and were crystallized in outrageous public scandals like this one. In a culture historically rooted in the land, in real estate—which generated much of the state's capital—social boundary making would continue to evoke painstaking demarcations of tangible physical sites.

The Farish Street district—a removed, criminalized place in the dominant discourse—yielded unreliable truth tellers, Democrats argued.[146] Acknowledging and sharing in this construct, Republicans produced official voices to document Allain's condemnable presence in the space. Police officers—the only individuals with legitimate rationales for traversing the zone; indeed, the surveillant authority—had seen Allain there. They testified to his activity. Such testimonies, it seemed, didn't require the technological confirmation of the polygraph.

That August of 1983 patrol officer Randy Clark saw Bill Allain apparently speaking to Donna Johnson: "There was a black male prostitute by the name of Donald Johnson in the immediate vicinity of his vehicle . . . standing right beside the vehicle at the driver's window." Narcotics agent J. C. Guy and vice investigator William Gardner also placed Allain in the suspect district, as they promulgated an official, if precarious, terminology for their transgendered objects of surveillance. Guy carefully observed Allain before stopping him, five years prior, on Farish Strèet: "He was in a small car and he was over talking to one of these people of the evening. . . . To the best of my recollection there was a female prostitute or a he-she talking to him. . . . I pulled the blue lights on him and I pulled him over. . . . I probably informed him that he was obstructing the traffic [and] I told him he could leave." More recently, Gardner witnessed Allain driving throughout the area, and he recalled that at the corner of Mill and Oakley, "one of these male-female impersonators, or he-shes, whatever—attempted to flag him down."[147]

The *Clarion-Ledger*'s report of these sworn statements helped construct an "inner city area" where the sordid events occurred. The area was mapped by discrete street names and characterized by "street solicitation." It was occupied, at least in "the evening," by "male 'drag queens,'" "female prostitutes," "he-shes." Yet the true innermost city, the downtown core, the oldest section of Jackson, was the adjacent business district. And by the 1980s the only residential single-family dwelling in the business district was the governor's mansion. Ironically, the inner city—which dominant discourses increasingly cast in marginal relationship to white suburbia—was residential address of both abnormal, nonrepresentative citizens and the most respectable of citizens, the governor. And, it was presumed, *his* family.

The business district was the daytime milieu of Billy Mounger, Victor Smith, Bill Allain, *and* Nicole Toy and Devia Ross. Over lunch their paths crossed in the pecking order of the service industry. Mounger and Smith—with offices in the prestigious Deposit Guaranty and Capitol Towers Buildings, respectively—surely dined on occasion at the Walthall, Ross's place of employment; Allain at the Sun-N-Sand Motel restaurant, where Toy washed dishes. The Sun-N-Sand was a hybrid space, situated on the Lamar Street edge of both the business and Farish Street districts. The only motor hotel within walking distance of the new Capitol, it housed rural and small-town delegates to the state legislature and served as a site for illicit sex—the two of which functions often overlapped, as we have seen.[148]

Such overlap—the daily temporal shifts in urban spatiality—unsettled many white middle-class Mississippians. Allain addressed their fears and explicitly attempted to allay them: "I used to live in that area [the hybrid zone between downtown and Farish Street] because it was within walking distance of my office. But believe me, all I ever did was walk or drive through it." "Allain lived in Sterling Towers, an apartment building," the newspaper helped, "across the street from the [predominantly white] Mississippi College School of Law."[149] Yet the papers did not report that Allain had moved out of Sterling Towers as early as 1978 to a Stanton House apartment (in which maintenance workers apparently found gay erotica).[150] To travel home to Stanton House on Morningside Street from either his law office on Congress Street or the attorney general's office on High Street, Allain would have to drive a few blocks east and several blocks north, a mile in all. The Farish Street district lay to the west.

Republican interests were served by a spatial linking of Allain to this tenderloin district. Press accounts distanced Mounger, Smith, and Clement from this geographically proximate realm by reinscribing vertical striations of race and class. Each member of the group had "a plush office with an impressive view from the upper floors of Jackson's tallest office buildings."[151] They literally were above it all. Yet, as reporters saw it, their great wealth made their motives suspect in conducting the investigation. The group's milieu was called into scrutiny as well. So Mounger, for example, never revealed the extent of his remove from the discursively constructed sex district, the very real income disparities not only between him and the sex workers, but also between him and the vast majority of Mississippians. Mounger's home stood three and a half miles outside the downtown core in the Woodland Hills section, an in-town automobile suburb driven by white flight in the 1940s and 1950s. Situated on a sprawling lawn of magnolias, hollies, and pines, Mounger's two-story, three-chimneyed, white-brick Georgian residence of rambling additions mimicked a rural plantation architecture of lingering cache in upper-class (sub)urban housing.[152] If, to the average Mississippian, Devia Ross lived in another world, so did Mounger—though under consumer capitalism, his was an enviable, if resentment-inducing, world.

The memory and the continuing reality of racial segregation—the daily interaction of whites and blacks in hierarchical work settings; the nightly division of whites and blacks into partitioned residential sectors—informed the creation and maintenance of libidinally segregated spaces, of heteronormative terrain and what Gordon Brent Ingram calls "queer-scapes."[153] The group could be made aware of queer worlds through the innocent encounter between a straight, wealthy (and notably) female client and her gay, working-class service provider—the hairdresser. Allain, on the other hand, was suspect for multiple reasons. While he may have engaged in paid service relationships with race and class subordinates, such *sexual* favors were historically *taken* by powerful whites. Also, the Allain scandal summoned up the dangerous crossings of night work and queer sex—when work moved outside of temporal bounds and where persons ventured beyond spatial bounds. In the wrong place at the wrong time, Allain was too close to his race, class, gender, and sex underlings.

No, Allain's backers countered. The charges were simply too "far out." Homosexuality was elsewhere. As Republican Victor Smith averred: "People realized that that [unnameable] kind of stuff happened in San Francisco. People in Mississippi were shocked that people from here were leading that [unnameable] kind of life."[154] The task for Republicans was to expose and thereby partially shape a queer world, casting it as both here *and* there. It was among us, but in a distinct cordoned-off zone. Allain had crossed the safety of the dividing line. Worse, his seemingly same-sex, gender-ambiguous, interracial relations served to blur and confuse—to queer—the primary social distinctions that many white Mississippians held dear.

White leaders of the Democratic Party felt that "people in Mississippi" didn't want to be exposed. Voters didn't want to know. Republicans' "Farish Street fantasy" was too vile.[155] Reporters and voters joined in the cadence, Democrats agreed with Republicans, that the incidents were—in words that must have hurt and maybe amused Ross, Toy, Johnson, and thousands of other queer Mississippians as they read the papers—"sickening," "repugnant," "frightening," "disgusting," "filth," "slime."[156] But Democrats went a step further than the Republicans. It was all *too* outlandish, they said, to believe. It was as unimaginable as it was unnameable.

Allain's principal backers, themselves rich oilmen, clarified the matter. More than the alleged activities, the allegations were reprehensible—and incredible. "I think that the allegations are so far out," Natchezian John Callon of Callon Petroleum said, "that it's difficult for me to believe that they have any validity." David New, a Natchez oil producer who contributed $22,000 to the Allain campaign, said, "It makes me sick at my stomach. I have known the man for twenty-five years, and I can't believe it." Besides, he had Allain's word of honor. In language that eerily recalled, almost verbatim, Billy Mounger's encounter with Jon Hinson three years prior,

New said Allain "looked me squarely in the eye and said 'David, it is not true.'"[157]

Pitted against one another were white cultural, political elites—the oil aristocracy, a new landed gentry not of agriculture but of extraction. Their gaze settled on a minute, undervalued section of real estate on the edge of Jackson's downtown core. The queer sex practices and queer people there, Democrats and Republicans agreed, were incompatible with the class privilege and power prerogatives of high elective office. Republicans accused the Democratic candidate of consorting with black transgender sex workers; Democrats accused Republicans of consorting with black transgender sex workers. As Democratic Party chair Danny Cupit put it, for Republicans "to take the word of *somebody like that* and give it any degree of credibility defies reason and logic."[158] That Republicans were gay baiting Mississippi First, a progressive political action committee, further hurt their credibility.[159] Claude Ramsey, the head of the state AFL-CIO, concurred. "I don't think the people will buy this crap," he said. "The whole thing is unbelievable."[160] Even independent gubernatorial candidate Charles Evers, who stood to benefit from the mudslinging, called the charges "un-Christian," "unpatriotic," and "unbelievable."[161]

Still, some believed. According to Kirk Phillips of the Mississippi Gay Alliance, many queer Mississippians believed.[162] But queer voices receded, were denied legitimacy, as the state's major public figures battled it out. "Only this is certain," wrote *Greenwood Commonwealth* publisher John Emmerich. "One side is telling an enormous lie."[163]

How then to tell the truth of sexuality? If confession had failed in the Hinson affair, would accusation prove reliable? Was the truth ultimately knowable?

The Allain campaign insisted it was, if Mississippians relied on the right sources. As one television advertisement cautioned, "There's a new word in our campaign for governor." Shifting the focus of electoral attention, the word was not *queer*, but rather—in all capital letters—"*SMEAR.*" The inexpensive graphic then enumerated the dubious credentials of those "who[m] the smear merchants would like us to believe":

Three male prostitutes.

Each with criminal records.

Each admittedly bribed $300 each and $50 a day.

"Mississippians are a lot better and a lot smarter," the voice-over concluded. "And we're going to elect a good man governor: Bill Allain."[164]

Good men were best measured by good women. Again reminiscent of the Hinson scandal, Allain's ex-wife Doris Rush went before the cameras on the candidate's behalf. Appearing in another campaign television commercial, she extolled Allain's virtues and questioned his opponent's integrity.

> I have watched in disgust as the Bramlett campaign has tried to smear my former husband. I know that the charges they are making about Bill are not true. You know a man well when he is your husband. There is no finer, more upright, more honorable man than Bill Allain, and don't let anyone tell you anything different.[165]

Allain told reporters that the marriage ended amicably in 1970, after more than five years, because "I was a workaholic."[166] Mississippi newspapers were loath to mention the divorce petition. In it, Rush declared that, in the words of the *Washington Post*, "Allain ceased having marital relations with her shortly after the wedding."[167]

Mississippians wanted proof. Ever-elusive facts could be nailed down, it was thought, through the wonders of technology. Polygraph testimony, despite its flaws, promised hope in this Foucaultian "great chase after the truth of sex."[168] While the Allain scandal left Mississippians wondering who they could believe, a faith in science was unshaken.[169] Since the pretense of ignorance normally at work around queer sexuality had been shattered by the accusations; since queer sex had been pushed to the fore; since Mississippians' habits of dissembling—an everyday cultural practice— had been brought to light and denaturalized by the scandal, truth would have to be obtained via technology.

One after another, players in the drama lined up for polygraph examinations. Ross, Toy, and Johnson passed lie detector tests sponsored by both the group and the *Clarion-Ledger*. But even as the newspaper's editors noted a polygraph's inconclusiveness and inadmissibility in Mississippi courts,[170] Bramlett challenged his Democratic opponent to take a test, and Allain acceded. Allain promised only that his attorney would arrange an exam before the election, now less than two weeks away. Allain nonetheless criticized the procedure. Individuals like Ross, Toy, and Johnson—who were "deluded" into thinking they were women, he said—could score well regardless of the truth.[171]

The group's attorney Bill Spell insisted that state attorney general Bill Allain submit to an "independent, third-party" examination.[172] The *Clarion-Ledger* supported this line of reasoning. Otherwise, "a private test . . . keeps it in the hands of [Allain's] own campaign and keeps the findings controlled by the candidate."[173] As election day neared, Bramlett stepped up the pressure. He pledged to withdraw from the race if Allain could pass three independent lie detector tests. A "bipartisan" group of ten businessmen from across the state urged both Allain and Spell to take lie detector tests. Headed by Yazoo City native Owen Cooper—a former Mississippi Chemical Company executive, former Southern Baptist Convention president, and longtime Democrat—the ten proposed that Spell and Allain take tests immediately, "with the hope of dispelling the uncertainty which hangs over this election," only six days away. The *Meridian Star,* however, said there wasn't enough time; the election should be postponed pending a grand jury investigation, "so that voters may know the truth before they go to the polls." [174]

Five days before the election, Allain released his polygraph results. Called a "sham" and an "insult" by Bramlett, they purportedly demonstrated that Allain was not "a homosexual," that he had never "committed a sex act with another man"—two precise linguistic constructions full of loopholes. For maybe Allain, like so many sexual nonconformists, had nonetheless concluded that he was not a homosexual; maybe too he had "deluded" himself into believing that Ross, Toy, and Johnson were women.

Allain further produced statements from Donna Johnson's parents, J. V. and Bettye Johnson of Rankin County. The Johnsons said they recognized their son was a homosexual in eighth or ninth grade; they sent him for counseling and then for psychiatric evaluation at the state hospital at Whitfield. Despite their efforts, they said, Donald Johnson had become a "habitual liar," a "drug addict," and a thief. He was "totally unstable." [175] Thus, the Allain scandal was a scandal for the members of the family-hood as well. Ross, Toy, and Johnson—apparently cut off from their parents, living in the inner city—publicly stood in stark contrast to the Johnsons' prototype of husband and wife, a wholesome rural household of normative familial life.

Bill Spell took the suggestion of Owen Cooper and the ten. On the Saturday before the Tuesday election, he took a polygraph test supervised by four journalists. He passed. [176] All the members of the group—Billy Mounger, Victor Smith, and Neal Clement—offered to take tests. [177] To reporters, Mounger reiterated his genuineness of purpose. He said he wanted to "make amends for the Jon Hinson episode." Besides, he declared, the Allain incidents made "Jon Hinson look like Prince Charming." [178]

Anxious for conclusions, Mississippians questioned the polygraph process but rarely the polygraph itself. Democratic and Republican supporters quibbled over the character and credentials of the varied polygraph examiners, the subtleties of the questions posed, rarely acknowledging that a lie detector, rather than a device for uncovering an essential truth, more precisely was an instrument in the production of truth. Sexual behavior and, in particular, sexual identity eluded even the most sophisticated of truth-telling technologies.

Bill Allain canceled most of his campaign appearances and quietly awaited the election.

Meanwhile, Devia Ross, Nicole Toy, and Donna Johnson remained sequestered in motels. Since their daily routines were not reported by the press at the time, I imagine that they marveled from afar as their roles in the scandal dwindled. In many ways, the governor's seat hinged on their testimony, but increasingly the old-guard white political establishment dominated the media discourse. The sex workers rarely if ever met the wealthy oil executives supporting Allain and the wealthy oil executives supporting Bramlett. Soon, however, they would encounter Victor Smith.

Victor Smith must have experienced pangs of guilt. While "nobody in this state would think that Billy Mounger" had pursued the investigation "out of spiritual reasons,"[179] Smith ostensibly held to a higher moral aim. Smith was born in 1930 and born again in 1971. In addition to oil speculation, he invested in a lucrative segment of the popular religion market.[180] In addition to the rituals of mainline Protestant denominations to which the overwhelming majority of Mississippians belonged—Baptist, Methodist, Presbyterian—"spiritual phenomena" in the state flourished "outside formal church institutions" as well.[181] Through his Maranatha Christian bookstores, Smith supplied Mississippians with the tools necessary to keep the faith and, in the directive known as the Great Commission, to spread the gospel to others. Maranatha served not only as an outlet for Nashville—"a combination Mecca and Vatican of the South, the center of Baptist and Methodist denominational life and a great religious publishing center";[182] it also carried any number of items produced through nonecclesiastical channels—audiotapes, daily devotional guides, wedding planners, religious clothing and trinkets—along with multiple versions of the Bible. By aiding Mississippi consumers in their quest for religious truths, Victor Smith profited handsomely. He had a significant financial interest in converting heathens.

As the election loomed, Smith decided that the Great Commission extended even to black male transvestite prostitutes. He would fly down to Baton Rouge, their current hideout, and "witness to them and turn their lives around." At least partially aware of the deep divides of race, class, gender, and sexuality, the white Smith took three black lay leaders with him. Perhaps they could convince Ross, Toy, and Johnson to turn from their evil ways. Devia Ross was astounded: "There we were in all this political campaign and thing, and they were talking to us about saving our souls."

Victor Smith was shocked, too: "All they wanted to talk about was money." It seems Spell and the Pendleton agency were doling out the living expenses in careful, meager increments, to keep the three in line. Smith guessed he "saw their point," and promised to look into it.[183]

Devia Ross was fed up. She felt she and her friends were being used. By the time they got to a Monroe, Louisiana, motel, the sex workers were thinking about calling it quits and going home. After all, Spell had told them they would only be away for a few days. Now, three weeks later, they seemed trapped. Their money was sometimes withheld; their requests were met with threats. As Nicole Toy describes it, their Pendleton detective-chaperon "went to telling us about how we would get sued if we were to pack up and leave and all this kind of carrying on." On the other hand, the detective said they were free to go, if they had the means. He "bust in the room, and he went to talking about 'Get your stuff,' you know. 'Y'all leave.'" Ross asked how they would get back to Jackson. He shouted, "Hell, hitchhike. Catch a bus. Do whatever you want to do." After that, Toy said, "we eventually, you know, settled down." [184] Resignation set in; they waited out the election, captives in the motel.

ALLAIN WON. On 8 November 1983, he garnered a "landslide" 55 percent of the vote, compared to Bramlett's 39 percent.[185] As longtime political observer Bill Minor put it, the queer allegations "only cost him five points in the election." Indeed, without irrefutable evidence—as when police caught Hinson in the act—Mississippi voters felt as Minor did even fourteen years after the scandal: "I don't *want* to believe it." [186]

In January 1984, two months after the election, Ross, Toy, and Johnson reversed their stories. Allain's attorney produced new lie detector results, showing that the three *now* "were telling the truth [by insisting they] lied about the allegations in October." The *Clarion-Ledger* asked to administer yet another polygraph examination to each of the three. They declined. "No, we will not take additional tests on anything," Nicole Toy declared. "We are trying to end this thing. We want it to be over. We do not want our names in the paper anymore." [187]

They had been deceived. They were bitter; they were unemployed. Bill Spell "used us and used us," Toy said. "This is not fair. I lost my job [at the Sun-N-Sand Motel restaurant] over this and can't pay my bills. They promised us this would not happen." [188] (Of the reversal, Bill Spell said, "We expected this to happen, rather than them acting like normal human beings.") [189] Bill Allain broke his promise as well. From the moment the scandal broke, he swore he would be vindicated in a slander proceeding.

He never filed the lawsuit. He served a four-year term characterized as quiet, low key.

"We all [are] liars," Neil Bartlett observes.[190]

GERALDO RIVERA CAME to town. The flamboyant investigative reporter—known throughout the country for his television antics—professed a unique access to the truth. He would reveal "why people did what they did, and whether what they did was truthful."[191] His segment, "Anatomy of a Smear Campaign: Low Down and Dirty," for the ABC television news-magazine 20/20, purported to exonerate Allain, as it participated in the homophobia of those Rivera decried. Rivera offered only one new testimonial, a "surprise interview" with Betty Mitchell, who said she once had been "involved with" Allain for four years. Now married, she "had a box full of love letters and poems and things" that Allain had written. "That man was a normal man in every sense of the word," she told a prime-time TV audience. "He was romantic. We had a good sex life."[192]

In his Jackson Sheraton Regency hotel suite, Rivera prepped Devia Ross in a five-minute pretaping interview. Ross said her initial allegations were true. She had had sex with Allain. Rivera was incensed. He yelled at Ross; he grilled her on camera. Ross walked out. Convinced she was telling the truth, an observer for the *Clarion-Ledger* called out to her: "Devia, are you going to walk home?"[193]

In the car culture that was rural, suburban, and urban Mississippi, Ross and her friends were marginalized, forced by deprivation to hustle a "ride" or a "date." Their heels their only means of transport, they lacked the physical and social mobility at the heart of American success ideology. In a striated socioeconomic system, structured by race, class, gender, and sexuality, they personified the most dispossessed and consequently the most suspect typologies. They shouldered the uneven burdens of an unjust order; they labored in menial jobs that enabled lives of ease for Billy Mounger and his ilk.

Ross was an unequal participant in social discourses such as the Allain scandal, which reflected and created notions of the commonsensical and the ridiculous, the normal and the outcast, the safe and the dangerous. She contributed generously to the family-hood but served as the nemesis in heterosexist depictions of white middle- and upper-class family life in Mississippi. Relegated materially and metaphorically to the liminal spaces of the inner city, her life and livelihood called hegemonic structures into question yet simultaneously eased the fears of the powerful, convinced as they were that her realm existed apart from (indeed, as justification for) their own. Minoritized queer sexualities could be contained and constrained within space, they lulled themselves into believing.

EXACTLY TEN YEARS after election day, in the early morning hours of 8 November 1993, former Walthall Hotel employee and Bill's Club entertainer Devia Ross was found shot at the corner of Mill and Monument, in her neighborhood, the Farish Street district. She died at the hospital. Bill Spell said, "As I remember him, he was a rather pathetic creature. . . . It's tragic when anybody gets shot, but his whole life was a tragedy." Spell felt he had done all he could for his former associate. After all, he said, once the election was over, "we got him a job at a fast-food place."[194]

Such places, Bill Spell assumed, were the logical domain for men like that. Such assignations Bill Spell and his crowd felt entitled to make. But again and again, queer Mississippians contested these notions. As David Harvey notes:

> Social relations are, in all respects, mappings of some sort, be they symbolic, figurative, or material. The organization of social relations demands a mapping so that people know their place. Revolutionary activity entails a remapping of social relations and agents who no longer acknowledge that place to which they were formerly assigned.[195]

Four decades of queer life show that marginalized Mississippians individually and collectively resisted—and sometimes were complicit in—the allocations and positionings of hegemonic forces. In their struggles against the often oppressive structures of church, state, and science, they occasionally accepted their "place" but more often made and remade spaces all their own. Maneuvering through the relations of everyday life, they established networks of interaction and sites for homosex, frequently within the very community institutions and built environments predicated on heterosexist privilege—the home, the church, the school, the workplace. Questioning received wisdom, scrutinizing the taken-for-granted, queer Mississippians reflected on and often rejected discursive conventions, exposing powerful mythologies like the homosexual suicide and homosexual homicide narratives as the realities of a homo*phobic* homo*cidal* schema—a logical oppressive outgrowth of the inequitable play of capital.

Yet the great variety of ways in which Mississippians experienced and acted on queer desire demonstrates the difficulty of fashioning a *we* to which *I* and all these historical actors can belong. Even for a given historical moment, the label *queer Mississippian* poorly conveys the complexity and diversity of the lives I have grouped under this rubric—individuals as different along lines of race, class, gender, sexuality, and region as are Devia Ross, Bill Allain, Nicole Toy, Donna Johnson, Jon Hinson, and others in this chapter and in this book.

Over time some queer Mississippians evinced the classical trajectory so well documented by American lesbian and gay historians to date: They acknowledged and acted on their desires; they moved to Jackson (or perhaps an out-of-state city); they became part of an urban gay culture as they self-identified as gay; they became involved in sustainable institutions like the Metropolitan Community Church; and they joined an increasingly nationalized political movement through organizations such as the Mississippi Gay Alliance. But most queer Mississippians followed other routes. They crafted lives of myriad types in mostly rural spaces. The stories of those lives I have only begun to elucidate. But in the process, I have inevitably altered notions of myself and my place as I have attempted to differentiate my fellow queer Mississippians across time and space. I see now that at the intersection of the heteronormative and the queer, the gender conforming and defiant, across the multiple contours of race, class, and region, queer Mississippians have variously managed to endure. They have planned, created, re-created, and sustained adaptive forms to insure that—despite the difficulties, whatever the impediments—they functioned and moved in a world they could call home.

Epilogue

TOO MANY QUEER STORIES end in death. Too many queer stories end with AIDS.

I bring my history to a close in 1985, in part because that's when the human immunodeficiency virus took hold in Mississippi to such an extent that queer lives and queer networks were irrevocably altered—as were, of course, all lives and cultures, though in different ways. The year 1985 also marked the end of a sweeping demographic trend. Urbanization—a movement characterizing much of twentieth-century America—was held in check. In human terms, that meant that the majority of Mississippians would continue to live in the countryside—in small-town and rural spaces. While many still picked up and left Mississippi, even greater numbers returned or settled anew. Most, of course, never left in the first place.

One such native, as we have seen, is a man I call George Albright. In the late 1990s Albright continues to live and work in rural Jones County, in his family home, on his family farm. He continues to *live* with HIV and *work* for social change.

IN 1994 GEORGE ALBRIGHT agreed to a tape-recorded interview with a volunteer at the American Red Cross in Hattiesburg, Mississippi. The tape was deposited with the Mississippi Oral History Program at the University of Southern Mississippi. The director of that program suggested I listen to the tape when he heard about the nature of my project.

The interview demonstrates cultural barriers like those I experienced in enlisting black Mississippians as oral history narrators. Generally speaking, African Americans seemed reluctant to participate in my project, cautious about revealing the names of other persons (regardless of assurances of anonymity), less likely to invite me into their homes, less likely to speak with me at length. For reasons well exemplified by the historical events chronicled here (particularly, I recall the interrogations by Bill Higgs and other white Mississippians in chapter 4; the interrogations of Devia Ross, Nicole Toy, and Donna Johnson in chapter 7), many African Americans rightly are wary of white middle- and upper-class interlocutors.

The Albright interview is perhaps further fraught by differences of gender and sexuality. Despite posing numerous questions about Albright's intimate and sexual relations, the young white interviewer does not reveal her own sexuality—as I found it helpful and necessary to do, in order to build trust. Though her questions, in print, appear intrusive and manipulative (as indeed all our questions are), what the reader cannot hear is her soft, gentle, and reassuring voice, the voice of an individual attempting connection, attempting to locate shared concerns—in short, empathizing.

. . .

Question: Going back to high school, you talked about having your friends, and they later became your drinking buddies. What about dating?

Albright: We really didn't have much time to date in high school, because working on a farm took a lot of our time. When we came in from school in the afternoon, we had chores. In the fall we had to get the cotton out of the fields, the corn had to be gathered, and the sugarcane had to be cut down and ready for syrup. It really kept us pretty busy.

Q: A very busy life. When you were out of high school, did you then find time to date?

A: Not really. I was mostly working or with the boys, drinking.

Q: Right. Would you call yourself, when it comes to dating and relationships with other people, personal relationships with one other person, I should say, would you call yourself a late bloomer?

A: Yeah, I would.

Q: Have you had a serious relationship before in your life?

A: Oh, yeah. Back in probably about, around '88, '89, '90. Had three, back-to-back, which I thought were mistakes. Later on down the line I found out they were mistakes. But I didn't regret anything.

Q: Right. So you had three. Can you tell me about them?

A: Yeah, well, I thought I was going into a relationship where the person was going to treat me like I wanted to be treated. Then after I got into it, I found out they were only out for what they could get. They thought, at the time, since they knew I was HIV, they thought I was probably getting a disability check, and they could get that. Once they found out that I wasn't, then they dropped me like a hot potato. They were only in it for the money. I didn't see it that way. I thought they really cared until I found out what they were after.

Q: Was the second relationship similar?

A: The second and third one were pretty well the same thing.

Q: So, going back prior than that, you really didn't date much.

A: No, I didn't really date much, because like I say, coming up I didn't really have time from the chores I had to do, trying to help my neighbors and friends out, you know, in the community, helping them out, trying to get their crops in and do our chores too. It took a lot of my time.

Q: Right. So when you went into your first serious relationship in life, you were already HIV-positive.

A: Yeah.

Q: I'd like to go back to prior to those relationships and back to the day you found out you were HIV-positive. Can you tell me how you found out about the fact that you have the virus?

A: Yeah, it was in 1987 around the fifteenth of August. I was admitted to the Methodist Hospital in Hattiesburg with pneumocystis pneumonia. Of course I didn't know it was pneumonia until about three weeks later, when my family doctor, who just happened to be walking down the hall of the hospital—I had been in the hospital three weeks running a high temp of a hundred and five, which the nurses there and the doctors couldn't break—and she happened to see my name on the door and come in and ask me what was the problem. I told her I was running a high temp and I had a real bad cold. She asked me would it be alright to run the antibody test. And I told her yeah. And then that's when I found out it was positive.

Q: What did that feel like when you got the news?

A: At first, you know, I thought my world had come to an end. I had to regroup, step back, and take an inventory of my life. Figure out how I came in contact with it. Go through the proper channels, notifying my partners from the military, all the people I had sex with over those four years.

Q: Do you know how you acquired it?

A: Not up until the first part of this year. It came to me in a dream, in a vision, where I got it from. I found out later the person that infected me is deceased now, 's been deceased now about four years.

Q: She has. Hmmm. What did you know about HIV and AIDS the day you found out you had it? How much did you know then?

A: I knew quite a bit about it, because I had been reading a lot of material on it. And I had been hearing a lot on TV about it. . . . I was doing a lot of studying on it.
. . .

Q: When you contracted HIV, did you know enough about it to protect yourself? Or did you think that it was something that you couldn't get? Or did you choose not to? Or did it just never cross your mind? What were the circumstances?

A: Like Magic Johnson, I thought it couldn't happen to me. That only gay people could get it. Those were the first thoughts that crossed my mind, because that's what they were first saying. Later I found out that wasn't so. I figured it couldn't happen to me because I was an athlete and I took good care of myself.

Q: Right. Who was the first person you told?

A: The first person I told was my father.

Q: And how did he react?

A: Well, he shocked me, because he told me we were all going to die of something, that it wasn't the end of the world. Don't let it get me down. Hang in there.

Q: What was your first emotional response?

A: Why me? That's basically what hit my mind. Why me? Or why not somebody else?

Q: Were you angry?

A: At first I was angry. But after about a year and a half, I learned to turn my anger and frustration into positive and hopeful thinking and learn as much as I could about the disease to help others.

. . .

Q: What about your family. Did they all know?

A: I told my father. My mother knew before I did, because my doctor had told me that if it came back positive, she [the doctor] was to be the one to tell her because my mother was a heart patient. She said a sudden shock like that could make her have a heart attack. Another heart attack would probably be it, because her heart was so weak. It took them awhile to accept me, but once they did they became very supportive.

Q: [Your community, your neighbors, your church.] Tell me about them now in your life.

A: A lot of them, after they found out, you know, some of them left and some of them stayed. Only the true friends, as I called them, were the ones that stayed. They don't treat me any different. They still treat me the same. . . . Of course I've done some AIDS lectures at the church where I was raised. . . .

Q: So you're pretty open about having the virus, about telling people that you are HIV-positive.

A: Right, because I've been on TV and radio here. . . . My first appearance in public was in 1989. . . . Once I told them that I wasn't gay, that I had gotten it through multiple sex partners, then they kind of relaxed a little bit. But then they wanted to stereotype me as what you call a gigolo or a woman's man, which—I'm just like anyone else. I just made a mistake and got caught.

. . .

Q: How has it affected your personal relationships?

A: Well, it cost me some relationships. When I told the person I first met or another I was HIV-positive, a lot of them walked away. One or two said it didn't really matter, but eventually it did. Of course the relationship I have now with my friend I think is great. I wouldn't trade anything for it.

Q: So you have a serious relationship with someone now?

A: I'm in the process of a serious relationship.

Q: You're in love?

A: Yeah, that's basically it.

Q: In your other potential relationships, you've been very honest? This person knows that you are HIV-positive?

A: Right. You know, I figure it's better if everything's out. That way—she'll know up front, then there wouldn't be no fallbacks later on. She wouldn't have nothing to throw up in my face later on, well you didn't tell me, or something.

Q: Even though she's accepting of this fact, that you're HIV-positive, do you think that it will affect your long-term relationship with her?

A: No, I don't think so.

Q: What about children?

A: Children? I have one daughter who's going to be eight years old October the fourth—which I haven't seen in a couple of years.

Q: Are you going to go see her?

A: As quick as I find where she's at.

. . .

Q: How has your circle of friends changed since you found out you were HIV-positive?

A: I have more friends who are what you would call probably gay or lesbian than I did before, because at that time I had a closed mind to them, where now my mind is more open because I found out that we're all equal. We're all human beings.

. . .

Q: What are your ambitions right now? What are your goals?

A: Right now my goal is to educate as many as I can. Help stop the spreading of HIV by doing more education and prevention. And also someday, hopefully, start my own task force.

Q: Where have you found the most support?

A: I've found the most support probably in the church. Churches are now beginning to open their doors. They want people who are HIV-positive to come in and talk to their members, because they're finding out that they have a lot of church members, they have family members who are testing positive or dying from AIDS. At first they closed the doors. Now they're beginning to open them up.

Q: Did you have immediate support from your church when you found out you were HIV-positive or when they found out?

A: Not at first. It took awhile. Probably about four or five years before they really accepted it. Once another person tested positive, I think that's what really made them sort of open the doors.

. . .

Q: And now you speak in your church.
A: I speak there or anywhere really.
. . .

PROBLEMS OF IDENTIFICATION. These problems lie not necessarily with
George Albright or men like that in Mississippi. They exist for us observers
and interpreters compelled to label, analyze, categorize, and—inevitably—simplify.

As George Albright responds to the first question posed above, his motives appear to diverge from those of the interviewer. They diverge from
my own. Elsewhere in this text, in chapter 2, I rely on these words Albright
spoke to help elucidate the nature of agricultural labor in rural Mississippi.
I present the words in edited format, a smoothed-out life story, condensed,
giving the illusion of an unmediated, "authentic" account. Here, when it is
paired with the interviewer's query, Albright's description of farm work,
we might venture, resembles a circumlocution, a technique of indirection.
The interviewer wants to discuss Albright's dating habits. Albright, perhaps, does not.

Is George Albright engaged in habits of dissembling when he repeatedly
refers to three former partners in the third-person plural, as a collective, as
"they"? When he speaks of them as "one or two"? When he speaks of a
particular individual as "the person"? When he chooses to speak not of the
individuals but of the "relationships"? The "second and third ones"? Or
when he speaks of his current partner as "my friend"? These phrases might
suggest an unwillingness to accommodate the interviewer's wishes. They
might recall speech patterns characteristic of an earlier historical period, of
a culture of quiet accommodation, when the suspect feigned innocence and
the authority feigned ignorance. The phrases just might function foremost—as some queer readers of this text surely will appreciate, for whom
this technique maybe will resonate—to obscure the gender of the partner.

When faced with almost irrefutable traces of queer sexuality, ordinary
Mississippians in the mid- and late twentieth century often insist on their
right to not know. Adamantly, they maintain that they don't *want* to believe
certain accounts. George Albright's interviewer seems to participate in this
will to ignorance, a will to normalcy. When Albright describes "the person"
who infected him, he hesitates. His voice drops to a near-whisper, slurred
beyond my recognition, to an "s." The person, Albright mumbles, "'s been
deceased now about four years." [Ha]s been deceased? [She]'s been deceased? [He]'s been deceased? The interviewer, present as the words are
spoken, perhaps hears accurately. "She has," the interviewer confirms.

"Hmmm." Perhaps, on the other hand, she hears—as human beings are wont to do—what she wants to hear.

Or maybe Albright engages in a pronoun gender-switching characteristic of gay camp. From this point forward in the interview—after first resisting interrogations about his sex life, having now gendered his partner(s) as feminine—Albright asserts his difference from, but his newfound kinship with, "what you would call probably gay or lesbian" people. He further asserts the geographical remove—the rural/urban split—of AIDS (and gay) discourses. He casts AIDS as elsewhere, as he describes how he notified his (non-gender-specific) "partners from the military," those he had sex with during his only extended period of residence outside Jones County, in the navy. The implications are not unlike those of dominant strategies that cast homosexuality as elsewhere.

Indeed, gay and AIDS discourses constantly suggest one another, though not solely due to the epidemiological factors that prompted higher incidences of AIDS among gay men early in the crisis. Gays and AIDS respectively—and in tandem—call up the queer. As George Albright's narrative demonstrates, to be among the first diagnosed with HIV or AIDS in Mississippi is to be queered, to be marked as other, regardless of stated or implied sexual orientation. Still, the rhetoric of gay identity politics easily affixes to AIDS interrogations. And since African Americans too suffer higher incidences of HIV and AIDS, such rhetoric and interrogations are complicated in Mississippi by noxious traditions that promote white scrutiny of black lives and African American answerability to whites, traditions that depict black sexuality as diseased and infectious. (Recall the former Sovereignty Commission director's racist warnings, in chapter 4, about venereal disease among blacks.) Albright's interviewer asks if he has been—and in the process compels him to feel that he should be—"pretty open about having the virus." She lauds his being "very honest" with his partners about his HIV status. Through television and radio appearances, by public affirmations of self in varied settings including this interview, Albright comes out of a closet.

American AIDS educators in the 1990s attempt to shift the onus off of gay men, as they advise against labeling (and thereby stigmatizing) "risk groups" in favor of delineating (and thus universalizing) "risk behaviors." Despite any efforts to the contrary, however, particular behaviors are valorized, such as monogamy, while others are demonized, such as sex with multiple partners. As we see, in gay and AIDS identity politics, normalizing forces are ever at work. But the language of risk groups and risk behaviors is likewise suggestive in the ways its assumptions share in those of another important queer discourse: the articulation of gay identities as distinct from queer acts. Both today and in the past, notions of the queer help us undo and reconceptualize the existing state of things, the limitations of gay identity politics.

QUEER ACTS, AS this study has shown, were well incorporated into the structures of daily life in Mississippi, especially at midcentury. Individuals who engaged in queer acts often didn't identify as gay. Mississippians such as George Albright felt little connection to an urban world of so-called independent living, crafted around sexual affinities but likewise demarcated by hierarchies of race and gender performance. Albright exhibited allegiances foremost to family members, those who first learned of his illness and now support him in it; and to his community of faith, with which, after four to five long years of perseverance, he has fashioned a new understanding. Like the black Mississippians who rejected the tenets of a white-controlled gay church, George Albright shapes an identity firmly rooted in his "home church," as it is often called. His home, his local community, his church.

Uninteresting and perhaps counterproductive is the project of certifying any individual as gay—as "true" to some "fixed" "inner" core being. As this book should demonstrate, the truth of sexuality is often elusive and mutable. Genders and sexualities in mid- and late-twentieth-century Mississippi prove fluid, both adhering to and defying myriad means of classification. We all (can and should) frame the questions differently. Clearly same-sex genital contact alone doesn't denote queer sexualities. What constitutes proof of sexual contact—today and historically? What about gender nonconformity of other sorts? How do race and place affect sexual and gender meanings? Isn't sexual role as distinct from sexual object-choice more transgressive in certain places and times? Aren't nongenital romantic relations between men, such as kissing, often more culpable than genital relations? Isn't the number of partners sometimes more salient to surveillant authorities than the gender of a partner? Aren't these questions themselves limited and limiting? Aren't there innumerable patterns and behaviors we've yet to adequately articulate?

A Note on Interviews

Interviews ranged in length and formality from brief conversations, sometimes by phone, to exhaustive oral histories tape-recorded over several hours, even days, usually in the home of the narrator. Below I have provided the dates and places where the interviews occurred or, in the case of telephone interviews, the locations of the interviewees. In many cases, electronic mail or, more commonly, postal correspondence clarified and expanded upon these interactions. I have not attempted to document all those secondary exchanges below.

The stories of some narrators are given lengthy exposition in the text. These large excerpts are not set off in block quotes and are not interrupted by ellipses. The reader should assume that the narrative represents selected portions of an edited life history.

At first, I begrudgingly accepted some narrators' unwillingness to use their real names, wedded as I was to contemporary notions of pride and outness. By the end of the project, I encouraged anonymity. In these interviews, many individuals acknowledged participating in sexual acts still considered felonies in the state of Mississippi and many other parts of the United States. I am happy to aid and abet their acts of civil disobedience. I likewise changed the names of eight narrators (denoted by asterisks) interviewed by the Mississippi Oral History Program, University of Southern Mississippi, Hattiesburg, from which I obtained transcriptions and tapes.

I chose pseudonyms by consulting a list of the most common surnames in Mississippi. I assigned names of roughly equal prevalence. This means that my pseudonyms will correspond—as the real names of these narrators do—to the names of many Mississippians, living and dead. These coincidences are both unintentional and intentional. I don't mean to "malign" the "good name" of anyone; I do mean to show that "we" are a part of every community.

That said, these narrators represent myriad sexual persuasions and affiliations, from the most normative to the most marginal over time. I have spoken with a variety of interviewees for many different reasons, not just to instantiate queer identities or queer sexualities.

With the appropriate permissions or under the relevant professional standards, I have used the real names of public figures and of some interviewees who provided only cursory information or corroboration. I do not distinguish between real and fictional names below or in the text. Proper names of all third parties referred to in these interviews, with the exception of public figures, have been changed.

Place-names have not been changed, here or in the text.

Interviews

*Albright, George, Hattiesburg, Miss., 9 September 1994

Alexander, Thomas, Jackson, Miss., 26 June 1998

Anderson, Libby, Jackson, Miss., 7 July 1997

*Baldwin, Jill, Hattiesburg, Miss., 2 August 1993

Bernard, Allen, Sunshine, La., 25 September 1993

Bolton, Victoria, Madison, Miss., 16 June 1994

Busby, Harold, Birmingham, Ala., 22 June 1996

Childress, Ben, Atlanta, Ga., 4 September 1993; Washington, D.C., 2 March
      1994; 21, 24 March 1997

Cooper, Isaac, Jackson, Miss., 12 February 1997

Corley, Carl, Zachary, La., 29 July 1997

Dudley, Betty, Jackson, Miss., 16 June 1994

Ensley, Phil, San Diego, Calif., 8 August 1998

Foreman, Ed, Vicksburg, Miss., 18 May 1996

Garrett, Bonita, Atlanta, Ga., 24 February 1996

Garvey, Patrick, Washington, D.C., 18 July 1998

Greene, Anthony, Atlanta, Ga., 15 February 1996

*Hartley, Kerry, Hattiesburg, Miss., 21 July 1993

*Hechinger, Andy, Hattiesburg, Miss., 27 July 1993

Herrington, Ted, Hattiesburg, Miss., 13 January 1996

Holmes, Joe, Brandon, Miss., 18 May, 6 July 1996

Howard, Sr., John, Brandon, Miss., 22 March, 23 December 1996

Hughes, Jimmy, Jackson, Miss., 17 May 1996

*Hunt, Melvin, Hattiesburg, Miss., 22 July 1993

Ingalls, Mark, Clinton, Miss., 15 June 1994

Janacek, Delia, Jackson, Miss., 18 September 1997

Jeffries, Darryl, Brandon, Miss., 6 July 1996

Jones, Vince, New Orleans, La., 21 July 1998

Jordan, Stephen, Jackson, Miss., 7 April 1996

Knight, Ronald, Terry, Miss., 7 April, 19 May 1996

MacArthur, Bill, Natchez, Miss., 15, 16, 25, 26 May 1996

Minor, Bill, Jackson, Miss., 15 July 1997

Nesbit, Sylvia, Jackson, Miss., 17 September 1997

Phillips, Thomas Hal, Corinth, Miss., 25 November 1994; 18 July, 27 December 1995

Plant, Chuck, Jackson, Miss., 18 May 1996

Powell, Jeremy, Atlanta, Ga., 3 June 1996

Riley, John, Chicago, Ill., 6 January 1995

Rivers, DeAnn, Jackson, Miss., 12 August 1997

Salario, Blaise, Baton Rouge, La., 25 July 1997

Sandifer, Eddie, Jackson, Miss., 29 July 1998

Sawyer, Randall, Marietta, Ga., 21 March 1996

Smith, Fred, Jackson, Miss., 1 July 1997

Smith, Rickie Leigh, Pearl, Miss., 14 January 1996

Spencer, Fitz, Natchez, Miss., 15, 16, 25, 26 May 1996

Switzer, Kathy, Jackson, Miss., 28 March 1994

Terrence, Jan, Oxford, Miss., 21 June 1996

Tillman, Lottie, Jackson, Miss., 13 January 1996

Tillman, Ward, Jackson, Miss., 13 January 1996

*Ulner, Frederick, Hattiesburg, Miss., 22 July 1993

Walls, Kelly, Atlanta, Ga., 20 April 1994

Watson, Florence, Baton Rouge, La., 25 July 1997

*Watson, Stan, Hattiesburg, Miss., 1 July 1993

Weiss, Burton, Berkeley, Calif., 4 February 1996

Wilkinson, Stuart, Atlanta, Ga., 23 February 1994

Woods, Jake, Atlanta, Ga., 12 February 1994

*Young, Cindy, Hattiesburg, Miss., 4 August 1993

Carl Corley Bibliography

(in chronological order of publication)

Pulp Fiction

A Chosen World, PL524 (Agoura, Calif.: Pad Library, 1966), 187 pp.

My Purple Winter, FL1 (San Diego, Calif.: Publishers Export Co., 1966), 159 pp.*

The Scarlet Lantern, FL3 (San Diego, Calif.: Publishers Export Co., 1966), 158 pp.*

Star Light Star Bright, PL537 (Agoura, Calif.: Pad Library, 1967), 188 pp.

A Fool's Advice, FL9 (San Diego, Calif.: Publishers Export Co., 1967), 156 pp.*

Fallen Eagle, FL11 (San Diego, Calif.: Publishers Export Co., 1967), 155 pp.*

Faces in Secret, HES101 (San Diego, Calif.: Publishers Export Co., 1967), 159 pp.

Brazen Image, FL17 (San Diego, Calif.: Publishers Export Co., 1967), 155 pp.*

A Lover Mourned, FL24 (San Diego, Calif.: Publishers Export Co., 1967), 188 pp.

Sky Eyes, FL28 (San Diego, Calif.: Publishers Export Co., 1967), 153 pp.*

Satin Chaps, FL31 (San Diego, Calif.: Publishers Export Co., 1968), 155 pp.*

Attala Rose, C504 (San Diego, Calif.: Publishers Export Co., 1968), 272 pp.

Jesse, FL33 (San Diego, Calif.: Publishers Export Co., 1968), 156 pp.*

The Purple Ring, FL39 (San Diego, Calif.: Publishers Export Co., 1968), 150 pp.*

The Different and the Damned, SP19 (San Diego, Calif.: Publishers Export Co., 1968), 167 pp.**

C: Classic
FL: French Line series
HES: Human Experience series
PL: Pad Library
PR: A Pleasure Reader
SP: Special Documentaries

*   cover art by author
**   published anonymously
***   identified in Norman bibliography; further data unavailable
****   same manuscript as *Cast a Wistful Eye*; slightly different pagination

Cast a Wistful Eye, FL41 (San Diego, Calif.: Publishers Export Co., 1968), 153 pp.*
Black Angel, FL47 (San Diego, Calif.: Publishers Export Co., 1968), 148 pp.*
Trick of the Trade, 101-26, 1968***
Easy Ride, FL77 (San Diego, Calif.: Publishers Export Co., 1970), 160 pp.
The Hustling Place, 1027 (El Cajon, Calif.: Regency, 1970), 158 pp.****
Swamp Angel, PR295 (San Diego, Calif.: Greenleaf Classics, 1971), 156 pp.
Jail Mate, PR297 (San Diego, Calif.: Greenleaf Classics, 1971), 154 pp.

Nonfiction

The Agony of Christ (Baton Rouge, La.: Carl Corley, 1967), 89 pp.
History of the Acadians (Baton Rouge, La.: Carl Corley, 1968), 31 pp.
Carl Corley's Illustrated History of Louisiana (Eunice, La.: The Eunice News, 1981), 343 pp.

Population of Selected Mississippi Communities, Towns, and Cities

	1950	1960	1970	1980
Belzoni	4,071	4,142	3,394	2,982
Biloxi	37,425	44,053	48,486	49,311
Bovina	*	*	*	*
Brandon	1,827	2,139	2,685	9,626
Brookhaven	7,801	9,885	10,700	10,800
Carrollton	475	343	295	338
Clarksdale	16,539	21,105	21,673	21,137
Cleveland	6,747	10,172	13,327	14,524
Clinton	2,255	3,438	7,289	14,660
Columbia	6,124	7,117	7,587	7,733
Columbus	17,172	24,771	25,795	27,383
Corinth	9,785	11,453	11,581	13,839
Crystal Springs	3,676	4,496	4,195	4,902
D'Lo	516	428	485	463
Eastabuchie	*	*	*	*
Edwards	1,002	1,206	1,236	1,515
Electric Mills	*	*	*	*
Ellisville	3,579	4,592	4,643	4,652
Escatawpa	*	1,464	1,579	5,367
Fayette	1,498	1,626	1,725	2,033
Flora	655	743	987	1,507
Florence	313	360	404	1,111
Flowood	*	486	352	943
Forest	2,874	3,917	4,085	5,229
Gloster	1,467	1,369	1,401	1,726
Greenville	29,936	41,502	39,648	40,613
Greenwood	18,061	20,436	22,400	20,115
Hattiesburg	29,474	34,989	38,277	40,829
Hollandale	2,346	2,646	3,260	4,336
Holly Springs	3,276	5,621	5,728	7,285

	1950	1960	1970	1980
Indianola	4,369	6,714	8,947	8,221
Itta Bena	1,725	1,914	2,489	2,904
Jackson	98,271	144,422	153,968	202,895
Kossuth	242	178	227	190
Laurel	25,038	27,889	24,145	21,897
Leland	4,736	6,295	6,000	6,667
Louise	479	481	444	400
Louisville	5,282	5,066	6,626	7,323
Loyd Star	*	*	*	*
McComb	10,401	12,020	11,969	12,331
Madison	540	703	853	2,241
Magee	1,738	2,039	2,973	3,497
Magnolia	1,984	2,083	1,970	2,461
Mantee	189	166	142	158
Meridian	41,893	49,374	45,083	46,577
Mize	439	371	372	363
Money	*	*	*	*
Montrose	222	169	160	120
Morton	1,664	2,260	2,672	3,303
Mound Bayou	1,328	1,354	2,134	2,917
Natchez	22,740	23,791	19,704	22,015
Oakley	*	*	*	*
Oxford	3,956	5,283	8,519	9,882
Pascagoula	10,805	17,155	27,264	29,318
Pearl	*	*	*	20,778
Pelahatchie	867	1,066	1,306	1,445
Philadelphia	4,472	5,017	6,274	6,434
Port Gibson	2,920	2,861	2,589	2,371
Portersville	*	*	*	*
Prentiss	1,212	1,321	1,789	1,465
Richton	1,158	1,089	1,110	1,205
Shaw	1,892	2,062	2,513	2,461
Shuqualak	714	550	591	554
Starkville	7,107	9,041	11,369	15,169
Summit	1,558	1,663	1,640	1,753
Taylorsville	1,116	1,132	1,299	1,387
Tchula	927	882	1,729	1,931
Terry	497	585	546	655
Tupelo	11,527	17,221	20,471	23,905

	1950	1960	1970	1980
Tylertown	1,331	1,532	1,736	1,976
Union Church	*	*	*	*
Utica	824	764	1,019	865
Vicksburg	27,948	29,143	25,478	25,434
Water Valley	3,213	3,206	3,285	4,147
Waveland	798	1,106	3,108	4,186
Wesson	1,235	1,157	1,253	1,313
Winona	3,441	4,282	5,521	6,177
Woodland	*	*	130	135
Yazoo City	9,746	11,236	11,688	12,426

* denotes unincorporated communities not itemized in U.S. Census figures.

Notes

Introduction

1. Minnie Bruce Pratt, "Identity: Skin Blood Heart," in *Rebellion: Essays, 1980–1991* (Ithaca, N.Y.: Firebrand, 1991), 32.

2. Gayle S. Rubin, "Thinking Sex: Notes for a Radical Theory of the Politics of Sexuality," in *The Lesbian and Gay Studies Reader*, eds. Henry Abelove, Michèle Aina Barale, and David M. Halperin (New York: Routledge, 1993), 23–24.

3. This literature is vast. Perhaps most influential has been John D'Emilio's essay "Capitalism and Gay Identity," first published in *Powers of Desire: The Politics of Sexuality*, eds. Ann Snitow, Christine Stansell, and Sharon Thompson (New York: Monthly Review Press, 1983), 100–113; see also his groundbreaking monograph *Sexual Politics, Sexual Communities: The Making of a Homosexual Minority in the United States, 1940–1970* (Chicago: University of Chicago Press, 1983); also, Michel Foucault, *The History of Sexuality*, vol. I, *An Introduction*, trans. Robert Hurley (New York: Pantheon, 1978), 43. Eve Kosofsky Sedgwick explores the Great Paradigm Shift in *Epistemology of the Closet* (Berkeley: University of California Press, 1990), 44–48.

4. David Harvey, *Justice, Nature and the Geography of Difference* (Cambridge, Mass.: Blackwell, 1996).

Chapter One

1. Mart Crowley, *A Breeze from the Gulf* (New York: Farrar, Straus & Giroux, 1974), 6.

2. Average daily traffic volume on state roads in Jasper County in 1957—the last year for which records are available—ranged from 230 vehicles on Mississippi Highway 528 to 1,060 on Mississippi 15. Thus, on average, five to twenty-two vehicles passed each hour in each direction; more during the daytime, less at night. *Traffic Volume Map, 1957 Traffic of Mississippi*, Mississippi State Highway Department, in Map Collections, Mississippi Department of Archives and History, Jackson, Miss.

3. Ted Herrington, interview by author, Hattiesburg, Miss., 13 January 1996.

4. For example, Herrington remembered the year of the incident above (1953) but did not mention the season. Because my experience of Methodist revivals in the 1960s and 1970s was that they invariably were held in the summer, I speculate that this episode took place in the summer and so "it's hot." Because air-conditioning was still a luxury option

on most motor vehicles, I further speculate that the car (or truck) windows were rolled down. Of course, it may have been raining.

5. Chuck Plant, interview by author, Jackson, Miss., 18 May 1996. References to feeling like "the only one in the world" or—at coming out—realizing one is "not the only one in the world" abound in oral history interviews with lesbians and gay men in America.

6. Fitz Spencer, interview by author, Natchez, Miss., 26 May 1996.

7. George Chauncey, *Gay New York: Gender, Urban Culture, and the Making of the Gay Male World, 1890–1940* (New York: BasicBooks, 1994); Esther Newton, *Cherry Grove, Fire Island: Sixty Years in America's First Gay and Lesbian Town* (Boston: Beacon Press, 1993); Marc Stein, *City of Sisterly and Brotherly Loves: The Making of Lesbian and Gay Communities in Greater Philadelphia, 1945–72* (Chicago: University of Chicago Press, forthcoming); Brett Beemyn, "A Queer Capital: Lesbian, Gay, and Bisexual Experiences in Washington, D.C. During and After World War II," in *Creating a Place for Ourselves: Lesbian, Gay, and Bisexual Community Histories.*, ed. Brett Beemyn (New York: Routledge, 1997); Elizabeth Lapovsky Kennedy and Madeline D. Davis, *Boots of Leather, Slippers of Gold: The History of a Lesbian Community* (New York: Routledge, 1993).

Broader surveys tend to focus on Los Angeles, San Francisco, New York, and Washington. Biographies, ethnographies, and other studies likewise treat individuals and events in those places: John D'Emilio, *Sexual Politics, Sexual Communities: The Making of a Homosexual Minority in the United States, 1940–1970* (Chicago: University of Chicago Press, 1983); Martin Duberman, *Stonewall* (New York: Dutton, 1993); Lillian Faderman, *Odd Girls and Twilight Lovers: A History of Lesbian Life in Twentieth-Century America* (New York: Columbia University Press, 1991); Eric Marcus, *Making History: The Struggle for Gay and Lesbian Equal Rights, 1945–1990: An Oral History* (New York: HarperCollins, 1992); Ina Russell, ed., *Jeb and Dash: A Diary of Gay Life, 1918–1945* (Boston: Faber and Faber, 1993); Randy Shilts, *The Mayor of Castro Street: The Life and Times of Harvey Milk* (New York: Saint Martin's, 1982); Stuart Timmons, *The Trouble with Harry Hay: Founder of the Modern Gay Movement* (Boston: Alyson Publications, 1990); Kath Weston, *Families We Choose: Lesbians, Gays, Kinship* (New York: Columbia University Press, 1991).

A notable exception is Allan Bérubé's impressive *Coming Out under Fire: The History of Gay Men and Women in World War II* (New York: Free Press, 1990). While Bérubé charts military life as experienced across a variety of locales, the postwar settling of veterans in major metropolitan areas is treated as a linchpin of late-twentieth-century urban gay culture.

8. John Howard, "The Library, the Park, and the Pervert: Public Space and Homosexual Encounter in Post–World War II Atlanta," *Radical History Review* 62 (spring 1995): 166–187; also, Allen Drexel, "Before Paris Burned: Race, Class, and Male Homosexuality on the Chicago South Side, 1935–1960"; John Howard, "Place and Movement in Gay American History: A Case Study from the Post–World War II South"; David Johnson, "The Kids of Fairytown: Gay Male Culture on Chicago's Near North Side in the 1930s"; Tim Retzloff, "Cars and Bars: Assembling Gay Men in Postwar Flint, Michigan"; Roey

Thorpe, "The Changing Face of Lesbian Bars in Detroit, 1938–1965"; all in *Creating a Place for Ourselves,* ed. Beemyn; also, Daneel Buring, "Softball and Alcohol: The Limits of Lesbian Community in Memphis from the 1940s through the 1960s"; Saralyn Chesnut and Amanda C. Gable, "'Women Ran It': Charis Books and More and Atlanta's Lesbian-Feminist Community, 1971–1981"; Katy Coyle and Nadiene Van Dyke, "Sex, Smashing and Storyville in Turn-of-the-Century New Orleans: Reexamining the Continuum of Lesbian Sexuality"; Kathie D. Williams, "Louisville's Lesbian Feminist Union: A Study in Community Building"; all in *Carryin' On in the Lesbian and Gay South,* ed. John Howard (New York: New York University Press, 1997).

9. See especially John D'Emilio's "Capitalism and Gay Identity," first published in *Powers of Desire: The Politics of Sexuality,* eds. Ann Snitow, Christine Stansell, and Sharon Thompson (New York: Monthly Review Press, 1983), 100–113.

10. I have relied on Donna Jo Smith's perceptive reading of Bérubé, "Queering the South: Constructions of Southern/Queer Identity," in *Carryin' On in the Lesbian and Gay South,* ed. Howard, 372–76.

11. See Scott Bravmann, *Queer Fictions of the Past: History, Culture, and Difference* (Cambridge, U.K.: Cambridge University Press, 1997).

12. David F. Greenberg, *The Construction of Homosexuality* (Chicago: University of Chicago Press, 1988), 468.

13. Bravmann, especially 3–14, draws significantly and usefully from the work of Martha Vicinus, among others; Kevin J. Mumford, *Interzones: Black/White Sex Districts in Chicago and New York in the Early Twentieth Century* (New York: Columbia University Press, 1997), 100–101, 115.

14. As Essex Hemphill (ed.) writes, "There was no gay community for black men to come home to in the 1980s." *Brother to Brother: New Writing by Black Gay Men* (Boston: Alyson Publications, 1991), xix. Jewelle Gomez notes, "The fallacy that homosexuality is 'white' has been used frequently to try to shame Blacks into 'recanting.'" *Forty-three Septembers* (Ithaca, N.Y.: Firebrand, 1993), 176. For further explications of the tensions between imagined sexual communities and "home" communities based on race and ethnicity, see Russell Leong, ed., *Asian American Sexualities: Dimensions of the Gay and Lesbian Experience* (New York: Routledge, 1996). Will Roscoe, ed., *Living the Spirit: A Gay American Indian Anthology* (New York: Saint Martin's Press, 1988).

15. Kennedy and Davis; Newton.

16. This argument might still have an essentialist ring. Yet my purpose is to disclose how this desire, seemingly available in all times and places, is differently constructed based on social context. That is, though I consider myself a social constructionist, I share some of the views of John Boswell, a scholar frequently maligned as "essentialist." Boswell insists that he does *not* support the notion that sexuality is "essentially independent of culture, . . . that society does not create erotic feelings but only acts on them." I build on my argument, with the help of Valerie Traub, later in this chapter.

The mired-in-the-quicksand debates over essentialism versus constructionism often are simplistically aligned with nature versus nurture arguments. Despite the recent popular press attention over seemingly different neurobiological traits among homosexuals and heterosexuals—such as Simon LeVay's *The Sexual Brain* (Cambridge, Mass.: MIT Press, 1993)—I am uninterested in a search for "causes" of homosexuality or heterosexuality. As Boswell well puts it, "I was and remain agnostic about the origins and etiology of human sexuality." "Revolutions, Universals, and Sexual Categories," in *Hidden from History: Reclaiming the Gay and Lesbian Past*, eds. Martin Duberman, Martha Vicinus, and George Chauncey Jr. (New York: Meridian, 1989), 36; see also Edward Stein, ed., *Forms of Desire: Sexual Orientation and the Social Constructionist Controversy* (New York: Garland, 1990).

17. Alfred C. Kinsey, Wardell B. Pomeroy, and Clyde E. Martin, *Sexual Behavior in the Human Male* (Philadelphia: Saunders, 1948); see also Regina Markell Morantz, "The Scientist as Sex Crusader: Alfred C. Kinsey and American Culture," *American Quarterly* 29 (winter 1977): 563–89. For a good overview of Kinsey's life work, see Martin Duberman's review of the problematic James H. Jones biography, *Alfred C. Kinsey: A Public/Private Life*, in *The Nation*, 3 November 1997, 40–43.

18. I don't want to speak monolithically of all American lesbian and gay historical scholarship to this point. Nor do I want to set up a straw man, a reductive portrayal of other arguments that easily can be put asunder. Yet I do see a number of the widely recognized major works as, at a minimum, unconcerned with specifying sexual acts. Among those, I would include Bérubé's *Coming Out under Fire*, Faderman's *Odd Girls and Twilight Lovers*, and D'Emilio's *Sexual Politics, Sexual Communities*. To be fair, the latter— D'Emilio's groundbreaking dissertation-turned-monograph—is billed as a political history. His subsequent survey with Estelle B. Freedman, *Intimate Matters: A History of Sexuality in America* (New York: Harper & Row, 1988), the definitive work in the field, locates and elaborates any number of sexual practices within and across the hetero/homo dyad.

19. Douglas Crimp, "How to Have Promiscuity in an Epidemic," in *AIDS: Cultural Analysis, Cultural Activism*, ed. Douglas Crimp (Cambridge, Mass.: MIT Press, 1988): 237–71.

20. Martin Duberman, *About Time: Exploring the Gay Past*, rev. ed. (New York: Meridian, 1991), 408.

21. Bérubé, 5–7; John Dittmer, *Local People: The Struggle for Civil Rights in Mississippi* (Urbana: University of Illinois Press, 1994), 13–14.

22. Regional and sectional biases are common in reporting and historical writing on AIDS in the United States, particularly as regards the South. See Meredith Raimondo, "Dateline Atlanta: Place and the Social Construction of AIDS," in *Carryin' On in the Lesbian and Gay South*, ed. Howard, 331–69.

23. Bureau of the Census, *United States Census of the Population, 1980; Statistical Abstract of the United States, 1996*. Generally speaking, rural populations are defined as those residing in communities and towns of twenty-five hundred persons or fewer and those residing outside of towns.

For a useful overview of agrarian life in the United States, see David B. Danbom, *Born in the Country: A History of Rural America* (Baltimore, Md.: Johns Hopkins University Press, 1995).

24. C. Vann Woodward, *Origins of the New South, 1877–1913* (Baton Rouge: Louisiana State University Press, 1951), ix.

25. Taylor Branch, *Parting the Waters: America in the King Years, 1954–63* (New York: Simon & Schuster, 1988), 828; Clayborne Carson, *In Struggle: SNCC and the Black Awakening of the 1960s* (Cambridge: Harvard University Press, 1981), 3; Richard Kluger, *Simple Justice: The History of* Brown v. Board of Education *and Black America's Struggle for Equality* (New York: Vintage Books, 1975), 774.

26. *Jackson State-Times*, 6 June 1961.

27. During the 1960s, American folk and popular music helped move Mississippi to the national margins. As Phil Ochs sang, "Here's to the land you tore the heart out of / Mississippi, find yourself another country to be a part of." Nina Simone: "Everybody knows about Mississippi, god damn."

At the 1964 Democratic National Convention in Atlantic City, courageous civil rights activist Fannie Lou Hamer of Ruleville expressed near disbelief at the level of brutality and injustice in her home state and posed the question to television audiences: "Is this America?" See Kay Mills, *This Little Light of Mine: The Life of Fannie Lou Hamer* (New York: Dutton, 1993).

28. Brick in *Cat on a Hot Tin Roof* (New York: Dramatists Play Service, 1958) and Sebastian in *Suddenly Last Summer* (New York: Dramatists Play Service, 1958) are but two.

29. See Daneel Buring, *Lesbian and Gay Memphis: Building Communities Behind the Magnolia Curtain* (New York: Garland, 1997). On New Orleans, see Coyle and Van Dyke. Also, see the fascinating but poorly documented entry by Lucy J. Fair (pseudonym for a male author) in the oft-discredited *Encyclopedia of Homosexuality*, ed. Wayne Dynes (New York: Garland, 1990), 892–96.

30. Ronald Knight, interview by author, Terry, Miss., 19 May 1996.

31. Ibid.

32. Patrick Garvey, interview by author, Washington, D.C., 18 July 1998.

33. Ted Herrington, who told me about this incident, thinks the minister lives to this day in California.

34. Howard, "The Library, the Park, and the Pervert." Ted Herrington remembered this incident without prompting.

35. Ben Childress, interview by author, Atlanta, Ga., 4 September 1993.

36. Bill MacArthur, interview by author, Natchez, Miss., 26 May 1996.

37. Estelle Freedman, " 'Uncontrolled Desires': The Response to the Sexual Psychopath, 1920–1960," in *Passion and Power: Sexuality in History*, ed. Kathy Peiss and Christina Simmons (Philadelphia: Temple University Press, 1989), 199–225.

38. Mary E. Odem, *Delinquent Daughters: Protecting and Policing Adolescent Female*

Sexuality in the United States, 1885–1920 (Chapel Hill: University of North Carolina Press, 1995), 14.

39. *Mississippi Code, 1972,* vol. 22, section 97-5-31, 237.

40. The historical literature on religion in the South—particularly on white Protestantism—is considerable and, until recently, mostly celebratory. Generally, it posits a greater religiosity in the South—measured by church membership, stated belief in God, and so forth—as compared to other parts of the country. An overview should begin with the work of Samuel S. Hill, particularly his edited *Encyclopedia of Religion in the South* (Macon, Ga.: Mercer University Press, 1984). His most recent work attempts to complicate the theory of southern religious continuity and homogeneity over time; it focuses on three related name groups—the Baptists, the "of God" bodies, and the "Christians": *One Name but Several Faces: Variety in Popular Christian Denominations in Southern History* (Athens: University of Georgia Press, 1996). See also Charles Reagan Wilson, ed., *Religion in the South: Essays* (Jackson: University Press of Mississippi, 1985). For an account published near the midpoint of this period, see Kenneth Bailey, *Southern White Protestantism in the Twentieth Century* (New York: Harper & Row, 1964). On African American religious traditions, see C. Eric Lincoln and Lawrence Mamiya, *The Black Church in the African-American Experience* (Durham, N.C.: Duke University Press, 1990).

41. D'Emilio, *Sexual Politics, Sexual Communities,* 20.

42. Rickie Leigh Smith, interview by author, Pearl, Miss., 14 January 1996.

43. Anne Fausto-Sterling, "The Five Sexes: Why Male and Female Are Not Enough," *The Sciences* (March/April 1993): 20–21. On transgender history, see Leslie Feinberg, *Transgender Warriors: Making History from Joan of Arc to Dennis Rodman* (Boston: Beacon, 1996).

44. Judith Butler, *Gender Trouble: Feminism and the Subversion of Identity* (New York: Routledge, 1990), 128–41.

45. Regarding transsexual: whereas the *sex* in the mid- and late-twentieth-century definition of *homosexual* refers both to sexual intercourse and biological sex—say, a homosexual likes to have sex with someone of the same sex (admittedly a reductive formulation)—the *sex* in *transsexual* refers to biological sex alone, specifically, a sense of a mismatch. Vernon Rosario shows how male-to-female (MTF or M2F) transsexuals, as now understood, have been described with the same language early sexologists used to depict a male homosexual: "a female soul caught in a male body." "From our current critical perspective," Rosario surmises, "nineteenth century descriptions of . . . inverts seem to confuse 'gender identity' and 'sexual orientation' (i.e., one's sensed core gender versus one's sexual preference in partners)." Vernon A. Rosario, II, "Trans (Homo) Sexuality? Double Inversion, Psychiatric Confusion, and Hetero-Hegemony," in *Queer Studies: A Lesbian, Gay, Bisexual & Transgender Anthology,* eds. Brett Beemyn and Mickey Eliason (New York: New York University Press, 1996), 37–38, 40–41.

46. Ibid. Sex-reassignment surgery, introduced at midcentury, so framed identity that transsexuals came to be referred to as *preop* or *postop*(eration). Indeed, the procedure's

ascendancy occasioned a chilling example of circular and surveillant medical logic: the psychiatric diagnosis of "gender identity disorder," as spelled out in the American Psychiatric Association's *Diagnostic and Statistical Manual of Mental Disorders* (DSM) was predicated on the "patient's" stated interest in or request for surgical intervention. "Therefore," as Rosario summarizes, "the medical definition of 'transsexualism' is codependent on its surgical treatment." Put another—rightly sarcastic—way: "It is as if 'appendicitis' could be diagnosed only if lower right quadrant abdominal pain were accompanied by the patient's insistent demand to have an appendectomy."

For an engaging and perceptive retelling of the Jorgensen story, see David Harley Serlin, "Christine Jorgensen and the Cold War Closet," *Radical History Review* 62 (spring 1995): 136–65.

47. Marjorie Garber, *Vested Interests: Cross-Dressing and Cultural Anxiety* (New York: Routledge, 1992). Most significantly, Garber sees "transvestism" as "a space of possibility structuring and confounding culture: the disruptive element that intervenes, not just a category crisis of male and female, but the crisis of category itself" (17).

48. Raymond Williams, *The Country and the City* (New York: Oxford University Press, 1973), 96.

49. Ibid., 1.

50. Quoted in George McKay, ed., *DiY Culture: Party and Protest in Nineties Britain* (London: Verso, 1998), 45.

51. Ed Foreman, interview by author, Vicksburg, Miss., 18 May 1996.

52. Randall Sawyer, interview by author, Marietta, Ga., 21 March 1996.

53. Valerie Traub, *Desire and Anxiety: Circulations of Sexuality in Shakespearean Drama* (New York: Routledge, 1992), 103.

54. Ibid. Emphasis added.

55. Ibid. Emphasis added.

56. Eve Kosofsky Sedgwick, *Epistemology of the Closet* (Berkeley: University of California, 1990), 44.

57. Michel Foucault, *The History of Sexuality,* vol. I, *An Introduction,* trans. Robert Hurley (New York: Pantheon, 1978), 8.

58. Ibid., 17.

59. As Foucault elaborates, "Silence itself—the things one declines to say, or is forbidden to name, the discretion that is required between different speakers—is less the absolute limit of discourse, the other side from which it is separated by a strict boundary, than an element that functions alongside the things said, with them and in relation to them within over-all strategies. There is no binary division to be made between what one says and what one does not say; we must try to determine the different ways of not saying such things, how those who can and those who cannot speak of them are distributed, which type of discourse is authorized, or which form of discretion is required in either case. There is not one but many silences, and they are an integral part of the strategies that underlie and permeate discourses." Ibid., 27.

60. Yet, the notion of silence as imposed by dastardly oppressors—or as inculcated in the cowardly oppressed—is clearly at work in the late twentieth century in AIDS and identity politics. "Silence," I have chanted with other ACT UP activists, "equals death."

61. Herrington. Also, Ward Tillman, interview by author, Jackson, Miss., 13 January 1996.

62. Jan Terrence, interview by author, Oxford, Miss., 21 June 1996.

63. Betty Dudley, interview by author, Jackson, Miss., 16 June 1994.

64. Victoria Bolton, interview by author, Madison, Miss., 16 June 1994.

65. Herrington.

66. Pete Daniel, *Standing at the Crossroads: Southern Life in the Twentieth Century* (Baltimore, Md.: Johns Hopkins University Press, 1996), 66.

67. I do not mean to suggest that either is a static state. Rather, conceptions of uncertainty and certainty, "false consciousness" and self-knowledge, are hardly binary and ever dynamic. These signifiers and the signified are always in flux.

68. See Freedman.

Chapter Two

1. Richard Wright, *Black Boy* (New York: Harper and Brothers, 1945), 227.

2. T. J. Fox Allen and J. A. Van Hoesen, *A Digest of the Laws of Mississippi* (New York: Alexander S. Gould, 1839), appendix, ch. 14, sec. 228. In more recently published statutes, *Mississippi Code, 1972*, the prohibition against unnatural intercourse (97-29-59) appears after the law forbidding a "stallion or jack . . . to be kept in public view or permitted to run at large."

In 1955 the sodomy law was ruled to cover heterosexual oral and anal intercourse as well as homosexual. *State v. Davis* (1955) 223 Miss 862, 79 So 2d 452.

3. Edward W. Soja, *Postmodern Geographies: The Reassertion of Space in Critical Social Theory* (London: Verso, 1989), 14. The foregoing discussion owes much to the emergent interdisciplinary scholarship often referred to as the new cultural geography. Most useful for my purposes is Tim Cresswell, *In Place, Out of Place: Geography, Ideology, and Transgression* (Minneapolis: University of Minnesota Press, 1996).

4. Benedict Anderson, *Imagined Communities: Reflections on the Origin and Spread of Nationalism*, rev. exp. ed. (London: Verso, 1991), 6.

5. See James W. Loewen, *The Mississippi Chinese: Between Black and White* (Cambridge: Harvard University Press, 1971).

6. My father remembers watching the Negro team from his hometown, Brandon, play the all-Choctaw team from Philadelphia, Mississippi, in 1946. John Howard Sr., interview by author, Brandon, Miss., 22 March 1996. Before African Americans were allowed to enroll at Mississippi's white institutions of higher education, Choctaws did. Jan Terrence, interview by author, Oxford, Miss., 21 June 1996.

7. James L. Cox, ed., *Mississippi Almanac: The Ultimate Reference on the State of Mississippi* (Yazoo City, Miss.: Computer Search & Research, 1995), 485.

8. This discussion of Mississippi's distinctive geographical regions and peoples is informed by James W. Loewen and Charles Sallis, eds., *Mississippi: Conflict & Change*, rev. ed. (New York: Pantheon, 1980), 15–26.

9. Dale Krane and Stephen D. Shaffer, *Mississippi Government and Politics: Modernizers versus Traditionalists* (Lincoln: University of Nebraska Press, 1992), 249–69. On black voting, see Frank R. Parker, *Black Votes Count: Political Empowerment in Mississippi after 1965* (Chapel Hill: University of North Carolina Press, 1990).

10. Neil R. McMillen, *The Citizens' Council: Organized Resistance to the Second Reconstruction, 1954–64* (Urbana: University of Illinois Press, 1971).

11. Krane and Shaffer, 114.

12. Ibid., 204.

13. Earl Black and Merle Black, *Politics and Society in the South* (Cambridge: Harvard University Press, 1988), 223.

14. Cox, 57.

15. Ibid.

16. Krane and Shaffer, 220.

17. Ibid., 208, 213. Cox, 227–28. Parker, 17. Cox derives much of his data from U.S. Census figures for the 1980s and for 1990. I find this almanac to be a very useful document in comparing Mississippi to other states and to national averages, even over the entirety of the period under discussion. Though I don't want to extrapolate backward, certain demographic trends are necessarily of such lengthy duration that vastly different ratios over the course of a few decades seem unlikely. Where other factors might suggest significant change over a short time, I attempt to address them.

18. Krane and Shaffer, 157, 174–75.

19. James W. Silver, *Running Scared: Silver in Mississippi* (Jackson: University Press of Mississippi, 1984), 74.

20. V. S. Naipaul, *A Turn in the South* (New York: Vintage, 1990), 158.

21. James C. Cobb, *The Most Southern Place on Earth: The Mississippi Delta and the Roots of Regional Identity* (New York: Oxford University Press, 1992), xi.

22. Tal Stanley, "The Place of Justice" (review of *Justice in the Coalfields*, film directed by Anne Lewis), *Southern Changes* 17 (fall/winter 1995): 29.

23. Aaron Betsky, *Queer Space: Architecture and Same-Sex Desire* (New York: William Morrow, 1997), 17. Betsky elaborates a bit on this reductive formulation as follows: "The purpose of queer space is again ultimately sex: the making of a space either for that peculiar definition of the self as an engine of sexuality or for the act of sex itself," 20. But Betsky's central narrative is, like so many others, a tale of the city. Implicit throughout is the notion that queer space can be found only in urban areas or, as he concedes, in "our suburbs and now our exurbs," 14.

Related biases and stereotypes of the rural are evident in a recent path-breaking work in queer geography, David Bell and Gill Valentine, eds., *Mapping Desire: Geographies of Sexualities* (New York: Routledge, 1994). In their introduction, the editors state that for rural lesbians and gay men, the "only openings for expressing their sexuality may come from episodic encounters in public toilets or highway rest areas or infrequent trips to neighboring towns' bookstores and porn cinemas," 8. While my research shows that these were indeed important sites of interaction, they weren't the "only" or even the primary ones.

Similarly, Jerry Lee Kramer's contribution to this collection, "Bachelor Farmers and Spinsters: Gay and Lesbian Identities and Communities in Rural North Dakota," 200-13, says more about the author's—indeed, the profession's—preconceived notions and interpretive frameworks than about the lives of rural Americans. It is perhaps Kramer and his colleagues, not necessarily his subjects, who would be engaged in a frustrated "search for identity and community."

24. Fitz Spencer, interview by author, Natchez, Miss., 26 May 1996.

25. John Brinckerhoff Jackson, *A Sense of Place, A Sense of Time* (New Haven: Yale University Press, 1994), 57. The ideological determination of architectural spaces is well addressed by Joel Sanders in his introduction to the edited collection *Stud: Architectures of Masculinity* (New York: Princeton Architectural Press, 1996), 13: "Although purportedly outside the domain of politics, the way buildings [and, I would add, other elements of the built environment] distribute our activities within standard spatial configurations has a profound ideological impact on social interaction—regulating, constraining, and (on occasion) liberating the human subject."

26. Andy Hechinger, interview by Mississippi Oral History Program, Hattiesburg, Miss., 27 July 1993.

27. See, for example, Christine Stansell, *City of Women: Sex and Class in New York, 1789-1860* (New York: Knopf, 1986). On the home as a site for middle-class heterosexual courtship, see John D'Emilio and Estelle B. Freedman, *Intimate Matters: A History of Sexuality in America* (New York: Harper & Row, 1988), 73-78. Though they largely ignore issues of sexuality, two very useful texts on housing in the United States are Kenneth T. Jackson, *Crabgrass Frontier: The Suburbanization of the United States* (New York: Oxford University Press, 1985); and Gwendolyn Wright, *Building the Dream: A Social History of Housing in America* (New York: Pantheon, 1981).

28. Darryl Jeffries, interview by author, Brandon, Miss., 6 July 1996.

29. Cox, 57-58. For a useful historical overview of manufactured homes—a popular housing option in Mississippi—see Allan D. Wallis, *Wheel Estate: The Rise and Decline of Mobile Homes* (New York: Oxford University Press, 1991).

30. Rosemary Daniell, *Fatal Flowers: On Sin, Sex, and Suicide in the Deep South* (New York: Holt, Rinehart, and Winston, 1980), 251-52.

31. Craig Claiborne, *A Feast Made for Laughter* (Garden City, N.Y.: Doubleday & Company, 1982), 20-21.

32. Daniell, 252.

33. Fitz Spencer, letter to author, Natchez, Miss., 20 March 1998.

34. Carl Corley, letter to author, Zachary, La., 18 March 1998.

35. Mark Ingalls, interview by author, Clinton, Miss., 15 June 1994.

36. Ed Foreman, interview by author, Vicksburg, Miss., 18 May 1996.

37. Mark Ingalls, letter to author, Jackson, Miss., 20 March 1998; Chuck Plant, letter to author, Jackson, Miss., 19 March 1998; Spencer, 26 May 1996.

38. Ingalls, 15 June 1994.

39. Ibid.

40. Spencer, 20 March 1998.

41. Jonathan Odell, letter to parents, in *Breaking Silence: Coming-Out Letters* (New York: Xanthus Press, 1995), 9–10.

42. Daniell, 252.

43. Ben Childress, interview by author, Washington, D.C., 21 March 1997.

44. Ronald Knight, interview by author, Terry, Miss., 19 May 1996.

45. Raymond M. Berger, *Gay and Gray: The Older Homosexual Man* (Urbana: University of Illinois Press, 1982), 44.

46. Ingalls, 15 June 1994.

47. Elizabeth Lapovsky Kennedy and Madeline D. Davis, *Boots of Leather, Slippers of Gold: The History of a Lesbian Community* (New York: Routledge, 1993), 57–58.

48. Ingalls, 15 June 1994.

49. John Howard, "Place and Movement in Gay American History," in *Creating a Place for Ourselves: Lesbian, Gay, and Bisexual Community Histories*, ed. Brett Beemyn (New York: Routledge, 1997), 218.

50. Neil Miller, *In Search of Gay America: Women and Men in a Time of Change* (New York: Atlantic Monthly Press, 1989), 182–85.

51. Stan Watson, interview with Mississippi Oral History Program, Hattiesburg, Miss., 1 July 1993.

52. Berger, 39–43.

53. Spencer, 26 May 1996.

54. Frederick Ulner, interview with Mississippi Oral History Program, Hattiesburg, Miss., 22 July 1993.

55. Carl Corley, letter to author, Zachary, La., 27 March 1998.

56. Keith Vacha, *Quiet Fire: Memoirs of Older Gay Men* (Trumansburg, N.Y.: The Crossing Press, 1985), 166.

57. Joe Holmes, interview by author, Brandon, Miss., 18 May 1996.

58. Charles Reagan Wilson, "Bible Belt," in *Encyclopedia of Southern Culture*, vol. 4, eds. Charles Reagan Wilson and William Ferris (New York: Anchor Books, 1991), 83.

59. Lincoln and Mamiya, *The Black Church in the African-American Experience* (Durham, N.C.: Duke University Press, 1990), 92.

60. Ibid., 106.

61. Cox, 89.

62. Samel S. Hill, *One Name but Several Faces: Variety in Popular Christian Denominations in Southern History* (Athens: University of Georgia Press, 1996), 15–43.

63. Willie Morris, *North toward Home* (Oxford, Miss.: Yoknapatawpha Press, 1967), 41.

64. Lincoln and Mamiya, *The Black Church in the African-American Experience*, 407.

65. Hortense Powdermaker, *After Freedom: A Cultural Study in the Deep South*, rev. ed. (Madison: University of Wisconsin Press, 1993), 234.

66. George Albright, interview with Mississippi Oral History Program, Hattiesburg, Miss., 9 September 1994.

67. Corley, 27 March 1998.

68. D. Michael Quinn, *Same-Sex Dynamics among Nineteenth-Century Americans: A Mormon Example* (Urbana: University of Illinois Press, 1996).

69. The feminization of churchgoing, observed in many locales, was compounded by the predominance of women in the Mississippi population—greater than in any other state, except one. Cox, 58.

70. Powdermaker, 283.

71. For a description of a mid-1960s Alabama high school version of the womanless wedding, see Minnie Bruce Pratt, *S/HE* (Ithaca, N.Y.: Firebrand Books, 1995), 159. As recently as 1998, my mother was a judge in a womanless beauty pageant to benefit the First United Methodist Church of Brandon, Mississippi. Betty Howard, conversation with author, Brandon, Miss., 20 May 1998.

On this topic, historian Pete Daniel generously shared materials and observations from his current research, for which I'm grateful.

72. Allan Bérubé, *Coming Out under Fire: The History of Gay Men and Women in World War Two* (New York: Plume, 1991), 97.

73. Pratt, *S/HE*, 13.

74. Ronald Knight, letter to author, Terry, Miss., 11 May 1998. For fictionalized, but at least partially autobiographical, accounts of homoeroticism and religion in rural south Georgia, including autoeroticism and homosex in sacred spaces, see Roy F. Wood, *Restless Rednecks: Gay Tales of a Changing South* (San Francisco, Calif.: Grey Fox Press, 1985), 22–32, 68–81, 139–44.

75. Corley, 27 March 1998.

76. Mark Ingalls, letter to author, Jackson, Miss., 31 March 1998.

77. Childress.

78. Lottie Tillman, interview by author, Jackson, Miss., 13 January 1996.

79. Ward Tillman, interview by author, Jackson, Miss., 13 January 1996.

80. Corley, 27 March 1998.

81. Miller, 186.

82. Harold Busby, interview by author, Birmingham, Ala., 22 June 1996.

83. Childress.

84. Gayle Graham Yates, *Mississippi Mind: A Personal Cultural History of an American State* (Knoxville: University of Tennessee Press, 1990), 270–73.

85. Wright, 119.

86. Max C. Smith, "By the Year 2000," in *In the Life: A Black Gay Anthology*, ed. Joseph Beam (Boston: Alyson Publications, 1986), 227.

87. Jeffries.

88. On interpretations of these verses, see Keith Hartman, *Congregations in Conflict: The Battle over Homosexuality* (New Brunswick, N.J.: Rutgers University Press, 1996), 42–45.

89. Charles Marsh, *God's Long Summer: Stories of Faith and Civil Rights* (Princeton, N.J.: Princeton University Press, 1997), 89, 113, 227–28.

90. Corley, 27 March 1998; Patrick Garvey, interview by author, Washington, D.C., 18 July 1998.

91. Watson. The story of David and Jonathan is found in the book of I Samuel.

92. Loewen and Sallis, 247. Moreover, Mississippi teachers were among the lowest paid in the United States, ranking forty-ninth on one scale at the end of the period. Krane and Shaffer, 206.

93. See David S. Cecelski, *Along Freedom Road: Hyde County, North Carolina and the Fate of Black Schools in the South* (Chapel Hill: University of North Carolina Press, 1994).

94. *A Statistical Summary, State by State, of School Segregation-Desegregation in the Southern and Border Area from 1954 to the Present* (Nashville, Tenn.: Southern Education Reporting Service, 1967), 20; Loewen and Sallis, 315.

95. John Howard, "'Doing God's Work': White Church Entanglement in the Southern Segregation Academies" (paper presented at the History of Education Society Conference, Cambridge, Mass., October 1992).

96. In 1960, for example, Governor Ross Barnett wrested control of textbook screening committee appointments from the state superintendent of education, naming "fiery segregationist[s] and citizen council supporter[s]" to the oversight bodies. *(New Orleans) Times-Picayune*, 17 September 1960. See also *Jackson State-Times*, 21 September 1960.

97. Leslie Harper Purcell, *Miracle in Mississippi: Laurence C. Jones of Piney Woods* (New York: Carlton Press, 1956), 104, 163–64. Jones's kowtowing to white authorities, his quiescence at a time when other black leaders demanded social change, are evidenced by the appraisal of one Sovereignty Commission investigator. Zack J. Van Landingham, memorandum to Governor J. P. Coleman, 25 September 1959, Sovereignty Commission Files, Mississippi Department of Archives and History (hereafter MDAH), Jackson, Miss. For a small-town white-owned newspaper's praise for Jones, see *Prentiss Headlight*, 2 April 1959.

98. Randall Sawyer, interview by author, Marietta, Ga., 21 March 1996. These Hinds County public schools, surrounding the state's capital of Jackson, were among the last in Mississippi to desegregate. See *Statistical Summary*, 20. Indeed, the Edwards Attendance Center, where Randall Sawyer's mother was a teacher, became the site for a by-then clichéd defiant state stand-in-the-schoolhouse-door. *Jackson Daily News*, 9 September 1970; *Clarion-Ledger*, 11 September 1970.

99. Eric Marcus, *Making History: The Struggle for Gay and Lesbian Equal Rights, 1945–1990: An Oral History* (New York: HarperCollins, 1992), 389.

100. Corley, 27 March 1998.

101. Daniell, 252.

102. Corley, 18, 27 March 1998.

103. Terrence.

104. Ibid.

105. Vacha, 163; Knight, 11 May 1998.

106. Daniell, 199.

107. Chamberlain-Hunt Academy is perhaps the only nineteenth-century private boarding school still in operation in Mississippi. As of 1967–1968, the *Chamberlain-Hunt Academy Cadet Handbook*'s meticulous list of rules offered no explicit guidance regarding homosexual interaction. But the final rule well suggested how officials might view such activity, as it evidenced the requisite hush-hush handling: "Any cadet breaking the rules of accepted social or *moral* behavior, whether the rule is written or *unwritten*, is subject to disciplinary actions." Emphasis added. Chamberlain-Hunt Academy Papers, box 3, MDAH.

108. Purcell, 74, 95–96, 224. Minutes of the Executive Committee, 20 November 1957; 30 August 1953; 26 October 1972; Piney Woods Country Life School Records, boxes 1 and 3, MDAH. For more on the history and operation of Piney Woods, see the four-page section devoted to the school in the "Historical and Development Edition" of the *Brandon News*, 21 September 1944.

109. Ingalls, 15 June 1994.

110. Toni McNaron, *I Dwell in Possibility: A Memoir* (New York: The Feminist Press, 1992), 116–17.

111. Betsky, 17.

112. Ibid., 16, 21.

113. McNaron, 116–17.

114. Ibid., 117.

115. Of the numerous civil rights histories that document these and related events, see especially two key works: John Dittmer, *Local People: The Struggle for Civil Rights in Mississippi* (Urbana: University of Illinois Press, 1994); and Charles M. Payne, *I've Got the Light of Freedom: The Organizing Tradition and the Mississippi Freedom Struggle* (Berkeley: University of California Press, 1995).

116. Cox, 292–93; *Statistical Summary*, 21.

117. Anne Moody, *Coming of Age in Mississippi* (New York: Laurel, 1968), 230.

118. Lottie Tillman.

119. Jess Stearn, *The Sixth Man* (New York: Macfadden, 1962), 150.

120. These are personal recollections. One of my coworkers in Jackson around 1980 told me about 1970s dorm life at his alma mater, Jackson State. I observed similar phenomena firsthand while briefly attending Millsaps College in 1981 and while visiting the University of Southern Mississippi on several occasions in the eighties.

121. Bonita Garrett, interview by author, Atlanta, Ga., 24 February 1996.

122. Isaac Cooper, letter to author, Jackson, Miss., 12 February 1997.

123. Lottie Tillman; Garrett; Terrence.

124. Jill Baldwin, interview with Mississippi Oral History Program, Hattiesburg, Miss., 2 August 1993.

125. Cindy Young, interview with Mississippi Oral History Program, Hattiesburg, Miss., 4 August 1993.

126. Kerry Hartley, interview with Mississippi Oral History Program, Hattiesburg, Miss., 21 July 1993; Cooper; Ward Tillman; Hechinger; Watson.

127. Watson.

128. Ulner.

129. Baldwin.

130. Cooper.

131. Vince Jones, interview by author, New Orleans, La., 21 July 1998.

132. Margaret Walker, *Richard Wright, Daemonic Genius: A Portrait of the Man, a Critical Look at His Work* (New York: Warner Books, 1988), 88, 310.

133. Stearn, 41.

134. Ulner.

135. The arrests occurred in a library men's room in 1986, as was reported in local and national media. I spoke informally with one of the arrestees in 1989.

136. See chapter 6.

137. Ulner.

138. On Mississippi State, Foreman.

139. Hartley.

140. Corley, 27 March 1998.

141. Albright.

142. Krane and Shaffer, 35, 213.

143. Ibid., 36, 58.

144. See Pete Daniel, *Breaking the Land: The Transformation of Cotton, Tobacco, and Rice Cultures since 1880* (Urbana: University of Illinois Press, 1985).

145. Harold Hodgkinson, *Southern Crossroads: A Demographic Look at the Southeast* (Greensboro, NC: SERVE, 1993), 33.

146. James C. Cobb, *The Selling of the South: The Southern Crusade for Industrial Development, 1936–1990,* 2nd ed. (Urbana: University of Illinois Press, 1993), 272–76.

147. Corley, 27 March 1998.

148. Rickie Leigh Smith, interview by author, Pearl, Miss., 14 January 1996.

149. Corley, 27 March 1998.

150. Watson.

151. Ingalls, 15 June 1994. Several oral history narrators knew Dr. Folk socially and/or were among his patients.

152. This is another personal recollection. During my youth, I overheard a conversation between my mother and one of the board members of this bank. At a time when white-owned banks had few black employees, it is conceivable that racial prejudice may

also have played a part in the decision. Interestingly, though I remember the conversation vividly, my mother does not remember it.

153. Miller, 185.

154. Hartley.

155. McNaron, 115–26; Young.

156. Ingalls, 15 June 1994.

157. Corley, 27 March 1998.

158. Plant.

159. Ingalls, 20 March 1998.

160. Bill MacArthur and Fitz Spencer, joint interview with author, Natchez, Miss., 26 May 1996.

161. Constance Curry, *Silver Rights* (Chapel Hill, N.C.: Algonquin Books, 1995), 188.

162. Reed Massengill, *Portrait of a Racist: The Man Who Killed Medgar Evers?* (New York: Saint Martin's Press, 1994), 8–9.

163. Krane and Shaffer, 204.

164. Erle Johnston, *Politics: Mississippi Style* (Forest, Miss.: Lake Harbor Press, 1993), 246–52.

165. Even as George Chauncey locates working-class homosex in the semipublic interstices of crowded tenements and boardinghouses, he does not situate sex within familial households, within the walls of the private home. See his richly detailed study *Gay New York: Gender, Urban Culture, and the Making of the Gay Male World, 1890–1940* (New York: BasicBooks, 1994).

Chapter Three

1. Dorothy Allison, *Two or Three Things I Know for Sure* (New York: Dutton, 1995), 2.

2. Carl Corley, letter to author, Zachary, La., 18 March 1998.

3. Ronald Knight corroborates and more definitively pinpoints the locations and approximate dates of operation of the two bars mentioned. Neither he nor Chuck Plant recalls the name of this bar, but Knight confidently places it at the corner of Pascagoula and Gallatin, exactly two blocks from the railway station, just a block off Pearl. According to Knight, the bar served gay male customers in the early to mid-fifties, though the owner—presumably Connie—was a lesbian. This must be the Cellar, mentioned in chapter 4 and located at the same corner of Pascagoula at Gallatin.

Though he didn't remember it by name, Knight placed the Tropic on Pearl near Lamar, as did Plant, albeit more tentatively. Knight remembers the interior exactly as Plant describes it. Ronald Knight, interview by author, Terry, Miss., 19 May 1996.

4. Chuck Plant, interview by author, Jackson, Miss., 18 May 1996.

5. Bureau of the Census, *United States Census of the Population, 1950, 1960, 1970, 1980, 1990.* Figures are for the city proper.

6. James L. Cox, *Mississippi Almanac: The Ultimate Reference on the State of Mississippi* (Yazoo City, Miss.: Computer Search and Research, 1995), 36.

7. John K. Bettersworth, *Mississippi: A History* (Austin, Tex.: Steck Company, 1959), 168–69.

8. Plant's interest and skill in music was apparent to his Central High classmates. In the school yearbook, *The Cotton Boll*, his photo was accompanied by the phrase "Where words fail, music speaks." Of the roughly 350 graduating seniors, "Chucky" was distinguished for his "enviable ability . . . to express himself through three languages—music, art, and Latin. The merriment of this red head," the yearbook writers added, "spreads to all those about him."

9. Carl Corley, letter to author, Zachary, La., 27 March 1998.

10. Laud Humphreys, *Tearoom Trade: Impersonal Sex in Public Places,* rev. enl. ed. (New York: Aldine de Gruyter, 1975). Lee Edelman, "Tearooms and Sympathy, or, The Epistemology of the Water Closet," in *The Lesbian and Gay Studies Reader,* eds. Henry Abelove, Michèle Aina Barale, and David M. Halperin (New York: Routledge, 1993), 553–74; and "Men's Room," in *Stud: Architectures of Masculinity,* ed. Joel Sanders (New York: Princeton Architectural Press, 1996), 152–61. See also Dangerous Bedfellows, eds., *Policing Public Sex: Queer Politics and the Future of AIDS Activism* (Boston: South End Press, 1996).

11. Knight corroborates the tearoom at the City Auditorium and remembers the raid there, as do many narrators.

12. John Howard, "The Library, the Park, and the Pervert: Public Space and Homosexual Encounter in Post–World War II Atlanta," *Radical History Review* 62 (spring 1995): 166–87. Stephen Jordan, interview by author, Jackson, Miss., 7 April 1996. Fitz Spencer, interview by author, Natchez, Miss., 26 May 1996.

13. Bureau of the Census, *United States Census of the Population, 1950.*

14. Mark Ingalls, interview by author, Clinton, Miss., 14 June 1994. Jordan likewise confirms these sites.

15. On American tennis professional Renée Richards, the male-to-female transsexual who underwent treatments in the seventies, see her autobiography, *Second Serve: The Renée Richards Story* (New York: Stein and Day, 1983).

16. On Dr. Benjamin P. Folk Jr., see chapter 5.

17. Rickie Leigh Smith, interview by author, Pearl, Miss., 14 January 1996.

18. Donna Jo Smith, "Queering the South: Constructions of Southern/Queer Identity," in *Carryin' On in the Lesbian and Gay South,* ed. John Howard (New York: New York University Press, 1997), 381.

19. Knight. For similar outlying establishments in Virginia—"honky-tonks" friendly to lesbians—from roughly the same period, see Bob Swisher, "City Lesbians 'Took Over,' Danced at Country Beer Joint," *The Richmond Pride* (April 1985): 6.

20. Author site observation, Jackson, Miss., 27 July 1997. On vice at motor courts and motels from the 1920s to 1940s, see Warren James Belasco, *Americans on the Road: From Autocamp to Motel, 1910–1945* (Cambridge, Mass.: MIT Press, 1979), 139, 148–49, 168.

21. Carl Corley, interview by author, Zachary, La., 29 July 1997.

22. Knight.

23. See testimony in *State of Mississippi v. Lawrence E. Burns,* No. 15636, Circuit Court of the First Judicial District of Hinds County, Mississippi, 29 November–1 December 1955, Mississippi Department of Archives and History (hereafter MDAH), Jackson, Miss. This case is discussed in chapter 4.

24. Corley, 27 March 1998.

25. Knight. Also, see note 3.

26. *The Lavender Baedeker* (San Francisco: Guy Strait, 1964), 1, 16. By comparison, there were several listings under Alabama. Eight years later John Francis Hunter, author of *The Gay Insider, USA* (New York: Dell, 1972), sent numerous query letters to Mississippi, but "got zero replies." *The Gay Insider* had several Alabama listings.

27. Joe Holmes, interview by author, Brandon, Miss., 18 May 1996.

28. Victoria Bolton, interview by author, Madison, Miss., 16 June 1994.

29. Randall Sawyer, interview by author, Marietta, Ga., 21 March 1996.

30. Anthony Greene, interview by author, Atlanta, Ga., 15 February 1996. Jeremy Powell, interview by author, Atlanta, Ga., 3 June 1996.

31. Frederick Ulner, interview with the Mississippi Oral History Program, Hattiesburg, Miss., 22 July 1993.

32. Ibid.

33. Melvin Hunt, interview with Mississippi Oral History Program, Hattiesburg, Miss., 22 July 1993.

34. Ulner.

35. Corley, 27 March 1998.

36. Ulner.

37. John Howard, "Place and Movement in Gay American History: A Case from the Post–World War II South," in *Creating a Place for Ourselves: Lesbian, Gay, and Bisexual Community Histories,* ed. Brett Beemyn (New York: Routledge, 1997), 213–14.

38. Ulner.

39. Cindy Young, interview with Mississippi Oral History Program, Hattiesburg, Miss., 4 August 1993.

40. Kerry Hartley, interview with Mississippi Oral History Program, Hattiesburg, Miss., 21 July 1993.

41. Neil Miller, *In Search of Gay America: Women and Men in a Time of Change* (New York: Atlantic Monthly Press, 1989), 182. Roey Thorpe, "The Changing Face of Lesbian Bars in Detroit, 1938–1965," in *Creating a Place for Ourselves,* ed. Beemyn, 166, 180 n. 5.

42. Isaac Cooper, letter to author, Jackson, Miss., 12 February 1997.

43. Bonita Garrett, interview by author, Atlanta, Ga., 24 February 1996.

44. Smith, 382.

45. Mark H. Rose, *Interstate: Express Highway Politics, 1939–1989,* rev. ed. (Knoxville: University of Tennessee Press, 1990; 1979), 31; Cox, 325, 373.

On postwar automobility in the United States, see Kenneth T. Jackson, *Crabgrass Frontier: The Suburbanization of the United States* (New York: Oxford University Press, 1985), 246–71.

46. Edward F. Haas, "The Southern Metropolis, 1940–1976," in *The City in Southern History: The Growth of Urban Civilization in the South*, ed. Blaine A. Brownell and David R. Goldfield (Port Washington, N.Y.: Kennikat Press, 1977), 176.

47. Tim Retzloff, "Cars and Bars: Assembling Gay Men in Postwar Flint, Michigan," in *Creating a Place for Ourselves*, ed. Beemyn, 243.

48. Ibid., 236, 243.

49. Henri Lefebvre, *Writings on Cities*, trans. and eds. Eleonore Kofman and Elizabeth Lebas (Cambridge, Mass.: Blackwell, 1996), 118–32. See also Lefebvre's definitive study *The Production of Space*, trans. Donald Nicholson-Smith (Cambridge, Mass.: Blackwell, 1991).

50. Dale Krane and Stephen D. Shaffer, *Mississippi Government and Politics: Modernizers versus Traditionalists* (Lincoln: University of Nebraska Press, 1992), 16. Interestingly, Mississippi delegates to Washington—Senator John Stennis and Congressman Will Whittington—initially resisted the interstate effort, convinced the system would be built to the detriment of two-lane farm-to-market roads. Rose, 36–38, 91–92.

51. Krane and Shaffer, 218.

52. Ibid., 233–34; "Mississippi: Stinging the Good Ole Boys," *Newsweek* 10 August 1987, 21.

53. Krane and Shaffer, 129.

54. Knight.

55. Greene.

56. Ed Foreman, interview by author, Vicksburg, Miss., 18 May 1996.

57. Cox, 325.

58. Hunt.

59. Hartley.

60. *Clarion-Ledger*, 2 December 1986.

61. Ulner.

62. *Clarion-Ledger*, 2 December 1986.

63. *The (Atlanta) Barb*, December 1976, Files of the Atlanta History Center Archives, Atlanta, Ga.

64. Powdermaker, 49.

65. William Armstrong Percy, III, "William Alexander Percy (1885–1942): His Homosexuality and Why It Matters," in *Carryin' On in the Lesbian and Gay South*, ed. Howard, 81.

66. Allen Bernard, interview by author, Sunshine, La., 25 September 1993.

67. *Jackson Daily News*, 30 August 1958.

68. *Traffic Volume Map, 1957 Traffic of Mississippi; 1978 Traffic Volume Map of Mississippi, Mississippi State Highway Department*, in Map Collections, MDAH.

69. Knight.

70. John Howard Sr., interview by author, Brandon, Miss., 22 March 1996.

71. Kendall Blanchard, *The Mississippi Choctaws at Play: The Serious Side of Leisure* (Urbana: University of Illinois Press, 1981), 45, 55–56, 98–99, 126. A masculinist read of *toli*

and related tribal games is Thomas Vennum Jr.'s *American Indian Lacrosse: Little Brother of War* (Washington, D.C.: Smithsonian Institution Press, 1994).

72. "Highway 80 League, Rules and Regulations, 1950," in the personal files of John Howard Sr.

73. Joe Holmes, interview by author, Brandon, Miss., 18 May, 6 July 1996.

74. Norman Hayner, *Hotel Life* (Chapel Hill: University of North Carolina Press, 1935), 6. Cited in Belasco, 149.

75. Ingalls.

76. John Brinckerhoff Jackson, *A Sense of Place, A Sense of Time* (New Haven: Yale University Press, 1994), 190–91. Also suggestive is Jackson's *Discovering the Vernacular Landscape* (New Haven: Yale University Press, 1984); and Michael Hough, *Out of Place: Restoring Identity to the Regional Landscape* (New Haven: Yale University Press, 1990).

77. Corley, 27 March 1998.

78. See *Scrapbook, 1938–1940*, box 1, Garden Clubs of Mississippi Collection, MDAH.

79. Jimmy Hughes, interview by author, Jackson, Miss., 17 May 1996.

80. Ibid. "Detail of Roadside Park No. 75, Hwy. #45 [ca. 1950]; Roadside Park No. 75 [1967]," Mississippi Department of Transportation, Jackson, Miss.

81. Hughes.

82. "Rest Stop Facility for Miss. State Hwy. Dept," Godrey, Bassett, Pitts and Tuminello, Architects, Mississippi Department of Transportation, Jackson, Miss.

83. "Roadside Park" [1967].

84. Hunt.

85. Knight.

86. Ingalls.

87. Plant. On the transformation of retailing and the implications for car culture, see the contributions of Lizabeth Cohen, Thomas W. Hanchett, and Kenneth T. Jackson in "AHR Forum: Shopping Malls in America," *American Historical Review* 101 (October 1996): 1,049–1,121.

88. For accounts of rest area and truck stop sex among rural Appalachians, see Abraham Verghese, *My Own Country: A Doctor's Story* (New York: Simon & Schuster, 1994), 115–16.

89. Ben Childress, interview by author, Washington, D.C., 21 March 1997.

90. Bolton.

91. Alan Lomax, *The Land Where the Blues Began* (New York: Pantheon, 1993), 340–43.

92. Vince Jones, interview by author, New Orleans, La., 21 July 1998. Corley, 29 July 1997.

93. Allan Bérubé, *Coming Out under Fire: The History of Gay Men and Women in World War Two* (New York: Free Press, 1990).

94. Ben Childress, interview by author, Atlanta, Ga., 4 September 1993.

95. Oye Apeji Ajanaku, "Discharge USN '63," in *In the Life: A Black Gay Anthology*, ed. Joseph Beam (Boston: Alyson Publications, 1986), 114–15.

96. Neil Simon, *Biloxi Blues* (New York: Random House, 1986).

97. Eric Marcus, *Making History: The Struggle for Gay and Lesbian Equal Rights, 1945–1990: An Oral History* (New York: HarperCollins, 1992), 333.

98. For example, all my attempts to verify the 1952 suicide(s) at Keesler were thwarted. Neither the base library nor any of the local newspapers could find press accounts. Older staff members had no recollection of the events.

A community oral history project, the Atlanta Lesbian and Gay History Thing, recorded numerous narratives of an event known by several as Black Sunday. Apparently, during a police raid of a gay party in a hotel or high-rise apartment, someone jumped out of the window to his death. Dates and locations vary, though they cluster around what is now called Midtown Atlanta, during the mid- to late 1940s and early 1950s. Because such events are rarely indexed as "sex crimes," as "sex" related, or even as "vice," they are very difficult to track down using traditional research methods.

99. Robert Coles, conversation with author, Cambridge, Mass., 5 December 1995.

100. Columbus B. Hopper, *Sex in Prison: The Mississippi Experiment with Conjugal Visiting* (Baton Rouge: Louisiana State University Press, 1969), 24, 37–38, 41, 91–94. See also David M. Oshinsky's incisive study *Worse than Slavery: Parchman Farm and the Ordeal of Jim Crow Justice* (New York: Free Press, 1996).

101. See John Dittmer, *Local People: The Struggle for Civil Rights in Mississippi* (Urbana: University of Illinois Press, 1994).

102. Charles M. Payne, *I've Got the Light of Freedom: The Organizing Tradition and the Mississippi Freedom Struggle* (Berkeley: University of California Press, 1995), 244.

103. Amber Hollibaugh, "Right to Rebel," in *Homosexuality: Power and Politics,* ed. Gay Left Collective (London: Allison and Busby, 1980), 205.

104. John D'Emilio, "Homophobia and the Trajectory of Postwar American Radicalism: The Case of Bayard Rustin," *Radical History Review* 62 (spring 1995): 80–103; see also Jervis Anderson, *Bayard Rustin: Troubles I've Seen: A Biography* (New York: HarperCollins, 1997).

105. Burton Weiss, interview by author, Berkeley, Calif., 4 February 1996. On the efforts of Weiss, his fellow students, and area residents, see Cornell-Tompkins County Committee for Free and Fair Elections in Fayette County, Tennessee, *Step by Step: Evolution and Operation of the Cornell Students' Civil-Rights Project in Tennessee, Summer, 1964* (New York: W. W. Norton, 1965).

106. In 1970 at least one gay white Mississippian viewed racial and sexual oppressions as linked. He worked in a latter-day "settlement house" for indigent blacks and demonstrated against the shootings at Jackson State. The incident at Jackson's historically black university had shocked the nation. During a period of heightened racial tensions, highway patrolmen and city police opened fire on campus protesters, killing two and wounding twelve. The FBI found that the officers shot at least three hundred rounds at the gathering. James W. Loewen and Charles Sallis, eds., *Mississippi: Conflict and Change,* rev. ed. (New York: Pantheon, 1980), 319–20.

107. Doug McAdam, *Freedom Summer* (New York: Oxford University Press, 1988), 219–21.

108. On migration into and out of the South, see Daniel M. Johnson and Rex R. Campbell, *Black Migration in America: A Social Demographic History* (Durham, N.C.: Duke University Press, 1981); Jack Temple Kirby, *Rural Worlds Lost: The American South, 1920–1960* (Baton Rouge: Louisiana State University Press, 1987). On Mississippi specifically, see Neil R. McMillen, *Dark Journey: Black Mississippians in the Age of Jim Crow* (Urbana: University of Illinois Press, 1989); and Loewen and Sallis, especially 330–36.

109. McMillen, *Dark Journey*, 258–60.

110. Loewen and Sallis, 331.

111. Greene; Sawyer.

112. Craig Claiborne, *A Feast Made for Laughter* (Garden City: N.Y.: Doubleday & Company, 1982), 72.

113. Randy Shilts, *The Mayor of Castro Street: The Life and Times of Harvey Milk* (New York: St. Martin's, 1982), 44–45.

114. Jonathan Odell, letter to parents, in *Breaking Silence: Coming-Out Letters* (New York: Xanthus Press, 1995), 9–10.

115. In describing Mexican and Mexican American homosexual behaviors, Tomás Almaguer uses Freudian terminology to draw the distinction between (1) sexual aim, the type of sex act, and (2) sexual object-choice, the gender of the partner. "Chicano Men: A Cartography of Homosexual Identity and Behavior," in *The Lesbian and Gay Studies Reader*, eds. Henry Abelove, Michèle Aina Barale, and David M. Halperin (New York: Routledge, 1993), 255–73; see also Joseph Carrier, *De Los Otros: Intimacy and Homosexuality among Mexican Men* (New York: Columbia University Press, 1995).

Both of these scholars see penetrative homosexual intercourse as similarly less transgressive among Mexican and Mexican American men. Ranging from sexual aim to sexual object-choice, analogous dyads might be penetrative/penetrated, insertive/receptive, active/passive (for Smith and, as we shall see, Knight, this reverses for oral sex), top/bottom, butch/femme, masculine/feminine, male/female.

Hector Carillo sees beyond these dyads, offering complicated matrixes of queer desire, as I similarly attempt to suggest here. "Globalization versus Locality?: The Formation of Contemporary Homosexualities in Mexico" (paper presented to Queer Globalization, Local Homosexualities: Citizenship, Sexuality, and the Afterlife of Colonialism Conference, Center for Lesbian and Gay Studies, New York, 24 April 1998).

116. Knight.

117. Steven Seidman, "Identity and Politics in a 'Postmodern' Gay Culture: Some Historical and Conceptual Notes," in *Fear of a Queer Planet: Queer Politics and Social Theory*, ed. Michael Warner (Minneapolis: University of Minnesota Press, 1993), 121.

118. Marcus, *Making History*, 388–90.

119. Ingalls.

120. Anonymous, "Seduced by a Younger Boy," in *My First Time: Gay Men Describe their First Same-Sex Experience*, ed. Jack Hart (Boston: Alyson Publications, 1995), 66–67.

121. Knight.

122. Will Fellows, *Farm Boys: Lives of Gay Men from the Rural Midwest* (Madison: University of Wisconsin Press, 1996), ix.

Chapter Four

1. Mab Segrest, *My Mama's Dead Squirrel: Lesbian Essays on Southern Culture* (Ithaca, N.Y.: Firebrand Books, 1985), 57.

2. Chuck Plant, interview by author, Jackson, Miss., 18 May 1996.

3. This discussion is drawn primarily from local press accounts and from the Mississippi Supreme Court case *Burns v. State* (1956) 228 Miss 254, 87 So 2d 681. Included with the supreme court briefs and decision are the trial court transcripts, *State of Mississippi v. Lawrence E. Burns*, No. 15636, Circuit Court of the First Judicial District of Hinds County, Mississippi, 29 November–1 December 1955, Mississippi Department of Archives and History (hereafter MDAH), Jackson, Miss.

4. Carl Corley, letter to author, Zachary, La., 15 September 1997.

5. *Jackson City Directory, 1955–1956* (Richmond, Va.: R. L. Polk & Co., 1956), 1:586, 4:39.

6. W. C. Dear, questioned by defense attorney W. W. Pierce, *State v. Burns*.

7. *Burns v. State.*

8. Ibid.

9. *Clarion-Ledger* (hereafter *CL*), 28 September 1955.

10. *Jackson Daily News* (hereafter *JDN*), 28 September 1955; *CL*, 29 September 1955.

11. *CL*, 29 September 1955.

12. *CL*, 29 November 1955.

13. On homosexual panic, see Eve Kosofsky Sedgwick, *Epistemology of the Closet* (Berkeley: University of California Press, 1990), 19–21. See also Gary David Comstock, *Violence against Lesbians and Gay Men* (New York: Columbia University Press, 1991).

14. John D'Emilio, *Sexual Politics, Sexual Communities: The Making of a Homosexual Minority in the United States, 1940–1970* (Chicago: University of Chicago Press, 1983), 50–51.

15. *JDN*, 29 November 1955.

16. Paul Stribling, questioned by defense attorney W. W. Pierce, *State v. Burns*.

17. James Roy Luke, questioned by defense attorney W. W. Pierce, *State v. Burns*.

18. Marcus Atkins, questioned by defense attorney W. W. Pierce, *State v. Burns*; C. E. Flanagan, questioned by defense attorney W. W. Pierce, *State v. Burns*.

19. Forrest Bratley, questioned by defense attorney W. W. Pierce, *State v. Burns*.

20. Willard Dougherty, questioned by defense attorney W. W. Pierce, *State v. Burns*.

21. Warren Koenig, questioned by prosecuting attorney Julian Alexander, *State v. Burns*.

22. Lawrence Burns, questioned by defense attorney W. W. Pierce, *Burns v. State*.

23. Leon Hendrick, instructions to the Hinds County Circuit Court jury, *Burns v. State*. Emphasis added.

24. *JDN*, 12 December 1955.

25. John Dittmer, *Local People: The Struggle for Civil Rights in Mississippi* (Urbana: University of Illinois Press, 1994), 57. See also Stephen J. Whitfield, *A Death in the Delta: The Story of Emmett Till* (New York: Free Press, 1988).

26. In all the oral history interviews for this project, the John Murrett trial is the only one of its kind mentioned from the 1950s. Nor is there any mention of police arrests akin to those of the 1960s, discussed in the next two sections.

27. Dittmer, *Local People*. Charles Payne, *I've Got the Light of Freedom: The Organizing Tradition and the Mississippi Freedom Struggle* (Berkeley: University of California Press, 1995).

28. Dittmer, *Local People*, 79. On the origins of the sit-in movements, see William F. Chafe, *Civilities and Civil Rights: Greensboro, North Carolina and the Black Struggle for Freedom* (New York: Oxford University Press, 1980).

29. See, in the order referred to here, Winthrop Jordan, *White over Black: American Attitudes toward the Negro, 1550-1812* (Chapel Hill: University of North Carolina Press, 1968); George M. Fredrickson, *White Supremacy: A Comparative Study in American and South African History* (New York: Oxford University Press, 1981); Deborah Gray White, *Ar'n't I a Woman? Female Slaves in the Plantation South* (New York: W. W. Norton, 1985); Joel Williamson, *The Crucible of Race: Black-White Relations in the American South since Emancipation* (New York: Oxford University Press, 1984).

For a contemporaneous assessment of the psychological dimensions of race and sex, still fresh with insight, see Lillian Smith, *Killers of the Dream*, rev. enl. ed. (New York: W. W. Norton, 1961; 1948). On formulations of the race traitor further tainted by queer sexuality, see Mab Segrest's compelling autobiographical account, *Memoir of a Race Traitor* (Boston: South End Press, 1994).

A useful overview of white liberalism in post–World War II Mississippi can be found in Tony Badger, "Fatalism, Not Gradualism: The Crisis of Southern Liberalism, 1945–65," in *The Making of Martin Luther King and the Civil Rights Movement*, eds. Brian Ward and Tony Badger (New York: New York University Press, 1996), especially 67–74.

30. Neil R. McMillen, *The Citizens' Council: Organized Resistance to the Second Reconstruction, 1954–64* (Urbana: University of Illinois Press, 1994; 1971). For a contemporary account of Citizens' Council activities, see Hodding Carter III, "Citadel of the Citizens Council," *New York Times Magazine*, 12 November 1961.

31. "Crime Report Reveals Menace of Integration," Association of Citizens' Councils, Greenwood, Miss., late 1950s. Mississippi Sovereignty Commission Files, MDAH.

32. Robert B. Patterson, letter to Hamilton Thornton, Saint Louis, Mo., 26 September 1960. Mississippi Sovereignty Commission Files, MDAH. For a brief interview with Robert Patterson, see Howell Raines, *My Soul Is Rested: Movement Days in the Deep South Remembered* (New York: Putnam, 1977), 297–303.

33. "To the States," Citizens' Councils of America, 1961. Mississippi Sovereignty Commission Files, MDAH.

34. Untitled flyer, Association of Citizens' Councils, Greenwood, Miss., undated. Mis-

sissippi Sovereignty Commission Files, MDAH; see also McMillen, *The Citizens' Council,* 183–88.

35. *Community Citizen,* 20 October 1960.

36. For an excellent study of the Student Nonviolent Coordinating Committee, see Clayborne Carson, *In Struggle: SNCC and the Black Awakening of the 1960s* (Cambridge: Harvard University Press, 1981).

37. *CL,* 25 May 1961. *JDN,* 25 May 1961. *Atlanta Constitution,* 27 May 1961.

38. *JDN,* 31 May, 6 June 1961.

39. *(Jackson) State-Times,* 31 May 1961.

40. *CL,* 25 May 1961.

41. *JDN,* 6 June 1961.

42. *JDN,* 29 June 1961.

43. *JDN,* 21 June 1961.

44. *JDN,* various dates, summer 1961.

45. *JDN,* 16 June 1961.

46. Ibid.

47. *JDN,* 22 June 1961.

48. Carl Corley, letter to author, Zachary, La., 25 April 1998.

49. Ibid.

50. *Rebel Underground,* October, December 1962; January 1963. Ole Miss Rebel Underground Papers, MDAH.

51. *JDN,* 29 July 1964.

52. Record of Rustin, Bayard, #33914, Pasadena Police Department, 21 January 1953. This record, along with a covering note from Citizens' Council operative Dick Morphew to commission director Erle Johnston, is one of several items on Rustin in the Mississippi Sovereignty Commission Files, MDAH.

On Rustin, see John D'Emilio's forthcoming biography, a portion of which appears as "Homophobia and the Trajectory of Postwar American Radicalism: The Case of Bayard Rustin," *Radical History Review* 62 (spring 1995): 80–103.

53. *CL,* 10 October 1968. The headline reads "SEX CRIMINAL ENDORSES MUSKIE."

54. *JDN,* 2, 3 July 1965.

55. *The Citizen* [Official Journal of the Citizens' Councils of America], February 1965, 11, 18.

56. Erle Johnston, *Mississippi's Defiant Years, 1953–1973: An Interpretive Documentary with Personal Experiences* (Forest, Miss.: Lake Harbor Publishers, 1990).

57. *JDN,* 7, 11 July 1965.

58. *JDN,* 11 July 1965.

59. *JDN,* 19 July 1965.

60. *Jackson Advocate,* 18 July 1964. For the variety of black and white press responses to the civil rights movement in Mississippi, see Julius E. Thompson, *The Black Press in Mississippi, 1865–1985* (Gainesville: University Press of Florida, 1993), 58–80.

61. *The Citizen*, February 1965, 11.

62. Tom Scarbrough, "Clay County," memorandum to files, 25 May 1965, 2. Mississippi Sovereignty Commission Files, MDAH.

63. *The Klan Ledger*, April 1965. Mississippi Sovereignty Commission Files, MDAH.

64. Charles Marsh, *God's Long Summer: Stories of Faith and Civil Rights* (Princeton: Princeton University Press, 1997), 64. With the exception of Bowers's phrase "the whores of the media," the words are Marsh's.

65. *Harvard Crimson*, 4 March 1964.

66. Phil Ensley, interview by author, San Diego, Calif., 8 August 1998.

67. Tom Scarbrough, "Mount Beulah or Southern Christian Institute, Edwards, Miss.," investigation report, 31 July 1962. Mississippi Sovereignty Commission Files, MDAH. For another, sympathetic take on Bill Higgs from the period, see Clarice T. Campbell, *Civil Rights Chronicles: Letters from the South* (Jackson: University Press of Mississippi, 1997), 76, 78, 79, 81.

68. Steven F. Lawson, *Black Ballots: Voting Rights in the South, 1944–1969* (New York: Columbia, 1976). Parker, *Black Votes Count*.

69. *JDN*, 3 February 1961.

70. A. L. Hopkins, "Robert L. T. Smith, Sr.," investigation report, 16 May 1961. Albert Jones and A. L. Hopkins, "Investigation of Tarl Brooks," investigation report, 21 December 1961. Mississippi Sovereignty Commission Files, MDAH.

71. R. M., "March 28 Meeting of Interracial Group at Saint Andrews Episcopal Church," 13 June 1961. Bob Moses, letter to James Dombrowski, New Orleans, La., 5 June 1962. Scarbrough, "Mount Beulah." Mississippi Sovereignty Commission Files, MDAH.

72. Complaint, *C. E. Shaffer, et al. v. Citizens' Council Forum, et al.*, United States District Court for the Southern District of Mississippi, Jackson Division, January 1961. Mississippi Sovereignty Commission Files, MDAH.

73. *General Laws of the State of Mississippi*, 1956, ch. 365, 520–24. Cited in "Sovereignty Commission Agency History," finder's guide. Mississippi Sovereignty Commission Files, MDAH.

74. McMillen, *The Citizens' Council*, 140.

75. *(New Orleans) Times-Picayune*, 8 January 1961. *JDN*, 11 January 1961. *CL*, 13, 18, 23 January; 25 February 1961.

76. *CL*, 13 January 1961.

77. *Holmes County Herald*, January 1961.

78. *CL*, 13 January 1961.

79. Albert Jones, letter to Wilburn Hooker, Lexington, Miss., 7 August 1962. Mississippi Sovereignty Commission Files, MDAH.

80. "Statement of Minnie Pearl Collins," 22 June 1962, in Tom Scarbrough, "Yazoo and Humphreys County," investigation report, 6 July 1962. Mississippi Sovereignty Commission Files, MDAH. *CL*, 10 June 1962. *(Memphis) Commercial Appeal*, 10, 25 June 1962.

81. Tom Scarbrough, "Sunflower, Yazoo and Holmes Counties," investigation report, 13 September 1962. Mississippi Sovereignty Commission Files, MDAH.

82. Ensley. *CL*, 10 June 1962. *(Memphis) Commercial Appeal*, 10 June 1962.

83. Albert Jones, itinerary for investigator A. L. Hopkins, 17 June 1962. Mississippi Sovereignty Commission Files, MDAH.

84. *Clarksdale Press Register*, 19, 20 June 1962. *JDN*, 19, 21 June 1962. *(Memphis) Commercial Appeal*, 19 June 1962. *CL*, 21 June 1962.

85. *JDN*, 19 June 1962.

86. Ibid. *Clarksdale Press Register*, 20 June 1962.

87. *(Memphis) Commercial Appeal*, 25 June 1962.

88. "Statement of Minnie Pearl Collins."

89. *JDN*, 19 June 1962.

90. William Dewey Peters, questioned by Tom Scarbrough [handwritten notes], undated [1962]. Mississippi Sovereignty Commission Files, MDAH. In 1962 Mound Bayou staged Diamond Jubilee celebrations to mark the seventy-fifth anniversary of its founding. Peters was arrested in 1961.

91. James A. Schnur, "Closet Crusaders: The Johns Committee and Homophobia, 1956–1965," in *Carryin' On in the Lesbian and Gay South*, ed. John Howard (New York: New York University Press, 1997), 132–63.

My analysis here is indebted to Steven Lawson for framing this and related phenomena more broadly as a culture of investigation.

92. Original Bill for Divorce, *Mrs. Elizabeth Burt Higgs v. William L. Higgs*, Chancery Court of the First Judicial District of Hinds County, Mississippi, No. 61542, 6 July 1962. The divorce was later granted, after Bill Higgs refused to answer. Final Decree of Divorce, 21 September 1962. Mississippi Sovereignty Commission Files, MDAH.

93. Mrs. Paul Brannon, letter to Virgil S. Downing, Jackson, Miss., 29 July 1963. Virgil S. Downing, "Horace A. Nelson," investigation report, 23 January 1963. R. M., "March 28 Meeting." Mississippi Sovereignty Commission Files, MDAH.

94. A. L. Hopkins, "Trial of Attorney William Higgs," investigation report, 18 February 1963. Mississippi Sovereignty Commission Files, MDAH.

95. Ibid.

96. Ensley; Bill Minor, interview by author, Jackson, Miss., 15 July 1997.

97. Hopkins, "Trial of Attorney."

98. *Harvard Crimson*, 4 March 1964.

99. James W. Silver, *Mississippi: The Closed Society* (New York: Harcourt, Brace & World, 1963), 97–98.

100. Minor.

101. James W. Silver, *Running Scared: Silver in Mississippi* (Jackson: University Press of Mississippi, 1984).

102. Virgil Downing, "William L. Higgs and Associates," investigation report, 31 July 1963. Mississippi Sovereignty Commission Files, MDAH.

103. *CL*, 29 October 1963; *Harvard Crimson*, 4 March 1964; *The Nation*, 13 December 1965, 460–62; *JDN*, 29 July 1966, 26 May 1967.

104. Ensley. In 1998 Phil Ensley unsuccessfully petitioned the Mississippi Supreme Court to posthumously reinstate Higgs to the bar. I'm grateful to Phil Ensley for generously sharing his research and reflections on Bill Higgs.

105. Dittmer, *Local People*, 122, 459 n. 5.

106. Payne, *I've Got the Light of Freedom*, 244–45, 295, mentions both the Higgs incident and the Aaron Henry incident, to be discussed, in his impressive study of Mississippi organizing. While he refuses explicit judgment on either, he frames them within broader discussions of the trials and tribulations *unfairly* visited upon movement activists and volunteers. Both Payne and Silver, *Mississippi*, 97, note the timing of the Higgs arrest.

107. Aaron Henry, "Inside Agitator," unpublished autobiography written with Bill Silver, undated [1965?], box 1, series I, subseries B, folders 2–5, Aaron Edd Henry Papers (hereafter AEHP), Lillian Pierce Benbow Room of Special Collections, Coleman Library, Tougaloo College, Tougaloo, Miss.

In the Henry Papers, pages 211–30 of chapter 12, "The Diabolical Plot," chronicle these events. I have a slightly different version, labeled chapter 11 and numbered 9–29, graciously annotated and provided to me by Henry's biographer, Constance Curry. This quote, 9–10.

108. For additional sketches of Henry, I have relied on *Jackson Advocate*, 11 January 1979; *Sunbelt: Black Life in Mississippi* (April 1980): 18–19; *CL*, 5 November 1993; *New York Times*, 21 May 1997.

109. *Jackson Advocate*, 11 January 1979. Minor.

110. Silver, *Mississippi*, 212. "I was somewhat embarrassed," Silver wrote on another occasion, "when Aaron Henry hugged me in the presence of photographers" at a civil rights meeting at Tougaloo College. Reporters from the *Clarion-Ledger*, Silver worried, had taken note. Silver, *Running Scared*, 58.

111. Evans Harrington, letter to Aaron Henry, 2 October 1972, box 76, series V, folder 1307, AEHP.

112. "Diabolical Plot," 15–17.

113. Ibid., 19.

114. Ibid., 19–20.

115. *CL*, 24 October 1972.

116. "Diabolical Plot," 11. Included with the Mississippi Supreme Court case records, *Henry v. State* (1963) 253 Miss 263, 154 So 2d 289, are the trial court transcripts, *State of Mississippi v. Aaron E. Henry*, No. 29, County Court of Bolivar County, Mississippi, 21–22 May 1962, MDAH.

117. *Henry v. State*. "Diabolical Plot," 21.

118. "Diabolical Plot," 23.

119. *Henry v. Collins, Henry v. Pearson* (1965) 380 US 356, 85 S Ct 992.

120. *Henry v. Mississippi* (1968) 392 US 931, 88 S Ct 2276, 20 L Ed 2d 1389.

121. Dittmer, *Local People,* 122. George Alexander Sewell and Margaret L. Dwight, *Mississippi Black History Makers,* rev. enl. ed. (Jackson: University Press of Mississippi, 1984; 1977), 85.

122. *Newsweek,* 30 March 1998, 15.

123. As of March 1999, the twenty-two-year-old lawsuit to unseal the Sovereignty Commission files still had not resolved the fate of a few remaining records, including those on Aaron Henry, who died before completing a privacy claim. See *CL,* 21 May 1998.

Given that several documents in the closed files have been indexed under the name Sterling Lee Eilert, it's clear that the incident was at least monitored by the Sovereignty Commission. Given their aggressive pursuit of Bill Higgs and innumerable others, a much more active role in the Henry case seems likely.

124. "Diabolical Plot," 23.

125. Gerald Epworth (pseudonym), letter to Aaron Henry, 17 April 1972, box 76, series V, folder 1301, AEHP.

126. Henry's draft reply was handwritten directly onto the letter from Epworth. Henry may have never sent it. Epworth, whom I contacted by telephone, says he does not remember receiving such a response from Henry. Nor does he clearly remember the circumstances of their meeting, though he assures me that as to the obvious sexual overtones in the letters, "none of that came up" between them in person.

Apparently distressed by my call, he later contacted my academic chair, insisting such inferences could not be published. However, under current professional standards, the letters are open to use. In fairness to him, I use a pseudonym and omit his current place of residence. Gerald Epworth, interview by author, 20 May 1998.

127. *CL,* 24 October 1972; *JDN,* 24 October 1972.

128. L. W. McCaskill, letter to Ronald Goldfarb, 22 October 1972, box 76, series V, folder 1305, AEHP. In folder 1304 is an undated (1972) press account of McCaskill's indictment in federal court for selling drugs to an undercover agent.

129. Aaron Henry, letter to Ronald Goldfarb, 25 October 1972, box 76, series V, folder 1305, AEHP.

130. *CL,* 2 November 1972.

131. *Jackson Advocate,* 6 June 1985.

132. Ibid.

133. Dates range from 1984 through 1986, boxes 82–84, series V, folders 1375–1401, AEHP. They include correspondence forwarded from Henry's home and Fourth Street Drug Store, both in Clarksdale. Preprinted labels, likely applied by Noelle Henry, instructed the postal service to forward each piece to Aaron Henry at the Sun-N-Sand Motel. The room number was not specified.

134. These messages likewise range from 1984 through 1986. Most supportive of my argument are the messages found in box 83, series V, folder 1391, AEHP. Many are written

on the same type of imprinted message pad clearly utilized by Sun-N-Sand staff. See for example, Aaron Henry, dictated telephone message to Pedro Erwin, Room 132, 31 October 1985, 12:30 P.M.: "Dr. Henry had to go to Hattiesburg. Will be back late tonite [sic]."

Also in these folders are undated handwritten messages from Henry to Erwin, apparently left in the motel room. One from 1984 is written on a Ramada Inn pad and perhaps predates their residence at the Sun-N-Sand or indicates that Pedro sometimes accompanied Henry on his travels: "Pedro, I will be back by 6 P.M., Aaron." The other, also from 1984, is written on a three-by-five-inch index card: "Pedro, I am in the dining room. Come on up, Aaron." Box 82, series V, folder 1375, AEHP.

135. These checks, drawn on the State Mutual Federal Savings and Loan Association, Jackson, Mississippi, appear in box 83, series V, folders 1388 and 1390, the latter of which contains a complete monthly statement, April to May 1985. This latter folder also includes a monthly Visa statement for Aaron Henry, on which is listed a $351.45 charge to Sun-N-Sand, 15 January 1985.

136. Minor.

137. For corroboration of the two arrests described—in Clarksdale and Washington, D.C.—and for details of the two others—in Jackson (see *CL*, 9 September 1976) and Florida—I have relied on the testimony of respected journalist Bill Minor. Though generally friendly to and politically aligned with Henry, Minor was once involved in litigation against him. The resultant investigation further illuminated these four arrests.

138. Delia Janacek, interview by author, Jackson, Miss., 18 September 1997. Janacek played with the symphony from its founding in 1944 until 1989. In addition, I have relied on numerous items in the Jackson Symphony Orchestra, 1944–1959 Subject File, MDAH. See particularly, "Jackson Symphony Orchestra, History and Significance" (1952), "Jackson Symphony Orchestra, 1956–1957," and "Jackson Symphony Orchestra: The First Twenty-Five Years" (1969).

139. Janacek.

140. *JDN*, 16 February 1959.

141. Sylvia Nesbit, interview by author, Jackson, Miss., 16 September 1997.

142. According to the Jackson Police Department records manager, his staff's inability to locate *detailed* records of these events suggests not that they didn't happen. Not long ago, a man arrested on "similar charges asked to see his own file," which was no longer there. Often such files were cleansed. In the 1965 cases, the official presumes that Russell and others were "corralled," held in "temporary confinement, and let go." Thomas Alexander, interview by author, Jackson, Miss., 26 June 1998.

Sketchy reports not made available to me, but relayed verbally by Alexander, did confirm that Russell, an elected official, and two other men were arrested at the City Auditorium on 29 July 1965. Also, in their daily tally of police arrests, the *Clarion-Ledger* counted four for "disorderly conduct." *CL*, 2 August 1965.

143. Alexander.

144. *CL*, 9 August 1965. *JDN*, 9 August 1965. Emphasis added.

145. Harvard Sitkoff, *The Struggle for Black Equality, 1954–1980* (New York: Hill and Wang, 1981), 199.

146. *CL*, 3, 6, 8, 9 August 1965.

147. *CL*, 5 August 1965. An astonishingly similar editorial cartoon by a *Jackson Daily News* staffer, almost two decades later, depicted a slender queer figure—explicitly marked as gay—in tight pants and flip-flops. See chapter 6.

148. Janacek.

149. DeAnn Rivers, interview by author, Jackson, Miss., 12 August 1997.

150. Frederick Ulner, interview with Mississippi Oral History Program, Hattiesburg, Miss., 22 July 1993.

151. Ibid.

152. Ulner remembers rumors that the Johnson aide committed suicide. As with the Jackson raids, I've seen no official records of the arrests nor corroboration of the suicide.

153. On massive resistance, see Parker, 34–77.

154. Edmund White, reading at the Regulator Bookshop, Durham, N.C., 18 September 1997. See his novel *The Farewell Symphony* (New York: Knopf, 1997).

155. Again Chuck Plant's remarks are typical. Eddie Sandifer makes explicit the tri-state comparison in Smith, "Queering the South," in *Carryin' On in the Lesbian and Gay South*, ed. Howard, 382.

156. For a similar argument about working-class white communities in a small peripheral South city, see Diane Wood Middlebrook, *Suits Me: The Double Life of Billy Tipton* (Boston: Houghton Mifflin, 1998), 18–19.

157. Parker, 30.

Chapter Five

1. Herman Raucher (screenwriter), *Ode to Billy Joe* (Burbank, Calif.: Warner Brothers, 1976). I have relied on the videocassette (Burbank, Calif.: Warner Home Video, 1992). A slightly different version of this dialogue can be found in the novel: Herman Raucher, *Ode to Billy Joe* (New York: Dell, 1976), 217–18.

2. As previously suggested, a number of social constructionist historians date the emergence of the modern homosexual—an identity-based rather than behaviorally based individual—around the close of the nineteenth century. See John D'Emilio, "Capitalism and Gay Identity," in *Powers of Desire: The Politics of Sexuality*, eds. Ann Snitow, Christine Stansell, and Sharon Thompson (New York: Monthly Review Press, 1983), 100–13; Lillian Faderman, *Surpassing the Love of Men: Romantic Friendship and Love between Women from the Renaissance to the Present* (New York: William Morrow, 1981); Michel Foucault, *The History of Sexuality*, vol. I, trans. Robert Hurley (New York: Pantheon, 1978); and David M. Halperin's illustratively titled *One Hundred Years of Homosexuality and Other Essays on Greek Love* (New York: Routledge, 1990).

Accounts of suicides by homosexuals begin to appear in the medical literature and in fiction around the same time. See numerous accounts described in Jonathan Ned Katz, ed., *Gay American History: Lesbians and Gay Men in the U.S.A.* (New York: Thomas Y. Crowell, 1976), an indispensable work in queer history.

An analysis of homosexual homicide narratives might begin with Lisa Duggan's perceptive account of one geographically proximate (Memphis) lesbian murder narrative: "The Trials of Alice Mitchell: Sensationalism, Sexology, and the Lesbian Subject in Turn-of-the-Century America," *Signs* 18 (summer 1993): 791-814, soon to be released in book-length form.

Higher incidences of suicide among today's queer youths are theorized in Eve Kosofsky Sedgwick, *Tendencies* (Durham, N.C.: Duke University Press, 1993), 1-2, 154. Also useful, though it does not address gender nonconformity, is Eric Rofes, *I Thought People Like That Killed Themselves* (San Francisco: Grey Fox Press, 1983). Note that the imprecise category of "people like that"—deployed by Rofes—does not seem to be regionally specific, though I find it well encapsulates discourses and conceptualizations of, by, and about queer Mississippians.

In her novel *Strange Fruit* (New York: Reynal & Hitchcock, 1944), 243, Georgia writer Lillian Smith narrates a similarly ambiguous female gender (and presumably sexual) nonconformist and also represents a popular linkage between homosexuality and child molestation. A southern mother warns her daughter, "There're—women, Laura, who aren't safe for young girls to be with. Of course you are young and inexperienced. . . . There're women who are—unnatural. They're like vultures—women like that."

3. For the sheet music, see Bobbie Gentry, *Ode to Billy Joe* (New York: Larry Shayne Music, 1967).

News writers and critics have used differing spellings of the protagonist's name, as have the primary creators of the legend. Gentry's original draft lyrics—handwritten on two lined sheets of a yellow legal pad—carry the title "Ode to Billy Joe" but refer to "Billy Jo" throughout. These and other Gentry papers are on deposit at Archives and Special Collections, John Davis Williams Library, University of Mississippi, University, Mississippi. The album was titled *Ode to Billie Joe* (Hollywood, Calif.: Capitol, 1967). The subsequent novel and movie versions refer to "Billy Joe." I use "Billy Joe," but I leave quoted passages intact. Such spellings carry gender connotations: Whereas "Billie Jo" could be used for a female, "Bobby Lee" would not be an unusual name for a male southerner. "Bobbie Leigh" might be the most "feminine" of spellings.

4. Through her Los Angeles agent, I arranged for an interview with Gentry by phone from her residences in Savannah and Atlanta. I spoke with her very briefly, set up a time for a follow-up call, after which she failed to answer her phones or respond to my voice-mail messages.

Gentry's early biography is drawn from the *Clarion-Ledger* (hereafter *CL*), 28 August, 1 October 1967; 17 April 1968; 9 August 1976; the *Jackson Daily News* (hereafter *JDN*), 23, 28 August 1967; the *Tupelo Daily Journal*, 7 February 1983; "Down Home with Bobbie Gentry," *Life* 63 (10 November 1967): 99-101; and "Bobbie and Billie," *Newsweek* 70

(28 August 1967): 81–82. Geographical descriptions are adapted from James W. Loewen and Charles Sallis, eds., *Mississippi: Conflict and Change*, rev. ed. (New York: Pantheon, 1980), 15–17, 20.

5. See Pete Daniel, *The Shadow of Slavery: Peonage in the South, 1901–1969* (Urbana: University of Illinois Press, 1990; 1972).

6. Directed by King Vidor, the film was originally released by Twentieth-Century Fox. The videocassette version (Farmington Hills, Mich.: CBS/Fox Video, 1983) contains the following notes: "Ruby Gentry is a tempestuous girl who lives in the southern swampland. Hopelessly in love with Boake Tachman, a refined man from one of the better southern families, she is brokenhearted when Boake marries a more respectable girl. Seeking revenge, she marries a wealthy businessman and uses his money to wreak havoc on Boake's life."

7. *CL,* 28 August 1967.

8. Gentry, "Ode to Billy Joe."

9. "Bobbie and Billy," 82; *JDN,* 23 August 1967.

10. *JDN,* 23 August 1967.

11. Ibid.

12. *CL,* 28 August 1967; *JDN,* 28 September 1967.

13. *JDN,* 23 August 1967.

14. *CL,* 1 October 1967. On Greenwood LeFlore, for whom the city and county were named, see Loewen and Sallis, 52.

15. *(Memphis) Commercial Appeal,* n.d. [August 1967]. Bobbie Gentry Subject File, MDAH, Jackson, Miss.

16. "Bobbie and Billy," 81.

17. "Bobbie's Billie's Bundle," *Time* 90 (1 September 1967): 50–51.

18. "Down Home."

19. *JDN,* 17 July 1972; *CL,* 24 July 1972.

20. *JDN,* 28 September 1967, 26 November 1967; *The (Carrollton, Miss.) Conservative,* 5 October 1967; *CL,* 13 June 1968, 26 May 1985.

21. "Bobbie Gentry, Damone, Rockers Form Companies," *Billboard* 80 (16 March 1968): 10; Marty Bennett, "Bobbie Gentry's Fiscal Wizardry," *Variety* 251 (7 August 1968): 43.

22. Bennett.

23. I draw attention to Nabors's television role in *Gomer Pyle, USMC,* because the blurring of fictional and real-life personas proves emblematic of the movement from modern to postmodern representation in sixties and seventies American culture. And because that is indeed how he was known to most Mississippians. Famous as the North Carolina simpleton from *The Andy Griffith Show* who was shipped off to join the marines (ergo, his own spinoff sitcom), the Sylacauga, Alabama, native Jim Nabors was nonetheless building a successful singing career. An early record album traded on the bumpkin TV role: *Shazam!*

Jim Nabors, Star of the CBS Television Network Series, Gomer Pyle, U.S.M.C., sings You Can't Roller Skate in a Buffalo Herd and Other Immortal Favorites (New York: Columbia, 1965). Soon, however, he would be admired for his country music, gospel, hymns—particularly Christmas songs—and operatic interpretations. He would go on to have his own television variety show, *The Jim Nabors Hour* (1969–1971). Still, he was best known as Gomer. After her 1968 concert appearance at Mississippi State University, when Gentry evaded questions about her love life, one reporter persisted: "What about Gomer?" To which Gentry replied, "Well, Gomer and I are very close friends. There is no burning romance between us." *Grenada Sentinel Star,* 11 March 1968.

Biographical data on Nabors can be pieced together from a variety of books on *The Andy Griffith Show:* Dan Harrison and Bill Habeeb, *Inside Mayberry* (New York: Harper-Collins, 1994); Richard Kelly, *The Andy Griffith Show* (Winston-Salem, N.C.: J.F. Blair, 1984; 1981); Stephen J. Spignesi, *Mayberry, My Hometown: The Ultimate Guidebook to America's Favorite TV Small Town* (Ann Arbor, Mich.: Pierian Press, 1987). See also Tom Whitfield, "Museum in Ala. Hometown Pays Tribute to Jim Nabors," *Atlanta Journal-Constitution,* 23 November 1995.

24. These rumors circulated in the Mississippi of my youth—the 1970s. That Nabors was suspect is evidenced by a *People* magazine feature from 1994 describing his life-saving emergency liver transplant. The liver failure was brought on by complications from hepatitis B, a virus common among gay men (though not so delineated in the story). Still, at a time when stars like Rock Hudson and athletes like Magic Johnson had to account for the ways in which they acquired HIV, the reporters unselfconsciously questioned Nabors's veracity: "Doctors say it would be unusual, but not impossible, to contract the disease as Nabors believes he did"—from tainted water in India. Tim Allis and Joyce Wagner, "Preserving Mr. Pyle," *People* 41 (15 April 1994): 69–71.

25. *JDN,* 19 December 1969; "Bobbie Gentry Weds Wm. Harrah in Reno," *Variety* 257 (24 December 1969): 41.

26. *JDN,* 10 August 1970. Though reported as Gentry's first, the Harrah marriage may have been her second. On 29 October 1968 the *Clarion-Ledger* and *Jackson Daily News* reported Gentry's engagement to Kelly Gordon, her Columbia producer. She would marry country music artist Jim Stafford—best known for his single "Spiders and Snakes"—in 1978. *JDN,* 16 October 1978. In 1980 Gentry was said to be living with her infant son and separated from Stafford. *Columbus (Mississippi) Dispatch,* 18 May 1980.

27. Herman Raucher, *Ode to Billy Joe* (New York: Dell, 1976); Cobbett S. Steinberg, *Film Facts* (New York: Facts on File, 1980).

28. "'Billy Joe' Will Premiere June 3 in Jackson, Miss.," *Boxoffice* 109 (10 May 1976): 11; "WB Seminars Promote 'Ode to Billy Joe,'" *Boxoffice* 109 (17 May 1976): 9; *JDN,* 3 June 1976.

29. Janet Maslin, "Cornpone," *Newsweek* 87 (21 June 1976): 77.

30. Jay Cocks, "Summer Clearance," *Time* 108 (20 September 1976): 80.

31. *San Francisco Chronicle,* 29 June 1976. Other reviews noting the film's "authentic-

ity" include *Film Bulletin* 45 (April 1976): 10–12, 15–19; *Independent Film Journal* 78 (25 June 1976): 14; and *Philadelphia Magazine* 67 (August 1976): 56.

32. Patrick Snyder, "Max Baer Crosses Tallahatchie Bridge," *Rolling Stone* 220 (26 August 1976): 13.

33. Jonathan Rosenbaum, "Ode to Billy Joe," *Monthly Film Bulletin* 43 (August 1976): 170. Emphasis added.

34. Jenny Craven, "Ode to Billy Joe," *Films and Filming* 23 (November 1976): 31–32. Emphasis added.

35. "Ode to Billy Joe," *Variety* 283 (9 June 1976): 23.

36. Joe Holmes, interview by author, Brandon, Miss., 6 July 1996.

37. *JDN*, 12 August 1975.

38. Vito Russo, *The Celluloid Closet: Homosexuality in the Movies*, rev. ed. (New York: Harper and Row, 1987), 22.

39. *Variety* 283 (9 June 1976). Gentry encouraged this representation, calling the plot "a Romeo and Juliet situation, because the two families don't want the kids to get together." *CL*, 3 June 1976. Yet, of Billy Joe's family members, we only see the father, very briefly, as he looks for his dead son. No mention is made of the McAllister family's displeasure with the young couple.

40. Gary Jane Hoisington, "Why I Didn't Go to See 'Billy Joe': A Non-Review," *(Boston) Gay Community News* 4 (4 September 1976): 9.

41. Steve Warren, "What Made Billy Joe Jump?" *The Advocate* 95 (28 July 1976): 42–43; Thom Willenbecher, "'Ode to Billy Joe' is Ode to Machismo," *Gay Community News* 4 (4 September 1976): 9, 11.

42. Paul Trollope, "Ode to Billy Joe," *(Toronto) Body Politic* 26 (September 1976): 26.

43. Kelly Walls, interview by author, Atlanta, Ga., 20 April 1994. Emphasis added.

44. John Riley, interview by author, Chicago, Ill., 6 January 1995.

45. Ben Childress, interview by author, Washington, D.C., 2 March 1994.

46. Jake Woods, interview by author, Atlanta, Ga., 12 February 1994.

47. Stuart Wilkinson, interview by author, Atlanta, Ga., 23 February 1994.

48. Billy Joe threw Bobbie Lee's rag doll Benjamin off the bridge—flatly symbolic of her loss of innocence. Alas, this plot element didn't readily foretell the answer to the second question, as many had long assumed it would.

49. Viewers knew from verse five of the song that, a year later, "Brother married Becky Thompson; they bought a store in Tupelo."

50. Barksdale was played by Mississippian James Best, who had roles in a number of Hollywood films.

51. Local resident Simpson Hemphill made his screen debut as Brother Taylor. *JDN*, 10 August 1975. Jake Woods remembers Hemphill as a lifelong bachelor who threw lavish cast parties for his fellow players in the Greenwood Little Theater. His home was large, Woods recalls, for only one person.

52. As we have seen, another body would be pulled from the Tallahatchie River two

years after the date of the legend. In 1955 black teenager Emmett Till was tied to a piece of machinery and dumped into the river. He had been lynched for allegedly "talking fresh" to a white woman in Money, Mississippi. The trial, which resulted in acquittals, drew international media attention. See Stephen J. Whitfield, *A Death in the Delta: The Story of Emmett Till* (New York: Free Press, 1988).

53. Eve Kosofsky Sedgwick, *Epistemology of the Closet* (Berkeley: University of California Press, 1990), 1.

54. Ibid., 86–90.

55. Henry Nash Smith, *Virgin Land: The American West as Symbol and Myth* (Cambridge: Harvard University Press, 1978; 1950), ix.

56. Richard Slotkin, *Regeneration through Violence: The Mythology of the American Frontier, 1600–1860* (Hanover, N.H.: University Press of New England, 1973), 5.

57. Mark Ingalls, letter to author, Jackson, Miss., 20 March 1998; Chuck Plant, letter to author, Jackson, Miss., 19 March 1998; Fitz Spencer, letter to author, Natchez, Miss., 20 March 1998.

58. Fitz Spencer, interview by author, Natchez, Miss., 26 May 1996.

59. On Phillips's identity and career, see my introduction to the most recent reprint edition of Thomas Hal Phillips, *The Bitterweed Path* (Chapel Hill: University of North Carolina Press, 1996).

60. Thomas Hal Phillips, *The Bitterweed Path* (London: Brown, Watson Ltd., 1966).

61. Thomas Hal Phillips, interview by author, Corinth, Miss., 27 December 1995. On the 1963 and 1967 gubernatorial campaigns of Republican Rubel Phillips, see Erle Johnston, *Politics: Mississippi Style* (Forest, Miss.: Lake Harbor, 1993), 150–58, 194–98.

62. Thomas Hal Phillips, *Kangaroo Hollow* (London: W. H. Allen, 1954), 69.

63. Ibid., 188.

64. Thomas Hal Phillips, interview by author, Corinth, Miss., 25 November 1994.

65. The story of Jonathan and David is found in the book of I Samuel.

66. Hubert Creekmore, *The Welcome* (New York: Appleton-Century-Crofts, 1948).

67. Mark Keller, "Hiram Hurbert [sic] Creekmore," in *Lives of Mississippi Authors, 1817–1967*, ed. James B. Lloyd (Jackson: University Press of Mississippi, 1981), 108–111.

68. *New York Herald Tribune*, 21 November 1948.

69. *New York Times Book Review*, 21 November 1948.

70. Plant.

71. Ronald Knight, interview by author, Terry, Miss., 19 May 1996.

72. Creekmore suffered a blistering (and in retrospect, comical) indictment of his first novel *Fingers of Night*—released in paperback as *Cotton Country*. Titled "Dregs of South Pictured Again," the Memphis *Commercial Appeal* review bemoaned Creekmore's subject matter: "violent sex repressions, adultery, murder, threatened lynchings, not to mention poverty and oppression. . . ." Warning that the author "threatens some day to come back to Mississippi to live," the critic signed her piece, "Emily Whitehurst (Mrs. Phil Stone), Oxford, Miss." 19 May 1946.

73. This is Patrick Cather of Birmingham, Alabama. I am deeply grateful to him for this and any number of other leads and suggestions in my work.

74. *CL/JDN*, 25 September 1960.

75. Ibid.

76. Lee Server, *Danger Is My Business: An Illustrated History of the Fabulous Pulp Magazines: 1896–1953* (San Francisco, Calif.: Chronicle Books, 1993), 18. Also useful is Richard M. Ohmann, *Selling Culture: Magazines, Markets, and Class at the Turn of the Century* (New York: Verso, 1996).

77. Ibid., 79. On female audiences specifically, see Tania Modleski, *Loving with a Vengeance: Mass-Produced Fantasies for Women* (New York: Routledge, 1984). This is a useful text for tracing sadomasochistic impulses in sexual fantasy, impulses that become apparent in Corley's work.

78. Server, 89.

79. Roger Austen, *Playing the Game: The Homosexual Novel in America* (Indianapolis, Ind.: Bobbs-Merrill, 1977), 178, 196–97 n. 30.

80. Server, 30.

81. Woody Haut, *Pulp Culture: Hardboiled Fiction and the Cold War* (London: Serpent's Tail, 1995), 3.

82. Diane Hamer, "'I Am a Woman': Ann Bannon and the Writing of Lesbian Identity in the 1950s," in *Lesbian and Gay Writing: An Anthology of Critical Essays*, ed. Mark Lilly (Philadelphia: Temple University Press, 1990), 50. Also on Bannon, see Suzanna Danuta Walters, "As Her Hand Crept Slowly Up Her Thigh: Ann Bannon and the Politics of Pulp," *Social Text* 23 (fall/winter 1989): 83–101.

83. Hamer, 68–70.

84. John D'Emilio, *Sexual Politics, Sexual Communities: The Making of a Homosexual Minority in the United States, 1940–1970* (Chicago: University of Chicago Press, 1983), 132–34.

85. Ibid., 135.

86. Austen, 215–19. Tom Norman, *American Gay Erotic Paperbacks: A Bibliography* (Burbank, Calif.: Tom Norman, 1994), 1.

87. Austen, 153.

88. Ibid., 178–84.

89. Tracy D. Morgan, "Pages of Whiteness: Race, Physique Magazines, and the Emergence of Public Gay Culture," in *Queer Studies: A Lesbian, Gay, Bisexual and Transgender Anthology*, eds. Brett Beemyn and Mickey Eliason (New York: Routledge, 1996), 288.

90. *Daddy and the Muscle Academy* [video] (Los Angeles: Tom of Finland Foundation/Filmitakomo Oy, 1991). Written and directed by Ilppo Pohjola.

91. Plant.

92. D'Emilio, *Sexual Politics, Sexual Communities*, 136.

93. Again, I relied on Patrick Cather of Birmingham and on John Durham and Mike Pinkus of Bolerium Books in San Francisco. Over time these antiquarians gathered the

bulk of his novels. Only a handful of American libraries have begun to assemble these and other throwaway pulps in their special collections and archives.

94. Pierre Bourdieu, *Distinction: A Social Critique of the Judgment of Taste*, trans. Richard Nice (Cambridge: Harvard University Press, 1984), 484.

95. Ibid., 471.

96. Ibid., 474.

97. *JDN*, 7 November 1954; *CL/JDN*, 25 September 1960.

98. Bourdieu, 474.

99. A bibliography of Corley's works is appended to this study. According to Norman (8), one pulp critic speculates that Corley's work also appeared under the pseudonym Dennis Drew. Only one Drew title, *Like Father, Like Son* (HES 102) [San Diego, Calif.: P.E.C., 1967], turns up in OCLC's electronic World Catalog of library collections. It was not, I learned, written by Corley.

100. Norman, 6.

101. Truman Capote, *Other Voices, Other Rooms* (New York: Signet, 1948), 153. As described in this Corley novel, "Cafe Demonde" seems to be located on the site of New Orleans' actual Café du Monde, now a chain located at tourist destinations throughout the United States. Corley's spelling—and the alternate he uses five paragraphs later, "Cafe DeMonde"—may be a reference to the demimonde. Or, as is common in pulp fiction, they may simply be misspellings.

102. For historical accounts of homosexual activity in rural (Texas) camps of the Civilian Conservation Corps, 1933, see Martin Duberman, *About Time: Exploring the Gay Past*, rev. ed. (New York: Meridian, 1991), 149–54.

103. D'Emilio, *Sexual Politics, Sexual Communities*, 135.

104. *The Complete Reprint of Physique Pictorial* (Cologne, Germany: Taschen, 1997). All subsequent references to *Physique Pictorial* are taken from this three-volume work. Most early issues have no page numbers.

105. Norman, 9.

106. These appear in, respectively, the August 1953, spring 1955, fall 1957, December 1953, and January 1960 issues of *Physique Pictorial*.

107. Morgan, 289.

108. *Physique Pictorial* (October 1953). These images have antecedents in nineteenth-century paintings of European American women and infants captive among Native American tribes. See Julie Schimmel, "Inventing 'The Indian,'" in *The West as America: Reinterpreting Images of the Frontier*, ed. William H. Truettner (Washington, D.C.: Smithsonian Institution Press, 1991), 162–65.

109. *Physique Pictorial* (December 1953).

110. Homi K. Bhabha, "The Other Question: The Stereotype and Colonial Discourse," *Screen* 24 (1983): 18. Kobena Mercer, *Welcome to the Jungle: New Positions in Black Cultural Studies* (New York: Routledge, 1994), pp. 133–34; see also pp. 176–84.

111. "Sir Prise Publishers Present Paintings and Drawings by Carl Corley," n.d. promotional flyer, in files of the author.

112. Bourdieu, 482.

113. For the misogynistic strains of this thinking, see page 186 of *A Chosen World*.

114. Emphasis added.

115. Angela Weir and Elizabeth Wilson, "The Greyhound Bus Station in the Evolution of Lesbian Popular Culture," in *New Lesbian Criticism: Literary and Cultural Readings*, ed. Sally Munt (New York: Columbia University Press, 1992), 95–113.

116. *Jackson City Directory, Baton Rouge City Directory,* and *Baton Rouge Suburban Directory* (Richmond, VA: R. L. Polk & Co.), for each of the years in question. Also, *South Central Bell Telephone Directory for Greater Baton Rouge, La.*

117. Blaise Salario, interview by author, Baton Rouge, La., 25 July 1997.

118. Ibid.

119. Florence Watson, interview by author, Baton Rouge, La., 25 July 1997.

120. Carl Corley, conversation with author, Zachary, La., 25 July 1997.

121. Carl Corley, interview by author, Zachary, La., 29 July 1997.

122. Salario.

123. Now on deposit at Special Collections Library, Duke University, Durham, N.C., are the Carl V. Corley Papers. Included therein are, among other items, copies of all the pulp novels, many unpublished typescripts, and original artwork—including the Sir Prise Publishers posters and a "sketch of Cisco aboard the ship 'Rixie' for invasion of Guam, July 1944." Also in Corley's scrapbook is a photograph of (Cisco) Tomlinson, R-2, Scout, Texas.

124. Hains's biography I have drawn from several sources: *JDN*, 14, 15, 27 July 1975; *CL*, 20, 21 July 1975; *(Memphis) Commercial Appeal*, 15 July 1975. Also, a number of oral history narrators mention him.

125. *JDN*, 22 January 1957.

126. *JDN*, 19 August 1957.

127. *JDN*, 9, 17, 21, 24 September; 10 October; 26, 28 November; 3, 7 December 1956; 10, 13 March 1959.

128. *JDN*, 6 November 1960; Sam Cat, letter to Frank Hains, n.p., n.d.; Mrs. J. L. Shields, letter to Frank Hains, Tchula, Miss., 18 July 1961, box 21, Frank Hains Papers, Mississippi Department of Archives and History (hereafter MDAH), Jackson, Miss.

129. *JDN*, 25 February 1976.

130. *JDN*, 8 December 1964.

131. A survey of the literature might begin with David Bergman, ed., *Camp Grounds: Style and Homosexuality* (Amherst: University of Massachusetts Press, 1993).

132. *JDN*, 17 July 1958.

133. Novid Parsi, "Projecting Heterosexuality, or What Do You Mean by 'It'?" *Camera Obscura* 38 (1998): 168.

134. *JDN*, 1 September 1958.

135. Jackson Little Theatre program, *Cat on a Hot Tin Roof*, 4–14 February 1959, folder 31, Frank Hains Papers, MDAH.

136. *JDN*, 24 April 1959.

137. *JDN*, 28 September 1956.

138. *JDN*, 2 October 1956.

139. *Lincoln County Advertiser*, 10 January 1957.

140. "New Picture," *Time* (24 December 1956): 61; "Should It Be Suppressed?" *Newsweek* (31 December 1956): 59.

141. Arthur Knight, "The Williams-Kazin Axis," *Saturday Review* (29 December 1956): 22.

142. Harry Hewes, "The Boundaries of Tennessee," *Saturday Review* (29 December 1956): 24.

143. "New Picture."

144. *JDN*, 5, 6, 10 January 1957.

145. Chon Noriega, "'Something's Missing Here!': Homosexuality and Film Reviews during the Production Code Era, 1934–1962," *Cinema Journal* 30 (fall 1990): 35. Note that this article's title restates the words of Tennessee Williams or, more precisely, his character, Big Daddy, from *Cat on a Hot Tin Roof*. Big Daddy insists that Brick's inability to have amorous relations with his wife doesn't add up, his excuses don't make sense. What's missing, what Brick won't say, is what the movies seemingly can't say—and what the reviews subsequently do say.

146. *JDN*, 18, 19, 21 July 1965.

147. *JDN*, 15 July 1965.

148. Jackson Little Theatre program, *Bernardine*, 3–13 December 1958, folder 16, Frank Hains Papers, MDAH.

149. Eddie Sandifer, interview by author, Jackson, Miss., 29 July 1998.

150. The much-debated 1968 off-Broadway play, *The Boys in the Band*, by Mississippian Mart Crowley, was produced as a musical in 1969, made into a successful film in 1970, and successfully revived on Broadway in 1996, again occasioning considerable discussion. For those reasons, I forgo discussion here.

151. *JDN*, 14 July 1975.

152. *CL*, 20 July 1975.

153. *CL*, 22 February 1976.

154. *CL*, 19 September 1976; *JDN*, 19, 22 September 1976.

155. *JDN*, 27 July 1975.

156. *JDN*, 25 February 1976.

157. *JDN*, 15 July 1975.

158. Cathedral of Saint Andrew, "Order of Worship," 23 March 1988, Benjamin Perry Folk Jr. Subject File, MDAH. Biblical passages are taken from the New Revised Standard Version.

159. *CL*, *JDN*, 21, 22, 23 March 1988. For an early biography of Folk, see the entry in

The Story of Jackson: Biographical Sketches of the Builders of the Capital of Mississippi (Jackson: J. F. Hyer Publishing Company, 1953), 426–28; see also the obituary in *The Northside Sun,* 14 April 1988.

160. Mark Ingalls, interview by author, Clinton, Miss., 15 June 1994; Rickie Leigh Smith, interview by author, Pearl, Miss., 14 January 1996.

161. *CL/JDN*, 23 March 1988.

162. *CL*, 23 March, 14 April, 20 May, 27 August, 7 September 1988.

163. According to records at the Mississippi State Penitentiary at Parchman, John W. Tyler died of natural causes in 1994 at the age of thirty.

Chapter Six

1. "Vote for Aaron E. Henry for the Mississippi State Legislature, November 2, 1971," Files of Aaron Henry, Mississippi Department of Archives and History (hereafter MDAH), Jackson, Miss.

2. Don Sanders, "Christianity's Intolerance of Gays," *This Month in Mississippi* 9 (December 1982): 20–21.

3. "Metropolitan Community Church of Jackson," *This Month in Mississippi* 10 (October/November 1983): 17.

4. On Mattachine and on Randy Wicker's involvement, see John D'Emilio, *Sexual Politics, Sexual Communities: The Making of a Homosexual Minority in the United States, 1940– 1970* (Chicago: University of Chicago Press, 1983), 125, 158–61.

5. "New Homophile Organization," *The Ladder* 8 (May 1959): 7.

6. Eddie Sandifer, interview by author, Jackson, Miss., 29 July 1998.

7. "Expose Short-Haired Anti-Intellectual Queers," *Kudzu* 1 (12 November 1968).

8. "Heavy Hog," *Kudzu* 1 (17 December 1968). On the official backlash against *Kudzu* and its staff, see *Clarion-Ledger* (hereafter *CL*), 10, 11 October; 19, 20 December 1968; 31 May 1970.

9. Martin Duberman, *Stonewall* (New York: Dutton, 1993), 190–221. On the GLF in New York, see Terence Kissack, "Freaking Fag Revolutionaries: New York's Gay Liberation Front, 1969–1971," *Radical History Review* 62 (spring 1995): 104–134.

10. David Hayward, "Where Were You in '72? Atlanta Was Proud and Gay," *The Gazette* (n.p., n.d.; 1981).

11. Darrell Yates Rist, *Heartlands: A Gay Man's Odyssey Across America* (New York: Plume, 1993), 267–69. For more, see "History of the MGA," *This Month in Mississippi* 9 (September 1982): 20.

12. Donna Jo Smith, "Queering the South: Constructions of Southern/Queer Identity," in *Carryin' On in the Lesbian and Gay South,* ed. John Howard (New York: New York University Press, 1997), 382.

13. Rist, 267.

14. Joe Nix, "Jackson Gay Community Speaks Its Mind," *Reporter* 20 (30 January 1975): 1.

15. *ACLU/Memos* (Newsletter of the American Civil Liberties Union of Mississippi), January–February 1975.

16. Nix.

17. *(Jackson) Steppin' Out*, 4 November 1977.

18. *Workers' World*, 21 October 1977; see also *The Anita Bryant Story: The Survival of Our Nation's Families and the Threat of Militant Homosexuality* (Old Tappan, N.J.: Revell, 1977).

19. *Workers' World*, 18 June 1977.

20. Nix, 10.

21. Ibid.

22. Ibid. The white owner of Mae's regularly put off all my attempts at an interview. Though accounts differ, many narrators assume that he and/or his family likewise owned the black bar, Bill's.

23. "Jackson Police Department Personnel Complaint," 28 September 1976, Files of the Mississippi Gay Alliance (hereafter MGA), MDAH. See also *CL*, 30 September 1976.

24. Mary Ramberg, letter to John Buggs, Washington, D.C., 18 March 1977, Files of MGA, MDAH.

25. *Jackson Daily News* (hereafter *JDN*), 14 September 1979. In his groundbreaking study *Tearoom Trade: Impersonal Sex in Public Places*, rev. enl. ed. (New York: Aldine de Gruyter, 1975), 46, 64, sociologist Laud Humphreys shows that men interested in homosexual encounters in public places only make overtures to those who indicate, through various in-group signals, a willingness to participate.

26. *JDN*, 14 September 1979.

27. *Mississippi Gay Alliance v. Goudelock* (1976) 536 F 2d 1073; see also Defendants' Brief, *Mississippi Gay Alliance and Anne Debary v. Bill Goudelock, Mississippi State University, et al.*, United States Court of Appeals for the Fifth Circuit, No. 74-4035, Files of MGA, MDAH.

28. Nix, 1.

29. "Mississippi Gay News," *This Month in Mississippi* 8 (December 1981).

30. *JDN*, 23 August 1974.

31. Sandifer.

32. Joe Holmes, interview by author, Brandon, Miss., 6 July 1996.

33. *Worker's World*, 29 December 1983.

34. Earl Black and Merle Black, *Politics and Society in the South* (Cambridge: Harvard University Press, 1987), 62, 69.

35. The following discussion of Perry's life and early MCC history is informed by his two memoirs: Troy D. Perry with Charles L. Lucas, *The Lord Is My Shepherd and He Knows I'm Gay* (Los Angeles: Nash Publishing, 1972), and Troy D. Perry with Thomas L. P. Swicegood, *Don't Be Afraid Anymore: The Story of Reverend Troy Perry and the Metropolitan Community Churches* (New York: Saint Martin's Press, 1990); see also *Mobile Register*, 8 June 1997.

36. Perry and Swicegood, 28.

37. Ibid., 35, 42.

38. Ibid., 36.

39. Ronald M. Enroth and Gerald E. Jamison, *The Gay Church* (Grand Rapids, Mich.: William B. Eerdmans Publishing, 1974), 41.

40. Ibid., 140.

41. Ibid., 106.

42. Ibid., 137.

43. Thomas Furman Hewitt, "The American Church's Reaction to the Homophile Movement, 1948–1978" (Ph.D. diss., Duke University, 1983), 289.

44. Ibid., 291.

45. Ibid., 292–93. Interestingly, Hewitt cites Rev. Dr. John R. Claypool of Jackson —no relation to Denita, later mentioned—as one of the more "compassionate, nonjudgmental" members of the Baptist leadership, 307.

46. Ibid., 263–64; Ward Tillman, interview by author, Jackson, Miss., 13 January 1996. The full statement reflected conflict among the church's clergy and lay delegates. Among the more conciliatory yet patronizing statements: "Homosexual persons no less than heterosexual persons are individuals of sacred worth. All persons need the ministry and guidance of the Church in their struggles for human fulfillment, as well as the spiritual and emotional care of a fellowship which enables reconciling relationships with God, with others, and with self. Further we insist that all persons are entitled to have their human and civil rights ensured." For an account of the floor debate, see Bruce Hilton, *Can Homophobia Be Cured? Wrestling with Questions That Challenge the Church* (Nashville: Abingdon Press, 1992), 84–86.

47. Hewitt, 268.

48. *JDN*, 15 June 1979; *CL*, 17 November 1984.

49. Robert Nugent and Jeannine Gramick, "Homosexuality: Protestant, Catholic, and Jewish Issues; A Fishbone Tale," in *Homosexuality and Religion,* ed. Richard Hasbany (Binghamton, N.Y.: Haworth Press, 1989), 26.

50. David Greenberg, *The Construction of Homosexuality* (Chicago: University of Chicago Press, 1988), 468.

51. Hewitt, 63.

52. Ibid., 260.

53. Ward Tillman.

54. Ellen Rosenberg, *The Southern Baptists: A Subculture in Transition* (Knoxville: University of Tennessee Press, 1989), 89.

55. Ted Herrington, interview by author, Hattiesburg, Miss., 13 January 1996.

56. Vince Jones, interview by author, New Orleans, La., 21 July 1998.

57. J. Kathleen Bills Harder, "The Role of the Local Pastor in the Political Mobilization of Evangelical Protestants" (Ph.D. diss., University of Maryland, 1988), 62.

58. Thomas Hal Phillips, interview by author, Corinth, Miss., 27 December 1995.

59. Janet Watson and Tommy Ross, "Afterword," in *Rural Gays and Lesbians: Building*

on the Strengths of Communities, eds. James Donald Smith and Ronald J. Mancoske (Bing-hamton, N.Y.: Harrington Park Press, 1997), 114–15.

60. Frederick Ulner, interview with Mississippi Oral History Program, Hattiesburg, Miss., 22 July 1993.

61. Perry and Swicegood, 267.

62. *CL,* 6 February 1983.

63. *CL,* 28 March 1983.

64. Kathy Rudy, *Sex and the Church: Gender, Homosexuality, and the Transformation of Christian Ethics* (Boston: Beacon Press, 1997), 6–8.

65. Mike Wells to "Family Member," 7 March 1982 [*sic;* 1983], Files of MGA, MDAH; *CL,* 12 March 1983; *(Memphis) Commercial Appeal,* 12 March 1983. Subsequent quotes are from the Wells letter.

66. *JDN,* 23 March 1983.

67. *CL,* 28 March 1983.

68. *CL/JDN,* 5 June 1983.

69. Don McGregor, "The Homosexual Church," *Baptist Record* (April 1983).

70. Kathy Switzer, interview by author, Jackson, Miss., 28 March 1994.

71. *(Memphis) Commercial Appeal,* 12 March 1983.

72. "Mississippi Gay Alliance; The Moral Majority Is Neither," 27 April 1983, Files of MGA, MDAH.

73. *CL/JDN,* 5 June 1983.

74. *CL,* 13 March 1983.

75. *JDN,* 22 March 1983.

76. Ibid.

77. Ibid.

78. Ibid.

79. *CL/JDN,* 5 June 1983, shows the video as still yet to be produced. No further references to television or radio spots appear in the Files of MGA, MDAH. Kathy Switzer remembers seeing the clips on a Jackson evening news telecast. Mike Wells declined my request for an interview.

80. *JDN,* 22 March 1983.

81. *CL/JDN,* 5 June 1983; *JDN,* 6, 7, 8 June 1983.

82. D'Emilio, *Sexual Politics, Sexual Communities,* 52.

83. This is not a reference to Troy Perry, but rather Mississippian Ken Martin, mentioned below.

84. Darryl Jeffries, interview by author, Brandon, Miss., 6 July 1996. It's important to note that this memory was unprompted. It arose within the context of the narrator's broader life history. At this point in the interview, I had not mentioned religion or spirituality.

85. *CL/JDN,* 5 June 1983.

86. Switzer.

87. "Metropolitan Community Church of Jackson," 17.

88. Switzer.

89. James L. Cox, ed., *Mississippi Almanac: The Ultimate Reference Guide on the State of Mississippi* (Yazoo City, Miss.: Computer Search and Research, 1995), 53.

90. *JDN*, 28 April 1983.

91. Meredith Raimondo, "Dateline Atlanta: Place and the Social Construction of AIDS," in *Carryin' On in the Lesbian and Gay South*, ed. Howard, 355.

92. *CL/JDN*, 5 June 1983.

93. Switzer.

94. Sandifer.

95. *CL*, 4 July 1998.

96. Sandifer.

97. *CL*, 4 July 1998. Though much of the Mississippi Gay Alliance files are on deposit at the Mississippi Department of Archives and History in Jackson, Eddie Sandifer donated portions of his personal papers to the private, gay-owned, and sporadically staffed ONE/International Gay and Lesbian Archives in Los Angeles. Though I left repeated messages at ONE/IGLA over a two-month period requesting an appointment, my calls were never returned. Queer Americans considering a bequest of historical materials should weigh the benefits of gay community repositories against the advantages of better-funded and increasingly queer-friendly university and state archives, which adhere to professional standards of preservation, access, and public accountability.

Chapter Seven

1. Tennessee Williams, "Desire and the Black Masseur," in *One Arm and Other Stories* (New York: New Directions, 1948), 86.

2. Jon Hinson, "Statement of Congressman Jon Hinson," 8 August 1980, in Jon Hinson Subject File, Mississippi Department of Archives and History (hereafter MDAH), Jackson, Miss.

3. *Clarion-Ledger/Jackson Daily News* (hereafter *CL/JDN*), 9 August 1980.

4. *CL*, 7 August 1979.

5. *CL/JDN*, 9 August 1980.

6. *JDN*, 18 August 1980.

7. Ibid.

8. *Capital Reporter* (hereafter *CR*), 11 September 1980.

9. On the public/private binary, see Eve Kosofsky Sedgwick, *Epistemology of the Closet* (Berkeley: University of California Press, 1990), especially pages 109–121.

10. For a compelling explication, see John Patrick Diggins, *The Lost Soul of American Politics: Virtue, Self-Interest and the Foundations of Liberalism* (Chicago: University of Chicago Press, 1986).

11. On the open secret, see Sedgwick, *Epistemology of the Closet*.

12. *CL/JDN*, 17 August 1980.

13. *CL*, 9 August 1980.

14. Michel Foucault, *The History of Sexuality*, vol. I, trans. Robert Hurley (New York: Pantheon, 1978), 59.

15. The most notable from the period is Pat Califia's essay "Public Sex," reprinted in her collection *Public Sex: The Culture of Radical Sex* (Pittsburgh: Cleis Press, 1994), 71–82.

16. *CR*, 11 September 1980.

17. *CL/JDN*, 16 August 1980.

18. *CR*, 11 September, 12 October 1980.

19. *CL/JDN*, 16 August 1980.

20. *JDN*, 20 August 1980.

21. *CL/JDN*, 17 August 1980. Emphasis added.

22. *CL*, 28 August 1980.

23. *CL/JDN*, 16 August 1980.

24. Novid Parsi, "Don't Worry, Sam, You're Not Alone: Bodybuilding Is *So* Queer," in *Building Bodies*, ed. Pamela L. Moore (New Brunswick, N.J.: Rutgers University Press, 1997), 104.

25. Ibid.

26. Ibid., 105.

27. *CL*, 6 September, 7 October 1980.

28. *JDN*, 9, 10 October 1980; *(Memphis) Commercial Appeal*, 10 October 1980; *CL/JDN*, 12 October 1980.

29. *CL/JDN*, 12 October 1980.

30. *CL*, 2 October 1980. According to this latest statement, the Hinson campaign deduced that Singletary would have been informed through Hinson's 1978 Democratic opponent, John Hampton Stennis. Indeed, a resident of the Fourth District recalls that the Stennis campaign was rumored to have known the Hinson incidents but chose not to disclose them. The staffers felt it unnecessary given Stennis's comfortable lead in the polls. They also felt such mud-slinging might backfire. Fred Smith, interview by author, Jackson, Miss., 1 July 1997.

31. *JDN*, 22 October 1980.

32. Parsi, 103.

33. See chapter 6.

34. *JDN*, 19 August 1980.

35. *Tylertown Times*, 21 August 1980.

36. *JDN*, 1 October 1980.

37. *JDN*, 6 October 1980.

38. *CL*, 7 August 1979.

39. *CL/JDN*, 16 August 1980.

40. *CR*, 16 November 1978.

41. Ibid.

42. "Congressman Jon Hinson," Jon Hinson Subject File, MDAH.

43. Kathy Rudy, *Sex and the Church: Gender, Homosexuality, and the Transformation of Christian Ethics* (Boston: Beacon Press, 1997), 55.

44. Ibid., 37.

45. *JDN*, 25 August 1980.

46. *CR*, 11 September 1980.

47. *CR*, 27 November 1980.

48. *CL*, 9 August 1980.

49. *CL*, 6 November 1980.

50. *CL*, 7 March 1980; *CR*, 11 September 1980; *CL/JDN*, 12 October 1980.

51. *CL/JDN*, 12 October 1980.

52. *CR*, 25 September 1980.

53. "For Mississippi and America Jon Hinson Speaks Out," Jon Hinson Subject File, MDAH.

54. *Jackson Advocate*, 7 June 1979.

55. *JDN*, 12 June 1979.

56. *CR*, 2 November 1978.

57. *CL*, 13 October 1980; *JDN*, 30 October 1980.

58. Jim Furch and Ralph Lord, cochairs, Finance Committee, Congressman Jon Hinson Campaign, Letter to "Friend," Jon Hinson Subject File, MDAH.

59. *CL*, 23 December 1979.

60. *CL*, 6 November 1980.

61. *CR*, 21 February 1980.

62. *JDN*, 17 July 1980.

63. Of the numerous accounts of Reagan's coattails, Earl Black and Merle Black point to the particular appeal among white southerners. *Politics and Society in the South* (Cambridge: Harvard University Press, 1987), 315. Also, *The Vital South: How Presidents Are Elected* (Cambridge: Harvard University Press, 1992), 349.

64. *CL*, 6 November 1980.

65. *CL/JDN*, 12 October 1980.

66. *CL*, 6 November 1980.

67. *CL/JDN*, 12 October 1980.

68. Neil Bartlett, *Who Was That Man? A Present for Mr. Oscar Wilde* (London: Serpent's Tail, 1988), 84.

69. Judith Butler, *Gender Trouble: Feminism and the Subversion of Identity* (New York: Routledge, 1990), 138–39.

70. *CL/JDN*, 8 February 1981.

71. *JDN*, 5 February 1981.

72. *CL*, 6 February 1981.

73. Ibid.

74. *CL*, 20 February 1981.

75. *CL*, 11 February 1981.

76. *Washington Blade*, 6 February 1981.

77. *CL*, 5 February 1981.

78. Ibid.

79. *CL*, 6 February 1981; *CL/JDN*, 14 March 1981.

80. *CL/JDN*, 14 March 1981.

81. Rudy, 8.

82. Robert Bauman, *The Gentleman from Maryland: The Conscience of a Gay Conservative* (New York: Arbor House, 1986).

83. *CL*, 6 February 1981.

84. *CL/JDN*, 15 March 1981.

85. Smith.

86. William Armstrong Percy III, "William Alexander Percy (1885-1942): His Homosexuality and Why It Matters," in *Carryin' On in the Lesbian and Gay South*, ed. John Howard (New York: New York University Press, 1997).

87. *JDN*, 13 February 1981.

88. Ibid.

89. Unsigned letter to Donald J. Devine, Director, U.S. Office of Personnel Management, [February 1981], Jon Hinson Subject File, MDAH.

90. *CL*, 6 February 1981.

91. Joel Williamson, *The Crucible of Race: Black-White Relations in the American South Since Emancipation* (New York: Oxford University Press, 1984). For visual depictions of these and other stereotypes of African Americans, see Marlon Riggs's trenchant documentary film *Ethnic Notions*.

92. Bartlett, 29.

93. *CL/JDN*, 15 March 1981.

94. *CL*, 29 May 1981; *Washington Post*, 29 May 1981.

95. *CL*, 3 January 1984.

96. *CL*, 2 September 1980.

97. *CL/JDN*, 13 March 1994.

98. *New York Times*, 27 July 1995.

99. In Jackson during the summer of 1983, "She Works Hard for the Money" was number one on the playlist at Jack's Saloon, number six at Bill's Disco. *This Month in Mississippi* 10 (June/July 1983): 13.

100. *JDN*, 26 October 1983. There are no extant Walthall Hotel employee files for this period. Libby Anderson, interview by author, Jackson, Miss., 7 July 1997.

101. Leon E. Pettiway, *Honey, Honey, Miss Thang: Being Black, Gay, and on the Streets* (Philadelphia: Temple University Press, 1996), 18, 34, 42.

102. *CL*, 9 November 1993.

103. Jeremy Powell, interview by author, Atlanta, Ga., 3 June 1996. On drag in the South during the early 1980s, see Jere Real, "Dragtime: Dressing Up Down South," *The Advocate* 373 (4 August 1983): 46-50.

104. Pettiway, 18, 36.

105. *JDN*, 26 October 1983.

106. Ibid.; *1983 Jackson City Directory*, 3:32.

107. Of Thomas W. Hanchett's work, see, for example, *Sorting Out the New South City: Race, Class, and Urban Development in Charlotte, 1875–1975* (Chapel Hill: University of North Carolina Press, 1998); also, "Black Residential Patterns in the Urban South, 1860–1960: A Typology of Change" (paper presented to the American Historical Association, Atlanta, Ga., 5 January 1996). On Atlanta, see Ronald H. Bayor, *Race and the Shaping of Twentieth-Century Atlanta* (Chapel Hill: University of North Carolina Press, 1996). A compelling account of racial segregation patterns in the city, it forgoes analysis—as do all works of southern geography—of sexual minority communities.

108. *CL*, 26 October 1983.

109. Ibid.

110. Ibid.

111. *JDN*, 26 October 1983.

112. *CL*, 26 October 1983. Emphasis added.

113. Ibid.

114. Ibid.; *CL*, 13 April 1984.

115. *CL*, 26 October 1983.

116. *(New Orleans) Times-Picayune*, 6 November 1983. I don't mean to discount the efficacy of gossip. As Eve Sedgwick says, citing Patricia Meyer Spacks: "I take the precious, devalued arts of gossip, immemorially associated in European thought with servants, with effeminate and gay men, with all women, to have to do not even so much with the transmission of necessary news as with the refinement of necessary skills for making, testing, and using unrationalized and provisional hypotheses about what *kinds of people* there are to be found in one's world." Sedgwick, *Epistemology of the Closet*, 23. Emphasis in the original.

117. *CL*, 26 October, 2 November 1983; *Washington Post*, 5 November 1983.

118. *CL*, 15 January 1984.

119. Ibid.; *JDN*, 26 October 1983.

120. *1983 Jackson City Directory*, 3:286, 3:384; *JDN*, 26 October 1983.

121. Pettiway, xxv. Pettiway describes the site of his study as a "large urban center." It appears to be Philadelphia.

122. *CL*, 26 October 1983.

123. Pettiway, xxxviii.

124. *CL*, 30 October 1983.

125. Ibid.; *CL*, 26 October 1983.

126. *JDN*, 26 October 1983.

127. *CL*, 26 October 1983.

128. David Harvey, *Justice, Nature and the Geography of Difference* (Cambridge, Mass.: Blackwell, 1996).

129. *CL*, 26 October 1983.

130. What was "conceivable"—I'm attempting to show—was quite limited and phal-locentric, at least in this arena of public discourse. For other possibilities, for other ways of characterizing sexual difference and thereby "disrupt[ing] many forms of the available thinking about sexuality," see Sedgwick, *Epistemology of the Closet*, 25–26.

131. *CL*, 26 October 1983.

132. Ibid.

133. Though the case *Loving v. State of Virginia*, 1977, originated elsewhere, it was applied to miscegenation statutes in several states including Mississippi. Robert Sickles, *Race, Marriage, and the Law* (Albuquerque: University of New Mexico Press, 1972), 64.

134. *CL*, 26 October, 2 November 1983.

135. *CL*, 13 October 1983.

136. *CL*, 24 October 1983.

137. *CL*, 12 October 1983.

138. *CL*, 24 October 1983; *JDN*, 24 October 1983.

139. "Not Just a Fighter, but a Winner!" Bill Allain Subject File, MDAH; also, Bill Allain, Letter to "Friend," Bill Allain Subject File, MDAH.

140. *CL*, 15 March, 4, 19, 28 August, 11 September 1983.

141. "Not Just a Fighter."

142. *(New Orleans) Times-Picayune*, 6 November 1983.

143. The descriptor "Republican kingmakers" was used disparagingly by Governor William Winter. *CL*, 5 November 1983.

144. Homi K. Bhabha, "Are You a Man or a Mouse?," in *Constructing Masculinity*, ed. Maurice Berger, Brian Wallis, and Simon Watson (New York: Routledge, 1995), 58.

145. Andrew Parker, "Unthinking Sex: Marx, Engels, and the Scene of Writing," in *Fear of a Queer Planet: Queer Politics and Social Theory*, ed. Michael Warner (Minneapolis: University of Minnesota Press, 1993), 22.

146. The *Jackson Daily News* supported this argument. In referring to Ross, Toy, and Johnson—each of whom had confessed to felonious sexual acts—the newspaper's head-line offered a shimmering statement of the obvious: "3 MALE PROSTITUTES IN CASE ALL HAVE CRIMINAL RECORDS." *JDN*, 26 October 1983.

147. *CL*, 2 November 1983.

148. See chapter 4 on Aaron Henry.

149. *CL*, 28 October 1983.

150. *CL*, 30 October, 27 November 1983. City directories show Allain's residence ad-dress as 170 E. Griffith Street, Apt. G4 [Sterling Towers] as of 1977, and 970 Morningside Street, Apt. B6 [Stanton House] from 1978 through 1983. See *Jackson City Directory* for each year, pages 2:12, 2:12, 2:12 (1979–1980 combined issue), 2:13, 2:12, 2:12.

151. *CL*, 2 November 1983.

152. Mounger's home stood at 3833 Old Canton Road. *1983 Jackson City Directory*, 2:612.

153. Gordon Brent Ingram, "Marginality and the Landscapes of Erotic Alien-(n)ations," in *Queers in Space: Communities, Public Places, Sites of Resistance*, ed. Gordon Brent Ingram, Anne-Marie Bouthillette, and Yolanda Retter (Seattle: Bay Press, 1997), 28–29, 461 n. 8.

154. *CL*, 2 November 1983.

155. *CL*, 5 November 1983.

156. *JDN*, 26 October 1983; *CL*, 30 October, 10 November 1983.

157. *JDN*, 26 October 1983.

158. *CL*, 27 October 1983. Emphasis added.

159. See the editorial in Mississippi First's newsletter, *First Edition* 2 (November 1983), Mississippi Gay Alliance Subject File, MDAH. A contemporaneous letter to District 72 voters from the "Concerned Citizen's [sic] Committee" attempted to link Mississippi First to the Mississippi Gay Alliance and its "toothless leader"—a reference to Eddie Sandifer. Mississippi Gay Alliance Files, MDAH. When "the group" first approached television stations about running advertisements of the accusations against Allain, it called itself Concerned Citizens for Responsible Government, Victor Smith, chair. *CL*, 2 November 1983.

160. *JDN*, 26 October 1983.

161. *CL*, 26 October 1983.

162. Joe Herzenberg, "Gay-baiting in Southern Politics," *Southern Exposure* (September/October 1985): 17. Oddly, the state's principal gay periodical, *This Month in Mississippi*, made no mention of the scandal in its pages.

163. *CL*, 30 October 1983.

164. "Smear," William A. Allain commercials, 1983, Political Commercial Archive, University of Oklahoma, Norman, Okla. Additional Allain campaign television advertisements, including those portraying his "fighting" image, can be found in this archive.

165. *CL*, 27 October 1983.

166. *CL*, 26 October 1983.

167. *Washington Post*, 5 November 1983.

168. Foucault, 79.

169. That faith produced a "real" embodiment of Donna Haraway's theoretical cyborg—a "coupling between organism and machine." The polygraphed individual, a human strapped to truth-telling equipment, was indeed "a condensed image of both imagination and material reality." It dissolved the mind/body split, yielding an altered superbeing, gauged in its veracity. While the polygraphing individual struck fear as an apocalyptic figure of control, the cyborg subjects of surveillance could (and did, we shall see) shatter the illusion of universal truth, even as their very mechanism promised to find out (rather than make) the truth(s). *Simians, Cyborgs, and Women: The Reinvention of Nature* (New York: Routledge, 1991), 150.

170. *CL*, 27 October 1983.

171. *CL*, 28 October 1983.

172. *CL*, 29 October 1983.

173. *CL*, 31 October 1983.

174. *CL*, 27 October, 3 November 1983.

175. *CL*, 4 November 1983; *JDN*, 4 November 1983.

176. *JDN*, 7 November 1983.

177. *CL*, 5 November 1983.

178. *CL*, 2 November 1983; *Washington Post*, 5 November 1983.

179. The words were spoken by Danny Cupit, chair of the state Democratic Party. *CL*, 26 October 1983.

180. *CL*, 2 November 1983.

181. Charles Reagan Wilson, *Judgment and Grace in Dixie: Southern Faiths from Faulkner to Elvis* (Athens: University of Georgia Press, 1995), xvi.

182. Ibid., 6.

183. *CL*, 22 January 1984.

184. *CL*, 15 January 1984.

185. *JDN*, 9 November 1983; *(Memphis) Commercial Appeal*, 10 November 1983.

186. Bill Minor, interview by author, Jackson, Miss., 15 July 1997. Of course that "evidence"—being caught by police—is refutable as well. Indeed, I and perhaps other queer Mississippians would put less faith in police technologies of truth than other Mississippians might.

187. *CL*, 15 January 1984; *Washington Post*, 16 January 1984.

188. *CL*, 15 January 1984.

189. *CL*, 16 January 1984.

190. Bartlett, 84.

191. *JDN*, 29 March 1984.

192. *CL*, 13 April 1984.

193. *CL*, 15 April 1984.

194. *CL*, 9 November 1993.

195. Harvey, *Justice, Nature and the Geography of Difference*, 112.

Index

ABC (American Broadcasting Co.), 281, 296

accommodationism, xi, xix, 81, 188, 239, 249, 261, 304; as ending after adolescence, 43; and the church, 56, 244; as transformed by the civil rights movement, xvii, 166, 170–73; in college, 66–67; in fiction, 190; of gender experimentation among boys, 18, 21, 45, 59, 76; and Frank Hains, 224; and Aaron Henry, 161, 165–66, 171–72; and the homophile movement, 232; and the law, 141–42, 166; in Mississippi, 141–42; and the police, xix, 81, 133–34, 167; and the press, 282; of sexual experimentation among boys, 43; and silence, 32, 184, 262; and the Southern Baptists, 242; and white gay bar culture, xv; in the workplace, 73. *See also* ignorance: pretense of

Ace, 210

ACT UP/Gran Fury, 116

Adams, Joy, 270

adult theaters/bookstores, 96, 258, 259, 263, 269

AFL-CIO, 291

African Americans, 17, 37, 42, 46, 70, 76, 79, 227; and accommodationism, 161, 165–66, 171–72; in Atlanta, 120; and bars, xvi, xxiii, 96, 98, 99, 102, 236, 278–79; and church, 49–52, 54, 55, 72, 153, 158, 294, 303–304, 306; and the civil rights movement, xv, 51, 56–57, 58, 64–65, 118, 129, 142–66, 170–73, 255;

and class, 73–74; and college, 64–66, 147, 151, 157; and cross-race sexual relations, xvi, 73, 105, 119, 162, 165, 272, 275–78, 280, 283–85, 290; in the Delta, 176; and elective office, 150, 163, 269, 271; and the family-hood, 282, 285, 293, 296; and farming, 70–71, 300–301; and gay organizations, 239; and gay spirituality, 231; and gender transgression, 79, 117–18, 158–59, 172; and the Great Migration, 13, 119–20, 176; and HIV/AIDS, 305; and the homophile movement, 232; and Jackson housing, 279–80; and lynching, 118, 141, 142–43, 277, 350n.52; and the Metropolitan Community Church, 253; and the military, 117; and mobility, 101; in Negro baseball leagues, 37, 322n.6; neighborhoods, 101; physique-art depictions of, 210–11; and the police, 105, 152–63, 237, 280, 288; population of, 37; and prison, 117–18; representations of, 181, 192, 204, 213–14; and roads, 104; and same-sex dance, 113–14; and school, 56–57, 58–59, 61; and sex work, 280, 281–82; and Smith Park, 236; and suburbanization, 96–97; white interrogations of, 152, 154–55, 156, 159–63, 171–72, 281–83, 292–95, 299, 305; and work, 72, 73–74. *See also* race; racial segregation; racism

African Methodist Episcopal (AME) Church, 50

Agony of Christ, The, 207, 219

367

Made in the USA
Coppell, TX
07 October 2020